The Prophet of Paradise

J. Harris Anderson

Amanda,
wishing you many exciting chases of one kind or another.

The Prophet of Paradise

A Paradise Gap Novel

J. Harris Anderson

Blue Cardinal Press • Philomont, Virginia

Published by
Blue Cardinal Press
Post Office Box 182
Philomont, Virginia 20131
www.bluecardinalpress.com

This novel is a work of fiction. Names, characters, places, organizations, business establishments, events, and incidents are either products of the author's imagination or are used fictitiously.

Library of Congress Control Number: 2013920397

Trade Paperback
ISBN-13: 978-0-9911645-0-9
ISBN-10: 0991164504

Copyright © 2013 by J. Harris Anderson

All Rights Reserved

"Shall We Dance?"
Copyright © 1951 by Richard Rodgers
and Oscar Hammerstein II
Copyright Renewed
Williamson Music (ASCAP), an Imagem Company, owner of publication
and allied rights throughout the World.
International Copyright Secured. All Rights Reserved.
Used by Permission.

First Edition

Cover design by Carol Gana
Cover photo by Karen Monroe (www.middleburgphoto.com)
Back cover photo by Anne Whiting (www.annewhitingphotography.com)

For Ellen
“A-wooooo!”

Acknowledgements

Many generous and thoughtful people contributed their time, talent, and expertise toward the crafting of this novel.

Fellow authors Karen Myers (www.perkunaspress.com) and Jan Neuharth (www.huntcountrysuspense.com) were indispensible guides through the labyrinth of the modern publishing world. Their patience with an endless string of questions and eagerness to offer knowledgeable counsel were of immeasurable value. I am deeply in their debt.

A team of advance readers soldiered through a voluminous stack of manuscript pages and provided both helpful critique and inspiring encouragement: Marion Chungo, Diane Ingoe, Scot Litke, the Ryans (Dale, Bill, Priscilla), and Jenny Young.

A nod goes to David Zincavage for his help in tracking down "The Foxhunter's Faith" and to the late Jimmy Young for knowing it existed.

The finished packaging of the printed version owes its eye-catching allure to the design skills of Carol Gana, the photographic genius of Karen Monroe (Middleburg Photo) and Anne Whiting, and the artistry of Dagmar Cosby (for the Blue Cardinal Press logo). The accompanying website (www.bluecardinalpress.com) was created by Scott Coughlin and Chris Comeau of IDI Multimedia.

Marion Maggiolo of Horse Country Saddlery (www.HorseCountryLife.com) deserves a special word of appreciation. For nearly two decades she has given me the opportunity to distill the multi-hued essence of foxhunting to fit the confines of the printed page for *In and Around Horse Country* and other related publications. Such an apprenticeship is a rare opportunity, and one for which I am most grateful.

Given this incredible support team, the fault for any errors that may still appear within these pages lies solely with the author.

Finally, one individual stands out as the person without whose support, encouragement, patience, and counsel none of the above would have been possible: Ellen Flynn, my life partner. She carries the burden of that role with a giving spirit and a loving grace that exceeds all reason.

Reader Advisory

This book contains strong language and adult situations. It is intended for a mature audience. Reader discretion is advised.

Cast of Characters

An alphabetical listing (by last name) of the characters can be found at the back of the book.

The steel axe...is not only replacing the stone axe physically, but it is hacking at the supports of the entire cultural system...With the collapse of this system of ideas...there follows an appallingly sudden and complete cultural disintegration...Without the past, the present could be meaningless and the future unstructured and uncertain.

"Steel Axes for Stone–Age Australians," Lauriston Sharp, 1952

****

Faith is the substance of things hoped for, the evidence of things not seen.

Hebrews 11:1

Chapter 1

Crutchfield County, Virginia
Friday morning, September 2
The Visions Begin

THE HEAVY HEAT of late summer lingered in the Piedmont. Horsemen scheduled their exercise rides early before the air turned to steam and the sparrow-sized horseflies massed for full assault. Thumper Billington rode out from his home, Montfair, shortly after sunrise. Cantering down a shady tunnel through the pine woods, he saw Ryman McKendrick walking across the open field ahead.

McKendrick's appearance showed he'd taken a tumble. He walked stiffly, with a limp in his left leg. His hardhat sat askew on his head. Grass stains smudged the back of his white polo shirt. A smear of gritty soil slashed across one cheek of his blue jeans.

"Ry," Billington called out, "you okay?"

Ryman stopped and turned to face the approaching rider. Billington knew well the unfocused look of a concussion. He'd seen it dozens of times on the faces of others, a few times in his own mirror.

"Damnedest thing," Ryman said. "Biggest deer I've ever seen. A buck. Must have been at least a twelve-pointer, maybe fourteen. And this thing—something in the middle of its rack. Couldn't tell what."

Thumper dismounted and gave Ryman a critical assessment. "Deer spook, huh? Anything broken?" He lifted a hand, three digits raised. "How many fingers am I holding up?"

"Sumbitch flew out of the woods. I mean he really flew. Like airborne. Right in front of my horse. What was that thing? Shiny. Like it was hanging between his antlers."

"Ryman, listen to me. What day is it?"

"I musta gone over the horse's head. I was riding Colby, that youngster just off the track. Probably never seen a deer that close before." Ryman looked around. "Musta hightailed it home. Or he could be halfway back to Charles Town by now."

"Okay, Ry, you got yourself a royal concussion. We can skip the President of the United States question." Thumper pulled out his cell phone. "I think we'd better arrange for a trip in the red light limo."

"And there was this mouth." Ryman's eyes suddenly regained their focus and he grabbed Thumper's arm before he could push the 911 button. "It was, like, floating above me. I was on the ground, on my back. And I could see the mouth, with the lips moving, trying to tell me something. But I couldn't hear any sound. And it wasn't human. I... I remember thin lips, black maybe, and square teeth." He released his friend's arm and the unfocused gaze returned. "Where's my goddamn horse?"

"I'm sure he went back to the barn. I'll get you home. Then we'll get you checked out."

Ryman's hand shot forward again and blocked Thumper's second attempt to push the button. "You were holding up three fingers, it's Friday, and the President of the United States is your typical asshole who says one thing, does another. Half the country thinks he's God and the other half thinks he's a commie."

"Damn, that was a quick recovery."

"I probably do have a concussion. Hell, just another day at the office, right? But I really did see this, Thumper. Huge goddamn deer, enormous rack. And something else. It all happened so fast. I was galloping along the edge of the woods over by Caleb's Forty and this sumbitch just came outta nowhere, right in front of me. Next thing I knew I was on the ground, horse was gone. When I sat up, the deer was standing across the field, looking at me. The sun was shining off some strange thing, like it was... sort of... suspended above its head. I stood up to get a better look and the damn deer just... disappeared."

"I don't know, Ry. A nasty head bump can come back to bite you later."

"Shit, Thumper, I've had a lot worse than this. So have you. I'm awake and standing upright, ain't I? Besides, I don't have time for all that medical crap. I gotta get to town, run some errands, then get to the shop."

Billington put his cell phone away. "All right. But I'm escorting your ass back home."

During the long walk to the McKendricks' place, Fair Enough Farm, Thumper kept Ryman's bruised brain engaged with light banter, discussing the success of the summer exercise program for their horses and hounds. Joint-masters of the Montfair Hunt, the most important concern to both men was that the informal season of the foxhunting calendar was scheduled to begin the following morning.

The conversation drifted in and out of lucid exchange. At times Ryman spoke with clarity of a specific hound, a promising new entry, and his expectations of how well the hound would hunt. Then he mumbled the same remarks about the deer that spooked his horse, the height of its leap, the size of its rack, his glimpse of some strange object between its antlers, and the image of moving lips floating above him as he lay on the ground. He then looked around, wondered where his horse was, and the loop—hound, deer, leap, rack, mysterious object, moving lips, where's my horse?—repeated.

They found the young Thoroughbred outside the Fair Enough barn. It hadn't taken him long to learn where his new home was and the pull of the herd guided him back. The only damage was a broken set of reins.

After untacking and turning the horse out to pasture, Ryman limped toward his F250.

"You sure you're okay to drive?" Thumper asked. "Looks like it's not just your head that got smacked."

"Ah, hell, I'm fine. Back's a little sore. Hard damn ground to be landing on. Nothing broken though. Got some ibuprofen in the truck, gotta hit the ABC store for some scotch to wash it down with. That'll fix me up."

"Maybe the errands can wait. Have Nardell keep an eye on you. If you were having hallucinations, you probably have a more serious concussion than you realize."

"They weren't hallucinations. Anyway, Nardell's got appointments this morning and I got things I gotta do. I'll see you at kennels tomorrow morning, bright and early."

Thumper watched as Ryman drove down the dusty road leaving Fair Enough Farm. He could only hope in some vague way that his friend would not pass out behind the wheel. Neither of them were praying men. Chasing foxes was their faith, scotch whiskey their savior's blood, ham biscuits their wafers. Their "Hallelujah!" was "Tally-ho!" and "Amen" was "Gone to Ground."

Chapter 2

DANELLA KERNAN ROCKETED through the hotel lobby and bounced onto the chair across from Janey Musgrove.

"How was the flight down from New York?" Janey asked.

"Fine. You know, it seems like every time I come to Virginia, they've put up three more buildings around here. A few more years, and Tysons Corner will be as crowded as Manhattan."

"Only without the charm," Janey added.

"Right. Sorry, but I'm on a pretty tight schedule, and I know you have a morning class to teach. So let me get to the point. What I'm hearing back from editors is that the subject matter has been played out. It was amusing at first, and your approach was fresh and entertaining. But after two books, what's left to cover? The pitch for a third just isn't flying."

"Maybe I can tweak it," Janey said. "Find some angle that gives it a different spin."

"Look, as your agent I want you to succeed. But, honestly, I don't think it's the angle so much as the material. I mean there are only so many ways you can write about fringe religions. You did a great job on your first two books. But how many times can you go to that well? New religions just aren't popping up every day."

"There are still others I haven't covered." Janey's eyes brightened behind her thick glasses as she recited examples from her latest research. "There's the Church of the Jedi Knights. Some people consider it a parody but others are taking it as a serious religion. There's a new movement in Argentina that worships a famous soccer player as a god. Doesn't that relate to the way many sports fans feel about their idols? Just the use of the word 'idol' suggests a form of worship."

"All very good and interesting points. But is there enough to flesh out an entire book? Something original enough that you're not just rehashing the first two? Maybe you should consider submitting more journal articles, or just focus on your academic work for a while. The job at George Mason is going well, isn't it?"

"Yes, okay, I guess. But I'm a long way from getting tenure. They could drop me from the faculty whenever they want."

"You keep plugging away on your research. When you've built up a sufficient amount of new material, or come up with a new angle, we can try again."

Janey's gaze drifted around the lobby. Deep in thought, she only vaguely noticed a set of old-fashioned foxhunting prints on the wall. The hotel's décor paid homage to the horse-centered past that had once thrived in that area.

"A new angle…" Janey mused.

"That might help," Danella said. "Something more timely perhaps. Or something a wider audience could relate to. Santeria was interesting, particularly your coverage of the controversy over animal sacrifice. Wicca and the typical New Age belief systems are easy to classify among the 'fruit and nuts' set. I did find the section about the natives in New Guinea who worship Prince Philip amusing. But the politically correct forces are making it difficult to write anything that appears to belittle 'primitives.' We have to respect their society even if they believe the Royal Consort is their white-skinned god." Danella could not suppress a smirk at the recollection of the photo in Janey's second book of a small, nearly naked South Seas islander, a deeply reverent look on his aged face, cradling a portrait of Prince Philip in one arm, a British flag draped over the opposite shoulder.

As they rose to leave, Janey looked again at one of the hunting prints. This time it caught her attention. Several bewhiskered gentlemen wore scarlet coats and top hats. Ladies sat mounted in sidesaddle finery. The huntsman stood at the center with a pack of hounds gathered around his horse. An enticing bucolic scene rolled off into the distance, verdant fields festooned with freshly cut haystacks.

Janey absently waved a hand toward the print. "Isn't that lovely?"

Danella was already running tight for her next appointment, a clandestine meeting with a former Capitol Hill staffer pitching a tell-all exposé. She paused momentarily by Janey's side, the fifty-something firecracker literary agent and the forty-ish professor/author, both diminutive and trim, one sporting the latest New York chic daytime business fashion, the other in slightly ill-fitting discount outlet garb and practical shoes.

"Yes, lovely," Danella agreed, and then started toward the door.

Janey remained in place. "I think I might like to have lived back then. It must have been a gentler time, people lived closer to nature, were more in touch with real life, not all the artificiality we have around us today."

Danella stopped and took a half step back. "Yes, a wonderful period to have been alive… if you were a white male who owned property and had been born into the right family. None of those ladies were allowed to vote, racial segregation was the law of the land, even slavery in some areas, medical science hadn't advanced much beyond the Middle Ages, high infant mortality, no social welfare net. But, as you said, none of today's artificiality to worry about."

A Mid-Westerner by breeding and a pragmatist by nature, not inclined to bathetic sentiment, Janey chuckled at her own naivety. "Well, okay, maybe not back then. Still, though, these folks would have made an interesting cultural study. But I guess I'd need a time machine for that."

"No, actually, you wouldn't. There are people who still do this. And not far from here."

"Really? Do you know them?"

"Only one of them. As it happens, you know him too. Or at least met him once, at my Christmas party last year. I'm sure you've seen his name on my website. Thaddeus Billington."

"Rings a bell. History?"

"Yes, US history, politics, that sort of thing. He's from a very old Virginia family, lives somewhere out in the hinterland on a big estate." Danella adopted an aristocratic British accent. "Rides to hounds, doncha know."

"People who still do this sort of thing, and in the twenty-first century. Mmmm, maybe there's something… some angle that..."

"Let's not lose sight of the fact that your field is comparative religion, specifically of the fringe variety. You're not a cultural anthropologist."

"Yes, you're right, of course. Well, I'll think of something, some new angle to make publishers sit up and take notice."

"I'm sure you will."

Chapter 3

RYMAN MCKENDRICK STARED at a decorative box on a shelf in the Warrenton Alcoholic Beverage Control store. The box contained a bottle of Glenfiddich Ancient Reserve Single Malt ($84.80/750 ml). He held a liter bottle of Bowman's blended scotch whiskey ($11.95) in his hand. The clerk recognized him as a regular customer, an aficionado of fine scotch, an occasional purchaser of top shelf brands when he was feeling flush, but lately settling for the blended cheap stuff. Ryman remained in the same spot for a long time, mesmerized by the Glenfiddich package.

"Can I help you with something?" the clerk asked.

"Did you know 'Glenfiddich' means 'Valley of the Deer' in Gaelic?" Ryman asked without taking his eyes off the label.

"Um... yeah, I think I mighta heard that somewhere."

"Looks like an eight pointer to me."

"Huh?"

"That stag." Ryman pointed to the Glenfiddich logo, the image of a red stag's head. "I counted them, only eight points. Mine had at least twelve. Maybe fourteen. It happened so fast, hard to tell. Plus there was that... what the hell was that thing?"

The clerk, a retired paper-pusher trying to stretch his meager pension with a part-time state job, began to think through the drill on how to refuse service to an inebriated customer. The sight of Ryman's well-muscled, heavily veined arms, the sleeves of his polo shirt stretched taut around his biceps, caused the clerk to earnestly hope a physical confrontation could be avoided.

He took a few light sniffs, trying not to be too obvious in his attempt to detect any telltale odor coming off Ryman: manly sweat, hay, horse manure, leather cleaner, diesel fuel. No trace of alcohol.

"A stag," Ryman muttered to himself. "Never occurred to me."

"Are you all right, sir?"

Ryman looked down at the bottle of Bowman's in his hand. "Well, as Daddy would say, looks like cheap booze and ugly women this weekend." He flashed a friendly smile at the clerk and walked to the checkout counter, no hint of a stagger, just a slight limp in his left leg. The clerk breathed a sigh of relief and followed.

****

The image of the stag continued to rumble around in Ryman's thoughts as he drove due west, away from the gravitational pull of Warrenton and back into the still-rural terrain of Crutchfield County. He saw the Glenfiddich logo. He saw the deer that knocked him off his horse, then the vision of a mouth floating in the air above him, thin black lips moving over square teeth. These images percolated in his mind as he traveled along Paradise Turnpike, the winding two-lane road that followed the old east/west Indian trail through the foothills below the Blue Ridge. The absence of centerline markings required drivers to estimate their own lane space, more a gentleman's agreement than a hard boundary. No curbs bordered the roadside. The pavement simply ended and the surface transitioned to either steep banks or deep ruts.

Just past the intersection with Montfair Lane, where a left turn toward the south led to the Billington and McKendrick farms, Ryman rounded a sharp curve. An approaching Mac Tools delivery truck drifted over toward Ryman's side of the road. Both drivers hit the brakes and swerved their vehicles sharply. Tires squealed and a head-on collision was averted by inches. Ryman's truck went up the bank to his right. The delivery truck barely missed rolling down the steep hill on the opposite side of the road.

Ryman was able to stop his truck before it reached the sharpest slope of the bank, only just avoiding a rollover himself. He rested his head on the apex of the steering wheel and took a couple of deep breaths. When he raised his head, there, on the crest of the slope directly in front of him, silhouetted against the cloudless summer sky, was the buck that had spooked his horse that morning. There were thousands of deer in that part of the state. But Ryman had no doubt this was the same one. Chest out, head erect, it was the biggest buck he'd ever seen. And there was still something in the center of its rack, directly above its head. He squinted to get a better look. The late morning sun's reflection bathed the object in a whitish aura. It couldn't be a natural part of the buck's antlers. This was no ordinary deer. And why had it just appeared again, staring down at him like that?

Something about this image seemed familiar—a proud stag, a glowing object above its head. His concussed brain could not process the data. It was in there somewhere, but the file would not open.

A door slammed shut and the sound caused Ryman to glance in his sideview mirror. He saw the other driver coming toward him. When he looked back up the hill, the deer was gone.

Ryman jumped out of his truck and scrambled up the bank to where the deer had been standing.

"Hey, man!" the other driver called out. "You okay? You can't leave the scene. Where you going?"

Ryman did not answer. He reached the crest of the hill and looked in all directions for some sign of the buck. There was little cover where it could have hidden, mostly open fields, the nearest tree line a hundred yards away. Yet there was no sign of the animal, only a couple dozen grazing Black Angus.

"What do you want, damn it?" Ryman called out. "Where the hell did you go?"

"I just wanted to be sure you were okay, man. I'm right here."

Ryman looked down toward the road and saw a confused deliveryman staring up at him. He glanced back toward the fields, but he saw no trace of the buck. With a resigned slump he made his way down the embankment. "Yeah, I'm okay. You?"

"Fine. Probably got some things spilled around, but no biggie. Damn country roads you people got out here."

"You oughta be used to 'em by now." The driver had been making regular stops at McKendrick and Sons until recently. A problem about some payments in arrears led to the service being stopped. Ryman wasn't sure of the details; he left those concerns to his father and the shop's bookkeeper.

"You sure you're all right?" the deliveryman asked. "What were you doing climbing up the hill there?"

"Huh? Oh, just thought I saw something. Musta been mistaken. I gotta get to the shop. See ya, man."

As Ryman continued on, his thoughts returned to visions of stag heads. But now another image appeared with them, the Mac Tools logo, its rounded red "MAC" letters brightly displayed on a white background. Tools—something about tools. He wondered how badly the tools had been tossed around when the driver swerved to avoid him. Serve the son-of-a-bitch right for cutting off the service. Well, it wasn't the driver's fault. Just following company orders. Made it inconvenient, though, not having tools delivered right to the shop. Something about that prickled at Ryman's thoughts.

Stag heads and the Mac logo were still with him as he cruised into Paradise Gap.

The "Gap" portion of the name referred to a crimp in the mountains above the village. It may have served as a suitable crossing for the more vigorous frontiersmen. But it was too steep and rocky for wagons and the heavily laden settlers who followed. More commodious routes into the Shenandoah Valley were chosen, paved roads followed, and the "gap" quickly reverted back to a tree-covered crease.

The provenance of "Paradise" was less certain. Some preferred the mythology that the landscape—rolling foothills sweeping away from the picturesque mountains, plus the fertile soil and abundant game—inspired an obvious Edenic comparison. Another less romantic but possibly more accurate story held that the first trapper to cross at the crease was named Jedidiah Paradise. Jed found a life of commerce more to his liking than that of trailblazer and so established a trading post at the base of the mountains' eastern slope. When the westbound traffic took other paths, the enterprise folded. But a small settlement had already formed around it and, if for no other reason than the inclination of Virginians to resist change, it remained. Although no metropolis by any measure, the village achieved a respectable solidity and a degree of self-sufficiency as an oasis of service and social cohesion for the surrounding farming community.

At the east end of the village sat the General Store, frequented by the locals more for gossip than groceries. Most of the items on the rustic wooden shelves looked like they had been salvaged from a 1950s bombshelter pantry. A portion of the store's scanty profits came from the extensive selection of wines, many from nearby Virginia vineyards, and microbrews more notable for their amusing titles than their taste.

Ryman drove past the store, toward the west end of the village, past Crutchfield County Bank, the post office, a tiny Methodist church, auto service center, two antique/junk shops, the fire-and-rescue station, and a smattering of houses interspersed here and there in a range of architectural styles from authentic colonials, three of them complete with National Historic Site plaques, to brick ramblers, rudely out of place among the gracious older homes. One of the more stately houses served as a bed and breakfast, owned by a retired couple who, fortunately, did not have to depend on a steady stream of guests to survive.

The occasional day-trippers from the ever-encroaching suburbs stumbled upon the village and lingered for an hour or so to soak up the Mayberry-like quaintness and imagine what life must be like where neighbors actually spoke to each other.

On the far end of Paradise Gap, official population 347—a number subject to decrease on any given day, considering the age of several residents and the occupations of others—was McKendrick and Sons Farm Implements. Ryman parked his truck and unfolded himself from the cab. Even before he reached the shop's front door beads of sweat began to form on his bare arms and the back of his tanned, deeply lined neck. With Labor Day Weekend just ahead, the entire Piedmont was one enormous hothouse.

Chapter 4

FERGUS MCKENDRICK, RYMAN'S father, and Muriel Hudkins, secretary-receptionist-bookkeeper-housemother, sat at their adjoining desks in the cramped office they had shared for more than forty years.

"Here are the paychecks," Muriel said as she handed him three envelopes.

"Where's yours?" Fergus asked.

"The same place it's been for the past two months," she replied.

"I told you, Muriel, you gotta stop skipping your check."

"I will not put this business in the red any farther than it already is."

"You let me worry about that."

"I'm sure you are worrying about it. I'm just not going to add any more to your worries."

"You can't just go on not taking your pay. And things will turn around soon. We've been through tough times before."

"I truly pray that things will turn around soon. Yes, we've seen difficult times before, but this situation is serious. Mister Sensabaugh called yesterday. They're getting impatient at the bank."

"Bing's never let me down. He'll understand we just need a bit more time."

"Bing's retired. Bob runs the bank now."

"I know that."

Muriel caught a faint question skim over her boss's face.

"But Bing's still got some say, don't he? He's—what they call it?—chairman meritorious."

"Chairman emeritus."

"Yeah, that." Fergus hunched his shoulders, then pulled them back, stretching his chest into a wide barrel. "Seems I got a belch here I can't get up. Must be that cheap warehouse coffee you been buying." He withdrew a faded bandana from his hip pocket and wiped his brow. "And is it just me, or is the AC on the fritz again?"

"I'm sorry, but there isn't any money for your expensive special blend of coffee. It feels fine in here to me, but if the air conditioning is not working properly, we'll just have to live with it for now. We're in arrears with Jessup HVAC. And other suppliers are threatening to cut us off. Mac Tools already has. The John Deere franchise could be in jeopardy."

"Oh, everyone just needs to be a little more patient. Better times will be here soon."

"Things aren't like they used to be. No sir. Times have changed. It's a shame in many ways. But that's how it is."

"Well, at least y'all get to knock off early for the weekend," Fergus said. "Me and Ryman can hang around in case any customers show up."

The conversation stopped at the sound of the front door opening. Ryman's footsteps echoed in the empty showroom.

"You get that wrench Bar needed?" Fergus asked as Ryman entered the office.

Now Ryman realized why the sight of the Mac Tools truck had troubled him. He'd been so focused on the Glenfiddich label that he'd forgotten his main reason for driving into town. He briefly considered fibbing to his father, covering his mistake by telling the old man that they didn't have the correct wrench at Tractor Supply. So why hadn't he gone to Home Depot, Southern States, or the Farmers Coop? Why hadn't he called to ask Bar if there was another tool that would do the job? No way out. He had to own up to it. "Sorry, Daddy, I completely forgot. Lots on my mind this morning."

"Damn, boy. I don't suppose you forgot to go to the liquor store?"

Ryman did not answer.

"No," Fergus said, shaking his head, "I didn't think so. Bar ain't gonna be happy."

Ryman stood silently, a fifty-six year old man in the pose of a petulant child.

Fergus rose, wiped his forehead again, stretched out his left arm, then brought a fist to the middle of his chest, trying to bring up that reluctant belch. Muriel pretended to busy herself with an accounting task. The old man looked more closely at his son. Something about Ryman's eyes did not seem right, a distant dullness in them. "You okay, boy?"

"Fine, Daddy."

"You sure?"

"Took a spill this morning. Deer spook. No big deal."

"You riding that young chestnut we got from the track last week?"

"Colby, yeah. But I can't say it was his fault. Damn deer jumped right in front of us. Big buck, huge rack." The light began to return to Ryman's eyes. "Just flew right out of the woods. Surprised us both. I went off over his head, but no harm done." The more he recounted the event, the more animated he became. Muriel halted her paperwork pantomime and stared up at him. He was now pacing back and forth in the tiny office, his head cocked to one side, as if trying to work out a puzzling question.

"And there was something... damn, I wish I'd gotten a better look. What the hell was it? Right in the middle of that huge rack. Could it have been... ? No, no way. But it did kind of look like… And then the Glenfiddich stag. 'Valley of the Deer.' Son-of-a-bitch. Never occurred to me. Then I'm driving back and damned if he isn't there again, right after the Mac Tools guy ran me off the road. Or maybe I just imagined it. When I went after him he... he just... "

"Ry!"

The sound of his father's voice jolted him out of his reverie.

"You ain't all right, boy. You got yourself a helluva concussion. You shouldn't a drove all the way to town. You leave your truck… damn." He placed a hand on his abdomen. "I do believe that cheap coffee's given me a powerful dose of indigestion. You leave your truck here and I'll run you home after I hand out the paychecks. C'mon with me, boy."

At eighty-five Fergus was the force behind McKendrick and Sons, a big man with a contagious enthusiasm for life. He sported a wavy mane of silver hair and his huge smile had lost none of its luster, thanks to top quality dental work. He moved with the self-assurance of a man who had seen combat; the scarlet tails he wore to the annual hunt ball were decorated with his medals from the Korean conflict. Other than his brief, youthful stint as a US Marine, he never wanted to live anywhere but Paradise Gap or do anything other than succeed his father into the farm implement business, as McKendrick men had done since his great-grandfather started the company in 1885.

When Fergus wasn't bedazzling a customer with the wonders of the latest developments in John Deere technology, he threw himself into his other passion—chasing foxes around the Virginia countryside, another tradition handed down over several generations within both the McKendrick and Billington families.

Ryman shared his father's love of mounted hunting but not the old man's dedication to the sales and service of farm implements. He was, though, equally happy to have never left Paradise Gap, other than that year and a half at Bridgewater College. After three semesters he became convinced a college education would be of no benefit to him. Given his GPA and spotty attendance record, the school's administration readily agreed.

Ryman followed his father from the office into the showroom filled with unsold merchandise, devoid of prospective buyers. The space had the unnatural feel of a museum display. The sound of thick-soled shoes on the bare tile floor rattled around the motionless pieces of equipment, a dozen empty padded yellow seats waiting for butts that might never come.

Before they reached the swinging door into the service bay, Muriel stepped out of the office, purse and car keys in hand. A severely prim and proper woman, she was a matron of the African Methodist Episcopal Church. Their building sat a half mile outside the village, the vestige of a time when mingling the races for an act as personal as worship services was not condoned. Not much had changed in that regard. Sunday mornings were still the most segregated hours in America, none more so than in Crutchfield County.

"I'll be leaving now," she said. "Have a pleasant holiday weekend. See you on Tuesday." Muriel was well schooled in the social graces and proper speech, her diction always perfect, her grammar correct. She steadfastly guarded herself against allowing even one "y'all" or "ain't" to escape her lips. It wasn't easy, working around such heathens, hearing the Lord's name abused and the Queen's English mangled every day.

From the service bay came the sound of clattering metal, a tool tossed in anger. "Goddamn piece a shit! Who the fuck designs these sorry ass machines? For Christ-fucking-sake, I ain't never gonna get this cocksucker finished. What were y'all thinking, putting the clutch way the fuck up there?"

The question was rhetorical. There was no one else in the bay except Bar Reinhardt, head mechanic.

Muriel tried not to flinch. With a "Hmmph!" she turned and left.

Fergus and Ryman headed on through the swinging door that led to the service bay. The showroom's aura of fresh tires, clean metal, and bright expectations gave way to the practical aroma of diesel fuel, heavy lubricants, sweat, and swear words that still hung in a menacing cloud over Barstow "Bar" Reinhardt. Bar alone was menacing enough. At six-four and two-eighty he made the McKendrick men look "medium." But his size was secondary, relatively normal even, compared to the wide, jagged scar where his left eye and ear had once been. The remaining eye swam in a pale blue pool, its opaque lightness a glittering contrast to the grotesque absence of its partner. He wore grease-stained white bib overalls, no shirt underneath, and heavy Red Wing work boots. His upper body showed a thick matting of red hair over his fair, freckled white skin. A spreading patch of gray peaked out over the top of the bib. What remained of the hair on his head was also a mix of red and gray. The thinning patches fore and aft threatened to convene amidships.

He looked up as Ryman entered the service bay, an expectant glint in his one good eye.

Fergus gave Ryman a poke in the arm. "You'd best tell him."

"Ah, Bar, man, I'm sorry," Ryman stammered. "I didn't get that wrench."

"Why the hell not?" Bar began to straighten up from his crouched position.

"Oh, well, I guess I... kinda forgot."

"You forgot to go? Or you went on your liquor run and forgot the tool?" Bar got bigger with each word as he raised himself up to full height. Ryman tried to make himself smaller.

"Look, man, I'm sorry, just had a lot on my mind. I'll run back right now and see if I can get it."

"You ain't driving nowhere," Fergus said, grabbing Ryman's arm as he started to turn away. "Ry got hisself bonked on the head this morning. Seems a deer spooked his horse. He's a little confused still."

"Damnedest thing. See, this big buck just flew outta the woods... "

"You go ahead and wrap up for the day, Bar," Fergus continued. "I'll call Preston and tell him his bush-hog won't be ready for a few more days. The... uh... part we had to order didn't show up. Damn UPS, or something."

Bar shook his head in disgust and trudged off to his workbench.

Fergus and Ryman continued on through the open bay door. A picnic table sat off to the side of the small paved area behind the service bay, its wooden planks so badly splintered only those with thick pants or bad judgment dared sit at it. Two men leaned against the table's edge. Neither wore thick pants.

Recently past the ordeal of his fortieth birthday, Miles Flanagan retained his former jockey physique. His skin was tanned and weathered, his face rutted with frown lines. His dark, close-cropped hair showed the first hint of salt among the pepper. He wore a faded red polo shirt that strained across his chest and biceps, then billowed loosely around his narrow waist. A scuffed pair of paddock boots peaked out from below his faded jeans.

The other man, Conway Purvis, barely twenty but several inches taller than his co-worker, wore his unnaturally blonde hair long and stringy. If his skin was tanned, it was impossible to tell as much of it was covered with intricate tattoos. He wore a black tee shirt emblazoned with a Norse warrior wielding a battle ax beneath the name of the Southern rock band Molly Hatchet, the song title "Flirtin' With Disaster" in ornate script across his belly. His greasy jeans hung low on his hips. As the McKendricks approached, Conway took a quick last drag on his Marlboro, dropped it onto the hard packed bare soil, and crushed it with the sole of a Red Wing boot, the same model Bar wore but several sizes smaller.

"Here ya go, boys," Fergus said brightly as he handed them their paychecks. "Don't spend it all on booze and women," he added with a wink and a smile. "Save a bit to fritter away foolishly."

Neither man smiled back. They'd heard the same line countless times, and hadn't thought it particularly funny from the start. It became even less so as the size of their paychecks dwindled.

"Sorry there ain't nothing else for y'all to do today. Might as well get a jump on the weekend though. Don't do anything I wouldn't do. And if you do, name if after me."

Miles and Conway left separately, sullenly, exchanging no wishes for a pleasant holiday weekend, and Fergus and Ryman went back into the service bay.

"Looks like another weekend of cheap booze and ugly women for you, Bar," Fergus said as he handed him his check. "Sorry it ain't more."

Bar didn't bother to look at the amount. He just folded the check and stuffed it into a pocket of his overalls. "Well, boss, ain't that a bitch."

Fergus's grin turned to a grimace as his left arm shot out again. He twisted it as if trying to work out a cramp while his right hand went to his chest, the palm flat over his heart. "Damn... coffee... " The grimace became surprise, his eyes wide, head up. His left hand landed on Bar's sweaty bare shoulder, his right clutched at his chest. He looked straight at Bar, then his legs crumpled and he toppled over onto a pile of discarded lawnmower tires. His frozen gaze stared sightlessly up at the corrugated metal roof.

Ryman had never seen anyone die before. Bar had, but not for a long time. Bar knelt down and felt for a pulse. Then he looked up at Ryman and said, "I don't reckon it'll make much difference, but we'd better call 911."

Ryman remained frozen, staring at the body of his father. "Shouldn't we do CPR or something?"

"You know how to do that shit?"

"Just what I've seen on TV. Pump his chest and stuff."

Bar's one working eyebrow arched. He stood up, pulled his cell phone from a pocket of his overalls, and jabbed the 911 key with a beefy, oil-blackened finger. Just before the operator answered, he turned to Ryman and said, "Looks like you're the boss of this place now. Ain't that a bitch." Then back into the phone he said, "Huh? Uh, no, ma'am, not you. Appears we got us a dead man here. McKendrick and Sons, 235 Paradise Turnpike, west end of Paradise Gap. Am I sure he's dead? Well, he could be takin' hisself a noontime nap here in this pile a wore out tires. But my money's on dead. Do I know CPR? Shit, lady, I cain't hardly spell CPR. Anyone else here? Just Ryman but he don't look so good hisself right now. And I sure ain't doing no mouth-to-mouth on his ugly ass. Yeah, I think you're right. We'll wait for the amb-lance."

Chapter 5

THE PENTAGRAM AND circle tattoo on Nardell Raithby's left breast declared her recent allegiance to Wicca. She was certain she'd finally found a belief system suited to her unique talents and perspectives. Over the fifty-four years of her life she'd been Born Again (then unborn again, if that's possible), tried Landmark (the price of admission exceeded her humble means), flirted with Scientology (too intense even for her), wanted to convert to Judaism (turned out to be harder than *Fiddler on the Roof* made it look, and she didn't really feel chosen to be among the Chosen People), considered Mormonism (felt even less comfortable around the squeaky clean LDS folks), and lived briefly with a Hindu but when he abandoned her so did her interest in Eastern religions (she never could get her arms around Hinduism anyway).

Nardell's jill-of-all-trades employment pattern paralleled her smorgasbord approach to religion. She'd been a riding instructor, saddle fitter, nutritional supplement sales rep, photographer, store clerk, pet sitter, writer, and a washer/repairer of horse blankets.

The owner of the print shop in Warrenton was always happy to see her at the counter because it meant another batch of business cards and promotional flyers. The latest ones described her services in equine massage, aroma and crystal therapy, and interpreting the past lives of horses.

On this Friday morning she was at Cecelia Broadhurst's estate, Kimber Farm, in the company of barn manager and groom Dorcas Stanhope.

Dorcas had no patience for what she considered Nardell's voodoo nonsense. She had her doubts about Nardell's massage skills as well, given how recently this new career had been launched and the absence of any professional credentials. All Nardell had to do was produce a stack of business cards declaring herself an equine massage therapist and anyone willing to hire her did so at their own risk, and that of their horses.

The horse people in the local community knew Nardell and her spotty background. Yet many felt a compassionate urge to support her in whatever endeavor she attempted, a civic duty if not outright charity.

Cecelia Broadhurst was in the vanguard of that magnanimous crowd. Dorcas, having only arrived from Florida two years earlier and not exactly flush with cash herself, did not share her boss's indulgent attitude toward Nardell's erratic career path. But as the great lady's employee, she had no choice but to do as instructed.

Cecelia maintained fifteen horses on her estate, enough to keep Dorcas busy seven days a week. Her charges ranged from young animals just starting their training for the foxhunting field to aged retirees who had done their duty and now enjoyed a life of ease in the pastures of Kimber Farm. Most, though, were seasoned hunters of prime age. It was the responsibility of Dorcas Stanhope to keep those horses fit and ready for the highly polished toe of Cecelia's boot to slip into the stirrup and be off for a perfect ride.

Dorcas had one other duty. It had been the deciding factor in her landing the job. Cecelia was the benefactress of the local junior riding program, her own private undertaking for children who wanted to ride cross country and learn about foxhunting. The matron of the manor had little direct involvement in the workings of the program herself. She provided the facilities and mounts for those who needed them and left the actual schooling and organizing to her barn manager.

When the previous manager opted to get married and leave Virginia, Cecelia found no shortage of willing applicants. What distinguished Dorcas Stanhope's resume from the others was her service to a hunt in Florida known for its strong juniors program. The recommendation from the club's master had been an exercise in guarded wording, complimentary but not glowing with praise. Cecelia chose to disregard that and hired Dorcas anyway.

After two years, she'd found no cause for complaint. Dorcas was conscientious, and the children responded to her well.

Dorcas reclined against a stall door and watched as Nardell leaned toward one of Cecelia's hunters and worked her strong fingers into the animal's muscles. As much as Dorcas wanted to find fault, her knowledge of equine physiology told her that Nardell knew what she was doing.

Other than an age difference of fourteen years, with Dorcas on the younger end, both women showed the results of a lifetime spent working on and around horses. Their skin, more cured than tanned, was stretched a bit too tightly over hard, sinewy muscles and steely bones that supported 115 pounds on a 5'6" frame. Nardell wore her chestnut brown hair in a long French braid while Dorcas preferred a short crop for her sandy blonde curls. Both moved with the swagger of a bantam-weight boxer, a confidence bred by decades of working with beasts ten times their size. Their everyday wardrobes consisted of breeches, polo shirts, and paddock boots, all well-worn but functional for daily duties. They owned make-up and at least a few dresses, but cosmetics served no purpose in their working life and only the rare special occasion called for ladylike attire. Their finest and most expensive clothing was reserved for formal hunting days.

"There we go," Nardell said as the horse hung his head down and moved his mouth in a soft chewing motion. "All that tension's easing away."

Dorcas could not disagree that the horse was responding positively. "He does seem to be enjoying the rubdown."

"What I do is more than just a rubdown," Nardell replied with a spark of indignation in her deep brown eyes, the shade of well-used saddle leather soaked in whiskey. "It's about releasing the energy and getting the horse in touch with his aura, where he can be in harmony with his past..." Ryman's ringtone sounded from her cell phone. "I'd better take this. Hello? Oh, oh dear! Are you okay? Of course, I'll meet you there. I'm at Cecelia's. I'll leave now. Okay. Love you. Bye."

She looked at Dorcas, her eyes wide and moist. "I have to leave."

"Oh, my God. What is it?"

"It's Ryman's father. Ryman says it looks like a heart attack, a big one. He thinks... he thinks... I have to go, meet him at the hospital... sorry, I can't finish... have to reschedule…" She gathered up her crystals and incense, hustled out to her mud-splattered, dinged-up, faded green Subaru Outback, and took off, leaving Dorcas in the barn aisle, watching Nardell's tires fling stones from Kimber Farm's neatly pebbled driveway.

Dorcas led the horse back out to pasture. She held her composure, enough to prevent the perceptive animal from sensing her swelling distress. Her steps faltered as she returned to the barn. Knees became rubber by the time she reached the office door. Once inside, she stumbled across the room, collapsed into the desk chair, and let the tears flow where no one, not even the horses, could see or hear.

Chapter 6

THUMPER BILLINGTON'S ATTENTION was far away from his early morning encounter with Ryman. A generous offer from a respected publication had him cloistered in his study, crafting an article on *The Life and Morals of Jesus of Nazareth,* known more commonly as *The Jefferson Bible.* A condensed cut-and-paste rearrangement of Biblical text, Jefferson selected the passages he thought instructive and deleted those that referred to miracles, the supernatural, Christ's divinity, or resurrection.

Although not a theologian, Billington was a recognized authority on the Founding Fathers, particularly the Virginians. He had authored half a dozen well-received books on such topics as the Constitution, the Presidency, and the Supreme Court. His most widely read work was a biography of his late father, who served eighteen terms in the House of Representatives.

The appeal of this assignment was mainly for the intellectual stimulation. The money was pocket change. The Billington portfolio and landholdings negated any need for actual labor. The Montfair estate was the largest privately owned parcel in Crutchfield County and had belonged to the Billingtons since Colonial times.

The estate employed a core staff of four full-time workers—two married couples who lived on the property—plus a variety of hourly workers and contract farmers who raised beef cattle and grew corn, soybeans, wheat, and hay. Five horses occupied the historic stone barn, which had been home to more than a dozen riding and driving horses before the proliferation of motorized vehicles and farm equipment.

The current residents were off-the-track Thoroughbreds who had transitioned from racing to foxhunting: Lenny (short for Leonard Slye), Thumper's number one field hunter; Ozzy, a youngster just starting his transition from race track to hunt field; Minnie Dee and Trisky, his daughter Elizabeth's horses who, with her away at college, were mostly ridden by Thumper's wife Shelagh (herself then away attending to family business in Ireland); and Bee, an all-purpose mount who had been too thick and slow to make it on the track but proved to be a sane, steady fellow no matter who was on him or what he was asked to do.

The property also held the kennels, stables, and huntsman's residence for the Montfair Hunt. The current huntsman, Crispian "Crispie" O'Rourke, shared the small house with his significant other, Patti Vestor, and the two of them shared their lives with sixty-some working foxhounds and four staff horses, also ex-racehorses.

Among the staff mounts, Crispie's number one was Kashmir, a strikingly handsome dark bay. Nimby, an unremarkable but reliable chestnut, was his alternate. On the Tuesday and Saturday hunts Patti rode Pennywise, a feisty strawberry roan mare (whose color closely matched Patti's reddish-blond hair and pink, freckled complexion). Her Thursday mount was an aging gray named Lap Dance (by Big Woody out of Tiny Dancer), most likely in his final season as a staff horse.

Four staff horses, particularly with one nearing the end of his career, was a thin number for a three-day-a-week hunt in the demanding Montfair country, with its rolling terrain and numerous jumps. Thumper had his eye on a few prospects. Bolstering the number of mounts for the staff would be especially important when Shelagh returned and resumed her duties assisting the huntsman as a whipper-in.

Thumper's concentration was broken by a rapping sound. He looked up to see Crispie standing in the doorway.

"Sorry if I'm interruptin', Boss. You wanted me to get with you about plans for tomorrow marnin'." A newly naturalized American citizen, Crispie wished to soften his Galway brogue. But the occasional lapse into his native vernacular still occurred.

"Right, right." Thumper stood up and walked around to the front of the massive mahogany desk that dominated the study. He motioned Crispie to one of the leather club chairs in front of the stone hearth. "Something to drink?"

"Water would be fine."

"Yes, of course." Thumper opened the small refrigerator hidden behind the bar front in the corner of the room and grabbed a bottle of water for his guest and a Diet Coke for himself.

As Thumper plopped down into the adjoining chair, Crispie withdrew a folded piece of paper from his shirt pocket. "I've made up the draw list for tomorrow. Fourteen and a half couple, mostly veterans, but there are two and a half couple of puppies I want to take. Beamer, Boston, Hempstead, Harkness, and Westward."

"Hempstead's a bit of a babbler, isn't he?"

"A wee bit, yes. But I tink... er, think he has a good nose and a decent voice once he gets to work. We need to see if he can get past the babbling, or if that's gonna be a problem. I'll be taking out most of our steady, seasoned hounds."

"Conman?"

"Maybe not yet. We had some trouble with him last season, going off on his own. Might wait a bit on bringing him."

"Okay, I'm with you. All the puppies have looked pretty good on deer."

"Aye, they have. Deer are 'specially thick but the puppies have been payin' 'em no notice. Not a-tall."

"Nope, not a-tall," Thumper said, mimicking the lingering trace of Crispie's accent. "Although Ryman's young Thoroughbred took notice of one this morning. Pitched him off and gave him a good bonk on the head."

"Is he all right?"

"I hope so. He was certainly concussed, but by the time I left him he seemed to be functioning okay. You know Ryman, thickest damn skull in Crutchfield County, possibly in the whole state of Virginia. Still, though, I wish he hadn't insisted on driving to Warrenton. He was still mumbling to himself about the deer when he drove off."

"Those deer are mighty thick indeed. Gettin' inta Patti's garden somethin' fierce. Eatin' everything in sight, knockin' stuff down. Even took out a piece a that nice fence I put up for her. 'Carse, could be other things gettin' in there. Rabbits I'm sure. Raccoons and possums likely."

Crispie took a swig from the bottle of water, a frequent appurtenance since he'd taken the pledge several years before. "Um… is there any update on when Shelagh… er, Mrs. Billington… will be back? Nardell can fill in as the third whip for now, but I reckon she'll return to back-up status once the missus comes home."

Thumper took a sip of his soda. "It seems the missus will be staying on the Old Sod for awhile longer. Needs more time to wrap up her father's affairs than she'd thought." He noticed a tightness in the Irishman's mouth, as if trying to hold his tongue. "What? Have you heard something from your sister?"

"Ah, nothin' really. Only that Mrs. Billington is getting in some pre-season hunting while she's there, exercising the hounds, carrying the horn in her father's place while the hunt looks for a permanent replacement."

"Really? She hadn't mentioned that, only that there was so much to sort out with her father's estate, taking up all her time."

"I'm only passin' along what me sister mentioned."

Thumper's cell phone rang. The screen showed Ryman as the caller. "Hey, Ry. What? Is that a siren I hear? You okay? Jesus Christ, I told you not to drive... What? Oh, man, I'm sorry. Right, I'll meet you there. You're not driving are you? Bar's there? Good. Have you called your mother? Yeah, sure, I'll pick her up. No, of course she shouldn't be driving alone."

He clicked off the phone. "Fergus McKendrick just suffered what looks to be a massive heart attack. He's being rushed to the hospital, although Ryman doesn't seem to think there's much hope."

"Holy Mother a God," Crispie whispered and crossed himself. He muttered something else that Thumper, although fluent in Latin and passably familiar with Gaelic, could not make out.

The two men stood but remained in silent reflection for a long moment, the only sound the whir of a weed trimmer off in the distance, one of Thumper's hourly workers keeping the place shipshape.

Crispie was the first to speak again. His hesitant tone revealed his discomfort at the question that had to be asked. "D'ya tink… well, I mean… do you think we'll still hunt tomorrow? What with Mister McKendrick maybe dyin' an' all?"

"A good question. But too soon to say. Best to assume for now that we'll hunt as planned, see how things develop."

Thumper looked up at the portrait of his great-grandfather, the imposing visage of Thaddeus Augustus Billington the First. The painting hung above the stone hearth, the focal point of the room. "What do you think Fergus would have wanted?"

"Me?" Crispie asked, not sure if Thumper was addressing him or the portrait.

"Yes, you."

"Well, sir, I tink Mister McKendrick woulda wanted us ta go huntin'."

"I tink you're right."

Crispie followed Thumper into the kitchen where Natasha Nutchenko was preparing lunch. Her gray hair was secured in a tight bun and her summer house dress clung to her pale, ample flesh. She sang a snappy Polish children's tune as she worked. She once tried to explain the lyrics to Thumper, something about a man from Krakow, seven horses, a rusty sword, a red woolen cap, and I'll kick your ass if you mess with me. He could only assume his years spent studying the Classics left him bereft of the ability to understand Polish folk culture.

"I'm sorry," Thumper said, "but I'm going to have to skip lunch today. An emergency's come up."

"No, but you cannot skip lunch. I am vorking all morning on special chicken salad, your favorite."

"Your chicken salad is every bit as delicious even days later."

She was not appeased. "Lettuce is vilting, valnuts is soft, celery not crisp." She planted her palms on the counter and hung her head. "Fine. Run off to emergency. What is problem?" She looked over at Crispie. "Hound is needing toenail trimmed?"

"It seems Fergus McKendrick's had a heart attack," Thumper told her. “I’m on my way to pick up Mrs. McKendrick, take her to the hospital.”

The annoyance drained from her broad face, replaced by shocked dismay. She bowed her head again, crossed herself, and muttered something in Polish. “I am sorry. Yes, yes, of course chicken salad can vait.”

The two men left through the mud room. Crispie drove the staff truck back to the kennels while Thumper piloted his car down the long main drive of Montfair, wondering if the woman he was on his way to pick up was now a widow.

Chapter 7

ASTRID STEVENSON GRIPPED the back of Shelton McKendrick's head, twining her fingers through Shelton's thick hair, a mass of tangled curls, savoring her partner's youthful passion and skillful technique. She was cruising blissfully toward climax when Shelton's phone rang.

"Don't answer it," Astrid ordered, trying to prevent Shelton from reaching the phone on the bedside table.

Shelton looked up with a teasing grin. Large hazel eyes twinkled above Astrid's trim abdomen. "That's my father. Maybe I'd better see what he wants."

"Like hell. He can leave a message." She pressed the back of Shelton's head, urging her lover to continue.

Shelton gave a couple of licks that sent Astrid's back arching and prompted a deep moan. "Maybe I should put it on speaker so he can enjoy this too."

"Well, aren't you the pervert. Looks like my lucky day."

Shelton got back to business in earnest and soon afterward the two of them sat together reclining on the pile of pillows propped against the bed's headboard.

A three thousand mile separation—Astrid on the East Coast, Shelton on the West—made for a difficult relationship. It took some maneuvering for Astrid to arrange her schedule to be in San Jose and for Shelton to keep a clear calendar for those days. But the efforts paid off.

Astrid, petite and vivacious, wore her jet-black hair short, emphasizing her sharp features. At forty-three no one would question her if she claimed to be several years younger.

Shelton Louise McKendrick, tall and broad shouldered, could pass for anywhere from twenty-five to forty-five. For one generation after another the McKendrick genes produced large men with features that, while not handsome in the classic sense, were not unpleasant and tended to improve with age. Those genes did not discriminate based on gender and the McKendrick women were only barely distinguishable from their male relatives. From an early age Shelton eschewed make-up, most jewelry, and high heels. She went for understated attire in muted colors and flats that kept her height barely south of six feet. Her one ever-present adornment was a small medallion on a gold chain around her neck, the medal of Saint Hubert. Astrid assumed it was some church-related trinket from Shelton's childhood. She had not yet asked what it really meant and Shelton had not offered to tell her.

"Do you really have to fly back today?" Shelton asked. "It's a holiday weekend after all."

"I wish I could stay longer, but there's no holiday for me. I'll be in the office all weekend catching up on everything that's fallen behind while I've been out here. The new Costa Rica project is taking shape, but still needs work. Then I'm off to Dallas next week. I really should have grabbed the redeye home last night, but…" She snuggled closer to Shelton. "…I figured I'd allow myself a little mini holiday."

"I've got a full schedule of appointments next week too. I have to drive almost to Vancouver for some of them."

"You know," Astrid said, "the offer still stands for you to come work with me. You could move back to DC, take over all the affiliate relations. I could spend more time on other parts of our mission if I had someone I can trust running that function."

"It's tempting. But I really do enjoy my job. I feel like being a rep for veterinary pharmaceuticals is my way of helping animals."

"You could help them even more if you accepted my offer. I mean, People Against Cruelty to Animals is nationwide. And soon to be international once we get the Costa Rica branch up and running."

"Or," Shelton suggested, "you could move the headquarters out here. This area's pretty friendly toward PACA's mission."

"I know. But I have to be close to Washington. And… I don't know… a West Coast address, especially in the San Francisco area, might make some people think we're a wacky, leftist organization."

"Which you kind of are." Shelton reached over for her phone as Astrid gave her a playful poke in the ribs. "Guess I'd better see what my father was calling about."

"Sheltie Lou," Ryman's recorded voice began, "ah, look sweetheart, I'm afraid I got some bad news. Me and Bar are at the hospital and... well... you see... I know this is gonna be hard... but... "

With her head right next to Shelton's, Astrid could hear the conversation without need of speaker mode.

Bar's voice was audible in the background. "Tell her, dammit. Or gimme the phone and I will."

"Um... here's Bar."

"Oh, for Christ sakes," Bar said in disgust. "Sheltie Lou, your grandpa's had a massive heart attack, keeled over in the service bay a couple of hours ago. We ain't got the official word yet, but I don't reckon it looks very good. Will be a damn miracle if he pulls through. I expect you'll want to get back here, get out to the farm, be with your grandma. She's always been sweet on you. Not so much on your old man. Cain't say as I blame her."

"Gimme the damn phone back," Ryman said. "Look, sweetheart, sorry to have to break the news to you this way. I know you been traveling a lot lately, can't hardly keep up with you these days. But gimme a call when you get this, let me know where you are and how soon you can get here."

Shelton clicked off the phone. She took two deep breaths and said softly, "My grandfather's had a heart attack. Looks bad."

"I'm so sorry." Astrid squeezed Shelton's bare arm. "I should have let you answer the phone. That was selfish of me."

"You didn't know. It's okay."

"Are you close to your grandfather?"

"Yeah, pretty close."

"There's a family farm?"

"Yes, out in Crutchfield County. That's where I grew up."

"You never mentioned you were a farm girl."

"I'm not anymore. City girl now." She looked down at Astrid nestled beside her, one graceful arm tightly wrapped across Shelton's substantial torso. "With city girl tastes." She tried to raise a smile but it did not succeed. Instead, the reality of her grandfather's situation began to set in and tears flowed. "Fergus... he was my hero... always loved me as I am... big and ugly... I liked greasy machines instead of dolls... overalls more than dresses... he never judged. I thought he'd live forever."

Astrid rose up and cradled Shelton's head against her naked body. "Shelton, you're not ugly. And dolls and dresses are just stereotypes. You're your own woman and you should be proud of it." Her mouth turned up into a mischievous grin and she tousled Shelton's hair. "'Course, you are kinda big. But I like that about you."

Shelton showed a glimmer of a smile through her tears.

"This farm, are there animals on it?" Astrid asked.

"A few."

"Such as?"

"Well, horses mostly. And a couple of dogs."

"No food stock then…"

"Look, that's just where I grew up. I'm away from all that now. Three thousand miles away. Although I guess I'm going to be making a trip back there. I hope I can get there before… before…" Shelton started to tear up again.

"I'm sorry about your grandfather," Astrid said. "You let me know if there's anything I can do, if you want me to be with you at the hosp..."

"No!"

Astrid released Shelton, surprised by the response. "Is there a problem with your family? They do know about your sexuality, don't they?"

"Yeah, they know. They're okay with it. Well, most of them anyway. It's just that, well, I mean you're busy and everything. I don't want to impose, that's all."

"Sure, of course. Whatever you're comfortable with." Astrid swung out of bed, reached for her robe and wrapped it snuggly around her. "Guess we'd better get going," she said, all business now. "I've got a long flight ahead of me." She started toward the bathroom but then stopped, turned around, and cocked her head provocatively. "There is one other thing."

"What's that?"

"*Sheltie Lou*?"

Shelton groaned.

"Maybe you're still more of a farm girl than you thought."

When Shelton finished dressing, she lifted her Saint Hubert's medal from the bureau. She held the small gold medallion in her hand and looked at the image on the front: a man in bishop's robes flanked by a hound on one side and a deer with a glowing cross between its antlers on the other side. She then turned it to the inscription on the back. It showed a date from twenty-seven years before, when she was five years old, the first time she rode with the hunt on Thanksgiving Day, Blessing of the Hounds. She and her father stayed in the back, Ryman held the lead-line to her pony, and gave her a running commentary on what was happening.

What little girl wouldn't have gladly traded places with her that day? Her own pony, being safely led by her father in his scarlet coat, her grandfather larger than life at the head of the field, the brisk autumn air in her lungs, hounds baying and horses galloping. It all seemed so perfectly natural to her then. It was what everyone she knew did. Except for her mother and grandmother who stood off to the side at the blessing, casting disapproving looks. She thought then that life everywhere was like her life in Crutchfield County. It took awhile for her to find out otherwise.

She slipped the chain around her neck and followed Astrid out the door.

Chapter 8

FERGUS MCKENDRICK MADE a bold move when he hired a young Muriel Hudkins as his bookkeeper. The civil rights movement was in full force then. But it made little difference in the daily lives of most people in Crutchfield County, black or white.

Three candidates applied for the bookkeeper job. It was clear that Muriel had the best qualifications: a two year degree from a business school in Richmond, three years experience as bookkeeper for a furniture store there, excellent references, a polite and professional manner, and, because of her recent marriage and move back to Crutchfield County, the need for local employment and a consequent willingness to work for the modest salary Fergus offered.

Over the next four decades Fergus and Muriel shared a cramped office and a productive working relationship. Their interaction away from the shop was limited. Each made visits to the other's home on special occasions, and each felt equally uncomfortable.

Muriel not only applied her financial skills to keeping McKendrick and Sons' books in perfect order but she applied the same discipline to her personal finances. She and her husband Ben saw all four of their children graduate from college. Two of them went on to earn advanced degrees. All four got well away from Crutchfield County.

As a widow living alone Muriel's attentions became even more focused on the AME Church of Paradise Gap. She was stuffing prayer cards into the programs for Sunday's service when Ryman called.

"Muriel, I'm sorry to bother you at home, but I figured you'd want to know right away. My father's had a heart attack. His chances don't look very good."

"Oh, my dear Lord."

"Me and Bar are at the hospital now. He collapsed at the shop shortly after you left. The paramedics got there quick as they could, tried their best. But they didn't sound too encouraging."

"Sweet Jesus. Mister Ryman, I'll start praying for your father right now. And I'll get the church prayer chain started. There's wonder-working power in prayer. Yes there is."

“Oh, yeah, of course. Well, I appreciate that. I’m sure it will help a lot.”

“Mister Ryman, you let me know what else I can do. How’s your dear mama holding up? Does she need anyone to come sit and pray with her?”

“Ma? Ah... no... I reckon Ma will be fine. Mister Billington’s bringing her to the hospital now. I’ll buzz you back when I have more to report. Meanwhile, y’all get that prayer thing going.”

“I’m already calling on the Lord to sustain you and your dear mama. And asking that He be merciful to your daddy.”

“Right. Thanks.”

Chapter 9

RYMAN MCKENDRICK WAS in his teens when a large, badly scarred, rough looking character with one hauntingly pale blue eye showed up at Fair Enough Farm. The man told Fergus and his wife Rhetta that he'd served in Vietnam with their son Teedy, that Teedy had often talked about the family homestead and the farm implement business. He said they'd talked about that the night before the mortar assault wiped out the entire platoon, every man killed except Barstow Reinhardt.

Bar said he'd been drifting around since the war, kind of lost. He found himself in Virginia, thought he'd stop by and pay his respects. And, by the way, he was looking for work and was pretty handy when it came to fixing mechanical things.

Fergus could not turn away a brother Marine and, yes, maybe he could use some help at the shop, part-time anyway. And no one was using the old hunter's trailer back in the woods if he needed a place to stay until he found something suitable.

Ryman's mother did not hear these offers. She'd gone into a shaking fit, turned deathly ashen, and retreated upstairs to her bedroom the moment Bar mentioned Teedy and Vietnam in the same sentence. She had a few comments to make to Fergus later, although by then the deal had been struck and Fergus McKendrick would never go back on his word. Certainly not to a fellow Marine, and a wounded vet at that.

Four decades later Barstow Reinhardt had worked his way up from part-time assistant to head mechanic at McKendrick and Sons, he still lived in the old hunter's trailer, and Rhetta still made every possible effort to avoid the sight of him. No one dared even mention his name in her presence.

The half dozen people in the hospital's emergency department waiting room, however, could not help but notice the sight of Bar Reinhardt as he and Ryman were ushered in by a patient aid volunteer, an elderly woman in a blue smock. Bar's bulk flowed over the chair he settled into. The others waiting for news of their loved ones and friends could not decide whether to stare at his bare upper torso, only partially covered by the soiled once-white bib overalls, or the monstrous scar slashing through the left side of his face. Averting their eyes did not lessen the force of his presence as the air in the small windowless room was instantly overpowered by the scent of diesel fuel, hydraulic fluid, industrial hand cleaner, and workman's sweat. There was an incongruity to Bar's presence in a hospital waiting room, that whoever was in the ER was more likely his victim than his loved one.

Nobody took much notice of Ryman, the man with the sad green eyes who slouched into the chair next to the deformed, smelly giant. He was what you would expect to see in such a place; lean, sharp-featured, tanned, his short brown hair touched with gray and matted from the tractor cap he'd just removed, his chin bristly with three-day-old stubble. Ryman's polo shirt, jeans, and paddock boots identified him as more horseman than farmer, only a slight distinction in the community. He'd likely been in this waiting room a few times before as the result of someone's unpleasant encounter with a horse or piece of farm machinery. And while his scars were not as visible as Bar's, it was a good bet he'd been the patient himself more than once.

A woman hushed her young son, avoiding the uncomfortable if honest question the child asked about the scary looking man. "Let's take a walk," she said brightly, as she arose and led the child down the hallway.

Anticipating the outcome of their reason for being there, Ryman said, "What's taking them so long? The old man's dead. You know he's dead, right?"

"Looked dead to me," Bar replied. "And I've seen a good bit of dead."

Hearing this, a middle-aged man also arose and decided a walk would be a good idea.

"Something just occurred to me," Ryman said.

"Whazzat?"

"You were with my brother when he died, and now you were with my father when he died."

"Reckon I'm bad luck for you McKendrick men. You'd best watch yourself around me."

Ryman noticed one of the few remaining people in the room, a young man also dressed in farmer/country/workman attire. Unfazed by Bar's presence, he took a long swig from a bottle of Mountain Dew.

"I sure could use a drink," Ryman said.

"When couldn't you?" Bar replied.

"Did you know 'Glenfiddich' means 'Valley of the Deer?'"

"You don't say?" Bar looked at Ryman, surprised by this unexpected remark.

Ryman's gaze drifted off to the opposite wall, settling on a spot just above the Mountain Dew-swilling fellow's head. "It's a stag on the label.

'Valley of the Deer.' That stag this morning could have sent me to the Valley of Death. It was almost like he was *trying* to knock me off the horse. Then he just stood there looking back at me. That mouth. That must have been the mouth! That sumbitch was talking to me."

"Probably sayin' what a fuckin' idiot you are."

Ryman continued musing to himself, as if Bar wasn't there. "I couldn't hear anything. No words, not even a sound. Just saw those lips moving. But not human lips. The deer's lips! What was he trying to tell me?"

"How about that your old man was gonna kick the bucket in a few hours and you were gonna be left with a business that's about to go into the shitter."

"And that thing between his antlers. What was that? It was so bright, the sun shining on it. Too much glare to make it out." He looked at Bar, his eyes wide with conviction. "You wouldn't believe it. Biggest damn rack I've seen in years. Had to be at least twelve points, maybe fourteen. You'd have thought we'd seen a buck like that before, not just show up out of nowhere. You ever seen one with a rack that big around here?"

"A fourteen pointer? You sure?"

"Well, maybe. At least twelve, though."

"I mighta seen one that big maybe twenty years ago or so. Frank Worsham bagged a fourteen pointer in... lemme see... '89 maybe."

"Right, exactly. And nobody knows the deer herds in Crutchfield County like you do. So if you've never seen him and I've never seen him, where the hell did he come from?"

"Maybe from some fuzzy corner of your scrambled brain. Sounds like you got a pretty good bonk on the head this morning."

"No, I'm sure I saw him. And then again driving back from Warrenton. Standing up on the hill right in front of me after the Mac Tools guy damn near hit me head on."

"You didn't mention that."

"Yeah, well, things got a little hectic around the shop this afternoon, didn't they?"

Bar let this remark pass and sat in quiet reflection. "Ain't gonna be the same without old Fergus around," he said.

"You're telling me?"

"Well, it ain't like he was in the prime a life. Christ sakes, Ry, the man was eighty-five. He had to go sometime. Y'all did set up some kinda plan, right? Make a smooth transition from him to you? The old man had some life insurance, right?"

"I'm not sure about all the details."

"You're not sure." There was a note of disdain in Bar's voice.

"That wasn't my area."

"No, your area's been mostly spending more time with horses and hounds than you did at the shop, being the big time master of the hunt. Sportin' and boozin' your life away."

"You're sure a big help here at my time of loss. Aren't you supposed to be comforting me, preparing me for the news that's going to come through that door any time now, some ER doc bearing the sad report that the old man is gone, too late, nothing they could do?"

"I ain't the comforting type, you know that. I just tell it like I see it. And I see you needin' to get a grip on what's real. Now more than ever."

Ryman stared across the room again. "Maybe I do need to cut back on the booze."

"They say alcoholism is hereditary."

"Yeah, you get it from having kids."

"Very funny, dumb ass. I never seen your old man take a drop. Everybody around here knew Fergus didn't touch the stuff, nobody ever questioned it. 'Course, for all I know your old lady could be sauced up to her eyeballs every damn day. Maybe you got the gene from her."

"No, Ma doesn't drink either. But Daddy used to, back before you showed up. There's still a liquor cabinet in the living room, where he kept a few bottles for his friends when they came over to the house. Hell, I don't think any of that stuff's been touched in years. When I was a kid, though, I can remember Daddy knocking back the sauce and getting real loud. Then he'd start being really happy one minute, loved everybody, and the next minute he'd go off and want to punch some guy's lights out. Did it a few times too. Back then nobody went to jail for throwing a punch. The sheriff sort of winked at country boys getting into it. Hell, most of the times shit like that happened he was there too, letting the men punch each other and roll around some before he waded in and pulled them apart. But all that changed after Teedy died." Ryman looked down at the floor. "Lots of stuff changed after Teedy died."

The two men sat in silence for several minutes. Ryman was the first to speak again. "I was in the bank the other day and Bob Sensabaugh asked me to step into his office for a private chat. He said if we don't start paying down our line of credit, they may have to call the note on the shop."

"Cain't say I'm surprised. What would your old man have done in that situation?"

"Well, if it was Bing still running the bank, I guess he'd smooth talk him into giving us more time."

"So why didn't you smooth talk Bob into that?"

"'Cause Bob ain't like Bing. And I ain't Fergus McKendrick. I'm just the spare son he got stuck with after the number one son went off with you and got himself blown up."

"Yeah, well, that was a long time ago. We all got scars. Life's gotta go on."

Ryman's cell phone rang. "It's Thumper. Yeah? Okay, ten minutes? Ma's with you? Thanks, I'll let him know. I'm in the ER waiting room. No, no word yet. See ya in a few."

"Reckon I'd best get going then." Bar stood up just as the woman and her son returned. The little boy gazed up at this creature who appeared to have stepped out of a bedtime story about giants, ogres, and trolls. He couldn't decide between fascination and repulsion. "Hey there, little feller," Bar said with what passed for a smile, a thin line of brown teeth revealed by slightly upturned lips, a friendly gleam in his crystal blue eye. The boy leaned hard against his mother's leg. Bar turned back to Ryman. "Wish I could stay to give you that comfort you so badly need. Guess you'll have to get that from the crazy old ba... I mean from your dear old mama. Gimme a call when it's official, just for the hell of it."

"Yeah, sure, I will. Thanks... well, for... you know... everything and all."

Bar smiled down at the little boy again, nodded politely to the mother, and left.

The room seemed suddenly spacious and airy, although Bar's pungent odor lingered. The occupants were all relieved to see him go. All except Ryman.

Relief for him arrived minutes later when a slender woman wearing dusty jeans, paddock boots, and a pink polo shirt with upturned collar dashed into the room. Her long chestnut hair, arranged in a frazzled French braid, trailed behind her. Ryman jumped up to accept Nardell's embrace.

"Oh, honey," Nardell said, "I'm so sorry. Any more news?"

"Still waiting. But from the looks of things, I don't think there's much hope."

"Oh, there is hope. You have to believe that."

"I dunno. He looked pretty bad lying there in that pile of tires. And the way the paramedics were working on him... "

"I don't mean like that. I mean that Fergus is progressing to his next level. If he has passed on from this life, he's resting in Summerland now, preparing for the next. He led a good life here, he grew in wisdom and good works. That will be a great help to him in the... "

"Yeah, okay, whatever." He motioned for Nardell to sit. As she did, her polo shirt fell open enough to reveal part of her new Wicca tattoo. The little boy caught sight of it, as did the Mountain Dew-swiller. The little boy wondered why the lady had painted this picture on herself. The young man thought this wasn't a bad looking woman for her age. He'd happily grab hold of that tattooed tit and enjoy the ride any day.

His reverie was interrupted when Thumper entered the room, accompanied by Ryman's mother. At eighty-one Henrietta "Rhetta" Keane McKendrick retained enough evidence of her youthful beauty to confirm the stories that sixty-some years ago she had been the most sought after catch in Crutchfield County. Her green eyes, identical to Ryman's, were bright and alert, able to hold the viewer in their mesmeric spell no less as an octogenarian then when a dozen bucks had eagerly courted the feisty young beauty. She did not believe in cosmetic subterfuge, never had either the patience or the need for it. Her hair was now gray and close-cropped; she cut it herself. Wrinkles, yes, there were wrinkles, but a good twenty years behind the curve where most women would have been at her age.

She marched into the waiting room, erect and in charge. "Well?" she demanded of Ryman. "Is he dead or not?"

Ryman jumped up at his mother's entrance. "I'm pretty sure so, Ma."

"Pretty sure? Is that all you got? Pretty sure? Who's in charge around here?"

Ryman's roommates all sat staring at the demanding old woman barking questions. The little boy assumed he was now in the next chapter of the fairy tale, the one where the wicked witch/stepmother/evil queen makes her appearance. Except those characters do not wear blue jeans and white blouses with embroidered flowers. At least the giant dressed for his part.

Thumper interceded on Ryman's behalf. "I'm sure someone will be here as soon as there's something to report. There are procedures that have to be followed... "

"Fine," Rhetta snapped. "Bad enough y'all didn't think I could drive here myself, like I'm some decrepit old lady. If it weren't for my po-lite nature, I'd a kicked Thumper down the front steps when he was trying to manhandle me into his damn car. Well, y'all can wait here like a bunch a lumps. I'm gonna go find someone who can tell us what's goin' on."

She turned and started back out the door, almost knocking over the young woman coming the other way. The woman was wearing ER scrubs.

"Excuse me," she said, deftly dodging Rhetta's assault. "I'm looking for the McKendrick family."

"That's us," Rhetta said. "I'm Mrs. McKendrick."

"I'm Doctor Chua. Would you care to sit down, Mrs. McKendrick?"

"I can stand," she replied.

The doctor looked at Ryman. He nodded. She took a breath and said, "I'm sorry, we did everything we could... "

Chapter 10

THE MCKENDRICK FARMHOUSE, a sprawling two storey wooden frame building, sat nestled on a low rise along the eastern base of the Blue Ridge Mountains. Although substantial by most standards, the acreage of Fair Enough Farm was barely a fourth of the Montfair property. Located about five miles outside the village, it was still a working farm but those doing the farming were no longer McKendricks. Contractors leased parcels of arable land throughout the area. They had the specialized equipment and access to the crop and livestock markets to make for a profitable venture. Most years anyway.

An old wooden barn, sorely in need of a fresh coat of paint, housed five horses: Ryman's two Thoroughbreds (including the newly arrived youngster Colby), Fergus's two Thoroughbred/Percheron crosses, and Nardell's feisty little Arab/Quarter Horse cross, the sole mare of the herd. Several other outbuildings were in varying states of disuse and decay. A small stone cottage located at the base of the rise below the main house served as home for Ryman McKendrick, Nardell Raithby, and an old retired hound named Wycroft, whose blood ran strong through some of the best hunters in the current Montfair pack, the highly praised W line.

The interior décor of the main house represented "country" in the genuine sense, not the imagination of a city-raised designer with a vision of what "country" should be. "Country" in Crutchfield County meant old, battered, stained, wobbly, and mismatched. Any given piece of furniture had likely been around so long no one could recall its exact provenance. "Redecorating" was a foreign concept. Rooms were furnished over time not so much by intent as by accumulation.

One item that stood out among the clutter was an eight-by-ten color photo in an ornate antique gold frame. It showed a man in his Marine dress blues, a slew of medals on his chest. Every eligible young fellow in Crutchfield County spent two years fervently praying that Fergus McKendrick would not come back alive from Korea, leaving Rhetta a widow in need of a man to care for her. Their hopes were crushed when the big man returned and took up family life with his beautiful bride and young son, Tavish Dougal (always referred to by his initials, hence

"Teedy"). Soon thereafter a second son, Ryman Hamish, arrived.

Rhetta and Thumper entered the living room to find the first wave of mourners already assembled: Crispie O'Rourke and Patti Vestor; Mildred Preston, Montfair Hunt's third and most junior joint-master, and her husband Doctor Josh Preston; club secretary Marva Henderson; Muriel Hudkins (looking extremely prim, proper, and uncomfortable); and The Reverend Doctor Daniel T. Davenport, pastor (or "vicar" as he preferred to be called) of St. Cuthbert's-in-the-Woods Episcopal Church.

Rhetta found herself assaulted by a barrage of hugs and expressions of condolence. She accepted the gestures stiffly, a reaction not unnoticed by the assembled grievers who took the cue to allow her space.

Patti, Mildred, Marva, and Muriel had brought snacks. Light munching and awkward conversation filled the time until Ryman and Nardell arrived, their delay caused by the need for her to drive him back to the shop to retrieve his truck. While there, he made up a handwritten sign and hung it on the shop's front door: "Closed Due to Death in the Family. Will reopen for business soon."

Once they were settled in, Thumper called for everyone's attention. "I'm sorry to have to trouble you all with this, especially you, Mrs. M., but we need to decide on our plans for tomorrow. Thanks to Marva's diligent work the word has already gotten out to the hunt members and," he glanced over at Reverend Dan, "apparently to the community at large. I'm sure everyone's wondering if we're still going to hunt in the morning. We need to make that decision now, get out an email, and update the message on the phone monitor. Crispie and I have already discussed our thoughts, but we need to hear from you, Rhetta. Whatever you're comfortable with, that's what we'll do. Everyone agree?"

All heads nodded.

Rhetta looked at those before her, one by one, her face stern, her eyes steady. "Y'all want to hunt? Go ahead and hunt. Makes no difference to me." She turned to Thumper and added, "I have to use the ladies' room. May I be excused?"

"Of course." When she was gone, Thumper turned to Ryman. "Sweet as ever, Ry. And we were afraid your father's death might cause her to go to pieces."

Ryman tried to avoid eye contact with anyone else. He looked out the window and said, "Not much daylight left. I've got to squirt some ointment in Token's eye. He got himself a scratch the other day. I'll be right back."

"Real quick before you do that," Thumper said, "what are your thoughts about hunting tomorrow? You've got as much say in this as anyone. Certainly as much as her." He jerked a thumb in the direction of the hallway down which Rhetta had gone.

There was a murmur of agreement among the others.

"Ah, gee, I guess... lemme think." He paused for a moment, sorting through the pros and cons in his still-rattled brain. Then a memory floated to the surface. "It was during hunt season when the news about Teedy arrived. Damn, now that I think about it, it was the day before Blessing of the Hounds. You remember that, Thumper?" Billington nodded. "Daddy never flinched. He said his son had done a Marine's duty and paid a Marine's price. He'd died to keep us free and we should honor his sacrifice by exercising that freedom. I wasn't sure what my brother dying was keeping us free from. Still ain't, really. Anyway, my old man and yours went on ahead with the Blessing and the day's hunt." He looked down the hall. "Ma wasn't too pleased about that. Ain't been too pleased about much since."

He glanced out the window again. "I'm losing daylight. Gotta get that horse's eye doctored."

Nardell jumped up. "I can do it, sweetheart. Just tell me where you left the ointment."

"No, that's okay, darlin'. Easier for me to do it. I reckon the question is what would my old man want? Well, he did a tractor salesman's duty and paid a tractor salesman's price. He died to keep our fields bush-hogged and our crops harvested. We should honor his sacrifice by riding our horses over those fields tomorrow. I say we go hunting."

Chapter 11

RYMAN WENT OUT the back door and toward the barn. Along the way he was joined by the old hound Wycroft.

"Hey, Wy. Coming along with Ry? You and me buddy, Wy and Ry."

He could swear the hound was smiling at him, understanding the word play.

A tube of medication in one hand and a lead-line in the other, Ryman headed for the pasture. He found Token grazing at ease. (As a colt, the horse had been the only dark bay in a field of adult grays.) Between the horse's accepting nature and Ryman's skill at treating equine ailments and injuries, the eye ointment was applied in seconds.

The job done, Ryman stood with the horse and hound, gazing up at the western sky, enraptured by the sunset. A fringe of pink glowed along the mountaintops and faded into a dark scarlet above as the last flickers of light played in the clouds. After fifty-six years of watching sunsets from Fair Enough Farm, Ryman still appreciated the splendor of an evening like this. He'd seen a few sunsets from an urban vantage point and they were all a pale imitation of what a ripping good one looked like in the country, absent the weakening influence of city light pollution.

Ryman recalled that his father always enjoyed a good sunset. But Fergus McKendrick would never see another one. The sense of loss flooded over Ryman and he felt terribly alone. It was obvious from an early age that his brother would be the one to fulfill their father's expectations, that Teedy would carry the family name and honor forward. Teedy embraced that role eagerly, which left Ryman free to go his own pleasure-seeking way, avoiding responsibility whenever possible, accepting the role of spare son and frivolous little brother.

Teedy's unexpected decision to quit college, forego his student deferment, and join the Marines surprised everyone, no one more than Rhetta who did her best to dissuade him. Fergus, although opposed to the move at first, came to accept it as his son's patriotic duty. Proud of his own service, Fergus could hardly forbid his son from following him into the Corps. But it was the Vietnam conflict that escalated the situation from a philosophical debate over the merits of military service to the stark reality that this could be a life-or-death decision.

The mortar shell explosion that took Teedy's life, and Barstow Reinhardt's eye and ear, sent a rippling tide of consequences from a nameless rice paddy all the way back to Paradise Gap. Much changed after that. But some things remained the same. Ryman was too set in his ways, his outlook on life too ingrained, for him to step into Teedy's now vacant role. And no one else questioned that. Parents, family, and friends all accepted the fact that the real son was gone, only the spare, frivolous son remained.

Ryman turned around toward the eastern horizon. A string of headlights gleamed along Montfair Lane. Vehicles turned into Fair Enough Farm, drivers parked anywhere they could around the house. The county was turning out in force to express their condolences.

"Well, I reckon I'm the boss of McKendrick and Sons now," Ryman said aloud. He looked down at Wycroft. "And the farm too. Ain't that a bitch." The hound took a step and leaned his head against Ryman's leg. "A major bitch for me anyway." He reached down and scratched Wycroft behind the ears. The hound leaned in harder. "Shop's seriously in the red. The farm's getting by, but it's not producing like it used to. A good year is breaking even. Looks like I'm going to have to get serious about some things, old guy. No easy retirement for me, like you got. Hell, I might even have to step up, be a man, and make Nardell an honest woman." He gave the hound one more hard scratch. "Nah, I ain't going that far."

An image formed in Ryman's imagination, a bowl of some sort. He felt Wycroft's doleful brown eyes staring up at him. "Damn, you haven't been fed yet, way past your chow time. Sorry, old guy, guess we'd better get... "

There was a whirl of motion behind him. Something rock hard struck him on the side of his head and he felt himself tumbling over. He saw Token's legs brush past him, felt the whoosh of fast-moving hooves as they missed his falling body by a fraction of an inch. He landed on the hard earth of the pasture, a dusty patch of ground after the long summer drought. He came to a stop lying on his stomach, covered with red clay dust, a pounding pain just above his temple where Token's boney head had hit him. The horse had spooked to one side, the hound to the other. Both had now stopped and faced toward the same spot, looking at something on the other side of the pasture.

Ryman lifted his head and found himself staring at the buck. The deer was in the pasture with them. His entrance in the dimming twilight had startled the horse. Ryman dared not move. Although the light was fading, he could still see well enough to get a good look at this animal. He quickly counted the points. Yes, a fourteen-pointer. The object between its antlers was gleaming white. He could make out a vertical shaft with what appeared to be a circle near the top. It was not attached to the antlers in any way Ryman could see. It seemed to be suspended in the air, as if floating above the deer's head.

What was it that seemed so familiar about that image?

"Who are you?" Ryman whispered. "What do you want?"

This was mostly to himself. He did not expect an answer. But the deer's mouth moved, as if in response. Did he hear something? A muffled noise, like "hhhbbtt"? He glanced over at Wycroft to his left, then at Token on his right. Both hound and horse continued to stand motionless, eyes fixed on this strange apparition. Had that sound come from one of them? Token snuffling maybe? No, it seemed to come from the direction where the deer stood. "Hhhbbbuutt." Louder this time, and clearly from the deer.

From his left came another sound, with a questioning lilt, "Hhhnnnt?" Wycroft stood at attention, stern aloft, his eyes bright and focused on the deer. "Rrrrnnn?"

Ryman's head began to throb. He wanted to lift his hand and rub the spot where Token had struck him but was afraid the motion would scare off the deer. The mouth moved again. "Hhhbbbbuuuttt."

To his left again came, "Rrrrnnnn?" and Wycroft start to move a foot forward.

"No," Ryman whispered to the hound. "Leave it."

Wycroft relaxed, no longer ready to launch himself at the deer. But he did not break his stare off this tempting quarry.

Token, accustomed to sharing his turf with other harmless herbivores, became comfortable with the deer's presence and went back to grazing. The movement of the horse's head down toward the ground broke the stand-off. The deer looked away from Ryman and toward the horse. When he did, Wycroft shot forward, baying in full cry and off to the chase. The deer was away in two leaps, over the pasture fence and into the dark woods.

Ryman leapt to his feet. "No! Leave it! Wycroft, leave it!"

The hound stopped.

"Wycroft, come," Ryman ordered and the hound returned to his master. "You know better than to run deer. Especially that deer."

"Hhhhnnnttt?"

The hound's mouth did not move, and Ryman could not be sure if this was an audible sound or only something he heard in his aching head. But he was sure he heard something. Did it come from Wycroft? No, he told himself. Too weird.

"Hhhhnnnntttt?" More insistent this time.

Now an image formed in Ryman's imagination. Hounds running. He was among them, part of the pack. He recognized the terrain, their own hunting country. He even recognized some of the hounds around him, but every one of them was either dead or retired, like Wycroft. Now he saw Wycroft and the others as they were in their hunting prime, running hard, joyfully in pursuit of their prey.

Chapter 12

THE MORNING MEETING with Danella Kernan churned in Janey Musgrove's mind throughout the day as she taught her comparative religion classes at George Mason University. She arrived home in the early evening and walked from her car with a few plastic sacks of groceries she'd picked up for the long, lonely weekend. In the courtyard formed by four apartment buildings, two teams of Pakistanis were engaged in a spirited cricket match. Janey had to skirt around the edge to avoid interfering with the action.

From the open windows of the apartments she passed came a symphony of scents as residents prepared their evening meals: Chinese five spice, North African harissa, Indian curry, Guatemalan cardamom.

She heard an equally varied array of languages: Spanish, Hindi, Farsi, Mandarin, Arabic.

For most of Janey's neighbors in Fairfax County, Labor Day weekend had little meaning other than that schools were closed on Monday and many people did not have to go to work that day. Their holidays followed different calendars—spiritual observances unfamiliar to Christian culture and historical events of importance to nations other than the United States.

Though still technically in her native country, Janey was a world away from her hometown in Chippewa County, Minnesota. The loneliness began to overwhelm her and the grocery bags felt like concrete blocks in her tired arms. She had traveled to several exotic locales around the world to study minority religions, from the Pacific South Sea Islands where Prince Philip reigns as a god, to the Kalahari Desert where the San Bushmen have practiced the mystical beliefs tied to their hunter/gatherer lifestyle for millennia.

But these had always been observation expeditions, a few weeks to study the native culture, interview the locals, experience the unique flavor of the area, and attempt to grasp what they believed and why they believed it. Then it was back to the States and a resumption of her academic pursuits in her own environment.

Now she felt that she was the one being observed, that hundreds of people from distant parts of the world had traveled to Northern Virginia to see what her life was like. Only they weren't going back home. They were here to stay. They looked upon *her* unquestioned customs and beliefs with speculation and amusement. "Labor Day?" If it's a day for labor, why is everyone not working? Whose labor are you celebrating? The more she thought about this, the more she questioned her own acceptance of this holiday. She wondered how many Americans, born and raised in the US, knew anything more than that it meant schools were closed and most people did not go to work, just like the Pakistani cricketers, looking forward to a day off on Monday with no idea why.

After trudging up to her third floor flat, she dumped the groceries on the kitchen counter and gazed out the window at what to her was a foreign sporting match being held in her own front yard. It had been the blandness of Chippewa County that inspired her to specialize in fringe religions, to study people whose beliefs and values were so strikingly different from what she considered "normal." In Clara City, where she grew up, everyone she knew was white and most were Lutheran. The main extent of diversity was whether someone's ancestors were Norwegian, German, or English. No one there questioned the point of Labor Day, nor did anyone ever wonder how it came to be. The phrase "Pullman Strike" might spark a faint glimmer of recognition among the most erudite of the populace. But few, if any, could have explained the connection between the labor unrest of the 1880s and the three-day weekend the entire United States now observed.

Yet the holiday had become firmly entrenched in American culture, signifying the end of summer (pointless to those who measure the seasons by southern hemisphere cycles), the start of a new school year (relevant only because it had once been necessary for children to work on the family farm all summer), the kick-off of the professional and collegiate football season (a misnomer to those who considered "futbol" a game in which one actually manipulates the ball with one's foot). To ladies of Janey's mother's generation, it meant the last day of the year when it was socially acceptable to wear white.

It occurred to Janey that Labor Day in the US meant no more to the cricketers than Pakistan's Labour Day meant to her. Neither had a religious connotation. Yet they both provided an element of cultural cohesion, requiring only that the celebrants corporately agreed that it was a holiday worthy of their observation.

Was there a potential premise there? Rather than trying to milk fringe religions for a third book, perhaps a study of secular holidays around the world, what events inspired their inception, what gap had grown between the original impetus for the observation and the unrelated practices that had been adopted (such as celebrating the strength of the national workforce by doing no work)?

She heard shouts of exultation from some of the cricketers outside. She had no idea what they were saying, but the tone and fervor suggested something along the lines of "God is on our side!"

Chapter 13

RYMAN STUMBLED INTO the living room, his shirt and jeans stained with dirt, his cap cocked to one side. The number of people in the house had increased fourfold. The crowd filled the living room and spilled out into the front hallway.

"What the hell happened to you, boy?" Rhetta asked.

"Damnedest thing," Ryman muttered. "Too weird. Too fucking weird. One strange fucking day."

Muriel stiffened.

"You watch your damn language in this house, boy," Rhetta ordered.

Nardell hastened to Ryman's side. "Are you okay, sweetheart?"

"Huh? Oh, yeah, sure, sure. Just fine. Just... damn, it's all too weird. I need a drink."

"Don't look like he needs a drink to me," Rhetta observed. "Likely he's got some 'shine stashed out there somewhere, drank a few pops to his old man's memory, and fell down the hill. Damn fool. Patti, come help me get them sandwiches ready. We got more people to feed." Patti obeyed and followed Rhetta to the kitchen.

Ryman pushed Nardell aside and teetered toward the liquor cabinet.

"Thumper, Crispie!" Nardell said, aghast at the welt on the side of Ryman's head. "He's been hurt. Do something."

Thumper moved to block Ryman's path. "Ry, what happened?"

"Screw this cheap-ass Bowman's crap," Ryman said. He reached around Thumper and started searching through the dust-covered liquor bottles. "Where's the good stuff? I know the old man kept some top shelf scotch in here for his special friends. Ah, here it is," he said, lifting the chosen bottle. He filled a glass and took a sip.

"Ryman," Thumper said again, firmly this time, "tell us what happened. Are you okay?"

"Weird, Thumper. Fucking weird. I need a few minutes."

"Sure, sure." Thumper nodded toward Crispie who came to Ryman's other side.

"Maybe ya'd best sit down, Master. Here, let me help ya," Crispie said as he grasped Ryman's forearm.

Ryman looked down at Crispie's hand and jumped as if a live wire had touched him. "Holy shit!" He dropped his glass and it shattered into pieces. Scotch splashed across the rug.

Ryman grabbed Crispie's hand. "What's that?" he demanded, pointing to a large ring on Crispie's finger, an ornament Ryman had never seen before.

"It's... it's something me sister sent me," the startled Irishman replied. "She said it would help keep me from forgettin' the Old Sod now that I'm fully American."

Ryman held Crispie's hand up and stared closely at the ring. A large silver base supported an oblong black stone on which was set an ornate white cross with a decorative circle at the intersection. "The design. What's this design?"

"It's the Celtic Cross," Crispie replied, surprised at the strength of Ryman's grip, the intensity of his gaze, and the urgency of his question. "Supposed to be a symbol of Ireland, or the Catholic church in Ireland, or some such thing. I'm not sure exactly."

Ryman continued to stare at the ring, turning Crispie's unwilling hand at different angles. "That's it! That's fucking it!"

Thumper reached over and put his hand on Ryman's. The distraction allowed Crispie to jerk his hand free. "What is it, Ry?" he asked gently.

"The buck! That's what's between the buck's antlers. I knew I'd seen it somewhere, but I couldn't get a good enough look at it. But now I know. It's a goddamn Celtic Cross, or something like that. A cross anyway, hanging right between his rack. Like the one on the Saint Hubert medal. Son-of-a-bitch. What do you think that means, Thumper?"

"I don't know, Ry." He adopted a calm, non-threatening tone, as if he were a shrink trying to talk down a distraught patient. "What do *you* think it means?"

"Damned if I know. But that sumbitch has been following me all day. Flipped me off a horse this morning. Then he's there along the side of the road when I almost got smashed by the Mac Tools truck. Like he knew I was coming. Then my old man drops dead. And now this. Talking. He was talking. Wycroft too. Not real words. But sounds. And then... like I was a hound, like I was Wycroft. Running with the pack. This is too fucking weird, Thumper."

"Ry, you're under a lot of stress." He motioned toward Josh Preston and gently led Ryman toward a large stuffed chair. "And it looks like you've had another blow to your head. Two in one day, not good. Here, sit down, rest a bit. Let Josh have a look at you."

"My drink... I spilled... "

"S'okay. I'll get you another one in a minute."

Josh Preston, a family practice physician, began to give Ryman a thorough going-over.

Rhetta returned carrying a tray of food. Patti trailed behind with another. Nardell and Marva were on the floor collecting the broken bits of glass and trying to soak the scotch up from the rug with paper napkins.

"What the hell happened here?" Rhetta asked.

Nardell looked up. "Oh, just an accident. Someone dropped a drink."

"That someone wouldn't be my clumsy fool of a son, would it?"

"He's hurt. He's not himself," Nardell said.

"Yeah, right." She held out the tray to those standing around her. "Sandwich anyone?"

Chapter 14

A GROUP OF dedicated foxchasers showed up the next morning for the seven o'clock meet at the Montfair Hunt kennels. Two-dozen followers left their homes in the predawn hours—virtually the middle of the night to some—to arrive as early as six thirty for final preparation and to assure they were not tardy.

A gauzy mist hung over the fields, lying heaviest in the low areas, blurring the sunrise into a diffuse glow. The insistence of the sun, though, would soon dispel every visible trace of vapor and temperatures would rise quickly under a bright summer sky. The horse flies were already starting their search for fresh blood and the scent of strong insect repellent merged with the aroma of mowed grass and oiled leather.

Bing Sensabaugh was among the first to arrive. At the admirable age of eighty, he rarely missed a day of hunting, particularly after he retired and turned the reins of Crutchfield County Bank over to his son Bob. The hunting gene skipped a generation as neither Bob nor his wife Kitty rode to hounds. But Bing had placed his grandchildren, Baden and Beatrice, under the tutelage of Dorcas Stanhope. She pulled in driving Cecelia's massive van, laden with horses for the patroness and her groom and ponies for several eager children.

A few die-hard traditionalists—most notably Bing Sensabaugh—refused to hunt in anything more casual than a hacking jacket with shirt and tie. Most others opted for the comfort of a polo shirt, a nod to practicality on the warmer mornings. Even so, the shirts were expected to be clean and tidy. They could be of any hue except red, the color reserved for staff.

Ryman McKendrick's polo shirt was neither clean nor tidy. The collar was frayed, one button was missing, and it was more wrinkled than a Shar-Pei puppy. It may have been the requisite red once, but had faded to a sickly salmon pink. The condition of his boots and breeches were no better. His eyes were bleary, flecks of sleep crust clung to his lashes.

Nardell caught Thumper's disapproving assessment of her partner's slovenly condition. She rode over to confer with him in private. "I'm sorry, Master. Neither of us slept worth a damn last night. Every time he dozed off he started mumbling crazy stuff like, 'That's it! A cross!' and 'What does it mean? What do you want?' Then he'd wake up, get out of bed and pace around, raving about that deer he claims to have seen. Went on like that all night. It's a miracle either one of us is here this morning. Maybe the decision to hunt today wasn't such a good idea."

"Well, too late now," Thumper said. "Can't disappoint these folks who've made such an effort to be here. But if you want to take him home and skip it, that's okay. We'll go on without you. Dorcas has brought some of her best students. They could help whip-in."

"No," she said, "Ryman and I will hunt. I doubt I could get him to go home anyway. But I'm worried sick about him. He's not thinking clearly, no telling what he might do. And the last thing he needs is another blow to his head. I just hope it's a short morning, without much action." Her face, pale from the night's disruptions, flushed and she tried to correct herself. "Oh! I shouldn't say that. Never wish for a bad hunting day, right? Sorry, Master."

"That's okay. Under the circumstances, I can't say I'm not of the same mind. May my ancestors forgive me."

Nardell moved off to help Crispie and Patti keep hounds packed up as Thumper rode over to a very distracted-looking Ryman McKendrick. Mildred Preston joined them for the pre-hunt confab.

Crispie sat mounted at the center of the pack, twenty-nine well-trained foxhounds obediently gathered around his horse, looking up expectantly at their leader, awaiting his signal. Patti flanked the pack on Crispie's right, Nardell took her position on the left. Ryman's job was to follow along as drag whip when the pack moved off.

"Scent's likely to be best down below," Thumper said. "Let's cast into the covert at Gretchen's Bottom."

"There's no fox in Gretchen's Bottom this morning, Thumper," Ryman replied with matter-of-fact confidence.

"Sure of that are you, Ry?"

"Sure as my old man's lying on a slab."

"A rather grim analogy."

"I'm telling you there's a big red, a fine brush with a white tip, just waiting for us on the far side of your eastern stone wall pasture."

"Ry, there's no actual covert there. We've had cattle in that pasture all summer, still a couple dozen head there now. Any scent that might have been there will be badly foiled. And it's right along the road. If, in the unlikely event hounds do strike, there's a good chance the big red you say is there will head north toward the road. Then what?"

"He won't."

"Look, I understand you're still a little fuzzy from yesterday. I mean, two concussions and all you went through, but... "

"Josh said it was likely only one concussion, from that spill in the morning. And not all that bad really. The second was just a bump. And he didn't see anything all that wrong with me. No worse than usual anyway."

"What do you think, Mildred?"

"I agree with you, Thumpah," she replied, her sharp New England twang a striking contrast to the soft Virginia drawl of her companions. "Very unlikely we'll find where Ryman wants to go. Sorry, Ry, but I think Thumpah's right."

"C'mon, give me this one, will you? I've got this... I dunno... this sense about it. Kinda like I could see the fox, or that something's telling me to cast hounds there. What have we got to lose if I'm wrong? A little time? Then if nothing happens, we lift hounds and go to Gretchen's Bottom."

"What do we have to lose, you ask?" Thumper shot back. "Well, like I said, if you're right about the fox and he takes hounds north, we could be chasing the pack across the road and out of our country."

"He won't."

"Yeah, sure. And if you're wrong, we lose time, and that is a consideration. Scent's going to lift quickly once the mist burns off. And where you want to go is the opposite direction from Gretchen's Bottom."

"Look, guys," Ryman said, positioning his horse closer still and lowering his voice, "do this for Fergus. We're supposed to be honoring my old man this morning. This is how I'd like to honor him. Maybe it's him that's telling me to do this."

"And maybe it's minor head trauma," Mildred snapped.

"Damn, Ryman," Thumper said, "playing the Fergus card. That's kinda low."

"I'm really sure about this, Thumper."

"Well, I'm not. Neither is Mildred. I'm afraid you're outvoted, my friend. It's our responsibility as masters to show our followers good sport as best we can. These folks didn't get up at oh-dark-hundred so you could try some harebrained plan because a bump on the head makes you think you're getting messages from some mysterious deer, and now an apparently unseen fox as well, or maybe your late father." He looked over at Crispie. "Mister O'Rourke, we're going to cast in Gretchen's Bottom this morning, as planned."

"Aye, Master. Should be a lively one waiting for us there on this fine marnin'."

Thumper turned back to Ryman. "If hounds don't find there, maybe we'll consider your suggestion for the second draw." He then addressed the group of mounted followers. "Good morning everyone. Welcome to the start of another season of cub hunting. Great to see all these eager faces here so early in the morning. Just one quick thing before we move off. As I'm sure everyone's heard, our long-serving senior master passed away yesterday. So this morning's hunt is in his honor and I'm sure y'all join me in sharing our condolences with Ryman."

A chorus of "Hear, hear" arose from the crowd.

"It's too early to have any details about funeral or memorial services, but we'll let everyone know as soon as that's all pinned down. The sun will be burning off scent soon, so we'd best get to it. I'll be leading the jumping group. Mildred will lead the non-jumpers. Mister O'Rourke, let's go hunting."

Crispie led hounds off to Gretchen's Bottom, a popular hangout for the local foxes and, as the name suggests, a low-lying area along a creek where the ground was likely to be moist, a helpful element for good scenting. Hounds worked hard, eager to find a line and give chase. Crispie encouraged his pack with his lilting, musical calls: "Leu in, me beauties! Leu in! Get 'im up now. Where's 'e at? Where's 'e at? Warwick, me brave lad, get 'im up! Hempstead, leu in the covert now."

Patti, Nardell, and Ryman held their posts, flanking the covert, ready for the action to begin. The field of followers stood a short distance off, watching, listening, and waiting. And waiting. And waiting.

One hound opened with a tentative note. But it was Hempstead, the young entry who tended to babble. Still, though, everyone drew to attention, hoping to hear the rest of the pack join in. Not so much as a whimper was heard to confirm a strike and even Hempstead went silent again.

After fifteen frustrating minutes, with the mist almost completely burned off, the sky now clear and bright, Crispie turned to Thumper. "Sorry, Master. Doesn't look like Charlie's been here lately. How 'bout we try the Cistern Covert?"

Ryman cantered in from his sentry position. "Thumper, you said if we didn't find here—and I told you we wouldn't—we'd try... "

"I said we'd consider it."

"Look, I was right about Gretchen's Bottom, wasn't I? The field's getting impatient. And, like you said, it's our job to show good sport. I *know* that big red is still... "

Thumper cut him off. "Crispie, let's draw to my eastern stone wall pasture."

"I'm sorry, Master?"

"You heard me. Lift your pack and let's get to it. Of course, if hounds happen to strike a line on the way there, we'll go with it."

Ryman did not catch the quick wink Thumper gave the huntsman.

"Aye, Master." Crispie blew the pack in to him and moved off toward the east.

"It's the right call," Ryman said as he turned to resume his position as drag whip.

"It's also a long hack from here to there," Thumper replied. "If hounds hit along the way, your big red will just have to wait."

Not one hound threatened to open on the march from Gretchen's Bottom to Billington's eastern stone wall pasture. A confused group of followers mumbled and sweated as they hacked along past half a dozen well-known coverts (from the French "couvert" and pronounced "cover" by English-speaking foxhunters).

No one who knew a smidgeon about foxhunting would cast hounds where they were headed. An open field, mostly flat, it held three-dozen head of cattle. Their droppings coated the ground with an odiferous foil that would easily mask other scents, including that of a fox. The stone wall enclosing the pasture stood three feet high all around, topped by a stake-and-rider rail fence that added another foot. Montfair Lane ran along the eastern edge, the service road leading to the Montfair barn and outbuildings bordered the south. To the north were woods that offered shade for the cattle and beyond that a wire fence completed the enclosure. There was a gate from the adjoining pasture to the west and next to it an old jump, a twelve-foot wide span where the wall was slightly lower. After years of disuse, several cracks and holes appeared where stone and mortar fell away. A wooden pole rested above the jump, cradled in the vee notches of the timber rails, to dissuade adventurous cows from jumping out.

No one was more surprised than Crispie that his hounds had not roused a fox on the long hack to this unlikely spot. Now he was unsure what to do.

"No need for the field to go in, Thumper," Ryman said. "Charlie's going to get up and head north-northwest."

"How can you be so sure about that, Ry?"

"Beats the hell of me, man. I just... well... something's telling me... crap, I can't explain it. And, yes, I could be wrong. But I haven't been so far. If you're still willing to give this a shot, you and Mildred hold the field right here. Crispie and me'll put hounds in, y'all just wait and get ready to run hard."

"Christ sakes, Ry, this is the damnedest thing I've heard in all my years of foxhunting. But you're just risking looking really stupid so have the hell at it."

Ryman rode forward and dropped the rail from atop the old jump. He told Crispie to bring hounds on and follow him, then jumped the wall and cantered toward the far side of the pasture. Crispie shook his head but did as he was told. Halfway across the field Ryman stopped and turned his horse facing north. Crispie and the pack stopped just behind him.

There, trotting casually out from the sparse woods, directly toward them, was a large fox, sporting a lustrous red coat, black points, and a bright white tip on the brush. Its size suggested it was a male: a dog fox. He stopped when he saw the scene before him, two mounted riders and twenty-nine foxhounds staring at him. Everyone stood motionless for several seconds. The fox was not ruffled by the encounter. Instead, he turned to his right—north-northwest. Ryman couldn't be sure but a split second before the critter took off, he thought he saw the fox wink at him.

The run that followed was, in the estimation of all participants fortunate enough to have been out that September morning, the best opening cub hunt anyone could recall. The big red led them on a twisting, turning chase through the prime part of their hunting country. For nearly a full hour he never threatened to run out of the territory and managed to keep hounds just close enough to hold his scent without putting them at a loss. Mildred and Thumper kept their followers perfectly positioned to follow the action, always within sight of hounds and privileged to have multiple views of Sir Charles himself as he worked his wily way through the rolling fields and woods of the Montfair estate.

Finally deciding he'd given his pursuers enough sport, the fox went to ground in a familiar den in—of all places—Gretchen's Bottom.

Crispie dismounted and blew the wavering call of "Gone to Ground," cheering his hounds and praising them no end for their excellent work. The followers, exhausted but thrilled, joined in the accolades. Flasks were passed around and quickly drained.

As Crispie was drawing hounds away from the hole, a flash of red and white caught everyone's attention. The fox had bolted from the den's backdoor and was away again.

A member of the field shouted "Tally-ho!"

"No!" Ryman commanded. "Leave it. Let him go."

Crispie sprang back onto his horse and looked at Thumper.

"Ryman's right," he said. "We've had enough sport for one morning. Horses and hounds are at their limit. Let him be."

It was a short hack from Gretchen's Bottom back to the kennels. All hounds were on and once safely back in the kennel yard, Ryman and Nardell took their leave for the hack back to Fair Enough Farm.

"Guess we'll be headin' home now," Ryman said. "You'll excuse us if we don't hang around for the tailgate."

"Wait one damn minute," Thumper ordered. He and Mildred rode over and intercepted Ryman before he could go. "What the hell just happened here?"

"Why, we just had a great morning of sport," Ryman said casually. "Isn't that what we're out here for?"

"You know damn well what I mean. How did... how could you have possibly... ?"

"Look, man," Ryman said, his offhand tone turning more serious, "I'm as freaked about this as you are. Shit, I expect I'm freaked a lot more because it's my brain that's all scrambled with this stuff. It's gotta have something to do with that damn deer. But beats the hell out of me why... or how. Maybe it was just a one-time shot. You know, lucky guess."

"Yeah, maybe," Thumper said.

"Ryman," Mildred asked, "could you... like... see the fox in... in your mind... or did you... just how did you know?"

"I wish the hell I could tell you, Mildred. I really do." He looked at his watch. "I gotta go. We're having a staff meeting at the shop. We need to discuss what happens next, now that the old man's gone. Wish I had some visions about that too, instead of just where to find a fox to chase."

Chapter 15

"'SCUSE ME," RYMAN said as he slid behind Nardell in the tack room and reached across her to hang his bridle on the hook above the sink.

She leaned back into him. "Hmmm," she murmured, "is that a hunt whip in your breeches or are you just glad to see me?"

He pressed harder against her. "It does seem I'm... ah... kinda stimulated."

She turned to face him, keeping her body tight against his and wrapping her arms around his waist. An inviting smile brightened her face as she looked up at him. "What time did you say you have to be at the shop for the staff meeting?"

"One o'clock. Plenty of time yet."

"This was an amazing morning. That was really something how you knew where that fox would be, and which way he'd go. Like you could tell what he was thinking."

"Aw, shucks, ma'am. 'Tweren't nothing."

"Can you tell what I'm thinking?"

"I've got a pretty good notion."

"I'm still stoked from that chase."

"Are you now? Well, maybe we need to do something about that?" He slid his hands down to her buttocks and pulled her even more firmly to him. She felt him hard and eager.

"Sure you have time? I don't want you to be late for your meeting."

"Hey, I'm the boss now. What are they gonna do? Fire me?"

"And you're not too tired? You didn't get much sleep last night. And you did some hard riding this morning."

"I feel like I got a good bit of hard riding left in me."

Her smile widened. "I can clean all the tack later."

"Excellent idea. Race you to the sack."

They dashed through the door of Ryman's cottage. Sweat-soaked polo shirts were discarded as they rushed toward the bedroom. Both of them were down to boots and breeches as Nardell flopped onto the bed and lifted her legs. Ryman tore at the laces of her brown field boots, yanked one off and tossed it over his shoulder, then did the same with the other. He wasted no time sliding off her socks, breeches, and panties.

"Now you," Nardell said as she jumped up, turned Ryman around, and pushed him down onto the bed.

Rather than hurrying, she took her time, teasing the laces loose, slowly sliding off his right boot an inch at a time. Ryman's cock was so hard and throbbing by this point that he had to undo his breeches to relieve the pressure. Nardell's eyes popped at the sight of his erection.

"Wow, looks like you did have a hunt whip in there," she said.

His left boot still on and his breeches down around his thighs, he reached up and grabbed her arms. "C'mere, now," he said as he pulled her to him.

She straddled him and he thrust inside her. She leaned back and let out a low moan. "Think you can hold that as long as that fox kept up the chase?"

He took in a breath and let it out slowly. "Seems I may already be about to go to ground."

She moved forward and placed her hands on his chest. "Try to keep... "

His cheeks swelled as if he were about to blow a gasket and his eyes widened. "I... can't... ahhhhhh!"

His orgasm sent her bouncing as if she were sitting atop a green-broke colt. Watching him climax only fanned the flames of her own passion. She closed her eyes as the realization that he would now go limp caused a shudder of disappointment. Maybe she could coax him into being late for his meeting, long enough for him to recover and go at it again. Of course, she could always resort to the vibrator in the nightstand drawer after he left. But it wasn't the same.

She opened her eyes and looked down to see him grinning broadly up at her. He wasn't even starting to retract. His erection remained as insistent as when he'd first entered her.

"Appears this chase ain't over yet," he said as he began to move his hips.

Nardell leaned back again, taking his penis into her as far as it could go. She couldn't remember when he'd been this hard and thick. Every drop of blood in his body must have collected in that one appendage. He was probably so dizzy from the lack of blood flow to his brain that he couldn't even remember he'd already finished. During their courtship it was not uncommon for him to have two or sometimes three orgasms over the course of a few hours of love-making, taking some time to recover between each one. But as routine domesticity set in, the once-is-enough pattern had taken hold. It was still good sex, perhaps better, she thought, than most people their ages were having. But at times she missed the passion and heady pleasures of their courtship days.

Even then, though, she'd never experienced anything like this. It was as if he hadn't climaxed at all, that he could go on like this for however long she wanted until she was fully satisfied.

She threw her head back and met his thrusting with a slow, purposeful undulation. "No... this chase... is not... over. Tally... freakin'... ho... oh... oohhh... ooohh."

Chapter 16

A HEAVY POUNDING on the front door sent Ryman sitting bolt upright in bed. Nardell lay beside him, still sleeping soundly. Another burst of pounding started her stirring.

"Whazzat?" she mumbled.

The cottage door opened and the clumping sound of thick boots echoed off the bare wooden floor.

"C'mon, boss man!" Bar cried out. "Get your ass in gear. Time to rally the troops."

Ryman looked over at the bedside clock. "It's only twelve fifteen," he called back. "Meeting's not till one."

"You don't wanna to be the last one to show up. Makes it look like you don't respect your people. I gotta stop at the General Store on the way, get some pastries. And we gotta get the coffee perking."

Ryman found a pair of jeans among the pile of clothes on the floor and slipped them on. Nardell rolled over and fell back into a deep sleep as he softly closed the bedroom door and stepped into the living room.

"By the way," Bar said, "while you been napping Sheltie Lou called. She said she's been trying to reach you all morning but you weren't answering your phone and you ain't returned her messages."

"Oh, crap. I always turn the phone off when I'm hunting, must have forgot to turn it back on." He picked up his phone from the end table where he'd tossed it when he and Nardell were racing to the bedroom.

"Yeah, well, since she couldn't raise you, she buzzed me. I told her she hadn't missed much not getting hold a you, that you been acting even crazier than usual."

"Thanks. Always nice to have your support. Especially where my only child is involved."

"Hey, dumb ass, ain't me raving about some damn deer you claim to have seen, thinking the sumbitch is talking to you."

"Guess I'd better call her back before we go," Ryman said, pulling on the same polo shirt he'd worn hunting that morning, now even more wrinkled after lying in a damp heap for a couple of hours.

"You can call her on the way to the shop. She was asking about plans and stuff, if she should drop everything and fly back. I told her there was no need for that, nothing she could do just now. You'd let her know as soon as things are lined up. And are you really gonna wear that shirt?"

"What? Why not?"

"'Cause you're supposed to be the goddamn boss now. You should at least try to look like one. And besides, I can smell it from over here."

"Guess I should present a more professional image, like you."

Bar wore his standard uniform of grease-stained white bib overalls with no shirt. "I ain't the boss man. I'se jist de step-an'-fetch-it tool boy. Now go put on a halfway clean shirt and let's get the fuck outta here."

****

Ryman sat at his father's desk, Bar in the visitor's chair facing him.

"Sit up straight," Bar ordered, "and get your shit together. You are now *the* McKendrick of McKendrick and Sons. You got employees to think about. They need reassurance, need to know what's going on, that this leaky ship we're all sailing on ain't gonna sink and leave 'em stranded."

"Shit, Bar, *I* don't know what the hell's going on. How am I supposed to reassure them? Reassure you? You're an employee too." Ryman rubbed his head. "*You* want reassurance from me?"

"Not me, you dumb fuck. If I needed reassurance from the likes of you, I'd be one sorry ass son-of-a-bitch. It's the other three I'm thinking of. Bad enough the business is going down the shitter. Now your old man, the only thing that was holding it together, is gone. Muriel, Miles, and Conway probably all spent a troubled night wondering what's gonna happen now."

"They ain't the only ones," Ryman mumbled. "What am I gonna tell them?"

"You're gonna tell 'em that everything's gonna be okay. The shop's gonna be closed for a few days, out of respect for Fergus's memory. You're gonna say what an important part of the community McKendrick and Sons has always been, and you're gonna do everything in your power to see that continues to be so. You're gonna thank them for their loyalty and tell them you're gonna do your best to live up to the example your father set for you. You're gonna tell them that funeral arrangements haven't been finalized yet but you'll let 'em know as soon as they are. And then we're all gonna sit around, drink coffee, eat some pastries, and swap stories about your old man. And, Ryman, one more thing."

"What's that?"

"You're not gonna say one damn thing about that fucking deer. You hear me?"

"Yeah, yeah, I hear you."

The others arrived. Muriel took her seat at her desk, Miles and Conway sat in the remaining two visitors' chairs, filling up the small office to capacity.

"I want to first thank y'all for coming," Ryman began. "Sorry to have interrupted your holiday weekend. But... well... I reckon this is... y'all know..."

There were murmurs of agreement and dismissals of any thought of inconvenience, given the circumstances.

"If we all pull together," Ryman continued, "we can get through this." His own words sounded foreign to him, stilted and artificial, a talentless actor reading a hackneyed script. "I know it's a shock to everyone, losing the old man so suddenly. It's going to be tough without him around. But we're all professionals. And we know how important this business is to us all, and to this community."

The only one in the room who looked professional was Muriel Hudkins. Her Saturday attire was no different than her weekday business uniform, only slightly less formal than her Sunday church dress. Muriel never wore slacks, only skirts and dresses, with hems no higher than mid-calf. She wore starched long sleeve blouses with the collar secured and only modest jewelry, the most prominent piece of which was a simple gold cross hanging from a delicate chain around her neck. Her hair was always perfectly trimmed. She made no attempt to hide the gray and now, at sixty-seven years old, there was only a hint of the original black left.

Bar, Miles, and Conway showed no trace of a professional bone between the three of them. The only addition to Bar's attire since the day before was a sweat-stained, oil-streaked John Deere tractor cap that had once been a bright green but was now sun-bleached to a limey pastel. Miles and Bar also wore essentially the same garb as before, having only changed their shirts; Miles to a baby blue polo embroidered with "Delaney Racing Stables" on the left breast, Conway to a black tee shirt with a white skull and cross bones set above the printed slogan "Work Is For People Who Don't Know How To Plunder." Miles had brought in a brown paper bag and set it down on the floor beside his chair.

Everyone sat in uncomfortable silence for a long, tedious moment. The troops weren't getting the reassurance Bar felt they needed. Before he could embellish on what Ryman had so inarticulately tried to say, Miles spoke up.

"Community my ass. Wouldn't matter a good goddamn to anyone else in Crutchfield County if this place closed up."

Muriel flinched at Miles's misuse of the Lord's name.

"Well, maybe you're right about that," Ryman said. "But would it matter to you?"

Miles thought about that for a few seconds. "Yeah, well, I guess so. I mean, it's not like I'm getting lots of hours making deliveries, am I? Or up to my ass in customers at the parts counter. But I ain't earning enough off exercise rides to get by, so what little I've been making here matters. Not a lot of other jobs around just now. Not even grunt work 'cause the Mexicans have taken it all."

"Okay, so there's one vote for trying to keep this ship afloat," Ryman said. "Leaky though it is. I think I know where Muriel and Bar stand. But feel free to chime in if you want."

"Hell, boss man," Bar said, "you know I'm in. 'Course, I don't need the money like these sorry-ass sons-of-bitches." He pointed toward Miles and Conway. "Working here is just a hobby for me. But I'm gettin' kinda old to be finding a new interest, so if only to keep from becoming a bored member of the idle rich, yeah, I'd like to see this leaky ship keep on sailing awhile longer."

The four men all turned to Muriel.

"I've been working here," she began quietly, "at this same desk, in this little office, for forty-three years come this October. The Lord has been my strength and my shield in all that time. My strength to be here every day, no matter what—sick children, my husband's passing—right here, doing my job. And He's been my shield against the blasphemy, profanity, and obscenity that spews out of your mouths day in and day out. I pray for each of you every night. Yes, I do. I pray the Lord will reveal His light to you, that you will see the danger your souls are in, repent, and turn to Him. It's likely I'll go home to be with the Lord before that happens with any of you. But I love each of you in the Lord, as difficult as that is at times, most times, and He wants me here to minister to you if your day of repentance ever comes."

Four men squirmed in their seats, unprepared for this sermonette. In all her years at McKendrick and Sons, Muriel had never spoken of her faith so openly.

She looked at Ryman. "Your father was a good man. Not a perfect man, to be sure. And as far as I know he never accepted Jesus as his personal savior. And that causes me to grieve this morning for his eternal soul. But I pray God will have mercy on him for his acts of kindness. I've sat here and watched your father help people in more ways than any of you ever realized. Money out of his pocket to help someone, that was always his way. Paying his employees from his personal funds when there wasn't enough in the till. If a farmer needed credit, had to have a new part or a repair job to get his crops in and didn't have the cash, Mister McKendrick carried him for it. Most paid him back in full. A few didn't but he never went after them, never aired their failings in public."

She turned her attention to Bar. "He took you in when you came back from the war, gave you a place to live and a job to do. He was as much a father to you as he was to his own kin. All your blustering doesn't impress me. I know you loved him. Yes, I do.

"And when I came to work here..." She paused and her voice caught slightly. "There was only one thing that mattered to him and that was if I could do the job. I showed him I could and that was all he needed to know. There weren't many men like him in this part of Virginia back then. And although he was as blasphemous, profane, and obscene as the rest of you heathens, I never once heard him use... well, let's just say he kept his foul language on a non-personal basis.

"Mister Ryman, you were just a kid when I came to work here. But now you're the boss. If you can strive to be as good a man as your father was, I'll work as hard for you as I did for him. That's all I've got to say."

Ryman, Miles, and Conway all looked down at their hands in their laps. Only Bar sat looking at Muriel. He pushed the cap back on his head, smiled broadly, and nodded. Then he turned to Conway. "Well, that just leaves you, you little pervert."

Conway shot a scowl at Bar. "Um, well, y'know, the pay's been pretty... bad around here. I didn't know anything about Mister McKendrick paying us out of his own pocket, if that's what he's been doing. But if he was, um... I guess that was pretty nice of him. But, y'know, I gotta think about my future... if I want to be a tractor mechanic all my life. I mean... if there's even gonna be tractors around here that long." Conway was struggling on two fronts. One, he was uncomfortable speaking in this setting, with people old enough to be his parents or even grandparents. Two, he was doing his best to avoid using any words or phrases from his standard lexicon that might rankle Muriel's sensibilities. He wasn't sure exactly what the difference was between blasphemy, profanity, and obscenity—it was all just "cuss words" to him—but trying not to make any such utterances slowed his usually halting speech down to a painfully difficult stammer. "I got a… a cousin working for Jessup Heating and Air Conditioning. He said there might be an opening for an apprentice. I wasn't gonna say nothin' till I looked into it. But, well, y'know, y'all are being so honest about things, so... well, I guess that's kinda where I'm at with this. I ain't been doing much around here lately but handing tools to Bar. Not enough work to keep even him busy, let alone the both of us. So... like, if they are hiring at Jessup... I mean..."

"Certainly," Ryman said, relieved that at least one employee might opt to leave and help reduce the flow of red ink. "A career in the HVAC field would be a great opportunity, and Jessup is a fine company. How about we just leave it for now that you're still with us for the time being, but are considering other options?"

"Yeah, like, I guess so."

"Okay, good. Well, that makes four of us in for sure, one who may be moving on if the opportunity presents itself. I think that makes a forum."

"Quorum," Muriel corrected.

"Yeah, that. Well, whatta ya say we dig into these pastries Bar picked up?" He reached into the bag and pulled out an apple Danish. "Share a few memories about my old man, kinda honor the old days here at McKendrick and Sons and usher in the new era."

Miles reached down and picked up the brown paper bag from beside his chair. "And I've got just the thing to do the honoring and the ushering with." He pulled a dark square-shaped bottle from the bag.

"Holy shit!" Bar exclaimed. "I don't fucking believe this."

Muriel's face drew so tight it looked like it might crack.

Forgetting Muriel's presence, Ryman lapsed back into his standard jargon. "What the fuck is that?"

Conway just grinned, shook his head, and pointed at Miles. "You, my friend, are a true badass."

"What?" Miles said. "It's a bottle of Jäger. I thought that would be a good way to honor the old man, him being such a big hunter and all. Is there a problem?"

"Yeah," Bar said, "there's a big goddamn problem. First of all, it's a little early to be drinking anything. Secondly, Jägermeister for Christ sakes? You want us all to be shitfaced before two o'clock in the afternoon? This is no way to honor the old man's memory. Third of all, the last thing we need is for..." He looked over at Ryman, who clearly did not understand what was going on. "Gimme that." Bar reached out a large paw to grab the bottle away from Miles. But the smaller, athletic man was too fast for him. Miles jumped up, knocking his chair over, and moved the bottle so Bar's swipe missed. He then clutched it tightly to his chest.

Bar got up and stood next to Miles, looking down at him, his one eye ablaze with menace, as if at will Bar could send forth a shaft of cerulean flame that would reduce Miles to a pile of smoldering embers. Bar could see the shadow of fear pass across Miles's face as he gazed up at the massive, mutilated, angry man towering over him. "Fuck you," Miles said with as much bravado as he could muster.

"Gimme that right now or I'll break your..."

"Wait a minute!" Ryman said. "What is that?"

"What's what?" Miles asked, relieved to have Ryman distract Bar from his impending assault.

"On the bottle. That picture." He flipped his hand toward Miles. "Give it here."

Miles handed him the bottle and then looked up at Bar with a "so there" smirk. Bar cocked his hand back feigning a smack to Miles's head, but then grunted and sat back down.

Ryman stared at the label on the bottle of Jägermeister. It showed a stag's head, with a twelve-point rack. Between the antlers was a bulb-shaped golden globe inside of which was a white cross with glow lines radiating out around it. "That's him," he muttered. "On a goddamn bottle of booze." He held the bottle up with the label facing toward Bar. "Do you see this?"

"Yeah," Bar sighed, "I see it. I was hoping you wouldn't."

Ryman's furrowed brow asked why.

"Because..." Bar waited for Ryman to figure it out.

"Oh, yeah, right. I wasn't supposed to talk about the deer."

"What deer?" Conway asked.

"Never mind," Bar snapped.

"But this is different," Ryman countered. "This is totally different. This is no fucking coincidence."

Muriel stood up. "That's it. I've heard enough." She looked at Ryman. "Like I said, your father was no saint when it came to his language. But even he wasn't this bad. I'm ashamed of you. And all of you going on like this is too much."

"I... I didn't say anything... b-bad," Conway protested.

She smiled at the pimply faced, stringy haired, heavily tattooed white boy. "No. No you didn't, Conway. And I appreciate that. At least there's one gentleman left among this group of heathens who can keep a civil tongue. And now it looks like you may be leaving us. These reprobates may not miss you if you go, but I will." She turned back to Ryman. "I mean no disrespect, Mister Ryman, but I assume the meeting is officially over. I have no stomach for any pastries, and I'm not sure any of you would appreciate my stories about Mister McKendrick. I know I wouldn't appreciate any of yours. So if you'll excuse me..." Clutching her purse close to her chest, she moved toward the door.

As she passed Bar he leaned his chair back and grinned at her. "Have a nice day."

"Hmmph," and she was gone.

Ryman asked Miles, "Why did you bring this?"

"Um, like I said, because your old man was so big into hunting, You know, master of the hunt for all those years. 'Jägermeister' means 'master hunter' or something like that. At least that's what someone told me. I don't speak any Dutch."

"It's German, you fucking idiot," Bar said. "But he's right about the 'master hunter.' There's an old myth that it contains elk blood. That's bullshit. But it is some powerful stuff. It can even knock me on my ass after a couple bottles or so."

"Yeah, right," Miles scoffed. "A couple bottles of that stuff and you'd be dead."

"My point exactly, smart ass."

Ryman rotated the bottle, trying to read the words printed around the outside edge of the label. "What's this say?"

"How the hell should I know?" Bar replied. With a smirk at Miles, he added, "I don't read Dutch."

"Maybe there's a message here," Ryman said.

"You've gotten enough messages lately. How about we just consider this meeting adjourned. If no one wants any pastries, I'm taking them home. I paid for the damn things."

Miles and Conway both waved them off. "Take 'em, man," Conway said. "I ain't hungry. But, shit, a shot of that Jäger wouldn't be a bad idea."

"Nobody's having any goddamn Jäger in here," Bar said. "If you and dumb ass wanna go someplace and get shitfaced on your own time, that's your business. But not here."

"Yeah, okay man. Whatever."

Ryman placed the bottle down next to the computer monitor on his father's desk and starting punching something into the keyboard.

"What the hell are you doing now?" Bar asked.

"I'm Googling 'Jägermeister,' see if I can find out what this says."

"Oh, crap." Bar turned to Miles and Conway. "Looks like we're on our way to Crazytown, fellas. I may have to put up with this shit, but y'all don't. If you wanna take off, now's your chance."

Miles folded his arms. "I want my bottle of Jäger back."

"It'll be here waiting for you. Give you some incentive to show up for work when we reopen."

"Screw that. No telling when that will be. And it's my fucking bottle."

"Here," Ryman said, setting the bottle on the edge of the desk within Miles's reach. "I just needed to make sure I spelled the name right. Got it."

Miles and Conway stood up. Miles took the bottle and gave Bar a defiant look. Conway was already through the door and pulling out a Marlboro when Miles said, "See you at the funeral."

"Try to show up sober," Bar replied.

"Try to take a bath. And find a shirt." Miles pulled the office door closed before Bar could respond.

"Holy shit!" Ryman said. "Hey, man, listen to this. Wikipedia's got the scoop. It says the words around the label are from some poem written by a German guy back in the 1800s. It gives a loose English translation: *This is the hunter's badge of glory, That he protect and tend his quarry, Hunt with honor, as is due, And through the beast to God is true.*" Ryman continued to gaze at the screen. He scrolled back up to study the image of the label on the Wikipedia page. "Son-of-a-bitch, Bar, this fucker looks just like the deer that was stalking me yesterday. And the cross between his antlers. Mine has more of a Celtic cross, sort of a circle around it, like the one on Crispie's new ring. But it's pretty fucking close."

"Ry, deer do not stalk people. *We* stalk them. It's a predator-prey kinda thing."

"Yeah, I know. But this sumbitch was stalking *me*. Might still be. How else would you explain him showing up three times in one day?"

"I don't suppose it's dawned on you that no one else has seen this supposed deer, that this could all be just a figment of your scotch-soaked imagination, the Ryman McKendrick version of pink elephants."

"That was no damn pink elephant that knocked me off the horse. More like the goddamn deer was aiming right for me. Then taunting me the other two times. And that thing between his antlers. Like this." He pointed to the image on the screen. "I thought the Glenfiddich thing was something. 'Valley of the Deer.' But that's nothing compared to this. Then Crispie's sister sends him a new ring that's the same shape as what I saw. And why would Miles show up this afternoon, of all afternoons, with a bottle of Jägermeister?"

"Oh, I dunno. Because he's as bat-shit crazy as you are?"

"Or because this is all fitting together. Someone or something, some force or other, is trying to tell me something."

"Look, man, you had one hard damn day yesterday. Enough to stress anyone out way beyond the breaking point. You need to chill out. 'Course, you gotta get your old man's funeral planned. And for that you gotta deal with the crazy old... well, at least you'll have Sheltie Lou to help you."

That distracted Ryman's attention from the computer screen. "Yeah, makes it a little easier to deal with Ma when Sheltie Lou's around. When I called her on the way here, she said she's taking the redeye Tuesday night, be here sometime on Wednesday."

Bar brightened. "Hey, now that it looks like the little pervert is leaving, maybe Sheltie Lou would like her old job back."

"Yeah, right. After all that college, a high-paying sales job, wearing clean clothes every day, like she's really gonna come back here, hand you tools, and be a grease monkey again."

"She always loved working here."

"As a kid, yeah. But she's a grown woman now. Got her own professional career. And her own life, three thousand miles away from the likes of us."

Bar stood up. "Well, shit-for-brains, if you're just gonna sit there and stare at that screen, I'm gettin' my ass outta here. I got better things to do than waste my time with you. I got hungry birds to feed."

"You find some fresh carrion?"

"Always plenty around if you know where to look."

"You spoil those damn birds. They can fend for themselves, y'know."

"Sure they can. But I like having 'em around. Everyone should have pets. You have your horses and hounds, I have my vultures."

"Whatever."

Bar collected his pastries and left.

Ryman sat staring at the image of the Jägermeister label and reciting the lines of the poem to himself, "*This is the hunter's badge of glory, That he protect and tend his quarry, Hunt with honor, as is due, And through the beast to God is true.*"

Chapter 17

THE MCKENDRICKS HAD played second fiddle to the Billingtons for nearly two centuries. The Billingtons had a substantial head start, by more than a hundred years, thanks to a land grant from George II in return for favors to the Crown from the Fifth Earl of Hemsly, Lord Billington. The fifth earl sent his fourth son, rendered a useless appendage through the practice of primogeniture, off to the New World to oversee the holdings in the Colony named in honor of the Virgin Queen. Over the next three hundred years the property that once extended, in theory, from the Blue Ridge Mountains to the Ohio River dwindled to slightly less than four thousand acres; a mere speck of the original, but still a handsome and valuable hunk of real estate.

A Billington antecedent chose the name "Montfair" for reasons known only to himself (or possibly herself as Billington women never quite fit the mold of dainty, submissive Southern belles). What was clearly chronicled in the family records, however, was the impressive string of manipulations, double-dealings, questionable legalities, an occasional stroke of genius, a revolution, occupation by an invading army, the resultant post-war financial devastation, and a rare incident or two of actual heroism that kept the property in Billington hands. The hands of the thirteenth descendent to whom Montfair passed belonged to Thaddeus Augustus "Thumper" Billington, IV, JD, PhD, MFH.

While the Billingtons were establishing their dynasty on Virginia soil, the McKendricks were scratching out a living as peasant farmers in the Scottish Highlands, roughly in the vicinity of Inverness. It would be another hundred years before Lachlan McKendrick packed up his few belongings and, with the sturdy missus and several wee tykes in tow, struck off for a better life across the Great Waters. The final overland leg of their journey stopped at the eastern base of Virginia's Blue Ridge Mountains, at a small village named Paradise Gap.

Devout Presbyterians who believed in hard work, diligence, and frugality, the McKendricks prospered in their new home. When they were able to dress well enough, they became Episcopalians.

The plum fruit of their prosperity was secured the day Fingal

McKendrick, grandson of Lachlan, purchased seven hundred acres of prime farmland from a cash-strapped Josiah Billington, Thumper's great-great-uncle.

Standing along the property line, with the Billington manor house visible on a distant hilltop, Fingal turned back to take in the view of his newly acquired land. "It may not be Montfair," he said. "But it's Fair Enough."

****

The first trailer arrived at Fair Enough Farm shortly after six o'clock Tuesday morning. By six-thirty there were more than a dozen rigs parked in the field directly across from the McKendricks' house. Most of those riding that day were the dedicated regulars with both the stamina and the free time to go foxhunting at such an early hour on a weekday morning. One of those was Cecelia Broadhurst who arrived in her Mercedes while Dorcas pulled a two-horse trailer with the mounts for her and the boss. Cecelia's horse for the day was an experienced, level-headed animal. Dorcas was assigned to one of the "greenies" that needed much more mileage under a groom's skillful hands.

Thumper was not among this ardent band of hunters. He was in Charlottesville, preparing to enlighten a specially selected group of law students on some of the more arcane intricacies of the US Constitution.

Among those present for the morning hunt were a few unexpected participants, hunt members who did not usually make their first appearance until later in the season, when the meet times moved to more accommodating hours such as nine or ten o'clock. Word had spread about Saturday's hunt, although Ryman's performance was reported with varying degrees of accuracy. Some who missed that day's sport had been sufficiently intrigued by what they heard to set their alarms for four a.m., pull on their boots and breeches, stumble out to the barn in the predawn darkness, load up their horses, and arrive at Fair Enough Farm just as the sky was lightening to a soft summery pink. If there was to be another chase like the one on Saturday, they wanted to be part of it.

Rhetta did not usually bother to see the hunt move off, even when hounds met on her front lawn. While Fergus was marshaling everything and everyone to order, great master that he was, she'd be in the kitchen working on her second cup of coffee and dashing through the crossword in the *Crutchfield Courier*.

This morning, though, she ventured out onto the porch. Abel the Boxer, her constant companion, trotted behind her. Rhetta's presence caught everyone's attention, especially Bing Sensabaugh's. The moment of recognition that passed between them was awkward and fleeting. It was he who quickly turned his eyes from hers and pretended to adjust a loose keeper on his horse's bridle.

Ryman also took note of his mother's appearance. As she stood looking over the group of riders assembled under the ancient oak trees, he steered his horse toward her.

"Nice of you to come see us off this morning, Ma."

"Only thing I'm here to see 'off,' boy, is that you and your damn friends stay 'off' my flower beds. At least I could count on your daddy to keep all those yay-hoos where they belong, not let 'em come across the drive onto the house side." She stared down at Ryman and craned her neck to make a point of looking at his horse's feet. "Like where you're standing now."

"Oh, sorry, Ma. I forgot. I'll..."

Rhetta's attention was distracted by the sight of a truck rolling down the main driveway, between the front lawn and the field where the trailers were parked. Bar Reinhardt sat at the wheel of his mint-condition '72 F-100 pickup, a two-tone job in aqua blue and bright white. "Where's he going at this hour?" Rhetta asked.

"Oh, I reckon he's heading to the shop."

"What the hell for? The shop's closed, ain't it?"

"Well, yeah, we're not open for business, because of Daddy and all. But there's some repair work to get finished up so he said he'd go in and get it done. Josh Preston's waiting for his bush-hog, mowing's falling behind. Bar said he doesn't mind doing it on his own time."

"How's he going to get in when neither you nor your daddy are there to open up?"

"He's got his own key."

"He what?"

"He's always had a key to the place. Daddy gave him one years ago. Lots of mornings he's the first one there. If you'd taken some interest in the place, you'd have known that."

Her eyes flickered with hazel-tinted sparks. "Don't you sass me, boy. I got more interest in that business than you realize. And it's just like you and your old man to trust that no good... to let him run loose in... Damn, your old man was an even bigger fool than I thought. And you ain't no better." She turned and stomped back toward the front door, Abel at her heels, calling over her shoulder as she went, "And get your damn horse away from my flower bed!"

Ryman returned to the lawn where the other riders were gathering. Crispie, Patti, and Nardell had the pack in place, off to the side, awaiting the start of the day's sport.

Ryman rode up alongside Mildred, who turned to him and said, "Any idea where that fox from Saturday's run is hanging out this morning? Or was that just a fluke?"

Ryman did not answer immediately. He looked back at the house, where he assumed his mother had taken up her usual position in the kitchen. He surveyed the scene around him, noticed some of the new faces among the followers, took note of how eager hounds were to be off to the game. He then turned to Mildred and replied, "We must through the beast to God be true."

With a jerk of her head she asked, "What's that supposed to mean?"

"I'm not sure myself. But I haven't been able to get that line out of my head for the past three days."

"Did you make that up?"

"No. Something I... I just stumbled across the other day. A poem, by some old German guy."

"I didn't know you were into German poetry. Always thought you limited yourself to books with lots of pictures."

Crispie rode over to the two masters. "Where shall we cast?"

Ryman sat up erect in his saddle, and stated in an oratorical tone, "Mister O'Rourke, you must earn the hunter's badge of glory, you shall protect and tend the quarry."

"Master?" Crispie said.

"It seems Ryman has discovered old German poetry," Mildred explained, unable to conceal a sneer. "You know what a terrible effect that can have on the mind of someone whose idea of high poetic art is the naughty limerick."

Addressing them both, Ryman continued, "We shall hunt with honor as is due, and through the beast to God be true."

"Master, I'm afraid I don't follow you. Maybe you shouldn't be huntin' this marnin'. Could be those bumps on the head from Friday are still plaguin' you."

"I'm fine, Mister O'Rourke. Cast your hounds in the Blackberry Covert. Charlie's waiting for us there. Or, I should say, Charlene in this case."

"Um... Master, that's high ground, likely to be dry as a bone. Maybe a low lyin' spot, down along Stoney Creek..."

"Are you the Master, now, Mister O'Rourke? Or do I still hold that title?"

Crispie and Mildred were both surprised by the sharpness of Ryman's remark.

Sensing their reaction, he softened to his usual easy manner. "I'd like to try Blackberry Covert first. I can't explain it, but I've got the same feeling I had Saturday. And I was right then, wasn't I?"

"Aye, master, that you were." Crispie looked to Mildred who shrugged and nodded her concurrence.

"He even knows it's a vixen," she said, rolling her eyes in disbelief. "How can we refuse?"

"All right, then, Master. Blackberry Covert it is."

"Good. You won't be disappointed." Ryman checked his watch. "I need to make a couple of announcements, then we'll be off." Crispie returned to his hounds as Ryman addressed the crowd. "Hark! Hark, please." All eyes turned toward him. "It's wonderful to see such a great turnout this morning. I hope your efforts are rewarded with some good sport. One quick announcement about plans for my father's memorial service..." Ryman's attention was distracted by a rider having trouble with his horse. The animal was tossing its head and backing up. The rider became increasingly unsettled, unable to determine the cause of the horse's discomfort. "There will be a private family service on Friday," Ryman continued. The horse was now backing into other horses, shaking its head with escalating force. The rider, a man rarely seen at a weekday hunt, was apologizing profusely as others tried to avoid the fiasco.

Ryman broke off from his announcements. "Les, what seems to be the problem there?"

Lester Peterson had only three seasons of foxhunting experience and was no more than a moderately competent rider on his best days. He called back in a shaky voice, "I don't know, Master. He's never done this before." It was only the man's long, slender legs and natural athleticism that kept him from being unseated. His lack of horsemanship left him bereft of any idea about what could be causing this behavior.

Ryman sat motionless for several seconds, the one calm person among a growing scene of turmoil on the lawn. Finally he said, "Hop off, Les. And remove that bridle."

Relieved at the chance to dismount, Les quickly swung off and, holding the reins around the horse's neck, unfastened the bridle as fast as he could, a difficult task as the horse continued to object to some unseen annoyance. Once the bridle was off, the horse shook his head twice more, then relaxed.

"Is that his regular bit?" Ryman asked.

Les examined the bit. "Holy crap! Oh, geez, I must have grabbed the wrong bridle."

Ryman rode over and took a closer look at the bit. "Not only that, but this one's rigged wrong. It's upside down, so the port's jabbing him in the tongue. This bit's way too severe for that horse. Any horse really. And by rigging it incorrectly the pressure's even worse."

"I'm sorry, Master. We'd been using this on another horse. And he didn't object."

"Some horses will put up with more crap than others. The other horse must be the stoic type. Or has a mouth of iron. But this sensitive fellow here wasn't about to accept that thing poking him in the tongue."

"I guess I must have still been half asleep when I was loading the tack. But... how did you know that was the problem?"

Ryman looked at the horse for a few seconds, then pointed his whip at the animal. "He told me."

"He what?" Les asked. "How... you mean... like, by the way he was shaking his head and all?"

"Yeah, that too. You got another bit with you?"

"Um, no, afraid not."

Ryman turned to Nardell. "Honey, would you run back to the barn and get Clyde's bridle? That should fit this fellow okay. And it's a light snaffle, won't cause him any discomfort."

Nardell trotted off to get the bridle, a piece of tack used on one of Fergus's horses. The question of what to do with the pair of big chestnut draft crosses, Clyde and his partner Dale, had not yet been addressed.

"We can wait a few minutes, can't we, Crispie?"

"Aye, Master. Wouldn't want Mister Peterson to miss out on this marnin's sport, after all his efforts to be here this early."

"Thank you, Master," Les said. "I appreciate that. Um... you think he'll be okay in a snaffle? I've never ridden him in something that light. He can get a little strong, especially in the hunt field."

Ryman again turned his attention to the horse. The animal jerked his head up, pricked his ears forward, and fixed his large, bright eyes on Ryman. Man and animal remained motionless, looking at each other. Everyone watched in stunned silence. Finally Ryman said, "He'll be fine. Don't pull on him. The reins aren't a safety strap. Keep a little contact, but stay light in his mouth. Use your leg and your seat, easy with your hands. That's what he wants." He then broke off his gaze from the horse and looked at Peterson. "Besides," he said with a wide grin, "we're going to run the hell out of both of you this morning. You'll be two tired but happy hunters by the time we're done."

He turned to face the crowd once again. "Now, if I may continue, there will be a public memorial service for my father this Saturday, as part of the day's hunt. We'll meet on the lawn next door at Montfair. Although we'd usually go much earlier, we're setting the time for nine o'clock to allow more folks to attend, both mounted and on foot. Reverend Davenport will conduct the service and others will share a few remembrances of my father. Then we'll move off to hunt. Might be getting a bit warm by then, but maybe we can still get in a decent chase to honor our late master before the temps get too steamy. Hope y'all can be there. I'll be leading first field this morning, Mildred will lead second."

Nardell arrived with the bridle. Peterson remounted and found his horse now obligingly calm. He turned to club secretary Marva Henderson, who was on Trooper, her always well-behaved Appendix Quarter Horse, and said quietly, "How the hell did he do that? Is he that good of a horseman? It was like... like he could read the horse's mind."

"Could be he's that good," she replied. "The man's been around horses since the day he was born, seen a lot in his life, surely has more tricks in his bag than all the rest of us here combined. But that thing on Saturday..."

"Yes, I heard all about that. That's why I took this morning off, got up in the middle of the night to be here. And grabbed the wrong damn tack in the process."

Ryman turned to Crispie and said, "Mister O'Rourke, Blackberry Covert if you please. Let's go hunting."

"Blackberry Covert?" Marva whispered. "High and dry? That can't be right."

Crispie took the pack down the lane that led to the interior of Fair Enough Farm. As hounds trotted past Ryman's cottage, a tremendous racket came from within. Wycroft was locked inside to prevent him from joining in on the hunt. He usually raised no more than a mild objection, a mournful howl or two, then settled in on the old leather sofa to rest his arthritic joints and dream of bygone days afield. But today he was in full voice and scratching furiously at the door in his efforts to get in on the action.

Three hounds—Warwick, Wasted, and Winfield, descendants of Wycroft and similar in voice—stopped in their tracks and looked back, distracted by the plaintive howls. Patti spoke sharply, "Get on to him!" All three obeyed immediately and resumed their places in the pack trotting in a tight knot at the heels of Crispie's horse.

Hearing the ruckus, and imagining the damage being done to his home, Ryman pulled up and signaled those following him to halt. He turned toward the cottage and stared at the door. The intensity of the howling gradually decreased. The scratching stopped. As Ryman continued to direct his gaze at the door, the howls softened to a whimper. The sound of creaking furniture springs could be heard through the open window, then silence.

Ryman moved on. Those following him murmured among themselves about what they'd just seen.

The route to Blackberry Covert took the hunters toward the high ground along the back edge of the McKendrick property. This required the first field to jump half a dozen obstacles—coops, stone walls, post-and-rail fences—while the second field came along through the nearby gates.

Marva Henderson and Les Peterson rode in the first field. After the sixth jump, Marva commented to Les about how nicely his horse was behaving. She'd seen the pair many times before and had always made it a point to stay as far away as possible given the horse's unruly manner and Lester's lack of control.

"It's like he's a different animal," Les said. "Ryman was really right about the bit. And about my hands too, I guess."

"Something's certainly calmed him down. Or maybe it's you who's calmed down and you're channeling that to the horse."

"Could be that too. Is what I've heard about Saturday's hunt true?"

"If you heard that Ryman insisted on taking hounds to a place where the chances of getting up a fox were statistically zilch, and we then got up a big red who ran us around like a demon for almost an hour, then you heard right."

"Yep, that's what I heard. Think he can do that again?"

"Well, he's already covered the part about going to a really tough place to get up a fox. As for what happens after that, I guess we'll soon find out."

"Hark, please!" Ryman commanded, quieting the chatter going on behind him. He reined his horse to a halt on a small knoll a short distance from a mass of brambles and scrubby trees—Blackberry Covert. It was the highest point on Fair Enough Farm, a perfect spot from which to view the surrounding countryside. It was also the least likely place to find a fox on this warm, dry morning. No rain had fallen for a month, not unusual for August and early September in the Virginia Piedmont. But the lack of moisture combined with the high temperatures that often reached the mid-90s by day and only slightly moderated at night drove most of the wildlife to lower, cooler, moister areas. Furthermore, even if a fox were found in this unlikely spot, hounds would have a hard time following as the fox's scent would quickly evaporate.

Even the least experienced of those out hunting this day knew such elemental points. Questions and comments were quietly mumbled among the riders as they sat and watched the huntsman cast hounds.

Crispie blew a short note on his horn, the signal for the pack to leave him and go into the covert. "Leu in! Leu in the covert. Get 'im up, me beauties," he called to his hounds. "Where's 'e at? Get to 'im now."

Nardell took a position to one side of the covert, Patti to the other, where all points could be seen and the fox detected if it broke into the open.

That seemed to be a big "if" as a hound's voice rose tentatively, with a questioning lilt: "Could this be a line of scent?" Then silence. This repeated several times, with different hounds hesitantly giving voice only to go quickly silent.

Crispie was about to ask Ryman if he was ready to give this up and try the moist bottom land along Stoney Creek when Patti's yell echoed off the hilltop. "Tally-hoooo!" She removed her hunt cap and held it out at arm's length, pointing away from the backside of the covert. "Gone away!"

Crispie raced around to where Patti was pointing, just as the whole pack burst into full cry and came surging from the brambles, hot on the scent.

Ryman's fox of the day decided it was time for the game to begin.

Les Peterson got his wish. And Ryman's prediction again proved true. The fox, a small, light colored vixen, stayed ahead of the pack by just enough distance to keep them on the scent but safely away from her brush. Hounds faltered on the line twice when the fox led them over patches of rocky ground where her scent would not hold. Both times she stopped, sat down, waited patiently for hounds to regain the line, then trotted on calmly when the chase resumed. Although still a youngster, she'd played the game several times during the previous season and quickly learned the routine. She knew her speed, cunning, familiarity with every secure hideout in her domain, and her store of tricks for foiling scent would keep her safely away from the comparatively deficient hounds and bumbling horses and riders. Though greatly outnumbered, she was in control and accepted her role with full awareness of her superiority.

The fox stayed on higher ground, enticing her pursuers by dashing across open fields in full view, then cutting into the woods and out of sight, only to appear a few minutes later sprinting through another field. Those following hounds that morning could not recall when they'd seen more of a fox during the chase. Even a fleeting view was a thrilling moment. This was a feature-length wildlife documentary.

Patti paced the action on the right, staying abreast of hounds but not interfering with the interplay between pursuers and quarry. After forty-five minutes at a steady pace, hounds in full cry much of that time, she saw the fox turn her way. She was then bordering a neighboring landowner's pasture filled with grazing Black Angus cattle, enclosed by a high tensile wire fence that offered neither gate nor jump for mounted riders. The owner, Frank Worsham, opened his land to hunting later in the season, after his beef cattle had gone to market. But at this early point he did not want anyone riding through his stock fields.

If the fox continued on her path, she would run under the fence and be lost to the followers. Patti would then have to stop hounds and force them to break off the chase. This would require every shred of skill she could muster—position her horse correctly to face the oncoming hounds, use her voice and the crack of her whip to lift their heads from the line of scent, and, as a last resort, go to her pistol and send a noisy blast of birdshot into the air to stress the seriousness of her commands. If she succeeded, the pack would transition from a mob of feral hunting canines in hot pursuit of prey to three-dozen obedient house pets. If she failed, the hounds would surge past her, become trespassers on land to which the followers had no access, continue on the chase without staff supervision, possibly put themselves at risk, at least require much extra work by the staff to get them safely back to kennels, and incur the ire of an accommodating landowner.

All this flashed through Patti's mind in an instant as she saw the fox turn toward the cattle field. There was one other possibility—get there first and turn the fox, send the quarry back into McKendrick property where the chase could continue.

Patti pressed her horse forward and raced to the point toward which the fox was heading. She reached the fence line before the fox got there and turned her horse to face the oncoming vixen. Twenty yards away the fox stopped. She'd put enough distance between herself and hounds to have a few seconds to spare without jeopardy. She and Patti stared at each other. Patti held her whip at the ready, prepared to send up a loud crack if necessary to convince the fox to take a different route. The fox looked beyond Patti to the cattle field, knowing she could elude hounds if she dashed past this minor obstacle and continued on, easily foiling her scent among the cow droppings. She then looked back in the direction she'd just come from. Hounds were pressing hard, still in full cry. She had only a second to decide.

As the pack came surging forward, the fox looked up once again at the human attempting to block her path. What did Patti see in that fleeting instant? A smile? A nod? Some jaunty devil-may-care pose? Whatever glimmer of recognition she caught, it was over in an instant. As hounds closed on their prey, the fox turned and ran straight into the pack, cutting a path through the middle, traveling so fast the hard running hounds were unable to react. By the time they realized what the fox had done, they'd overrun their target by a substantial distance, the fox was well clear of the pack and on her way in the reverse direction.

It took Patti several more seconds to refocus on her job. Hounds were casting about, their sterns aloft like so many antennae on a fleet of amusement park bumper cars, trying to relocate the line of scent that had seemingly disappeared into thin air. She was still slightly dazed when Crispie came riding up, closing the short lead hounds had gotten on him when the fox took them through a thick patch of deadfall and undergrowth. Ryman, Mildred, and two-dozen sweat-soaked but exhilarated riders were close behind.

"Report, please," Crispie barked at Patti.

"Strangest thing," she replied, looking past him to the spot where she'd last seen the fox melt back into heavy woods. "Through the pack.

Ran right through the pack."

"Who ran through the pack?" Crispie asked.

"The fox," Patti said.

"Where'd he go?"

"She. I'm sure it was a vixen, just like Ryman said. She reversed, fooled the pack, took off that way." She pointed her whip toward the fox's path.

"A vixen, you say?" Crispie's tone was skeptical. "Stopped for a chat, did she? Introduced herself?"

"Well, yeah, kinda. I don't know. It was strange. I had to stop her from getting into Worsham's cattle field, try to turn her to keep her in play. She... she stopped, looked right at me, turned around and ran back through the pack. Got clean away, left them all stumped as to where she went."

Crispie turned to Ryman. "Shall we try to regain the line, Master?"

Ryman, a huge grin on his face, replied, "I think this little lady has obliged us with enough sport for one morning. Horses are hot, riders have had a good run. You and Patti have both earned the hunter's badge of glory, you did protect and tend your quarry, did hunt with honor as is due, and through the beast to God were true."

"If you say so, Master," Crispie said.

"I do say so. Collect your hounds and let's go home."

Chapter 18

JANEY MUSGROVE WAITED in line at her bank in Fairfax, close to the George Mason University campus. She'd been in this branch many times but she'd never bothered to pay much attention to the décor. This morning, though, she noticed that the walls were decorated with prints similar to those in the hotel lobby—classic foxhunting scenes. Each image depicted men in scarlet coats, wearing top hats and sporting bushy side-whiskers. Ladies in elegant sidesaddle attire looked demure but in control of their well-muscled Thoroughbreds. In some prints hounds gathered around the huntsman's horse with the field of riders arrayed in a circle about them. In others the action was underway as hounds and riders streamed across the countryside, some riders in mid-tumble off their horses, others already on the turf, the rest galloping on hard after hounds.

Other than the hotel, where had she seen these images before? Now that she thought about it, they seemed to be pervasive in certain places. She'd seen similar prints in other bank lobbies and hotels, there was one in her dentist's waiting room, two in the apartment complex rental office. Was this a Virginia thing? Or perhaps common throughout the East Coast where riding to hounds was equated with prestige? Foxhunting, horseracing, and polo—sports synonymous with money and class. She didn't recall ever seeing foxhunting prints in Clara City, or anywhere else in Chippewa County or all of Minnesota for that matter. But maybe they had been there and she'd just never noticed them. She'd heard of foxhunting. Who hadn't? She'd also heard of regattas and yachting's America's Cup. But she'd never actually seen a yacht up close, and certainly didn't expect to ever be invited onto one.

Why did the foxhunting prints always show scenes from long ago? The only clips that came to mind from TV were period pieces on public television; a brief segment in *Upstairs, Downstairs* or *Downton Abbey*. You might see a modern photo of a racing yacht cutting through the water. Images of the British royals playing polo showed up in magazines. Horseracing's Triple Crown still made the mainstream news. But there were never any current portrayals of foxhunting, at least not to her recollection. That would suggest it was because no one did it any more.

And yet Danella Kernan said it still went on out in the Virginia hinterland where Thaddeus Billington lived.

Despite Danella's completely valid points about the difficulties and inequalities of the older time portrayed in the hunting prints, there was still an undeniable romantic allure about those scenes. Why else were they used so widely? Who wouldn't want to imagine herself a member of the gentry, the landed aristocracy, someone who could spend a morning riding to hounds, relax with a game of cards at the club through the afternoon, and then dress for dinner served in a glowing, candlelit dining room, attended by a staff of liveried servants?

Had Danella been with her, she would have quickly disabused Janey of those naïve misconceptions as well. But standing there alone, it was a pleasant escape to spend a few moments imagining that lifestyle.

"Next."

Janey's reverie was snapped by the sound of the bank teller's voice.

After completing her transaction, she placed a call to Danella.

Chapter 19

DANELLA'S CALL TO Thumper came while he was provoking a debate among his seminar students over the interpretation of "slavery" as enumerated in the Thirteenth Amendment of the US Constitution. An activist group known as PACA—People Against Cruelty to Animals—had devised a legal stratagem on behalf of "plaintiffs" they claimed were being subjected to "involuntary servitude." The wording of the Amendment does not mention "people" or "persons," only "the party." Thumper tossed out that grenade and sat back to enjoy the mental gymnastics demonstrated by the bright young minds entrusted to his care for a three-day workshop.

When break time arrived, he returned Danella's call.

"Do you remember Janey Musgrove?" she asked.

"Name rings a very faint bell."

"You met her at my Christmas party last year. Small, trim woman, early forties, thick glasses. She's written two books on fringe religions, teaching now at George Mason."

"Okay, kind of coming back to me. Must not have made much of an impression."

"Usually the case with brainy women of substance."

"And yet that's always been my type."

"Yeah, right. Look, I happened to mention to her that you're a foxhunter. She's working on a book concept about sports, more of a cultural study. She'd like to come out and observe you and your friends sometime."

"'Observe?' You make it sound like Margaret Mead visiting Samoa."

"How about 'watch' then? Would it be okay if she comes out to see what you all do out there? A favor to me and a help to one of your fellow Kernan Agency clients."

"I suppose, sure. You know I can't refuse my favorite agent."

"Thank you. And, I might add, your *only* agent. She's very excited about this. How soon can she come for a visit?"

"Hunting season has just begun, cub hunting anyway. Formal

season's a couple of months away yet. But, um, this may not be a good time right now. Our senior master just passed away on Friday."

"Oh, I'm so sorry."

"This week is pretty much a hectic rush to get ready for a private funeral Friday and then a huge public memorial service on Saturday which, I'm just thrilled to say, will be held at my place. And as if that's not enough, I'm in Charlottesville until Thursday teaching a special seminar class. So I'm trying to plan for a couple hundred people, about half of them turned out in their finest for a morning of foxhunting, arriving on my front lawn in less than a week. And I have to do much of it without being on site."

"Sounds like it will be quite an event."

"That it will. I hope anyway."

"The kind of event that, say, someone wishing to see what goes on in the world of foxhunting might benefit from attending. Possibly a once-in-a-lifetime opportunity."

"Ah… gee, Danella… I don't know. I'm going to be totally tied up with my duties hosting this thing. I won't have time to escort someone around who…"

"Oh, she won't need an escort. Janey can take care of herself. As long as she has your permission to be there, she'll just stay out of the way and observe… er, watch what goes on."

"Well, okay, as long as I don't have to play the gracious host. Maybe I can hand her off to someone else who won't be so encumbered. I'll email you the details and directions, you can pass them along."

"Wonderful. Thank you."

When he checked his email later, he found a report from Mildred detailing the morning's events. Ryman's behavior grew odder still. He'd started quoting lines from some obscure German poem, appeared to have the ability to communicate with horses and hounds, and insisted they draw from Blackberry Covert, despite Crispie's suggestion they cast along Stoney Creek. But darned if they hadn't enjoyed another morning of great sport.

****

"I would never ask you to lie, Elizabeth," Thumper said. "That would offend my gentlemanly sense of honor. Yet to ensure domestic tranquility, we must see to it that Natasha does not find out about this."

His daughter put on a suitably serious face. "She will never hear the truth from me. As far as I know, you have tasted nothing but cafeteria gruel during your entire stay in Charlottesville. Under pain of death and severe torture, I will reveal nothing about our lovely evening at the finest

French restaurant in all of central Virginia." She held up a three-finger pledge. "On my honor as a gentlelady."

"Good. How's your squab?"

"Marvelous. How's the rack of lamb?"

"Superb."

It was a radical, rebellious move when a Billington boy asked to be sent to the new "academical village" launched by a family acquaintance. Billington men had always studied at William and Mary. The boy's father acquiesced only because he had the deepest faith in the founder of this start-up operation, a Mister T. Jefferson. The boy who was allowed to attend the University of Virginia when the paint was barely dry and the mortar not quite set was Thumper's great-great-grandpapa, father of Thaddeus the First.

An unbroken succession of Billington men attended The University from then onward. (Among the FFV set—First Families of Virginia—no further citation was needed; *The* University sufficed.) For the first one hundred and fifty-one years of the school's existence, Billington women were denied admission. That changed in 1970 when co-education arrived.

Thumper's two sisters, Myrna and Claudette, followed their mother in attending Hollins, as young women of her family, the Crutchfields, had done for almost as long as Billington men had been attending U.Va. A new tradition began when Elizabeth became the first female Billington to attend Mister Jefferson's Academical Village. On this evening she was just beginning her third year, moving into the full pursuit of her major concentration in political philosophy, policy, and law.

Assessing his only daughter across the table, Thumper had to admit that she was not a raving beauty—her nose a bit beaky, her chin slightly too sharp, and her hair an unremarkable mousy brown. A slender figure, devoid of curves, disguised her physical strength and natural athleticism.

He did, though, appreciate her charming energy and the dancing sparkle in her mahogany brown eyes. Those were the qualities that drew him to her mother and which he now saw smiling back at him from across the tiny table.

After giving her the inside scoop on every professor in her discipline, which ones to cultivate as mentors and which ones to avoid as know-nothing blowhards, Thumper moved on to the passing of Fergus McKendrick and its aftermath.

"How's Mrs. McKendrick holding up?" Elizabeth asked.

"Like a rock. It's Ryman I'm worried about."

"Not taking his father's death well? I can understand that."

"If only it were that simple. I'm concerned he may have some serious mental problems. Maybe from all those years of hard drinking, maybe from one concussion too many, or maybe... I don't know... just finally going off the deep end."

"That bad? What's he doing?"

He told Elizabeth about the supposed sightings of a big buck with something resembling a Celtic Cross between its antlers, how Ryman claimed to be hearing voices or sounds from animals, getting visions of where foxes were, even though both times had been in the last places any sensible hunter would have cast hounds. Yet, oddly enough, both times he was dead right, even down to the fox's gender.

"And now," Thumper concluded, "he's quoting some obscure German poem. Mildred looked it up and says it's on the label of the Jägermeister bottle, of all the wacky things."

"Maybe not so wacky."

"How do you mean?"

"There's a stag with some sort of cross thing over its head on the Jäger label."

"How would you know that?"

"You don't want to know."

Thumper thought about that for a moment. He remembered the grain alcohol bashes of his youth, basically paint thinner mixed with Hawaiian Punch in a trashcan and stirred with a broomstick. No, he probably didn't want to know why his sweet, innocent daughter, surely destined to be the Chief Justice of the United States one day, was on such intimate terms with the Jäger label artwork.

"So that's the connection," he said. "He must have seen it in the liquor store after he got bonked on the head last Friday."

"If he's been drinking Jäger, that would explain a good bit of his behavior."

He gave Elizabeth a narrow stare, trying to convey the appropriate aura of parental disapproval.

She smiled back demurely and took a dainty bite of squab. "This is excellent. Want a taste?"

He nodded and she placed a forkful in his open mouth.

"Mmmm, delicious. I'd offer you a bite of my lamb but I'm a selfish bastard and intend to eat it all myself."

"I figured," she said, reaching over and taking a large chunk of lamb off his plate.

"I just hope Ryman can get through these next few days," he said, watching her slowly savor the exquisite lamb. "When I'm not in class, I'm on the phone or email every spare minute getting things organized for Saturday. Lousy damn time Fergus picked to drop dead."

"Some people just have no consideration," she agreed, reaching over and snagging another piece of lamb. "Too bad Shelagh's not here to help you. Why isn't my new mommy back home yet? I miss her so."

"Sure you do. She says she's got more details to wrap up on her father's estate. But, well, Crispie's sister reports that she's finding time to hunt the old pack in her father's place." He fondled his wine glass and watched the red liquid swirl around. "Just between you and me, I'm beginning to suspect that she might not be coming back at all. It was always her dream to take up the horn from her father. But the old guy just didn't seem to want to quit. So she came over here looking for greener pastures."

"Well, she certainly found them, didn't she?"

"But then her old man up and dies. Thoughtless old bugger."

"As I recall, he wasn't much older than you."

"That depends on what the definition of 'much' is."

Elizabeth's obvious pleasure at this news transitioned to a show of concern. "Are you okay with this? I mean, like, you guys have only been together a couple of years. You're not, like, all depressed over it?" He saw and heard a glimmer of her as a teenager, talking to her classmates at the Foxcroft School about someone breaking up with a boyfriend. She was still in a transitional phase of life, at the critical turn of twenty-one, no longer a child, more mature than many at her age, but not quite ready to take on that Chief Justice job.

He sighed and pursed his lower lip. "No, I'm not, like, all depressed. I realize now that our union was a mistake, for both her and me. I'm ashamed to admit that it was a mid-life lark by an aging old fool. I should have just made it a fling, something that would have played itself out. But you know me. Gentlemanly honor, eh?"

She reached across the table, took his hand, and any lingering trace of teenage shallowness melted away into earnest sincerity. "You are a good man, Thumper Billington. I'm proud to call you my father. You're no fool and you have nothing to be ashamed of. I'm sorry it didn't work out for you. She did not know or appreciate the real you, she only wanted what you have, and it's something she never will."

"She'd have never gotten Montfair under any circumstances. That will only go to you no matter..."

"That's not what I meant. I'm talking about integrity." She released his hand and sat back, erect and perky. "So now let's celebrate." She caught the server's attention. "Please bring us two of the biggest, sloppiest, most decadent thing on tonight's dessert menu."

"Geez," Thumper said, "I've got to be able to fit into my white breeches on Saturday."

"Well, if you'd rather skip the dessert here, I think I know where I can find a bottle of Jägermeister."

"No, no! A big sloppy dessert will be just fine."

Chapter 20

SHELTON CAUGHT THE redeye Tuesday night and by mid-day Wednesday she stood in the Fair Enough Farm kitchen helping Rhetta work through a pile of dirty dishes.

Abel lay comfortably curled on his bed in the corner. With a half dozen dog beds positioned throughout the house, wherever Rhetta was the four-year-old Boxer was sure to be close by.

"I can't believe all these people have been coming over to pay their respects," Shelton said as Rhetta handed her another plate to dry, "bringing you food, then hanging around eating half of it, and not even offering to help clean up."

"They offered. But I don't like no one else messing with my kitchen. They don't know where things go, how to do a proper hand-washing job. Everyone's got dishwashers nowadays, flat forgot how to do things on their own. So I ran 'em all out, rather do it myself."

Rhetta looked up from her plate scrubbing to see Shelton's lip quivering. Shelton exclaimed "Oh, Grandma!" and fell against the smaller woman, almost knocking her over. She pressed her considerable weight on her grandmother and wept.

"There, there child." Rhetta patted Shelton's back with a soaking wet hand. She tried to pull away without being too forceful, but Shelton had her in an iron grip. "Hush now. You're just all wore out from that long flight. I reckon you didn't get much sleep. You just be strong, like your granddaddy was. He didn't ever break down over someone dying. Even when you'd a thought he should have." Shelton started to go limp and the weight was too much for Rhetta to hold up. She struggled to push Shelton toward a kitchen chair. Abel leapt up, barked and bounced around them. He wasn't sure if they were playing or fighting, but if his mistress was in danger, he was ready to help. The two women shuffled clumsily a few paces across the floor. Rhetta maneuvered Shelton close enough, then pushed with all her strength. Shelton collapsed onto the chair.

Satisfied that Rhetta was safe, Abel returned to his bed and flopped down with a grunt.

"I... I know," Shelton said through her sobs, trying to regain her composure, wiping her eyes with the back of her hand. "I loved him so much. He was my hero."

"Hero. Yeah, he was a hero. Even had the medals to prove it." She went back to washing the dishes.

Shelton sat slump-shouldered. She pulled a paper napkin from the holder on the table and blew her nose. "I know how it was between you two. I don't know why. But that was your business." She looked around the kitchen, down at the floor. "I can remember when I was little, playing in here while you and my mother sat and drank coffee, talking about Grandpa and Daddy. You all probably didn't think I was listening. Boy, could the two of you go on. I think my first full sentence was, 'Men, can't live with 'em, can't shoot 'em.'" She smiled lightly and shook her tangled locks.

"Still as true today as it was then," Rhetta said.

"Oh, I don't think all men are that bad."

"That's because you've never lived with one. And you don't own a gun."

"Women can be just as bad. Some of them anyway."

"I suppose that's true. That fiery little redhead you lived with a while back, I recall she gave you fits."

"Ericka. Yes, she did. Probably a good thing I don't own a gun."

"I haven't heard about anyone else lately." Rhetta paused her scrubbing and looked over her shoulder at Shelton.

"Oh, no one in particular just now. Work's so busy and all. Not much time for socializing really."

"New job's going well then? You like what you're doing?"

"Oh, yeah, it's great. Just busy. Lot of traveling, vets' offices all around the Pacific Northwest. Hard to keep a relationship going when I'm on the road all week." Shelton grabbed another napkin and dabbed her eyes. "You know, Grandma, it's always meant a lot to me that you... and Grandpa too... never judged... never had a problem with... that part of my life."

Rhetta turned back to the sink. "Child, your mother had enough of a problem with it for all of us. Didn't see no reason to pile it on. Not like anyone with a lick a sense shoulda been surprised. You ain't the first to go that way, won't be the last. More important things to worry about in this life."

Shelton sat up straight and pulled her hair out of her face. "Oh, my God. My mother. I guess I'll have to call her, tell her about Grandpa. And... oh Christ! I suppose she'll want to come to the funeral."

"You don't need to worry about that now, child. As I recall, she pretty much swore off all us McKendricks when she left here. Said it was us that drove you wrong, encouraging you to act more like a boy than a girl. Vowed she'd never set foot on the farm again. So I don't expect she'll show up all teary at your grandpa's service."

"You think?"

"Hell, child, I don't see where you even need to call her at all. When was the last time you heard from her?"

"Been awhile."

"Awhile?"

"Fourteen years."

"I think there's some kind of limit on how long someone can quit being your mother and still have any rights to that. What do they call it? A statue of stipulations?"

"Statute of limitations."

"Yeah, that."

Chapter 21

MAKING HIS WAY through the mass of mourners at Mossback's Funeral Home in Warrenton, Thumper nodded to Muriel Hudkins, turned out in proper mourning attire complete with hat and gloves. She stood perfectly poised, politely listening as Luella Starett, owner/operator of the Paradise Gap General Store, related a bawdy tale about Fergus. Muriel held her composure and responded with the requisite "Oh, my. You don't say? Dear me." at the appropriate intervals. Thumper could tell she'd rather be most anywhere else and he commended her inwardly for her devotion and fortitude.

He then came upon two couples standing along the edge of the crowd. All four looked equally uncomfortable. The two ladies—one beefy and pale, the other small and dark—wore their most somber church dresses. The men—one thick and balding, the other wiry with a head of coarse black hair—tried not to look too out of place in their ill-fitting jackets and mismatched ties.

Thumper made it a point to thank the Nutchenkos—Natasha and Voytek, his housekeeper and farm manager—and the Ledesmas—Javier and Bettiana, his head groom and stable caretaker—for coming to pay their respects.

Moving on, he came to Grantham Meisner, executive director of NAFCA, the North American Fox Chasers Association. Kirsten Kettering, Grantham's significant other, stood at his side.

"What's up with your joint-master?" Meisner asked, not bothering with any sorrowful references to the deceased.

"Not sure what you mean. I've been away the past three days, drove straight here from Charlottesville. Has Mildred been misbehaving again?"

"I don't mean Mildred, and you know it. We'd heard the sport was off to a good start—an exceptionally good start—so Kirsten and I went out this morning."

"And I hope you weren't disappointed."

"With the sport? Hell, no. It was fabulous, first rate. But, Ryman… well, he didn't quite seem himself. He was going around reciting a poem, something about 'The hunter's badge of glory,' holding his hand up like he was making the Boy Scout pledge. Very strange look in his eyes."

"He's probably just still rattled by his old man's death. I wouldn't worry about it. The main thing is the sport was good."

"Incredible," Kirsten said. "I've never run and jumped so much during the first week of cubbing. I'll be stiff for a month."

Coming from a professional horse trainer who rode no fewer than six horses a day, Thumper took that as particularly high praise for the Montfair pack. "Well, then, who cares if my joint-master is acting a little strange? Even for him."

Turning from Grantham and Kirsten, Thumper found himself facing a tall, elegant lady of indeterminate age. Cecelia Broadhurst was ten years Thumper's senior. Thanks to good genes, an athletic lifestyle, and excellent cosmetic surgery, she could have passed for his junior by an equal amount. She'd been married four times, each husband a better catch than the one before. The final hubby had passed away just north of ninety, leaving Cecelia the bulk of his considerable fortune. His legacy included a specially designed climate-controlled building that housed his collection of twenty-two classic MG automobiles. An admirer of Cecil Kimber, the legendary designer of the original MG motorcars, the late Mister Broadhurst named his Virginia estate in the man's honor.

To help offset the appearance of being nothing more than a hugely successful fortune hunter and now idle rich member of the Virginia uppercrust horsey set, Cecelia dabbled in real estate. She was aligned with a firm that specialized in multi-million dollar country estate properties. The allure for Cecelia, though, was not so much the potentially hefty commissions as it was the access the job provided to the local gossip grapevine.

"Cecelia," Thumper said, taking her heavily bejeweled hand, "good of you to come."

"For our senior master? Of course I'd be here to pay my respects. But I do bring apologies from Dorcas. She said she wasn't feeling well, asked me to convey her condolences to the family."

"Sorry to hear that. I hope it's nothing serious."

"You do know her father passed away recently?"

"No, I hadn't heard that. I suppose that makes Fergus's death a bit hard on her."

"I'm sure she'll bounce back, just needs some time to come to terms with this. As we all have to do eventually."

"Tell me about it."

A flush of red appeared along Cecelia's high cheekbones. "Oh, well, yes, I suppose a bit more difficult for some than others. I'm sorry."

"Long time ago, and well behind me now. Tonight the focus is on Fergus. I'd better get in the receiving line before Ryman's hand falls off."

Fergus lay in state, his wavy silver hair perfectly coifed, an artificially healthy color on his face. He was dressed in full formal hunt attire: scarlet coat, canary vest, white stock tie with gold pin, white breeches, black boots with brown tops. His hunt cap rested in the crook of one arm, his whip in the other.

Rhetta, Ryman, and Shelton were stationed to one side of the casket, greeting the mourners as they filed past. When Shelton saw Thumper, she excused herself, made her lumbering way through the packed room, grabbed his arm, and led him out into the hallway where the crowd was slightly less dense.

"What's wrong with my father?" she demanded.

"Nice to see you too," he replied.

"He's saying something like, 'Hunter's badge of glory,' to everyone who comes through the line. Grandma's told him to stop it twice now but he just keeps doing it. Shaking hands and muttering that phrase as if he was saying, 'So nice of you to come.'"

"Your old man had a nasty bonk on the head last Friday. Two of them in fact. And seeing your grandfather keel over dead right in front of him probably didn't help any. I thought he'd be back to his lovable old self by now. Appears he's not."

"And he keeps asking people if they've seen a deer. Something about a big buck, huge rack, and a cross-shaped thing. Everyone's starting to look at him funny, I can hear the buzz going around the room. You'd better get him out of there before Grandma loses..."

"That's enough, goddammit!" Rhetta's voiced exploded from the viewing room. "Ain't you got no respect for your own father? If you won't stop your damn babblin', then get the hell out of here. I won't have you embarrass this family any more! Where the hell's Sheltie Lou?"

Thumper tucked in behind Shelton like a halfback following a blocking lineman and stayed close as she cleared a path through the startled crowd.

They reached the casket to find Ryman in his petulant child stance, Rhetta in full harridan mode, a hand on one bony hip, the other pointing toward the exit.

"Grandma," Shelton said in a hushed tone, "let's not have a scene. Daddy's been under a lot of pressure the past few days, what with his head trauma and all."

"Pressure and head trauma be damned," Rhetta snapped back. "Comes a time when a man's gotta stand up and be a man. And if he cain't, then he needs to go act like a crazy fool somewheres else."

Thumper took Ryman's arm and started to lead him away while Shelton tried to restore order, soothing Rhetta and shooing her back into her assigned spot. The buzz in the room turned to silent stares as Thumper guided Ryman out. He found an empty office along the back hallway and plopped Ryman down into a chair.

"Ry, this has to stop. Or you at least need to get some control. This is not the place, not the crowd to be..."

"But, Thumper, I can't get that poem out of my head. And that deer keeps haunting me. I've got to find him, track him down, figure out what this is all about..."

He started to rise from the chair and Thumper pushed him back down. It felt like shoving a sack of feathers.

"You're not going anywhere. You have an obligation to your father. And if not to him, considering it's likely he's not aware of what's going on just now, then certainly to your mother and daughter. You've got two options this evening. You can either pull yourself together, march back in there, take your place in the receiving line, and address people in a manner proper for this occasion. Or you can excuse yourself as being under too much strain and have Nardell drive you home."

Ryman sat for a long moment, his head down and shoulders hunched. "You wouldn't believe the sport we had while you were away," he said. "Foxes up on the first cast, wonderful runs, great hound work..."

"I know. Mildred emailed me her reports. But that's got nothing to do with this evening..."

"And then after the hunts..." His head came up, he flashed a devilish grin, and his eyebrows danced. "Hoo boy! It's just... Nardell and me are like... newlyweds. Or kids. Can't wait to get home... or wherever..." His eyebrows did a quickstep on that remark.

"Ah... well... Mildred's reports didn't say anything..."

"It's all about the 'Hunter's badge of glory,' don't you see. About hunting with honor as is due, and through the beast to God..."

"Ry, I think we've got a more serious issue here than I'd imagined." Thumper leaned close to him and took a sniff. "You haven't been into the sauce this evening, have you?

Ryman looked up with an innocent sheen on his face. "No, not a drop. Maybe later, after all this. But not before."

Thumper saw no hint of falsehood in Ryman's eyes. "Good. But something's going on in that banged-up brain of yours. Do you think you can deal with the rest of this evening in a halfway normal fashion?"

Ryman stood up, squared his shoulders, twisted his neck, and straightened his tie. "You betcha."

"No more 'Hunter's badge' crap?"

"Not a word."

"Nothing more about that deer?"

"Scout's honor," he said, holding up the three-finger pledge.

"All right, then. Let's get you back where you belong. But if you drop the ball again, you're on your own, pal. And God help you if you piss off your dear mother a second time this evening."

"Been pissing her off all my life," Ryman said. His shoulders lost a touch of their firmness. "No reason tonight should be any different."

"Yes," Thumper snapped back, "tonight should be different. It's your old man's wake, for Christ sakes. Just get through tonight, the funeral tomorrow, the memorial service before Saturday's hunt. Then you can go as fucking bonkers as you want."

"Promise?"

"Cross my heart."

"Deal."

Miles Flanagan and Conway Purvis accosted them in the hallway. Miles managed to find what marginally passed as a dress shirt and bedecked it with a tie he'd picked up at the thrift shop for fifty cents. The shirt was three sizes too big and the tie, a swirling paisley pattern thirty years out of fashion, was encrusted with an angled slash of pea-green stain. In place of his everyday jeans he wore a rumpled pair of khaki Dockers. He'd at least knocked some of the mud and manure off his paddock boots. Conway did not feel the need to costume himself in anything more than a clean tee-shirt, absent any artwork or slogans, and jeans that were somewhat less grease-stained than his work uniform. This, by Purvis standards, constituted formal attire.

Ryman greeted them in a polite, level manner. "Miles, Conway. Thanks for coming. I'm sure my father would have..."

"When are we going back to work?" Miles demanded.

Conway's stance softened some when he saw the painfully surprised look on Ryman's face.

"Can... can we talk about that later? I need to get back to the receiving line and..."

"And we need to get back to work," Miles interrupted. "We've lost this whole week already. And you ain't said nothing about whether or not we're gonna get paid for the days the shop's been closed."

"Well, it won't have been a full week," Ryman pointed out. "Monday was a holiday anyway."

"Yeah, a *paid* holiday. At least your old man always paid us for national holidays. 'Cept Martin Luther King Day. Although I suspect he paid Muriel for that one. So me and Conway, we need to know. Are we gettin' paid, and when are you gonna reopen the shop?"

"Look, Miles," Thumper said, taking a half step forward, "now's not the time..."

"This ain't no concern of yours, *Mister* Billington. Besides, you ain't exactly got the best track record as an employer."

"Now see here, Flanagan..."

Ryman put a hand on Thumper's arm. "It's okay, Thumper. I got this one. You boys show up for work bright and early Monday morning, back to business as usual."

"What about our pay for this week?"

"Regular paychecks next Friday."

"This week too?"

"This week too."

"The Monday holiday?"

"Yes, the full week."

They stood in an uneasy foursome for several long, awkward seconds. Conway wanted to get outside for a smoke. Miles showed a lingering hint of skepticism as he sized up Ryman. Finally satisfied that he'd gotten what he came for, Miles turned and marched down the hallway. Conway obediently followed.

"I don't know why you put up with that impertinent little loser," Thumper said.

"I reckon Daddy felt sorry for him. Seems nobody wanted him riding their horses anymore. I guess Daddy figured he'd be better off behind the parts counter than in the saddle."

"Well, he might still be riding for me if I hadn't caught him mistreating my horses. Will you be able to make good on what you just told him?"

"C'mon," Ryman said. "I've got mourners to greet."

Chapter 22

THE BODY LAY along the shoulder of Paradise Turnpike, a plump doe obligingly whacked by a fast-moving vehicle, killed instantly, and not more than a few hours dead. Bar shooed away a pack of complaining crows, gathered the deer's hooves together, and with a smooth motion swung her into the bed of his truck.

He pulled up next to a spot about fifty feet from his trailer, an area littered with bones and tufts of hair. Grabbing the deer again by the legs, he flung the carcass away, rivaling an Olympic hammer-thrower for the distance the body flew before landing with a dull *thunk* on the hard ground. A stirring sound was already beginning to emanate from the thick woods that surrounded his home.

"Woooo whoooop!" Bar called out. "C'mon, my lovelies. Wooooo whoooop!"

A large black bird, its dark wrinkled head devoid of feathers, white tips at the ends of its two-foot wingspan, came gliding down from the cover of a tall pine. Another followed, then two more. Others soon came on. Each one circled down in a graceful spiral and landed beside the waiting carcass.

"There ya go, kids," Bar said. "Reggie, Maude, Gertrude, Heathcliffe. Dig in. Ah, here's Heckle and Jeckle now. And Tweety close behind. Enjoy your dinner, my friends."

Bar drove the rest of the way to his trailer and hauled himself inside. It offered sparse living space, especially for a man his size. A bed filled one end, what passed for living quarters the other, with a tiny kitchenette and bathroom between. The bathroom consisted of a single enclosure that served as both toilet and shower stall. The toilet drained out to a sewage tank, a water tank next to it fed the shower and kitchen sink. A propane tank provided fuel for the two-burner stove and enough heat in the winter to keep him from freezing to death, if just barely. The only semblance of contact with outside civilization was the electric power line. It wasn't there when Bar moved in. He'd gotten along with kerosene for light, had no need for anything that required electricity. But once it became apparent that this was going to be Bar's permanent home, Fergus insisted on running the line back to the trailer. Fergus paid for the installation, and ever since the little bit of electricity Bar used was a tiny indistinguishable portion of the overall Fair Enough Farm electricity bill.

Amid the mismatched second-hand (in some cases third- or fourth-hand) furniture, a few old photos, and other scattered memorabilia was one item oddly out of place: A relatively new, topgrade laptop computer, perched on a dented aluminum tray stand.

Bar grabbed a beer from the half-sized fridge, twisted off the top, and sat down at the computer. He brought up a website and began browsing through the information, taking a pull on his beer every minute or so. He moved to another website, then a third. The information he read did not register. He went back two, three, even four times rereading the same details. Nothing stuck.

He should have gone to the viewing. He knew it would have been the right thing to do. As uncomfortable as he would have felt, he should have done it for Fergus. He glanced around the trailer. Look at all he did for me, he thought. Even after... well, that was a long time ago. Of course, *she* would have been there. But he didn't necessarily have to deal with her. She'd be stuck there by the casket. He could have just popped in, made a brief appearance, then left. At least folks could confirm he'd paid his respects. Not like anyone could have missed seeing him.

Too late now. Be dark soon. The others will be getting back to the farm before long.

He stood up, drained his beer, took another from the fridge, and went outside. The warm September evening air was heavy with pine scent. Lightning bugs flashed their mating display across the open patch of ground between his front door and the woods. Mosquitoes buzzed around him, drawn by the scent of blood under his exposed flesh. He sat down in a rickety lawn chair, reached beside it, pulled up a plastic bottle of insect repellent, and gave himself a good sprits.

The birds were already well along in their methodical devouring of the deer carcass. Bar sat sipping at his beer and thought about the cycle of life. Everything dies, one way or another, some sooner, some later. Fergus had come to the end of his cycle, after a good long run. Are such things meant to be? Or is it all just random chance and means nothing? Would things have been different if he'd pulled the trigger a split second sooner? Was what happened destined to be or could he have changed the course of things? No way to ever know. But I'm still here, he thought, and many other better men are not. One in particular.

One less deer out in the woods now too, but still plenty more. Maybe that one Ryman saw. If he really did see it. Damn fourteen-pointer? With some crazy-ass cross thing between its rack? Ryman's out of his fucking head. Must be the strain of his old man dropping dead. And all those whacks on the brain. Damn fools, riding horses, running after hounds, chasing foxes around. Never could figure that. And all that fancy dress, their silly-ass traditions.

He sat watching the vultures pick the carcass clean as he worked on his beer.

Now here are animals that serve a purpose. Nature's perfect janitors. Ugly things to most folks. Disgusting creatures. But wouldn't the world be a mess without them, doing their job, cleaning up the remains when some other critter's time comes? And it comes to all.

He raised his bottle and said aloud, "Reggie, Maude, and all my fine ugly, disgusting darlings, here's to ya! Bone apple teet!"

Chapter 23

THE REVEREND HERBERT K. Laudermilk served St. Cuthbert's-in-the-Woods for close to four decades. He was the ideal parson for an Episcopal church in foxhunting country: soft-spoken, erudite, mannerly, a gentle comforter, confident in his faith while never one to force his beliefs on others. He seemed to be a man constantly bemused by life, always aware of the ironies and injustices of this world, yet hopeful that there was some benevolent force at work that would eventually reveal itself and he would understand it all. One evening, alone in the parsonage study, he laid his head down and left this world to find out if that benevolent force does exist.

In his stead, the diocese sent a much-traveled fellow, the Reverend Doctor Daniel T. Davenport, who presented all the outward appearance of an English country vicar: tall and slim except for a rounded paunch, with sagging shoulders, pallid skin, an aquiline nose hinting at aristocratic breeding, salt-and-pepper beard and hair constantly in need of a trim. His unkempt eyebrows curled up at the ends into little bushy horns and rings of circles drooped beneath his bored brown eyes. He often had a pipe clenched between his yellowed teeth, which gave his clothes the perpetual scent of charred hedge clippings rotting in an abandoned fireplace. He pronounced the word "been" as "bean," his Mini Cooper ran on "petrol," he wrapped his leftovers in "aluminium foil," and he watched Masterpiece Theater on the "telly."

The real Dan Davenport was born and raised in Portage, Indiana, the son of a sheet metal mechanic father and store clerk mother, neither of whom finished high school nor had been any farther away from Portage than Kankakee. Young Dan parlayed his studious habits and Anglophile fascination into a career in the clergy, got out of Portage as quickly as possible, earned a doctorate in theology and spent the next twenty years bouncing around a succession of parishes, never finding a home quite suitable for his unique proclivities.

The foxhunting world, populated as it is by many who excel at affectation of one form or another, suited him well. The few remaining congregants at St. Cuthbert's had no particular problem with a

Midwesterner of humble origin recreating himself as a theological scholar from the Shires.

Had Father Herb conducted Friday's private service for Fergus McKendrick, it would have been an entertaining, uplifting occasion, a balanced blend of spiritual reflection, humor, and praise for the heroism and good works of the deceased. Instead the specially invited attendees were stuck with Reverend Dan, who clumped up the few steps to the pulpit. His haggard visage dripped with saintly solemnity.

St. Cuthbert's consisted of a modest white wooden structure, situated on a side street off Paradise Turnpike. A large window behind the pulpit allowed a sweeping view of the rolling countryside. The mourners could at least enjoy the scenery while pretending to listen to the sermon.

In the back right corner sat Muriel Hudkins, arrayed in her best funeral turnout—black dress, black hat, and even black gloves, the picture of respectful propriety. Directly across from her to the left, occupying a substantial portion of the back pew, sat a most uncomfortable Barstow Reinhardt. Muriel could not remember the last time she'd seen him wearing a shirt any earlier than late November. On this occasion he wore a long sleeve denim work shirt, wrinkled but mostly clean. His bib overalls appeared to be new, not a spot or stain anywhere on them. Muriel thought she could see a price tag sticking out from one side. A rarely used black patch covered the scarred remains where his left eye had been blown away.

Muriel's attention snapped back to the pulpit where Reverend Dan began with his opening prayer.

"Everliving God, who didst call thy servants Aidan and Cuthbert to proclaim the Gospel in northern England and embued them with loving hearts and gentle spirits: Grant us grace to live as they did, in simplicity, humility and love for the poor; through Jesus Christ, who came among us as one who serves, and who liveth and reigneth with thee and the Holy Spirit, one God, now and forever. Amen."

No one recalled much of what was said thereafter. But many did enjoy the view out the window.

****

As the small crowd moved to the McKendrick section of the cemetery for the interment, Bar kept a careful distance and left as soon as the first shovelful of dirt landed on the casket lid.

Ryman's attention was directed toward the surrounding woods rather than at his father's casket. He scanned the tree line, searched the pastures. If he could have turned around to survey the fields across the road from the church without incurring a sharp poke in the ribs from Rhetta, he would have done so.

Thumper stood slightly behind him and to one side. He could see Ryman's head swiveling and caught the hawkish glint in his eye when he turned toward him. He tried to send positive thoughts into his friend's disturbed brain. *Hold on, Ry. Just a couple more days and you can go stone crazy about your deer sightings and hunting visions. Just not here, not now. Hold on, old buddy.*

Ryman managed to get through the graveside service and the small group shuffled in a quiet huddle to the parking lot.

"That was some excellent sport your hounds showed yesterday," Grantham said to Ryman.

Ryman brightened at the remark. "You betcha! Best ever. Y'see, it's all about the hunter's ba..."

Thumper cleared his throat.

"... um... I mean... it's about the *huntsman's*... ba... er... *ability*... to... ah... have his pack in such great shape... and, well, Crispie here has done a wonderful job."

Thumper gave Ryman a nod of approval.

"It's not just about Crispie," Mildred added. "Oh, sure, he's doing a heckuva job. But Ryman's the one who just seems to know..."

"Say," Thumper broke in, "maybe we'd all better get going. Lots of people coming in this afternoon, much to do to get ready for the memorial service tomorrow."

"Well," Grantham said, "now that you mention it, I've still got some tweaking to do on my remarks."

"Okay, then." Thumper turned to Reverend Dan. "Padre, very nice service."

The priest grimaced at the flippant form of address. "Thank you, Professor Billington. Such a loss to our community, this fine man."

Ryman opened the passenger door to his truck and gave Nardell his hand as she climbed in. He whispered something in her ear, she scrunched her shoulders and giggled. He slammed the door closed and did a high-stepping dash around to the driver's side.

Mildred and Josh did a double-time to their car. He also opened the door for her and upon closing it practically vaulted over the hood and into his seat.

Crispie and Patti headed the other way toward the staff truck, his hand on the small of her back, urging her to make haste. He didn't bother to get the door for her but was shifting into reverse before she had her door closed.

Thumper stood in the parking lot, trying to process what he'd just seen—most odd for people departing from a burial service.

"Reckon we'd best get going too," Rhetta said to Shelton. "I could use some help picking out what to wear tomorrow."

"Sure, Grandma," Shelton replied.

As Rhetta turned toward Shelton's car, Bing stepped forward. "Henrietta?"

She stopped cold and whipped around to face him. "Been a long time since anyone's called me that." Her expression was a mix of smirk and smile.

"I haven't had a chance to offer my personal condolences." He gestured awkwardly toward his son and daughter-in-law. "From all of us, really. Never known a better man than Fergus. We all share your sense of loss."

"I bet you do." The smirk deepened, the smile faded. She turned and continued toward the car. "C'mon, Sheltie Lou. I got a whole pile a clothes on the bed for us to go through."

Chapter 24

IT WAS A given that the proper public send off for Fergus had to be tied to a hunt. Everyone involved in planning the event agreed that, despite the warmth of early September, formal kit must be required—scarlet coats for those so entitled, black for all others. There would be some sweaty hunters attending the memorial service and participating in the hunt to follow. But anything more casual would not convey the pageantry the event demanded.

It was impossible for Thumper Billington to put a firm figure on the number of hunts he'd seen move off from the Montfair estate house over his lifetime. Several hundred at least. He could not, though, recall ever seeing as big a crowd on his front lawn as there was the morning of Fergus McKendrick's memorial service. Pillars of the foxhunting community came from as far away as California. Hunters from one tip of the Atlantic Seaboard to the other were there. Many had trailered in their own horses, some were mounted on loaners or hirelings. Others opted to remain on foot, either unable to have a horse on site or as part of that revered group of hunters emeriti who because of age, infirmity, or injury (or, in many cases, a combination of all three) no longer ride to hounds.

The Paradise Gap B&B was booked solid within an hour of the official announcement of the memorial service. Every hunting-friendly farm in Crutchfield County, and into the surrounding counties as well, opened their guest rooms and pastures.

The local non-hunting contingent turned out in mass. Everyone knew Fergus McKendrick and all felt an obligation to pay their respects.

It became apparent early in the week that Fair Enough Farm could not handle this onslaught. So Thumper offered Montfair, enlisted his staff to pitch in, and hired some additional muscle for the special event. He felt like he was managing the foxhunting version of Woodstock.

He instructed the landscaping crew to do the best trim job on his front lawn, all twenty-two acres of it, they'd ever done. Parking arrangements for cars and horse trailers had to be made. A stage was erected and a public address system set up. A section for the standing crowd was cordoned off, another for the mounted hunters. Hounds were bathed and groomed to present their finest appearance, as were the staff horses. Thumper engaged his most reliable caterer and gave her carte blanche. One table was laid out with three-hundred Saint Hubert medals, one for each guest to take as a memento. Tents were set up over the food service area.

Scanning the expanse of lawn from the columned portico of the main house down to the stone pillars at the entrance off Montfair Lane, it was impossible to look in any direction without seeing a plethora of scarlet coats. A dozen photographers, half of them pros, including one who had flown in all the way from Wales (at Thumper's invitation and expense), the others talented amateurs, circulated among the crowd. Moving between the mounted riders were another dozen helpers, each carrying a silver tray with an assortment of beverages—port, sherry, orange juice, and apple cider—in small cups. Thumper rounded up as many silver stirrup cups as he could muster, between the family's collection and loaners from other hunt members. But the servers ultimately had to resort to paper cups to accommodate everyone, a painful but necessary bow to convenience and modernity.

Thumper was going over final details with the caterer when a vaguely familiar woman approached.

"Mister Billington?"

"At your service."

"I'm Janey Musgrove. Danella Kernan, my agent, well, actually *our* agent, said it would be okay if I..."

"Oh, yes, yes, of course. Glad you could come." He did his best to force a smile.

Thumper caught sight of Chet Henderson, Marva's husband, along the edge of the driveway, organizing the car-followers. Although not a horseman himself, Chet knew as much about the sport as most of those who rode, a good bit more than some. He was the perfect escort for Janey.

An extensive caravan was shaping up for this special day. Non-riding spouses and significant others, hunters emeriti, riders recovering from injuries, and the battalion of photographers were all eager to follow the action and witness the spectacle in its full splendor afield.

"Let me introduce you to someone who can help make sense of this for you," Thumper said as he caught Janey by the arm and guided her along. Janey's eyes widened behind her thick glasses and her feet—improperly shod in open-toed flats, ill-suited for a day in horse country—barely touched the pebbled pathway as Thumper half-guided, half-dragged her over to Chet. "Janey Musgrove, may I introduce Chet Henderson, renowned leader of the Montfair Hunt Truck Brigade. Chet, Janey is a fellow member of the Kernan Agency client team. Never seen a foxhunt before. She'd like to find out a bit about what we do, and see how it's done. May I entrust her to your expert care?"

"Most certainly, Master," Chet replied. "I'll see to it she has a front row seat when the action starts."

"Thanks. Ms. Musgrove, sorry I can't spend more time with you just now. But please stay for the post-hunt refreshments and perhaps we can chat some then."

With that, he marched briskly along the edge of the crowd, acknowledging greetings with a quick smile and a cursory wave. Javier Ledesma stood by the stage steps where he held the reins of Thumper's horse, Lenny, and waited for the master's arrival. The horse's dark coat gleamed. His mane was perfectly braided, thanks to the nimble fingers of Javier's wife Bettiana. His eyes were bright and alert, his neck arched, nostrils flared. The strange sights of a stage, speakers, tents, and vehicles, plus the bustle of more than two hundred people around him had every fiber in his highly bred body on full alert.

Ryman arrived, having ridden Token over from Fair Enough Farm. He dismounted and handed the reins to Javier. Both horse and rider looked drained and distracted.

"Buck up there, m'friend," Thumper said, giving Ryman a chuck on the shoulder. "Just a wee bit longer and this will be over. We'll go have us some sport, then some refreshments. Look at all these folks who've come to honor your old man. Quite a legacy."

Ryman looked out at the crowd and his face tightened even more. Still staring at the mass of people, he said, "Old Whitehouse Covert this morning."

"What?"

"That's where we'll draw."

"That's not what we agreed on. We discussed this with Crispie yesterday. We're drawing to Gretchen's Bottom. There's plenty of open ground there for the field to view hound work. We've had no rain yet, need to stay in the low-lying areas if there's going to be any chance of sport."

"No fox there, Thumper," he said, holding his gaze out toward the crowd.

"Another one of your visions?" Thumper said with increasing frustration. Grantham Meisner was looking down from his seat on the platform. His brow furrowed and he pointed at his watch.

"Vision?" Ryman replied. "Hell, I dunno what you'd call it. Vision, sense, something... someone... speaking to me." He bowed his head and kicked at a clump of grass clippings with the toe of his boot.

"Shit, Ry. I told you, just knock this crap off until this is all over. We're drawing to Gretchen's Bottom. There are too many people here, lots of whom have come from far away at great effort and expense to honor your old man. It's likely to be a short enough hunting day as it is with scent rising everywhere. I'm not going to risk spoiling the day for all these folks because of these harebrained... feelings... or whatever it is you're having."

Ryman turned to face Thumper, a glint of challenge on his troubled face. "I've been right the last three times haven't I? You saw it last Saturday. And Mildred told you about Tuesday's and Thursday's hunts."

"Okay, I'll give you that. But maybe the third time was the charm and now you're done. You can't keep this up forever without hitting it wrong eventually."

"Maybe. But it won't be today."

"No, it probably won't be. If we draw to Gretchen's Bottom, that is."

Grantham cleared his throat and jabbed at his watch with increased emphasis. He jerked his head, signaling for them get up on the platform and get the show started.

"C'mon," Thumper said, "Our audience awaits." He pushed Ryman up the steps and they took their seats.

Thumper, Ryman, Rhetta, Shelton, Grantham Meisner, and the Reverend Doctor Davenport were seated on the stage. Grantham was assigned the opening remarks, Thumper would go second, Ryman third. Reverend Dan was slated to be the closing speaker and that would be the cue for Thumper and Ryman to leave the stage, mount their horses, and join Mildred at the front of the hunting field.

As Thumper turned the podium over to Ryman and took his seat, he could see moisture forming on the back of Ryman's neck, enough to dampen his stock tie. Ryman stammered through his speech, pulling at the cloth wrapped tightly around his neck with increasing frequency as the time wore slowly on. His voice was scratchy and his lips dry by the time he concluded.

Ryman wrapped up to mild applause and a mumbled mass utterance of "Hear, hear." He and Thumper then descended from the platform, mounted their horses, and took their positions. In proper respectful fashion, all gentlemen removed their head coverings. Ryman dripped with sweat. Beads flowed down his face, into his eyes, and left dark dots on the lapels of his scarlet coat.

"You okay, Ry?" Thumper whispered as Davenport blathered away in his singsong fake British tone, something about ashes and dust.

"Yeah, sure," Ryman croaked in response.

"I dunno, buddy. You don't look so good. Maybe you should skip the hunt this morning. Lot of strain on you, man."

"No! I have to hunt this morning."

A few bystanders turned to look at the source of this remark, stated a little too loudly for the circumstances.

"And," he continued, turning to Thumper with a lowered voice, "we *have* to draw to Old Whitehouse."

"Nope, not happening."

"For my old man's sake then."

"You already tried that low shot once. Not working today."

"And noooow," Reverend Dan intoned with oratorical flair, "let us conclude with the story of Saint Hubert, the patron saint of hunters."

Ryman and Thumper stopped their argument and gave their attention to the speaker.

"Hubert was reportedly a great lover of pleasure and his chief passion was the chase, to which he devoted nearly all his time. According to the legend, Hubert was afield one morning, participating in the chase of a deer on horseback with his famous hounds."

Ryman swayed in his saddle. He stared vacantly at a point just above Davenport's head.

"As he was pursuing a magnificent stag," the clergyman continued, "and in a clearing in the forest, the animal stopped and turned. Hubert was astounded at perceiving a crucifix suspended between its antlers..."

The circuit of Ryman's swaying motion increased. Sweat cascaded down his face, soaked his coat, and left spots on his white breeches.

Every hound in the pack stood at attention. Thumper felt Lenny tense up and prick his ears forward. All horses there—more than a hundred of them—did likewise. Not one hoof moved, not the slightest jig, tails did not swish at flies. The animals stood like statues, eyes riveted on the swaying figure of Ryman McKendrick.

Limply waving one arm for emphasis, Reverend Dan prattled on, "... while he heard a voice from the figure of Christ say, 'Hubert, unless you turn to the Lord, and lead a holy life, you shall quickly fall into the abyss of Hell!'"

Ryman dropped the reins and put his arms out to his sides, palms up. His hunt cap, tucked under his arm, fell to the ground with a bounce and rolled away. He tilted his head back and closed his eyes. Token did not move a muscle.

"Ryman!" Nardell called out from her position with the pack. "Oh, my God! What's wrong?"

Ignoring her outburst, Davenport approached his conclusion. "Hubert dismounted immediately from his horse, fell prostrate on the ground and asked, 'Lord, what would you have me do?'"

Ryman went slack. Thumper reached out to steady him but was too late. Ryman fell backward. His bare head thumped onto Token's rump, then he rolled off to one side and landed face down on Thumper's neatly trimmed front lawn.

Chapter 25

A COLLECTIVE GASP arose from the crowd of onlookers, followed by a rumble of murmurs and exclamations of wonder.

Javier was immediately in place to take the reins as Thumper leapt off Lenny.

Token stood as if guarding his fallen rider.

All hounds kept their eyes on Ryman's prostrate figure. Several of them whined softly.

Nardell, Mildred, and Josh were also off their horses and joined Thumper in a circle around Ryman. All four pulled out their cell phones and started to call 911. Seeing this, Thumper ordered the others to stop, said he'd handle that, and gestured for Josh to render aid.

From the stage came the sound of heavy footfalls as Shelton's flat soles smacked across the platform and cascaded down the steps. Grantham followed her at a pace that suggested frustration more than panic.

"Daddy!" Shelton cried, pushing past the others and kneeling beside her father, almost knocking Josh over as he tried to check Ryman's vital signs. She placed her hands on Ryman's shoulder blades and shook him forcefully. "Daddy! Oh, my God! What's wrong? What happened?"

"Best not do that," Josh said, regaining his balance and attempting to restrain Shelton. "Could be dehydration, possibly heat stroke. We need to get him out of these heavy clothes and cool him down. Help me roll him over."

"No!" Nardell shouted. "What if he has a neck injury? You shouldn't roll a person over..."

"Nardell," Josh interrupted, "I'm the doctor here. His neck's okay. I watched him fall. The critical thing is to get him cooled down."

Shelton and Josh rolled Ryman onto his back while Thumper engaged the 911 operator.

Ryman's eyes were closed and blades of freshly cut grass clung to his sweat-soaked face and clothing.

As Josh started to unbutton the coat, Ryman's eyes popped opened. His right arm moved in a scarlet blur and he grabbed Josh's hand with a crushing grip.

Everyone startled back at the unexpected movement. Josh winced at the pressure on his hand.

"Don't," Ryman said, quietly but with a commanding tone.

"Ryman," Josh said, trying to wrench his hand away, "you're not well. Could be heat stroke. We need to get you out of these clothes, cool you down. This is serious. Listen to me."

"No, Doc, you listen to me. I'm fine." He released Josh's hand and rose to his feet in one smooth motion. He'd stopped sweating, which Josh knew to be another sign of heat stroke. But the anguished expression was gone from his face. In its place was calmness, an air of authority with an aura of gentle compassion. He brushed the grass blades from his coat, reached into the back pocket of his breeches, withdrew a bandana, and wiped off his face. "Sorry to have troubled y'all," he said matter-of-factly, as if nothing had occurred worse than a mild sneezing fit.

"Ryman," Josh replied sternly, "you're *not* fine. Heat stroke is serious. It can be fatal, cause major organ damage. One of the symptoms is strange behavior, including hallucina..."

"Nothing like that going on with me, Doc." Ryman straightened his coat and retrieved his hunt cap from the ground. He placed the cap back on his head and gave it a couple of quick pats. "Everything's in perfect working order." He looked around at the two hundred faces staring at him (not counting the thirty-seven foxhounds and one hundred horses who all continued to focus on Ryman). "Sorry folks, just a passing dizzy spell. Everything's okay."

He grasped the left stirrup on his saddle and started to lift a leg to remount Token. Thumper pushed Preston aside and grabbed Ryman's arm to stop him.

"No hunting for you today, buddy. You're taking a short trip in the red light limo, get yourself checked out. They'll be here any minute."

Ryman froze with his foot halfway up to the stirrup. He locked his eyes on Thumper's with penetrating intensity. His usual downcast manner was gone, his natural reticence to make direct eye contact replaced by a laser-like, green-tinted gleam. His arm felt like a steel shaft under Thumper's hand.

"I'm afraid your red light limo pals will be disappointed." He brushed his friend aside and swung up onto his horse. "We need to get this morning's sport started. Lots of folks here, like you said. Don't want to disappoint them."

The others joined Thumper in a group protest. Only Rhetta and Reverend Dan remained where they were, she seemingly miffed and embarrassed by her son's behavior, he perturbed at having the brilliantly crafted summation of his remarks interrupted. His displeasure increased when he realized Ryman was calling for the hunt to begin, foreclosing the chance for him to regain the crowd's attention and leave them wowed by his theological genius. He tried to press on to his conclusion but no one paid a sliver of attention.

Ryman dismissed the ardent attempts to dissuade him from hunting, or being on a horse at all. "Hiccup's over," he said. "Y'all better get back on your horses if you don't want to miss the sport." He turned to Crispie and raised his voice. "Mister O'Rourke, shall we draw to Gretchen's Bottom?"

Javier gave Thumper a leg up onto Lenny. "Gretchen's Bottom?" Thumper said. "What about your insistence on Old Whitehouse."

"Plans have changed. Would have been too long and too hard a chase from Old Whitehouse. There's a more suitable customer waiting for us at Gretchen's Bottom. It's all been arranged."

"What's been arranged? What the hell are you talking about?"

Ryman ignored the questions and rode over to the front of the stage. He stepped lightly from Token's back directly onto the platform. The horse stood stock still at the spot where Ryman dismounted. Reverend Davenport stood agape at the podium, frozen in mid-sentence. Ryman gestured politely for him to move aside, stepped up to the microphone and said, "I reckon enough's been said about my daddy. I'm sure what he'd want now is for all of us to have a bit of sport. And that's just what we're going to do. Let's go hunting!"

He gracefully remounted Token and signaled to Crispie. The huntsman blew a short note to call his hounds to order and moved off.

The others who had dismounted scrambled to get back on their horses and follow along.

Bar Reinhardt was off to the side, safely out of Rhetta's line of sight, leaning against his truck. He gave a special whistle and Shelton turned her head at the sound, a familiar note but one she had not heard for many years. Checking first to see that her grandmother wasn't watching, she went to him and they climbed into the truck.

Ryman rode up to Nardell along the left side of the pack. "Honey," he said, "would you mind riding drag today? I need to be up with hounds."

She looked at him with a dazed expression, still baffled by his behavior, deeply concerned for his well-being. "Okay... yeah, sure," she replied. She turned her horse and fell in behind the flowing procession of huntsmen, hounds, and whippers-in, Patti on the right, Ryman now on the left.

Thumper and Mildred led their fields of followers, about equally divided into the jumpers following him, non-jumpers behind her. Dorcas Stanhope shepherded her flock of a dozen juniors in the jumping field.

Cecelia Broadhurst fell in with Mildred and served as mother hen to another dozen young kids not quite ready to handle the challenging jumps around the Montfair country.

Gretchen's Bottom had originally been selected as the first draw for a number of reasons. It was a short hack from the Montfair front lawn, far enough to give the riders time to loosen up, enjoy the scenery, and prepare for some sport, but not so far as to dissipate the stamina of hunters and horses on a warm morning. It consisted of a low-lying wooded area along a strong creek where scenting was likely to be better than on higher and drier ground. Positioned toward the interior of the Montfair acreage, a fox breaking covert from there could be chased in any direction. The ground sloped gently upward away from the creek into open fields where an audience of a hundred mounted riders could easily fan out. A farm road ran along the hillcrest, allowing those following in cars and trucks an equally full view of the action in the woods below.

Every vehicle was crammed to capacity—front seat, back seat, and truck bed—except for one. Bar kept his truck away from the main caravan when everyone loaded up. He waited until the procession was underway before falling in at the rear, accompanied only by Shelton.

"I'm worried about Daddy," she said.

"You damn well should be," Bar replied with a grunt. "Been acting bat-shit crazy for a week now since he got wacked on the head and your granddaddy died. You ain't seen but a bit of it."

"I've seen enough, between the way he was acting at the viewing the other night, and now passing out this morning. We need to get him to a doctor."

"Maybe he'll listen to you. Won't take no counsel from me. Imagine that?"

"I have to fly back home tomorrow. I don't know when I'll have a chance to talk to him."

"Back 'home' is it? Hell, California ain't your home. Maybe it's time you realized that and came back here where you belong."

"I… I don't feel like I belong here anymore. I did when I was growing up maybe. Although I don't think I realized it at the time. But I've been gone too long, got another kind of life now."

"You think your old man's gonna step into your granddaddy's shoes and keep the shop going? We might just as well lock the doors and take down the sign now."

"Please don't make me feel guilty about that. I know how much the shop means to you… and to others. It's just that I… I just can't…"

"Yeah, you're right. I'm sorry for tryin' to dump that on you. We'll get by somehow, I reckon. Or, if not, well, what the hell, I can retire and live off my fabulous investment portfolio, use my Social Security just for beer money."

"I'd hate to think what would become of all the tractors in Crutchfield County if that happened," Shelton said with a wisp of a smile.

The vehicles ahead all came to a stop along the crest of the hill overlooking Gretchen's Bottom.

"Looks like they're gonna try to get some action up," Bar said.

Crispie brought the pack to the hillside just above the wooded tree line. Patti moved off to a sentry position on the right, Nardell took a spot to the left where each could report if either of them viewed a fox. Ryman remained beside the pack, rather than fanning out to a sentry point as a whipper-in should do. Crispie was about to raise his horn to his lips and blow for the pack to leu in when Ryman stopped him.

"One second," Ryman said. As Crispie held his horn in mid-rise, Ryman surveyed the pack. Every hound's head turned toward him. Ryman singled out one hound in particular and set his gaze into the deep brown eyes. Bred and trained by Crispian O'Rourke, the Montfair hounds responded best to commands given in his voice. Ryman's Virginia drawl took on an Irish lilt. "Aye, Warwick, that's me lad. Y'know what to do then." His eyes traveled over to another hound. "Wasted, yes, that's the ticket. Good lass. Hempstead, none a that now."

He looked up from the pack and stared into the woods. He then closed his eyes, bowed his head, and mumbled something to himself. Crispie managed to catch the last few words, "... through the beast to God is true."

Ryman straightened up in the saddle and motioned for Crispie to cast hounds. The huntsman blew a short note and thirty-seven tricolor foxhounds surged into the covert as one body.

Not one of the five score spectators assembled on that hillside had ever seen better hound work. Ryman remained in the same spot, quietly watching and listening as Crispie trotted back and forth along the tree line, encouraging his hounds. "That's it, me beauties! Get 'im up now! Where's 'e at?"

Trilling cries arose from the pack as first one hound and then another picked up traces of that addictive scent, the musky odor of *vulpes vulpes* for which centuries of careful breeding had attuned their incredibly sensitive noses. Deeper still, the scene embodied the drama of the age-old bond between human, hound, and horse. The eager baying of three-dozen canines turned loose to seek their prey reverberated off the theater-style hillside and sent shivers of excitement up and down the spine of every onlooker. A hundred horses watched the wooded stage below, ears pricked, feet planted four square, waiting for the split-second signal that the chase was on.

Ryman remained in his position as if the conductor of a grand opera.

The living pageant portrayed the oldest strain of human memory, a link to the time when man first married the agile speed of the horse with the natural hunting drive of the dog. Somewhere the specter of an ancient ancestor, warmly clad in animal skins, his belly full thanks to his skills afield, raised his bow in exultation and exclaimed, "Hunt good!"

Right on cue, the cry of hounds rose into a chorus, swelling in a Rossini-like crescendo as Ryman dropped the reins and lifted his arms, holding his hunt whip aloft as if it were a baton.

One voice rose above the pack. Warwick, the principal tenor, displayed his talents in a brilliant aria. Wasted, his sister, joined in, filling the role of mezzo-soprano. Young Hempstead, who showed promise as a baritone, accepted his duty as supporting member of the troupe. Not one discordant note of babbling was heard from him. As the performers reached their climax, a shrill cry sounded from the wings as Patti sang out, "Tally-hoooooo!"

Act Two: The Chase is On.

And off they went. At Ryman's command Token surged forward into the woods, right behind Crispie and Kashmir. A trail cut through the trees, across the creek, and continued on a short stretch to where the woods ended on the far side of the covert. A post-and-rail jump guarded the trail's exit into the open pasture beyond. Thumper fell in behind Ryman at a respectful distance so as not to crowd huntsman and staff in their efforts to show good sport. Fifty riders followed him as they splashed through the creek, cantered briskly along the trail, and soared over the jump.

Mildred took her half of the followers down the tree line to another trail that led to a gate, easily opened from horseback to minimize delay for the non-jumpers. What time Mildred lost in having to take her people around jumps she made up for with a blazing pace on the flat. Riding behind Mildred Preston was not for sissies, even if her followers were spared the challenge of the Montfair country's stiff, unforgiving, stone and timber fences.

As Lenny landed smoothly over the post-and-rail, Thumper caught a glimpse of the fox sprinting toward the crest of the hill ahead, the pack in full cry close behind. The thrill of the chase was momentarily sullied by Thumper's concern that this might be too much for some of the hunters, overdressed as they were, many horses not yet in top condition.

He quickly shook that thought away. Too late now. Charlie was up, hounds were hot on the line. There was a good ruckus going on behind him, with so many riders in the field, several of them vying for position, trying to get to the front. As master and field leader, whatever havoc happened behind was not his concern when hounds were running. The job was to keep his followers in view of the action, show them the excellent work of hounds, and have them there at the end when the fox went to ground or slipped away from the pack and left hounds at a loss. If there were fifty at the start and five at the finish, so be it.

On this morning, though, each time Thumper took a quick glance over his shoulder he saw that everyone was still there, most of them smiling broadly, many showing splatters of creek mud and coatings of dust on their coats, a few with smudges across their faces as well.

After thirty minutes of exhilarating non-stop pursuit, he began to worry that they really were going to overdo it. The fox's circuit resembled the route they'd taken the previous Saturday when that big red took them from the edge of the Montfair boundary safely into the heart of their territory. Could it be the same fox? Quite possibly. Yet no one dropped out, no one came off, not even one horseshoe was lost. Jump after jump, field after field, trail after trail, they continued on at an even pace, not overly taxing for any horse or rider, but enough to keep the adrenaline flowing steadily. The cry of hounds was constantly in their ears, the pack nearly always in sight, and, at suitable intervals, there was a striking reminder of what this was all about when the obliging fox gave everyone a view of his handsome self.

When it finally appeared that a few riders were beginning to falter, Thumper heard the hounds' cry change. The insistent baying of the chase—long, open notes blended in a harmonic melody—switched to the shorter, higher pitched, questioning whine that signals a fox has gone to ground.

He pulled up on a rise in the middle of an open field and there, just inside the tree line below, the pack was gathered around a neatly secure den, a small rock pile guarding a cozy hiding spot, a slit between the rocks perfectly sized to permit nothing larger than a fox to enter. Warwick, Wasted, and Hempstead were at the center of the pack, each trying to get a nose into the small hole, alternately lifting their voices and calling the fox to come back out and play. Others rolled on the leaf-covered ground around the den entrance. A few flitted around the outskirts searching for scent, hoping it had been a trick and the fox was still afoot, or another was nearby to start the chase anew.

Crispie hopped off his horse, handed Kashmir's reins to Ryman, went to the hole, leaned over, and blew "Gone to Ground." He cheered the pack for their excellent work. "Good lad, Warwick. And Wasted, me fine lovely. Hempstead! I knew ya had it in ya. Well done, lad, well done. Hayfield, Harkness, Challenge, Conman, fine hounds all of ya!" He patted heads and scratched ears. All hounds smiled up at him, proud of themselves, enjoying the praise of their leader.

Just as when they started, the followers were again positioned in a theater-like setting, looking down at the spectacle of the chase's end. Patti and Nardell flanked the pack to the right and left, Ryman remained in the middle. He let the reins of Crispie's horse drop and turned Token to face the crowd gathered along the hillside above him. Kashmir waited patiently for Crispie's return.

Addressing the audience, he said, "I hope everyone's enjoyed this bit of sport. We could go on all day like this if we chose. But I reckon this is enough for most of y'all." He flipped open the cylindrical case secured to the front of his saddle, withdrew his father's old flask, and raised it high. At this signal the audience members all reached into cases or pockets, pulled out their flasks, and lifted them in response. His face beaming, Ryman recited his new Jäger-mantra in a stentorian voice: "This is the hunter's badge of glory, that he protect and tend his quarry, hunt with honor as is due, and through the beast to God is true!" His eyes traveled from one end of the line of mounted riders to the other, then came back to Thumper and Mildred who were side-by-side at the midpoint. Ryman lifted his flask higher still and called out in exultation, "To Fergus!"

The hills rang as a hundred voices called back, "To Fergus!"

Chapter 26

MONTFAIR'S FRONT LAWN was abuzz with exclamations of "I'll be damned," "I can't believe he did that," and "Most amazing thing I've ever seen," interspersed with eruptions of laughter and whoops of pleasure. Old friends embraced, shook hands, and smiled broadly. The crowd throbbed with *bonhomie.*

Only when Rhetta came along, cutting through the crowd with Shelton hovering on one side, Elizabeth Billington on the other, did the *joie de vivre* cease. The guffaws and giggles gave way to somber expressions of "So sorry for your loss," "My deepest sympathies," and "If there's anything I can do," as the stern-faced old woman in black marched by. As soon as she'd passed and the parting wave closed behind her, the merriment resumed.

She came to a group where Bing Sensabaugh stood amidst a swarm of admiring ladies.

"... so I'm lying there on the ground," Bing said, "my horse gone off to God knows where, Henrietta comes riding by, looks down at me—I swear to God this is true—and says 'If you think I'm stopping to pick up your sorry ass, you've got another think coming. Hounds are running!' And off she galloped, leaving me to..."

He stopped in mid-sentence when he caught Rhetta's stare boring a hole through him.

Hands on hips, she demanded, "What makes you think you can tell stories on me, Harry Sensabaugh?"

Buoyed by the support of his adoring posse, the awkwardness of the previous day's post-funeral encounter was gone. With his usual confident ease and a polite smile, he replied, "Public domain, Henrietta."

She did not expect such calm defiance. "What's that supposed to mean?"

"It means no one has exclusive rights to the stories of our lives: yours, mine, or anyone else's. Unless what I'm saying isn't true, you have no cause to object."

She took two steps toward him. He did not budge.

"I'll object if I damn well please."

"Object all you want. But did you or did you not leave me lying on the ground, my back badly wrenched, my horse gone, no one else around, and ride on after hounds?"

"That... that was forty years ago."

"Forty-two to be precise."

She turned to Shelton. "What's he mean, 'public do-main?'"

"Um, well, I guess, like, common knowledge, or something." Flustered by Rhetta's request for her input, Shelton gave Bing a pleading look asking for confirmation.

"Something like that," he said.

"You cain't go talkin' 'bout me like that. It's... it's... whatcha call it? Phi-landerous."

Elizabeth leaned over to her and whispered, "Slanderous."

"Yeah, that."

Bing took a step forward and his flock of admirers assembled into a tight mob behind him. One lady remained at his side and held a firm grip on his left arm. His tone softened as he said, "Henrietta, I'm truly sorry for your loss. I know Fergus loved you deeply, and I'm sure you loved him... in your own way. He was a good man. And he will be missed."

She stood mute for several seconds, intent on holding her stern composure. The barest trace of a tremble tugged at one corner of her mouth. Then, in a voice more accusatory than conciliatory, she said, "I reckon you do know a thing or two about love and loss, Harry Sensabaugh. Just don't go preaching it at me."

She turned and walked away. Shelton and Elizabeth followed, casting questioning glances at each other. Positioned between her two young attendants, Rhetta appeared to have grown smaller.

Thumper, standing in front of the food service tent, said to Reverend Dan, "I appreciate your contribution to this morning's service, Padre. It seems your words had a powerful effect on Ryman. What is it the Bible says about the word of God being sharper than a double-edged sword?"

"'For the word of God is quick, and powerful, and sharper than any two-edged sword, piercing even to the dividing asunder of soul and spirit, and of the joints and marrow, and is a discerner of the thoughts and intents of the heart.' Hebrews 4:12, King James Version."

"I'm impressed."

"What? That I'm a doctor of theology and I can actually quote Holy Scripture from memory? What do you think I've been doing the past twenty-some years?"

"No, of course… I didn't mean… well, that's not necessarily one of the more frequently quoted… and yet you… well, you just shot that right out."

"You, Professor Billington, are a student of the law and I would never be surprised at your ability to call up a legal reference, no matter how arcane. You might allow me the same consideration for my area of specialty."

"It was meant purely as a compliment, Padre. Sorry if it came out sounding wrong."

"I might also mention that 'Padre' is not an appropriate form of address for …"

"Oh, look! Here's someone you might want to meet." Janey Musgrove was wandering through the crowd and Thumper took the opportunity to call her over. "Well, what do you think of all this?"

"It's fabulous! Everything I'd imagined and more. A week ago I thought this had all died out, that no one still did it. And yet here you all are, so much pageantry, such tradition. And what a thrill watching from the hillside when the dogs were looking for a fox to chase. It was like… like a play… with music… or maybe more like a movie, like a costume drama."

"I'm glad you found it worth the trip out here to our little corner of the world."

"May I come again?"

"Of course, any time."

"Next Saturday?"

"Well, sure, if you'd like. But I must warn you there won't be a display like this. Not unless another one of our masters happens to drop dead in the next couple of days. We'll be back in our regular informal mode, no fancy coats, some folks just wearing polo shirts. Oh, and now that I think about it, I recall Chet said something about being away next weekend, taking care of his mother who's going into a nursing home. So he won't be there to lead the car-followers. But perhaps someone else will fill in that day."

"I don't want to impose," she said.

"Not a problem. Come on out and we'll see what we can do."

"Perhaps I could escort you that day," Reverend Dan offered.

"Oh, goodness, excuse my manners," Thumper said. "Janey Musgrove, may I introduce the good Reverend Doctor Daniel T. Davenport, vicar of St. Cuthbert's-in-the-Woods, shepherd over a flock of misfits and miscreants sorely in need of his ministrations."

Janey needed no help pinpointing Reverend Dan's denomination. The clerical collar worn over a faded lavender shirt, frayed brown herringbone sports coat with suede elbow patches, and unkempt beard said "Episcopalian" loudly enough. The scent of pipe tobacco enhanced the "vicar" image in her mind.

"Actually," Dan said, "we've already met once before. And may I say how much I enjoyed your books. Yours is a subject I've always taken an interest in myself."

"I'm afraid I'm a bit embarrassed," Janey confessed. "I'm sure we've met, but I can't quite place the occasion."

"George Mason University, last fall. I attended the talk you gave about your second book. I, too, find the lesser known, definitely non-mainstream belief systems to be quite fascinating. We had a lovely chat afterwards, over the weak tea and stale biscuits they served."

"Oh, certainly, now I remember. What a coincidence. Your parish is nearby?"

"Yes, in the local village. When might your fans see your next book?"

"No time soon, I'm afraid. There aren't many other fringe religions beyond the ones I've already covered. And, unfortunately, there just don't seem to be new ones springing up every day. So I'm looking into another topic, a sports idea, how that can have a religious-like connotation for many people."

"Indeed it can," Dan said with a note of disgust. "I find myself in competition with billion dollar sports enterprises for people's attention on what used to be considered 'The Lord's Day.' Puts a poor, humble vicar like myself at a significant disadvantage."

"I'm sure your parishioners prefer to worship with you than attend some garish, boisterous sports event," Janey said.

"Or at least arrange their schedules to do both," Thumper added.

"Yes, well, one can always record a sporting event and watch it later. The Lord prefers that we worship Him in real time." Dan reached into his coat pocket and withdrew a card. "My contact information. Call me if you'd like to accept my offer for next Saturday. I'm sure I won't do nearly as good a job as Chet, but I've learned a thing or two about the byways in these rustic parts. Perhaps we could meet in the village that morning, spare your car the rigors of traversing our rough country roads."

"If it's not too much of an imposition."

"Certainly not."

Thumper noticed Bing strolling toward them accompanied by an unfamiliar lady. "Now here comes one of the most sporting gentlemen you'll ever meet." He introduced Bing to Janey.

"And," Bing responded, "may I introduce my friend Marie Hardesty, from the Brookside Hunt down in southwestern Virginia."

Thumper took her offered hand lightly. "A pleasure to meet you. I know the masters there very well. In fact, I believe I saw them earlier, come to pay their respects to Fergus."

"Yes, several of us from Brookside came up with them. My first time out with Montfair. What a day! I haven't felt this… this vibrant in years." She squeezed Bing's arm and smiled at him with a glow that struck

Thumper as suggestive of an interest in something more than casual friendship.

"Turns out," Bing added, "that Marie and I have several things in common: mutual acquaintances, foxhunting, widowhood, grandchildren, the banking business."

"Are you a banker too?" Thumper asked.

"My husband was."

Bing explained further. "He and I knew each other through the Virginia Bankers Association. Wonderful fellow."

"Now, Professor Musgrove, here is someone worthy of your studies; the venerable Harry Sensabaugh, known to all as 'Bing.' A recent inductee into the octogenarian club and still dashing all about the countryside chasing foxes."

Bing flashed a modest wave of his hands. "Been doing it so long I could probably lapse into a coma and my body would still stay on the horse by sheer force of habit."

"Bing's grandfather was one of the original members when my great-grandfather founded the Montfair Hunt."

"That must have been quite a long time ago."

"You could say that," Thumper replied. "Two centuries ago, by some count."

"Feels that way to me some days," Bing quipped.

Marie gave him another arm squeeze accompanied by a sweet smile. "But not today, I'll bet."

He returned the smile and patted her hand. "Nope, not today."

Marie asked Janey the standard question foxhunters pose at a hunting event when introduced to someone in plain clothes: "Do you ride?"

"No, not lately anyway. I rode some as a kid. And I've done some trekking on horseback into remote areas for some of my professional work. But certainly nothing like you folks do. You all must be excellent riders to do this."

Marie scoffed. "Hardly. You're thinking of the dressage queens and show hunters. Most of us out here just hang on and hope for the best."

Thumper and Bing affirmed Marie's remark with a synchronous "Amen."

"Well, look who's finally arrived," Thumper said when he saw Ryman's truck cruising up the driveway.

As Ryman emerged from his truck, conversation stopped and all heads turned. Someone started clapping. Others picked up the cue and a burst of applause, heightened by cheers and whistles, rumbled across the lawn.

He bowed deeply with one hand across his abdomen and the other against the small of his back, still playing the conductor's part. After taking several bows, he spied the pile of Saint Hubert medals on a nearby table. Reverend Dan stood close by, like a street peddler displaying his knock-off wares. It appeared he'd had no customers. Ryman strode over to the medals. Nardell trotted behind in the role of adoring acolyte. He motioned for Davenport to step aside, lifted the medals from the table, divided them into two groups, gestured to Nardell, and slid the chains over her outstretched arms.

Ryman slipped one medal from Nardell's arm and turned to the person closest to him, an old friend of Fergus's, a hunter emeritus who'd driven up from North Carolina for the service. Ryman placed the chain over the man's head, raised his right hand in the three-finger scout salute, and said, "The hunter's badge of glory." He moved on to the next person and repeated the ceremony. This continued as he and Nardell worked their way through the entire crowd. Those yet to be reached stood silently awaiting his arrival. Those who had received their medals watched with reverent respect as he moved on. Some fondled the small coin-like objects, a few murmured softly to those beside them.

One person who looked anything but reverent was Bob Sensabaugh. The other family members—Bing, Kitty, thirteen-year-old Beatrice, and sixteen-year-old Baden—along with Marie Hardesty all willingly accepted their medals and smiled back at Ryman as he saluted each of them. Bob waved a hand, refusing to have the chain placed over his head. Bing and Kitty playfully encouraged him. They suggested it was all in the spirit of this special day, that he shouldn't be rude to Ryman. Bob acquiesced. But he stood stiff and stonefaced during the brief ceremony. He removed the medal and slipped it into his pocket as soon as Ryman and Nardell stepped along to the next recipient.

This turned out to be Dorcas Stanhope. As Ryman placed the chain over her head, she threw her arms around him and pulled him close. "I'm so sorry about your father," she said, tears welling up in her eyes. "If there's anything… anything I can do…"

Ryman stood frozen with his hands behind her neck, surprised by the force of her embrace and the expression on her face—part sorrow, part invitation.

Nardell moved in closer to Ryman's side. "We appreciate your concern," she said, emphasizing the plural. "We'll let you know if we need help with something."

Dorcas ignored Nardell and continued to gaze up at Ryman. "You're still coming tomorrow, aren't you? I mean, if you need time to be alone, we could reschedule. But the kids…"

"Oh, right," Ryman said. "Tomorrow, the kids. A talk about proper turnout and etiquette." He took the opportunity to lift his hands from around her neck and extricate himself from her embrace. He straightened his vest and jacket and said, "Yes, certainly, I'll be there. Wouldn't want to disappoint the kids. Well, um…" He held up the three-finger salute, grinned foolishly, and said, "a badge of glory to you. May the beast be true."

As they moved on, Nardell hissed into his ear, "It's 'through the beast to God is true.' And what's this about talking to the kids tomorrow?"

"Sorry, with all that's been going on, I guess I forgot to tell you. Dorcas asked me to give a short presentation about turnout and stuff to the kids."

"You know I have appointments all day tomorrow."

"Right. Well, it's no big deal. I'll just pop over to Cecelia's, have a chat with the kids there, and be back home."

"Fine." Nardell turned to look at Dorcas, who was fondling her new Saint Hubert medal, and bumped into Ryman's back when he stopped to greet the next person.

"Brother Peterson!" Ryman exclaimed. "Here's a badge of glory for you!"

Rhetta, Shelton, and Elizabeth joined Thumper, Janey, and Dan along the front of the food tent watching this strange spectacle.

Thumper underestimated the number of Saint Hubert medals needed, mostly because Ryman was awarding them to everyone, including grooms, catering crew, and the Montfair house and farm staff who'd come to pay their respects. Even the sound system technicians got medals and Ryman's Jäger-blessing. By the time he and his sore-armed assistant worked their way through the entire assembly back to where they started, there were only six people yet to be so blessed.

Ryman didn't seem to notice, but there were only four medals now held in Nardell's weary hand.

He came to Shelton first. "A special one to go with the one from your first hunt," he said, placing the chain over her head. He took a half step back and gave his daughter the salute and blessing, executed with the military formality of a French general awarding the Croix de guerre. Then to Elizabeth he said, "And a new one for you, too." She obediently bowed her head and accepted the gesture. Another salute and blessing.

He then took a sidestep and found himself facing his mother.

"Think you're some big stuff now, dontcha?" Rhetta said. "Gallivantin' all around here, actin' like you're the King of Siam or somethin'."

He started to deflate under her withering stare. But then he caught himself, held his head erect and threw out his chest. "No, Ma. It's not about me. I'm just the messenger. But it's a message I'm honored to bear."

"You try puttin' one of those things on me, boy, and I'll kick your shins in. I ain't in no mood for this foolishness."

"As you wish," he replied with a shrug. Stepping away from Rhetta, he said, "Might as well go to this lady here." He found himself looking into the face of a bewildered Janey Musgrove. "I don't believe we've met. I'm Ryman McKendrick, servant and messenger of our blessed Saint Hubert."

"Janey… Janey Musgrove, guest, um, of Mister Billington, and friend of Reverend Davenport."

"Well, friend Janey, welcome. And may the blessings of Saint Hubert be upon you." He slipped the penultimate medal over her head and recited the Jäger-blessing accompanied by a salute. He refrained from embracing her, but simply nodded and moved on to Thumper.

"No, really," Thumper protested, "that's okay. I'm sure there's someone else here who hasn't gotten his yet. And that's the last one." Thumper was about to say it should go to Reverend Dan, but before he could utter that thought, Ryman had already slipped the chain over Thumper's neck.

Ryman, his face wreathed in a beatific glow, grabbed Thumper by the shoulders and said, "Thank you, my friend. None of this would have been possible without your help. You are a true servant of Saint Hubert, and of me, his messenger and heir."

Thumper heard an indignant splutter mumbled to his immediate right. It sounded something like, "Bloody hell!" blurted in a blended accent somewhere between Hampshire and Terre Haute.

Ryman stepped back, raised the salute, and intoned in a slow-cadenced voice dripping with gravitas, "*This* is the hunter's badge of glory, that he *protect* and tend his quarry, hunt with honor as is *due*, and through the *beast* to God is true!" He then grabbed Thumper's hand in a vice-like two-fisted shake. "Hallelujah, Brother."

He released Thumper's hand, turned around to face the crowd, now back to their own merry-making, lifted both arms and said, "My people!"

"That's it!" Rhetta exclaimed. "Completely off the deep end. You know any good shrinks?" she asked Thumper. "This boy needs a serious head adjustment. If you're really his friend, you'll get him off his high horse and back down to earth where he can be of some use." She grabbed Shelton by the arm. "C'mon, Sheltie Lou. You don't need to see your poor daddy this way. Let's get on home, child."

Shelton obeyed, but as Rhetta pulled her along she kept looking back over her shoulder, staring in tortured confusion at her father.

Reverend Davenport slunk off toward the parking area carrying an unopened magnum of champagne. He reckoned he'd earned it.

"I'm starving," Nardell said, using her massage skills on her own forearms, briskly kneading first one then the other. "C'mon, ladies, let's get something to eat."

Nardell and Elizabeth flanked Janey and the three of them hustled off to the food tables.

"Brother McKendrick," Thumper said, "may one of your people have a word with your Holiness?"

"Nothing holy about me, Thumper. I'm only the vessel chosen to carry the message."

"And what exactly is that message, your not-so-Holiness?"

"Why, that we must through the beast to God be..."

"Yeah, yeah, I get that. Ry, this is even freakier than I'd imagined. I've seen some strange stuff in my day. But never anything like this. Why did you decide to go to Gretchen's Bottom when you regained consciousness? What the hell was going on that made you pass out?"

"It's difficult to explain."

"Try."

"No, not just now. Maybe when I've had some time for it all to set in. It's still kind of a blur. I know what I felt, what I saw. But it's hard to put it into words. Words that would make sense to you anyway."

"Then maybe you at least can explain this. When I asked why you told Crispie to take hounds to Gretchen's Bottom, you said something like, 'It's been arranged.' What did you mean by that? What had been arranged?"

"What you wanted."

"What *I* wanted?"

"You wanted there to be a fox in Gretchen's Bottom. And you wanted a good run, but not too long and hard on this hot morning. Isn't that what you got?"

"Of course I wanted that. But you never know what will happen once you're afield."

"Can't you?"

"C'mon, Ry, you've been at this game as long as I have. There's never been any way to predict exactly what live quarry is going to do."

"Not unless... oh, what's the point? Perhaps you will understand in time. But there's no use trying to explain it to you now. I'm only beginning to understand it myself. You wanted to get up a fox from Gretchen's Bottom and that's what you got."

"And maybe Crispie and I were right that it was the best place to cast hounds and your idea about switching to Old Whitehouse was bunk."

Ryman's grin showed a trace of condescension. "Yeah, perhaps it was just a load of bunk, and you were right in the first place. If it makes you feel better to believe that..."

"Honey," Nardell interrupted, "you should get something to eat."

She held a plate heaping with the excellent fare being served under the tent.

"Wow, looks great," Ryman exclaimed. "Now that you mention it, I could use some grub." He placed a hand on Thumper's shoulder, more lightly this time, and smiled warmly. "Thanks, Thumper. You're the best for doing all this. I owe you big time." He started to walk off toward the serving tables but stopped, looked back, held up the three-finger salute, and said, "Badge of glory, my friend. Badge of glory." He then spun around and floated away.

Janey Musgrove glided to Thumper's side. They both watched Ryman cruise through the buffet line, alternating between scooping up food and raising the salute to everyone he passed. "Is this a normal part of your foxhunting practices?" she asked.

"No, it is not."

A male voice agreed. "It most certainly is not."

Thumper had not been aware of Grantham Meisner's approach.

"Most odd behavior on the part of your joint-master," Grantham said.

"Yes," Thumper replied, "most odd indeed." He turned to his guest for the introduction. "Janey Musgrove, may I present Grantham Meisner, executive director of the North American Fox Chasers Association, my very dear, old friend and cousin."

Janey arched an eyebrow at the mention of "cousin," a seeming inconsistency with the man's faint but noticeable British accent.

Thumper caught the look. "Grantham's mother and mine were related, on the Crutchfield side of the family. She married a Brit, to the great dismay of us Colonials, and the result of that union was the wisp of a fellow you see before you."

Janey shook the hand of a man who stood no more than 5' 8". Although he appeared to be the same age as Billington, he retained the wiry build and erect posture of a gymnast. Or perhaps a jockey.

"A pleasure to meet you," Grantham said. Turning back to Thumper, he continued, "What was all that nonsense with the Saint Hubert medals? And that 'Badge of glory' poem he keeps reciting. I'm concerned Ryman may be under too much strain. Perhaps a holiday is in order, some quiet time for him to relax, get back to his old self."

"I'll suggest that to him. But you know how stubborn he can be."

"Well, at least see what you can do to rein him in. This is not the sort of behavior that represents foxhunting well."

"Precisely what I was just telling Ms. Musgrove." Addressing Janey, he said, "Look, about next Saturday, perhaps it would be best if you held off just a bit. It seems we have some… um… internal issues to address. I wouldn't want you to get the wrong impression about our sport, to think you're seeing a true representation of foxhunting when what you're really seeing is... is... well, let's call it an outlier."

"Outliers make for interesting reading."

"I'm sure they do. But what's happening here... well, to tell you the truth, I don't really know what's happening here."

Chapter 27

A TEASING HINT of autumn's musk perfumed the air, a September evening fit for open windows and a night spent basking in the tingling foreplay of fall. Ryman and Nardell declined the invitation to dine with Thumper and his houseguests at Montfair. Instead, the duties of the day fulfilled and the symphony of the morning's hound music still playing in their heads, they returned to the Fair Enough cottage.

As Ryman closed the door, Nardell placed herself before him and said, "Are you sure you're okay? I was terrified when you passed out and fell off Token."

He reached toward her neck, unhooked her stock pin, and slowly slid the shaft through the soft white material. "I've never been better." He began to untie her stock, slipping each strand out from the knot with gently playful tugs. "And I plan to keep getting better still..." He pulled the unbound tie from her neck, held it aloft, and let it fall to the bare wooden floor. "... now that I know what I've been called to do."

She caught the hungry look in his eye and felt the lingering strains of the morning's sport pulsate anew. She reached up and began to undo his pin and tie. "And what"—*tug*—"is it"—*tug*—"that you've been called"—*tug*—"to do?" The end of the stock slid through the knot. She held one end of the long piece of cloth in each hand and worked it back and forth, rubbing it against the nape of Ryman's neck and reeling him in toward her with each pull.

When she'd placed his lower body against hers, he slipped his hands around the small of her back and held her tightly. "To do what Saint Hubert would have me do."

She leaned back and began unbuttoning his canary vest. "And what is that?" she purred.

He removed his hands from her back and started unbuttoning her vest. "Restore the faith."

"Restore"—*pop*—"the faith"—*pop*—"of what?"—*pop*. His vest fell open.

"The true"—*pop*—"faith"—*pop*—"of"—*pop*—"... of..." His hands faltered. "Well, I'm not quite sure yet. But there's a true faith, and it's up to me to see that it's restored."

She pressed into him again. "It seems something's already been restored."

He moved on to unbuttoning her hunting shirt. "I've gotten so worked up on these past few hunts, I'm gonna have to have the tailor make some extra room in all my breeches."

"I know exactly what you mean," she said, working on his shirt. "I can't wait to get you home. Or wherever," she added with a wink and a waggled eyebrow.

She unbuttoned his shirt in synch with his movements to undo hers.

"Ry," she whispered, "tell me what you're seeing."

"I see you, in all your naked loveliness, enjoying me, in all my manly..."

"Yes, I see that too." She closed her eyes and shivered in anticipation as he reached around and unsnapped her bra. "But I mean when... when you're seeing... whatever it is you're seeing... or hearing... or feeling."

He cupped one breast in his hand, leaned over, and began tracing his tongue in a circle around the areola. The skin surrounding her Wicca tattoo was still reddened, but she was oblivious to any soreness. She felt only the electrically moist circuit of his tongue, the hardening of her nipple, and the insistent swelling in his breeches.

"I see"—*lick*—"the game"— *lick*—"I hear"—*lick*—"the voices"—*lick*—"I feel"—*lick*—"the chase."

He spun her around and pushed her forward with his hands on her hips.

The motion took her by surprise but she went along willingly as he began to move her around the room.

"Hounds get up and the game is on," he said, quickening the pace as he guided her in a figure eight between the furniture.

Wycroft lifted his graying head from the sofa and watched the two humans, one chasing the other.

"I am with the hounds," Ryman said, "among the pack. The scent fills my nostrils and drives me forward." He leaned over, placed his nose against her bare back at the spot where her eagle wings tattoo met the waistline of her breeches, and inhaled sharply. The touch sent another jolt through her and a soft moan floated around the cottage and out into the evening twilight. "But the fox is cagey and knows her stuff." He stretched out his arms, pushing her farther ahead of him. "Where's she at?" He stopped moving and lifted his head, looking left and right. "Ah, but she's just playing with us. The game's not over."

Nardell turned her head and looked back at Ryman, a sly smile on her face. She now fully understood where this was going.

"Yes!" he shouted. "There she is. A-woooooo! A-woooooo! The pack's in full cry! Forrard! Forrard to the chase!" He moved closer to her and resumed navigating her through the room, faster now, with sharper twists and turns. "A-woooooo-woooo-woooo! I'm running with the pack! I feel the horses coming on behind, pounding, pounding, pounding! The horn cheers me on! Ta-ta-ta-taaaaaa! Ta-ta-ta-taaaaa!"

Wycroft leapt off the sofa and join the simulated chase. His own "A-woooooo" harmonized with Ryman's horn imitation.

Nardell now took over choosing the path. Rather than letting Ryman guide her, she led him through the small cottage, from the living room into the kitchen, through the dining room, down the hallway past the bedroom to the rear door where she made a sharp turn that almost caused him to lose his grip. He held on as she doubled back and trotted along the hallway and into the living room, casting grinning glances back at him. Her frazzled French braid bounced like a vixen's brush. Wycroft loped along with them, baying enthusiastically, dancing around Ryman's legs.

Ryman worked his hands from Nardell's hips around to the front and unfastened her belt and the clasp of her breeches. Then, keeping one hand on her hip, he undid his breeches, never losing the rhythm of the chase.

Two more courses through the living room and, quickening the pace to an energetic canter, she made a line for the bedroom.

Ryman swung the door closed behind him, shutting out Wycroft whose baying intensified as he scratched frantically at the door.

Nardell was about to dive straight onto the bed but Ryman tightened his hold on her hips and stopped her halfway so that she landed bent forward over the edge. He yanked down her breeches, then his. With their boots still on and breeches around their knees, he thrust himself into her from behind.

"A-woooooooooo!" he sang out as he burst inside of her, the thrill of the chase culminating in an explosive orgasm.

"Yip, yip, yip, oooohhhhhh!" she called back.

"A-woooo, a-wooooo, *scratch, scratch, scratch,"* Wycroft added.

****

For the next several hours woos and yips, giggles and gasps, moans and sighs, howls and scratches poured from the open windows of Ryman's cottage. In an upstairs bedroom of the main house, Rhetta struggled to block out the distraction. She was curled in her easy chair, a bookcase to one side, a small cabinet to the other, a large TV facing her from across the room. Abel reclined on his dog bed close to his mistress's chair.

Everything in the room was Rhetta's alone; her furniture, her books, her TV, her clothes in the closet, her sheets on the bed, her dog at her feet, her bottle of brandy secreted in the cabinet. She and Fergus adopted the separate bedroom strategy decades before. His passing caused no significant disruption to her routine. It was simply as if a long-time housemate had moved out.

She was reading Theodore Sturgeon's *Venus Plus X*, plucked from her bookcase crammed with dog-eared paperbacks, the collection heavily comprised of aging Sci-Fi, most of them read several times over. For the occasional palate cleanser, one section contained a small supply of historical romances.

Shelton, scheduled to fly back to California early the next morning, said a friend who lived closer to the airport offered to let her stay there that night. Rhetta loved her only grandchild, but after sharing the house with her for three days she was relieved to see her drive away.

The harder Rhetta tried to focus on the fictional world of a distant time and place, the stronger the press of reality became. What was going on in Ryman's cottage? She knew damn well what was going on. But why? There had been some rutting sounds back when he and Nardell first took up together. But they faded out after awhile and their relationship seemed to be more like a typical middle-aged couple. Nardell had her quirks, Rhetta thought. But Ryman needed someone to keep an eye on him, and better Nardell than Rhetta.

What had gotten into that boy? All this talk about "Hunter's badge of glory," parading around like he was something special, falling off his horse in front of everyone that morning. Must have been drunk, only thing that could explain it. That early in the morning, and at his own father's memorial service. Shame on him. But he seemed okay when he came to. Everyone was talking afterward about what a fabulous morning of sport they'd had, and praising Ryman for it. And the way he'd stood before her when she refused the Saint Hubert's medal. Wasn't like him not to back down. And all this carousing with Nardell. Poor girl must be getting worn out by now.

A lull in the cottage disturbances allowed Rhetta's return to Sturgeon's imagined realm of Ledom. But she did not get past more than a couple of paragraphs before a loud "A-woooooo!" erupted through the night air, Ryman's voice at first but then Wycroft joined in. The duet bayed with gusto, their blended voices cadenced to the sound of pounding booted feet and clacking hound paws on a bare wooden floor. Nardell joined in with another chorus of "Yip, yip, yip, yeeeee!"

Abel lifted his head and barked a questioning, "Woof, woof, woof?"

"Hush now," Rhetta said sternly. "Don't you go joining in on this foolishness."

He laid his head between his front paws, grunted, and tried to go back to sleep.

She read the next sentence three times, then closed the book, reached for the remote control, switched on Turner Classic Movies and found that one of her favorites from *The Thin Man* series was playing. Another escape to a distant time and place, to a world so unlike Fair Enough Farm.

Watching Myrna Loy glide across the screen, Rhetta remembered her first encounter with the woman destined to become her long time next-door neighbor, the elegant, well-bred Cyril Celeste Crutchfield. They met during a foxhunt when Rhetta was riding as a groom for a prominent member of the club and Cyril, visiting on a break from school, admired Rhetta's skill handling the unruly horse. Rhetta's outwardly assured demeanor hid her inward awareness of the social chasm between them. Cyril, the Hollins-educated debutante descendent of a First Family of Virginia, engaged to Thaddeus Augustus Billington, III, heir to the largest landholdings in their part of the state. Rhetta, one of nine siblings from the hardscrabble Keane clan, her eight years of schooling considered sufficient for one destined to be a farm wife and member of the merchant class, risking her neck for a few dollars to train the misbehaving horse of a wealthy fat man.

But during their awkward encounter after the hunt, in which Cyril Celeste tried to be polite and Henrietta Keane wished she was somewhere else, the subject of Hollywood came up. How surprised Rhetta was to find that CeeCee Crutchfield shared her star-worshipping enthusiasm for heroes of the silver screen, past and present. When CeeCee revealed that if she had a daughter some day, she planned to name her either Myrna or Claudette and a son would be Humphrey Clark, the seeds of sisterhood were firmly planted.

Cyril made good on her threat regarding the girls' names. But her husband drew the line on the name for their middle child, his only son and heir.

Many of the movies on Rhetta's and CeeCee's fan list were still new when they first met, others had yet to be made. Now, though, they were all considered "classics." Thank goodness for Ted Turner and TCM that allowed Rhetta to relive those times before every other word of dialog consisted of foul language, when a sex scene required only a come-hither smile and a closing bedroom door, married couples slept in twin beds, people who were shot or stabbed did not bleed, and a perfectly choreographed song-and-dance routine could break out at any time.

Ah, the musicals. How Rhetta loved the musicals. And CeeCee was the only one she could share that with. But some of her imaginings were not suitable to share even with her next-door neighbor and fellow wife of a Montfair Hunt joint-master. On many a Sunday morning, ensconced in the McKendrick pew at St. Cuthbert's-in-the-Woods, Rhetta sat in thrall as Harry Sensabaugh's beautiful bass-baritone voice stood out in the tiny choir. Since his days in the high school glee club, his singing ability inspired comparisons to another crooner named Harry, last name Crosby, which led to Harry Sensabaugh being tagged with the same nickname: "Bing."

All during Reverend Laudermilk's sermons, Rhetta would imagine an entire musical production starring Bing, with her in the female lead role. Never mind that Rhetta couldn't carry a single note nor dance one step. But, then, Bing Sensabaugh's wonderful vocal skills would never know any fame beyond Crutchfield County. Still, it was fun to imagine. And the good Reverend's sermons never made much sense to her anyway. Looking back now, so many years later, perhaps she should have spent more time listening to Reverend Laudermilk and less time fantasizing about singing and dancing with Bing Sensabaugh.

For a brief instant, Rhetta saw a glimmer of CeeCee reflected in the TV screen, a passing shot of a background character who bore a striking resemblance. The death of Thumper's mother had left a larger hole in Rhetta's life than did the passing of her own husband.

She turned up the TV volume to maximum in hopes the snappy repartee between William Powell and Myrna Loy would drown out the sounds wafting up from Ryman's cottage.

****

Astrid Stevenson was waiting at the Thai restaurant in Arlington, a two-block stroll from her condo, when Shelton arrived.

"Lots of people show up for the service?" Astrid asked after Shelton settled in and drinks were ordered.

"Huge crowd." Shelton gazed at Astrid whose dark eyes glimmered in the dim restaurant light. It had only been a week since they'd been in each other's arms in San Jose. But Shelton felt a sharp longing to be back in Astrid's embrace, to feel that hard, tight body under her hands, playing her lover like a finely tuned instrument.

"So it was... what... speeches, remembrances about your grandfather, and then everyone standing around eating, drinking, talking? That sort of usual memorial service stuff?"

"Um, yeah, pretty much that. Our next-door neighbor put out a huge spread, made it really special. Tons of food, lots to drink." Shelton thought about riding around with Bar, following the hunt and watching the action from his truck. It had been several years since she'd been on a horse, following hounds. Other pursuits —college, graduate school, and a job three thousand miles from Crutchfield County—had pushed that part of her life aside.

Now, though, stirrings from that abandoned past were kindling a growing flame. She'd watched with rapt attention as hounds trotted into the covert, the field of riders arrayed on the hill, their horses eager to be off to the chase. With Bar's detailed knowledge of the terrain, he was able to position his truck to afford Shelton a splendid view of the action without interfering with the progress of the hunt. Few among the mounted group ever noticed the presence of the old truck parked along a farm road or perched among a stand of trees on a hilltop that afforded a sweeping view of the countryside.

Astrid was talking, telling Shelton about her meetings in Dallas. She stared at Astrid's lips. They smiled at one point, frowned at another, then pouted in thought as Astrid searched for the right word, a word Shelton wouldn't hear anyway. The sound of Crispie's horn, the melody of his voice, the music of the hounds—that incredible operatic performance it seemed as though her father was conducting—rang again in her ears.

And then the chase! Off and away, the fox breaking covert and dashing across the open field, the pack in full cry and close behind. A hundred horses pounding after them. Pounding, pounding, pounding. The horn cheering on hounds, *ta-ta-ta-taaaa, ta-ta-ta-taaaa*!

Memories of adolescence flooded over her. Her earliest sexual stirrings had been on the back of a horse, as a young girl, following her father and grandfather as they raced around the Virginia countryside after the Montfair hounds. Her first girlfriend had been a fellow member of the Crutchfield County Pony Club. The smell of horse sweat, wet hounds, and oiled leather were inextricably linked in her memory to sexual pleasure. All that stimulation, absent from her life for the past several years, had been visited upon her this day, reminding her where she was from and who she really was. She was only pretending to be a city girl.

Shelton fondled the two Saint Hubert medallions around her neck. She then hoisted her glass and downed her cocktail in one gulp.

"Well," Astrid was saying, "I told the head of our Dallas affiliate that if he couldn't handle the job, I could easily find someone who…"

"Tell ya what. Let's skip dinner, get back to your place."

Astrid stalled in mid-sentence. There was something different, something new, in her young lover's demeanor, an eagerness she had not seen before. The infectious enthusiasm was impossible to resist. She caught the waiter's eye. "Check, please!"

****

As excited as she was about what she'd witnessed that day, Janey did not think it would be appropriate to call Danella on a Saturday evening. She was brimming with the desire to tell someone. But who else other than her devoted agent would understand and appreciate what this could mean?

Sitting at her computer, she looked at the family photo she kept beside it—father, mother, her three brothers and their wives, several nieces and nephews, and an assortment of dogs, most of them Boxers. They were all living happily in Minnesota. Her parents still ran the family-owned furniture store in Clara City. The high-end new furniture sales were down but thanks to the foresight to maintain an extensive selection of used pieces and budget-priced accessories, the business was getting by. Her brothers had all gone off to college, as she had. Unlike her, though, all three stayed in the state and settled not far from their hometown, close enough that family gatherings could be easily held without anyone having to travel very far.

Anyone but her, that is.

Had the wanderlust she felt at twenty been real? Or just an imagined youth-fueled desire to break away from the mundane? Did she launch herself on the right career trajectory, a gypsy existence of travel and exploration? She'd built a solid career studying people whose lives and beliefs were as different from life in Clara City as any existence on the same planet could be.

And where had it gotten her? A doctorate, two published books—well-received but hardly bestsellers—and an untenured teaching job at a respected, albeit second-tier, university.

It had also gotten her a tiny apartment in Fairfax, Virginia, a county with the second highest median household income in the country and the rents to match. Her associate professor's salary would have gotten her a four-bedroom house in the best part of Clara City. But, then, there were no jobs for someone with her narrow skill set back there. And the thought of returning to her pre-college job keeping the books for the Musgrove Furniture Emporium offered no appeal.

Looking at the photo, she wondered who she missed most, her human family or the dogs? Her traveling made it impractical to keep pets. There was no one she knew well enough to entrust with the care of an animal companion when an assignment called and she was on a plane to track down another subject for her studies. It might be just a few states away, or it could be on the other side of the globe. Regardless of the destination, she'd be gone for awhile, long enough that pet care—for so much as a goldfish—would be a burden.

Of course, if there was a significant other to hold down the fort, things might be different. But that had not worked out for her. There was that one chance, years ago, and thinking about it brought back the smell of Reverend Davenport's pipe smoke.

She had to admit she liked the odor. It reminded her of the time she spent studying the Odinani beliefs of the Igbo people of West Africa. Another research fellow—an actual Brit, not a shred of affectation about him, brilliant yet self-effacing—smoked a similar blend. She'd not smelled that scent since they'd parted company at Djibo Airport in Burkina Faso. She wondered, as she now did with increasing frequency, what would have happened if she'd accepted his offer to return to the UK with him. It wasn't a formal proposal. More like a proposition. Her Midwestern Lutheran values, reinforced by the sound of her mother's voice over the poor phone connection, led her to decline the invitation.

She'd often wondered since if she'd correctly heard her mother say, "Don't go with him." Cell phone service in that part of Burkina Faso was then non-existent. With the static over the outmoded landline, her mother might have said, "You'd be a fool if you don't go with him."

But by the time that thought formed, it was too late. He was gone and the window of opportunity had closed. She'd never had the courage to ask her mother for clarification. Better to believe she'd done the right thing.

She turned her attention from the photo back to her computer screen and reread the notes she'd entered about the morning's experience. It was too soon to tell for sure if this was the spark she'd been looking for, but the possibilities were bubbling around in her inventive brain.

No one back in Minnesota would understand what this might mean, if there was something here to base another book on. It would be impolite to phone Danella on this weekend evening. But an email would be all right. The gist of the note she sent off to her agent was: "Foxhunting and religion… who knew? Saint Hubert sends his regards. More field research to come, will keep you posted."

****

A thick cloud of pipe smoke enveloped Dan Davenport. He was alone, as usual, so the toxic atmosphere was no threat to anyone else. He worked steadily through the magnum of champagne he'd carried off that morning. The more he swilled, the harder he puffed. He'd already refilled his pipe bowl twice; his humidor and tools were at the ready if he needed another fill up.

What was Ryman McKendrick up to? Bad enough he interrupted Dan's carefully crafted eulogy, an inspiring and respectful homage to a man he barely knew. No way to get the crowd's attention back after Ryman passed out, fell off his horse, then to everyone's surprise sprang back up and appeared to be a changed man.

Dan took a swig of champagne.

And then he steps onto the platform, right off his horse, and shoos me away from the podium. The nerve!

Another swig, and a long puff.

But then those shenanigans with the Saint Hubert medals, declaring himself to be the saint's messenger and heir. Blasphemy! Heresy! Apostasy!

A longer swig and a quick puff.

The worst of it was that I didn't get to deliver my pitch on behalf of St. Cuthbert's. What an opportunity that would have been. All those people, surely impressed with my godly eloquence, so many of them searching for a harbor in this tumultuous life.

Swig. Puff.

And St. Cuthbert's so in need of members. It would have been the perfect combination of... of...

Another swig would help, and a thoughtful puff. He formed his mouth into a circle and watched the smoke billow out in a dense gray swirl.

Of... call and response. Yes, call and response! I would have given the call, and there would have been a joyful response. The pews of our humble little building would have been filled the next morning. And those aggravating board members would see that the fortunes of St. Cuthbert's were turning. That I'm the man for the job, and will be for many...for many...

Swig. Light puff.

For... many... years... to... come!

He accentuated each word with a stab of his pipe stem.

But noooo!

A swill this time. No puff.

That bloody McKendrick! Messed it up, he did. Stole my audience. A thief, that's what he is. Stole all those eager souls right out from under me. God does not like a thief. Thou shalt not steal. And... and...

Another swill, a jab of the pipe stem.

And... Thou shalt have no other gods before me. Woe unto him who leads my people astray! Woe!

Dan lifted the champagne bottle and found it empty. The room started to swirl. He gripped the arms of his chair and tried to keep from spinning up to the ceiling, through the haze of pipe smoke.

Whoa!

****

Dorcas huddled in her barn loft apartment. She sat on the bed, knees to her chest, arms around her legs. Her phone lay on the bed beside her. She glanced down at the text message on the screen. "Miss u. Coming to

VA. c u soon."

How did he find her? Someone in Florida must have given him her number. Or maybe he'd heard that her father had passed away and paid a visit to Arkansas, expressed his condolences to the bereaved and asked, Oh, by the way, where's his daughter these days?

He was always good at getting people to do things for him, especially young women. And if they didn't cooperate, he had other ways to get what he wanted.

After two years, she thought she was safe. He'd done enough damage. He was not her responsibility. She couldn't save him, couldn't fix him. She'd tried. She just wanted to be free of him, free of all that past. Florida had been the last straw for her. He'd cost her the job there. She was lucky to land this new job. Luckier still that she could continue to work with children.

But now he'd found her. And one day, probably soon, he'd appear and it would all start again. Unless there was some other way, some way she could turn the tables on him, and be rid of him for good. She had to think clearly and consider her options.

****

Grantham Meisner rolled out of bed and pulled on his robe.

"Where are you going?" Kirsten asked. "The evening is young. And I'm feeling... well, I'm feeling pretty young myself. And you were incredibly stoked. You didn't burn off all that energy already, did you?"

"Stoked? Yes, I'm still stoked as you say." Grantham retained just enough of his British accent to reveal his true heritage to the astute listener. A life spent traveling the world for both sport and business had softened the edges of his native London tongue. "It's just that... that I can't help but wonder what happened today."

Kirsten sat up, reached out, and placed a hand on his arm. "You mean about Ryman?"

"Precisely. Oh, the sport was splendid. The entire day was marvelous, such a wonderful turnout for old man McKendrick. And this..." He nodded toward the bed. "...well, that goes without saying."

"But now you seem troubled."

"A bit, yes. Very odd behavior, don't you think? All that parading about, reciting that bloody 'Badge of honor' stuff. Even worse than he was at the weekday hunts. I'm worried about him. Perhaps his father's death has unsettled him more than we realize."

"I'm sure he'll be fine. Just give him a little time and everything will be back to normal."

"I suppose."

"Although…" She rose up to a kneeling position along the edge of the bed and slipped her arms inside his robe. "…I wouldn't object if some things didn't go back to normal." She gripped his buttocks with both hands and gave a firm squeeze.

His robe fell to the floor as he pressed her back down onto the bed. "A double badge of honor for me then."

"How about a triple?"

****

The trick to playing host to out-of-town visitors is to create the appearance of throwing one's home open to anyone in need while being highly selective about who one actually takes in. Thumper's mother taught him that social tightrope-balancing act. As a result, four carefully chosen couples—one each from Georgia, Texas, New York, and Montreal—occupied the spare rooms in the main house.

With Crispie and Patti included, Elizabeth out for the evening with her friends, and Thumper in his stag condition, eleven people sat down in the formal dining room to a dinner prepared by Natasha's talented hands. Two helpers hired for the evening from the catering staff were present; one to serve and one to clean up. Natasha had only to concentrate on her cooking and then soak up the praise afterward.

Everyone patted their bellies as they waddled from the dining hall into the living room. Thumper played bartender, whipping up anything requested, no matter how exotic, with professional flair.

Crispie and Patti claimed exhaustion from the day's exertion and asked to be excused for the remainder of the evening. After much appreciation was expressed for the morning's outstanding sport, they withdrew. Thumper noticed, though, that neither showed any visible trace of wear as they hastened to the door, arms around each other's waist. Patti whispered in her partner's ear. Crispie nodded vigorously in response.

When Thumper offered cigars from his humidor, only one other gentleman accepted. Times have certainly changed, he thought. In his father's day the men would have removed themselves to the study for stogies and brandy while the ladies chatted in the parlor. Now Thumper found few takers to join him in a fine smoke, fewer still willing to honor the practice that once had men discussing serious matters of state or commerce in one room while the gentle ladies tittered over domestic niceties in another. Of course, as the father of a future Madam Chief Justice of the United States, he knew he had to let those old customs go at some point.

His old friend from Georgia, Garland Williams, accepted the offer of a Davidoff Grand Cru Number One. The Williams family owned most of

Petersville, Georgia, a comfortable feudal arrangement predating the time when a Williams ancestor served with a Billington antecedent in an upstart body called the Continental Congress.

To avoid offending the others, they carried their smokes outside. Small talk and aimless meandering took them to the farm road between the main barn and kennel complex.

"Your hounds did an incredible job today," Garl said. "They're impressively sharp for so early in the season. Most packs aren't up to that hunting standard until at least mid to late October, if not even into November."

"Crispie's done a helluva job. He was a great find to take over the pack when Ivan died."

"Ah, dear old Ivan. He was the Montfair huntsman for—what?—forty-some years?"

"Forty-three."

"You and your old man were damn lucky to have him. And for so long too. Y'know, I've often thought," Garl said with a sly grin, "if I ever found my wife was having an affair with the huntsman, I'd keep the huntsman and fire the wife."

"Yep. It's not easy finding a good huntsman these days. Damn few of the old American breed left. Most of the good young ones are Irish or English imports."

"Speaking of things young, wifely, and Irish, when's your lovely bride coming back? I'm surprised she's not here for the start of cub hunting."

"Ah, well, in this case it seems the master's the one who might be fired."

Williams took a long drag on his cigar and blew out the smoke slowly. "You don't say. Wanna talk about it?"

"Not much to say, really. Seems her long-term priorities don't include yours truly. Better to be huntsman with the old pack back home than to linger as Mistress of Montfair."

"You seem to be taking it okay."

"C'mon, Garl, you know it was a stupid ass move on my part in the first place."

"I dunno, Thumper. A lot of us guys were taking second looks at our old wives. Sally somehow seemed a lot more wrinkled and saggy when Shelagh entered the room. And, man, does she have a great..."

"A-wooooo!" A howl went up from the kennels. One hound stirred and threw his tongue.

"Sounds like Warwick," Thumper said. "Must be some critter passing by that caught his attention."

Garl sniffed the air. "Fox maybe? Hard to get a good line on scent with all this cee-gar smoke."

"A-wooooo! A-woooooo!" Some other hounds joined in, and soon most of the pack was stirring.

They walked on closer to the kennels.

"Might be a fox playing around," Garl suggested, "Knows the hounds can't get him when they're kenneled up."

"I don't think so," Thumper said as they drew nearer to the huntsman's cottage. "Listen."

With the hounds momentarily quiet, they picked up a sound from the cottage, a high-pitched squeal trilling off into a giggle. This was followed by deep grunts in a rhythmic cadence.

As another squeal erupted, this one even higher, hounds rejoined their chorus.

Garl looked at Thumper and grinned. "Exhausted are they? Bullshit."

"Can't say I blame Crispie for choosing Patti's private company over lolling around with old farts like us."

"Maybe we should be heading in." He gazed thoughtfully at the cigar between his fingers. "It's been a long day. And I should see how Sally's doing. Likely she's about to pass out too."

Thumper gave his old friend a knowing eye. "You don't look a bit tired to me. Thinking maybe Sally's not so wrinkled and saggy after all?"

He smiled broadly. "Something like that. It's strange, but I've felt somehow... stimulated all day."

"Stimulated? You mean, as in 'horny?'"

"If y'all want to put it in such a crass way. You'd think I'd be worn completely out, what with the long drive up here, getting everything ready this morning, that fabulous hunt, and—oh boy!—that enormous dinner. Not to mention your wizardry behind the bar, and now this pleasant stroll and a fine smoke. And yet..."—he looked at the cottage where the glow from one faint light threw suggestive shadows on the shades—"... well, not that I don't enjoy your company and appreciate your hospitality, old pal, but what d'ya say we hightail it back to the house?"

He took off at a brisk walk. Thumper did his best to keep up with Garl's longer legs and greater motivation.

Feigned exhaustion turned out to be a handy excuse for all. In less than a minute after Garl stepped into the living room, stretched widely, yawned cavernously, and proclaimed his need to hit the hay, four couples had politely, if quickly, taken leave of their host and retired to their separate accommodations.

Thumper found himself uncomfortably alone. The party was over, only a hollow echo of the gaiety and companionship that had filled the room moments before remained in his ears. Surrounded by an army of empty glasses, he gazed at cushions that still bore the imprint of his guests' behinds. He wondered if this was what a non-believer would feel like if he happened upon a revival meeting at the moment of the Rapture. His guests had all ascended to their private heavens, leaving him trapped in his own Tribulation.

A few months earlier he'd have been the first to suggest they call it a night, played the part of the tired host, and then sprinted up the stairs after his nimble young wife, reinvigorated by the sight of fiery red locks cascading over her lily white shoulders, her perfectly rounded breasts rising to the feel of his eager lips, his calloused old hands sliding around the curves of that great...

Well, best not go there, he thought. He'd been nothing more than a stepping-stone along her way to a greater goal. And now some young, muscular Mic was likely romping her, probably to her greater delight.

It may have been his imagination, but he thought he heard the sound of creaking bedsprings ringing throughout the house.

He switched off the downstairs lights and went up to his empty room, where he slept not a wink.

****

Though much fainter than they were in Rhetta's bedroom, the noises coming from Ryman's cabin were still audible to Bar Reinhardt. He sat in his bent, frayed lawn chair as the deepening coolness of the evening washed over his mass of flesh. One strap of his overalls was unhooked, the bib draped diagonally across his abdomen. The laces of his untied Red Wing boots dangled lazily down to each side. The six-pack of Budweiser plunked on the ground beside him was down to three bottles.

The vultures returned to their treetop perches, sated from the latest feast provided by their benefactor, the body of a goat that had died of heart failure. Some people familiar with Bar's practice of collecting carrion for his "pets" found it at best spooky and at worst a suggestion of a gruesomely psychotic streak. But several of the local farmers, when faced with the need to dispose of downed livestock, found Bar's willingness to haul away the carcass a handy convenience. Either way, it made no difference to Bar what anyone thought of his fondness for large, ugly, ungainly, flesh-eating creatures.

It would be awhile before the night air cooled the inside of the trailer enough for him to sleep. He wondered if Ryman and Nardell would still be going at it by then. How long had it been since he'd known the feel of a woman? Long damn time. Since before he showed up at Fair Enough Farm. He'd had a few after he returned to civilian life. But it took a special kind of woman to deal with his disfigurement, rendered even more daunting by his size. They mostly fell into two categories: they either had a thing for freaks, or they required payment for their services. A few, as it turned out, were missing some parts themselves.

He'd spent a couple of years drifting around, squandering his disability pension, getting into bar fights when some asshole made a crack about his scars or insulted his military service. He remembered the day he made his decision. It began with him cooling off in a small town jail somewhere in Northern California, waiting to go before the judge on another drunk-and-disorderly. The judge turned out to be a former Marine who'd lost an arm at Bataan. He gave Bar a firm lecture on dishonoring the Corps, chided him for wasting his life, told him to be thankful that at least he'd come back alive when so many others hadn't, stop feeling sorry for himself and get on with being a useful member of society. He empathized with what Bar was feeling. He'd gone through it himself, knew the pain and frustration. But life demanded more of him. The Corps demanded more of him.

Bar remembered how the judge looked down at him, kindly yet stern, and said, "I have two eyes, but only one arm. So I use what I have. You've lost an eye and an ear, but you've still got both hands and fine strong arms. I suggest you stop using them to beat up people in barrooms and put them to productive use."

Two weeks later Bar Reinhardt knocked on Fergus McKendrick's door.

And now the man who had taken him in, given him a place to stay, and the chance to live up to the judge's counsel was gone.

This had sure been one crazy-ass week, between Fergus dropping dead and Ryman's strange behavior. Fergus's death was a surprise, coming so unexpectedly. On the other hand, Bar thought, the man was eighty-five. Gotta figure anyone that age could go at any time, whether fast or slow. Still, though, it sure threw a wrench into things. What will it be like when the shop reopens on Monday? Will Ryman step up and take command? Or will he still be babbling on about that goddamn deer, talking his nonsense about some badge of glory crap?

Either way, it didn't make all that much difference to Bar. Shop or no shop, he'd be okay. He didn't give a damn what happened to Miles. The little fool's employment problems were mostly his own doing, a result of his sour attitude and hot temper. Not good traits to assure long-term job security. It might even be better for Conway if the shop did fold. Speed him on his way to an HVAC apprenticeship, a better future than handing tools to Bar and waiting to take over as head tractor mechanic. And it was about time Muriel considered retiring anyway, spend more time on her church activities, go visit her kids and grandchildren.

What mattered most to Bar was staying where he was, his little oasis in the woods, his birds to feed, no one barking orders at him to pour fire on an unseen enemy, no mortars exploding around him, no mangled human bodies hurling through the air, no searing hot shrapnel ripping through his face. What had the lieutenant seen that he hadn't? If he'd acted seconds sooner, would he have had the VC in his sights in time to stop the mortar assault? He was the best shot in the unit, the only one to achieve the coveted expert ranking. He might have even made it into the elite sniper corps if he hadn't been so big and lumbering. Hard to conceal yourself when you're six-four and, even in his trim youth, a well-muscled two-thirty. The snipers were all little guys, more like the enemy, better adapted to jungle warfare. The jungle was the wrong place to send clumsy American farm kids and clueless city boys.

By the time he'd raised up from cover and started firing, it was too late. Did he hit any of the enemy? Maybe. He'd never know whether or not he'd taken someone's life. All he knew was that everyone else around him was dead and he was reeling from the ripping pain in his head, wondering how much of his face was left. He heard the choppers swooping in just before he lost consciousness. He'd always remember that sound, the *whoosh-whoosh-whoosh* of the rescuers arriving to drive back the enemy. What ghastly fate would he have met if the VC had overrun their defenseless position and found him badly wounded but still alive, alone among shredded body parts in a blood-soaked field? Hurrah for the choppers, scattering the oncoming attackers, hovering over him like a protective shadow, the comforting sound — *whoosh-whoosh-whoosh* — like the wings of a large, floating bird circling in to feed on fresh carrion.

****

Long after Bar had drifted off into a sweaty sleep, Shelton and Astrid were still awake, snuggled together on the sofa, vaguely watching an old movie, basking in the afterglow of an exhilaratingly athletic session in Astrid's bed.

"You're always good," Astrid said. "But tonight you were amazing. Where were you hiding that passion, and those incredible tricks?"

"I guess I just missed you a bunch this past week."

"We've gone a lot longer than that without seeing each other. Something got you really revved up."

"Maybe just being back in my old girlhood environment, seeing old friends, thinking about… about, y'know, those first times, how you felt—scared, confused, but… somehow… right."

"Well, if that's it, you should visit your old girlhood haunts more often." She nestled closer to Shelton. "In fact, maybe you should live closer to your girlhood haunts. And to me. The offer to take over the affiliate relations job still stands."

"It's tempting. At least the moving closer part. But, well, I'm not so sure about the job. It might be, y'know, awkward, us working together."

"I think we'd make a helluva team. But if you wouldn't be comfortable…" Astrid shrugged. "Sure would be nice having you live close by though."

As they settled back to watching the movie, Shelton's thoughts drifted into vague concerns about the incompatibility between life in Crutchfield County and the mission of People Against Cruelty to Animals. She cast a sideways glance at the enchanting woman curled up beside her. Perhaps there was some way that Shelton could have her cake and, so to speak, eat it too.

Chapter 28

THERE WAS NO outpouring of new attendees at St. Cuthbert's the following morning, only the few dedicated souls who came more because of structural habit than spiritual hunger. Of this sparse group, only four were under the age of fifty: Bob and Kitty Sensabaugh and their two children. Baden and Beatrice would rather have been anywhere else. But Bob was firm in his commitment that his children should be raised in the tradition of the faith that had sustained several previous generations of Sensabaughs. The kids acquiesced in exchange for afternoon transport to Kimber Farm, where they could ride with Dorcas and hang out with their friends.

Bing Sensabaugh, the indulgent grandfather who understood their discomfort, sat with the children and flashed the occasional furtive wink. He, too, could think of other places he'd rather be than suffering through another hour under the droning voice of Dan Davenport. There was, though, that structural habit thing. He'd spent his Sunday mornings in this building since he was even younger than his grandchildren. But it was different back then. The church was a more significant component of the community. He could recall at least one pastor from his boyhood days who rode to hounds. And, of course, there was the choir. He'd hoped his grandchildren might have rekindled that aspect of worship. They were both blessed with beautiful voices, and Baden was showing considerable promise as a talented guitarist as well. But while they submitted to their father's insistence that they attend Sunday morning services, neither had the slightest interest in performing boring church songs before a bunch of doddering old people.

Bing's attention was caught by the sound of several gasps from his fellow parishioners. He looked up to see Reverend Dan approaching the pulpit. The man never looked well, but this morning his usual haggardness had taken on a cadaverous pall. His eyes floated limply above folds of loosely wrinkled skin. Neither the hair on his head nor on his face had felt a comb that morning. His tongue repeatedly flicked at his dry, cracked lips. He moved with an unsteady gait, listing to first one side, then the other. He paused when he reached the first step to the elevated pulpit, grasped the rail, and tried to steady himself. When he lifted one foot, he started to tilt backwards and only his grip on the rail kept him from falling over. With a labored effort he heaved himself up onto the first step and then hauled his aching body the rest of the way.

Once in place, he gripped the sides of the lectern and looked out at what appeared to be a swirling sea of faces staring up at him. He thought for a moment his prayer for increased attendance had been answered. Then he realized there were only a third as many people there as his blurred vision led him to believe.

"Do you think he's sick?" Beatrice asked her grandfather.

"He's certainly not well," Bing whispered back. "Could be coming down with a touch of the flu."

"Brown bottle flu, more likely," Bob said in disgust. "I saw him walking off with a magnum of champagne yesterday. Looks to me like he downed the whole thing."

Dan was aware of the murmuring in the pews, but steeled himself to get through the service. He did so with difficulty, stumbling over his own words, losing his place at several points as the printed characters on his note pages squiggled in and out of focus. Five minutes after he began, the water glass under the lectern was empty. A few minutes more and his mouth felt like it was stuffed with gauze. His lips cried out for moisture but his swollen tongue could deliver no relief. He was revisited by the waves of nausea that plagued him throughout the night and left him facing the morning with no more than a few pitiful moments of sleep.

His performance at least provided the parishioners with a break from the typical dreariness of a Davenport lecture. Had he been his regular self that morning, several in attendance would surely have dozed off before he reached the halfway point of his sermon—a detailed Cartesian refutation of Spinoza's teleology. Instead, rather than his words having their expected somnambulant effect, his behavior inspired riveted attention. Baden and Beatrice passed notes to each other placing bets on when he would puke.

It was generally his listeners who were thankful when one of Dan's sermons ended. This morning no one was more thankful than Dan himself.

He took his place by the door and greeted each person as the attendees shuffled out into the late morning warmth. Several heads jerked back when the poisonous fumes of Dan's breath assailed their nostrils. As bad as he looked, he smelled even worse.

Bob sent Kitty and the kids on ahead while he and Bing waited until everyone else had left. As the final parishioner scuttled off to the parking lot, waving a hand before her nose, Dan turned to find himself facing the father-and-son team. He knew what was coming, and it was the worst possible morning for what he was about to be told.

Bing went first. “Reverend, we appreciate your devotion to Saint Cuthbert’s. And that was a very, um, interesting sermon this morning. But I’m afraid we’re reaching a critical point. The archdiocese is leaning on us pretty heavily. If things don’t start looking up soon, we may have no choice.”

“I have prayed fervently for guidance,” Dan replied. “And I truly believe this dark time shall soon pass.”

“The time for praying is gone,” Bob said. “It’s time for action. We’ve been in the red too long. The diocese won’t continue to bail us out any longer. Membership has plummeted, the offerings are almost nil, and the youth group has folded.”

“It is difficult, in these modern times, to impress upon children the importance of spiritual develop…”

“It’s always been difficult,” Bob countered. “That’s no excuse. It’s simply a matter of presenting it in a meaningful way to young people. Father Herb had that gift. You, I’m sorry to say, don’t.”

“Look, Reverend,” Bing said, his tone more patient than that of his son, “it may just be that this isn’t the right match. You’re a bright guy, you certainly know your stuff, and we’re sure you’re as committed to seeing the church survive as anyone. But it may be time to face up to the reality that our little parish out here in the sticks has reached an end. That pains me greatly, as I know it does you, Bob, and everyone else for whom this church has meant so much.” He paused to look up at the vaulted ceiling with its rough-hewn cross-timber supports, then out the large window behind the pulpit.

He thought about his days in what was once a thriving youth group, when he acquired his nickname, and all the years he lived up to that moniker as the anchor of the church choir. He was married in this building. Six generations of Sensabaughs had been christened and baptized at St. Cuthbert’s altar. Bob, Bing’s only child, had been active in the youth group under the direction of Reverend Laudermilk. Bob idolized “Father Herb,” as he was affectionately known, an influence so strong that Bob even considered the priesthood before opting to enter the family banking business. And the funeral for Loretta, Bing’s wife of over fifty years, was held here. She was buried in the graveyard, not far from the McKendrick’s plot where Fergus now lay.

The thought of Saint Cuthbert’s demise filled him with sadness, as if the end of its life would signal the approaching conclusion of his own. He’d always taken comfort in the seeming permanence of Paradise Gap’s long-standing institutions: McKendrick and Sons, the General Store, Crutchfield County Bank, Montfair Hunt, and Saint Cuthbert’s-in-the-

Woods. He'd managed to keep the bank going into his son's generation, and hoped it would be so for his grandchildren as well. McKendrick and Sons would likely have gone under had he not extended generous credit terms to Fergus at critical times. And, up until now, the church had at least managed to scrimp along. But time was running out and the disturbing image of a shuttered Saint Cuthbert's drew uncomfortably close to reality.

"The fact is," Bing said, "if we don't see significant improvement by the end of this year, we'll have no choice but to call it quits. The property will go on the market to cover our arrears and pay back the diocese. And you'll be reassigned."

"That's okay, Reverend," Bob said. "You're used to packing up and moving on. How many churches does this make now that you've been assigned to?"

"*Mmmph*-teen," Dan mumbled, looking down at the floor.

"What's that? I believe it's sixteen now, counting Saint Cuthbert's. Quite impressive. And you've got many more years of ministry service ahead. You might make the Guinness Book of Records yet."

"Let's not get personal here, son," Bing chided. "I'm sure the Lord has a plan for the good Reverend and if he wants him in some permanent place, serving another congregation, that time will come."

"And woe unto them when it does," Bob declared.

Walking to their cars, Bing said, "There's no need to be so judgmental about this. Maybe Davenport, in hindsight, wasn't the best choice. But lots of churches are struggling these days. And this is a pretty small community."

"No smaller than it's always been. And the church was doing fine until this stuffy, know-it-all guy showed up. I was against his appointment in the first place, you might recall."

"We didn't have much choice, though, did we? He didn't impress me a lot either, but the diocese forced him on us. And they've been covering his salary since he got here."

"And look what they've gotten for their money."

"We still have a few months left. Maybe things will turn around."

"Come on, Dad. You know as well as I do that's not going to happen. Not with this guy in the pulpit. And now it looks like, on top of everything else, he has a drinking problem."

"First time I've ever seen him that way. Maybe he really is sick, and it just looked like a hangover."

"Sure. And I'm the King of Siam."

Bing placed a hand on his son's shoulder. "I'm afraid you're probably right. And it's a damn shame."

"Yes, a damn shame."

****

Ryman wore his full cub hunting kit—tweed hacking jacket, Oxford shirt, silk tie, tattersal vest, beige breeches, and brown field boots—for his presentation to the juniors on proper turnout and etiquette.

"And so, kids," he said in summation, "when we faithfully observe these customs, we honor this wonderful sport that we're all privileged to be part of. But most of all, most importantly, we honor our blessed Saint Hubert. He provides us with the bounty we enjoy, the foxes to chase, the horses to ride, the country where it all happens. Will you honor Saint Hubert children?"

They all nodded and a few mumbled, "Yes."

"Good. Then let's close with the Badge of Glory pledge." He held up the three-finger salute and the children did the same. Ryman led them in the Jäger-blessing, pausing after each line for the kids to repeat the words.

Dorcas had been standing in the background, impressed with Ryman's detailed knowledge of the topic and his easy manner with the juniors. As he made his closing remarks and led them in the pledge, she stepped forward. "Thank you, Master. That was wonderful. And now, kids, it's time for tack cleaning. Everyone to the tack room." She shooed them away. Turning back to Ryman she said, "The Saint Hubert bit at the end there, is this something new?"

"New? Anything but. He's the foundation of our sport, the force behind everything we do. He's been pushed aside for too long, just a funny little figure on a medal that no one ever thinks about. But that's going to change."

"And you're going to change it?"

"Well, I guess so. I'm not sure how yet. But Saint Hubert will reveal the way."

In the two years Dorcas Stanhope had known Ryman McKendrick, she'd never seen him—felt him—so vibrant. He emitted an alluring power when he spoke of Saint Hubert. His face glowed and a captivating energy radiated from his body.

She stepped closer to him and placed her hands on his chest. His body felt rock-hard to her touch. "How does Nardell feel about this?"

"Oh, she's with me one hundred percent. And soon others will be too. You, maybe?"

She slid her hands down to his abdomen and fiddled with a vest button. "I might be willing to be with you."

"Hallelujah!" He raised his arms and stepped back. Dorcas stumbled forward slightly as he moved away and started toward his truck. "Saint Hubert be praised. Well, I gotta run. This has been great. You're doing a heckuva job with these kids. Keep up the good work. Saint Hubert is surely pleased."

Chapter 29

BAR LEFT FOR work a few minutes early on Monday morning, fully expecting he'd have to get Ryman roused up and moving. When he reached the cottage, Ryman's truck was already gone. Arriving at the shop, he found it parked in Fergus's old spot. He stepped into the office to find Muriel at her desk, working through the stack of mail—half condolence cards and half late payment notices—that had piled up while the shop was closed. Ryman sat at his father's desk, staring at the computer screen and clacking away on the keyboard. Any expectation that Ryman was getting his act together faded when Bar noticed Ryman's attire: the full cub hunting kit, with his tweed jacket hung over the back of his chair.

"Going hunting today?" Bar asked. "Not even gonna stick around the shop and pretend like you're working for a change?"

"I plan to be here all day," Ryman replied.

"Uh huh. Well, you musta forgot what it is we do here. The sign says 'Farm Implements, Sales and Service.'"

"Right. I'll do the sales, you do the service."

"What exactly you plannin' to sell in that get-up?"

"It's what Saint Hubert would have me wear. A mark of my office, you might say."

A sharp "Hmmph!" came from Muriel. She went on opening and sorting the mail.

"Your 'office?'" Bar asked. "What the hell's that supposed to mean?"

Ryman looked at Bar with a calm, steady gaze. "I have been called to be The Restorer of the Faith."

Muriel's second "Hmmph!" was louder than usual. Bar glanced over at her and their eyes met for a troubled moment.

Ryman's focus returned to the computer screen. "Did you know that the earliest form of religion was developed by primitive hunting tribes, way back in the Neolilith period?"

Muriel couldn't stop herself: "Neolithic."

"Yeah, that."

"For Christ sakes..." Bar blurted out. He caught the gentle throat-clearing from Muriel, but pressed on anyway. "Here I thought you were looking up ways to improve sales, maybe checking out the John Deere merchant site for some marketing ideas. And instead you're..."

"I thought Sheltie Lou said she could handle the marketing stuff."

"She offered to *help*, dumb ass, not do it all. She said she could write up some promotional crap, maybe make up a website, send out some emails when she has some spare time. For Cris... for crying out loud..." Muriel smiled and nodded slightly. "... first you spend most of your life depending on your old man to run things, and now you expect your daughter to bail your ass out, even though she's three thousand miles away and busy as hell with her own career."

"I have other things to think about."

"Like what?"

"It should have been so obvious before. It took three appearances from Saint Hubert's stag to make me realize..."

They all looked up at the sound of the front door opening. Miles and Conway always came in through the service bay side door. The sound of human steps mixed with the padding of dog paws of the tiled floor.

"Okay, Mister Salesman," Bar said. "Looks like you're on duty."

Ryman arose, put on his jacket, adjusted his tie, and stepped out of the office. He found Frank Worsham waiting in the showroom, his Golden Retriever at his side.

Worsham took note of Ryman's attire but said nothing. Although not a horseman or foxhunter himself, he'd lived around the breed his whole life and knew it was pointless to question their behavior. No matter how odd something might seem to others, foxhunters always gave the same pat explanation: Tradition.

Worsham handed an envelope to Ryman. "Figured it was time to get my account settled up. Got a decent price on my beef cattle. Been a good haying season. Corn market ain't looking too bad right now either. Sorry I wasn't able to catch up on this before your old man... well, you know. Ain't many left like Fergus. Being a farmer himself, he understood how the cash flow works. Same when Bing ran the bank. Bob doesn't quite understand how you gotta work with the cycles. Well, you know all that, don't ya?"

Ryman opened the envelope and looked at the amount of the check. Miles and Conway would get their pay that day. Muriel too if she'd agree to take it, maybe even some of what she'd been refusing to take the past few months.

Bar stepped out of the office, leaving the door ajar, and exchanged greetings with Worsham.

"I think you'll find nothing's changed here at McKendrick and

Sons," Ryman said. He folded the check and slipped it into his jacket pocket. "We've always been the farmer's friend, and we'll continue to be."

"Good to know that." Worsham reached down and stroked his dog's head. "Matter of fact, me and Merle have been thinking about upgrading to a new tractor." Ryman and Bar knew Merle was the dog, Worsham's constant companion and best friend, named for his favorite country/western performer. "Ain't that right, boy?"

The dog looked up and gave Worsham a loving grin.

Ryman noticed something uneasy in the dog's eyes.

"We've been checking out the new models online," Worsham said. "Kinda leaning toward one of those large frame 7830s."

Bar's attention perked up at this remark. He knew what the 7830 sold for, just on the base price. Add in some extras from the long list of options, and you'd be talking some serious money.

Worsham pulled a piece of paper from his pocket. "Wanna talk to you about that, Ry. See what kinda deal we can come to. I got a list of the options I'll need." He looked pointedly at Ryman's clothing. "Unless you're just heading out for a ride or something."

Ryman did not reply but stood looking down at Merle.

"No, no," Bar said, taking a step forward and placing a hand on Ryman's shoulder. Worsham's list of extras looked pretty long. "The boss man ain't goin' nowhere. Nothin' he'd rather do than make a deal with you on a new 7830. Ain't that right, boss man?"

Ryman, a deep frown on his face, broke his gaze away from the dog and looked at Worsham. "Frank, you need to get Merle to the vet. Right away."

"What are you talking about, Ry? Merle's in perfect health."

"How's he been doing getting in and out of your truck lately?"

"Huh? Well, okay I guess. Maybe a little slow sometimes. But, y'know, it's a big truck and he ain't getting any younger."

"He's only five, Frank."

"You keep pretty close tabs on other people's dogs, do you, Ry? Know exactly how old everyone's pets are?"

Muriel had been half listening to the banter. But the sharpness of Worsham's remark brought her to full attention.

"Look, Ry," Bar said, "I'm sure Mister Worsham takes good care of Merle. If he needs to be checked by the vet, Frank'll see to it. Ain't that right, Frank?"

"Yeah, sure, Bar. Merle's my best friend. I wouldn't let anything happen to him."

"So," Bar continued, "how about we get back to that tractor Mister Worsham's interested in. Y'know, Frank, I've read some really good reviews about the 7830. *Tractor Magazine* said it's quite a machine, said there's nothing on the market better for handling..."

Merle arose from his seated position at Worsham's side, walked over to Ryman, and leaned a hip against Ryman's booted leg. His canine grin faded and he gazed up at Ryman with the most serious expression his always-happy Retriever face allowed. "Woof!"

Worsham and Bar both stopped and stared down at the dog.

"He doesn't usually go to other people," Worsham said.

"Probably just Ryman's scent," Bar offered dismissively. "Got all that hound odor on those clothes. Merle ain't used to smelling that in here. Anyways, like I was sayin' about the 7830..."

"Woof!" The bark was more insistent this time. Merle kept his big brown eyes on Ryman.

"Right now, Frank!" Ryman ordered. "Get him to Doctor Carlyle immediately. Tell him to check his left hip. You ain't got time to be jawin' with us about tractors."

Muriel arose quietly and crept to the door to assure she didn't miss a word.

"Woof!"

"Ry," Bar said out of the corner of this mouth, "let Frank take care of his own dog. You got a big sale standing right here in front of you."

Ryman ignored Bar, took Worsham by the arm, and started leading him to the front door. Merle trotted along with them, barking enthusiastically. "I'm not selling you any tractors today, Frank. You got something more important to do. You and Merle, straight to Doc Carlyle's, tell him to check out..."

Worsham pulled his arm free and stood firm. "Have you lost your mind, McKendrick? I heard some things about how you've been acting since your daddy died. And I saw you pass out and fall off your horse at the memorial service. I figured it was just the shock of losing your old man. But now I ain't so sure. You think you got some power to sense something's wrong with my dog just by standing there? You must have a bunch of goddamn screws lose. Maybe I shouldn't be thinking about buying a new tractor from a crazy man. Not sure I shoulda even given you that check. No telling what you're likely to do with the money."

Ryman pulled the check from his jacket pocket and held it out to Worsham. "Fine. Take it then. Saint Hubert will provide."

Bar could see the amount of the check as Ryman offered it to Worsham. "Ryman! For Christ-fucking-sake! Let's just all take a breath and settle down a bit. Merle don't look like he's gonna keel over or nothing. I'm sure we can talk some business, then if Frank wants to run his dog to the vet's..."

Worsham looked at the check in Ryman's hand with narrowed eyes and pursed lip. He was strongly tempted to reach out and take it. A lot of other things he could do with that money. Like maybe go to White's Equipment in Warrenton and make a down payment on a new Kubota M135X instead of that John Deere 7830. And the word around Paradise Gap was that McKendrick and Sons might not be around much longer anyway. But instead he slipped his hands into the pockets of his jeans. "No. You keep that check. It's what I owed your father. And I always pay my bills. No man can ever say different about me. What you do with the money is your business. Long as it settles my account, that's all I care about."

Ryman nodded and slipped the check back into his pocket.

Bar and Muriel shared sighs of relief.

"Okay," Bar said, "now, like I was sayin' about the reviews on the 7830 large frame..."

Ryman cut him off. "Still not selling you anything today, Frank. I won't be a party to what happens to Merle here if he doesn't get seen. Like you said, as long as I've done what's right on my end, what you do with it is your choice. Good day to you then." He turned and walked back to the office, calling over his shoulder in a stiffly formal voice, "Mister Reinhardt, I expect you've got work waiting for you in the service department."

Muriel scrambled to get back to her desk before Ryman reached the office door.

"Um, look, Frank," Bar said, "Ry's been under a lot of stress the past week or so. Not just his daddy dying, but he's had some bumps to the head too. I'm sure he'll be fine shortly. Why don't I put some of them reviews together and get them over to you. I think you'll find the 7830, with the right options, would be the perfect choice for your..."

Worsham continued to stare at the closed office door. "Damnedest thing I ever seen."

"Woof?"

He looked down at Merle. "You're right, boy. Let's get outta here." Man and dog departed, without taking any further notice of the large man left hanging in mid-sentence.

Bar remained frozen in a daze for several seconds. Then he came to life and stormed into the office. Azure sparks shot from his eye, the scarred skin on the left side of his face pulsated with a crimson glow. "What the hell are you doing?" he demanded. His voice shook the walls in the tiny office. Muriel gripped the edge of her desk to keep from being unseated by the sheer force of Bar's threatening presence. "Jesus-H-*Fucking*-Christ!" Muriel's grip tightened. "Do you know what the sale of a 7830 would mean to us right now? And, holy shit, you were gonna give him back that check for..."

"Oh, that reminds me," Ryman said casually. He withdrew the check from his pocket and handed it over to Muriel. She released one desk-gripping hand to take it and her eyes widened when she saw the amount. "Please run this down to the bank when you're done with the mail. And then make out paychecks for everyone. Full salaries for last week, the Monday holiday too. And I hope you'll finally cut a check for yourself now."

Bar stood open-mouthed, his head swiveling back and forth between Ryman and Muriel. Ryman looked up at him and said calmly, "You were saying..."

"I... I was saying... oh, what's the point." His angry stance sagged and he threw his hands up. "We're fucked." Muriel's knuckles grew purple on the one hand that still gripped the desk's edge. "If we weren't going down the shitter before, we sure as hell are now. Some fine fucking salesman you are. Our best damn customer walks in here, hands us a golden opportunity, and you insult the man over his dog and run him out." He turned to Muriel. "Maybe it's time me and you thought about retirement after all. Don't look like either one of us is gonna have a job to come to much longer anyway."

"I will stay here as long as I am needed," she replied. "And perhaps I'm needed now more than ever." She looked over at Ryman who had resumed his research on ancient forms of hunting-centered worship. She then looked back up at Bar. "Perhaps you are too."

"Me? Hell, not much service work as it is. Won't be none at all after dumb ass here runs off the few remaining customers we got."

"I'm not talking about service work."

"Then what the hell are you talking about?"

"I... ah... well, I heard the conversation just now." She released her grip on the desk and put her hands up in protest. "I was not eavesdropping. No sir. I would not do such a thing. But you left the door open and I couldn't help but hear what was said."

"So you heard shit-for-brains run off Worsham over some stupid-ass stuff about his dog?"

Muriel did her best not to flinch.

Ryman chimed in, without taking his eyes off the computer screen. "Nothing stupid-ass about it. The dog has a tumor on his left hip. It's small now, but causing him pain, makes it hard for him to get in and out of the truck. At least that's what he told me. Worst of all, it's close to the femoral artery. If it moves slightly, well… Don't worry, Worsham will be back, once he realizes I'm right."

Bar and Muriel shook their heads.

"What I heard," Muriel said, "was that someone around here has the potential to be a good salesman."

"Well, it sure as hell ain't him!" Bar said.

"No, it seems it's not Mister Ryman. It's you."

"Me? Hell, Muriel, who's gonna buy shi... stuff from me? I'm a back room guy. Best kept out of public view."

"Nonsense. The Lord gives us each talents. And he also gives us obstacles. It's our duty to use those talents to the fullest and to overcome our personal obstacles. That's how I've lived my life, and the Lord has blessed me. One of your obstacles has been a small patch of your skin. My greatest obstacle has been all of mine. But, with the Lord's help, I have not allowed that to hold me back."

Bar sank down into a visitor's chair. The legs creaked under his weight. "Jesu... geez-o-pete. I got religion talk comin' at me from all sides. I reckon I should expect it from you. It's dumb... it's the boss man here I didn't figure going all religious on us."

"Mister Ryman seems to be experiencing a difficult time just now. I'm praying fervently for him. Yes I am. And for his dear mama too."

This elicited a "Hmmph!" from Bar.

She leaned across the desk and said in a whisper, "It's blasphemy, don't you know. The Apostle Paul says in the Book of Galatians, chapter one, verse eight, 'But though we, or an angel from heaven, preach any other gospel unto you than that which we have preached unto you, let him be accursed.' Oh, yes, I'm praying hard for Mister Ryman's soul."

Mister Ryman continued clacking away on his keyboard.

"Perhaps," Muriel said, "you should consider applying your talents in more ways than just fixing things. And do so while young Conway is still with us to take on more of the service work."

Bar sat back and thought about this. He looked at Ryman, still focused on the computer screen. "You listening to this, boss man?"

"About you being the salesman? I think it's a wonderful idea. You know more about our products than anyone. And with your winning personality and striking good looks, we'll have customers lined up out the door. Besides, I got other things to do."

"So we've noticed. That's kinda the problem."

"Well, sounds like a win-win to me." He broke his gaze away from the monitor and looked at Bar as if seeing him for the first time that morning. "Um, you might want to think about putting on a shirt though."

They heard the service bay side door slam shut followed by the sound of Miles and Conway walking through the showroom. Miles stepped into the office, Conway close behind.

"Gonna be some staff changes around here, fellahs," Ryman announced. "Conway, we'd like to ask you to hold off on the move to Jessup HVAC for now. Looks like we're gonna need you for more service work."

"Um, why's that?" Conway asked.

"Bar's gonna be handling sales."

A loud chortle came from Miles. "Are you serious? Turn this... this *freak* loose on the pub... URK!"

Bar shot up with surprising speed and had Miles by the throat before he could finish. "How about I do some freak work on you, you little runt." He held Miles off the ground with one hand, reached into a pocket of his overalls with the other and pulled out his keys. He slipped a key between two thick fingers and pointed the makeshift weapon close to Miles's face, just above his left eye. "Wanna know what it feels like to be missing some parts?"

All Miles could do was claw helplessly at Bar's arms, kick out with his feet, and make choking "Urk!" sounds. His eyes widened into abject fear as Bar dangled the key above his face.

"Oh, my dear Lord!" Muriel shouted.

"Bar," Ryman said calmly, "put Miles down. That's no way for our new executive sales manager to behave."

He let go of Miles and the small man crashed to the floor in a heap, grasping at his throat and sucking in deep breaths. "I'm... *gasp*... gonna... *gasp*... fucking... *gasp*... kill you... *gasp*!"

"Yeah, that's what they all say," Bar scoffed and slipped his keys back into his pocket. "What you're gonna do, you little shit, is show some respect. And you'd best hope I do a better job selling stuff than our wacked-out boss man. 'Cause if I don't, we're all down the tubes and you won't have a job here. And with your employment history, I'm not sure you'll last very long without aid from the McKendrick Benevolent Welfare Fund."

Miles stood up, still rubbing his throat, and glared at Bar. Then he looked over at Ryman. "You gonna let him get away with this? He coulda killed me."

"Nah, he wouldn't have killed you," Ryman replied. "Put you in a coma maybe. Poked out your eyeball. Although, come to think of it, he was saying something about needing some carrion for his pet vultures."

"Him?" Bar said. "Not enough meat on him to feed one bird let alone the whole flock."

"Very funny," Miles snarled. "What a bunch of assholes I'm stuck working with." He gave his throat one last rub, threw back his shoulders, and addressed Ryman. "You gonna make good on your promise to pay us for last week? Or are you so wacked-out you don't remember that? Or just flat ain't got the money?"

"Matter of fact, Muriel is just about to leave for the bank to make a nice fat deposit. And she'll have everyone's paycheck ready at the end of the day."

Miles looked over at Muriel for confirmation and she nodded back. "Well, maybe there's some hope for this place yet. Even with *this*..."—he jabbed a thumb at Bar — "... taking over sales."

Ryman stood up and straightened his vest.

Miles took note of the attire. "Why you wearing your hunting duds?"

"It's the mark of my new off..."

"Never mind," Bar interrupted. "Ryman's got other priorities he needs to focus on. So it's up to the rest of us to keep this leaky ship afloat."

"Right you are," Ryman said. "And I suggest y'all get to it. Muriel, off to the bank. Miles, Conway, work awaits."

When the others were gone, Ryman gave Bar a chuck on the arm and said, "You can do this. Saint Hubert is with you."

"Saint Hubert my ass. But you're right. I can do this. And do you know why?"

"Why?"

"'Cause I got enough sense to not go running off a customer like Frank Worsham when he's standing right in the showroom, ready to do a deal on one of the biggest tractors we can handle. Don't take no great sales skills to know that. But you know what it does take?"

"No, what?"

"It takes not being all wacked-out, thinking you can talk to animals, that you're the next fucking messiah. You need to get yourself some help, pal."

"Bar, Bar, Bar. You don't understand now. But you will, I'm sure. Saint Hubert will show you the truth."

Ryman placed his hand on Bar's shoulder. Bar knocked it away.

"Don't give me that shit. If you knew a goddamn thing about history, you'd know messiahs don't usually meet a very happy end. You're likely in for a whole heap of grief."

Ryman smiled warmly. "I'm no messiah. I'm just a messenger."

"Yeah, well, messengers don't fare too well neither."

"I'll be fine. Don't you worry about me." Ryman sat back down and returned to his online research. "Did you know that 'The Art of Hunting' in Latin is 'Ars Venatica'? And the English word 'venery' can mean either hunting or sexual intercourse. Ain't that fascinating?"

Bar shook his head. "Fucking goddamn fascinating." He leaned over the desk and put his face an inch away from Ryman's. "I'll tell you one more thing, boss man." His voice was low and steady. "You ever speak to me again the way you did in front of Worsham, calling me *Mister Reinhardt* in that haughty goddamn tone and telling me I got work waiting in the service department, and you'll think crucifixion is a fucking picnic."

Ryman's saintly demeanor wavered as Bar turned and stomped out of the office.

A ping from the computer signaled the arrival of an email. It came from a sender Ryman did not recognize, with an odd subject line: "Blasphemer Beware."

> Those who mock the True Church will suffer retribution for their perversion. And for every innocent soul you lead astray, the hotter will the fires of hell be for your eternal punishment. Repent now!

Must be some crazy spammer crap, Ryman thought, some wacko thinking God's telling him to send out holy emails. Poor delusional bastard.

Threats of crucifixion and hellfire. Well, after all, it *was* Monday morning.

Ryman shrugged and resumed his study of the phrase "Ars Venatica" and the intriguing double meaning of "venery."

Chapter 30

THE BUZZ ABOUT the remarkable quality of sport shown by the Montfair hounds spread through the membership and to fellow enthusiasts from neighboring environs as well. A few who had traveled from afar to attend the memorial service for Fergus arranged to stay over to enjoy what everyone expected would be another splendid morning of fox chasing. Thumper counted nearly four times the number of trailers normally seen for an early season Tuesday morning hunt.

He sought out Marva Henderson and found her just about to mount Emmie, her number-two horse. "Looks like we're going to have to enforce the guest limit," he said. "We can't tell the members not to come, but we may have to get serious about keeping down the number of guests."

"I'll get an email out as soon as I get home," Marva said. "Oh, my God! Will you look at that?"

He followed her pointing finger to see Ryman McKendrick, the picture of the most properly turned out cubbing foxhunter, leading a horse from around the back of his trailer. Rather than Token, he'd brought Colby, the inexperienced young Thoroughbred. In place of his slovenly polo shirt and stained breeches, he wore essentially the same outfit he'd worn to the shop the day before. His polished brown field boots gleamed in the early morning sunlight. His face, frequently speckled with three-day stubble, was clean-shaven. Rather than his usual gait—slouching along in an unhurried shuffle—he strode forward with erect posture and a lively bounce.

Nardell appeared behind him similarly attired, a pale blue show shirt with a matching patterned stock tie the only nod to gender specificity. She had applied a modest touch of make-up, a rarity for her, especially on a hunting day, and her French braid was neatly encased in a hairnet and tucked up under her helmet. With her tattoos concealed by the prim attire, she was the image of the aristocratic lady foxhunter. Instead of the compact gray mare Gabby, Nardell's Arab/Quarter Horse cross, a heavy chestnut gelding was backing down the trailer ramp—Fergus's favorite mount, the draft cross Dale, partner of the late master's other mount,

Clyde.

Both horses were spotless—bathed, brushed, and polished to a high sheen. Every piece of tack was immaculate, the leather freshly oiled and the metal parts shining. There wasn't even a speck of dust on the horses' hooves.

Only one element broke the otherwise stunning perfection: They both wore their Saint Hubert medals around their necks, dangling over their ties. Thumper also noticed an important piece of equipment was missing from their saddles—their staff radios.

The elegance of their turnout was even more striking as they began to mingle with their fellow hunters, all of whom, except Bing Sensabaugh and Marie Hardesty, wore polo shirts on this warm September morning. When the rest of the group from Brookside Hunt returned to their home turf following Saturday's memorial service, Marie accepted Bing's offer to extend her stay at his farm and enjoy a bit more sport.

The Montfair masters and staff convened for the pre-hunt confab. Hounds cavorted about, relieving themselves, limbering up for the sport to come.

"Pretty spiffy turnout, Ry," Thumper said. "You two look swell. My great-grandfather would be pleased."

"As much as I respect the memory of your great-granddaddy," Ryman replied, "it's Saint Hubert I aim to please. It's to honor him, and the sanctity of the sport, that Nardell and I are turned out according to our office."

"Your 'office?'"

"I am the Restorer of the Faith. And Nardell is my helper."

"And just what faith would that be?"

"Well, I'm still trying to work that out. But, Saint Hubert be praised, I'm getting a pretty good handle on the basics."

"And those basics include... ?"

"By honoring the sport, we honor Saint Hubert. That's what's meant by 'Hunt with honor, as is due.' And, ultimately, 'Through the beast to God is true.'"

"The good Saint Hubert was partial to Jägermeister, was he?"

"It's simple. We protect and tend our quarry, so we can earn the hunter's badge of glory." He lifted the medallion hanging around his neck and kissed it reverently, but with a hint of sensuality in the way his lips caressed the small disc. Dropping it from his hand, he continued, "And the reward of that glory extends to other aspects of our life."

"Amen!" Nardell added, her eyes heavenward and a serene smile on her painted lips.

Ryman maneuvered his horse so he was snugly beside Thumper and said in a low voice, "Did you know 'venery' can mean both 'hunting' and 'sexual intercourse?'"

"As a matter of fact, I did know that. Although I hadn't thought about it for quite awhile."

"Well, let me tell you my oldest, bestest friend, that ain't no—whatcha call it?—linguistical accident. Seems that the better the one kind of venery, the better the other kind too."

Thumper caught a fleeting exchange between Nardell and Mildred, some unspoken communication that appeared to endorse Ryman's point.

He thought about his stroll with Garl Williams, what they heard from Crispie and Patti's cottage, followed by the possibly imagined sound of roiling bedsprings in every spare room of his house while he laid awake in an empty boudoir. "I wouldn't know about that," he said curtly.

"Oh, yeah, right," Ryman replied sheepishly. "But, well, y'know..." He sidled in even closer and continued in a suggestive whisper. "... lots of single ladies in this club, and around these parts. Not that many eligible men. If you and Shelagh are through, well, just look around at all this available..."

"So your Saint Hubert is into both strong drink and promiscuity? Sounds like you've found a very obliging god to serve."

Ryman recoiled back in embarrassment. "No, man, it's not like that. And, hey, I don't recall you living like a monk after you and Gloriana split up."

"True, I did enjoy some liaisons *after* the divorce was final. But my honor as a gentleman does not permit me to engage in such dalliances while I am technically married to another. You know how I feel about that."

"Yeah, right, you and your gentlemanly honor, The University Code and all that. Well, suit yourself. I hope your honor is keeping you comfy at night."

"That's none of your goddamn business," Thumper snapped back, getting more impatient with each exchange. "And, by the way, it seems you and Nardell were so focused on pleasing Saint Hubert with your turnout that you forgot your staff radios."

"Didn't forget 'em. We don't need to rely on crutches like that. We trust in Saint Hubert and he'll show us the way. In fact, I'd prefer we all ditch the radios. They can only take away from the hunter's badge of glory."

"Look, Ry, you know I've got my reservations about these things." He placed a hand on the hefty piece of electronic equipment strapped to the front of his saddle. "But we have to think about the hounds' safety, if nothing else. Same goes for the tracking collars."

"I'd like to see those tossed too," Ryman said. "Saint Hubert won't allow any harm to come to our hounds. By using radios and tracking collars, we're dishonoring the sport, dishonoring him. Where's your faith, Thumper? What would your great-grandfather say about all this electronic gear?"

"To tell you the truth, my faith isn't in you right now, and it's certainly not in your conjured up image of some obscure figure who lived thirteen hundred years ago. And as for my great-grandfather, I think if two-way radios had been available in his day, he'd have been all for using them. Same goes for tracking collars." He looked around at the trucks and trailers. "And nice big trucks to pull fancy horse trailers over paved roads. And cell phones. And ambulances. And air conditioning. And email to keep in touch with our members. Tradition's one thing, practicality's another."

"And faith is above all."

"Hoo boy! Where are you coming up with this stuff?"

Ryman turned to Mildred and pointed at her radio. "How about leaving that worthless hunk of metal and wires behind. You haven't needed it lately anyway, have you?"

Her first reaction was to grip the radio in a protective squeeze. But then she realized Ryman had a point. "No, I guess I haven't, now that you mention it. But, gosh, I don't know..." She gave Thumper a questioning look.

"Your call," he said, scoffing at the whole concept. He noticed the large group of followers were done with their prep work and ready to go. "Enough of this. We've got people waiting. If y'all don't want to use your radios, fine. The less chatter on these things the better. But I'm not leaving our huntsman and hounds without help if there's a problem. We have a responsibility..."

Ryman rolled his eyes and cut off Thumper's lecture before it began. "Hey, Crispie," he called out. "What do you say we all toss the radios today. Let Saint Hubert be our guide and our *senior* master here can just prattle on to himself for a change?"

"That's enough, Ryman!" Thumper ordered, positioning his horse to block Ryman's path as he started to move away toward Crispie and Patti.

Several of the waiting followers perked up at the outburst.

Lowering his voice, he continued, "We're done with this. It's time to go hunting. I won't have you causing another scene in front of our members."

Ryman smiled calmly. The annoying glow of righteous peace wreathed his well-groomed face. "Okay, Thumper, whatever you say. You're the senior master now. So where shall we draw this morning?"

"You're asking me? I'm surprised you haven't come prepared with a vision of where the fox would be obediently waiting for us."

"Your call this morning. Saint Hubert and I have confidence in you,

Brother."

"Damn nice of you. And of Saint Humbug, too."

"Saint Hubert."

"So you say. Okay, then, my plan was to draw to Coon Tree Hollow. How do you and Saint Humpty-Bump feel about that?"

Ryman's visage shined with patient forbearance. "An excellent choice." Turning to Nardell, he said, "C'mon, sweetheart. Let's go hunting."

As they trotted off, Thumper called over to Crispie, "Mister O'Rourke, Saint Howzit-Hang approves our plan to draw to Coon Tree Hollow." He could see Ryman gaze skyward, mumble something to himself, lift his medallion and kiss it as he moved off to his position with hounds.

****

Bar Reinhardt stepped into the office and stood before Muriel, dressed in the same outfit he'd worn to the funeral service, right down to the black eye patch. He pulled at his shirt collar, trying to keep the irritating denim fabric at bay. "How do I look?" he asked.

"Like the picture of a perfect tractor salesman," she replied. "Just one thing I'd do differently." She motioned for him to come stand beside her, which he obediently did. She reached into her desk drawer and withdrew a pair of scissors. Bar's eye widened as she approached him. "Hold still now," she said. *Snip*. "There. That's better." She tossed the price tag in the trashcan and slipped her scissors back in the drawer.

"Oh, for Chris… ah… geez. I ain't bought any new clothes for awhile. Forgot about price tags and shi... stuff."

"Would you like some coffee?"

"Yeah, sure... um, it ain't the stuff that killed Fergus, is it?"

"I beg your pardon?"

"Oh, ah, nothing... just joking. He was saying... when... when he... thought he had like... indigestion or somethin' from the coff... oh, never mind. Yeah, sure, coffee would be great."

As Muriel poured a cup for him, Bar squeezed into the boss man's chair. He looked as uncomfortable as a Pentecostal preacher at a gay pride parade. At the sound of the showroom door opening, he stood up so fast he almost spilled the whole cup of coffee on his sparkling new white bib overalls.

"Customer," he said with a dry mouth.

Muriel placed a hand on his arm. "You can do this. Don't think of it as selling. Mister McKendrick never did. Think of it as helping people with their equipment needs. The Lord has allowed you many, many years to develop your knowledge, back there in the service shop. No one knows this equipment like you do, from the inside out. Just find out what someone needs, then make the right match. That's all there is to it."

Bar felt like he was being sent off to his first day of kindergarten. He took a deep breath, wedged himself between the two desks, and stepped through the office door to begin his new career.

****

As Bar Reinhardt was preparing to make his first deal as Executive Sales Manager of McKendrick and Sons, the current "son" was adding a fifth notch to his growing record of incredible hunting days. Thumper's ambivalence grew in direct proportion to Ryman's success. Certainly, he wanted to show good sport for members and guests. But with each outing like the one this day—hounds hot on the scent, three foxes playing a tag-team game that kept the action moving all morning—the chances of keeping the number of riders to a manageable level, and Ryman's head from swelling to the size of a Clydesdale's butt, diminished sharply.

Hounds had been in full cry, with halloas and tally-hos ringing across the countryside. The staff radios had been silent throughout the morning.

They hacked back to the meet after the final fox decided it was time for the fun to end and ducked into a convenient fox-sized drainpipe. The chatter among the followers sounded like a gaggle of schoolgirls on a trip to the mall. Even the men among the group spoke in elevated tones, their voices tittering almost as high as the ladies'.

"Oh-my-GOD! Did you see what that fox did?"

"Never saw anything like it!"

"How many fences do you think we jumped?"

"I lost count somewhere after the first twenty."

"I'm not even *tired*!"

"I think my horse could go another hour at least."

"I'm so glad we decided to stay a few more days. Honey, can we put off going home until Friday? Get in one more day of this fabulous sport?"

"I'll make the arrangements, my love."

A lavish spread appeared at the tailgate, nothing planned, just a spontaneous potluck outpouring of food and drink.

Thumper noticed Ryman and his Assistant Restorer of the Faith were absent from the spread. He took a stroll among the maze of trucks and trailers to assure they were okay. Coming around the corner of a large gooseneck rig, he saw the dressing room door of Ryman's trailer swing open. Ryman emerged in the doorway. His head swiveled back and forth in a lookout motion. His hair was mussed, his tie sharply askew, his vest gone, and his shirttail halfway untucked.

Thumper pulled back quickly behind the nearby trailer and then peered cautiously around the side.

Ryman stepped down to the ground, turned back to the open door, and said, "Okay, coast is clear. Everyone's at the tailgate."

Nardell appeared in the doorway, in a similar state of dishevelment. "Catch me!" She leapt into his waiting arms and wrapped her legs around his waist. Grinding against him, she said, "Sure you don't want to go back in for a little more. Just a quickie?"

"You know I do," he replied with a leering grin. "But we'd better not. The congregation's waiting for us. We must do our honors to Saint Hubert."

Her grinding action intensified. "Oh, c'mon. Only take a minute. I'm sure Saint Hubert won't mind."

He leaned his head back and closed his eyes. "Oh, you bad, bad woman. How you do tempt this old boy." He cocked an ear toward the tailgate area and listened to the sound of merriment ringing through the pasture. It was apparent the party wasn't going to break up any time soon. "Hell yeah!" he said. "The congregation ain't going anywhere."

He tossed Nardell back into the dressing room, jumped in after her, and slammed the door.

****

Blessed relief flowed over Bar when he entered the showroom to find his first customer was Frank Worsham.

Worsham took note of Bar's attire but, as he did when Ryman appeared the day before wearing his hunting duds, said nothing. Must be some new dress code around this place since Fergus died, he thought.

Bar noticed something different too. Merle was not with Frank.

"Ryman here?" Worsham asked. "I gotta talk to him."

"He's hunting. Afraid you're stuck with me."

"Oh, yeah, I forgot they've started back up again. Had a lot on my mind lately."

"You okay, Frank? And where's Merle? He ain't... I mean... he's okay...?"

"That's what I wanted to talk to Ryman about. Damnedest thing. After we left here yesterday, Merle kept acting real funny, whining and barking at me. He never does that. When we got home, he wouldn't get out of the truck. Refused my commands, just sat there whining. Now, I ain't saying I believed Ryman for a damned minute. But his foolishness or not, something wasn't right with Merle. So I got back in the truck and we went straight to Doc Carlyle." He paused and looked out the showroom window to where his F350 dually was parked. Bar could see no sign of Merle in the truck. "Damnedest thing."

"What Frank? Is Merle okay?"

"Doc said it was a tumor, on his left hip, very small, but enough to cause him some pain, especially for something like getting in and out of the truck. Said we caught it just in time. Could have hit the femoral artery and then… but he'll be fine. Needs a few days rest, is all. How could Ryman have known that?"

Bar gave his shirt collar a couple of tugs. Every thread of denim fiber began to prickle at his skin. He felt the band of his eye patch constrict, pressing hard against his swelling head. He wanted desperately to pull off both his shirt and eye patch. But he was stuck in his new uniform, the goddamn Executive Sales Manager, dutifully dressed for the part. "I dunno, Frank. Lucky guess maybe?"

"Seems unlikely. Maybe he saw Merle do something that I'd missed. Y'know, Ry's spent his whole life around all those hounds. Probably knows more about canine anatomy than most vets do. I've had dogs all my life too. But just one or two house pets at a time. Ryman grew up around—what?—sixty, seventy working hounds always in the kennels. I'm thinking that had to have something to do with it."

Another surge of relief flowed over Bar thanks to Worsham's well-reasoned explanation. "That's gotta be it, Frank. Hell, tell you the truth, Ryman knows a lot more about dogs than he does about tractors. He's sure spent more time around them. Lots more. So, yeah, makes sense that he could pick up on some little glitch, some way Merle was moving that only his eye would see, what with all that experience of watching how dogs move." The prickling sensation on Bar's skin eased and the tension on his eye patch relaxed. He was happy to resume his conviction that the boss man was totally wacked out, that Ryman's visions of a mystical talking stag were merely the product of his addled brain and his seemingly miraculous diagnosis of Worsham's dog was nothing more than a clever trick of observation.

"Just one thing," Worsham said.

"What's that?"

"Ryman didn't see Merle move until after he'd said there was something wrong. Merle had been sitting at my feet up till then. Ryman didn't see him struggling to get out of the truck, didn't see him walk until Merle got up and went over to him."

The prickling on Bar's skin started up again. "Yeah, well, maybe he's so good he could just tell by the way Merle was sitting. Anyways, it's all turned out okay, right?"

"Right. And I reckon I owe Ryman an apology. And my thanks."

"Well, I can pass that along to him when I see him. Or you could come back later and try to catch him. Cain't say exactly when he might get here though."

"I was also hoping to do a little business with him." Worsham reached into his pocket and pulled out his list of tractor requirements.

Bar's mood brightened.

"I've made up my mind to go with a new 7830. Thought about maybe looking at a Kubota at White's. But, well, after what Ryman did for Merle and all, that tipped it in y'all's favor. Still gotta sort through all the options, make sure I get the right package for what I need. And see what kinda price we're looking at. Guess I'll have to come back when Ryman's here."

"No need for that," Bar said. "Lemme see that list." Worsham handed him the paper and Bar gave it a read, muttering to himself, "Uh huh; right; nope, don't reckon you'll need that; this one's good; uh huh, good call there; maybe not this one, depending on a couple of other possibilities. Well, Frank, you've certainly done your homework. I think you're gonna be real happy with your new 7830. How about we step into my office and get everything worked out?"

"*Your* office, Bar?"

"We ain't had time to get out the press release yet. It was decided just yesterday that I'm taking over the sales function here. Seems Ry's a bit too busy with some other things just now. So I reckon y'all are stuck with me."

Now Worsham understood the shirt, clean overalls, and eye patch. He stood for a moment assessing the man before him. He'd known Bar Reinhardt from the time Fergus hired him as a part-timer. No question Bar was a first-rate mechanic. Never known a better one. Looking at Bar in a fresh light, Worsham saw that he was more than just a wrench-turner. He knew tractors, studied them, possibly even loved them. They were his life. Who better to help him put together the new package for his 7830.

"Okay, Mister Salesman. Let's step into your office and do this deal."

****

Thumper slunk back to the tailgate where Bing was holding court. A covey of ladies pressed tightly around him, every one of them in blissful delight watching each gesture and expression with twinkling eyes, ooohing, aaahing, and giggling at the precisely correct moments to accompany whatever amusing tale he was spinning. The scene reminded Thumper of bobby-soxers gathered around a '50s pop idol. Marie Hardesty out-shined all the others in her rapturous gaze at old Bing Sensabaugh. Cecelia Broadhurst competed for a close second.

"Sing something for us," Cecelia said.

"Better yet," Bing countered, "let's all sing something. Who knows 'The Huntsman's Rouse?'"

Only Marie raised a hand. "I do."

"Wonderful. A duet then."

She moved to his side, they each took a deep breath, and broke out in song. His rich bass-baritone, nearly identical to that of the more famous Bing, blended easily with her competent soprano. The jumble of horse trailers in the pasture formed a makeshift amphitheater.

The hounds are all out and the morning does peep,
Why how now you sluggardly sot!
How can you, how can you, lie snoring asleep
While we all on horseback have got, my brave boy,
While we all on horseback have got.

The first verse served as a warm-up, a chance to feel out each other's vocal proclivities and respond to the nuances of tone and inflection. The second verse flowed with noticeably improved confidence and comfort.

I cannot get up, for the overnight's cup
So terribly lies in my head.
Besides, my wife cries, my dear, do not arise.
But cuddle me longer abed, my dear boy,
But cuddle me longer abed.

On those last two lines, Marie sidled closer to Bing and gave him a theatrically exaggerated wink of the eye. This sent up a chorus of hoots and hollers from the crowd.

The two singers, now smoothly performing as one, rolled into the final verse with vigor.

Come, on with your boots, on your vapours a pox!
Nor tire us with longer delay.
For the cry of the hounds and the sight of the fox
Will chase all dull vapours away, my brave boy,
Will chase all our vapours away.

The boisterous applause and cheers startled some of the horses in the nearby trailers.

Thumper was so engrossed by this spontaneous outburst of song that he didn't hear the bootsteps approaching from behind. When Ryman's hand landed heavily on his shoulder, he jumped a foot.

"Wasn't that just wonderful?" Ryman exclaimed.

"About time you two got here," Thumper said dryly, massaging his shoulder. "Problem at the trailer?"

"No problem a-tall," Ryman replied. "Just continuing to enjoy this wonderful day of sport, like all our good friends here." Ryman strode over to Bing and pumped his hand. "Well done! Well done! Saint Hubert is surely pleased!"

"Oh! Oh!" Mildred shouted. "I know one we can all sing. 'Don't Fence Me In.' Let's sing that."

Thumper's reluctance to join in had nothing to do with his singing ability, or reputed lack thereof. (Whenever asked to participate in a sing-along, he demurred with the excuse that his singing voice fell somewhere between two tomcats wrestling on a tin roof and Henry Kissinger snoring.) It was the annoying gaiety—fueled by the intoxicating aroma of rampant pheromones mingled with the scent of horseshit—that had him flummoxed.

Joyfully, if imperfectly, harmonizing in song, no one took notice of the senior master's departure.

Chapter 31

THE FOLLOWING MORNING Rhetta and Abel entered Fergus's study. She found Ryman seated at his father's desk, an open book in his hand, several stacks of books arrayed around him. He leaned back in the swivel chair, his boots propped on the desktop.

"What the hell are you doing?" she asked.

"Research."

"Research on what?"

"*Notitia Venatica*." He held up a well-worn leather-bound volume and read from the frontispiece. "'A treatise on foxhunting, embracing the general management of hounds, etcetera, etcetera.' By Henry Thomas Alken, 1784 to 1851. The old man put together quite a library over the years." He waved a hand at the dozens of books on the shelves. "Some of these must go back to my grandfather, maybe even before him. Never had much interest in them m'self... until now."

"Get your goddamn feet down. Show some respect."

Ryman shrugged and swung his boots off the desk.

A quizzical cloud passed over Rhetta's face when she noticed his attire. "This... this ain't a hunting day, is it? And if it is, what are you doing here at this hour?"

The thought that he'd caught his mother off guard, made her think she didn't know what day it was, gave Ryman a glimmer of satisfaction. He waited a long moment before answering. "No, it's Wednesday. Not a hunting day."

This did not erase Rhetta's confusion. "Then why the hunting kit? And how come you're not at the shop? It's after nine o'clock."

He tugged at his vest. "The mark of my office. And Bar's got the shop covered."

She had no idea what he meant by the first remark. But the second comment lit her short fuse. "Boy, you've been told not to mention that name in this house! And what... ?" Confusion returned to mix with her anger. "... what do you mean *he's* got the shop covered."

"Ba... um, *he's* handling sales now. Conway's doing most of the service work, under Ba... under the supervision of the new sales manager, former head mechanic. Muriel's got the office under control, same as she did all the years she worked for Daddy. They don't really need me. Which leaves me free to focus on what I'm supposed to be doing."

"Have you lost your goddamn mind?"

"Some folks seem to be of that opinion," he muttered.

"You made that... that monstrosity the sales manager?"

"You might be surprised to know he sold a 7830 to Frank Worsham yesterday, with damn near every option available. Biggest one day sale we've made for a long damn time." Turning back to his book, he added offhandedly, "Bigger than Daddy made the past few years."

She stepped to the front of the desk and smacked the book from his hand.

"Hey!" he exclaimed. "This is a valuable old book. You mighta broke the spine..."

"I'll break your goddamn spine if you don't get your ass into that shop this minute and put things right! Hide that good-for-nothing freak in the back where he belongs. And keep an eye on that prissy little colored woman. Her and all her damn Jesus talk. She's just been waiting for the opportunity to steal the place blind. And now with your daddy gone, and you without the sense to be there watching..." Rhetta shook so violently she could no longer form words. She planted her hands flat on the desk and glared at Ryman. She expected him to wilt under her assault, slink out of the house, and go do as he was told. It had always worked before.

Instead, he calmly retrieved *Notitia Venatica* from where it had landed on the edge of the desk, brushed it off, and set it on the stack of other old books beside him. "You misjudge these people, Ma. Saint Hubert knows they are good souls. I know they are good souls. Known them pretty much all my life in fact. You won't even mention the name of one of them, and the other you see maybe twice a year, Christmas and some other special occasion. And even then you barely have two words to say to her. So what do you know about them?"

"You'd best not sass me, boy. You forget who owns this farm now. And who decides who lives here and who don't."

"Where I live is of no consequence. Saint Hubert will provide. He's called me to my mission and I have faith it will be fulfilled."

"Saint... what? Who? Your mission?" She stumbled back and dropped into the chair in front of the desk. "My boys. One defied me and got hisself killed. Now the other's gone stark raving mad. Lettin' freaks and coloreds take over the family business, thinkin' he's got some kinda holy goddamn mission." Ryman continued to sit calmly, the picture of self-assured peace. "What's going to happen to us? I guess it'll be the poor house for me. And the looney bin for you. I tried to raise you right, I truly did. I guess it was all a waste a time."

"Sorry, Ma. That's not going to work either. And I'd appreciate it if you wouldn't use such terms when referring to the fine people who are now running McKendrick and Sons."

"Fine people you say? Well, we'll see about that. Just don't come whinin' to me when it all goes to hell 'cause one's scared off all the customers and the other's stole anything that ain't nailed down. Fine people? Whether they are or not, I'll tell you one thing they sure ain't. They ain't McKendricks. That's what the sign reads, boy. 'McKendrick and Sons.' You're the McKendrick, and you're the son. It's you that's supposed to be there running things, making the sales, keeping an eye on them others."

"I may be a McKendrick, but I ain't the son."

"What? A course you're the son. You gone so batty now you don't even know who your own parents are?"

"What I mean is that I'm not *the* son, the son who was supposed to take over the business. That was Teedy. That's how Daddy saw it, and Teedy knew it. We used to talk about that, how he liked hanging out at the shop, working on stuff, talking to customers. He loved the tractor business as much as Daddy did. At least he loved the idea of it. Never got much chance to actually do it. But if he'd come back from the war, or not gone in the first place, he'd have made that business into something to be proud of. And likely had a whole bunch of sons to keep it going. Me? I never cared much for the tractor business. And there won't be any more 'sons.' So we might as well start phasing out the 'McKendrick' part too."

"If your daddy could hear such talk. If he weren't already dead, that kinda nonsense woulda killed him for sure. That business meant everything to him. Nothing more important to him than carrying on the family legacy, like his daddy and all the others before them."

"You're wrong, Ma. There was something else just as important to him." He placed a hand on a stack of books. "This. Daddy had two passions, selling tractors and chasing foxes. And he had two sons, one who was supposed to carry on the first passion, the other to carry on the second. Something went wrong with the tractor part. I reckon I'll never know what made Teedy decide to go off to that crazy-ass war. Sure wasn't any need for it. And he'd never said a damn thing about wanting to be a soldier."

Rhetta's mouth tightened and she turned away.

"Anyways, I was too young to know much about what was going on then. But I do know this, thanks to Saint Hubert and what he revealed to me through that stag: It's my destiny to carry on Daddy's foxhunting legacy. And the way to do it," he said, patting the stack of books, "is all right here." He arose, lifted an empty cardboard box from the floor, and began packing the books, citing authors as he lifted each one. "Higginson,

Mackay-Smith, Thomas, Beckford, of course. Everything Surtees wrote. Newer stuff too. Robards, Fine, Foster."

"Yeah, your daddy liked foxhunting. Big deal. Foxhunting don't pay the bills. Mostly just a drain on what little we already got. Maybe if he'd put more time into the business instead of riding all around the countryside three damn days a week most of the year, the business woulda done better." She stood up and pointed an accusing finger at her son. "And you'd best get this notion out of your head and get serious about your responsibilities. You'll be singing a different tune when I have to sell this place and you got no place to live. Maybe you and your girlfriend and your big freak pal can all move into a little trailer somewheres. Serve you right."

"I have faith that Saint Hubert will provide, that he will guide me..."

"Stop that talk, boy! There ain't no goddamn Saint Hubert and he ain't guiding you nowheres but to ruin."

Ryman opted not to point out the illogic of that statement.

Rhetta continued, "You're making it sound like foxhunting is some kinda religion. Your daddy mighta been crazy about it, but it weren't no religion to him."

"Wasn't it? Going through his books this morning, it occurred to me that that's exactly what foxhunting was to him. Check this out." He picked up *The Foxhunter's Bedside Book*. "From 'The Foxhunter's Faith,' at the close of Article Two: 'He that shall say that the day will be a bad scenting one, or in any manner endeavor to prophesy evil is an abomination.'" His finger skimmed down the page. "'He who talks loudly or leaps unnecessarily is an abomination... or who in any way causes inconvenience to any hound or hunt servant is an abomination.'" His finger wandered back up the page. "I like this one. 'It is acceptable that those of experience shall, at all times, give explanation and encouragement by word and deed to all young persons, so that foxhunting may continue in the land from generation to generation." He snapped the book closed and dropped it into the box. He then picked up *The Songs of Foxhunting*, held it out for Rhetta to see, and pointed at the title. "What do you think these are if not hymns?"

Her face turned ashen and her attack mode waned. "I know all about those," she said.

"Oh, right. There was a time when you were into it as much as Daddy was. Y'all used to sing some of these songs after a hunt, or when folks came over to the house. Seems I kinda remember Bing leading things with that great voice of his, you playing the piano."

"That was a long time ago. Don't matter to me now. What matters is you putting foxhunting on the same level with religion. I may not be much for church-going, but I know that what you're saying would be called blasphemy by lotsa folks. And saying it was your own departed daddy's religion makes it even worse. If there is a hell, you could rot in it for saying stuff like that."

"But foxhunting *was* Daddy's religion, Ma. It was his faith, the whole foundation and structure of his life. He was more than just a local master of foxhounds. He was like... like a bishop, sort of, guiding others, keeping the faith pure, acting like a missionary bringing new people into it. And I see in all these books that there's a whole belief system that goes back centuries. Hell, I even found out that people back in the Stone Age based the first form of religion on hunting."

"Well, we ain't in the Stone Age no more, are we? Only stones around here are the ones you got in your noggin."

Ryman chuckled and shook his head. "Probably some rattling going on in there. But not so much that I can't hear what I'm being called to do. It's been forming for a few days, but going through Daddy's books this morning made it all clear."

Rhetta sank back down into the chair, limp and frustrated. "All right, boy. If it'll shut you up, I'll humor you just this once. If it ain't to act like a decent man, take care of your family's business, and do right by your mother, just what is it you think you got this calling to do?"

He straightened his vest, lifted his Saint Hubert medal to his lips and kissed it. He then announced, "I have been called to revive the world's first true religion, the foundation of everything that's inside us, that makes us part of the natural world; the chase, the challenge, the risk, and the reward. It's what it means to be alive, in every way. I have been given a special gift. I can see and sense things others can't. Like the fact that Abel's waiting for a treat from that blue jar on the shelf behind me."

Rhetta had been slouching, her eyes half-closed, twirling a hand loosely as Ryman spoke. But at this last remark, her head jerked up and her eyes widened. "What? There ain't no treats in here. Abel only gets treats from me. Fergus never let him even come into his study."

"That's what you think. Abel and I know better. Don't we, fellah?"

"Woof!"

Rhetta stared at her dog, who was now standing, wagging his stub of a tail, and panting eagerly at Ryman.

"Daddy knew you didn't want anyone else giving Abel treats, so he'd love only you. That's why he made a show of keeping the dog out of here. Fact is, Abel would sneak in here anyway and Daddy would give him treats when you were off somewhere else." He reached toward the shelf and placed his hand on the blue ceramic jar.

"Woof!"

"How the hell do you know that? Your old man tell you, did he? Musta thought it was funny, pulling one over on the old gal, spoiling her dog just for spite."

"Wasn't about spite. He loved Abel too. He just couldn't show it around you 'cause you'd get jealous. And, no, Daddy never told me. Abel did."

"Woof! Woof!" His thick body was wiggling now from nose to tail, anticipating what was coming from the familiar blue jar.

"Here ya go, boy." Ryman finally withdrew a treat and tossed it to the dog.

Rhetta gazed in astonishment as Abel scarfed down the goodie. "You're lying. Your old man told you, and I'm sure the two of you got a good laugh about it."

"Believe what you want, Ma. The power is real. I didn't ask for it. And I don't know how it works, exactly. But with Saint Hubert's blessing, the world will realize the true path." He lifted the box of books. "Well, I got a lot more research to do. Best get outta your hair." He started toward the door.

"A church of foxhunting," Rhetta mused, reaching down and rubbing Abel's head. "Craziest damn thing I ever heard."

"Might seem crazy now, Ma. But I know you'll come around in time, and join us in the Venatican faith."

"Vatican?"

"No, Ma. Ve*nat*ican. A follower of the Ancient and Venerable Church of Ars Venatica."

He turned and left the room.

Rhetta stared at the empty doorway.

Abel stared at the treat jar. "Woof!"

Chapter 32

THE "OFFICE" IN Ryman's cottage consisted of a room barely larger than a closet. Nardell arrived home Wednesday afternoon from a day of massage therapy appointments to find Ryman hunched over the computer. Every surface in the tiny space was covered with open books and pages of notepaper.

"What's all this?" she asked.

"Our Holy Scriptures, the assembled work of foxhunting's theologicals."

"Theologians?"

"Yeah, that."

"Where you'd get all this stuff?"

"From my father's library. The old man collected every book he could find about the sport, from the classics to the latest works. It's all right here, everything we need to spread the word. Saint Hubert has provided."

"Indeed he has." Nardell picked up *Songs of Foxhunting* and began flipping through the pages. "Wow, look at all these songs. 'A-Hunting We Will Go,' 'John Peel,' 'Rouse, Boys, Rouse,' 'The Hunting Day,' 'Drink, Puppy, Drink.' Lyrics, sheet music. Cool."

"Better than cool, my darling." He took the book from her and held it to his chest. "Upon these books we will build our church. Saint Hubert knows that I'm just a messenger. No way I could come up with all this on my own. But many others have been hard at work over the centuries laying down the foundation. One in particular recognized that foxhunting is a form of religion, whether people realize it or not." He set down the songbook, reached for *The Foxhunter's Bedside Book*, and turned to a page marked with a sticky note. "From 'The Foxhunter's Faith.' 'He who, of his own freewill, goes home before the hounds do, or who is displeased with the day, or who is not fully uplifted, joyful, and thankful because of the day, is an abomination.'" He snapped the book closed and lifted a hand in praise. "Hallelujah!"

Nardell picked up the songbook again and leafed through it. "Lot of songs in here I don't recognize. But some I've heard, like 'John Peel.' She squared her shoulders and began to sing.

Do ye ken John Peel with his coat so gray?
Do ye ken John Peel at the break of day?
Do ye ken John Peel when he's far far awaaaaaay?
With his hounds and horn in the mor-or-ning.
Twas the sound of his horn called me from my bed...

He reached out and slipped the book from Nardell's hands. "That's lovely, darling, just lovely."

"You don't care for my singing, do you?"

"That doesn't matter. The point is to make a joyful noise."

"You didn't look very joyful just now."

"I'm sure Saint Hubert would be pleased."

"Okay, fine, so I can't sing. I don't recall you having such a hot voice either."

"No argument there. But we know someone who does."

"Bing?"

"You betcha. I remember him singing all these songs. Everyone would join in, but you could always hear Bing above the others, hitting the notes just right even when the rest didn't. Sometimes we'd have a little a cappella sing-along in the field after a hunt. Sometimes we'd gather in the house and my mother would play the piano. Or if she wasn't around there was usually somebody who could play. Not so much these days. Folks have stopped doing that sort of thing. I guess in the old days we had to find ways to entertain ourselves. Now you can listen to whatever you want whenever you want, people all going around with earphones on, locked in their own private world."

He closed the songbook and set it down.

"But we'll change that," he avowed. "We'll get folks communing again, sharing the joy of the sport, lifting their voices in praise."

"Even those of us whose voices aren't very joyful?"

"Maybe you can accompany us on the kazoo." Ryman tried to dodge the smack he knew was coming. But there wasn't enough space in the cramped room to evade Nardell's blow.

Chapter 33

AFTER AN INVIGORATING Thursday morning of sport, Crispie and Voytek Nutchenko, the Montfair farm manager, attended to the hounds as Patti took care of the horses. By noon hounds were settled, lounging in the cool shaded enclosures, well protected from the midday heat. Nimby and Lap Dance, hosed off, rubbed down, and thoroughly examined for any signs of strain or injury from the morning's chase, were turned out in a paddock adjoining the fan-equipped stalls. They were free to either graze outside or retreat into the cool enclosures where an automatic fly spray system made the environment even more comfortable.

His kennelman duties finished, Voytek went off to attend to other chores around the farm. Crispie and Patti retreated into the staff office where the window air conditioner was at full blast. The chill sent a shudder through Patti as it hit her sweat-soaked polo shirt.

"Geez," she said, "I didn't realize how wet this shirt is."

Crispie did realize that, and had been enjoying the sight of it clinging to his partner's nicely shaped figure as they went about their post-hunt tasks.

"I'd better get into something dry," she said, pulling off the damp shirt.

This caused Crispie to take even more notice with Patti stripped down to her sports bra, tight breeches, and brown boots. Her strawberry blond hair, enclosed in a hair net under her hunt cap throughout the morning and then subjected to the rigors of hound and horse chores, gave her the appearance of a woman ravished. She balled up the wet polo shirt and launched it into an arched shot. It landed with a swish in the dirty rags hamper next to the blanket-covered sofa.

"Are ya sure this doesn't need to come off too?" Crispie asked, hooking a finger beneath the bra strap.

She smiled over her shoulder, but lifted a dry tee shirt from a wall hook and slipped it on. "Maybe later," she said as she glided past him and took a seat at the huntsman's desk. "I want to make some notes about how the puppies did this morning while it's still fresh in my head." She brought up a file on the computer and began to type in her thoughts.

Crispie stood behind her. He looked over her shoulder and tried to read what she entered.

"I think Hempstead's getting past his babbling problem," he offered.

"Uh huh," Patti said, focusing on her report.

"It's the master's babbling I'm concerned about."

"Uh huh."

"All this talk about 'the hunter's badge a glory, protecting and defending the quarry.' What sart a blather is all that?"

"Uh huh."

"And that thing with me ring t'other night." He raised his hand and looked at the ring. "Getting all warked up over seeing this. Going on about some bloody deer. Makes ya wonder if he might be losing it."

"Uh huh."

"Still, though, I gotta admit we've had the best couple weeks a spart I can ever recall. Here or with any other hunt I been with. Certainly the best start a cub hunting ever."

"Is that so?"

"You're not listening to a thing I'm saying, are ya?"

"Sure, of course I am."

"A carse you're *not*. No mind, though. Reckon it's me that's babblin'." His eyes drifted from the computer screen to Patti's neck and the top of her shoulder exposed beneath the loose fitting tee shirt. Soft, pale, freckled skin just below his lips. He'd watched her several times that morning, racing with hounds, piloting Lap Dance over challenging fences as Charlie Fox led them on a splendid chase.

The temptation was too much. He leaned down and nibbled the side of Patti's neck. At first she squealed and jerked away. But the tingle his lips sent through her body lingered. Visions of the morning's run flashed in her mind, watching Crispie cheering the pack onto their fox, noting his effortless horsemanship, his long legs secure against Kashmir's sides, one hand holding his hunt whip and a light touch on the reins, the other placing his horn to his lips and blowing the thrilling strains of "Gone Away" as they raced across the verdant countryside. These thoughts stirred her even more and she bent her head to expose her neck, inviting him to nibble away. Her squeals of delight mingled with Crispie's low rumbling growls as his tongue and teeth worked lightly along her compliant skin.

Voytek walked the pasture fence line just outside, making notes of needed repairs. He heard strange sounds coming from the huntsman's office, escalating in intensity. First the sound of a barking vixen, then a lone baying hound. Hounds in kennels picked up the strain and soon the whole pack was in full chorus. Unsure if someone was in distress or if a confused fox might have strayed into the office and was wreaking havoc,

Voytek went to investigate. As he drew closer the sound of creaking furniture springs blended into the cacophony, the percussion timed in rhythm with the vixen barks.

Voytek reached the office window and his advance stopped cold there. Crispie sat on the sofa. Patti straddled him, her back towards the window. Both were naked. Crispie held his hunt horn in one hand, the other cupped around Patti's butt cheek. The springing stopped momentarily as Crispie took the mouthpiece end of his horn and moved it lightly around Patti's breasts, down her midline, across her abdomen, then back up again. She threw her head back and moaned softly as the cool metal traced across her bare skin. Looking past her shoulder, Crispie caught sight of an astonished Voytek Nutchenko staring through the window. He shot a quick grin at the voyeur and, with the hand cupped on Patti's ass, gave him a thumbs-up.

A red-faced, flustered farm manager stumbled away from the kennels, trying to remember what he'd been doing there in the first place.

****

Dan tracked down Janey's email address through the university's website: Haven't heard from you about Saturday, coming out to follow the hunt. Still interested?

Janey replied: Mr. Billington gave me the impression it might be better if I waited a while before coming out again.

Dan: That's odd. Did he actually say you couldn't come? I've never heard of anyone being banned from car-following. Unless you're an anti-hunting type who plans to sabotage their sport.

Janey: Of course I'm not. No, he didn't say outright I couldn't come, just seemed to think this wasn't the best time for me to be observing what they do.

Dan: Seems like you should be the judge of that. You, after all, are the researcher and author.

Janey: I was fascinated by what I saw last Saturday. I'd certainly like to see more. Do you really think it would be okay?

Dan: I do. We'll be careful to stay out of the way, not interfere with anything.

Janey: If you think it's all right. When and where should I meet you?

Chapter 34

THUMPER SAT ALONE at the dinner table on Friday evening, hunched over his plate, contemplating the letter from Shelagh's barrister. He absently pushed around a piece of salmon, topped with Natasha's scrumptious dill sauce, thinking more about Shelagh than about his devoted housekeeper's lovingly prepared food. Focused on the implications of the letter, he failed to notice the sound of her approach.

"Vhat is this?" she demanded, seeming to materialize at his side. "Food is not good? Something is wrong vith salmon? Sauce is bad? And potatoes. You are not even touching potatoes!"

He snapped into an erect posture and speared a large piece of pink, perfectly cooked fish. "No, no, everything is wonderful. I was just caught up in my thoughts." He began to shovel food into his mouth, smiling between bites and emitting muffled sounds of ecstasy.

She eyed him suspiciously. Then she noticed the letter. "This is vhat's upsetting you, no?" She picked it up and skimmed through the contents. "Hmmph! Silly, silly girl. I am sorry you are sad from this. But you vill be much better off if she is not coming back." She patted his arm. "There. Is good you are eating. Vill keep you strong and healthy."

"I may need my strength for tomorrow. No telling what stunt Ryman is going to pull this time."

"Yes, I am hearing much about this."

"You know about his 'church' idea? All his talk about Saint Hubert?"

"Oh, yes. Crispie is telling Voytek, Voytek is telling me. Everyone knows."

"And…?"

"Bah! Is… how you say it?… blasfemia, yes?"

"Yes, blasphemy. Some seem to agree with you. But others are lining up behind Ryman, supporting his antics."

"Voytek is telling me the things Crispie says Mister Ryman is able to do, that he is talking to animals, that even foxes are speaking to him. Is devil's vork."

"Mmm, well, I don't know about that."

"Oh, yes. Is devil's vork that leads pipple from true church. Mister Ryman is risking his soul, and souls of all who follow him."

"I'll be sure to point that out to him tomorrow morning." He picked up the letter. "Isn't your church opposed to divorce?"

"For Catholics, yes. But you are not Catholic, so is okay." She patted his arm again and smiled sweetly. "I am bringing dessert now."

"Just a small piece. I'm already having trouble getting my trousers buttoned."

"Bah!"

Chapter 35

REVEREND DAN STEERED his Mini Cooper into Fair Enough Farm at six-thirty Saturday morning. An eager Janey Musgrove occupied the seat beside him. She emerged from the car carrying a video camera and a large notebook.

As Janey arranged her gear, another rig pulled in, driven by Bing Sensabaugh with Marie Hardesty riding shotgun. Their two horses snuggled cozily in the trailer.

Dan caught sight of Rhetta standing on the front porch, Abel on guard beside her. "We should first make our manners to the hostess," he said, and they walked across the lawn to greet Rhetta.

"Good morning, Mrs. McKendrick," he called out cheerfully. "Lovely to see you on this fine morning."

Rhetta did not look pleased to see him. "If you're here for donations, Preacher, you're wasting your time."

He chuckled and scoffed at her remark as if it were meant as a joke. Janey guessed it wasn't and slowed her approach to the porch.

"Ho, no, no," he said. "I'm just escorting my friend, Professor Musgrove here, to follow the hunt. You might remember her from last Saturday. She attended your husband's memorial service."

Rhetta gave Janey a critical assessment. "Nope, cain't say I recall. You a foxhunter too, girlie?"

"No, ma'am. Never saw one before last week. I didn't think people even did this sort of thing any more."

"Some of 'em still do. The ones that ain't got no better sense."

"Well, I'm just here to observe."

"I reckon that means you got more sense than some others."

"What a big, handsome fellow," Janey said, pointing toward Abel. "He looks to be more the German than the American type."

"You know Boxers, do ya?"

"I grew up with several of them. Still three back home that I miss dearly."

"Woof!" Abel rose, trotted down the porch stairs, jumped up on Janey, and gave her a sloppy kiss. She embraced him and returned the affection.

Rhetta stood looking down at this exchange. "He don't usually do that with strangers."

"I guess he knows I'm a Boxer person."

"Mrs. McKendrick," Dan said, "I was wondering if you might be willing to share some thoughts about foxhunting with my friend Janey. I know a bit about the sport, but I'm sure it's barely a fraction of what you know."

"I'm sure it is, Preacher. But I ain't had nothing to do with it for a long damn time. I'm only out here to make sure none a them yay-hoos trample my flowerbeds. Then they can go on with their foolishness for all I care."

"Well, you see, Professor Musgrove would certainly benefit from your…"

"No, really," Janey said. "That's fine. We don't want to intrude. I'm just grateful you allowed us to be here on your property. Come on, Dan, we shouldn't bother our hostess any longer." She leaned over and gave Abel another embrace. "Bye, big fellah. Nice meeting you."

She turned and started to walk away. A reluctant Reverend Davenport followed. Abel stood watching her go, whining softly.

"C'mere, dog," Rhetta said, smacking a hand against her thigh.

The dog did not move.

"I said come *here*, dog."

Abel stayed where he was, his eyes on Janey as she and Dan walked back toward the trailers. "Woof!"

"Hmmm, you think so, do you?"

"Woof!"

"All right, then." Rhetta called out, "Hey, you two. Wait a minute."

****

Thumper rode over from Montfair on Ozzy, short for Ozymandias (by He's No Poet out of Across the Sands), a six-year-old gray Thoroughbred only recently retired from the steeplechase circuit. Making his debut as a field master's mount, the horse was on full alert as they approached the mass of trailers. Thumper had his hands full, mindful that the animal could explode at any moment. Ozzy had already worked up a lather around his breastplate just from the short hack between Thumper's barn and the Fair Enough parking field. He pranced at a sideways angle, his front end up, his feet light on the hard ground, ready to launch into a sprint. Thumper's calmness, firm legs, and soft hands offset some of the horse's edginess. He'd been on hundreds like this, many far more dangerous. He knew the horse would be fine once they moved off, comfortable in the lead where a well-bred racehorse wanted to be. To minimize the opportunity for misbehavior, Thumper arranged his arrival close to the scheduled time for the start of the hunt.

As he reached the center of the staging area and pulled alongside Marva Henderson, his attention was diverted from the jigging, pawing horse. Ryman rode among the trailers, handing out cards to everyone. One person after another took the offered card, looked at it quizzically, and nodded to Ryman as he held up the three-finger salute. Thumper looked the other way and saw Nardell doing the same. The two of them worked the crowd from opposite ends.

"What the hell is he doing?" he asked Marva.

"It appears he's passing out some kind of cards," she replied.

"I can see that," he said.

"Then why'd you bother asking me?" she snapped back.

Ryman and Nardell rode over to join in on the pre-hunt staff confab.

"Drumming up customers for the tractor business?" Thumper asked, pointing to the cards Ryman held in his hand.

"Not my concern these days. More important matters on my plate. Here."

He handed a card to Thumper. The "Badge of Glory" poem was printed on one side, above which was the title, "The Venatican Creed." On the other side it read:

The Ancient and Venerable
Church of Ars Venatica
Restoring the True Faith

"Nardell and me ran these off on the computer last night," Ryman said proudly. "This way everyone else can follow along when we recite the creed. The next batch will have the Celtic cross too. We haven't quite figured out how to do that yet."

"What the hell is this?" Thumper asked. "Might I remind you that the name of this club is the Montfair Hunt?"

"This is so much bigger than just our one club, Thumper. Saint Hubert wants me to spread the word to all. Besides," he added with a twinkle, "'Venatican' sounds much better than 'Montfairian.'"

Thumper was not amused. "You're playing fast and loose with something that's not fully yours to play with." He felt several pairs of eyes fix on him and decided it was not in his long-term interest to press the major landowner point. He might have reminded Ryman and his growing cadre of disciples that, when it came right down to it, their enjoyment of foxhunting in Crutchfield County was made possible mostly through the largesse of the Billington family. A little band of upstarts was threatening to mess with his comfortably established system of benevolent control. He wondered if this was how the Pharisees felt.

"What's this crap about reciting 'The Creed?'" Thumper asked

"Everyone here can say it along together," Ryman said, sweeping one arm widely at the scores of riders preparing to follow the day's hunt. "My people."

"This is all a joke, right?"

"No joke, Thumper. If we want Saint Hubert's blessing on our sport, we must through the beast to God be true."

Thumper looked over at Mildred for some support.

"Sounds okay to me, Thumpah."

This was not what he wanted to hear.

"Can't see it doing any harm," she added. "Just a quick recitation of those few lines, right Ryman?"

"Oh, yeah, sure," he said. "Well, maybe a few remarks, y'know, welcoming folks for being here, the usual opening announcement stuff."

Thumper wondered why Mildred was leaning toward Ryman's camp. She'd seemed especially perky the past few days, breaking out from her usual Boston Brahmin reserve.

"Fine," he conceded. "But keep it short." Maybe he could get some agreement from Crispie. At least he was the paid help and wouldn't want to displease the master at whose pleasure he served and on whose estate he lived. "Mister O'Rourke, I assume you don't want to keep your hounds waiting to be off. Do you have a plan for our first draw this morning?"

"Um, well, no, Master. I was… well, I figured Mister McKendrick would have another suggestion."

Ryman's newfound faith was infecting everyone, even a good Catholic boy like Crispie. Thumper was hopelessly outnumbered.

"May I remind you, Mister O'Rourke, that you are the huntsman of this pack. You know your country and you know your hounds. It's your responsibility to provide us with…"

"Whoa there, Thumpah," Mildred said. "No need to get on Crispie's case. We've all been going with Ryman's suggestions and he hasn't steered us wrong yet."

Between dealing with a wound up horse and arguing with his fellow hunters, Thumper hadn't seen the odd foursome milling around the edges of the trailers. Rhetta delivered a running commentary, pointing here and there, as Janey furiously alternated between videotaping and scribbling in her notebook. Dan and Abel followed silently along behind the two women.

No one took any particular note of Janey's presence. Videographers were a common sight at hunt meets. A few of the more knowledgeable Montfair members, however, noted the unusual presence of Rhetta

McKendrick, no one more so than Bing Sensabaugh.

"All right, fine," Thumper said, conceding his minority position. "Reverend McKendrick, where to?"

"The Cow Pen is the place to go."

Thumper could have cited multiple reasons, every one of them based on sound logic and decades of experience chasing foxes around the Montfair territory, why the Cow Pen was not a good choice. But he decided to let the True Believers hoist themselves with their own petard. "Cow Pen it is, then. And may the mighty Saint Humboldt shower his munificent blessings upon us, his devoted servants."

"Amen!" Nardell sang out.

Thumper shook his head and turned to address the crowd. "Good morning, everyone. Looks like another fine day for a bit of sport." Sensing the coming action, Ozzy's jigging escalated. Thumper had to turn him in a circle to keep the pent up energy from rocketing skyward. The horse needed to go, to move, to literally be off to the races. He was bred to run fast and turn left. Standing still in front of several dozen other horses, with a pack of hounds scrabbling around nearby, was not in his nature. "I'll be leading first field this morning… " Thumper said as he brought the horse back around to face the crowd. He had to pause as Ozzy spun again. When his circuit returned toward the front, he continued, "… my joint-master Mildred Preston will lead second." Mildred held up her hand to identify herself. Ozzy spun again and reared slightly. "And now, Mister O'Rourke, let's go…"

"Ahem!" Ryman cleared his throat with heavy theatricality.

"Oh, I almost forgot. My other joint-master would like to share a few words before we move off." He added *sotto voce* to Ryman, "Keep it short, your Holiness. I can't hold this fellow much longer."

Ryman moved Token alongside Ozzy. The young horse stopped spinning. Token stood like a rock as Ryman looked at the nervous gray. Ozzy's feet were instantly glued to the ground. His eyes softened, his head dropped. He emitted a gentle snuffle and began working his mouth in a light chewing motion. A surprised Thumper Billington now sat on a perfectly calm horse.

Ryman turned his attention to the crowd. "My good friends and fellow foxhunters, I'm honored and greatly humbled to have been chosen by Saint Hubert, our patron saint…"

"I thought Thumper was our patron saint," a deep male voice called out from somewhere in the crowd. Grins and chuckles tittered through the assembled riders.

Thumper smiled and doffed his cap in the direction from which the comment had come. When he looked that way, he saw a woman on foot out along the far edge of the crowd holding a video camera in front of her face. It was hard to see her clearly through the mass of mounted riders between them, but something about her looked familiar. He then caught sight of Rhetta standing beside her, Dan slightly behind. The woman lowered the camera and Thumper saw who it was. His smile vanished.

Ryman continued. "…to be his messenger and to restore the ancient faith of ars venatica. I'm sure y'all know that that's Latin for 'the art of hunting.' And so, by virtue of being dedicated foxhunters, every one of you here this morning is automatically a member of the Ancient and Venerable Church of Ars Venatica. Welcome, my brothers and sisters!"

"Amen!" Nardell exclaimed.

A few others—Mildred, Marva, Bing, and Marie among them—echoed back with an enthusiastic "Amen!" chorus. Most, though, looked genuinely confused, some bemused and some befuddled. A few talked among themselves, their comments animated with questioning gestures.

"And now," Ryman went on, "let us recite the Venatican Creed. If you'll all refer to the cards Nardell and me passed out earlier…" He waited while people reached into pockets and pulled out cards. Holding up the three-finger salute, he boomed out:

"This is the hunter's badge of glory,
That he protect and tend his quarry,
Hunt with honor as is due,
And through the beast to God is true!"

Roughly half of those in attendance went along with this. The combined effect was akin to a classroom of primary school children fumbling their way through the Pledge of Allegiance. A few nailed it perfectly, some tried earnestly to follow along, most self-consciously mouthed the words and wished it were over.

Janey stopped writing in her notebook and stood agape, her eyes huge behind her glasses.

"Don't write none a that down!" Rhetta commanded. "The boy's stark raving mad. Best we not blab that about, let him come to his senses first."

"That isn't a regular part of foxhunting?" Janey asked.

"That lunacy? Hell, no. More likely him and the huntsman would be sharing some dirty joke, or talking about how much they drank the night before. At least, that's how it was in my day."

"Now," Ryman said, "just before we move off to enjoy the bounty Saint Hubert has laid before us, I'd like to share a thought from 'The Foxhunter's Faith.'" He reached into his jacket pocket and withdrew an index card.

"A-*hem*!" Thumper interjected, a scowl on his face and a finger jabbing at his watch.

"Won't take but a minute, Thumper."

Thumper looked over at Crispie, expecting to receive the huntsman's endorsement that hounds were ready to go and should not be kept any longer. Instead, Crispie sat easily, smiling at Ryman. Hounds relaxed around him, not one stirred to be off to the chase.

"Some of y'all might be familiar with 'The Foxhunter's Bedside Book,'" Ryman said. "But I expect many are not. I found it in my late father's library and one piece jumped right out at me. Saint Hubert be praised!"

"Amen!"

Okay, Nardell, Thumper thought, enough already.

Rhetta threw up her hands in disgust and, with Abel in tow, marched back to the house.

"Written by someone identified only as a 'North-Country Hunting Parson,' nothing shows how our sport is truly a form of worship better than the ten articles of his 'Foxhunter's Faith.' I thought I'd share one of them with you this morning. And where better to begin than with Article One." He lifted the card and read from it. "'Every man shall present himself at the place of meeting quietly, suitably clothed, and in good time.' Now, there's some more stuff here about hacking to the meet, not driving tandem or using any manner of engine or machine, except by necessity. That may have had a purpose when this was written. But I believe Saint Hubert saw to it that the 'necessity' part was included to cover the way things are today. The important part, though, is that first sentence. We're all here to have fun, of course. But we should arrive quietly, recognizing the privilege Saint Hubert has blessed us with. We honor him and we honor the sport by being properly turned out and arriving on time. Sloppy attire and tardiness is rude to your fellow hunters and dishonors our beloved patron saint."

Slipping the note card into a coat pocket, Ryman said, "Well, my friends, I think that says it all."

"Amen!" Thumper shouted. "It certainly does. Thank you, Brother Ryman. Now what say we go chase some foxes?"

"Um… well, I wasn't quite finished, Brother Thumper. I was going to explain that many people seem to have forgotten those courtesies. And about how Saint Hubert wants us to be joyful and uplifting about…"

"Y'know, I just heard Saint Hubert speaking to me too. And he said he wants us to get going."

Ryman looked at Thumper quizzically. Was Thumper mocking him, or had his old friend also been visited with the spirit of Saint Hubert?

Thumper wasn't going to give him the chance to raise the question. "Mister O'Rourke, let's be off." Crispie snapped to attention, as did every hound, instantly eager to be away. "Draw to the Cow Pen, if you would."

He rode over closer to Ryman. "Plenty of mornings ahead for your preaching. Let's just not forget the real reason we're out here. And that all these people got up early and went through a lot of effort to ride to hounds, not to be your personal captive audience. Let's see that they get rewarded for their efforts."

Ryman let Thumper's intrusion pass without contest. "You're right. A long season ahead, plenty of time to instruct our flock in the proper ways to honor Saint Hubert and our blessed sport. See you at the Cow Pen." He started to ride off to take his position. But after a few strides he stopped, looked back, and said, "By the way, Brother Thumper, how's your new horse behaving this morning?" Before Billington could respond, Ryman squeezed Token into a trot and fell in behind the pack.

****

"This is where we go follow them in the car, right?" Janey asked.

Dan did not respond. He stood watching the hunters ride away. "Bloody hell," he finally muttered. "It's worse than I ever could have imagined."

"Dan, should we be going now? I don't want to miss a minute of this."

He remained motionless, his eyes riveted on the mounted band as they moved off into the distance.

"Reverend Davenport!" Janey said, tugging at his sleeve. "Do you know where they're going? Is there a way to get there by car? Dan!"

"Huh? Oh, yeah, well sort of. I think anyway. I've only followed them a couple of times before. And with someone else driving. But I think I know how to get there."

Janey started to doubt the knowledge of the sport Dan purported to possess. But whatever little he knew, it was more information than she had. He was her only guide and she'd have no chance to see what happened next without him.

They walked to his car and as Janey reached for the passenger door handle, a distressing sight caught her eye. The right rear tire was completely flat. "Uh, Reverend Davenport, I'm afraid we have a problem."

He came around to see what she was pointing at. "Bloody double hell. Second one this week. These roads are not built for this city-friendly car. Actually, they're not really 'built' at all. That's the problem."

She tossed her notebook and camera onto the front seat. "I'm pretty handy with a jack," she said, rubbing her hands together. "Maybe we can still catch up if we get it changed quickly."

"Well, I'm sorry to say that may take a bit longer than you'd prefer."

"I know some of these smaller cars have cheap jacks, hard to use."

She moved to the trunk and waited for him to pop it open. "Not very level ground here either. But it's solid." She stomped her foot on the hard packed earth. "Should hold okay. Can we get to it?"

"I'm afraid we cannot."

"Why?"

"An essential missing ingredient."

"You don't have a jack? No problem. There's bound to be one around here. I'm sure Mrs. McKendrick would let us…"

"I have a jack. What I don't have is a spare tire."

Janey stared at him. What kind of dolt had she teamed up with that he was driving around without a spare? Especially over these rough country roads.

Dan read Janey's expression of disappointment—more so in him personally than in the situation in general. "I do not typically go about minus a spare tire," he assured her. "Especially when escorting a lady such as yourself. The fault lies with the tire service center. As I mentioned, this is my second flat in a week. The other one was ruined, couldn't be repaired. But they were out of the size needed for this car, said it was on order and would arrive in a couple of days. By yesterday they still hadn't called to say it was there. And, while you can hire out an entire motor car, it seems you cannot hire just a tire." He smiled at what to him seemed a brilliant quip, complete with a bit of rhyme.

Janey was not impressed. "There's only one tire center around here?"

"Ah, most perceptive of you. There are indeed several. However, a member of our church owns this one, and he grants a generous discount in recognition of his humble vicar's boundless faith but limited funds."

Dan's explanation softened Janey's judgmental attitude. But it did nothing to ease her disappointment over not being able to follow the hunt. She was already starting to compose the opening chapter of her new book in her mind.

The farmhouse door opened and Rhetta stepped out onto the porch. She could see the flat tire, Dan and Janey looking at it helplessly. "Well, don't just stand there with your thumbs up your butts. Get the darn thing changed. I thought you were all hot to go follow the hunt."

"No spare," Janey explained.

"If that ain't the most worthless excuse." She stomped down the steps and strode over to the car. "Cain't you just pray over it and the Lord will heal the tire?" she asked Dan. "You preacher types are full of enough hot air to keep every tire in the county full, ain't ya?"

"A most amusing observation, Mrs. McKendrick," Dan replied.

"'Course even you could learn a thing or two from that crazy son a mine. Talk about your hot air. Hmmph!"

"Mrs. McKendrick," Janey said, "would you be able to drive us? Or let us use your car so we can follow the hunt?" She knew this was a bold request, asking a woman she'd just met to loan her a car. But she was desperate to continue her research. What was going on out there? The hunters were now well out of sight, off to who-knows-where doing who-knows-what.

Rhetta caught the pleading in Janey's eyes. "So, got yourself stuck 'cause some fool of a man didn't have enough sense to carry a spare tire." She studied Janey for a long moment. Finally she said, "I been there myself. Like I always say, cain't live with 'em, cain't shoot 'em. Likely we'd be better off without 'em." She paused again. "I reckon y'all can take mine."

"Oh, thank you," Janey enthused. "Why don't you come along with us? I could really benefit from your help, and your knowledge about what they're doing."

"Me? Nah, y'all just drive around and listen for the horn. You'll be fine."

Dan tried to reclaim a trace of his manhood. "I'm sure we will. I may have followed the hunt just a time or two, but I have lived around here for a few years and know the roads fairly well. As Mrs. McKendrick said, all we need do is listen for the horn. How hard could that be?"

A lot harder than you realize, Preacher, Rhetta thought. She reached into the pocket of her jeans. "Got the keys right here. C'mon."

They walked around to the back of the house. Janey tried to hurry them along. She stopped short when she saw the only vehicle parked there. Rhetta's "car" was actually a bright orange 1979 International Harvester Scout, one of the last ones made before production of the IH SUVs and pick-ups shut down.

"Y'all do know how to drive a stick, don't ya?" Rhetta asked, catching the hesitation from both Janey and Dan.

"Um, well, no," Dan confessed. "Actually, I'm afraid I don't. Hasn't ever come up before."

"How 'bout you, girlie?"

"Well, yes, sort of. But I'm not sure…" Janey had driven rougher looking rigs and could work a clutch with the best of them. But she now doubted Dan's ability to guide her to the action. The vehicle was secondary. It was Rhetta she wanted. "Are you sure you won't consider driving us. I know it's a lot to ask, but… please?"

Rhetta eyed Janey and Dan, then looked down at Abel standing next to her. "I expect I know what he thinks about the whole thing. Well, don't just stand there. Get in the damn car."

Chapter 36

WITH RHETTA'S INTIMATE knowledge of Crutchfield County's back roads and farm lanes, aided by her disregard for traffic laws and passenger comfort, she had her Scout positioned at a roadside overlook with a commanding view of the Cow Pen covert before the hunting field arrived there.

The foursome hopped out and stood looking over the sweeping view of the countryside.

"That field out there to the right," Rhetta said, "just past that thick stand a trees, is the Cow Pen. Used to be the place where the livestock would be held for the cattle truck. Ain't been used for that in years." She pointed toward a specific spot. "You can still see the remains of the old loading chute. All rotted out now, just a pile a timbers and boards, brambles and vines grown all over it. Makes a dandy hideout for foxes though. Good place to cast hounds, that and the stand a trees there to the left. 'Course, it's better when we've had some rain. Pretty dry and hard around here still, scentin' is likely to be tough. I'd a thought they'd go to lower ground to cast. But that crazy damn son a mine keeps takin' 'em to places like this."

"Do the hounds have to smell the scent?" Janey asked. "Are they sometimes able to see the fox and chase it by sight?"

"They're scent hounds, not sight hounds. A fox could be right in front of 'em—hell, right in the middle of 'em—and if they couldn't smell it for some reason, they'd pay it no mind."

Before Janey could ask another question, the hunt staff and hounds came into view, moving from the spectators' left toward their right, directly to the stand of trees. Janey lifted her video camera and zoomed in on Crispie at the front, the hounds packed up tightly behind him. Patti flanked hounds to one side, Ryman to the other, with Nardell bringing up the rear, assuring no hounds lagged behind.

As they moved toward the Cow Pen covert, the field came along at a suitable distance behind. Thumper was at the lead, three-dozen followers in tow. Crispie neared the covert and the followers halted. Patti and Ryman rode off to opposite sides. Crispie blew a short note on his horn and the pack surged into the small wooded area.

There was not one fox awaiting their arrival at the Cow Pen, there were two (a "brace" in hunting terminology). The hounds' strike cry went up almost immediately. It took only a few more seconds to realize it was a split. Half the pack followed the westbound fox, the other half opted for the one heading east. Patti was to the left of the covert, Ryman on the right. They tally-hoed simultaneously as both foxes emerged at the same instant.

Seeing the split, Crispie had to make the call and advise his staff what to do, which fox to follow and which half of the pack to stop. Ryman was well out of hearing range and still chose not to carry his radio. Patti had hers. Both foxes appeared to be heading in equally suitable directions to offer a good chase. Crispie started to press the "Talk" button to tell Patti to stop the split on her side. But he hesitated. Something was telling him not to do that.

Patti's urgent voice crackled over the radio. "Should I stop them? Crispie! Answer me!"

He took one more look toward the hounds on Ryman's side, all of them in full cry. The fox scampered at top speed. Ryman galloped to the side of the hounds and passed them. He appeared to be chasing the fox himself.

"Let 'em hunt," Crispie replied to Patti. "Ryman knows what to do." He then turned his horse toward Patti's side and sprang off in pursuit, blowing the notes of "Gone Away" and cheering hounds forward. "On to 'im, on to 'im!"

From their vantage point, the spectators on the roadside overlook watched as the fox on Ryman's side sprinted toward the old livestock chute. He reached it just ahead of Ryman, who then turned his horse around to face the oncoming pack. He did not yell for the hounds to leave the fox alone, did not crack his whip to get their heads up, did not reach for his pistol. He simply sat calmly and held up one hand.

The hounds stopped.

Rhetta's mouth dropped when she saw this.

Ryman then pointed in the direction where the other half of the pack was heading.

Hounds reversed and took off after their pack mates. Ryman cantered behind.

Rhetta continued to watch until Ryman and hounds were out of sight, into the woods heading west. "Damnedest thing I ever seen," she said.

"That was incredible!" Janey exclaimed as she lowered her camera. "Can we see more? Do you know where they're going?"

Rhetta did not answer. She continued to stare off into the western distance. "How'd he do that? Them hounds were hot. No one can stop hounds like that. Not in my day they couldn't."

"Mrs. McKendrick," Janey said. "Can we go? I'd really like to see more."

"Huh? Oh, yeah, sure. Sounds like the fox is turning north. Another good spot to view from up around there."

She returned to the Scout. Janey ran around and jumped in. Dan rolled his shoulders and shuffled toward the back door. He opened it and looked down at Abel. "After you." The dog jumped up on the seat, Dan folded himself in and Rhetta peeled off in a cloud of dust and gravel before he had the door closed.

In response to Janey's insistent questions, Rhetta continued a running commentary on how the sport was conducted "in her day."

After several such citations, Janey finally asked, "And when was your day, Mrs. McKendrick?"

"I ain't been on a horse for about forty years."

"Were you injured?"

"Me? Nah. Not much anyways. A few breaks here and there over the years I was ridin'. But nothin' serious."

"Then why'd you give it up, if I may ask?"

"You can ask, child. But I ain't got to tell you. Long story, long time ago. Best left alone now."

They rounded a sharp bend and Rhetta jammed on the brakes at the sight of Bing and Marie, mounted on their horses, in the middle of the road.

"Oh, thank goodness you're here," Marie said. "Bing's hurt his back. Can you give him a ride in to the meet?"

Bing was in obvious pain. But he said, "It's not that bad, just a little wrench. I can ride back."

Rhetta and her passengers disgorged from the Scout.

Marie slid off her horse and gestured toward Janey. "Here," she said, handing her the reins. "Hold the horses while I help Bing down."

Janey obediently stepped forward and did as instructed.

Marie stepped to the side of Bing's horse and offered to support him as he dismounted.

"No, really," he protested. "If we just walk back slowly, I'll be..." A grimace of pain contorted his face. "... fine."

"What happened?" Rhetta asked. "The old fool fall off again?"

"No," Marie replied. "He must have just turned the wrong way. We were running hard, fabulous chase. Oh, my God, what great sport! We came around a turn and his back just went out. We had to pull up and get to the road so we could hack back in. I'm sure glad you came along. He needs to get home and get ice on this as soon as possible."

"You some kinda doctor, are you?"

"No, but I know a thing or two about first aid and injured backs. My late husband had this happen all the time."

"Really, ladies," Bing interjected, "you're over…" Another grimace and Bing arched his back. "… reacting."

Marie motioned to Dan. "Come here and give me a hand. It'll probably take two of us to get him off the horse." She then looked up at Bing, one hand on his knee, the other on his hip. "You need to get off the horse now, sweetheart. The longer you wait, the worse it's going to get."

Sweetheart is it, Rhetta thought. "I don't know that he'll be any better off in my car," she said. "Ain't exactly an amb-lance. And it's a rough ride back to the farm."

"At least he can take the pressure off, lie down in the backseat. You can get him back quicker than if he walked the horse all the way in. And what if the horse stumbles and he comes off? Then it'll really be bad." She turned to Dan. "You hold his shoulders and I'll support the lower half. One, two, three…"

Bing conceded and dropped from the horse as carefully as he could. His helpers caught him and got him down feet first.

Marie took the reins of her horse from Janey and, finding a handy log along the side of the road, quickly remounted. She then took the reins of Bing's horse. "I'll pony his horse back," she said. "Thanks so much for doing this. See you back at the meet."

"Now wait just a damn minute…" Rhetta said.

But Marie was already gone, moving off at the trot, unable—or unwilling—to hear Rhetta over the clattering of eight hooves.

"I'm sorry about this, Henrietta," Bing said. "I really could have ridden back but she, well, she insisted and I…" He winced again.

"Get in the damn car," she snarled.

"Why don't you sit up front, sir?" Janey offered. "Or would you rather lay down on the backseat?"

"He can sit in the back with the other two," Rhetta ordered.

Janey chided herself for having interfered with the tribal dynamic. As a neutral observer, she was supposed to just let things play out as if she wasn't there so as not to taint her field research.

They all climbed into the Scout, Dan and Bing in the backseat with a very grumpy Abel between them.

"I reckon we won't be going on to see any more of the hunt," Rhetta said to Janey. "Looks like another lame ass man has messed up the plans."

"I'm okay," Bing said. "It feels much better being off the horse. I don't want to keep our guest…" Another grimace and contortion, this time accompanied by a groan, as the Scout bounced through a deep pothole. "… from seeing more of the action."

"You ain't okay, you damned old fool. Just sit there and shut-up. I'll get you back to the farm, leave you to your new girlfriend to get patched up. Then maybe we'll go back out and try to find the hunt."

"That's all right," Janey said. "I don't mean to be such a burden. Perhaps I can come back again. I understand this goes on regularly now for the next several months."

"Three times a week, till the end a March. Like these people got nothing better to do. 'Specially that no good son a mine. Bad enough he's always been more interested in chasing foxes than helping with the family business. You'd a thought his daddy dying might a changed that. But instead he's gone even farther off the deep end, blabbering away about Saint Hubert and his church idea. All stuff and nonsense."

Maybe stuff and nonsense, but it certainly piqued Janey's interest, particularly the phrase "his church idea."

The thought of Ryman's behavior caused Rhetta to tromp on the gas, which sent the Scout bouncing along the poorly maintained road like a kangaroo on a sugar high. Dan grasped whatever purchase he could find to keep from tumbling into Abel, who was having difficulty remaining upright himself. Bing gripped the edge of the seat with one hand, put the other to his mouth and bit the edge to keep from hollering out.

Janey thought about suggesting a slower pace might be better but remembered her role as neutral observer. Instead she said, "Hunting-based religion is considered by some to be the oldest form of belief system."

"You know about that kinda thing, do you?" Rhetta asked.

"I do. In a very simplistic sense, belief in supernatural forces is a way to mitigate the uncertainties of life. Hunter-gather societies depend on the availability of game and the hunter's ability to track and kill. Success depends on a blend of skill and luck. Hunters can improve their skills and increase the odds in their favor, like by riding horses and using dogs. But they need the aid of some unseen, unknown power to provide the luck. Without both, the tribe will starve."

"Don't look like no one's starvin' 'round here," Rhetta snapped. "And I ain't never ate a fox, but I hear they ain't very tasty."

"This is, of course, all new to me," Janey replied. "But it strikes me that it's about the rituals of hunting, not so much the end result. Like there's something embedded deep in our DNA that recalls the drive to hunt."

"Just as soon drive to the Safeway store. A lot easier than runnin' all 'round the countryside chasin' some critter you cain't eat anyways."

"Well, fortunately, we don't need to depend on that today. But it can be argued that society as we know it, possibly even language, evolved from early hunting cultures. People had to work together in a cooperative effort. And for that to happen, you needed to communicate and you needed some tribal structure about roles and responsibilities."

"Appears you've already done a good bit a thinkin' 'bout this."

"Professor Musgrove has written two books on the su…*ub*…ject of belief systems," Dan said as a particularly rough bounce broke up the word. "Excellent works, I might add."

"That a fact?" Rhetta asked. "You're some kinda writer then?"

"Yes," Janey replied, "some kind of, you could say."

"An excellent wri—*I*—ter. I thoroughly enjoyed both bo—*OO*—ks. Mrs. McKendrick, do you think we should be going a bit more slowly? Mister Sensabaugh appears to be in some discomfort."

"I'm just doing what his sweetheart asked. She wanted him delivered to the meet as quickly as possible, get him iced up. You doin' okay back there, Mister Sensabaugh?"

"I'm just… fine, Mrs. McKendrick." He bit harder on the fleshy edge of his hand.

Once back at Fair Enough Farm, Rhetta pulled to a stop along the edge of the field where the trailers were parked. "Ride's over," she said.

"Do you think we should deposit Mister Sensabaugh closer to his truck?" Dan asked

"This'll do, Preacher," Rhetta snapped back. "Everybody out."

Dan and Janey helped Bing out of the Scout. Rhetta remained behind the wheel with the motor running. By this point Bing could barely walk. Janey looked at the mass of trucks and trailers in the field across from the house. "Which one is yours, Mister Sensabaugh?"

"Silver and green rig, over there." He pointed toward the far edge of the field, quite some distance away.

Janey could no longer maintain her detached viewpoint. The man was in too much pain. "Perhaps he should rest in the house," she suggested to Rhetta.

"No!" Rhetta and Bing declared in unison.

Janey was taken aback by the fast and forceful dual objection. She reminded herself again of the researcher's need to remain aloof.

"Walking should actually help," Bing said through clenched teeth. "Not the first time this has happened. The old sacroiliac goes out on me every so often, ever since that fall I took when…" He tried to look over his shoulder at Rhetta but could not move his head that far. The attempt caused another ripple of pain to shoot up his spine. "Damn! Please, if you'll just give me a hand getting to the truck, I'll be fine. Marie should be back with the horses any time now. Thank you, Henrietta," he called out. "I appreciate the…"

She stepped on the gas and another cloud of dust and gravel erupted as she drove off.

"... lift."

By the time Janey and Dan had limped Bing over to his truck, Marie had returned. She quickly loaded the horses onto the trailer and jumped into the driver's seat. Bing was hoisted up into the passenger side and they drove off.

Janey and Dan walked back to Dan's car and stood looking at the flat tire.

"Do you have roadside assistance?" Janey asked.

"Afraid not. Meager parson's salary, you see. Can't afford such niceties." He reached into a jacket pocket, withdrew a pipe, and lit up.

No, thought Janey, but you can afford tobacco.

Dan's gaze shifted from the tire out to the site of Ryman's first Venatican church service. "What the bloody hell does he think he's doing? I mean, *really*, the Ancient and Venerable Church of Ars Venatica? It's sacrilege. A mockery. I've spent my entire life studying the most intricate points of theology and dutifully serving the Church. He gets whacked on the head and—hey presto!—he's the Messiah."

"More like a prophet, actually."

"Huh?"

"He claims to be speaking for Saint Hubert, more like he's the oracle than a deity himself. Which, technically, makes him a prophet."

"A prophet, huh? Ryman McKendrick, the Prophet of Paradise. I've been laboring here for over three years now, trying to keep our little parish going. It's not easy, you know. Attendance continues to decline. Some of the older, more faithful members have died off. And the young people aren't interested in church, too busy on their computers and mobile phones to have time for developing their spirituality." He pointed his pipe out toward the field. "And now I have to compete against... this!"

Janey placed a hand on Dan's arm. "If you recall from reading my books, this kind of thing doesn't usually last very long. Nor does it tend to draw many people away from mainstream beliefs. Those who buy into a new movement are typically lost souls searching for something other than what the traditional church has to offer. This will likely be just a passing fad. I mean, after all, how many people are there who can afford to keep horses and go foxhunting? The audience for this is particularly narrow."

"For the world overall, that's true. But in Crutchfield County, most everything revolves around foxhunting. Or is touched by it in some way. And Saint Cuthbert's-in-the-Woods is the closest thing there is to an official foxhunting church. At least it has been up till now."

Their attention was caught by the sound of a vehicle. An aged two-tone pick-up approached from the back of the McKendrick property. It came to a stop next to the disabled car and Bar Reinhardt stepped out.

"Got yourself a problem, Reverend?" Bar said looking at the flat tire. "Don't tell me you gone off without a spare again?"

"The tire center did not have a suitable replacement in stock," Dan explained. "They are awaiting its arrival." Dan took note of Bar's attire. "A little early in the season for you to be wearing a shirt. And clean overalls too. Attending another funeral this morning?"

"Very funny, Preacher. Nah, I got a good enough nap at the last one I went to. Thanks to the boss man going into competition with you, we've done a little rearranging at the shop. I'm now the executive sales manger at McKendrick and Sons Farm Implements." He turned to Janey and extended a hand. "I don't believe we've met. Barstow Reinhardt at your service."

Janey did a quick assessment. This fellow appeared to be a man of some authority, of superior ranking to the local vicar in the tribal hierarchy. Was it because of his size? Maybe his disfigurement served as an emblem of his warrior status? Both could be parlayed into valuable assets in primitive cultures. His hand was huge, calloused, and permanently stained from decades of contact with dark fluids. Yet his grip was politely mannered, firm but not crushing, held for just the correct few seconds and then gracefully released.

"Janey Musgrove," she replied.

"A pleasure to meet you. Got yourself stuck here with this lame-ass sky pilot?"

She recognized the military reference and a snippet of an old Animals song flashed in her mind. That might explain the scars. "Reverend Davenport was kind enough to escort me to follow the hunt this morning. I guess if he hadn't been doing that, this wouldn't have happened. So I suppose in a way it's my fault."

"Well, ain't you the understanding type. I suppose him not having a spare is your fault too."

"Can you help us?" Janey asked.

"Well, little lady, I don't just happen to have a spare on me that'll fit this piece of crap the Reverend calls a car. But if this one's fixable, I might be able to get it taken care of at the shop and have someone bring it back. What say we take a look?"

Dan was much less enthusiastic about Bar's help than Janey was. But she prodded him to pop the trunk and get out the jack. Bar quickly took over and had the tire off in seconds. He rolled the tire around in his massive hands and found the culprit, a screw embedded in the tread.

"How do you suppose that got there?" Janey asked.

"Probably come off one of the trucks that run up and down this road." He pointed toward Montfair Lane. "We got a lot of construction workers around here, some of 'em drive flatbeds and shit falls off."

"Can this be fixed?"

"Piece a cake. I'm on my way to the shop now. I'll have Conway patch it, and have Miles run it back when it's done." He dropped a heavy hand onto Dan's slack shoulder. Dan's knees buckled under the weight. "No charge, Reverend. My contribution to the Lord's work." Bar flashed a mischievous wink at Janey with his one good eye.

****

Janey and Dan were still waiting when the returning hunters came into view. The riders crested a distant hilltop and began the slow descent down to Fair Enough Farm.

Grantham Meisner pulled up alongside Thumper. "Damn him," he said. "He did it again."

"You're damning a good morning of sport? That doesn't seem right coming from the head of NAFCA."

"He's turning a hunt meet into a camp revival. What's next? He's going to start laying hands on people?"

Marva Henderson appeared on Thumper's other side. "What a great day!" she exclaimed, all smiles and good spirits. "I couldn't believe it when the pack split but then came right back together. I've never seen anything like it. It was almost like the foxes were working as a tag team. First the one gives us a heck of a chase and then we go back to the Cow Pen and darn if the other one isn't politely waiting for us in the old loading chute. So off we go again!"

Thumper rode on silently, thinking that Grantham to his right and Marva to his left typified the two camps into which people were forming: Pharisees and Followers. The Followers either held no position in the hunting hierarchy or, if they did, it was not an office on which they placed any great personal significance. Ryman was no threat and the sport was splendid. To the Pharisees, position mattered. For some it mattered a great deal. But to what lengths would the people in that camp go to protect their positions?

Grantham looked around Thumper to address Marva. "Doesn't Ryman's behavior seem a bit odd to you? I mean, really, the 'Ancient and Venerable Church of Ars Venatica?' What kind of nonsense is that? It's like he's trying to turn foxhunting into some kind of religion."

Marva replied with an air of mock innocence. "You mean it's not?"

"Of course not," he replied. "It's sport."

"To most, maybe. Just like for most people going to church is only something you do on Sunday mornings, not a central part of everyday life. But you two certainly take this sport seriously, almost as if it's your religion."

"Oh, that's absurd," Grantham protested. "We're just dedicated sportsmen who love good hound work and the thrill of the chase. There's no religious aspect to it."

"Really? Aren't the masters like clergy, the shepherds of your flock? You have special garments to signify your office and there's a customary way the members of your congregation should address you. How about blooding someone at their first kill? If that's not a form of baptism, I don't know what is."

She referred to the archaic tradition—increasingly rare, virtually extinct in many areas—of wiping streaks of blood on a person's cheeks and forehead the first time they attend a kill in the hunt field.

"You've even made foxhunting your full time career," she continued, still addressing Grantham. "You're, like, the head evangelist, leading the charge to protect the sport and win converts."

"All metaphor," Grantham said dismissively. "Okay, so maybe some of us are more dedicated to the sport than others. And for some it's become a profession. But it's pretty farfetched to suggest any of that rises to the level of a religion."

"Maybe not as farfetched as you think." With that Marva peeled away and rejoined the riders behind them. A rumble of happy chatter arose as people continued to discuss the pleasures of the morning's chase.

"This is where I get off," Thumper said. He turned a calm, well-behaved Ozzy for home while the others continued on toward the trailers.

Javier was waiting at the barn. With the horse in his groom's competent care, Thumper hopped into his car and drove the short distance to Fair Enough Farm. He arrived to find a level of exuberance he'd rarely experienced after a foxhunt. Marva had announced the tailgate as potluck and the members and guests responded with enthusiastic abundance.

Ryman stood at the center of the field, accepting handshakes and expressions of appreciation for the morning's sport. He repeatedly held up the three-finger salute and bestowed the Jäger-blessing on one person after another.

Janey Musgrove stood along the edge of the crowd catching it all on her video camera. Reverend Dan hovered at her side.

Thumper interrupted the recording session, took Janey by the arm, and guided her away from Ryman's Sermon-in-the-Field "A word, if you please."

Reverend Davenport started to follow.

"Excuse me, Padre, but I'd like to have a brief chat with Ms. Musgrove in private, if you don't mind. Why don't you help yourself to some refreshments?"

Dan stood silently, angered and embarrassed by the dismissal. After a few seconds' hesitation, he turned and stalked off to the food table.

When they were out of earshot of the others, Thumper turned to Janey and said, "I thought I'd asked you to wait until things had returned to normal around here before coming back."

Janey wasn't quite sure what it meant to be "senior master of the Montfair Hunt," but she knew Thumper was a personage not to be alienated if she wanted to continue her field research. "I'm sorry. Reverend Davenport said he thought it would be okay. I should have checked with you first. My apologies."

"Think you've found yourself another oddball religion to write about?" he asked. "And you just couldn't resist the opportunity."

"I avoid such judgmental terms. I simply study the various ways people express faith and find meaning in life."

"No one around here is looking for meaning. We're all just out for some sporting fun. Nothing more to it than that."

"Then we're on the same page. The premise for my book proposal is the role of sports in people's lives. This sport certainly appears to play a significant role in yours, and for all these others here."

"Don't try to bullshit me. You're not a sports writer. Your thing is wacky religions. And look what you just stumbled into." He waved a hand toward Ryman, who appeared to be arranging people into a choir. He gave a downbeat and a dozen voices broke out in "Here's A Health to Every Sportsmen." He could see Janey itching to capture this with her video camera.

She shrugged and assumed a disarming pose, suggesting she was totally willing to comply with any request he might make.

Thumper was only slightly familiar with her work. But the image of a small, dark, half-naked man with the British flag over his shoulder and a portrait of Prince Philip nestled in the crook of his arm sprang to his mind. He had a sudden mental picture of Ryman's face on the man's body, holding up his Saint Hubert's medal in one hand, the other formed into the Jäger-blessing salute. That was not the kind of publicity he wanted, either for the Montfair Hunt in particular or foxhunting in general.

"Look," he said, "this is just something we do in these parts. Been doing it since Virginia was a colony of the Crown."

Ryman's impromptu choir was just finishing the last lines of the first verse:

And may he ever cheerily
Each noble sport pursue,
If he takes his liquor fairly
And his fences fairly tooooo!

"Well, maybe we haven't been doing it exactly like this. What you're seeing this morning is not typical. My joint-master has been going through a difficult time. You know his father died recently. But maybe you weren't aware that it happened unexpectedly, and right in front of him. And he's also had some head trauma. We're all just humoring him until he gets through this rough patch. Perhaps it would be best, purely for reportorial accuracy of course, if you let this aberrant phase pass for him, and come back when everything's returned to normal. You'll see then that we're really just about some sport and camaraderie, nothing spiritual or religious going on here."

Janey nodded her agreement.

"Good. Well, I'm sure you need to get back to… wherever it is you came from."

"Fairfax."

"Yes, long drive, day's wearing on, and you must have gotten up very early to be here. I'll let you know when it's convenient for you to come again."

She reached into her bag for a notebook and pen. "I'll jot down my contact informa…"

"That's okay. I can get it from Danella." He took her arm and began guiding her toward Dan's car. "I'm sure the good Reverend Davenport needs to be going too. He must have a lot to do to prepare for tomorrow's service."

"Oh, well, you see, Dan's car had a flat tire. We're waiting for someone to fix it and bring it back. He drove me out here, I left my car in the village."

"Driving without a spare again, was he? Well, no problem. I have my car here. I'd be happy to run you back to yours."

More like run me off, Janey thought. "Oh, I wouldn't want to inconvenience you. And it looks like there's quite a party going on here. I don't want to take you away from all the festivities. I can just wait until Dan's ready, I'll stay out of your way."

"The party will still be happening when I get back. Please, my car's right over here."

"I should let Dan know I'm leaving."

"I'll pass along your regrets."

He tightened his grip on her arm and led her to his car. She had to admit Thumper's Jaguar sedan was a much nicer form of transport than Dan's Mini Cooper, although the air inside was quite chilly.

Dan Davenport suffered through two more hours of tailgate merriment, with Ryman the focus of everyone's attention, before Miles finally showed up with his repaired tire. Tales of the morning's sport were recited repeatedly. With each rendition, as the alcohol flowed, the pace became faster, the fences larger, the fox more wily, the hounds more keen. Songs were sung, Saint Hubert was praised. A gaggle of children, under the watchful eye of Dorcas Stanhope, stood off to the side, talking and laughing. Not one of them chatted on a cell phone or thumbed at text messages.

No one noticed Dan slip off when he saw Miles arrive in the McKendrick and Sons service truck. He patiently endured Miles's smart-ass mockery of his embarrassing situation in exchange for the man's help changing the tire.

Miles thought he was due some gratuity for his efforts, but Dan simply muttered a curt thank-you, crawled into his car, and sped away as fast as he could.

When he arrived at the parsonage, he went straight to his study and picked up the printed text of the sermon he'd prepared for the following morning. He thought of the hours he'd spent researching, drafting, polishing, and practicing his compelling consideration of the nexus between spiritual phenomenology and the Hegelian dialectic. He tossed the papers into the trashcan, sat down at his computer, opened a fresh document, and started typing.

****

Janey dashed through the door of her apartment and went immediately to her computer. Within minutes an email was on its way to Danella: Crank up the proposal machine. Book Three is on the way!

Chapter 37

A MUCH DIFFERENT Dan Davenport appeared before the St. Cuthbert congregants on this Sunday morning. He strode forward, head erect and shoulders square, then sprang up the steps to the pulpit. His eyes, aglow with righteous fervor, passed over the small audience, holding each person's gaze for a brief moment.

Everyone sat in silence, astonished by the mysterious change in the usually melancholy minister.

"My text this morning is taken from the Old Testament, the Book of Deuteronomy, chapter thirteen, verses one through three." His voice was strong and clear, the suggestion of an English accent gone.

"If there arise among you a prophet,'" Dan quoted, without looking down at any notes, "or a dreamer of dreams, and giveth thee a sign or a wonder, and the sign or the wonder come to pass, whereof he spake unto thee, saying, Let us go after other gods, which thou hast not known, and let us serve them; thou shalt not hearken unto the words of that prophet, or that dreamer of dreams: for the Lord your God proveth you, to know whether ye love the Lord your God with all your heart and with all your soul. The Word of the Lord."

And the people all replied, "Amen."

"My friends, false prophets are nothing new. As the verses I just shared with you show, our Lord has been warning his children not to be led astray since the earliest times recorded in the Old Testament. In fact, what is the very First Commandment?"

Bob Sensabaugh, surprised by the sound of his own voice, found himself saying aloud, "You shall have no other gods before Me."

"Yes, Brother Sensabaugh! Absolutely correct. The Lord knew, all the way back to the time of the Exodus, that there would arise those who seem able to work signs and wonders. And that some people would be taken in by what they see, forgetting the First Commandment and going after false gods. But we must not succumb to such enticements.

"You may be familiar with the story recounted in the fifth chapter of the Acts of the Apostles, where Peter and other followers of Christ were hauled before the Sanhedrin and told to cease preaching and performing miracles in the Lord's name."

Here Dan shifted into the role of a relaxed storyteller. The pulpit offered little space but, to the extent allowed, Dan strolled around, casually reciting the tale. "Gamaliel, a Pharisee and respected teacher of the Old Testament law, stood up and gave his colleagues the benefit of his wisdom. 'Let's be careful here, fellows,' Gamaliel said. I'm paraphrasing, of course," Dan added with a twirl of his hand. "'Remember some time back when a man named Theudas claimed to be someone special, and about four hundred men followed him? Well, Theudas was slain, his followers scattered, and nothing more came of it. Then another man, Judas of Galilee, came along and he also attracted quite a following. And what happened? Why, he also perished and his followers dispersed. So, my brothers,' Gamaliel told his fellow Pharisees, 'remember that these things are nothing new. And they all fade out after awhile… especially after the leader—how shall I put this?—*perishes.*'

"That was wise counsel two thousand years ago. And it still is. But how can we know today that someone who appears to work signs and wonders is a false prophet? Well, of course, one way is to assume that the days of prophecy are over. That is an enlightened approach, amply supported by scripture, and one I highly recommend. However, we know the failings to which human nature is prone, don't we?"

He paused and held a warm, indulgent smile for a few seconds.

"We know we should trust in the Lord and His Word. But that can become dry and boring, can't it?"

Several listeners vigorously nodded their agreement.

"Then someone who appears to have special powers comes along and—whammo!" He slapped his open palm on the lectern and several of the congregation's older members grabbed at their pacemakers. "How exciting! Something different, something that looks so real. It may be a faith healer, someone who can lay hands on a sick person and seem to cure them. It may be someone speaking in tongues, creating the impression that they're caught up in the spirit, channeling some angelic language. How about those who think their prayers can bring about miraculous changes in the weather? I'll bet the National Weather Service would love to hire them as consultants, wouldn't they?"

Nervous giggles tittered throughout the building.

Who was this strange preacher, and what had he done with the real Reverend Dan?

"Or," Dan continued, his demeanor turning from jocularity to grave solemnity, "it may be someone who claims to hear messages from saints or angels, someone who seems able to influence the natural world in an unnatural way. Miracles? Oh, maybe not miracles. Not at first anyway.

But, over time, as more and more people come to believe and follow, the stakes grow higher, the expectations greater. To what lengths will the false prophet then go to maintain his hold on those he has led astray? And what terrible future will befall those taken in by his deceit?"

Dan's voice rose to a crescendo on this last sentence. He stood with one robed arm raised, his face bright with indignation. He held that pose for sufficient effect, then swept his arm down and gripped both sides of the lectern. Leaning forward, he continued in a measured tone, "Oh, dear friends, do not be deceived. Yes, the Lord may allow such things to happen as a test of your love for His truth. Fortify yourself now with the power of His Word so that you will not be led astray. Follow not the false prophet, though he entice you and amaze you, though he appears even as an angel of light. Do… not… be… deceived.

****

When Thumper's cell phone rang Sunday afternoon, he was surprised to see Danella Kernan's name on the screen. He paused the TV so he wouldn't miss finding out how the Washington Redskins would work their magic to snatch defeat from the jaws of victory.

Getting right to the point, she said, "Thumper, I need your help with an important project."

"What can I do for you?"

"You can let Janey Musgrove do a piece about foxhunting."

"A piece?" he asked. "Or are we talking a book here?"

"A piece within a book."

"Another book about wacky religions?"

"No, not this time, not exactly anyway. It's more about… well, it's a sports concept."

"Yeah, so she told me. Come on, Danella. I've seen this woman's CV. Her doctorate is in comparative religion. She's not exactly Christine Brennan."

"The idea—and it's still rough at this point—is to consider the parallels and overlaps between sports and religion, particularly the overlaps."

"And where else is that more evident than out here in little old Paradise Gap where my redoubtable joint-master thinks he's the frigging prophet of Saint Hubert?"

"I don't know any details about that," she said.

He had a sneaking feeling she knew every detail about exactly that.

"But," she continued, "Janey is very enthused and I do believe she's on to something."

"What's she going to title it? 'Are you there, God? It's me, Cheesehead?'"

"Very funny. Actually, not a bad suggestion."

Yes, Thumper thought, Janey was on to something that could make her a pile of dough and make foxhunting look ridiculous, not only that foxhunters are a bunch of privileged snobs—"toffs" as the Brits would say—but that they actually think their rarified sport is on a par with religion. He was sure that would have Grantham Meisner scrambling to combat the negative publicity and set the record straight.

"Look," he said, "there are plenty of mainstream sports out there and lots of other lesser known ones she can focus on. Why bother with something as arcane as foxhunting? Hardly anyone out there among the reading public would be able to relate to that."

"No less," Danella countered, "than they could relate to inhabitants of a remote South Pacific island or the San of the Kalahari."

"So you're lumping foxhunters in the same box with the Prince Philip worshippers and naked Bushmen?"

"Of course not. Janey's idea is to… to… well, she's still working out the details. But I like the overall concept. She and I both think she's on to something."

Thumper looked at the image on the TV screen. He'd paused the game at the point where the 'Skins were about to attempt a field goal. The camera was on the crowd: people wore their team jerseys, most emblazoned with a specific player's name and number; others in outlandish costumes, variations on the Hogettes and similar get-ups; face paint; wigs; and, of course, the obligatory signs and banners extolling the merits of the home team warriors and proclaiming certain victory over the invading infidels. A few fans appeared to be engaged in fervent prayer, hands clasped, eyes heavenward, petitioning the Almighty to shepherd the airborne pigskin safely through the uprights. And all this on what used to be known in Christian circles as "The Lord's Day." Religion, indeed.

"So she's asked you to ask me to not run her off," he said.

"Something like that."

"Tell you what. How about I put her in touch with Grantham Meisner, and introduce her to some masters at other hunts, with my endorsement. If she wants a true picture of foxhunting, she needs to cover more than one club."

"That's a gracious offer and a practical suggestion. I'm sure she'll appreciate it. And, of course, I assume that means you're willing to include Montfair Hunt among those on the list."

"Um, no, that's not my intention. The offer is instead of, not in addition to. We're… well… Montfair is going through a… how shall I put this?... an awkward time just now. Our senior master died unexpectedly. His son, my joint-master, isn't handling the loss well. I don't think Professor Musgrove would get a true depiction of a typical foxhunting club by studying Montfair under these circumstances."

"Perhaps that's exactly what's needed," Danella countered. "How does a club handle difficulties like that? What motivates people to remain involved and committed to getting through the tough times? It's easy to be part of a group when everything's going well and people are having fun. It's the rocky periods that show what the members are really made of."

"I wouldn't say this is exactly a 'rocky period.' More like an aberrant phase, an outlier, if you will. And outliers only detract from a true understanding of the subject under study."

"Now you're sounding like a professor."

"Sorry. Let me take off my mortarboard and put it to you this way. I don't want this woman snooping around, taking notes, and reporting on what's going on out here. I don't know how much she's told you,"—he suspected a lot—"but we are not in normal Montfair Hunt mode just now. However, I'm sure it will pass soon, and then maybe I'll be open to her paying us a visit or two."

There was a pause on the line, during which he heard Danella take a long, deep breath. Having worked with her on numerous projects over several years, he knew what this meant. The light sparing was over. It was time to start throwing the serious punches.

"You know, Thumper, you're in a position to make or break this woman's career."

A heavy punch for sure. And he felt its well-placed sting.

"She didn't need me for her first two books," he replied. "And they did okay. She has an established track record now. And, I might add, the best damn agent in the business."

Ha! Take that uppercut to the chin, Kernan.

"Her second one didn't do as well. And the first wasn't exactly a bestseller. She's at that critical point, following her sophomore effort, where she has to prove she has the chops to keep going. Otherwise, it's flash-in-the-pan time."

"And I should care about this because why?"

"Because you're a good man, and because you've been there yourself. If you'll recall, we weren't sure your career would get past your second book. Had it not been for some influential support, it might have ended there."

A sharp right cross to the temple, and sparkles danced before his eyes.

"And now that you've made a success of yourself," she continued, "you want to see other serious, talented writers succeed. Here's a chance to do exactly that. Or condemn her to an adjunct professorship at a second tier school slaving away for a pittance of what someone with her skills and background should be making." She had him in the corner and was landing solid body blows. "Your choice, Thumper."

He felt his legs start to weaken.

"It's not just me, you know. I have a responsibility to the other club members. And to the broader hunting community. Anything that reflects poorly on Montfair sullies the image of foxhunting in general."

"There won't be any sullying here."

"How can you assure me of that?"

"This will be handled with sensitivity, the objective can be achieved without embarrassing anyone."

He wasn't ready to go down for the count, but was listening for the bell so he could retreat to his corner and recover his wind. "Sensitivity, you say. Like running a photo of a dark little man idolizing the Duke of Edinburgh?"

"No, more like when we worked on your father's biography and we skirted around a delicate issue involving the household help."

He dropped a knee to the canvas and heard the referee say *One, two...*

"Danella Kernan!" He bounced back up to rejoin the battle. "You're not possibly suggesting that certain information could find its way to inquisitive ears if I don't cooperate with this sports-as-religion idea, are you?"

"Certainly not. And, frankly, I'm surprised you'd even think such a thing after all the years we've worked together. A little hurt even."

It was a low blow, and he deserved to lose points for it.

"What I'm saying," she explained, "is that you and I have successfully dealt with touchy details before and still turned out a damn fine book. Your father's biography was well-received, and went a long way to further polish his already-stellar reputation. How many times do I hear people say that we need more men like Thad Billington in Washington, statesmen who put the good of the country above their self-interests? And much of that comes from how you crafted his definitive biography."

Perhaps, he thought. But Thumper was enough of a realist to know that the passing of time can help improve someone's image. And dying tragically in the crash of a small private plane, his lovely and devoted wife with him, while flying in bad weather to speak at a fundraiser for disabled children further contributed to the old man's saintly reputation. Covering that part of his bio was easy for him as a writer, if damn hard as a son.

Deifying dear old Dad put yet more points on Danella's card. He was on the ropes and flagging. It was his turn for the long pause and the deep breath. Danella knew she had him.

"All right, here's the deal," he said, trying to sound as authoritative as possible while preparing to concede defeat. "I'll need to approve whatever she writes, both in draft form and the final version. And if I choose to bring in anyone else, such as Grantham, for additional approval, I have the prerogative to do so. More to the point, if I'm not happy with the overall way Montfair Hunt or the sport in general is portrayed, it does not see the light of day."

"Agreed."

Ding! The round was over. He was still standing, but just barely.

His attention returned to the frozen TV screen. A flash of boyhood recollection brought back the memory of attending Redskins games at the old Griffith Stadium in downtown DC. His father was a friend of George Preston Marshall, team owner in those days, which meant special treatment and the best seats. Later, thanks to the family's friendly rivalry with fellow steeplechasing enthusiast Jack Kent Cooke, Thumper and his father were frequent guests in the owner's box at RFK. He'd not attended a game since his father died and Dan Snyder bought the team.

But he could vividly recall the passion that surged through the crowd, especially when Washington scored and the band played "Hail to the Redskins." Eighty thousand voices joined in. Everyone knew the words and the tune. It blew away anything the choir at St. Cuthbert's could muster, even with Bing Sensabaugh's impressive voice as the anchor.

He hit "Play" and the screen returned to life. The image moved from the cheering, chanting, praying crowd to the small, brown, oblong spheroid hurtling through the air toward the goalpost. It sailed several yards to the wrong side of the left upright. A collective moan arose from the fans. Prayers for help gave way to curses of disappointment. God, it seemed at that moment, was not on the home team's side.

****

It had been an excellent afternoon for the juniors at Kimber Farm. Dorcas led the children in a follow-the-leader game around the pastures and through the woods. The two oldest kids, Baden Sensabaugh and Missy Winslow, served as her aids to shepherd the younger ones along.

By late afternoon all her charges had been picked up by their parents, except for Baden and Missy, who volunteered to stay and help Dorcas with the evening stable duties.

When Dorcas entered the feed room, carrying a stack of empty buckets, she discovered why they were so eager to hang around. Missy leaned back against a stack of hay bales. Baden pressed himself against her. Their lips where locked in a passionate kiss and their arms held each other in a tight embrace. Missy had one booted foot wedged behind Baden's leg, pulling him in closer.

They leapt apart at the sound of a half dozen plastic feed buckets tumbling onto the concrete floor. The look on Dorcas's face—anger, pain, disappointment, fear—caused them to move even farther away from each other.

"H-here," Baden sputtered as he reached awkwardly for the fallen buckets, "let me help you with these."

"Leave…" Dorcas said, barely forcing the word out.

"No, that's okay," Baden said, stretching out a hand toward the nearest bucket, "I'll just pick these…"

"Leave now." It was more croak than command.

Deeply embarrassed and aware of how she'd disappointed Dorcas, Missy said, "Baden, let's go. I'll call my mom to come pick us up. We can wait outside."

They slunk past Dorcas, who remained just inside the doorway. No eye contact was made. When the kids were gone, she managed to take a few steps across the room and sat down on a hay bale. She took several deep breaths. As her composure slowly returned, she said aloud, "Don't let it happen again. It must not happen again."

Fear flared anew. The medicine cabinet. She had to check the medicine cabinet.

Chapter 38

MILDRED PRESTON DROVE home from Tuesday's hunt in a state of agitation. She'd been tempted and teased, her body joyfully vibrating to the strain of the huntsman's horn, the hounds' melodious cry, the heart-pumping sound of half a hundred hooves pounding over the turf. And then... nothing. All over. Wham, bam, thank-you, ma'am. Ryman and Nardell, Crispie and Patti, and several other couples cleared out as soon as possible. Dashing off to do... what? Bing's back was still bothering him, enough to prevent him from riding, but he came to the tailgate for some socializing. Marie had returned to Brookside, two hundred miles away. In her absence a gaggle of ladies lingered around Bing looking like they'd have gone home with him in an instant if he'd asked. To hell with husbands, boyfriends, or the fact that the man was eighty-freaking-years-old.

Mildred wished Josh could get away for weekday hunts. Trade-offs had been made when he decided to give up his stressful practice in Boston and move south where the pace was slower and the winters less harsh. Mildred had served for many years as master of a drag hunt in Massachusetts, where hounds followed an artificial line of scent instead of live quarry. She was enlisted into the Montfair leadership soon after the Prestons purchased a substantial piece of property in the hunt's territory.

At least Josh wasn't on call. He'd be home for the evening at a reasonable time. But, still, that was a few hours away. And Mildred could barely contain herself.

By early afternoon she couldn't stand it any longer. A remedy came to her mind.

****

Josh Preston arrived home to find a note, written in Mildred's hand, taped to the mudroom door: *You missed another amazing morning of sport, sweetheart. Although I can't replicate the full experience, maybe I can give you some inkling of how things went. And, if you're as successful at sticking with the scent as hounds were, you just might find the hunt's end even more rewarding.*

He entered the mudroom where he saw a piece of orange baling twine tied to a coat hook. Hanging from the twine was another note: *We hunted from Worsham's west hayfields. Opening cast into Skunk Hollow woods. Crispie had barely called "Leu in" before the fox got up and headed north, hounds in full cry, staff and field close behind. Past the cistern by Winter Creek (where it's always muddy), gave my boots a good splatter.* He looked down to see her field boots, speckled with reddish-brown Virginia soil, standing in their usual spot in the mudroom.

The line ran into the back hallway, where Josh saw several pieces of baling twine had been tied together. They led him to the kitchen where he found another note. *Past the double silos, still running hard, rounding the turn, Marva's stirrup leather broke. Good thing I always wear one as a belt, pulled mine off and tossed it to her, continued on.* The baling twine was tied to a bronze horse statue that sat on the kitchen's center island. A worn stirrup leather was draped over the horse's back.

The notated trail continued into the dining room. *Trying to make up for the time lost to Marva's mishap, I took a shortcut through the woods past the silos. Thicker than I expected. Didn't duck enough at one branch.* Mildred's helmet was hung over the tip of a ladder-back chair. There was a three-inch long rip in the black velvet cover.

From the chair the line ran into the front hallway where another note awaited. *Hounds splashed into Stuart's Run. Thought we'd lose here, water still deep in places. But that incredible Warwick continued to throw his tongue right across the stream, still had the line on the far side, the pack honored his nose and hardly missed a second of the chase. I hit the stream so fast that Lefty sent a plume of water up around us, soaked my socks.* Josh found a pair of damp socks hanging over a wooden bench in the front foyer.

His curiosity rose. He followed the orange line on into the living room. Another note was pinned to a stuffed ottoman. *Thumper took first field over the Grenville Road coop, I hopped off to get the gate. Leading Lefty through, hurrying to get back on and keep my followers in the action, I tripped over a rock and scraped my knee.* Resting on the ottoman were Mildred's tan breeches, one knee smeared with stains of grass and dirt.

Josh bent down and picked up the breeches. He looked back across the hallway into the dining room. Boots, belt, helmet, socks, and now breeches. A suspicion of what might be afoot formed in his mind. The growing pleasure of the pursuit caused a stirring somewhere lower.

The line now doubled back into the front hallway where it ran along the railing to the top of the stairs. Josh sprang up the stairs and found a note taped to the banister. *Fox turned, back toward Stuart's Run, then left-handed up the steep hill to Reynold's Ridge. Quite a dash up the hill, viewed the fox running effortlessly, well ahead of hounds. Shirt soaked by this point.* A red polo shirt lay in a crumpled heap on the banister.

Josh quickly followed the twine down the hall toward the master bedroom. Halfway along, the line looped around a wall-mounted light fixture with another note attached. *Even sweated through my bra!* A white sports bra hung from the light fixture.

There was just one stretch of line remaining, leading straight to the bedroom door. As he continued down the hallway, Josh slid the rough line through his fisted hand, a wide grin now on his face. The final note was taped to the door. *Fox put to ground in the rock outcrops on the ridge, Crispie blowing "Gone to Ground," happy hounds, all riders there, huge smiles, flasks passed. What a thrill! Came home tingling... wishing you'd been there... wishing... wishing... and now you are! Leu in!* As he reached to open the door, he found a pair of panties hanging from the knob.

Chapter 39

THE MOMENT BAR pulled into his front yard—if a patch of ground covered with nothing but bare earth and pine needles can be called a "yard"—he realized something was amiss. An inverted plastic five-gallon bucket sat beneath one window. It could have been put there for only one reason—so that someone could stand on it and look into his trailer. He found small shoe prints in the bare soil accompanied by the paw prints of a medium-sized dog. Then he saw the telltale tire marks and his suspicions were confirmed.

He made a quick check inside to assure that nothing had been taken or touched. Then he drove back up the rutted farm road to Ryman's cottage. Nardell answered his knock.

"Where's the boss man at?"

"I'm right here," Ryman called from his office.

"Any idea what your old lady was doing snooping around my trailer?" Bar asked from the living room.

"Huh? Ma was back at your trailer?"

"Ain't that what I just said? You both stupid *and* deaf? Cain't miss those Scout tire tracks. Appears she was looking in the windows, probably woulda been inside too if the door hadn't been locked."

"Me and Nardell have been gone most of the day. Just got home a couple of hours ago. If she was back there, it must have been before that."

"Well, next time you and your dear mama have some quality time, tell her to stay the hell away from my turf."

"Um, well, technically it is sort of her turf. I mean, she does own the whole farm, and everything on it."

"Fine, she's my landlady. But I know a couple of things about landlord-tenant laws and a landlord cain't just show up and enter the tenant's property without notice or being invited. So how about you remind her of that little detail."

"Sure. You betcha."

"Yeah, right," Bar scoffed. He walked into the kitchen and opened the fridge. "Thanks for offering. I believe I will have myself a beer."

He carried his beer down the hallway and peered into the tiny space where Ryman was seated at his computer, surrounded by a pile of open books and scattered note pages. Bar's presence more than filled the narrow doorway. "Whatcha working on in there, boss man?"

"Saturday's service."

"Saturday's what?"

"The second formal service of the Ancient and Venerable Church of Ars Venatica. I'll be preaching on Article Two from 'The Foxhunter's Faith.' Listen to this: 'Every man shall first salute and speak words of comfort to the huntsman and whippers-in, knowing full well that they have hard work to perform. He shall then count the hounds and examine them with great joy, but in a quiet manner. He shall then likewise cheerfully salute his friends. He that shall say that the day will be a bad scenting one, or in any way endeavor to prophesy evil is an abomination.'"

Bar turned to Nardell. "He's joking, right?"

"Not at all. Saint Hubert be praised!"

"You too, huh?" Bar took a long swig of beer. "Well, boss man, at least you got one disciple. Good luck getting more."

"There are already many, many followers of Saint Hubert," Ryman countered, "thousands who are members of the Ancient and Venerable Church of Ars Venatica. Venaticans for short. They just haven't been able to give their beliefs a name, or have a way to pull it all together. But thanks to Saint Hubert's revelations, starting with the visions he showed me of the Blessed Stag, the true church will soon be resurrected, the faith restored."

"This shit just gets deeper every day. The only right decision you've made since your old man croaked was keeping your crazy ass outta the shop. Which, in case you're at all interested, is still afloat, if just barely."

Ryman turned from the computer screen and looked at Bar. "How are things working out? You got everyone in the county set up with a new tractor yet?"

"One down—that would be Frank Worsham—several hundred to go—that would be pretty much everyone else within a hundred mile radius of Paradise Gap. Hell, I only been in the salesman's job a week. The 7830 Worsham's buying will help, but our take on that ain't enough to keep things going forever, or even cover what we're in the hole now. I called Sheltie Lou and she said she's trying to work up some marketing plans, get a website going. Taking time off for your old man's funeral has her playing catch-up on her real job. But she said she'd have some stuff ready soon."

"There, you see. Saint Hubert is providing for the shop, too."

"Saint Hubert my fat hairy ass! How about it was Saint Barstow who made the call, and Sister Sheltie Lou who agreed to invest her own time and talent in trying to help out the business that you oughta be running. That is, if you were in your right mind."

"Bar, Bar, Bar. My mind has never been righter. You must have faith that Saint Hubert will see to it that it all works out, just as he has planned."

"You need help, pal." He turned to Nardell. "Seems you could use a bit of head adjustment yourself. But, then, you always did have a screw loose. How's that new tat on your tit workin' out? Still got room on the other one for a picture of Saint Hubert? Or are you runnin' outta skin?"

Nardell's eyes widened and she shrank back, surprised and hurt by Bar's remark.

Ryman bolted up, letting the book on his lap fall to the floor. "Now wait just a damn minute. You can insult me all you want. I'm used to it. And mostly deserve it. But you leave her out of this or… or I'll…"

"Yeah? You'll what?" Bar did not move from the doorway. "You better think twice about fucking with me. I'm the only reason you're able to sit here on your ass making up your 'service.' If it weren't for me, and Muriel too, trying to hold the shop together, you'd either have to be in there running things yourself or stand outside and watch 'em taking down the McKendrick and Sons sign, and John Deere loading up all the equipment and hauling it away. I'm sure your daddy would be real proud of you then. And wouldn't your crazy old bat of a mama love to see you fall flat on your sorry behind."

Ryman's confrontational pose loosened. "Okay. I owe you that. But it still doesn't give you the right to insult Nardell. I'm the one Saint Hubert chose to restore the faith. She's just following my lead, because she believes in what I've been called to do."

"She does, huh? That right, Sister Raithby?"

"Yes, of course it is," Nardell said. "I believe in Saint Hubert, and I believe in Ryman's calling. I've seen his power. You'd believe too if you'd seen it." She put on a defiant face and thrust out her chest. "And maybe I just will get a tattoo of Saint Hubert on my other tit."

"Hopeless, both of you." Bar leaned in and tossed the empty beer bottle into Ryman's trash bin. "Thanks for the brewski. I doubt I can count on either one of you to keep an eye on my place when I'm at work. Too damn caught up in your Saint Hubert crap to notice what's going on around you in the real world." He stepped through the living room and stopped by the dilapidated leather sofa where Wycroft was comfortably stretched out. Bar reached down and patted the hound. "Maybe you'll sing out if the old bat and her ugly ass dog go sneaking around my trailer again. Unless you've gone totally wacko too."

Bar returned to his wooded oasis. He'd been so focused on the idea of someone invading his closely-guarded privacy that he'd forgotten to toss out the road kill from the bed of his truck.

"It ain't much, fellahs," he said as he heaved the carcass toward the vultures' feeding area. "Maybe the pickin's will be better tomorrow. But come on down and have a snack."

He watched the birds perform their slow, circling descent and muttered to himself, "I wish Ryman could communicate with you guys like he seems to be able to do with dogs and horses." He thought about what he'd witnessed between Ryman and Frank Worsham's dog. "Not that I believe any of that shit for a minute. Maybe I can train you to be attack vultures. Wouldn't that scare the bejesus out of the old bat if she comes messin' around here again? A whole swarm of my black beauties comin' after her."

Chapter 40

THE RAIN STARTED Wednesday afternoon. By the early hours of Thursday morning it was coming down in sheets. A tropical storm battered the East Coast. Its effects reached far enough inland to inundate much of the Mid-Atlantic, including Crutchfield County. Certain that Saint Hubert would not allow the Thursday hunt to be rained out, Ryman disagreed with Thumper's preference to cancel in advance.

He awoke at four a.m., two hours before the go or no-go call had to be made, at which point Marva would post the information to the membership. There seemed to be little need for that, though, as no one in his or her right mind would even remotely consider going out with hounds in these conditions. But, then, Ryman was clearly not in his right mind.

He slipped out of bed, went to his computer, and checked the radar. A weather miracle looked unlikely. Rain pounded a kettledrum chorus on the cottage's metal roof, the windows rattled, and the front door creaked.

Seeing the opportunity, Wycroft arose from his cushion in the corner of the bedroom and climbed up to take Ryman's spot next to Nardell. She rolled over and draped one arm across the hound. She made no distinction as to whether the lump she snuggled was human or canine. It was simply comforting to have a warm body to spoon with. Whether it was Ryman or Wycroft made little difference. In her deep slumber, Nardell's two male housemates felt and smelled about the same anyway.

The ping of an incoming email caught Ryman's attention. It was from the same unfamiliar sender who had sent him the "Blasphemer Beware" email the previous week. The subject line this time read, "Woe Unto Them Who Mislead the Innocent."

> "But though we, or an angel from heaven, preach any other gospel unto you than that which we have preached unto you, let him be accursed." Galatians 1:8. There is but one True Faith, and yours is not it.

Damn, Ryman thought, this poor sod must be up early too. Should I report this as spam? Nah, it's kind of amusing actually. Maybe I'll write him back, tell him Saint Hubert loves him, and that he's the one who should repent and accept the True Faith offered by The Ancient and Venerable…"

Boom! A flash of lightning, with a simultaneous foundation-shaking clap of thunder, exploded directly over the house.

Nardell awoke with a start. Seeing light in the hallway, she arose, slipped on her robe, and found Ryman clacking away on his keyboard.

"Are you sure you should be using the computer in this storm?" she asked.

Another bolt of lightning flashed, a bit farther off but still with enough force to brighten the inside of the cottage and send a shiver through the walls.

He stopped typing. His hands hovered over the keys. "Mmmm, I suppose you're right. But I'm sure Saint Hubert will move this storm off in time for us to hunt today."

"Ummm, I don't think so, sweetheart. The forecast last night said it was going to rain hard all day."

Ryman slumped in his chair and rubbed his face. "What would Saint Hubert have me do?'

"What would your father have done?" Nardell asked.

Ryman sat up straight. "Good question. He did always honor Saint Hubert in his own way, didn't he?"

"And would Fergus have taken hounds out in this?"

"No, of course not. No one hated to cancel a day's sport more than he did. But he always preached good stewardship over the hounds, the horses, and the land. It's one thing to put our own silly necks at risk. But we must maintain our duty to be responsible over what Saint Hubert has entrusted to us." He thought about this for a long moment, and then returned his hands to the keyboard. "I must make a note to preach about that."

"Quickly," Nardell suggested. "Then turn that computer off before the next lightning strike fries it."

Ryman did so, and a split second after he shut down the machine another lightning bolt hit and the power went out. He fumbled in the dark, found his cell phone, and called Thumper. Of course they were canceling. Yes, his power was out too. But the generators had kicked in and all was fine.

"Well, damn," Ryman sighed, switching off his phone. "No sport today."

"Not necessarily," Nardell said.

"What do you mean?"

She loosened the belt of her robe and let the front fall open. Ryman could only see her as a shadowy image in the darkness. But the message was clear enough.

She took a step toward him. "Didn't you tell me there are two meanings to 'venery?'"

"I did indeed," he said, standing up and slipping his hands inside her draping robe.

"Then maybe it's the other type Saint Hubert wants us to enjoy this morning."

"Blessed be his name."

She turned quickly and started down the hallway. "Yip, yip, yeeee!"

Ryman followed eagerly. "A-woooo, a-woooo!"

Chapter 41

BY SATURDAY CONDITIONS had improved enough for hunting to resume. The meet was at the Prestons' BoSox Farm. Josh wanted to name the place Green Monster Acres but Mildred felt that was too arcane a reference for those not steeped in the storied history of Fenway Park. She did, however, concede to his wish to name their five horses after Red Sox Hall of Famers: Lefty, Boggs, Hooper, Zimmer, and Yaz.

Thumper arrived to find Janey already moving through the crowd, her video camera humming as she interviewed one person after another.

To Thumper's thinking, there were way too many people there. Every hunt member was present, along with a dozen juniors under Dorcas Stanhope's leadership, plus an abundance of adult guests. Marva had her hands full keeping track of the attendance and collecting the caps—the fees non-members paid for a day's hunting.

Thumper found himself wishing for a less-than-stellar day. Although the additional income was helpful, too many riders hampered the enjoyment of the sport and caused excessive wear to the land. Perhaps a break in the action would dampen the enthusiasm and the numbers would return to more normal levels. The alternative was for Thumper to start enforcing the limit on guests, even turning some people away if too many showed up without having advance permission. That would be a last resort and a potentially ugly scene. Maybe there was some other way to weaken the enthusiasm without a confrontation.

The staff confab was just starting as Crispie, Patti, Mildred, Marva, and Nardell gathered around Ryman. It looked to Thumper like a team of basketball players, albeit mounted on horses, huddled around their coach, receiving instructions for the game about to start. Ryman reached out and placed a hand on Crispie's shoulder.

"O Saint Hubert," he intoned in a voice of supplication, his eyes heavenward, "may your blessings fall upon our Brother Crispian. May you instill your spirit within his breast, impart your vision to his eyes, your voice to his ears, your wisdom to his mind. May his senses be as those of a hound, his thoughts as those of the fox. May he bring honor to your name and help restore the faith, as is your holy mission. Amen!"

Thumper watched as Janey recorded this laying-on-of-hands ceremony with both her camera and notebook. But for his promise to Danella, he'd have sent her packing then and there. Instead, he did his best to ignore her and joined the other staff members. "So," he said to Ryman, "what's Saint Huey telling you this morning about where to cast?"

"Perhaps our blessed patron saint will speak through Brother O'Rourke this morning. I have laid hands on him and asked Saint Hubert to construe him with the blessed power."

"Do you mean 'imbue?'"

"Yeah, that."

Thumper turned to Crispie. "So, Brother O'Rourke, do you feel imbued? Or construed, for that matter?"

"Not sure what I feel, Master. Just kinda… well, strange actually."

Thumper saw Chet standing by his Land Rover, Reverend Dan next to him. Janey would have an excellent chance to see the sport that morning with the knowledgeable Mister Henderson as her guide. He had a flash of inspiration. "Y'know," he said to Ryman, "I've been feeling kind of strange lately myself. Haven't been able to put my finger on it, but I…well, I'm beginning to think Saint Hubert might be… how do I say this?... speaking to me too. Do you think that's possible?"

"Absolutely, Brother! He's been working through you in many ways. You just haven't realized it yet."

"Well, I think I'm starting to understand that now. Could you… would you… 'construe' me with the spirit?"

"Hallelujah! Welcome to the fold."

Ryman offered up the same petition he'd recited over Crispie. Thumper wasn't really listening. He was watching Janey chatting with two long-time members, recording their comments in her notebook as they regaled her with an animated account of the joys of foxhunting in general and, more recently, the blessings of Saint Hubert in particular. To endorse this, they each withdrew their Saint Hubert medals from inside their vests and proudly showed them to their interviewer.

She did her best to remain focused on the two people before her, but her attention was distracted by the sight of Thumper's bowed head, Ryman's hand on his shoulder.

The field was called to order. Ryman began with the Venatican Creed, followed by a well-received sermonette on Article Two. Thumper flinched when Ryman quoted, "He that shall say that the day shall be a bad scenting day, or in any manner endeavor to prophesy evil is an abomination." Then Bing, still ground-bound with a sore back, stepped forward and led everyone in singing "John Peel."

Thumper was surprised by the number of people who recited the pledge in full voice, many not even looking at the cards Ryman had handed out, and the strength of the assembled voices that joined in on the old song.

Being now "construed" with the spirit himself, Thumper mouthed along as convincingly as he could.

Janey eyed him suspiciously.

"Hallelujah!" Ryman said. "Time to get to the sport. Brother Thumper, where shall we cast this morning?"

"Oh, my goodness, you're asking me?" He tried to act surprised.

"Of course, now that you're construed with the spirit. Just let Saint Hubert guide you."

"Oh, okay. Well, ah, gee, let me think." He pretended to be deep in thought for several suspenseful seconds. "Um, how about Gryffyn's Corner?"

Ryman looked skeptical. "Ah, well, that's pretty deep into the country. And some boggy spots around there too. Shouldn't we stay up on higher ground? Closer to the roads? Been a long time since we've gotten a fox up from there."

"Gee, Ry, I can't explain it, but I have this… this sort of image or something, like that's where the fox is this morning. And it *is* on my land over there so if the boggy ground gets torn up, it's my problem."

Ryman smiled indulgently and nodded. "Okay then. It does appear you've been construed. Mister O'Rourke, let's draw to Gryffyn's Corner."

"Gryffyn's Corner?" Bing remarked as he climbed into Chet's SUV along with Janey and Dan. "No good way to get back there, even with four-wheel drive. Low ground, only wooded trails, soggy under most conditions, likely to be really deep after those heavy rains. Not where I'd have chosen to draw this morning. But, then, I'm not a master. Maybe Thumper knows something I don't."

Getting to Gryffyn's Corner was difficult for the mounted followers. Several fences had to be jumped along the way and the ground on the approach and landing sides got sloppier as each successive set of hooves churned it up. It was not a day to be stuck toward the back of the field. It was even harder on Mildred's non-jumping followers as there were few gates in that area so she had to lead her field on long, circuitous routes around the jumps and then canter or gallop through the slop to catch up.

In short order everyone except the field leaders was splattered with dark, oozing mud across their expensive tweed jackets, silk ties, and scrubbed faces.

An increasing rumble of gripes and groans reached Thumper's ears. It was precisely the music he wanted to hear.

After an arduous trek, they approached Gryffyn's Corner. It wasn't really a "corner" in the sense of an intersection, just a sharp bend in the wooded trail. Many years before a man named Gryffyn took a spill going around that bend, fell in an awkward manner, and broke a leg. As is customary in hunt country, the spot became known as Gryffyn's Corner.

Ryman circled around to the opposite side of the thinly wooded, low-lying area. The opportunities for a fox to conceal himself were slim; only a dull-witted critter was likely to be found there, if one at all. But just as Crispie was about to cheer his pack to "Leu in," one of the handsomest foxes anyone had ever seen appeared, as if out of nowhere. Surely a dog fox given his size and stance, he stood motionless among the sparse trees and cast a defiant, disdainful look at hounds. This startled them momentarily and the entire pack went silent, frozen in place. Then Warwick, ignoring the specter trying to stare them down, put his nose to the ground. His cry of "A-woooo! This is fox scent!" brought his mates back to their senses. They honored his strike with an enthusiastic chorus and took off on the line.

The fox, looking no more than mildly annoyed, turned and headed straight for high ground. Thumper led his followers through the stand of trees, out the other side, and moved along close behind Crispie and the pack. They only had to jump two fences with slightly trappy going and they were back on more appealing terrain, still damp from the recent rains but dry without being hard, soft without being deep.

The fox began to turn in a wide counterclockwise arc, keeping the network of farm roads that crisscrossed the area safely to his right. As the riders cantered along a hillside just below one of those roads, Thumper caught sight of Chet's Land Rover. Four figures stood along the roadside, enjoying a theatrical view of the action playing out below them.

The grumbles and groans from the followers ceased and when Thumper looked back over his shoulder all he saw were eager, smiling, mud-splattered faces.

Perhaps, Thumper thought, Saint Hubert had tricked the Pharisee at his own game. He immediately banished that idea from his mind. No, it was another case of pure dumb luck. Foxhunting is a gamble, not unlike playing the stock market. You make your best, most educated guesses knowing there will always be variables you can neither control nor predict. Sometimes you're right, sometimes not. And sometimes the chimpanzee with a dartboard does better than the Wharton grad. If Ryman had "construed" him with anything, it was only that he too could make seemingly inappropriate choices and the capricious nature of the sport might still turn the circumstances to the hunters' advantage.

Right or wrong, that remained his rationale.

****

Chet's Land Rover was a great improvement over Rhetta's Scout as a way for Janey and Dan to see the hunting action. The ride was rendered even more profitable by Bing's contribution to the narration. He essentially picked up where Rhetta's description of how a foxhunt was conducted left off and continued the thread in an unbroken line. Janey added several more pages to her rapidly expanding notes.

Chet knew enough to predict where the action was likely to conclude and drove to a roadside spot just above a frequently used den. He and his passengers heard hounds in full cry as they streamed through the woods on the far side of the field. He invited Janey and Dan to join him and Bing along the side of the road where they could more fully see what was about to play out before them.

Shivers raced up and down Janey's spine as the cry of the hounds grew nearer. Through the viewer of her video camera she could see glimpses of a fast-moving body here and there as the pack swept down through the thickly wooded hillside. Then, traveling at an oblique angle moving from right to left, a small red creature burst from the edge of the woods. Ears back and tail straight out, the fox dashed across the field, making a straight line for what looked like a rough mound of dirt. At the point where the fox was halfway between the tree line and the dirt mound, the lead hounds emerged from the woods, baying excitedly, tongues out, ears streaming, tails aloft. Within seconds the entire pack was in the field, thirty-three hounds working as one unified force.

Despite being outnumbered by such a huge margin, the fox still had control of the game. He'd eluded his pursuers to this point, thanks to his greater speed and his knowledge of every piece of tree bark and grass blade in his domain. Hounds and hunters had enjoyed a long enough chase and everyone was ready for a break. The fox knew just where to go for a well-deserved rest.

Janey's attention moved from the hounds back to the fox in time to see him reach the dirt mound and disappear from sight. He had used that abandoned groundhog hole more than once and knew it was secure and deep enough that hounds could not reach him there.

The pack flooded over the site moments after their quarry vanished. The tone of their cry shifted from the deep, resounding exuberance of the chase to the higher pitched whine of its conclusion. Some hounds made the futile effort of digging at the entrance. Some dropped to the ground and rolled, trying to soak up any vestiges of scent that might yet linger. Others scouted around the den, checking to see if there was a backdoor or if, perhaps, the fox was yet afoot and there was still a line of scent to follow.

Crispie rode up and swung off his horse. He bent over the den's entrance, blew the quivering notes of "Gone to Ground," and praised his hounds for their excellent work.

Janey lowered her camera and stood frozen, wide-eyed. Each note of the horn and plaintive whine of a hound sent another electric pulse through her body.

Thumper arrived with the first field, Mildred soon thereafter with the second. They formed a semicircle around the den, congratulated Crispie on the fine work of his pack, and withdrew their flasks for some much-needed refreshment.

Thumper had gotten so caught up in the pleasures of the chase that he'd completely forgotten his nefarious objectives for that morning. It was only when he tilted his head back to take a long swig from an offered flask that he caught the sight of four people standing at the top of the roadside bank along the field's edge.

His attempt to spoil the hunt and send Janey home empty-handed had failed. If anything, drawing to Gryffyn's Corner had been the perfect choice.

Ryman's hand fell heavily against Thumper's back, causing him to choke on the draught of port just then sliding down his throat.

"Hallelujah, Brother Thumper! You have indeed been construed with the spirit of Saint Hubert. Gryffyn's Corner! Who'd a-thunk it? What a thrill to see that our dear Saint Hubert is spreading his blessings to others."

"I… *cough*… don't think… *splutter*… it was… *hack, hack, hack*!"

"Oh, yes, of course, we must be humble. But you should rejoice in the spirit that our patron saint has construed upon you. All cares are banished by his loving kindness that gives us such an excellent morning of sport."

Thumper tried to respond. "You don't… *gulp*… understand. It was all… *cough*… I was just trying to… *hack*…"

Ryman squeezed Thumper's shoulder, lifted his other hand in the three-finger salute, and said, "Badge of glory, Brother. Today the badge of glory is all yours." He released his grip and rode off to bestow his blessings on Brother Crispie.

****

Thumper slid off Lenny at his trailer and was just starting to untack when Janey approached him.

"I'd like to thank you for allowing me to be here again," she said.

"Our agent knows how to make a compelling case," he replied, loosening the horse's girth. "I suppose that's why we're both fortunate to have her."

"She's been a great friend and supporter. The last thing I'd want to do is disappoint her."

"She explained my insistence on the right of review?"

"Yes, she did."

"Good. Then one way you can assure you don't disappoint her is to faithfully comply with that request."

"I fully intend to."

He continued removing Lenny's gear as he spoke. "My relationship with Danella has always been based on mutual trust and respect. We've never worried about putting things in writing because we each know the other's word is just as good, maybe better. I hope that will always continue to be so."

"As far as anything between the two of you that has to do with me, I can assure you it will." She spoke calmly, with a convincing air of certainty.

Thumper stood for a moment, his saddle slung over one arm. He gave her a careful assessment, then simply nodded his acceptance.

She noticed an oblong leather case strapped to the side of his saddle. "What little riding I've done has been mostly Western. Although I think some of the saddles I've used on treks into remote areas were Army surplus from the Spanish-American War. I'm not familiar with your English-style tack." She reached out and fondled the case. "What's in here?"

"Wire cutters. There's a good bit of old barbed wire around these parts, especially in the woods where fences used to be that have since fallen down. The wire can be hard to see in the undergrowth. It can be a nasty situation if a horse gets his feet caught in it. Always keep my Swiss Army knife handy, too. You never know what challenges might await out here in hunt country." He stepped into the dressing room of his trailer and placed the saddle on a rack, then switched on the pump to the water tank, pulled out the hose, and began washing off Lenny.

Janey moved briskly to avoid being sprayed. "I take it that what's occurring here, not being typical for a foxhunting club, is causing you some discomfort."

"Most perceptive of you."

"Of course, I have no frame of reference for what's typical and what isn't."

"I have enough familiarity with what's typical for the both of us. And, believe me, what you're seeing here is most definitely not typical."

"In what ways?"

He could see her straining to keep from committing the obvious faux pas of lifting her video camera to record his remarks. It was not the time to start interviewing the gatekeeper. He might yet have a change of heart and withdraw his support.

"In more ways than I can succinctly recite. And most of them would make little sense, given, as you aptly noted, your lack of reference. Suffice it to say for now that any resemblance between foxhunting and anything smacking of formal religion is purely coincidental. We may trot out Saint Hubert once a year or so for the sake of amusement. But what's happening here is way beyond that."

"Why do you think that is?"

"Look, Ms. Musgrove…" He brushed past her and reached for the sweat scraper.

"'Janey,' please"

"…I've conducted enough interviews in my career to know one when I see it. I told Danella I would not expel you from our midst. And I am the one person among this group who has the unquestionable prerogative to do so. But I did not agree to cooperate beyond that."

She smiled pleasantly and said, "I understand. I just wanted to thank you for your indulgence. Forgive me if I've been intrusive."

"Apology accepted." He fluttered a hand toward the tailgate spread. "Your time would be better spent among the faithful. That appears to be where all the action is."

A thick and boisterous crowd had formed around the tables. There was a considerable amount of pairing going on. Gentlemen placed their hands around ladies' waists. The ladies responded by leaning into their partners and smiling at them with a look that said, "You're on the right track, mister." Plates were heaped high with an array of delicacies and a flood of red plastic cups sloshed with intoxicating beverages.

The only contrast to this bacchanalian scene was the uncomfortable distance between Baden Sensabaugh and Missy Winslow. Dorcas alternated her disapproving gaze between the two teenagers and the unrestrained pairing going on among the adults.

Thumper finished wiping the excess moisture off Lenny, filled a water bucket, and hung up a hay net. He then reached into his truck and pulled out a cigar. "Mind if I smoke?"

"Of course not. This is, after all, your world, not mine."

"Did you get to see much of this morning's action?"

"Quite a lot. I even saw the fox twice. It's quite a thrill when you get to see the fox, isn't it?"

"Always is for me, even after all these years."

"When did you start foxhunting?"

"At the age of five, on a small pony with my father holding a lead-line for safety. But by the age of six I had no need for that, was on my own."

"Have you ever gotten hurt doing this?"

"A few times. But nothing serious, just some broken bones here and there, some concussions along the way."

"Is that typical?"

He took a long drag on his cigar and blew the smoke out in a slow stream. "Are we returning to interview mode?"

"Sorry. Just a habit, I guess. You understand."

"I certainly understand about habits." He looked at the cigar between his fingers. "I suppose you find this one to be particularly nasty."

"No, not really. I rather enjoy the smell. At least out here in the open. I did date a man once who smoked them quite a lot. Pipes too. It got pretty stuffy indoors. And his breath!" She waved a hand in front of her face and wrinkled her nose. "Oh, boy. It was all I could do to keep from gagging when he kissed me."

The thought of Janey kissing someone sparked the realization that she was not just a detached journalist, a neutral observer studying Thumper's cloistered world of foxhunting. Underneath the drab discount-outlet attire was a flesh-and-blood woman with a personal life that was, to him, a complete mystery. Had she been married before? For that matter, was she married now? The absence of a ring was not conclusive proof either way. He'd been addressing her as "Ms." and she'd offered no correction. Was she in a relationship? She'd obviously had at least one boyfriend in the past, an inconsiderate lout with a severe case of tobacco-induced halitosis.

"I'll put this out," he said, looking for an appropriate spot to snuff the stogie.

"Oh, no, please don't do that on my account. It reminds me of some of the tribes I've visited in South America where shaman use tobacco in their mystical and healing practices."

"You've been around."

"I've travelled some."

"And for all the exotic locales you've visited, here you are in plain old Virginia, USA, watching a bunch of toffs persecuting poor, innocent foxes."

"Exotic isn't only about place. It's also about practice. To me, this is quite exotic."

He returned to his cigar and they stood silently, watching the tailgate festivities. Bing was teaching an enthusiastic group the correct lyrics to "A-Hunting We Will Go."

"Mister Sensabaugh has a beautiful voice," Janey said.

"Bing? Yes, he certainly does."

"Good nickname for a singer. At least I assume it's a nickname."

"Yes, it is. And, as you might suspect, inspired by that other crooner of old."

"Speaking of nicknames… Thumper?"

"Not the same famous connotation."

"The little rabbit in *Bambi*?"

"Most definitely not." He tried to conceal his exasperation at being asked that question. But after so many thousands of times, it was hard not to let a hint of weariness show through.

"What then?"

"That, I'm afraid, is a piece of personal information revealed to none but a very select few."

Her face flushed. "Sorry, too personal."

"Totally legitimate question. I'm just… well… you see, being the fourth Thaddeus Augustus Billington, one will inevitably get pinned with a nickname of some sort. Mine serves its purpose. It just wasn't of my own choosing and the circumstances behind that are something I prefer to keep from the broader public. Not that the public actually gives much of a damn."

He knew exactly what Janey Musgrove was thinking at that moment: Who among the crowd here knows why he's called "Thumper" and how could she extract that information from them?

Their attention was diverted from the touchy topic of his nickname by a particularly loud burst of manly laughter and feminine squeals from the tailgate crowd.

"Come, Ms. Musgrove," Thumper said with mock formality as he took her by the arm and guided her toward the post-hunt celebrants. "Let us, the Scribe and the Pharisee, mingle with the harlots and publicans."

Chapter 42

THE CONGREGANTS WERE eager to see which Reverend Davenport would show up that Sunday morning: Hungover Dan, Fire & Brimstone Dan, or plain old Dreary Dan. Baden and Beatrice were hoping for Hungover Dan. He was the most fun to watch. They were disappointed to see an energetic man in flowing robes stride purposefully toward the pulpit and spring up the stairs with a lively bounce.

"My friends, there comes a time when we need to be reminded of the basics. Now, as you may know, I am not a follower of professional athletics. But I do admire good leadership. And who among us cannot help but admire that legendary leader of the gridiron, Coach Vincent Lombardi."

"Who?" Beatrice whispered to her brother.

"And what's a 'gridiron?'" Baden whispered back.

"Hush!" Bing said.

Dan continued. "Now, when Lombardi became the head coach of the Green Bay Packers, the team had not been doing well. It had been several years since they'd even had a winning season. At the first team meeting, Lombardi walked to the front of the room, looked at the men assembled before him, and held up a football." Dan lifted his arm high. "'Gentlemen,' he said to them, 'this is a football." Dan's arm came down with a dramatic flourish. "'We're going to get back to basics,' he told them. And I'm sure you know how things went after that."

Baden and Beatrice looked at each other and shrugged.

Dan raised his arm again. This time he held his Bible in his hand. "Ladies and gentlemen, this is our football, it contains our yard markers, our goalposts. We must be sound in the fundamentals. We must return to our touchstone when times seem troubling.

"And what could be more basic than the Lord's Commandments. I referred to the First Commandment last week. Today I will cover the Second Commandment." He placed his Bible back on the pulpit but did not look at it as he quoted the text.

"'You shall not make for yourself a carved image, or any likeness of anything that is in heaven above, or that is in the earth beneath, or that is in the water under the earth; you shall not bow down to them nor serve them. For I, the Lord your God, am a jealous God, visiting the iniquity of the fathers on the children to the third and fourth generations of those who hate Me, but showing mercy to thousands, to those who love Me and keep My Commandments'"

Dan then proceeded to regale his listeners with an artfully crafted sermon on idolatry, jealousy, iniquity, and mercy.

An hour later the charged up, if still sparse, group of parishioners went filing past an animated Dan Davenport who pumped everyone's hand as they left the church.

Bob Sensabaugh paused when his turn came. "Good sermon, Reverend. I wouldn't have thought to bring in a Vince Lombardi reference. Nice touch."

"Thank you, Brother Sensabaugh."

"Frankly, I'm surprised you'd ever even heard of the man."

"Ah, you must remember that when I was growing up in Indiana there was no professional football franchise in the state." Not only had the hint of an English accent vanished from Dan's speech, his native Mid-West tone was creeping back in. "Absent a home team, my father opted to root for the Packers. Why not the closer Chicago team I do not know. But for reasons of his own my father hated 'Da Bears.' Had my mother not forbidden it, there would have been a Vince Lombardi shrine in our house."

Driving home, Bing said to Marie, "All that talk of football, I couldn't help but think of an old Bobby Bare song during Dan's sermon." He sang a few bars of "Drop Kick Me Jesus Through the Goalposts of Life" with an exaggerated redneck twang.

"Faith and football," Marie said. "Religion and sports. Seems to be a spreading topic around here. It's a shame more people don't get to hear your beautiful voice, whatever you're singing."

"Yeah, well, maybe that will change one of these days."

****

Missy Winslow had just finished putting her tack away in the Kimber Farm tack room when Dorcas entered and closed the door behind her.

"I'd like a word with you, Missy."

The last thing Missy wanted was to be trapped in a room with Dorcas. "Look, Miss Stanhope, I'm really sorry about last week. It won't happen again."

"There's no need to apologize. I'm sure it wasn't your fault. What I wanted to talk to you about, well, I suppose it's more of a warning.

You're so young. There's so much you don't know about boys. About men. What they're really like. What they'll do. You have to be on your guard at all times."

"Baden's not like that. He's a real gentleman."

Dorcas stepped forward and extended a hand toward Missy. "Please, listen to me. I know. I've seen… I've seen… You may think someone's good, even like a brother. But you have to be watchful. Be careful about what you believe no matter what they tell you. And if they offer you…"

Missy stepped around Dorcas and reached for the door. "Okay, I will. I'm not a child. I can take care of myself."

"That's what many others have said."

"Look, if you don't want me here any more…"

"No! Please don't stay away. I don't mean to scare you. I care, that's all. I just care about you. Is that okay?"

"Yeah, sure. Can I go now?"

Dorcas simply nodded and limply waved a hand toward the door.

Chapter 43

BING WAS ONCE again the center of attention at Tuesday's tailgate. Spirits were high after another morning of excellent sport. Marie was back in Brookside but arrangements were in the works for her visits to extend far beyond the weekends alone. Absent her turf-protecting presence, a flock of ladies clustered tightly around Bing. He passed out sheets of paper to each one and then herded them into a group facing him. To his delight, several men wandered over and wedged into the back row.

"Excellent," Bing said. "I'm afraid I don't have enough song sheets for everyone, so some of you will have to share. All right then, here we go." He gave a downbeat and launched into the song. The lyrical phrasing and jaunty tune could have been penned by Gilbert and Sullivan:

A southerly wind and a cloudy sky
Proclaim the hunting morning.
Before the sun rises away we will fly,
Dull sleep and downy bed scorning.
To horse my brave boys and away, away,
Bright Phoebus the hills is adorning.
The face of all nature looks gay, looks gay,
'Tis a beautiful hunting morning.

Everyone sang out with gusto on the chorus.

Hark! Hark! Forward!
Tally-Ho! Tally-Ho! Tally-Ho!
Hark! Hark! Forward!
Tally-Ho! Tally-Ho! Tally-Ho!

Thumper and Ryman stood off to the side. The latter beamed at the impromptu show. The former wondered what the hell was happening to his great-grandfather's foxhunting club.

Thumper turned to Ryman. "You do realize that you've got this Saint Hubert thing completely ass-backwards?"

"What do you mean? I'm doing what he's called me…"

"Drop the bullshit for just a minute. Remind me how this fellow became a saint in the first place."

"C'mon, Thumper, you know the story."

"Yes, but I want to hear it from you, his chosen prophet."

"Um, okay. Well, he was hunting with his hounds, which he loved to do, and the stag appeared to him, the one with the cross above its head. And he heard a voice telling him to serve God."

"And then what?"

"Well, he started serving God and became a saint."

"And did he hunt any more after that day?"

"Um, well, I guess not. Y'see, he was so busy doing saint things…"

"Right. You've got the gist of it, but you're missing the salient point. The voice, supposedly of God, told him to give up his pleasure-seeking sporting ways. Now it seems like the voice you claim to be hearing is telling you to do just the opposite. Don't you find that just a bit contradictory?"

Ryman's brow furrowed as he thought about this. Then he suddenly brightened as the answer came to him. "Not contradictory, Thumper. It's the fulfillment."

"What?"

"Don't you see? Yes, Saint Hubert gave up hunting so he could serve the church. But after all these years, people have gotten too far away from the natural world. They've forgotten the truth. Religion's become just a bunch of mumbo-jumbo to most folks. Or they aren't interested in it all. And Saint Hubert's sad about that. So he's called me to bring people back, so they can be more in touch with the real world, with real human nature." Ryman smiled broadly and puffed out his chest, immensely proud of himself for coming up with such irrefutable logic.

Thumper shook his head. "You're something else. Think you've got this all figured out, do you?"

"Nah, not all of it. There's a bunch I'm still trying to figure out. But I think I've got the basics down pretty well. It's all about the exhilaration, that feeling you get when hounds are in full cry and the chase is on. That's what brings us closer to our real selves. Aren't you exhilarated, Thumper?"

"Exhilarated? When hounds are running, yes. But this other stuff that's going on…"

"Maybe if you had, y'know, a partner." Ryman gestured toward the ladies, many of them unattached, others wishing they were. He gave Thumper a wink and a nudge.

"Look, like I've told you, I'm still a married man until..."

"Yeah, yeah, whatever. Suit yourself." He walked away, stepped through the crowd around Bing, and pumped the song leader's hand. "Well done, Brother Bing! Well done! Saint Hubert is surely pleased!"

"Thank you, Brother Ryman."

"Y'know, I think it's time we got serious about a real Venatican choir. And I know just the person Saint Hubert has chosen to lead it."

Bing thought about this for a moment. There wasn't much hope of a choir reforming at Saint Cuthbert's. There would be few other chances for him to make use of his vocal talents while he still had them. A Venatican choir was better than nothing. "I'd be honored to, Brother Ryman. When shall we begin?"

"How about Thursday evening, at Fair Enough Farm?"

"I'll be there. May I bring Marie? And my grandkids too? They're both pretty talented. Beatrice has a beautiful voice, and Baden not only sings but plays the guitar as well."

"Saint Hubert be praised!" Ryman exclaimed, holding up the three-finger salute. "Our choir already grows by leaps and bounds, and across the generations. This is truly the work of our blessed patron saint. Yes, by all means, bring the kids. Bring Marie, bring whoever you choose. A badge of glory for all!"

"Oh! Oh!" Mildred shouted. "I know. 'The Music of the Hounds'! Let's sing that."

Thumper stood contemplating the scene before him. He knew the song, although it had been decades since he'd heard it sung. He remembered Bing forty years younger, standing next to the upright piano in the McKendrick's parlor. Rhetta played as Bing led the assembled revelers, his parents included. How had this practice faded out? The badge of glory BS aside, maybe bringing back the singing wasn't such a bad thing after all.

He found himself humming along, very softly, on the last verse.

Now when I'm dead, please bury me beneath that little hill,
So that when the hounds are running, I can listen to them still.
But just remember here on earth, I'll cook his goose, by zounds!
The man who says he doesn't like the music of the hounds.

Sirs William and Arthur, as well as Saint Hubert, would have been pleased.

Chapter 44

SEVERAL LOUD KNOCKS on Ryman's front door went unanswered.

"Maybe he's in the shower," Marie offered.

"Maybe," Bing agreed. "But Nardell should be here."

Marie grinned coquettishly and squeezed Bing's arm. "Maybe she's in the shower with him," she said softly enough that Baden and Beatrice, standing behind them, did not hear her.

That thought captured Bing's imagination for a moment. It had been a long time since he'd shared a shower with a woman. Perhaps when they returned to his place after the evening's choir practice…

He delivered two more sharp raps on the door. When that produced no response, he reached for his phone and called Ryman.

"Hey, Bing," Ryman said. "We're all waiting for you. Where are you?"

"I'm at your place. The question is where are you?"

"We're up at the main house. Didn't I tell you we were meeting here?"

Marie saw Bing's mouth tighten at Ryman's remark. "No, you did not say that. You simply said at the farm. I assumed you meant your cottage."

"Not enough room for everyone there. Besides, the piano's up here. Marva's got the sheet music all set up, I've printed off the lyrics. Get your butt up here, man. We need you."

Bing clicked off his phone and looked at his three companions. If it hadn't been for the kids, he'd have hustled Marie back to the car and headed home for a mutual scrubbing. But there stood Baden, guitar case in hand, and lovely Beatrice, her innocent blue eyes asking the obvious question, Why are we still standing here?

"It seems I misunderstood Ryman," Bing said. "We're meeting up at the main house. Everyone back in the car."

A minute later they were being ushered through the front door and into the living room. Marva sat at the piano, practicing the accompaniment to "John Peel." Baden went to her, uncased his guitar, and conferred with her on the song list for the evening.

The others gathered in the room, song sheets in hand, included Chet Henderson, Nardell, Mildred and Josh Preston. Sitting in a corner, no song sheet in hand, was Rhetta.

She broke her stare from a very uncomfortable Bing Sensabaugh and targeted her laser focus on Ryman. “You didn’t tell me *he* was comin’.”

“I’m sorry,” Bing said. “I thought we were meeting at Ryman’s. Don’t want to intrude. C’mon, kids, we’d better be going.”

Baden had just slung his guitar strap over his shoulder. He looked at his grandfather with bewilderment. Beatrice, always eager to show off her beautiful voice, flashed a pout at Bing that made his heart bounce a beat.

“You’re not going anywhere,” Ryman ordered. “You and the kids are our anchors. Without you we have no choir.”

“I appreciate that,” Bing replied, motioning to the children to come to him. “But you should have thought about, well… you know, there’s obviously some awkwardness and I don’t want to cause any…”

Rhetta caught the disappointed look on the faces of Baden and Beatrice. Her grandmotherly instincts overrode her personal feelings toward Bing. “S’okay,” she said, pushing up from the chair. “Y’all have your little songfest. Take over the whole damn house for all I care. Just leave me the peace of my own room.” She walked over to Bing and stood ramrod straight before him. “Sing your damn heart out, Harry Sensabaugh.” She looked at Marie, then turned back to Bing. “Didn’t take you long to get past Loretta dyin’.”

“It’s been five years, Henrietta. Life goes on, eventually. I realize the loss of Fergus is still new, but you’ll understand in time…”

“Don’t tell me what I’ll understand!”

Marie placed a hand on Bing’s arm. “I think we really should be going.”

Rhetta’s manner softened, but only slightly. “No, please, y’all stay.”

“I lost my husband three years ago,” Marie said. “I know what you’re going through.”

Rhetta’s smile reeked of insincerity. “You seem like a nice gal. But you don’t know shit. Well, y’all have a good time.” To Ryman she added, “Next time you want to have a singin’ session, have it somewheres else. C’mon, dog.” She left the room and, with Abel at her heels, trudged up the stairs, the image of long-suffering motherhood.

A prickling awkwardness hung over the room as Ryman marshaled everyone into position. Marva launched into her accompaniment, Baden followed on his guitar. The first pass at the song was stiff, sloppy, and disjointed. Ryman remained upbeat and encouraging. His enthusiasm began to dispel the pall that Rhetta had cast over the evening’s start.

After a few passes at “John Peel,” Rhetta was forgotten and the members of the first choir of the Ancient and Venerable Church of Ars

Venatica began to realize that, thanks to the Sensabaughs, they weren't going to embarrass themselves.

As the music drifted upstairs, Rhetta tried to shut out the sound and the memories it brought back. She was born into an age when electronic media was still in its adolescence and people—particularly country people—made much of their own entertainment. Her parents had known neither radio nor moving picture shows in their youth and thus carried on the tradition that every child born into the Keane family would learn to play a musical instrument. Rhetta did not so much choose the piano as it was chosen for her, her older siblings having already filled out the string section. Her talent was modest but her determination strong and with that she achieved sufficient competence to be the accompanist for the parlor songfests.

She still sat down at the old upright once in awhile and kept her fingers limber, but only when no one was around to hear. Her ears remained sharp enough to tell when Marva fell short, striking the wrong key or coming in a half-beat behind the tempo. The mistakes weren't all Marva's fault though. The piano was noticeably out of tune. But Rhetta could not bring someone in to correct that for fear word would get around that she still played. Only Abel was privileged to know that.

She switched on the TV in her room and was pleased to find that TCM was airing *The King and I*, with Deborah Kerr and Yul Brynner, filmed in 1956 when a white Russian from Vladivostok could play the King of Siam and no one questioned the casting. The opening strains of "Shall We Dance?" blended with the intro notes to "Drink, Puppy, Drink" rising from the room below. In Rhetta's imagination, Yul Brynner's bald head grew a wavy mane of sandy brown hair, neatly trimmed, and his thick features softened into the refined face of a young Bing Sensabaugh. About the time Deborah and Yul would have been cavorting in the palace, counting "One-two-three, *and* one-two-three" to the polka beat, Rhetta and Bing would have been part of the post-hunt crowd in the Fair Enough Farm living room, singing the same song the "choir" was now belting out. The room would have been filled with high spirits and the song tackled with gusto, the singers unconcerned with their vocal ability, just letting it rip with abandon, fueled by the adrenaline rush that lingered from the day's chase.

Only Rhetta cared about her cringingly bad voice, and thus kept silent, not only to spare herself from embarrassment but also to better hear Bing. He stood beside her at the piano, alternately leading the others and gazing down at her, his eyes bright with pleasure and his voice flowing over her with a resonance that vibrated to her core.

Then drink, puppy, drink
And let every puppy drink
That is old enough to lap and to swallow.

We've just been introduced,
I do not know you well;
But when the music started,
Something drew me to your side.

For he'll grow into a hound
So we'll pass the bottle 'round
And merrily we'll whoop and we'll holloa.

So many men and girls
Are in each others arms-
It made me think we might be
Similarly occupied.

The others in that long-ago room faded into the shadows and she was alone with Bing on the movie set soundstage. Now she was Deborah Kerr, in that gorgeous low-cut gown, prancing hand-in-hand with Yul/Bing.

Shall we dance?
On a bright cloud of music shall we fly?
Shall we dance?
Shall we then say goodnight and mean goodbye?
Or perchance
When the last little star has left the sky
Shall we still be together
With our arms around each other
And shall you be my new romance?

Swinging her hand in time with the music, Rhetta knocked the remote control from the arm of her chair. It landed on Abel's sleeping head. The dog awoke and jumped up with a start. The image on the screen returned to the original cast.

"Damn fools," Rhetta mumbled, bending over to retrieve the remote. "Sorry about that, dog."

Abel grunted in response, turned around three times, and plopped back down.

She pressed the volume up to maximum and the celluloid duet drowned out the sounds from below.

On the clear understanding
That this kind of thing can happen,
Shall we dance?
Shall we dance?
Shall we dance?

****

After dropping off the grandchildren, Bing was looking forward to getting Marie back to his place and maneuvering her into the shower.

"Was your affair with Rhetta before or after one or both of you were married?" she asked.

He was not expecting that. "What makes you think Rhetta and I ever had an affair?"

"A woman does not look at a man that way, or talk to him that way, unless she's… um… unless she's known him in a certain way."

"Rhetta McKendrick is not your typical woman. No telling what imagined slight she's turned into a horrible, unforgiveable offense. Ask anyone in Crutchfield County and they'll tell you the woman isn't right."

"I'm sorry. I suppose I shouldn't pry. Whatever happened I'm sure was many years ago."

"Assuming anything ever happened."

"Yes, assuming that."

Bing glanced at the dashboard clock. It was later than he'd have preferred. And, despite the luxurious comfort of his Cadillac Escalade, his back was still a bit sore. Perhaps the shared shower idea should wait awhile.

As they drove along the dark country road in silence, Bing thought back to the evening's practice session, standing beside the piano and singing "Drink, Puppy, Drink." In his mind he found himself looking down at the piano player. Marva's face morphed into Rhetta's, the Rhetta he knew so many decades ago, who always gazed up at him with those captivating hazel eyes, eyes that said, "I'd like to know you in a certain way."

On the clear understanding
That this kind of thing can happen,
Shall we dance?
Shall we dance?
Shall we dance?

****

Ryman ducked into his office for a quick email check before going to bed. A long list of new messages awaited. Several of them were from regular posters on Foxhunters Connected, an online discussion group for followers of mounted sport. Most sang the praises of what was happening at Montfair Hunt, including the sporting action they'd enjoyed that Thursday morning. Ah, the word was spreading. Saint Hubert was working through him to reach others who were then passing along the good news.

He noticed a different screen name among the list, the same one from which he'd received the two earlier messages warning him of blasphemy. This time the message was addressed to the entire Foxhunters Connected community, posted in response to someone's detailed description of the good spirits, singing, carousing, and especially the drinking that had gone on during the most recent tailgate.

> Micah 2:11 (from the New Living Translation of God's Word): "Suppose a prophet full of lies would say to you, 'I'll preach to you the joys of wine and alcohol!' That's just the kind of prophet you would like!"
>
> Ephesians 5:6 (Jerusalem Bible): "Do not let anyone deceive you with empty arguments: it is for this loose living that God's wrath comes down on those who rebel against him. Make sure you are not included with them."
>
> Do not be misled! God is not mocked. Open your eyes to the truth.

Ryman stared at the screen. This was no wacko spammer sending out doomsday messages at random. It had to be someone local, someone who knew what was happening with the Venatican Church. But who? Ryman had no idea how to trace something like this back to the source, if it was even traceable.

He had to trust in Saint Hubert. It was the power of the patron saint that was being questioned, not Ryman's. Ryman was just the vessel, only the messenger.

He vaguely remembered what Bar had said, something about messengers and crucifixion. A restless night awaited him.

Chapter 45

BAR WAS ALREADY at his desk when Muriel arrived Friday morning. His presence in the office differed only slightly from the familiar figure of Fergus she'd grown so accustomed to. Both were large men, both smelled of shaving cream and diesel fuel, both used drug store reading glasses to view the computer screen. The most striking difference was the way one side of Bar's glasses floated in space with no ear to support the frame and no eye to see through the lens.

"Worsham's money is about gone," Bar said.

"Are you looking at the bank statement?" Muriel asked.

"No. These are P&L projections. Any way you slice it, the P's are pretty slim, the L's are right high."

"I had no idea you were so proficient with financial software."

"Oh, it was mostly Sheltie Lou put this together. I just fed her some numbers to plug in." The ease with which Bar navigated through the spreadsheet belied his dismissal. "The point is, we'd best start showing some positive cash flow from this place soon or there ain't gonna be a need for any kind of software, nor hardware, nor no kinda ware."

"Yes, we have barely enough to pay Miles and Conway today. I'm sorry you have to go another week without a check."

"Ah, no problem for me. Like I've said, I'm just playing around here for a hobby mostly. I'd be bored in a week if all I was doing was jettin' around with the other idle rich types. Besides, who'd feed my birds if I was lollin' on the beach at Martha's Orchard?"

"Vineyard."

"Yeah, that." He leaned back and the wooden swivel chair creaked ominously under the strain. "Y'know, if something were to happen to Ryman, like a riding accident or some such thing, I suppose the shop would pass to Sheltie Lou."

"Yes, I suppose it would."

"Maybe that wouldn't be such a bad thing."

"Barstow! What are you suggesting?"

"I ain't suggesting nothing. Foxhunting's a dangerous sport. Hell, life's a dangerous game. I'm just saying maybe we should plan for some what-ifs. You know, think about some continuancies."

"Contingencies?"

"Yeah, that."

Chapter 46

SATURDAY WAS THE first Juniors Day of the season. The hunters met at Kimber Farm. Two-dozen young charges prepared for the morning's sport as Cecelia Broadhurst and Dorcas Stanhope fluttered among them, assuring all was well. The kids ranged from those just past toddler age, mounted on tiny ponies, to mid-teenagers on recently raced Thoroughbreds. Most every child there could ride circles around any adult present.

Ryman hustled his choir members into their formation and then addressed the crowd. "I'd like to introduce our first Venatican choir, who've been working hard to sing to the glory of our good Saint Hubert and the wonderful sport he provides for us. If you know the words or brought your hymnals, er, song sheets, please sing along with us."

Janey Musgrove and Dan Davenport stood off to the side observing. Janey videotaped while Dan scowled.

Ryman gave the downbeat and the choir launched into an acceptable rendition of "John Peel." It would have benefited from a piano accompaniment but Baden's confident guitar work helped. Some of the congregants joined in with enthusiasm, others muttered along, only a few remained silent.

The highlight of the performance was Beatrice's solo.

"This is an old folksong I found on the Internet," Beatrice said, her voice small but firm. "I don't know who wrote it, and I don't really know what all the lyrics mean. But I like it a lot. So... here goes." She closed her eyes, filled her lungs, then opened her eyes and launched a cappella into the fast-paced, bouncy ditty.

Ryman's chest inflated a bit more as Beatrice sang each line. Every note rang out as if a young Diana, goddess of the hunt, had descended and was blessing her worshippers with an auditory homage to the glories of the chase. When the last sweet, perfect note faded away, stunned silence enveloped the crowd. There were huge smiles and a few teary eyes.

Someone in the crowd broke the stillness with a cheer. At that signal, the entire assembly erupted into applause, whistles, hoots, and hollers. Kitty Sensabaugh beamed with delight and clapped as enthusiastically as anyone. Bob's arms remained folded across his chest.

When the cheering subsided, Ryman retook center stage. "And now let me share just a few thoughts on this Juniors Day from the 'Foxhunter's Faith.' This article says, 'It is acceptable that those of experience shall, at all times, give explanation and encouragement by word and deed to all young persons, so that foxhunting may continue in the land from generation to generation. He who thinks he knows, when he knows not, is an abomination.'"

Before Nardell could provide the punctuation, Cecelia shouted "Amen!"

"Thank you, Sister Cecelia. Now, if that isn't a clear call for welcoming juniors and doing everything we can to bring them along in the sport, I don't know what is. And notice this article says 'at all times.' Juniors Day is a great thing. And we'll continue to have them. But Saint Hubert would like us to make every day Juniors Day. Whether it's one young person riding along in the hunt field or several dozen, let every adult be mindful that your words and deeds are important. What you do and say can have a huge impact on how a young person learns about the sport, how they feel about what we do out here, and their desire to stay with it so, as the article states, foxhunting may continue in the land from generation to generation."

"Amen!" Nardell exclaimed, beating everyone else to the punch.

And the people—many of them anyway—said "Amen" back at her.

"Now," Ryman said, "let's go hunting."

Each staff member was paired with a junior. The rest of the kids rode in a bunch behind the field masters, the non-jumpers with Mildred and the jumpers with Thumper. His was by far the larger group. Every adult's heart was warmed by the sight of so many youngsters galloping across the fields, jumping fences that many adults would not attempt, unfazed by the occasional fall, eager to remount and continue on, and then gathered around the den when the fox went to ground.

There was plenty of that on this Juniors Day, whether through the unseen guidance of Saint Hubert or simply because the huntsman knew what he was doing, his hounds were fit and trained to a sharp edge, and the territory supported an ample population of healthy foxes willing to play the game. Whatever the reason, the hunters enjoyed several excellent runs throughout the morning and everyone returned to the meet in high spirits.

A crowd of children and adults stood around the food tables, swapping tales of their exploits amplified by peals of laughter and high-pitched outbursts of "Oh, my God!"

Dorcas and Marva bumped shoulders reaching for the same dessert tray.

"How's Chet's mother?" Dorcas asked. "Cecelia mentioned she wasn't doing well."

"She's not," Marva replied. "She's been moved into a nursing home. 'Skilled nursing facility' as they're now called. But we don't expect her to be there long."

"I'm sorry. You know, I lost my father recently."

"No, I hadn't heard. Did he live around here?"

"Arkansas, where I grew up. I… I hadn't seen him in many years. We had some disagreements."

Marva was suddenly grabbed around the waist from behind by her husband. Chet's demeanor did not reflect any sorrow about his dying mother.

"Hey, there, beautiful," he cooed into Marva's ear. "Wasn't that a fabulous morning?"

She reflexively pushed back against him. "It sure was."

"Just watching y'all from the car got me totally revved up," he said.

Dorcas snatched a second helping of dessert. "I'll leave you two alone then."

Chet was too busy nibbling on Marva's neck and she was too distracted by his touch for either of them to notice Dorcas slipping away.

Three people, though, did notice this scene as well as others like it at several points among the crowd. From their respective vantage points Thumper, Janey, and Dan watched as half a dozen pairs—Chet and Marva, Ryman and Nardell, Grantham and Kirsten, Mildred and Josh, Bing and Marie, Crispie and Patti—were all having trouble keeping their hands off each other.

Bob Sensabaugh was also scanning the crowd. He noticed Baden was nowhere to be seen. Slipping off to look for his son, he wandered through the mass of trailers until he reached the farthest edge of the field. He found Baden there, locked in a passionate embrace with Missy Winslow.

"What's going on here?" Bob demanded.

The teenagers sprang apart. Baden stared at his father in embarrassment, Missy swiveled her head looking for a way to escape.

"Is this what goes on here at Mrs. Broadhurst's when you're supposed to be riding horses? Is this why you're so eager to get here on Sundays after church?"

"Um, no, well, I mean, um, gee Dad, we were just… just, y'know…"

"Yes, I know perfectly well just what you were doing. And why you like hanging out here. Well, no more. Come with me. And you, young lady, I suggest you get back to your parents. You should be ashamed of yourself."

He grabbed Baden by the arm and forcibly dragged him along. When they reached the main gathering, where Beatrice was still soaking up praises for her solo, Bob growled at Kitty. "Get your daughter. We're leaving."

Kitty saw the humiliated look on Baden's face. He clearly wanted to be anywhere else than in his father's iron grip. "Why?" she asked. "What's wrong?"

"I'll explain on the way home. But I won't have my son bringing shame on this family. The whole atmosphere"—he waved his free hand around—"is leading our children down the wrong path, setting a terrible example for them. Beatrice! Come, now."

Bing saw the hurt look in his granddaughter's eyes and moved to intercede. "Gosh, Bob. Why not let the kids stay a bit longer. I mean, this is Juniors Day. It's all about them."

"All about them, is it? Letting them get away with whatever they want?"

"What are you talking about?"

Taking comfort in the protective presence of his grandfather, Baden spoke up. "Me and Missy Winslow were making out. Dad caught us."

Bing broke out in an amused grin. "Is that all?" He lowered his voice and gave Baden a wink. "Is she a good kisser?"

Baden relaxed, smiled, and gave Bing a knowing nod.

"Oh, great," Bob said, "just what I need from you, encouraging him. But I suppose that's where he gets it from."

Bing's jovial mood vanished. "What's that supposed to mean?"

Bob shot a disapproving look at Marie, then turned back to his father. "You could hardly wait for Mom to be in the ground before you started gallivanting around. And with the likes of her, already moving in, taking over as if she owns the place."

The color drained from Marie's face. Anger flared on Bing's. "Now you wait a minute. First of all, it's been five years since your mother passed, three since Marie lost her husband. You have no idea what it's like to be alone. And no right to criticize, especially not Marie. You apologize right now."

As their voices rose, all other conversation ceased and everyone focused on the family squabble.

"I will not. It's because of your influence that the kids are turning out like this." Bob looked at the crowd that had formed around them. "All of you. Carousing, carrying on, drinking, partying, singing. And while our church is fading into oblivion. Where are your priorities, Dad?"

Bob spotted Cecelia and Dorcas among the onlookers silently watching his tirade. "Is this the kind of thing that goes on here when responsible adults aren't around?" he asked them. "If it is, you won't be seeing my children here any more. I trusted you to set a good example."

Dorcas burst into tears and ran from the field.

Cecelia stood for a few seconds, watching her employee push her way through the crowd. She turned back to face Bob. "You have no idea what you've just done." She then followed Dorcas as she fled for the barn.

Dorcas's reaction had no affect on Bob. He turned his wrath on Reverend Dan next. "And look who's here too. Figure if you can't beat 'em, might as well join 'em, huh, Reverend? A lot more fun hanging out here than at our dull little church."

Dan took a step forward, his manner sure and his voice level. "Brother Sensabaugh, you're obviously upset. And I can understand why. But this is not the place to make a scene. You've already upset our hostess and Mrs. Hardesty. Perhaps you should apologize and then let the children enjoy their day. You can address this family matter at home."

"This is exactly the place to address this matter. It's because of this that our children are being corrupted and our church is failing. I'm not going to stand here and argue with you. You're right about one thing, this is a family matter. None of your goddamn business. And you can bet I'll deal with it at home. Which is where we're going, right now. Baden, Beatrice, get in the goddamn car. We're out of here."

The festive mood was irreparably broken. The hunters—young and old—drifted away and a somber progression vacated Kimber Farm. Ryman and Nardell waited until everyone else had left. When they finally prepared to head home, Ryman opened his truck door and found a song sheet lying on the seat. It was for "Here's a Health to Every Sportsman." Someone had drawn a thick red circle around the word "Health" and written a note above it: "Be careful for your own health."

****

Cecelia found Dorcas in her barn loft apartment, standing in front of the large plate glass window that provided a full view of the indoor arena.

"May I come in?"

A long, uncomfortable moment passed before Dorcas replied, her voice barely audible. "Sure."

Cecelia went and stood beside the younger woman. They both gazed down into the empty riding ring, staring at nothing in particular.

"Bob Sensabaugh is a jerk," Cecelia said. "No, that's too mild. He's an asshole. A royal, flaming, uptight prig of an asshole."

Dorcas relaxed slightly, and Cecelia was pleased to hear a mild chuckle.

Cecelia continued. "Totally wrong of him to criticize you. Me? That's another matter. I've been serving as a bad example to young people for decades."

"He wasn't wrong. I caught Baden and Missy kissing in the feed room. I tried to talk to her, to warn her. She didn't want to listen, didn't believe what I was trying to tell her. They're so young."

"Maybe not as young as you think," Cecelia said with a scoff. "Sixteen, raging hormones. C'mon, we've all been there. Some wish we still were. Bob's fooling himself if he thinks his son is going to behave like a Trappist monk. Baden's a handsome young man, very personable, a talented rider, and not a bad musician. In my day, that was a great formula for getting laid."

Dorcas stiffened at that remark.

Cecelia softened her flippant tone. "Look, your job is to teach the kids to ride, teach them about horses, hounds, and hunting. You're doing a fine job with that. We've got the most kids showing up since I started this program. But it's not up to you to be their mother hen when it comes to other things. That's up to their parents."

"I know. But I can't just let them do anything they want while they're here, can I? I mean, what if something happens? Something really bad?"

"Like what happened in Florida?"

Dorcas turned sharply and looked at Cecelia. "You know about that?"

"The master there is a good friend. Her reference letter was, well, I'd say it was guarded. I called her and with a little encouragement she told me everything."

"And you hired me anyway?"

"Of course. A nasty situation, certainly, and I understand why you had to leave. But I believe in second chances. Lord knows, I've had several of them myself. And third, and fourth." She put her arm around Dorcas and added, "Next time Bob Sensabaugh says anything insulting to you, tell the asshole to fuck-off. I'll back you up."

Dorcas leaned in to the motherly embrace. "Thanks."

****

"This Sunday morning," Reverend Davenport began, "we come to the Third Commandment. 'You shall not take the name of the Lord your God in vain, for the Lord will not hold him guiltless who takes His name in vain.'" Dan looked down at Bob Sensabaugh, who squirmed awkwardly and lowered his head.

Chapter 47

BY TUESDAY BOB'S harangue was mostly forgotten and the hunters enjoyed another satisfying morning of sport. No other unsettling messages appeared on Ryman's computer screen, nor on his truck seat, and he repeated his seeming ability to predict the location and direction of foxes when hounds went out again on Thursday.

As Ryman's streak continued, Thumper grew increasing conflicted. He needed some quiet time for reflection. He drove up to a remote location along the western edge of the Montfair acreage, an elevated spot just below the mountain ridgeline. Known simply as "The Cabin" to the residents of Crutchfield County, the building was originally a logger's shack that had been preserved, expanded, and renovated over the years. The small house sat at the end of an old logging road that imposed a bumpy, stressful drive even in a truck or SUV with four-wheel drive. But the peaceful seclusion and breathtaking view of the little village of Paradise Gap in the distance below and the endless expanse of the Piedmont stretching out to the horizon beyond was well worth the strain on both vehicle and passengers.

The east-facing view was especially compelling from the rear deck built over a deep ravine. Those prone to acrophobia were well-advised to avoid looking straight down over the edge. From that vantage point the deck appeared to be floating over the precipitous drop to the craggy terrain below.

A paddock formed by rough cross rails adjoined the building along one side. This allowed access on horseback with turnout for the animals while the riders engaged in other activities.

The Billington family maintained an open policy about The Cabin's use, allowing it to serve for a wide variety of purposes ranging from a base camp for the more adventurous deer hunters to a suitably spooky spot for Halloween parties. It was also the site of many unauthorized gatherings, whether one amorous couple or a few dozen revelers. But as long as the users respected the building and cleaned up after themselves, the Billingtons never objected. It was pointless to lock the place. A quick smash of a windowpane would allow access and an alarm would go unheard. Better to take a laissez-faire approach and trust the neighbors to use at least a modicum of care.

For the lone person in need of solitude, it was the ideal spot. And Thumper needed solitude. He dragged a folding canvas chair out to the deck, lit up a cigar, and enjoyed the view. He knew the contour of the land below him by heart. He could see every feature with his eyes closed. Yet he never grew tired of its beauty, particularly on an early autumn afternoon such as this one. The foliage was just beginning to turn, promising a brilliant palette of colors on the verge of full bloom. The Blue Ridge Mountains, misted by a faint haze of aquamarine, rolled off toward the north and south in a seemingly infinite series of softly rounded peaks.

Thumper Billington liked order and routine. This had led him to the classroom rather than the courthouse. Despite his father's wish that he follow the path to elected office, Thumper had no desire to endure the public scrutiny such a career demanded. He preferred to write about history rather than make it himself. Making history, as he knew better than most, tended to be a very messy process.

The revered traditions of foxhunting further supported his well-structured existence. He knew what he'd be doing at least three days a week from September through March. He even knew what he'd be wearing. In that respect, life at Montfair had changed little over four generations and the current squire of the estate took comfort in the steady, predictable rhythms of country living and sporting pursuits.

Now, though, his neatly arranged world was in turmoil, thanks to the imaginings of his lifelong friend and neighbor. Thumper didn't believe for one second that Ryman had received a special calling from a little known saint, even if it was the patron saint of hunters. But, despite that, he couldn't deny that something different was happening. Every hunting day had been exceptional—the best, most consistent run of sport he'd ever experienced. Was it because of Ryman, or was it just blind luck? With each passing day afield the ledger grew stronger in Ryman's favor, weaker on the side of luck.

The streak had to end at some point, Thumper told himself. Not that he wished for poor sport—heaven forbid! But a wake-up call was needed, something to infuse a dose of reality into what was happening. The Venatican Creed, a choir, Ryman's sermonettes on the Foxhunter's Faith, "construing" Crispie and others with the power of Saint Hubert, knowing without fail where the foxes would be and how they would run, too many people showing up for each hunt creating unmanageable crowds and damaging the land, Janey Musgrove collecting a mass of fodder for her next book—it all had to stop sometime.

One other manifestation of this movement troubled him—libidos everywhere appeared to be running at full throttle. From teenagers to grandparents, everyone was looking for some action, and finding it aplenty. The sound of roiling bedsprings echoed again in his ears.

Was he just grumpy because he had no outlet for the stimulation that resulted from so many days of great hunting action? Maybe if he let his closely guarded sense of honor flag just a bit and acted on the opportunities that were there for the taking, he'd be more willing to go with the flow. No, he knew he couldn't do that. The principle of fidelity was too deeply ingrained. He was fine with sex out of wedlock, as long as both parties were unattached and no vows were being broken. Was this a double standard? Probably, but one he could happily live with, as he had before his first marriage and then again between the dissolution of the first and the start of the second.

It looked like the second one would reach its conclusion in fairly short order, with the filings moving along without contest by either party. He should have known the marriage to Shelagh wouldn't work out and he chided himself for succumbing to the hormonal surges of a middle-aged fool trying to recapture his fading youth. But, man, he thought, it had its fun moments while it lasted. And did she ever have one great…

A stirring in the woods below caught his attention. He arose and stepped to the edge of the deck. Something was moving through the trees. He had to lean far out over the railing to see what it was. He could make out the vague outline of a body gliding through the thick pines, moving toward a short open expanse where run-off down the steep hillside had carved out a narrow gully.

There was a flash of brown as a big buck leapt from cover, cleared the gully, and disappeared into the woods again. It happened so fast Thumper saw little more than a blur. He saw enough to know that it was definitely a stag, with an exceptionally large rack. He was certain of that. But did he see something else? Little direct sunlight reached the ravine at that point. Was there a glimmer of something shiny, perhaps gleaming white, between the buck's antlers?

Thumper leaned as far over the railing as he could and strained to catch another glimpse of the animal. But it was gone, already deep enough into the heavy brush that there was no chance for a better view.

Had he seen Ryman's buck? Was there something above its head? No, it couldn't be, must have been a trick of stray light filtering between the pines. The woods were thick with deer. It could have been any one of a thousand big stags roaming the hills. Moreover, it was the start of the rut, when the alpha stags travel far and wide seeking to impregnate as many does as possible.

Thumper grinned and chuckled. "Hell," he said aloud, "even the damn deer are all pairing up and getting it on. Saint Humpty-Bump be praised!

Chapter 48

"CONMAN!" CRISPIE CALLED to one hound that was drifting a bit too far off. The hound begrudgingly turned and blended back in with the pack. "He was a problem at times last season," Crispie remarked. "Tended to go off on his own, babbled some, the other hounds learned not to honor him when he did that. Then, when we were hacking in, he took off a time or two, ran back out into the country. Took us a while to round 'im up."

"He's been much better so far this season," Ryman observed.

"Aye, that he has, Master. But I expect that may be due to how busy we've been, always some fox's brush to be hot after. I'm concerned, though, that if we have a slow day, he might revert back to those bad habits."

Ryman turned toward Conman and the hound's eyes locked on the human looking down at him from horseback. They remained like that for a long moment. Then Ryman nodded, smiled, and turned back to Crispie. "He'll be fine. This was to be his day to show you what he's got, that he can be a valuable member of the pack. He doesn't want to displease you. He's upset that you don't trust him."

"Is he now?" Crispie said. "All right then. Let's see if he can prove himself a warthy part of this magnificent pack o' hounds."

"Where shall we cast this morning, your Holiness?" Thumper asked.

Ryman sat up erect in the saddle and announced, "A fox will be found today in the hayfield just south of Cornelius Woods."

"Is that a fact?" Thumper said. "All right, then. How about we get going? Temperature's already starting to spike up. Pretty warm for early October."

"Not to worry. All will be fine." Ryman turned to face the Saturday morning crowd. "Just a few words before we move off. Article Four of The Foxhunter's Faith says this: 'Every man shall remember that the ground he passes over is not his own property. Whosoever uses not due care and consideration is an abomination.' Now, I'm sure everyone here knows that. Of course, someone might own enough land that he doesn't need to hunt on someone else's. But, dear friends, unless you're Thumper

Billington, you have to rely on the kindness of others to let you hunt across their land." He doffed his hunt cap to Thumper who returned a shrug and a sheepish grin. Several folks in the crowd chuckled, a few called out, "Hear, hear!"

Janey Musgrove zoomed her video camera in for a tight shot of Thumper's face.

"And even Brother Thumper rides across the land of others, such as the Hendersons' where we're meeting today and, on occasion, even your humble servant"—he placed a hand over his heart—"is honored with the presence of our senior master on McKendrick property.

"But for everyone else, Article Four means we must not assume that we can just show up and take advantage of such kindness, for if we do, we will soon lose that privilege. And we do not honor Saint Hubert when we disregard the articles of faith he has laid before us.

"So I must ask that everyone pay attention to this, and please—*please*—follow the proper procedures. There is a reason why we have to limit the number of guests. And Article Four clearly gives that reason. Every member in good standing is, of course, entitled to come out whenever hounds meet. But guests must—*must*—be granted permission in advance, and once we've reached the limit, that's it.

"Believe me, friends, the last thing I'd want to do is turn someone away on a hunting morning. But along with the blessings of Saint Hubert, we must also accept the duties he expects of us. We must be good stewards over all that he's entrusted to us, and that certainly includes the land. So be it hereby known to all our members, if you want to bring a guest, you must have permission. And for any guests who wish to come out on their own, the same applies. Otherwise, well, I'm afraid you'll find yourself the victim of Brother Bouncer, er, Brother Thumper here."

He leaned toward Thumper and said quietly, "Will that do?"

"That'll do, Ry, that'll do." Thumper turned to Crispie. "Mister O'Rourke, Cornelius Woods hayfield please!"

No fox was found in that hayfield. The first half hour was spent casting hounds around every inch of the field and a short distance into the surrounding woods. From time to time one hound opened tentatively, but nothing sustained. Conman stayed in the middle of the pack and never made a sound. Ryman and Nardell, both without their staff radios, remained off to the sides, aloof from the pack's struggles.

At one point Crispie rode close enough to Ryman for a brief exchange.

"Are ya sure about this, Master?"

"Patience, Brother, patience."

Crispie shook his head and rode on, encouraging his hounds with, "Where's 'e at? Get 'im up now. Get 'im up!"

But no fox got up.

Thumper could hear disgruntled murmurs behind him. They'd spent a frustrating thirty minutes standing along the edge of the field, doing little more than watching Crispie work the pack, searching in vain for the promised fox. The early October sun was now fully risen, the air thick and heavy. The riders—everyone turned out in full cub hunting attire of jacket, shirt, and tie—were broiling.

Crispie blew the call for "whips come in"—three quick blasts of the horn—and Thumper joined the staff for a confab. His face red and streaming with sweat, Crispie turned to Ryman. "Master, meanin' no disrespect, but that fox ya said would be found in this field seems to have made other plans."

"Indeed he has, Mister O'Rourke, indeed he has," Ryman replied.

"Then what should we do now?"

"Perhaps we should leave that to our *senior* master," Ryman suggested, pointing toward Thumper.

A flaw in Ryman's mysterious powers had finally emerged. Thumper was quick to resume command of what he considered mostly *his* foxhunting club. "Too open and dry here," he said. "We need to draw along the bottom, where it's cooler and damp. Mister O'Rourke, lift your hounds and let us hack through Cornelius Woods, down to the creek below Jubilation Ridge. I make no guarantee a fox will be found there." He shot a glance at Ryman. "I have been at this game for too many years to offer such assurances." Ryman showed no reaction to this remark. "But I do know how to improve the odds in our favor. And this open, hot field does not work to the hounds' advantage."

"Aye, Master," Crispie said. He blew a quick note to bring the pack to attention and huntsman and hounds trotted off into the woods.

Thumper followed behind, hopeful that some sport would be found ahead and those who had turned out that morning—members and guests alike—would be rewarded for their efforts.

They were not. It seemed every fox in that part of Crutchfield County was either sleeping in or on vacation. If there were any in the vicinity, none wanted to come out and play. Ryman's impressive run—whether through some briefly bestowed mystical power or just dumb luck—appeared to be over.

Thumper tried to provide his followers with a bit of entertainment, moving around to different vantage points as Crispie cast hounds from one covert to another. All he could manage were a few trots, a couple of short canters, and a smattering of small jumps. The horses were lethargic, bored by standing around, and when they did find something to jump, Thumper heard a succession of whacks as one horse after another jumped lazily and hit the top board with its hind feet.

After two more hours, Thumper decided to call it quits. He instructed Crispie to gather his hounds and head for home.

Ryman did not object. As they hacked back to the meet, he held his whip position, keeping hounds packed up behind Crispie, his face calm, even a hint of a smile starting to show.

"Watch Conman," Crispie shouted over his shoulder. They were two fields away from the trailers, the typical distance when the hound had bolted away the previous season.

"I've got him," Ryman called back.

At that, Conman drifted toward the rear of the pack, turned and faced Ryman. The hound let out a muffled "Woof?" The sound ended in a questioning lilt. Ryman nodded his head slightly, almost imperceptibly. At Ryman's nod, Conman bolted. He streaked past Ryman, his eyes sparkling, tongue hanging out to the side, long ears fluttering like ribbons in a breeze.

"Damn!" Crispie shouted. "Conman! Hold up, lad!" He put his horn to his lips and blew for the hound to return. Conman ignored him. "Hold up there! Bloody hell!"

"I'll get him," Ryman said. "Nardell, you'd better come with me."

Before either Crispie or Thumper could object, Ryman and Nardell were away, galloping after the fast-moving hound. They were quickly over a rise and out of sight, heading back in the same direction from which they'd just come, toward Cornelius Woods hayfield.

****

The mood at the tailgate gathering was less festive than it had been the previous hunting mornings. Several guests, citing the long distances they had to travel, excused themselves and pulled out without staying for any refreshments or socializing. Janey worked through the crowd and recorded the comments of those who remained. The responses consisted of the usual malarkey that follows a poor sporting day: you can't expect a home run every time at bat, blank days happen, it was still fun to be out enjoying the lovely countryside, better to be on a horse than stuck at work, tough scenting when the ground's dry, the heat and sun evaporate scent quickly, maybe there will be more rain soon and conditions will improve.

All true, of course. But, still, Janey could read the unmistakable sense of disappointment. Those who had been out every day since the first cub hunt of the season, when Ryman led them to Thumper's east stone wall field, had come out expecting more of the same. Others, persuaded by all the talk of the magnificent performances of the Montfair pack, made a supreme effort to attend, only to be led around for nearly three hours in sweltering heat on what amounted to nothing more than a trail ride in fancy clothes. And not even that great a trail ride.

Thumper's concern over Janey's presence eased now that Ryman had hit a blank day. Home run? Hell, he hadn't even gotten to first base. A complete shutout. That ought to take him down a few pegs. And, hopefully, that's where he'd stay. If all returned to normal, Janey could write whatever she wanted. He might even do the foreword, or at least a jacket blurb.

He was enjoying this thought when she came up to him at the tailgate table. There was a massive amount of food, but Thumper was the only one who seemed to have much appetite.

"So now you've seen what a hunting day can be like when dear Saint Humbug chooses to withhold his blessings," he remarked.

"Is that what you think happened?"

"No, of course not. Ryman's lucky streak just finally came to an end. It was a fun month, I'll grant him that. But he blew it this morning, got a bit too full of himself. Had to happen eventually. And I'm glad you were here to see it." He looked around the field at the remaining hunters and truck followers. "What happened to your constant companion, the Reverend Doctor?"

"He made some vague excuse about working on tomorrow's sermon. Between you and me, I think Bob Sensabaugh's outburst last week embarrassed him."

"Not surprised. Brother Bob made the poor Padre look pretty lame in front of several members of the church. Bing tells me Bob's still fuming over that silly incident with Baden and his girlfriend. He's gone so far as to forbid the kids from hunting. Damn shame."

"Like he thinks teenagers aren't going to make-out every chance they get."

"Had some experience along those lines, did you?"

"Of course. And I'm sure you did do."

"'Did'? What makes you think I'm not still having them? Well, the 'teenager' part aside."

"There does seem to have been a certain air about these post-hunt gatherings. How do I put it? Perhaps 'aphrodisiac' is too strong a word, but… titillating, maybe. Yes, a certain feeling of titillation."

"Noticed that too, have you?"

"We're both professional observers, aren't we? It's what writers do."

"I suppose. But with all the coupling that's been going on the past month, a blind, illiterate eunuch couldn't have missed it." Thumper looked around at the few people remaining. There was no hint of foreplay between any of them. The conversation was light and reserved, posture slumped under the heat and strain of the morning's tedious ride. "Now, though, it appears the tide of titillation has run out."

"What a shame."

"Enjoying it, were you?"

"Oh, I mean strictly from my observer's role. If everything now goes back to what you say is normal, it won't make for nearly as interesting a story."

"Just plain old foxhunting's not sexy enough for you?"

"Well, I don't really know now, do I? All I've seen is what you say isn't the norm. And that only from a distance."

"Tempted to hop on a horse and ride along?"

"Ummm, I don't know about that."

"You can't really get the full sense of the sport just watching from the roads. You have to be in the game to really know what it's like. I expect you've done some pretty risky things in your travels, faced some dangers to get to the heart of the story."

"Oh, I've had some rough rides. The trip down the Orinoco to reach the Yanomamö of the Amazon had its hairy moments."

"What? You've been down the Orinoco? That's the river that damn near killed Theodore Roosevelt."

"Traveling conditions had improved somewhat by the time I made the trip."

"Yeah, but still, if you could handle that, riding an old plug along in the hunt field should be a piece of cake."

"It would have to be really old and really pluggy."

"I have just the horse that fits that description."

"I'll think about it. I suppose it would be a chance to find out what actually happens out there. Even if what I've been seeing from a distance isn't the norm."

"I assure you that what you've seen this past month is *not* the norm. Take if from the esteemed Squire of Montfair, the redoubtable Thaddeus Augustus Billington the Fourth."

"Or, to those more in the know, 'Thumper.'"

"Yes, well, that too."

"I admit I've made some attempts to uncover the story behind your nickname. You've done an impressive job of, one, keeping the secret to a very select group and, two, securing the loyalty of those privileged few."

"It's good to have loyal friends."

"You do understand I'm not giving up."

"I'd expect nothing less from a fellow professional observer."

"I don't suppose I could persuade you to give in without a struggle?"

"And have that dark secret blabbed about in your next book? Now wouldn't that undo several decades of the obfuscation and subterfuge that it's taken to keep that information from public knowledge?"

"What if I promised not to publish it? Just to satisfy my own curiosity?"

Thumper's relief that Ryman's streak had ended and his hope that the Venatican Church would now wither and fade away was tainted with another thought, one he had not expected. He did not want foxhunting held up to the ridicule he feared would result if Janey's report focused on Ryman's aberrant behavior. Yet, as a fellow writer, he now felt a little twinge that she'd lost her main hook. Or at least the sharpness of that hook had been dulled by Ryman's complete failure that morning. And to accentuate the loss of his powers, Conman had run off, ignored Crispie, and blew right past Ryman.

Thumper noticed Crispie and Patti milling around. The other hounds panted in the trailer and the horses perspired in the mid-day heat. They needed to get back to the kennels. But where was the missing threesome? With no radios and their cell phones turned off, there was no way to reach them. It was not like Ryman and Nardell to be out this long bringing in one hound. Something was wrong, more than just the loss of Ryman's supposed powers. This was surely the end of the Ancient and Venerable Church of Ars Venatica.

Janey stood patiently waiting for Thumper's response as these thoughts ran through his mind. On an impulse, he said, "Tell you what. You ride along with us in the hunt field, prove yourself worthy of inclusion in the exclusive ranks of those who know about my nickname, and I'll spill the beans."

A jolt of exhilaration shot through Janey at this challenge. Her eyes sparkled behind her thick lenses. "You're on."

"Not so fast," Thumper cautioned. "There must be some metric to determine that you're truly deserving of this inestimable honor. You can't just grab mane and follow along for a few minutes, then pack it in and think you're done. No, no. Let's say three hunts. No, four. At least an hour each time, preferably all the way to the finish. You can ride in the second field behind Mildred." He gave Janey a visual assessment. "There's enough clothing in the Montfair attic for an entire troop of hunters. I think I can outfit you properly. What do you say?"

Janey stuck out her hand. "I say it's a deal."

Thumper returned the handshake. "Okay then. Deal."

They stood there, hands clasped together. The kick of Thumper's dare and the rush of Janey's rise to the challenge sent an electric spark through the air around them. Neither showed a willingness to release their grasp.

An Indian wrestling match might have ensued had Crispie not interrupted the stand-off.

"'Scuse me, Master, but don't you think we should maybe saddle back up and go lookin' for 'em?"

Thumper let Janey's hand fall. He stood facing her for a few more seconds before he turned and responded to Crispie. "Perhaps you're right. But it's not fair to leave the rest of the pack suffering in this heat. Patti can take her horse and the hounds back to kennels. Throw your saddle on Pennywise, I'll hop on Lenny, and we'll go see if we can find them. Then I can haul you and Pennywise home when we get back."

"I can't imagine why they've been out so long," Crispie said. "We know Conman can do this sart a thing. But I'd a tought… well… what with Ryman's ability to… to, y'know, sart a talk to animals an' all."

"Yes, well, perhaps yet more evidence that Ryman's mystical powers have left him."

"Maybe Saint Hubert's displeased with Ryman," Crispie suggested. "I suppose some might consider what he's doing blasphemy. I'm not particularly religious m'self. But I am a bit, well, superstitious I guess ya might say. Best not to tempt the fates, that's my policy."

"And a sound one it is," Thumper agreed. "Got a few pet superstitions of my own."

"Care to share any of them?" Janey asked.

"I'd love to. However, my number one superstition is, 'Never talk about your superstitions.'"

Movement off in the distance caught Thumper's eye. He gazed out toward the horizon and detected the image of two mounted figures. "Well, it appears blessed Saint Hubert has delivered our prodigals at last."

As Ryman and Nardell drew closer, Conman could be seen strolling casually along behind. None of them seemed to be in a hurry. As they came nearer still, Thumper noticed Ryman and Nardell looked disheveled. Nardell's hair had come undone from her hairnet. Their ties were loose and widely askew. Ryman's jacket buttons were misaligned with the holes. There appeared to be soil and grass stains on the knees of his breeches. Despite their untidy appearance, they both wore satisfied smiles.

Conman trotted over to Crispie and flopped down at his feet. Ryman slid off his horse and handed the reins to Nardell. As she led the horses over to their trailer, Ryman looked around and said, "Where'd everyone go? No tailgate today?"

"Do you have any idea how long you've been gone?" Thumper asked.

"Not really. Time doesn't matter when you're enjoying great sport."

"Is that what you've been doing? We thought you were trying to collect this one damn hound that didn't want to come in."

"No collecting required. We were all together the whole time."

Thumper threw up his hands in frustration. "I don't understand.

We've been waiting around here worried sick about you, all three of you. No radios or cell phones to reach you, no idea if you were safe. Bad enough the morning sport didn't happen, despite your confident-sounding prediction. But then Conman bolts, even though you were warned to watch him, and it takes two of you half the damn day to round up one stinking hound."

"Wrong on all points, Thumper," Ryman replied, still wearing an annoyingly complacent smile. "I said today was to be Conman's day and so it was."

"What about finding a fox in the Cornelius Woods hayfield?"

"And so we did."

"But…?"

"I said a fox would be found there today. I just didn't say when."

"For Christ sakes. This is absurd. And it looks to me like the two of you got into some kind of mischief out there."

His grin widened. "Oh, that we did. Nothing like a rousing good chase, fox gone to ground, just the two of us at the den, blood still pumping, a warm morning, soft ground. Had to do something with all that leftover energy. Conman dug. Nardell and me, well, we found another way to celebrate the chase's end." He nudged Thumper and flashed a wink at Janey.

"You were *hunting*?" Thumper asked.

"You betcha, just like I planned before we moved off, only a tad later. Y'see, this was going to be the day when Conman showed Crispie and all the rest of us that he truly does deserve to be part of our pack. Reynard was waiting for us in the hayfield, sunning himself atop a round bale. Conman would pick up the scent and hold the line alone, leading the pack on until the fox was roused and a splendid chase would follow. But then Crispie announced to everyone that he didn't trust Conman, didn't want him going off on his own. Embarrassed the poor hound in front of all his pack mates. So we decided to change the plan, let y'all see what happens when you don't trust Saint Hubert, when you don't have faith that your hounds are under his constant care."

"And then you went back out freelancing? Had your own private one-hound hunt, did you?"

"Precisely as planned."

"And you left everyone else waiting around, worrying about you, wondering if you all were okay."

"Had to be done, Thumper. Besides, it was really a double-win. You didn't want so many people showing up, so when Saint Hubert revealed his blessed plan for Conman, he also arranged for the whole morning to be slow, for no other fox to get up while you and all the others were out there. So when turnout is back to a level that makes you more comfortable, you'll have Saint Hubert to thank. Glory to his name."

"You're full of shit."

"Beg pardon?"

"I think you're making all this up. You were embarrassed that your precious Saint Hubert didn't shower his blessings on us this morning, because there is no Saint Hubert and no such blessings. Your luck finally ran out and you don't want to admit it. So you let Conman bolt, even though Crispie told you to watch him, and then you've been out there screwing around—figuratively and, it would appear, literally as well—until you thought it was time to come in and try to dupe us with this bullshit story. Well, it's not working on me."

Ryman laid a hand on Billington's shoulder. "Thumper, Thumper, Thumper. Where is your faith? Hasn't Saint Hubert shown you his power is real?"

The hand was quickly brushed away. "Don't give me that condescending attitude. I know you too well. You're not yourself, pal."

"I'm still me. It's just Saint Hubert working through me. You'll come to understand and believe in time. I know you will. But it's been a long morning and we need to get these horses home." He sauntered off toward his trailer, whistling merrily as he went.

Crispie had respectfully stayed out of the argument between the two masters. He watched Ryman climb into his truck and start it up. "Do you truly reckon it's back to normal now, Master?" he asked.

"Had to end sometime," Thumper replied. "And now, Ms. Musgrove, I too have a horse to get home to a comfortable pasture. But first, we should arrange for you to come to Montfair so we can get you outfitted for your new adventure and introduce you to your steed. The sooner the better."

"I'm afraid I have commitments the rest of this weekend. And I have classes to teach all week. Can we do it next weekend?"

"Saturday. We'll be hunting from the Prestons' that day. After a bit of morning sport, we can meet up at Montfair. Will that work for you?"

"Perfectly."

"It's a date then. Well… so to speak."

Chapter 49

WHILE REVEREND DAN was preaching on the Fourth Commandment—"Remember the Sabbath day, to keep it holy"—the foxhunters of Crutchfield County were more concerned about a late season hurricane moving toward the southeast coast. There was a chance it might hit Georgia and bounce back out into the Atlantic. But the likelihood was greater that it would hug the shore, continue to draw moisture from the ocean, and deposit downpours far enough inland to deluge Crutchfield County and keep hounds in kennels for both the Tuesday and Thursday hunts.

The storm was still well away from landfall by that October Sunday afternoon and conditions were pleasant as Dorcas led the juniors back to the barn at Kimber Farm. With Baden and Beatrice absent, Dorcas and Missy had their hands full shepherding the younger kids. Dorcas's relief at getting everyone back safely turned to shock and dismay when she saw a man leaning against the wall beside the barn door.

He appeared to be in his late thirties or early forties. His lean frame was covered by faded blue jeans, a plain black tee shirt, and a well-worn jean jacket. His sandy hair was cut in a haphazard style that suggested an effort to appear artistic. The avant-garde image was furthered by an attempt at a soul patch, a thin wisp of blond beard beneath his lower lip.

Dorcas vaulted off her horse. She handed the reins to Missy and said, "Take care of him for me, will you? And help the others get theirs untacked and hosed off. I'll be in the office if you need me."

She didn't wait for a response. Missy sat dumbfounded as Dorcas stalked across the barnyard toward the strange man. He straightened up, smiled, and started to offer a greeting. But before any words came out Dorcas had a firm hold on his jacket. She pulled him into the barn aisle, then into her office, and slammed the door.

"Why did you come here?" she demanded. "How did you find me?"

"Nice to see you too," he said flippantly.

"You've blown your last chance. I never want to see you again."

"Oooo, that's harsh." He strolled around the small office, nonchalantly taking in the décor, studying the walls bedecked with photos and ribbons from numerous horse shows. He poked at the objects on the desk. "Some old friends back home told me where you were. I thought you'd be happy to see me. It's been two years. You never even called."

"I know how long it's been. But it'll never be long enough."

"Wow, you are sore, aren't you? Would it help if I told you I've changed, that I've been to counseling? I'm a new man."

"You're lying. You haven't gotten any help. And you haven't changed a bit."

"Damn, you know me too well. Okay, busted." He chuckled, as if he'd done nothing more serious than left the toilet seat up. "So how's your little problem doing?"

"That's none of your business."

"Of course it is. I care about you."

"I think you'd better go."

"Go? I just got here. I came all this way to see you. All the way from Arkansas. You remember Arkansas, don't you? A shame about the old man. Sorry I wasn't able to get there in time for the funeral. Did you go?"

She shook her head.

"See. We're more alike than you're willing to admit. I've got my problems, you've got yours. Neither of us is perfect. The difference is that I'm honest about my imperfections. Even embrace them. You keep trying to deny yours. But the truth comes out. It always does."

"I wish you'd leave." It was only a whisper.

"And I wish you'd introduce me to that little piece of stuff you rode in with. What's she? Sixteen, seventeen? Just about right don't you think? Where do you keep that magic potion around here?"

Dorcas was across the small room in a split second and had the man by his jacket. The force of her assault knocked him back into the wall. Several photos fell, the frames and glass shattered as they hit the floor. Although four inches shorter than the man, she was stronger. Her fear and rage increased her power as the adrenalin surged. She pressed him into the wall and hissed, "Not again. Never again. I swear, I'll kill you if you ever try something like that again. I mean it."

From the look in her eyes, he had no doubt she meant it. "Kill your own brother? What would Daddy have said?"

"Don't mention him. He… tried. Tried with you, tried with me."

He could feel her grip slackening.

The office door opened. Missy stood looking in.

"I… I heard a crash. Is everything okay?"

"Oh, fine," the man said. "Clumsy me. I tripped. Dorcas was just trying to catch me. Weren't you, Dorcas?"

She released her hold on him, but said nothing.

Smoothing out his jacket, he continued. "Seems we both lost our balance and hit the wall. Sorry about the pictures."

Missy stepped forward. "Can I help you clean this up?"

He started to move toward her. "That would be nice. My name is…"

"No!" Dorcas brought her open hand into his chest and stopped him in his tracks. "You need to get back to the kids," she said to Missy. "We'll take care of this."

Missy stared in confusion, first at Dorcas, then at the man.

"Now. Go!" Dorcas demanded.

She backed out into the barn aisle, leaving the door open.

"Well," he said, "that wasn't very nice. Downright rude in fact."

"I can call the police."

"Oh, sure, go ahead. And tell them what? Your brother stopped by to visit and you attacked him? Seems like we have a witness who saw you pushing me against the wall. I never laid a hand on you. I know! Let's ask your boss to join us and we can both explain to her why you had to leave Florida in such a hurry."

"She knows."

"Oh, does she? The truth, the whole truth?"

"Yes."

"Maybe she needs to be filled in on a few more details. I doubt she knows everything. Not just about Florida, but maybe some details from your old Arkansas days."

A cold, stern voice sounded from the open doorway. "I don't care what happened in Arkansas."

Dorcas and her brother turned to find Cecelia looking at them.

"Ah," the man said, "you must be the mistress of the manor." He stepped forward and extended a hand. "Enoch Stanhope. Always a pleasure to meet a new friend."

"You have no friends here." Cecelia did not accept the offered hand. "I want you off my property and I want you to stay away from Dorcas."

"Well, now, she is my family. All I have left. You wouldn't deny me my one remaining bond of kinship."

"Consider yourself lucky I'm letting you go and not calling the law." She pulled out her phone. "You have two minutes to clear out."

A crowd of children had assembled in the barn aisle behind Cecelia. Missy stood at the front. Enoch held her in a predatory stare. Dorcas caught the shiver and look of fear on the young girl's face.

He turned to Dorcas. "Well, dear sister. It seems I'm outnumbered. Too bad. It could have been fun. Maybe some other time, some other farm. Remember, I'm not your only problem. Sooner or later, your other little issue will find you out. And so will I."

Cecelia stepped aside from the doorway to let him pass. The children stared as he walked to the parking area, got in his car, and drove away.

Chapter 50

THE OUTER EDGE of the hurricane dumped enough rain on Crutchfield County to keep hounds in kennels through the week. By Saturday the ground was still soggy but not enough to cancel another day of sport.

Ozymandias backed off Thumper's trailer and immediately went on full alert—ears pricked, head up, eyes rolling. It was his first visit to the Prestons' BoSox Farm. Overwhelmed by unfamiliar sights, sounds, and smells, Ozzy pranced around on the sodden turf as Thumper secured him to the side of the trailer. Quickly finishing the last preparation details, Thumper hopped on before the young horse slid into a meltdown and became completely unmanageable.

The horse settled down a bit with Thumper's relaxed, confident presence in the saddle. But he still had some rough spots to smooth out in his transition from racehorse to foxhunter.

Thumper found Ryman just mounting Clyde. "So your fervent prayers to the good Saint Hubey-doo were unable to thwart the storm and save us from canceling the weekday meets."

"You think I've lost my mojo, don't you?"

"If you mean do I think your story about last Saturday, that BS about 'Conman's Day,'..." Ozzy spun with lightning speed, spooked by the clattering of another trailer bouncing into the field. It was only because of Thumper's deeply ingrained muscle-memory, the ability to react by instant reflex, that he stayed on the flighty horse. "Steady, lad, steady," Thumper said soothingly as he stroked the horse's neck. The animal stood still but the tension in his muscles and the near-panicky gleam in his eyes showed that he could explode again at any second. "As I was saying, yes, I think your luck ran out last week. It's been fun, but the show's over."

Ozzy took several quick backward strides; Thumper had to give him a good squeeze with his legs to move him forward. He refrained from applying spurs or whip for fear of how the horse would react to such aids. With a project like this, slow and gentle was the way to go.

Ryman sat calmly on Clyde. He gave Thumper and the young horse a narrow-eyed assessment. Then he shook his head and said, "Nope, I don't think I will."

"Will what?" Thumper asked as Ozzy took another spin.

"Ye of little faith. Think I've lost my mojo, my luck's run out, huh? Okay, your choice. You and your handsome new gray are on your own." He moved Clyde forward and calmly walked away. "Have a nice hunt."

Thumper was too busy trying to keep his horse under control to ask Ryman what he meant, what he'd decided not to do.

The turnout that morning was notably lighter than the massive groups that had been showing up. Some may have been dissuaded by Ryman's admonition to request permission or risk being turned away. When that lecture was followed by a surprisingly and severely disappointing day of sport, the enthusiasm may have fizzled further. And while the hurricane had only toyed with Crutchfield County, compared to the damage it caused closer to the Atlantic Seaboard, the ground remained boggy in the low-lying areas and a few homes were still without power.

Any additional aftermath of the storm remained largely unknown. What unexpected obstacles might await along the hunt country trails? Would there be downed trees? Blocked jumps? Disturbed coverts? Flooded creeks? Some reconnaissance had been done and a few impediments removed. But there had not yet been time to examine every inch of the extensive Montfair Hunt territory. A detour or two had to be anticipated before the day was over.

Mildred's cell phone rang as she and Josh rode off from their barn toward the meet field. After a brief exchange, she hung up and turned to Josh. "Damn, that was Cecelia. She can't come tonight, something about her daughter having a relational crisis, needs mommy's shoulder to cry on."

"Well, more food and drink for the rest of us," Josh said, smoothing down an errant tuft of Zimmer's mane.

"We can't have eleven guests. I invited her as Thumpah's companion. He agreed that would be safe and respectful, little chance to set tongues wagging."

"I'm sure he won't mind being stag. It's just a dinner party among friends, everyone else will understand."

"*You* don't understand. It throws everything off, ruins the symmetry, the balance. We need anothah woman to make it work." They drew closer to the field where the riders were gathered. Mildred noticed Janey taking notes and snapping photos. "And I think I know just how to fix that."

She spotted Thumper off to the side of the field, working with Ozzy, keeping him away from the other horses, hoping to get the hunt started as quickly as possible. She trotted away from Josh and headed for Thumper and the wound-up gray. When she saw how the horse was behaving, she halted at a safe distance.

"Thumpah!" she called out. "I'm afraid Cecelia can't make it this evening."

"What?" Ozzy spun once and came back facing Mildred. "Oh, sorry. Well…" the horse spun again… "no problem. Should I bow out to keep the number even?" Another spin.

"Oh, no. I wouldn't want you to do that. I was thinking, well, if she's free, maybe Janey Musgrove would like to come in Cecelia's place. If that's okay with you, of course."

Ozzy froze. A child on a tiny pony had appeared from behind a nearby trailer. The horse stood transfixed by this strange sight. Other equines were not supposed to be that size. Something wasn't right. Only one thing for a high strung Thoroughbred to do. A warning buzzer went off in his brain; he wheeled around and tried to take flight from this scary apparition.

Thumper just managed to get the animal stopped before Ozzy either jumped over or crashed through the Prestons' pasture fence. Turning back toward Mildred, the horse barely under control, sweat streaming down Thumper's face and already soaking through his Oxford shirt and tweed jacket, he said, "Yeah, sure, whatever. I'm a little busy just now…"

"I don't suppose you gave that hoss any Ace," Mildred said.

"You know I don't use tranquilizers." The horse jigged sideways as Thumper tried to move him back toward the pony and child. The pony flashed Ozzy a look that clearly said, "Stupid Thoroughbred. Chill out and do your job."

"Well, your choice," Mildred replied. "Try to keep from breaking your neck before this evening. I don't want to have to go finding anothah date for Miss Musgrove."

"Who? A date? What did you…?"

But Mildred was already riding away to confer with Janey. "Miss Musgrove, I don't suppose by any chance you're free this evening, are you?"

"I have nothing special planned. Is there something I can do for you?"

"Josh and I are hosting a small dinnah party, nothing formal, just some friends getting togethah. We'd love to have you join us."

Janey thought back to her time spent with the Baka Pygmies of Cameroon. It was a significant turning point in her research when she was invited to sit with them for a meal of brush-tailed porcupine meat and caterpillar soup. After dinner, over the glittering light of the campfire, the old Healer, his dark eyes aglow, told her of Jengi, the forest spirit to whom they perform the Luma dance of thanksgiving following a successful hunt. From that evening on, Janey felt herself an accepted presence among the diminutive, primitive children of the jungle.

She answered Mildred with a humble nod. "I'd be honored."

That settled, and relieved that the required symmetry had been assured for her party, she went to join Ryman for the pre-hunt formalities. Thumper remained some distance away, still dealing with an over-stimulated horse.

"Can we get this show rolling?" Thumper called out in exasperation.

"All in good time, Brother Thumper," Ryman replied smoothly. "All in good time. Other matters to attend to first."

"Perhaps we could skip that this morning. Get right to hunting."

"Why Brother Thumper, what would your great-grandfather think? We must observe the traditions, mustn't we?"

"Traditions be damned in this case. I need to get this horse moving forward. He'll be fine once we're underway."

"He would have been fine if you didn't doubt… but, hey, it was your choice."

"I agree," Mildred said. "He should have given that animal a hefty dose of Ace. But, my goodness, that would be beneath the dignity of a Billington. Well, too late anyway now that the hoss is so excited."

"Yes, well, maybe that too," Ryman said. "But that's not really what I… oh, never mind. Either way, you're right. Too late. It's Thumper's problem, not ours." He turned to the assembled riders and harkened them to attention. "Good morning. It seems our blessed Saint Hubert saw fit to give us all a couple days off from hunting. But now that everyone's fully rested, it's time to once again enjoy the great bounty of sport he's laid before us. Today we come to Article Five from The Foxhunter's Faith…"

"Must you do that this morning?" Thumper called out. Waves of white lather flew from Ozzy's neck and chest as he pawed the ground and snorted in frustration.

"Sorry, Brother Thumper, can't hear you from way over there." He turned back to the group of riders before him. "I believe our senior master was adding his 'Amen' to our topic for this morning." A flutter of laughter passed through the crowd. "As I was saying, Article Five says this: 'He who talks loudly or leaps unnecessarily is an abomination. He who wears a macintosh on wet days or who uses any other device for making a mountebank of himself, or who in any way causes inconvenience to any hound or hunt servant is an abomination.'

"Now, I'm sure that most of you here already know what a 'mountebank' is. But I'm afraid this old country boy had to look it up to see what the word meant. Seems that, mostly, it's an old term for someone who climbed up on a bench and sold quack medicines in public places. But, as I've come to understand it, the word can also mean a flamboyant deceiver, someone who tries to trick people into believing something that's not true."

"Like," Thumper interjected as loudly as he could, "someone who deceives people with wacky ideas about a new religion."

Ryman turned to face Thumper. He set his gaze on Ozzy and the horse immediately stopped pawing and stood still. Ryman held his stare for several seconds, during which the horse did not move a muscle. "Yeah, that too," he said, then turned away, back toward the group of hunters. The moment he did so, Ozzy dipped a shoulder, spun around, and took off across the pasture bucking like a bronc at the National Finals Rodeo.

Janey and several others gasped in horror at the sight of Thumper clinging to the frantic, airborne horse. A less skilled rider would have been on the ground after the first buck. Thumper lightened his touch on the reins and squeezed his legs into the horse's sides, forcing the energy toward the front end rather than exploding upward from the rear. The pasture, however, was not large enough to vent all that power without blasting around the other horses, some of which were already starting to show signs of nervousness fueled by Ozzy's antics.

Zeroing in on the coop in the fence line at the far end of the pasture, Thumper realized he had no choice. It was a major error to ride out into the hunt country ahead of the pack and other followers where there was a risk of disturbing the game, fouling scent, and impairing the sport. No one knew that better than Thumper Billington. But an instant decision had to be made for the greater safely of all, as well as for his own. He pointed Ozzy toward the coop and the horse took it in full stride, landing as if he was on a steeplechase course, chewing up the turf as he sped off toward the open countryside.

"Looks like our senior master has decided to start the hunt without the rest of us," Ryman said. "Well, no problem. Maybe he and his wonderful new horse will get the foxes moving for us, save us the trouble of getting them up ourselves. Don't you agree, Brother Crispie?"

"Aye, Master. Although it looked to me that he's likely to be back at the Montfair barn before we even get movin'."

"I'm sure he'll get the horse stopped eventually. Now, where was I? Oh, yes, Article Five. Talking loudly, what we call 'coffee-housing,' leaping unnecessarily, which y'all know as 'larking,' or generally making a spectacle of yourself, disturbing others and causing inconvenience to hounds and hunt staff. It seems that kind of behavior is nothing new. We tend to think that foxhunters were much better behaved back in the old days, that too many people today don't take the sport seriously enough, are more interested in socializing, showing off, trying to look important by calling attention to themselves. Well, that all went on back in the time of our revered North-Country Hunting Parson who wrote these blessed Articles.

"And, in my opinion, the worst of the lot is what Saint Hubert would consider a mountebank, a deceiver. Maybe 'poser' is a good word for that. Someone who tries to look like a foxhunter but doesn't have the skill to back it up, can't control their horse, and isn't humble enough to admit it. That kind of behavior, my friends, is an *a-bom-in-ation*!"

A flash of gray off at the horizon caught everyone's attention. The crowd turned to see Thumper still trying to stop Ozzy as the horse raced across a distant field.

"Well, well," Ryman said, "speaking of someone who can't control his horse. There's a spectacle for you."

"I can't believe that," Mildred said. "Thumpah's never been unable to get a hoss stopped. Something must be terribly wrong. Maybe we should try to do something."

Ryman sat quietly and watched the gray heading for the woods where the trail led back to Montfair. "Perhaps you're right. I'm about done here anyway. A couple of quick hymns and we'll be off. Reckon it's best if Brother Thumper still has some horse left to lead the field." He stared out toward the runaway animal but said nothing. The horse began to slow down, from an out-of-control gallop to a brisk canter, to a gentle lope. At that point Thumper was able to regain full control. He turned Ozzy in a wide circle before they reached the woods and the horse continued to slow his pace to a trot and then to a calm, relaxed walk.

"Ah," Ryman said, "all is well. Saint Hubert be praised."

"Amen!" Nardell added.

"And now," Ryman continued, "if Brother Bing would be so good as to lead us in a song of praise to our glorious sport and the watchful care of blessed Saint Hubert, Brother Thumper should be back in time to lead y'all off to the chase. Unless," he added with a grin, "he and his horse have already had enough fun for one morning."

Thumper and Ozzy strolled back into the meet pasture just as the last verse of *The Huntsman's Rouse* was concluding:

For the cry of the hounds and the sight of the fox
Will chase all dull vapors away, my brave boy,
Will chase all dull vapors awaaaay.

"Quite a show there, Brother Thumper," Ryman said.

"Damnedest thing. I couldn't stop this sumbitch to save my ass. Haven't had an animal do that to me since I was eight years old on a runaway pony. Couldn't even turn his head to circle him. Single rein stop, lateral flexion, nothing worked. It was like some other force was driving him on, like I wasn't even there."

"You don't say."

"And then he just... something seemed to give and he settled down, came back fully under control. Damnedest thing."

"How about that? Amazing, isn't it? Well, you're back just in time. What say we go hunting? Mister O'Rourke, hounds please."

****

The storm had indeed left some destruction in its wake. But the foxes were still ready to play. A fluffy red got up on the first cast and gave the hunters a forty-five minute run. Ozzy was such a perfect gentleman that at times Thumper forgot which horse he was riding. He only realized he was not on Lenny when he noticed there was a gray between his legs, not his trusty, well-seasoned bay.

After a short rest as Crispie cast hounds into a covert of fallen trees taken down by the hurricane, the second fox bolted from his new hiding place and another merry chase ensued.

This customer, however, was wilier than his cousin and chose to use the storm's aftermath to heighten the stakes. He ducked into thick brush where none had been before, which caused hounds to struggle through the tangled debris. Crispie could find no way to get through. The deadfall that now blocked the path into the woods and the remnants of a wire fence made it too risky to try to find a way around the obstruction. He urged Pennywise on and raced along the edge of the tree line, hoping he could find a way through to stay with his hounds.

Thumper thought he knew a better way. Ordinarily he kept behind his huntsman rather than take a different line and risk interfering with hounds. But he opted to turn the opposite way and seek a path where he felt one might be.

He was right. A short distance along the tree line a trail opened up into the woods. It had seen little use the past few seasons and the overhanging branches and fallen logs showed the neglect. But it was passable, hounds were running just to the left of the trail, and Thumper was betting it would take him and his followers through the woods and into the clearing beyond where it appeared the fox was heading.

The path opened up more widely the farther the hunters rode into the woods. Thumper was able to maintain a canter, pacing the hounds as they coursed through the trees in full cry, hot on the scent. Everyone was focused on the captivating sight and sound of the pack. Thumper had them in the perfect position, a front row seat for the thrill of the chase. All eyes were turned to the left, enthralled by the spectacle.

The trail took a sharp bend to the right. Ozzy negotiated the turn with ease and Thumper barely noticed the change in direction as the hounds' trajectory curved the same way.

As hounds continued to arc toward the path the riders were

following, Thumper saw the fox just head of the pack. He was angling for the horses, preparing to make the bold move of running right in front of the lead horse, or even through the line of horses, putting all those cantering equines between him and the onrushing hounds.

Thumper had seen this done before. A smart, crafty fox has a deep bag of tricks to throw off hounds. He's a master of improvisation and can take advantage of an opportunity with perfect timing.

But Thumper Billington also knew how the game was played and was a worthy adversary for the sharpest fox. He pushed Ozzy forward, hoping he could head off the fox, prevent him from executing his evasive tactic, and keep him in play so the game would continue.

The fox was so close now, his scent filled Thumper's nostrils. In his haste and excitement, he did not notice the presence of another, stronger odor in the air. Nor, with his eyes on the fox, did he see the obstacle toward which he was racing, the other element of the fox's plan to evade hounds.

Ozzy, however, was aware of the foreign, frightening scent and when he saw its source dead ahead on the path, he slammed on the brakes and skidded to a sudden stop. Thumper's momentum propelled him forward, out of the saddle and onto the horse's neck. Ozzy then spun around and Thumper was flung to the ground.

He landed belly-down in a deep puddle on the trail. Covered in mud but unhurt, Thumper looked up just in time to see the fox dash across the trail ahead of him. The fox had executed his plan perfectly and won that round of the game. What Thumper then saw drove the breath from his lungs. A collective gasp rose from the followers.

Only a few yards away stood a black bear, a large sow with two cubs. She was not pleased.

Ozzy fled through the jammed up crowd of horses. He departed back down the trail, his steady manner melted into pure flight. His panic infected the other horses and the entire group joined in the retreat. None of the riders had the ability to stop their fleeing mounts. Thumper was left on the ground alone, his mud-splattered face pointed directly toward an angry *Ursus americanus*.

The North American Black Bear is generally not aggressive, more likely to avoid confrontation with humans if possible. But Thumper had put this old gal in a difficult position. And it was about to get worse as a pack of excited foxhounds, their quarry having just evaporated before their noses, arrived on the scene.

All parties froze in a tableau of fear. Hounds stopped short and sized up this unexpected visitor to the party. Thumper remained motionless, trying to appear as non-threatening as possible. The bear's small dark eyes locked on the earthbound human that had seemingly dropped from the sky right in front of her. The two cubs leaned into their mother's haunches, one on each side, waiting for her cue about what to do next.

Thumper realized the closest thing he had to a weapon was his Swiss Army knife in his hunt coat pocket. Unless Mama Bear needed her nails trimmed or a bottle of wine opened, that tool would be of no help. He resigned himself to his defenseless position.

Hempstead lifted one paw, cocked his head, and asked with a lilting whine, *What now?*

The bear's head turned to the hounds. Thumper was close enough to see her fur bristle and her muzzle curl into an angry snarl.

Hempstead took a step backward. The rest of the pack mimicked his move in choreographed unison.

Thumper slowly rose up to his hands and knees. The strange intruder now looked to the bear like an earth-encrusted quadruped that had risen from the bog before her.

Someone had to break the stand-off, but no one was willing to make the first move.

Something rattled in the woods behind the human and hounds. Thumper dared not turn his head to look for fear the movement would spark the bear to charge. The hounds seemed to sense this as well and each one remained still, staring forward at two hundred and fifty pounds of black dynamite that could burst toward them at any second.

The rustle grew louder, the sound of a body moving over the leafy forest floor.

The bear lifted her head and looked past Thumper and the hounds. Her eyes softened, the bristling fur smoothed, and her muzzle relaxed.

Every hound's head turned and followed her gaze.

Thumper heard a few gentle whines from the pack and could feel the tension ease. But he still didn't turn to see what was behind him. The bear could have been upon him in two seconds if she chose to charge and any sign of weakness or distraction could have set her off.

Another sound came from the opposite direction, behind the bear this time. Thumper knew this sound, the approach of horse hooves. He took a deep breath, relieved that help was on the way.

When the bear turned to see what was approaching from behind, Thumper took the chance to see what had made the first rustling sound. He caught a momentary glimpse of a brown body and the flick of a white tail as a big buck leapt into heavy brush and disappeared.

The noise grew louder from the other direction as Ryman cantered along the trail toward this unusual scene. As he calmly pulled the chunky draft to a stop, neither he nor Clyde seemed perturbed by what they'd encountered.

"Well, well, Brother Thumper," Ryman said, sitting with one hand on his hip, the other holding a loose rein. "Quite a day you're having. Your horse didn't want to hang around and play with Sister Bruin here? Looks like he took everyone else with him. Very bad manners."

"This is serious. The hounds are in danger. This sow could charge. No time for your smart-ass remarks."

The hounds shifted back to full alert, ready to spring forward at the slightest cue. The bear and her cubs swung around and backed off the trail, positioned now with Ryman to the right, the hounds in front, and a bog-bound Billington on the left.

"You're right," Ryman replied. "Gee, too bad I've lost my mojo. Otherwise I could have called on Saint Hubert to help you out here. But, oh well. Guess you're on your own." He started to swing Clyde away.

"Wait a damn minute! Mojo or not, you've got to help me out here!"

"Do I?" Ryman moved Clyde back to face Thumper and his ursine adversary. "Well, for the sake of our hounds, Sister Bruin, and her little ones, I reckon I should do something." He looked toward the hounds and said, "Settle now." Every hound softened its stance. Some sat, a few others laid down.

Ryman then faced the bear. He sat calmly, but said nothing. Clyde was just as relaxed, unfazed by the close presence of an animal that horses are genetically programmed to fear. After several seconds, the bear grunted—a long, guttural rumbling that sounded to Thumper like she was saying, *Well, excuse me for minding my own business in my own territory. Now, if you don't mind, the little ones and I will be on our way.*

She turned around and ambled off into the woods. The cubs trotted along on each side.

Before Thumper could say anything, he heard horses approaching, much louder than when Ryman appeared, and coming from behind him.

He stood up and saw his field of followers returning, Bing Sensabaugh at the front leading Ozzy. When Thumper looked back the other way, Ryman was gone.

****

Despite the smaller turnout, the tailgate gathering was even more boisterous than those of previous hunting days. The excellence of the sport that morning was reason enough for celebration. But few things ramp up the hoots and hollers like a bear encounter. The only one who did not participate in the tale-swapping recitations was the focus of the event himself. Thumper remained aloof, using the need to get Ozzy home after his harrowing experience as reason for an early departure. The repeated references to him as "The Davey Crockett of Crutchfield County" further fueled his desire to get back to Montfair, retreat to his study, and ponder the day's events.

Janey Musgrove caught up with him just as he was about to climb into his truck. "Are you sure you're okay? Bing said you took a nasty fall when the bear spooked your horse."

"Not nearly as nasty as it might have looked. Just a light tumble." He gestured toward his soiled attire. "Appears my clothing got the worst of it."

"It must have been frightening, left all alone facing that bear."

"She was probably more scared than I was. At least we were all equally confused. But it turned out fine. The bear and her cubs went one way, the hounds and I went another."

"That's all there was too it?"

"Pretty much."

"Well, I'm glad you weren't hurt. Um, look, about me coming to Montfair this afternoon, to try on clothes and meet the horse I'll be riding. Could we reschedule that?"

"Oh, yeah, sure. No problem. Another time."

"How about tomorrow?"

"Okay, that should work. Something's come up today then?"

"I have to get ready for tonight, drive back to Fairfax, get cleaned up and changed. You know, the things a lady needs to do before attending a dinner party."

"Oh, sure, I understand. Well, have a good time. I'll see you tomorrow. Call me when you're on your way."

"Aren't you coming?"

"Coming where?"

"The Prestons' dinner party."

Thumper tried to piece this information together. Yes, Mildred and Josh were hosting a dinner that evening. He was going to be seated with Cecelia Broadhurst. Had Janey been invited too? He didn't recall her being mentioned as one of the guests. He had an image of Mildred trying to tell him something before the hunt. But he was so focused on his unruly horse, he hadn't paid much attention to what she was saying. Something about Cecelia? Then Ozzy bolted and the rest of the day was mostly a blur.

Janey caught the puzzled look in Thumper's eyes and after a long pause she said, "Maybe it wasn't as light a tumble as you think. Let's get Doctor Preston to check you out before you drive home. You might have a mild concussion."

"I'm fine. I've had enough concussions to know one when I see it. And this isn't it. I was just… just, well, it's been an eventful day." He heaved himself up into the driver's seat and started his truck. Pointing toward the ebullient crowd around the tailgate table, he added, "You should be over there taking notes. Should be plenty of tall tales getting passed around. I wouldn't believe a tenth of what they tell you."

"And tonight? Should I discount everything I hear?"

"They say foxhunters drink before a hunt to make the jumps look smaller. And they drink after a hunt to make the jumps sound bigger. So, yes, as the evening wears on, turn up your BS meter accordingly. I'll see you then."

Chapter 51

JANEY'S SENSES WERE finely tuned to detect the subtlest clues that told of her subject's beliefs and values. Those sensitive receptors were overloaded with stimuli from the moment she passed under the Boston Red Sox flag mounted on a front column, lifted the brass fox head knocker on the Prestons' front door, and was ushered into the house. There was a smattering of BoSox trinkets here and there, enough to identify the occupants as devoted fans. But it stopped well short of creepy obsession.

The same restraint had not been applied to the foxhunting décor. Everywhere Janey looked there was something that screamed, "Foxhunters live here!" There were fox, hound, and horse sculptures—a mix of whimsical objects and fine art, from small knickknacks on shelves and tables to the impressive piece that dominated the kitchen's island counter. Framed prints, akin to those Janey had seen in the hotel and bank lobbies, adorned the walls, along with photos of Mildred and Josh on horseback—some formally posed for the camera, some action shots jumping fences—interspersed with group shots at social gatherings with everyone wearing hunting attire and clearly in high spirits.

There were throw pillows decorated with hunting scenes. The fireplace andirons were adorned with fox heads and a pair of Josh's old brown-topped boots stood on one end of the hearth, as if the hunter had just returned from a rainy day of sport. Quotes from Beckford's *Thoughts on Hunting* and quips from the comic novels of Surtees were stenciled along the ceiling border.

The powder room walls served as the canvas for an amateur artist's rendering of the local landscape, with mounted riders trotting behind the toilet and cantering above the sink. The hand towels were embroidered with the emblem of the Montfair Hunt.

Was this typical of a foxhunting household? Janey had no basis for comparison. Perhaps the Prestons were outliers, extreme in their expression of a foxhunting themed décor. Or perhaps this was standard, or at least not uncommon, among this narrow culture. Would the home of a golf enthusiast be similarly stuffed with elements of the sport? Tennis?

Cycling? Skiing? And, if so, would such an extreme display strike the objective observer as obsessive, an indication of an imbalance in the lives of the occupants?

A devout Christian might have a crucifix somewhere, perhaps the Praying Hands sculpture, maybe even a framed Bible quote or two. A Buddhist shrine in the living room would say a great deal about who occupied that space. A bag of golf clubs propped in a corner would at least serve as a conversation starter.

But the Prestons' home, from the hound head doormat to the boot-shaped beer steins, left not a scintilla of doubt about what the residents considered the central focus of their lives.

"You look lovely," Mildred said as she handed Janey a glass of wine. A mounted hunter followed a hound that chased a fox in an endless loop around the glass. Mildred took a step back for a full assessment of her last-minute guest. "Different spectacles, smallah and much more stylish. First time I've seen you wearing make-up. Just the right touch. Lovely dress."

Janey had stopped at an upscale mall in Fairfax on her way home that afternoon and, thinking of the royalties her next book would earn, splurged on the first non-discount-outlet garment she'd bought in years. "Oh, just something I picked up."

"Well, it's definitely you. Shows you actually do have a figure under those baggy clothes you usually wear."

"Baggy maybe, but functional for following you folks around all over the countryside. I don't think this little number would hold up very well under those conditions."

A rap of the heavy doorknocker caught their attention and they turned to see Josh open the door for Thumper. His style had not changed since prep school days at Woodbury Forest, from his tasseled loafers to his striped bowtie, with Oxford shirt, blue blazer, and corduroy trousers.

Bing gave a downbeat and on cue everyone burst out with, "Davey! Davey Crocket! King of the wild frontier."

Janey could see beyond Thumper's reddened cheeks and forced smile that he was a hair away from turning around and leaving. Before the assembled guests could get to "Born on a mountaintop…" she violated her observer's neutrality, moved quickly to his side and took his arm. "You look much better than the last time I saw you. You foxhunter types clean up well."

He allowed her to guide him toward the bar as the impromptu singing faded out. "Silly song," she whispered. "Wine?"

"Wine with dinnah," Mildred said, reclaiming her hostess role. "But he'll have scotch for now. I always keep a bottle on hand just for my joint mastah."

"At least I won't have to hide it from Ryman tonight," Thumper said.

"He and Nardell aren't coming?" Janey asked.

"Something with Nardell's mothah," Mildred explained. "Birthday, maybe? He didn't go into detail, just said they'd made anothah commitment, couldn't come."

Janey's disappointment at not having access to the principle target of her research was clearly visible, at least to Thumper.

"Just as well," he said, pouring himself three fingers of Talisker single malt. "I don't need to hear any more about… well, never mind. Plenty of good company here this evening. Old friends…"—he raised his glass to Mildred—"and new…" a tip to Janey, followed by a sip. He held his eyes on hers as she returned the gesture over the lip of her wine glass. "You fringe religion experts clean up pretty nicely too," he remarked.

As the evening twilight faded, Janey began to notice the scores of glowing candles strategically placed around the parlor and dining room. Had she overlooked something? Was there a Wicca-like component to foxhunting she'd missed? Some pagan tribute to the hunting gods?

But then, after observing the others and noting that she was the youngest person there, the reasoning became obvious. At a certain age, direct light became the enemy. Cosmetic surgery was not uncommon among the Montfair crowd. Janey had already seen ample evidence of that. But Mildred knew that replacing the harsh glare of bulbs with the forgiving flicker of candlewicks went a long way to improving everyone's appearance. Mix in some wine and other spirits, and the geniality flowed more freely.

The chatter around the dinner table quickly turned to the bear incident. Most of those present had been following Thumper when it happened: Bing, Marie, Grantham, Kirsten, Josh, and Marva. Mildred, leading second field, had taken her followers on a different route. Janey rode with Chet in his SUV.

"Never seen anything like it," Bing said. "Oh, I've had runaways before. I'm sure we all have. But this was mass horse hysteria. The best rider among us—and that sure wasn't me—couldn't stop his horse. It was like every mouth had turned to iron. They all drafted behind Ozzy, his reins flying loose and stirrups flapping against his sides, as he took off back down the trail. Funny thing, though, was that he seemed to know where he was going. There's not much of a clear trail to follow. And we've all seen loose, panicky horses take off into the woods, ignoring even well-worn trails.

"But I'm telling you, Thumper, that young fellow of yours… it was like he was leading us all out of there, away from the bear, as if you were still in the saddle doing just that yourself."

"Well, I guess y'all don't need me then. Maybe I'll take the day off next time and let Ozzy lead the field on his own."

"But then who would stare down the bear?" Marva asked.

Thumper's only reply was a dismissive chuckle.

Seated beside him, Janey could sense his desire to drop the bear talk. She could not, though, decipher why it bothered him. It seemed, even from her brief introduction into the foxhunting world, that this was the kind of event that would serve as fodder for countless retellings. And who better for that than a raconteur like Thumper Billington. If anyone could relate the events with style and wit, he certainly could. What was it, then, that unsettled him? The embarrassment of the master being tossed from his horse and dumped in a mud puddle? He didn't seem to mind being the butt of other stories, told with lighthearted good humor. Why not this one?

A change of subject was needed. "What did you all think of Ryman's sermon this morning?" Janey asked, addressing those around the table in general.

"Well, now I know what a 'mountebank' is," Marva said.

"Posers," Kirsten interjected. "I think he hit the nail on the head with that. They make a big deal about looking the part, trying to come off as country gentry. But as soon as their foot hits the stirrup, it all goes to hell. They can't control their horse, get in the way, can't keep up, make a lot of noise, interfere with hounds, get scared after twenty minutes and want to go in, all those things that mess up the sport for others."

"So," Janey said, "it seems that the Foxhunter's Faith articles Ryman is quoting have some merit."

This brought a pause for silent reflection around the table.

Grantham was the first to respond. "He's been making some good points. And people seem to be paying attention. The order in the field has been better than I've ever seen it. Even more amazing considering the number of people who've been showing up."

"Why do you think that is?" Janey asked.

This brought an even longer pause.

"Because," Thumper said tersely, "we have a well-respected hunt club with knowledgeable leaders, a topnotch professional huntsman, outstanding hounds, skillful staff, good country, and…" a nod toward Marva "… an honorary secretary who does her job properly, both in the field and otherwise. Any club blessed with those advantages shouldn't be surprised when we have a run of good sport and a field of followers who are consistently well turned out and correctly behaved.

"If Ryman, or anyone else, wants to ignore all that and claim what's been happening the past few weeks is attributable to some long-dead, little known saint, well, personally I think that's an insult to everyone else who's worked hard to make this club what it is."

No one was willing to challenge Thumper's point. He was right, of course, in every detail. But, still, they all knew there was something else happening, something more than Thumper was willing to concede. The sharpness of his remarks and the hardness in his eyes warned off anyone who might have been inclined to debate his point.

"Did you see how well little Alice did this morning?" Mildred asked, turning the discussion to juniors, a topic everyone could agree on. "For her first time off the lead-line, she was just as bold as the other kids. She's going to be a fabulous hunter."

The conversation drifted around to several other non-controversial topics, which allowed Thumper to relax and enjoy the evening. He was impressed by Janey's subtle interviewing skills as she harvested a wealth of information from her subjects without seeming intrusive. She benefited from the willingness of most foxhunters to talk about their sport and to educate those unfamiliar with its peculiar practices, parlance, and proclivities. After awhile, and with the wine flowing freely, he began to wonder how she'd be able to remember everything, devoid as she was of her video camera, not even armed with notebook and pen.

As Mildred was serving dessert and taking coffee orders, Janey tilted a bottle toward Thumper's wine glass. "Care for a bit more?" she asked.

"Please." He watched her pour, feeling warm and relaxed from two glasses of scotch before dinner and an indeterminate amount of wine during the four-course meal.

He found Janey to be a comfortable tablemate. As the years of marriage to Elizabeth's mother wore on, she became increasingly bored by talk of foxhunting, or much else that was of interest to Thumper. Shelagh wanted to talk about nothing else, and then mostly about the superiority of Irish sport compared to the watered down American variety. To her, most everyone on the west side of the Atlantic was a "poser."

In the glimmering candlelight, Janey's skin glowed with a rosy radiance. Her "dress-up" glasses revealed surprisingly long lashes. Her eyes, usually magnified to owlish proportions behind her "working" spectacles, were languid, dreamily half-closed.

"That'll do," he said when she'd filled his glass almost to the brim. He then took the bottle from her hand and tipped it toward her glass.

"I'd better not," she said. "I think I've already had a bit too much. And I have a long drive ahead of me still."

He kept pouring. "The Prestons have a guest room. I'm sure they won't mind. Tell me more about the cigar-smoking shamans of South America."

That bottle was done, and another partially drained, by the time the guests began to leave. The moment she stood up, Janey realized she'd made a big mistake. She'd let her guard down, compromised her objectivity, appeared weak in front of the subjects of her research, and would be risking a DUI or worse if she tried to drive home to Fairfax. But Thumper had been such a receptive listener, so eager to hear about her travels and exotic studies. And despite the amount of wine he'd consumed, not to mention the pre-dinner scotch, he did not seem in any way impaired.

He took her by the arm and steadied her toward the door.

Mildred noticed Janey's uneven step. "Oh, my goodness. I'm afraid we've been inattentive hosts. You're in no condition to drive, deah." She flashed a smile and a nod at Janey's impromptu escort. "But you're in good hands. Thumpah, take this young lady to Montfair and allow her the use of one of your many spare rooms."

Thumper did not object as Mildred hustled him and a woozy Janey toward his car.

"Oh, no," Janey protested, "I couldn't possibly impose. Maybe just a bit more coffee. And I can help you and Doctor Preston clean up. I'll be fine."

"Nonsense," Mildred replied. "You're not in any shape to clean up either. You'd break half my dishes."

They reached Thumper's Jag, he opened the passenger door, and guided Janey onto the plush leather seat. He closed the door before she could object any further.

"Don't you dare take advantage of this sweet young lady tonight, Thumpah Billington," Mildred said with mock sternness and a wagging finger.

"Why, Mrs. Preston," he said as he walked around to the driver's side, exaggerating his Virginia gentleman's drawl to comedic extreme, "y'all know the very thought of such an unchivalrous act would nevah so much as entah my mind. I am appalled you would even suggest such a thaing."

"Good. Now, tomorrow morning, well, that's anothah mattah."

"Right," he replied with a wink. "Gotcha."

Chapter 52

IT TOOK JANEY a few minutes to piece together the events of the previous night and realize where she was. She found herself in an unfamiliar bedroom. It was a corner room with windows on the north and east sides. Lying on her back, she could see a pattern of long, jagged cracks in the old plaster ceiling that brought to mind a map of the Amazonian Basin. She was in a twin bed, her new dress laid neatly on the other one. She looked under the covers and saw that she had slept in her bra and panties. Had she done so all night? Or had they been off at some point, and put back on?

No, the details came back to her. Thumper had been a perfect gentleman. He'd helped her upstairs, led her to this room, pointed out the nearest bathroom, showed her the spare robe hanging on the back of the door, told her to sleep as late as she wanted, and wished her goodnight with the impartial decorum of a hotelier.

She arose, slipped on the robe, and stood looking out the windows at the Montfair estate. Two-hundred-year-old oaks lined the half-mile long driveway. A huge bright red wooden barn, trimmed in white and supported by a stone foundation, dominated the left hand view. Several horses grazed leisurely in the adjacent pasture. Numerous smaller outbuildings were scattered around. The view beyond showed open fields dotted with round hay bales and beyond that the Piedmont lay shrouded in hazy morning mist.

It was a time warp moment, what the historical reenactors call a "period rush," as if she'd been dropped back into the 1800s, a small town Minnesota girl magically transformed to an Antebellum Southern lady.

She stepped out into the hallway and the smell of freshly brewed coffee drew her like a magnet to its source. The path took her to a sweeping spiral staircase. She padded in bare feet down the worn wooden treads, past dozens of painted portraits and aging photos—the gallery of Billington antecedents. She paused briefly at one eight-by-ten color photo of a family scene, two adults and three children mounted for a formal day of hunting. Father wore a top hat and scarlet coat, mother wore a black coat and derby. The kids, also topped with derbies, wore tweed jackets and jodhpurs. The children were arranged by age in front of the parents: a little girl on a tiny pony to the left, a boy of perhaps eight or nine on a larger pony in the middle, and next to him a girl a year or two older on a small horse. The quality of the photo and the vintage of some vehicles visible in the background placed the shot somewhere around the early to mid 1960s; about the time Thumper would have been eight or nine.

Janey continued to drift toward the coffee odor along a downstairs hallway, lined with still more paintings, photos, plaques, and other memorabilia. She noted the contrast between the Prestons' home and Thumper's. Theirs was nouveau, intentionally engineered to showcase a foxhunting image. His was the real deal, the ancestral home of genuine landed aristocracy. No one had consciously set about to create a foxhunting-themed décor. It just developed naturally over several generations, going back even before Thaddeus the First founded the Montfair Hunt.

Paying more attention to the wall hangings than to where she was going, Janey stumbled into the kitchen and stopped short at the sight of a large woman glaring at her.

"Who are you? Vhat are you doing here? Vhy are you not dressed?"

Janey was not prepared for this verbal assault. "I… I'm sorry…" she stammered. She wrapped the robe more tightly around her. "I was just… Thumper… um, Mister Billington invited me to stay over. We were at a dinner party last night, I had a long drive… he… he offered me a guest room."

"Guest room." The woman eyed Janey suspiciously. Her attire suggested she was going somewhere that required proper dress. Church, perhaps? It was, Janey remembered, Sunday morning. "Yes," the woman said. "Is wery comfortable bed in guest room. Big, soft, takes up most of room, no?"

"Well, no. The room I stayed in had twin beds. Rather small, actually. And a bit lumpy. At least the one I slept in."

"Ah, yes, that one." The woman's manner softened. Janey had passed Natasha's purity test. There had been no hanky-panky under the Montfair roof the night before.

Both women turned as they heard slippered footsteps cascading down the stairs. Seconds later Thumper appeared in the kitchen.

"I see you two have already met," he said.

"Only just," Janey replied. "Well, actually, we haven't even gotten to introductions yet."

"Sorry," he said to Natasha. "I should have alerted you about our house guest. But it was late, and a spur of the moment thing. Didn't want to disturb you. May I introduce Professor Janey Musgrove. Janey, this is Natasha Nutchenko, the force that holds the entire Montfair enterprise together."

Natasha brightened and extended a hand to the unexpected guest. "Professor, yes? Is good to have another professor in the house. Is nice to meet you."

"*Spotykać was*. Nice to meet you too."

Natasha's eyes widened. "You are speaking Polish?"

"*Mały*. Just a little."

"You have been there?"

"Briefly, a few years ago. Lovely country, so much history."

"History, yes. Not alvays good history. But much of it." She turned to Thumper. "Coffee is ready. Is also fresh rolls and fruit." She pointed to the center island where a plate of tempting breakfast rolls and a platter of assorted fruits sat. "The professor is staying for breakfast, yes?"

"Oh, no, I really should be going. I've imposed enough. Maybe just a quick cup of coffee, then I'd better hit the road."

"Nonsense," Thumper said. "Did you forget you were coming out today anyway to pick out your hunting kit and meet your horse? You've saved yourself an extra trip." He touched the lapel of the robe she wore. "And you're already undressed."

She pulled the robe tighter.

Thumper continued. "So let's have some breakfast and then plan our day. You haven't lived until you've tasted Natasha's homemade rolls."

"Well, maybe just one…"

"Good!" Natasha said. "Is nice you are staying for breakfast. I must be leaving for church. Voytek is vaiting in car." She moved to the mudroom door, then stopped to look back. Comfortably wrapped in house robes, Thumper in slippers and Janey's feet bare, he poured the coffee as she arranged two plates of rolls and fruit. She saw it as a satisfying scene of domestic harmony, something too long absent from Montfair's main house.

A car horn honked outside and she hustled out the door.

Thumper led Janey to his study where they sat in the two stuffed leather chairs and enjoyed breakfast.

"I can't thank you enough for your hospitality last night," Janey said. "I'm feeling quite embarrassed this morning. I don't usually find myself in that kind of condition. Haven't really since, gosh, not since early college days."

"You're in the big leagues now, sister. They say a group of foxhunters is really just a drinking club with a riding problem."

"I think I'd better try harder to keep my researcher's objectivity, not act like I'm actually part of that club."

"Oh, we're fine with having tee-totalers among us, as long as they're not puritanical prudes. I trust you're not one of those."

"By some standards, maybe I am. Still a lot of old-fashioned, mid-West, Lutheran values in my genes."

"Perhaps that will provide you with a strong enough foundation to resist being proselytized by Ryman's Venatican bullshit."

"This troubles you, doesn't it? Something happened yesterday, something about your run-in with that bear, that you don't want to talk about."

"Let's just say I'm still trying to sort out other possible explanations for these recent occurrences and Ryman's seemingly mystical powers."

"What might some of those other possible explanations be?"

Thumper took a few moments to gather his thoughts and consider whether or not to respond. Janey waited patiently, eyeing him with a neutral, non-threatening gaze over her coffee mug.

"Well," he said, "I figure they fall into three categories. First, coincidence, or simply pure luck. He says a fox will be waiting for us at a specific location, and when hounds get the fox up he'll run a certain way. And that's what happens. But was it because of some sixth sense Ryman has somehow developed—been 'construed' with—or was it just a lucky guess? Second, what I'd call specialized knowledge. Ryman's been at this game a very long time. Maybe he's just achieved a critical mass of miniscule but interrelated details that enables him to read signs that others can't—subtle clues of moisture, wind, ground conditions, clouds, sun, temperature, and such—and come up with the right call for where a fox will be and where it will go. He might not even realize that it's all just a result of thousands of days doing this over more than fifty years, but thinks it's some special gift he's suddenly been given."

A long pause spurred Janey to ask, "And the third category?"

"Despite my natural bent toward skepticism and rational thought, maybe—and it's a huge *maybe*—he did have these visions and there really is something supernatural going on here." He shook his head in disbelief that he'd even given voice to such thoughts. "I keep waiting for his luck to run out. I thought it had last Saturday. But yesterday… well, it seems he still has his mojo working."

"Did that mojo have anything to do with the bear incident?"

"Maybe. Maybe not. There might have also been… but, then, I can't really say for sure. It all happened pretty fast. And I was facedown in the mud part of the time. Anyway, it all worked out okay. And at least there aren't newspaper headlines this morning saying, 'Foxhunter Disturbs Mama Bear and Cubs, Gets What He Deserved.'"

"Is that what you're concerned about? Bad press?"

"Not everyone thinks foxhunting is such a great thing. We usually try to keep a low profile. Publicity tends to bring out the nut cases who think the Thirteenth Amendment applies to household pets."

"That's the one that ended slavery?"

"Yes, that one."

"And from the research I've done the past few weeks, I know foxhunting has been banned in the UK."

"Yes, well sort of anyway. It's rather complex how that's turned out. Basically, though, it was strictly a matter of class warfare, not a damn thing to do about protecting foxes. It's still legal to shoot them, trap them, poison them, or do any other form of harm to them. It's only illegal to chase them with hounds. And even that's still allowable under certain conditions. Simply a case of misguided city folks trying to stick it to those they consider 'toffs.' And now foxes are invading London, killing house pets, biting small children. Go figure.

"Fortunately," he continued, "there's less of that over here. But we still have enough people whose concept of wild animals is based on decades of Disney depictions where all critters think like humans, and some can even sing and dance. It's all fluffy and lovely… until they show up in your suburban backyard and eat your cats."

"And you're concerned the favorable attention Ryman is getting from foxhunting enthusiasts might have a flipside, that it could also draw attention from those opposed to what you're doing?"

"I can see where it might."

"Upstart belief systems always face opposition. The establishment does not like competition."

"Just ask the Pharisees, right?"

"Exactly." Janey's smile was spiced with a sparkle behind her stylish "dress-up" glasses.

"Let's hope Ryman doesn't end up nailed to a cross," Thumper said

"There are different forms of martyrdom, figurative crucifixion if not the literal kind."

"It didn't used to be like this. No one had to hide to fact that they rode to hounds. Hell, there were even a couple of Disney cartoons with Donald Duck and Goofy that poked fun at the sport, but in a good-natured way. If anything, foxhunting was seen as something to aspire to, one of those special privileges accorded to the jet set. And everybody wanted to be part of the jet set. Even further back, in my grandfather's time, it was just something country people did. Farmers wanted to keep the fox population under control to protect their poultry and smaller livestock. It served as a cohesive force for the community."

Janey's eyes wandered up to the portrait above the mantelpiece. "Is that your grandfather?"

"Great-grandfather, actually; Thaddeus Augustus Billington the First. All succeeding generations have him to thank for what we still have today."

"He amassed the family fortune?"

"No, it was already amassed long before. He preserved it when an invading army swept through here, destroyed and pillaged at will, and then established martial law upon their victorious conquest. Many prominent families fell into abject ruin. They had sunk much of their wealth into the cause for Southern liberty and were left with nothing, completely destitute.

"But Thaddeus the First was a crafty fellow. He was too old and infirm to fight, or so he let on. That allowed him to avoid the taint of enemy combatant. He used a mix of diplomacy and duplicity, with a possible dose of skullduggery, to straddle the fence between the defeated Confederacy and the conquering Union. He managed to hang on to all landholdings and had the foresight to transfer much of the family's financial resources to a friendly banker up north just before secession.

"About twenty years after the war ended, when at least some of the neighbors had rebuilt a semblance of normal life, he invited them to join him for some sporting diversion. Most folks around these parts kept a few hunting hounds. They'd all bring their hounds to a meeting location, most frequently the front lawn of Montfair, put them together into one pack, and go off in pursuit of foxes for a few hours. Thus the Montfair Hunt was born."

Janey rose and surveyed the room. He could see her writer's eye taking in the details that painted a picture of the room's occupant. It was clearly a man-cave—dark, dusty, and cluttered. The heavy mahogany desk predated Thaddeus the First, as did many of the other furnishings. The stone hearth dominated the room. The rough-hewn mantelpiece held an eclectic mix of family memorabilia. The deep green walls gave the space a sylvan feel, as if it were a hidden refuge in a shaded forest glade. Framed photos and assorted artifacts created a museum-like atmosphere. Most of the photos featured portraits of racehorses or hunting scenes.

Among the wall hangings was a brace of antique pistols mounted on a thick oak plaque. Thumper noticed Janey pausing to study them. "Carried by my great-great-Uncle Josiah," he explained, "younger brother of Thaddeus the First, in the War of Northern Aggression. Navy Colt .44s, a favored sidearm of cavalry troopers."

She nodded and moved on to the next group of photos. One caught her attention with a jolt of recognition.

"Is that who I think it is?" she asked.

"It is." He arose and joined her in front of the small black-and-white photo of a lady in hunting attire on a bay horse jumping a large rail fence. "She was a frequent visitor here after Jack died. The guest cottage was always open to her and whenever possible she came for hunting days with my parents. Until they… well, she didn't visit here much after… after…"

"I'm sorry," Janey said, placing a hand on his arm. "I remember the news story. Terrible tragedy. It must have been awful for you."

"It was going to be his last run for re-election. Thirty-six years in the House was more than most could have borne. But he wanted to serve one more term, and then retire. He shouldn't have tried to make it to that campaign stop. Lousy weather for flying, poor visibility. But he didn't want to disappoint his loyal constituents. And Mother insisted on going with him."

Janey stood silently beside him and allowed her host to collect himself.

"Well, anyway," he continued, "that's how I ended up becoming the Squire of Montfair, much sooner than I expected or would have preferred. How about you? Parents? Siblings?"

"Both parents living, three brothers. All still in Minnesota." She strolled along, viewing the other photos. Interspersed with the hunting and racing shots were numerous images of Thumper's grandfather with various dignitaries from his era (he served as Virginia's lieutenant governor in the 1930s) and even more of his father with, among other notable personages, every US President from Lyndon Johnson to Bill Clinton. "I'm the only one in my family who had an itch to see the world," she said. "It seems, though, that the world mostly came to you." She returned to the first photo. "We did not have former First Ladies visiting us in Chippewa County. Pretty dull existence, I'm afraid."

She moved to the fireplace and examined the assortment of items arrayed on the mantelpiece: a battered and tarnished old hunting horn, several small framed photos, a few figurines, and one object that seemed strangely out of place. "What's this?" she asked, pointing to a stone ax head.

He reached up and lifted the object, held it in his hand and considered it for a long moment. "Something my father brought back from Australia. He was on a Congressional junket, some political worthy presented it to him as a gift. Are you familiar with the story of the Yir Yoront?"

"Are you kidding? Who hasn't heard of Lauriston Sharp's study of what the introduction of steel axes did to the Yir Yoront?"

"Um, well, in my experience, hardly anyone has heard of that. In your world, that may be as common as a Mother Goose bedtime story. But in the broader culture, I've encountered very few people who know about this tribe, what happened to them, or the name of the anthropologist who told the tale."

"Is this a real Yir Yoront ax head?"

"We assume so. Perhaps the Aussie who gave it to my old man was pulling his leg, grabbed a paperweight off his desk as a last minute gift, figured the stupid Yank wouldn't know the difference. But we've always preferred to believe it's the real thing, one of the last ones made before the steel axes arrived and everything went to hell."

"May I… may I hold it?"

"Of course."

He handed the ax head to Janey and she stood cradling it in her hands as if it were a religious relic—which, in a sense, it was.

"I had a double major for my undergrad degree," she said, "religion and anthropology. I wrote my senior thesis on Sharp and the Yir Yoront. Never thought I'd have the chance to see an actual… one of the real…"

"Assuming it's real."

"Oh, it's real."

"How can you be so sure? We've never bothered to have its provenance checked."

"I can tell. I can just… well… it just *feels* real."

"Speaks to you too, does it?"

"What do you mean?"

"Oh, nothing. Silly thought. How about some more coffee?"

"Love some."

"Seems to be warming up a bit. What say we have our second cup on the side porch. Nice and sunny there. And maybe another roll, and just a bit of that delicious fruit."

The conversation ambled around various topics. She told of some harrowing experiences she'd had while traveling to undeveloped parts of the world to gather information for her books. He recounted stories of famous personages who had been guests at Montfair during his father's days in Congress, how some historic pieces of legislation had been hammered out on that very porch. She talked of her family back in Minnesota, he filled her in on his two children and his sisters, Myrna in LA and Claudette in Manhattan.

The absence of any adornment on Janey's left ring finger combined with not even a cursory reference to a spouse (past or present), significant other, or children told Thumper all he needed to know.

He noticed she'd eyed his wedding ring several times, but had said nothing. The moment was finally right.

"And *Mrs.* Billington?" she asked.

"As you know, my mother was on the plane…"

"Not *that* Mrs. Billington, the current one."

He held up his hand and looked at the ring. "I suppose she's still the current one. Which is why I continue to wear the ring. Gentlemanly honor, don't you know. Or maybe lawyerly prudence." He gave her a short explanation of the situation with Shelagh. "I expect this will be resolved fairly soon," he concluded, "but no definite timeframe yet."

"And the Mrs. Billington before that?" She added hastily, "If I'm not prying."

"Our twenty year union is best described by Rodney Dangerfield's line in *Back to School*: 'I'm an Earth sign. She's a Water sign. Together we made mud.'"

"Yet you stayed together for twenty years?"

"About nineteen years longer than we should have. She eventually had her fill of Virginia country life, went back to California, the Hollywood environs, where she belongs. Our son went with her. Our daughter, the future Chief Justice of the United States, stayed."

They heard a car pulling up the driveway and a few minutes later Natasha appeared on the porch.

"Ah, you are still here. Breakfast is good, yes? Perhaps you are staying for lunch too?"

Janey looked at her watch. "My goodness, I didn't realize it was getting so late. I hope I haven't overstayed my welcome." She stood up. "Here, let me help with that," she said to Natasha as she began picking up the mugs and plates.

"Oh, no, please. You are guest. You are not needing to help clean up. Is my job."

As they followed Natasha back to the kitchen, she began to sing her favorite Polish folk song, the one about a man from Krakow, seven horses, a rusty sword, a red woolen cap, and I'll kick your ass if you mess with me. To Thumper's surprise, and even more so to Natasha's, Janey started to sing along with her, word-for-word, in reasonably decent Polish.

Natasha stopped, turned around, and said, "You are knowing this song?"

"I visited an elementary school while I was there and the children taught it to me. We sang it over and over again, many times. I've never forgotten it."

Natasha stood staring at Janey with a pleasantly stunned expression. Finally she said, "You are coming back again, yes?"

"If Mister Billington wishes, yes, certainly."

"Mister Billington is wishing, yes," Thumper said. "But today's visit is far from over." He stood squarely in front of Janey and placed his hands on her robed shoulders. Feeling vulnerable, she wished she had on more than just bra and panties under the loose-fitting robe. His closeness, the pressure of his hands, the tang of coffee on his breath, rekindled the sense of intoxication she'd felt the night before. "Time to go upstairs. There's something else we need to do."

Natasha's happy grin turned into a curious scowl.

Janey tried not to look directly into Thumper's eyes. "Why, Mister

Billington, whatever do you have in mind?"

"Getting you ready to meet your horse, of course." He spun her around toward the hallway. "To the attic!"

Natasha breathed a sigh of relief and went about cleaning up the breakfast dishes.

Thumper led Janey from the kitchen, upstairs, past the bedrooms to a door at the far end of the hallway that Janey had not noticed before. Opening the door, he motioned for her to follow him up the narrow set of bare wooden stairs. They emerged into a large attic filled with a jumbled array of trunks, boxes, and more than two hundred years worth of Billington cast-offs.

"You're almost exactly the same size and shape as my younger sister. At least her shape before she moved to New York, got married, and had kids. Her entire riding wardrobe, from formal hunting kit to beat-up old barn gear, is stored away up here. Unlikely she'll ever be able to fit into it again. Might as well put some of it to good use."

Thumper rummaged through his sister's stuff and came up with a pair of worn but serviceable breeches, denim shirt, paddock boots, socks, half chaps, a faded Barbour jacket, and a helmet. "This will do for starters. Then we'll see about formal hunting kit."

"I thought you said the plan for today was to meet the horse. Why do I need all this just to meet him?"

"What? Did you think I meant say 'Hello,' rub his nose and give him a carrot? The only way to 'meet' a horse is to hop on and ride, see how well the two of you get along. C'mon." He hustled Janey down the attic stairs and dropped the load on the spare twin bed in the guest room. "I hope the boots aren't too tight. I'll call Javier and have him start getting the horse ready. Let me know if you have any problems with any of this stuff."

Fifteen minutes later Janey stepped into the hallway, feeling as out of place as she had among the Igbo people of Burkino Faso. Only there she'd at least been wearing her own clothes. The feel of a stranger's garments, tainted by the scent of the musty attic where they'd long been stored, heightened the sense of foreignness, as if she was not only wearing someone else's clothes but had put on another person's skin. The helmet, with its tight chinstrap, felt especially strange.

Thumper was dressed and waiting for her. He eyed her up and down, then grasped the helmet and twisted it back and forth. "That'll do. But you don't really need to have that on just yet. Unless you're afraid you might fall down the stairs."

She gratefully removed the strange headgear. "The boots feel a little odd. But I think I can manage to stay upright."

They proceeded to the main barn where Javier was brushing off a thickly built chestnut horse who stood calmly in the cross-ties, almost dozing. The animal looked enormous to Janey. But he seemed docile enough, with a kind eye.

"This is Buffoon's Ballet," Thumper said by way of introduction. "Bee for short. He's semi-retired now, a little too old to keep up with the long, fast-paced hunts that we usually have as the season moves along. But he's a steady old guy, knows his job, pretty much puts the rider on autopilot."

"I don't suppose we could start with something smaller."

"Nonsense. Actually, it's the smaller horses that are more likely to be difficult. Big guys like Bee tend to be the gentle giants."

"He's awfully wide."

"That's a good thing. You'll have to get waaaay over to one side before you can fall off."

When Javier had finished grooming and tacking the horse, Thumper motioned to Janey to put on her helmet and then led the horse out to the ring. Janey followed obediently—if somewhat apprehensively—behind.

Thumper gave her a basic introductory lesson. He moved her legs into the correct position, heels down and each aligned with hip and shoulder. He placed his hands on hers to guide her into the correct rein control and pressure, squeezing her hands to show how to communicate through the horse's mouth without pulling or jerking. He walked along beside Bee, his hand on Janey's thigh like a father preparing to release a child on her first two-wheel bike ride. He told her how to transition the horse into a trot and then stood back and watched her ride around him in a circle.

The animal's power flowed into Janey's senses. It took her a few minutes to grasp the rhythm of posting to the trot, but once she'd mastered that, the ride felt like floating along on a large wave.

"It's not about strength," Thumper said. "It's about balance and flexibility, sensing the creature underneath you and feeling the cues that pass between you and the horse. The best riders are the ones with the sensitivity to pick up on the subtlest signal and respond positively. When it's good it's like dancing. When it's great, it's like making love."

Janey wasn't sure if her blush was caused by Thumper's comment or simply the rush of this new experience. Either way, she liked it. And she wanted more.

When it came time to stop, Thumper stood next to the horse and said, "You did great. You may not have done much riding before, at least not much by our standards, but you definitely have a feel for it. You just might earn inclusion in the nickname club yet."

"I fully intend to do so. No matter what it takes."

"I admire your pluck. Now swing your right leg over his rump, then kick your left foot out of the stirrup and slide down with your right hip against the horse's side. I'll steady you. It's a long way down off this big fellah."

It was indeed a long drop, longer than Janey expected. She landed hard and began to stumble forward. Thumper caught her and pulled her toward him. She half-turned and found herself with her hands on his chest and his arms wrapped tightly around her waist.

He showed no inclination to release her.

Several seconds passed in silence before she pressed her hands against his chest and pushed herself back. Thumper read the signal and let her go.

As they walked to the barn, Janey stroked the horse's muzzle and said, "Interesting name, Buffoon's Ballet. From the Prokofiev work?"

Thumper halted in his tracks and looked at Janey. "You know that work? Nobody knows that work. Well, maybe about as many as know who Lauriston Sharp was."

"I like to listen to classical music when I'm writing. But how'd this big, lovely fellah get stuck with that name?"

"He was kind of a clown when he was a colt, a big teddy bear who loved to gambol around in the pasture. But being bigger than the other colts, he looked kind of silly doing it. My father was very knowledgeable about classical music. He came up with the name. It's not his registered name, but he's been just 'Bee' for so long I can't recall offhand what's on his Jockey Club papers. And his racing career lasted about half a furlong. It was quickly decided he was destined for a career somewhere other than the racetrack. The hunt field turned out to be much more suitable for his temperament and speed, or lack thereof."

They reached the barn where Javier was waiting to take the horse.

"You looked very good, ma'am," Javier remarked. "I was watching."

"Now that's high praise," Thumper said. "Javier is one of the best horsemen I've ever known. If Javier says you looked good, that's worth something."

"I don't know how I looked, but it certainly felt good."

Thumper turned to Javier. "What do you think? Is she ready for a little action in the hunt field?"

"Sure. Why not? Only way to know for sure is to go out and give it a try. Same as starting a green horse."

"Okay then," Thumper said. "Next Saturday you start earning your points to join the nickname club. Let's go get your cub hunting kit together. Back to the attic!"

Chapter 53

BOB SENSABAUGH GRIPPED Reverend Dan's hand and pumped it forcefully. "Excellent sermon. 'Honor your father and mother.' How timely that came up on your Ten Commandments list today."

"Perhaps more timely than you know." Dan held the offered hand firmly, not letting go when Bob was clearly ready to move along. "Would you mind staying for just a few minutes? There's something I'd like to discuss with you… in private."

Bob's brow knitted into a questioning wrinkle but he nodded his assent. "Sure. I'll just wait outside." He continued out the door where Kitty and the children waited in the churchyard.

When the last parishioner had taken her leave, Dan called Bob back inside the church. He strolled down the center aisle. An uncomfortably curious Bob Sensabaugh trailed behind. When they reached the altar, Dan said, "I wanted to catch you out of earshot of the children. Baden came to me yesterday to ask if I'd intercede on his behalf."

Bob's posture stiffened. "You? Intercede on behalf of my son? What about?"

"Look," Dan said soothingly, "I didn't seek this. I'm not one to interfere in family matters. Unless, of course, there's some direct connection to the church."

"And there is in this case?"

"It seems so. The gist of it is that your children are upset that you won't let them go foxhunting and have forbidden them to return to Mrs. Broadhurst's. Baden asked me if I'd talk to you about this, try to convince you to let them return."

"What business if that of yours? And what does it have to do with this church? If anything, I'd think you'd want to keep every child in Crutchfield County away from that travesty. Bad enough it's corrupting the morals of young people with all that carousing and carrying on. But with what McKendrick's doing… why, it's… it's blasphemy. Surely you don't endorse all that?"

"No, I don't. I find it very troubling as well."

"Troubling? Is that all? How about an outright perversion of the true faith? Shouldn't you be doing everything possible to try to stop this?"

"In my own way, I believe I am."

"Well, I certainly don't see it."

"And perhaps that's just as well."

"You said Baden's request had some connection to the church."

"Yes, he asked me to tell you that if you'll lift the restrictions, they'll be willing to sing in church on Sunday mornings."

Bob pondered this for a long moment before he replied. "A quid pro quo, is it? My sixteen year old son trying to bargain with me, and going through you as his mouthpiece."

"I felt it was my duty to convey the request, as the young man came to me seeking help. I am not advocating for or against him. As the parent—and one I know only wants the best for his children—the decision is yours. I won't deny that it would be a wonderful blessing to have those two talented young people enhance our humble services by raising their voices in praise to our Lord." He smiled warmly and revealed a hint of blue-collar upbringing Bob had never before seen in the pious Reverend Doctor. "Heck, I suppose you folks get a bit tired of hearing nothing but me prattle on about this-and-that every Sunday morning."

"I'll think about it, Reverend, and will pray earnestly for the Lord's guidance. I agree that I'd like nothing more than to hear my children singing in church. Maybe it would even inspire others and we could form a small choir. But the question is at what cost?"

"And for how long?" Dan asked. "I assume we're still on a track to wind this operation down soon."

Bob shrugged. "Oh, yes, that. Well, things have been looking up the past few weeks. Still a long way to go to be out of the woods. But attendance has been better and the offerings are on an upward trend."

"So I've noticed. But I'm leaving all that to the Lord. I'm just doing what I feel he's calling me to do. However things turn out, it's ultimately in His hands."

"Amen."

Dan returned a brisk nod and marched off to the rectory. His purple-trimmed white robe flowed around his gangly form.

Bob stood at the altar and watched him go. A quarter of a century earlier he'd envisioned himself wearing robes like that. He'd been sure the Lord was calling him to the ministry. It was as clear as if he heard an audible voice speaking to him. But he was the only heir to the family banking business. Both his father and grandfather pressured him to follow in their footsteps. They could not envision Crutchfield County Bank without a Sensabaugh at the helm. Neither, for that matter, could most residents of Crutchfield County. So he chose family duty over service to God.

Chapter 54

A SMALL GROUP turned out for Tuesday's meet. Bing was in Brookside helping Marie pack up the essentials required to make chez Sensabaugh her primary residence. Marva was with Chet attending to details for his mother's funeral. Grantham and Kirsten were at a meeting of North American Fox Chasers Association officials in their Northeast region. Work duties had finally caught up with several of those who had used up their leave to go chasing foxes on weekday mornings. Cecelia was showing a property to a prospective client, but Dorcas was there with one of her employer's young horses in training.

Crispie cast hounds into the first covert as Ryman directed. The pack opened almost immediately. But it was a different cry, not the familiar enthusiastic certainty of a hot line of fox scent; more frantic, excitedly unsure. Hounds surged from covert and ran to the right where Ryman held his position. He fell in with them and paced the lead hounds as they ran hard through the woods.

The odd cry continued, intensifying as they crested a small rise and flooded down the hillside. Ryman noticed that the line appeared to be straight, no ducking or weaving, no evasive moves. It also avoided obvious obstacles where a fox might squeeze through knowing the larger hounds could not follow. It remained in the woods, but did not veer into the heavier brush, so hounds and mounted riders could stay on the line.

Ryman began to suspect they were on a coyote. But when he focused on Hempstead, who was in the lead, he sensed a different message. Confusion blended with the drive of the pack. *Fox*, the hound told him, *but horse scent too.*

As hounds surged around a sharp bend in the trail, their cry rose into a frantic cacophony of baying—the crescendo that signals the climax of the chase, that the pack is about to be upon their quarry.

Then every hound fell silent.

Ryman rounded the turn and Token skidded to a halt, only just avoiding contact with several hounds. The sudden stop sent Ryman forward onto the horse's neck. His hunt cap slid down over his eyes. As he righted himself into the saddle and pushed the brim of his cap back, his first thought was of the hounds. He looked around Token's feet to assure no hound had been hit. None had. Each one stood four square, staring at the sight before them.

When Ryman finally looked up, he beheld a curious image. Hanging from an old wooden deer hunting tree stand in a sturdy oak tree was a large plush stuffed toy fox. A length of baling twine was tied around its neck and it swayed gently in the morning breeze. A piece of poster board was pinned across the toy's belly. It bore a message large enough for Ryman to read from where he sat:

Psalm 63:9-10:
But those that seek my soul, to destroy it, shall go into the lower parts of the earth.
They shall fall by the sword: they shall be a portion for foxes.
The Defender of the Faith

The others arrived and a jumble of horses stopped short just as Token had. No one came off, but several riders were jostled and a few only barely kept from tumbling out of the saddle. Hounds, horses, and hunters were all frozen in stunned silence, every eye on this strange figure and its unsettling message.

Crispie was the first to find his voice. "Drag line. Someone's laid a line of scent, from that first covert to this tree. They wanted us to find this. All of us."

"What do you think it means?" Ryman asked.

Thumper squeezed Lenny forward and drew up alongside Ryman. "It means someone has a problem with your Venatican church idea."

"But who? Who could have done something like this?"

"Someone who knows the territory, how to lay a drag line. And, apparently, knows at least one Bible verse. Or how to Google one to suit his needs."

Nardell joined them, her face the palest Thumper had ever seen it. "I'm calling the police," she said, pulling out her cell phone and turning it on.

"Don't," Thumper commanded.

Her finger hovered over the 911 key. "Why not? This is a threat. Whoever's doing this has to be stopped. And it's at least trespassing."

"Maybe so. But it's on my land, so I get to make that decision. And I say we don't need something like this getting blabbed around. We file a police report, it goes public. Do you really want to see this in the *Crutchfield Courier*? Or on the evening news?"

"Well, no, I don't want that... but... I mean, if someone's threatening Ryman..."

"Thumper's right," Ryman said. "Just some wacko acting out on his demented ideas." He smiled broadly and sat up in his saddle, head held high. "No worries, folks. Probably just some kids pulling a silly prank. Halloween's coming up soon, right? Just a little practice at how to scare people. Best no one mentions this. Okay?"

The small band of followers all nodded in befuddled agreement.

"Mister O'Rourke," Ryman continued, "let's lift hounds and get them on a real line of scent, have ourselves some sport this morning."

"That okay with you, Master?" Crispie asked Thumper.

"Yes, certainly. But we should get this damn thing down first." He moved Lenny over toward the hanging fox, pulled out his Swiss Army knife, and cut the twine. He handed the stuffed toy to Ryman. "Here. This can be the first relic when historians study the rise and fall of your Venatican Church. You should keep it in a place of honor."

Ryman took it and tied the remaining piece of twine to his pistol holster. "Thank you, Brother Thumper. I will treasure it always."

As Ryman started to move off, Thumper caught his arm and said quietly, "You know this is no silly prank. Someone means business. For your own sake, you need to back off from this Saint Hubert crap."

Ryman put on the bravest face he could. "Saint Hubert will be my shield. I must be strong, and I'll find my strength in him."

"You keep this up, and you just might find your grave. And hear this, my oldest, bestest friend—I won't let you take Montfair Hunt down with you. You got that?"

"Ah, ye of little faith. I pray that our blessed Saint Hubert opens your eyes to the truth. Or maybe next time, I'll just let the bear eat you."

Chapter 55

RYMAN DID NOT recognize the rapping on his cottage door. Unexpected visitors were a rarity. He set down *Notitia Venatica* on the corner of his cluttered desktop and went to see who was there. He found Dorcas Stanhope on his front step.

"May I come in?"

"Yeah, sure." He motioned her inside. "What brings you over this way?"

She walked in hesitantly and stood looking around the small living room. "What a nice place you have here. So cozy, in a comfy, homey kind of way."

"All Nardell's doing. It was pretty much a wreck when it was just me."

"A woman's touch always helps." She walked through the room, lightly fingering the furniture, absorbing the feel of the place. She closed her eyes. "But it's manly too."

Ryman remained by the door, watching her. "Is there something I can do for you, Dorcas?"

She came back to him slowly, placed a hand on his arm, and gazed up at him with a look of concern. "I'm worried about you. I know you and Thumper said not to mention anything about yesterday, that it was probably just a prank. But I don't think so. I think someone's not very happy with what you're doing."

Ryman scoffed. "Ah, I can't let something like that bother me. Saint Hubert has called me to my mission and I must push forward."

Her grip on his arm tightened and her expression took on a more anguished cast. "You could be in real danger. I'd hate to see anything happen to you."

"Uh, well, that's real nice of you. Maybe you could pray to Saint Hubert, ask him to keep me safe."

She moved closer to him and slipped her arms around his waist. "I will." Her voice lowered to a whisper. "I'd do anything for you. Anything."

Ryman knew well the look of a woman's invitation. She'd clearly come for more than just to express concerns for his safety. He responded involuntarily, sliding his hands to her lower back. He felt his crotch twitch as blood flowed and his undershorts became tight. She was an attractive woman, her body firm but compliant. Nardell was starting to show some age as the daunting mark of six-oh loomed just a few short years ahead. Dorcas retained a more youthful aura, maybe not college-girl-young but still well shy of AARP vintage. He recalled a Groucho Marx line Thumper was fond of quoting about Shelagh: "You're only as old as the women you feel."

She pressed against him closer, increasing his arousal. All he had to do was lean over and kiss her, and the rest would take care of itself.

Nardell had appointments late into the afternoon. Did Dorcas know that?

Hell, he thought, I'm not married. This wouldn't be breaking any vow. We never said we'd be…

Dorcas was tired of waiting. She raised up on her toes, placed a hand behind Ryman's head, and drew his face down to hers.

She tasted soft and eager.

He was just starting to slip his hands down to her buttocks when she suddenly pulled back and pushed him away.

"I'm sorry. I'm so sorry," she said. Her voice quivered and she covered her flushed face with her hands. "I don't know what… I just came here because I'm worried about you, that's all. Something just came over me. I'm so embarrassed. Please… please forgive me."

"Oh, sure, yeah. Me too. I shouldn't have… I mean, it was as much my fault. How about we just forget this? What do you say?"

She brushed away tears. "I'd better go. Shouldn't have come." She stepped around Ryman toward the door. With her hand on the knob, she turned back to face him. "I don't want you to fall by the sword, to be a portion for foxes. Just be careful, watch out for yourself. Okay?"

"Okay, I will."

As she closed the door and walked quickly to her truck, Ryman looked over at Wycroft. He'd been watching the whole encounter from his spot on the sofa. "What the hell just happened here?"

"Mmmph."

Chapter 56

THURSDAY'S HUNT SAW no weakening of Ryman's resolve nor blip in the run of fabulous hunting days. At least, to Thumper's partial relief, he reserved his sermonettes for Saturdays and with a relatively small weekday turnout he kept his opening remarks to a minimum, embellished by only a couple of quick songs before they moved off.

If those minor distractions were contributing to the pleasurable action that followed, then even the few remaining agnostics, Thumper among them, were willing to go along with the foolishness.

Thumper's problem now, though, was that the episode with Conman had not signaled the loss of Ryman's powers. Nor had he been rattled in the least by the appearance of the fox effigy and the Old Testament warning. But it had certainly rattled Thumper. Someone within their own community, someone who knew the country and could lay a drag line, was making threats against Ryman. How far would that person go? And who could it be?

Worst of all, what if Janey Musgrove had seen that? Or saw whatever happened next? Instead of the honest and dedicated academic she appeared to be, could she actually be a skilful manipulator worming her way into the hunting world to get a sensational scoop to boost her writing career?

A swelling tinge of regret now clouded his impulsive decision to suggest the nickname challenge. Had he been duped into paving the way for her to plant herself at the very heart of what she sought?

He could not go back on his offer. He'd made a deal and he'd stick with it. Anything less than that would be an affront to his sense of honor. But maybe Janey wouldn't find foxhunting to her liking. Few people launched right into the sport with so little preparation. Perhaps the first run would scare the bejesus out of her and she'd call it quits. That would be a double win: keep her to the safer confines of the car-followers and secure the secrecy of his nickname.

Saturday's meet was scheduled for a lesser-used fixture, a spot farther back toward the base of the mountains with heavier woods and fewer pastures or crop fields. This meant fewer fences to jump as there was little need to restrain livestock. That allowed the second field to stay close behind Thumper's jumping group. There were, though, several inviting log jumps along the trails. Mildred was not averse to taking her followers over most of them. The philosophy at Montfair Hunt was that anyone with the gumption to follow hounds, while perhaps being excused from the need to jump a four foot fence, should at least be able to take a horse over a moderately sized fallen log.

Janey Musgrove just might be in for more than she bargained for on her first-ever foxhunt. Or she might be revealed as something other than she appeared to be.

Thumper caught up with Mildred and Marva at the Thursday tailgate. "I have a guest coming out on Saturday. She'll be riding with you in the second field, Mildred. And as she's my personal guest, there will be no need to collect the cap fee."

"Personal guest?" Marva replied. "And just who might this be?"

"Janey Musgrove."

Both ladies perked up at that.

"Do tell," Mildred said. "I didn't realize she rode."

"Oh, yes. Well, some anyway. Not hunting, of course. I put her up on Bee last Sunday. She did fine. And old Bee is a great babysitter. I've loaned her some of Claudette's old gear. Fits her nicely."

"It'll be a pleasure to have her out with us," Mildred said. "I'll keep a watchful eye on her, make sure she doesn't get into any trouble."

Thumper's radar pinged on that remark. Did Mildred have suspicions about her too? "What do you mean 'trouble'? Do you expect her to do something, see something?"

"Whoa there. I just meant in case she has a problem, being unfamiliar with hunting. That's all."

"Oh, yeah, right. Gotcha. Well, she should be okay. Don't worry about any special treatment. I'm sure she'll keep up just fine."

As Thumper moved on to chat with other members, Mildred and Marva shared grins and giggles.

"Brilliant of you to have sent her home with Thumper," Marva said.

"Seems to have gone well, doesn't it. I wonder what else went on besides her riding Bee and rummaging through Claudette's old stuff."

"Yes, it does make one wonder."

****

Dorcas's cell phone sounded with its generic ring as she was hauling the horses back to Kimber Farm. She was always troubled by calls from unfamiliar numbers. After several rings, she steeled herself and answered the call.

"Dorcas, Bob Sensabaugh here. Got a minute?"

"Oh, yes, of course."

"First of all, I'd like to apologize for what I said a couple of weeks ago. I didn't really mean to criticize you. I was thinking more about Cecelia. If anyone's a bad influence on the kids, it's her. I'm sure you're doing your best with them, under the circumstances anyway."

"Thank you. Apology accepted."

"Good. I've decided to let Baden and Beatrice return to hunting and to your Sunday afternoon sessions. I hope that's okay with you, after the way I acted."

"Of course that's okay."

"Just one other thing. I'm trusting you to keep an eye on them, especially Baden. I assume Missy Winslow is still coming on Sundays."

Dorcas felt her stomach tighten. She couldn't tell Bob about finding Baden and Missy in the feed room. Could she keep them apart? Watch them at all times when they were under her care? And perform her duties with all the other kids at the same time? How could she guarantee that those two foolish teenagers wouldn't misbehave when she had ten other children to worry about, most of them much younger and in need of supervision for their own safety? Kimber Farm was awash with hiding places: feed room, tack room, tool shed, hayloft, empty stalls. And that was just the main barn. There was the equipment barn, several run-in sheds, an old carriage barn, silos—no end to the possibilities.

"Yes," she replied, "Missy is still coming."

"Well, I know Baden will be in good hands under your watchful eye. He and his sister will be there this Sunday. And they'll be hunting on Saturday. I'll see you then."

Watch Baden? Dorcas was worried about Missy. To hell with Baden. Missy was the potential victim. It's never the boy. Boys are the predators. They can do whatever they want and get off scot-free. Girls are the ones who have to be protected. It was easier not having Baden around. But now she'd have to be back on her guard. It was turning into Florida all over again.

Chapter 57

JANEY'S SECOND SLEEPOVER at Montfair was planned better than the first. She arrived Friday afternoon, dressed in Claudette's casual riding clothes and carrying her cubbing kit for the next day. To ease his own conscience, Thumper insisted on a short riding session in the ring and then a brief hack. At least that would allow him to honestly say his guest had ridden cross-country before. He didn't have to mention that it had been for no more than half an hour.

Javier had both Bee and Lenny tacked up and waiting in the ring. Thumper was impressed that Janey already showed more confidence than she had the week before. He also wondered if her claim to have had so little riding experience was on the level.

After thirty minutes he said, "Okay. You look ready. Let's hit the trail."

Thumper led her along a path that began behind the main house and climbed gradually through the woods to an open patch on the mountainside that overlooked the Montfair estate. The autumn foliage was at its peak of multi-hued splendor; a riot of rich red, mottled orange, oaky brown, matte yellow, and lemony green. A few hints of modernity—a farm road, some power lines, the tiny speck of a plane in the distant sky—broke the full effect of the time warp feel. But with a little squinting, Janey could muster the same Antebellum sensation she'd had the previous Sunday morning. Seated astride Bee, riding alongside the Squire of Montfair on his spunky Thoroughbred, further heightened that sensation.

Riding a horse opened an ancient, dormant connection to the natural world. She sensed each step, every subtle feature of the terrain. Unspoken communication passed between her and the animal, a flow of signals through legs, hands, and back; muscle reacted to muscle, blending the two sentient creatures into a functioning partnership; living flesh and bone moving over a landscape unaltered by the leveling influence of asphalt.

The ride ended too soon. But the sense of being in a different reality remained as she followed Thumper's instructions through the duties of untacking the horse, brushing him off, putting everything away in its assigned spot in the tack room, and then leading Bee out to his pasture. She lingered a moment before she released him through the gate. Her hand went to his soft, silky muzzle. "You're a good guy, Bee. I'll see you in the morning."

"You two seem to get on quite well," Thumper said. "You should be just fine tomorrow. And now, how about a cocktail before dinner?"

"Maybe just a light one."

"To the study then."

Cocktails in hand, they parked themselves in the leather club chairs before the stone hearth.

"You do bear a strong resemblance to your great-grandfather," Janey said, lifting her glass toward the portrait of Thaddeus the First.

"The Billington men have always resembled romance novel cover models. In fact, it is the family's belief that Fabio is a distant relative and owes his success to Billington blood."

Janey assessed her companion skeptically. Billington men were, in fact, slight of build and weak of chin, much better suited to author photos on the flaps of academic book jackets than the covers of bodice-ripping romance novels. She doubted Thumper had ever ripped a bodice in his life. But he exuded an allure she found appealing in its own way: intellectual heft combined with self-deprecating humility, gentlemanly manners, and uncompromising integrity.

Thumper rolled up the sleeves of his flannel shirt and Janey noticed his bare forearms glowed with a copper sheen, still tanned past mid-autumn. The well-defined muscling and prominent veins in his arms and hands did not match Janey's image of a scholarly lawyer and bookish academic. Perhaps he could do some serious bodice-ripping if he wanted to.

"Why foxes?" she asked.

"You mean why is that the quarry we choose to chase?"

"Yes."

"As opposed to, say, groundhogs, gophers, beavers, badgers, wolverines, or wombats?"

"Yes. Why did foxes get the honor?"

"Because foxes are sexy."

"Sexy?"

"Think about it. Foxes are cute, smart, elusive, and tricky. A fox will tease you and play with you, tempt you to come on and then disappear in a flash, only to pop up again two fields away, grinning slyly and waiting for you to resume the chase. If the hunters don't mess things up, the fox will give us a long, thrilling run, with twists and turns, near catches and misses. She'll keep you alert and focused, caught up in the action, every care of the world dispelled, wrapped up in a single-minded mission to stay with her to the end. Now, if I were to call you a vixen, you'd probably take that as a compliment, right?"

"I suppose so. Not that anyone's ever called me that."

"Maybe not to your face."

Janey's head jerked at the thought that someone might have described her that way. She didn't think there was anything vixen-like about herself.

Thumper continued on quickly. "But if I were to refer to you by certain canine, bovine, or porcine metaphors, your reaction may be less than pleasant."

"You bet it would."

"You're too young to remember the Jimi Hendrix hit 'Foxy Lady'…"

"Oh, please. I may have missed Woodstock, but that doesn't mean I'm not a fan of classic rock."

"I thought you said you were into classical music."

"Only when I'm working. Otherwise, I'm into classics of a different type. Janis Joplin, Fleetwood Mac, Heart."

"Really? Well, there may be hope for you yet."

"So you're saying foxhunting is simulated sex?"

"The 'heart' of foxhunting, and sex, is the thrill of the chase. And what is it that makes a chase thrilling? Two things: anticipation and challenge. Will a fox be found? Will she get up and give you a good run? Can you handle the pace? Can you respond to her cues and guess where she's going? Do you have the stamina to stay with her until she decides it's over? And, ideally, when it's done, everyone—riders, horses, hounds, and foxes—are all still in one piece, maybe a little tired and sore, but ready to rest up and go at it another day.

"Now take, for example, your typical groundhog. Groundhogs are easy to find, they don't run very fast or far, they don't tempt or tease, they don't show any pleasure in the sport, they just want it over as quickly as possible and then to be left alone. No chase, no thrill. If you want thrill, you need chase. And no creature is more fun to chase than a fox. All foxes are hard-wired for the chase. It comes naturally to them. It's what makes them so alluringly sexy. So… foxy."

"You've obviously put a great deal of thought into this."

"Been doing it pretty much my whole life, had some time to think about it, why we do it, why every year at this same time the old butterflies flutter around in my gut the night before a hunt. Because it's sexy."

"Foxhunting, religion, and sex. What have I wandered into?"

Thumper drained the last of his Talisker single malt. "What indeed, Professor Musgrove."

****

"That was a splendid dinner," Janey said as Natasha cleared away the plates.

"Thank you. And I am wery happy you are eating everything. You are too skinny. Like Mister Thumper. Birds, both of you."

"If I spend much more time here, I won't be skinny for long."

"Is good then. Mister Thumper must keep inwiting you, I vill keep cooking. Yes?"

Janey and Thumper replied "Yes" in unison and Natasha happily returned to the kitchen.

"She's a gem," Janey said. "You're so lucky to have her."

"That I am. And Voytek, too. It was a fortunate day for the Billingtons when the Soviet Union collapsed."

"How's that?"

"When Natasha and Voytek were teenagers they ran off and joined a small Soviet circus, two Polish farm kids looking to escape to something more exotic. Voytek cared for the animals, Natasha did the cooking. Wasn't quite the exciting life they'd envisioned. The circus happened to be playing in the DC area when everything back home went to hell. They were stranded here, at a loss for what to do. A friend of my father's at the State Department asked around for people willing to take in the refugees until something could be worked out about what to do with them. The Nutchenkos showed up here, able to speak only the most rudimentary English. My father found some use for them and they've been here ever since."

"Funny how things you never expect to happen just come out of nowhere, and there you are."

"Yes," Thumper agreed, "and there you are."

Yes, he thought, and here we are. Just the two of us, all alone in this big, empty house. The anticipation of tomorrow's sport already tingling to the tips of fingers and toes. Janey's large, soft brown eyes, unfettered by her oversized glasses, gazing invitingly across the rim of her wine glass.

He took a deep breath and let it out slowly. "So," he said, "I trust you'll find the guest room comfortable."

"Oh, I'm sure I will."

They both sat looking at anything but each other.

"It's odd, though," Janey said. "I've slept in some pretty wild places, from mud huts to stone caves to under the stars on the plains of the Kalahari. But when I woke up in that room the morning… you know, when you were kind enough to let me stay over… I had this feeling, some sense that there was something… or someone else… I don't know. Does that sound strange?"

Thumper arose and offered his hand. "Come upstairs with me."

"Oh… well, I don't think… I mean it's not that…"

"For a history lesson."

"Is that what you call it in Crutchfield County?"

"Trust me."

She took his hand and he led her upstairs, past his bedroom door and down the hall to the corner guest room.

"Lot of history in this room," he said as they stepped inside.

He paused and looked around the small space. Two tall windows provided a sweeping view to the north, two others to the east. It was dark now, the deep, undisturbed darkness of the rural countryside. In the autumn moonlight the vague outline of treetops formed a ragged border between earth and sky. The room's high ceiling allowed long shadows to play across the walls from the light of the single table lamp. The simple twin beds gave the room a dormitory feel, as if they were the last two stations in the attic sleeping quarters of a Victorian orphanage.

"Billingtons have been born in this room," Thumper said. "Billingtons have died here. You are the most recent guest in a long line of distinguished visitors, names you would surely recognize, from world figures to Tinsel Town play-actors. Perhaps, though, the spirit that lingers the longest is that of my Uncle Josiah."

"The one whose pistols are on the wall in your study, the Navy Colt .44s?"

"Yes, that Uncle Josiah. And very observant of you to remember that."

"It's what I do."

"You do it well." Maybe too well, he thought. "Anyway, the war left him a broken man, racked with injuries and in constant pain. He fell to drink, squandered his share of the family fortune that his brother had managed to preserve. Finally reached the point where he had to sell off his portion of the Montfair property to Ryman's ancestor. He then drank his way through that money pretty quickly too."

"A shame they didn't know about PTSD back then."

"Right. Or have developed better pain meds. This was Josiah's room when he became unable to live on his own, basically a family charity case. A difficult lot for a once proud, dashing young cavalier, considered in his youth the most eligible bachelor in Crutchfield County, possibly all of Virginia."

"Did… did he die in this room?"

"Yes."

Janey shuddered as a faint wisp of air tickled the back of her neck. She wanted to move closer to Thumper, to feel the reassurance of his flesh-and-blood presence. But that would have been an admission that she was not always as adventurous as he believed. And it would compromise her observer's neutrality. So she stood firm and asked nonchalantly, "Did the alcoholism finally do him in?"

"No," Thumper said. "A Navy Colt .44."

"Oh."

"Hey, it's late, big day tomorrow. Best we call it a night." He bowed deeply, in the fashion of a dashing cavalier, said "Sleep well," and left the room.

Chapter 58

HEADS TURNED WHEN Janey emerged from Thumper's truck at the Saturday morning meet. Thanks to Claudette's cast-offs, she looked like a seasoned hunter in a tweed hacking jacket, show shirt with choker collar, beige breeches, and tall brown field boots. The outward appearance may have been perfection, but inside she felt uncomfortably out of place and nervous under the assessing gaze of so many real foxhunters. The comments about "posers" at the Prestons' dinner party came back to her.

Mildred was on Yaz, named for BoSox great Carl Yastrzemski. She rode over and said, "You look great, deah. I'm so glad you're coming out with us. You stay right with me and I'll take care of you. Not to worry."

Thumper and Janey mounted quickly and joined the others.

"Once we move off," Thumper said, "I'm going to be pretty busy. You just put Bee right behind Mildred and stay with her." He reached over and patted her on the thigh. "Have fun. I've got to go to work now."

Ryman called the field to order and the disciples arrayed themselves before the Prophet of Paradise. Thumper was pleased to see that Baden and Beatrice were among the mounted riders. He noticed Reverend Dan standing with the car-followers, his eyes glued on Janey.

"Let us now consider Article Six from 'The Foxhunter's Faith,'" Ryman began. "I quote, 'If it is possible, let every true believer abstain from all meat and drink, save only such as is necessary to sustain life. Let the whole day be kept as a special fasting and strengthening of the mind for 'the chase.' In the evening he shall partake of suitable meat and drink, and on the evening after a good day he shall have a special allowance.' The Word of Saint Hubert, through the hand of his servant, the North-Country Hunting Parson. Amen."

Janey wished there was some way she could videotape this. If she survived the morning, she told herself, she'd have to see about rigging up a helmet-cam.

"Now, my friends," Ryman continued, "why do you think Saint Hubert is calling us to fast, or only take as much as needed to sustain life, before we go hunting?" He did not wait for a response to his question. "I see two reasons for this; one is immediate and personal, the other is broader, more about what we honor when we go forth to the chase. Let me explain.

"Maybe some of you folks here can eat a huge breakfast, climb on a horse, and go running and jumping around the countryside like we've been doing and not suffer any problems with that. But I think it's like how we were always told not to go swimming right after a meal. Strenuous physical exertion is best done on an empty stomach, or at least after only a very light amount of food or drink. Furthermore, I don't know about you folks, but for me there's nothing better after a hearty meal than a good nap. A nice full tummy, stretch out on the couch, let that good old digestive process chug along… Ho boy, I'm getting sleepy just thinking about it."

Ryman yawned broadly, with theatrical flare. He noticed a few stifled yawns among the crowd, uncontrollable reactions to the power of suggestion.

He resumed his sermon with a vigorous tone. "But that's not how we want to be when we're out here in this splendid country, partaking of the glorious sport Saint Hubert has laid before us. We want every particle in our minds and bodies to be fully awake and alert. We want to pick up every hint of scent: the musky wisp of the foxes we chase, that wonderfully sour scent of wet hounds, the tangy odor of horse sweat, the earthy smell of leather, all of it. We want our eyes sharp to see everything, from what's on the ground right in front of us to the movement of game on the far horizon to the flash of a hawk swooping over a field in search of its own meal for the day. We want our ears open to hear the huntsman's horn, the baying of the hounds, the pounding of our horses' feet, and the pumping of our own hearts in rhythm with it all.

"So, my friends, take a pass on that heavy breakfast. Have a light snack if you must. But keep your senses sharp for all the glorious stimulation that awaits you in the hunt field.

"Now, then, about the broader aspect of this Article. What we're doing out here is honoring what life was like for all but the most recent sliver of human existence. If our ancestors were going to eat, they had to gather things, grow things, or hunt things… or most likely all three. There were no grocery stores within an easy drive. Every day was a struggle for existence. Learning how to track down game was essential for survival. Whenever we're out here doing what we do, we're keeping that thread alive back to those who came before us, to those who struggled and persevered, kept the human race going and thriving so that we could enjoy all the luxuries and benefits we're blessed with today. We're not looking to kill foxes. It's just a game and they know it. We're all actors in a grand play, and the spirits of our forebears look upon us and are pleased. Saint Hubert be praised!"

Several congregants joined Nardell in a hearty "Amen!"

"And now," Ryman concluded, "let us be off to the chase. Mister O'Rourke, hounds please!"

And the morning's play began, with Janey Musgrove, former member of the ground-bound audience, now on stage and part of the supporting cast.

****

As the second field waited to fall in behind Thumper and his jumping group, Mildred announced to her followers that Janey was the senior master's special guest, out for her first foxhunt, and was to stay right behind the leader. What Janey did not realize was that Mildred was warning off a few members in particular who felt it was their privilege to ride right behind the master and fought each other for that position. She wanted no one getting between Janey and her and the tone of her voice—with the emphasis on *special* guest—made sure the usual thrusters got the message.

By now Janey was accustomed to Crispie's horn blowing and the spectacle of the hunt moving off. But it was a wildly different experience to be in the midst of the action rather than watching from the sidelines. She felt herself swept along as if in a flow of motion beyond her power. It was exhilarating and frightening at the same time.

Hounds struck quickly. Wise old Bee knew what the sound of their cry meant and Janey felt a jolt pulse through her as the horse snapped to attention. His muscles tightened and he shifted from a plodding gait to a feather-light prance. The twitching of his sensitive ears flashed a semaphore message to anyone who understood equine body language: "The game is afoot! Let's be off!"

Without a word—no "Here we go!" or "Everybody ready?"—Yaz sprang into a canter and Mildred moved off down the wooded trail, close behind those following Thumper in the first field. Janey's presence on Bee was a non-issue to the horse. As long as she didn't get in his way—pull on his mouth, try to turn him, ask him to do something he knew was wrong—it didn't matter to him whether the person on his back was a six year old child, a forty-some year old woman, an eighty-six year old man, or no one at all. As long as hounds sang, the horn blew, and the horse in front of him kept moving, he was going to follow.

As the riders picked up speed, the cool autumn air flushed Janey's cheeks. A light mist still hung in the woods and her glasses fogged over, giving everything around her a gauzy appearance, as if she were riding through an antique tintype photo.

The cry of the hounds intensified—a primal, frantic wail. If pure adrenalin made a sound, that would be it. Somewhere, just ahead of that screaming, semi-feral pack of hounds, Janey knew there had to be a fox. And the fox was in charge. There was no preordained script to follow, no predictable, practiced routine. The action would unfold as the fox dictated. The hunters could only follow where the fox took them. This was what Thumper meant—the thrill of the chase. Janey let herself go with the spontaneity, the challenge, the abandon to be carried along where the chase took her. She rejoiced in the physicality of it, the demand for reflexive action, no time to think, just respond.

Clods of mud flew up from Yaz's hoofs, splattering Janey and Bee. A quick glance behind showed a line of similarly muddied riders. Everyone had looked so neat and clean at the meet. But now appearance meant nothing. Get on with the chase, there will be time to clean up later.

There was only the urgency of pressing on, moving to the steady rhythm—dada-DAH, dada-DAH, dada-DAH—as the twelve hundred pound quadruped beneath her cantered insistently forward. Her breath came in quick gasps. Her armpits began to perspire under the tweed jacket.

She thought for a moment of her daily running workout. She was all alone when she ran, fighting the force of gravity with every step, pushing herself to keep going toward some arbitrarily arranged destination. There was no thrill to running, no game, no chase.

But here she felt a partnership with the horse, the freedom of sailing along in unison with another flesh-and-blood creature, the need to trust that he'll deliver her safely to the climax, no matter how long it takes to get there.

A log jump loomed ahead. It was child's play to first field. But when Thumper hopped over it, he wondered briefly what Janey would do. He knew under normal circumstances Mildred would go right over it. Would Janey follow? Or would that be the too-much point for her? As he moved on down the trail, he felt a pang of regret that he'd knowingly put her in this situation. It seemed like a good test when he'd first thought of it. Now all he could do was mutter to himself, "Take care of her, Mildred."

And Mildred did. She called back to Janey as they approached the log, "You okay with this?"

"As long as the horse is."

"He'll be fine. Grab mane and look up!"

Seconds later she felt herself lifted into the air, floating for a second, and then the mild impact as the old hunter landed on the trail and continued in his competent rhythm. More logs awaited and Janey found herself enjoying the rolling weightless experience, each one an exclamation point at just the right moment.

The chase went on, twisting through the wooded trails, past rocky slopes, splashing into muddy ruts, a few brief dashes through the high grass of fallow fields, and then back into the woods. Janey's stamina and leg strength served her well. She was happily cruising to the beat of the eternal pursuit, thinking only of the moment, giving herself fully to the experience.

She heard the tone of the hounds' cry shift into a higher pitch. The pace quickened. Bee stretched out and found a gear Janey hadn't expected was there. The hunters emerged from the woods into a wide field that led to a tree-covered rise on the far side. Hounds were now in a frenzy of passion, moving as one roiling mass toward that rise. Huntsman and whippers-in followed close behind, Thumper and his followers hard on their heels. Mildred gave Yaz his head and the horses behind burst into a full gallop.

Janey's eyes watered behind her thick glasses. As Thumper had shown her in the ring, she entwined a finger in Bee's mane and held on tight. She was nearing the limit of her endurance. But her body was not her own. It belonged to the creature under her. And he was not going to stop until the game was done.

The climax came at the rise.

Hounds swarmed a den safely tucked among tangled bushes. Their voices sang of the chase's end, joyful strains of victory tinged with a longing for more, a sadness at the knowledge that the thrill would soon ebb.

The riders formed a semi-circle around the den. Crispie dismounted and blew "Gone to Ground."

Janey had heard that horn call before from the distance of an observer. It had excited her then. But now, just a few yards away from the horn's bell—her heart pounding and her lips sucking the cool, moist air—those trilling, quavering, tickling notes put every nerve into a riot of giddy fever.

Smiling broadly, she collapsed forward onto Bee's neck and buried her face in the sweaty tang of his thick mane.

Thumper looked over and saw her, fearful at first that she was about to collapse. But then she pushed herself upright and he saw the satisfied grin. He guided Lenny over to her. "You okay?"

"Oh, my God. Absolutely okay. That was… amazing!"

He withdrew his flask and offered it to Janey. "Looks like you could use some refreshment."

She took the flask, a cylindrical glass bottle, and looked at the clear liquid within. "What's in it?"

"Oh, that's Crutchfield Creek Water." He made a surreptitious wave at Mildred who was about to offer a comment.

Janey took a swig. A burst of gasping and coughing quickly

followed. "Wa... water? That's... *cough*... that's *some* water."

Mildred shot a narrowed-eye at Thumper. "That's moonshine, deah. Shame on you, Thumpah, for tricking this young lady. And after she's done such an admirable job following hounds."

"Sorry," he said sheepishly.

Janey regained her composure. "No, no. That's okay. Just a part of the initiation I assume. Nothing compared to what I had to go through to be accepted by the Yanomamö."

Thumper started to reach for the flask but Janey declined to give it up. Instead she raised it to her lips and took another drink. Prepared for the sting, she did not flinch. "Ah, very fine water you folks have here in Crutchfield County." She flipped the flask's lid closed and handed it back to Thumper. With a triumphant tone she added, "One hunt down. Three more to go and your nickname secret is mine."

Thumper looked at his watch. "Not quite an hour yet."

"Well, let's go chase another fox then."

As Janey accepted the praise of other members of the field, many of whom did not expect her to do nearly so well, Thumper got Mildred aside. "I must say I'm surprised."

"She did incredibly well. I can't believe this is her first ever foxhunt."

"Yes," he said, "it does make one wonder."

****

Perhaps with his watchful eye on Janey the Neophyte, Saint Hubert decreed that one chase was enough for her first day. The rest of the morning was spent strolling around the countryside as hounds searched for another fox. But they found none.

When Janey and Thumper reached the trailer, he jumped off Lenny and positioned himself in a gentlemanly stance next to Bee as Janey prepared to dismount. She did so with confident grace, at least until her feet hit the ground. She was not prepared for just how much strength had been drained from her legs. She began to wobble and Thumper reached out to steady her. She was again in his arms, but showed no desire to push him away this time.

They were in that position when Bob Sensabaugh appeared. "Oh, excuse me. I didn't mean to interrupt."

They sprang apart. It appeared to Bob as a reenactment of the scene he'd come upon with Baden and Missy. Couldn't any of these people keep their hands off each other?

"No, no," Thumper said. "Just helping Janey get off. I mean... get off the horse."

"Yes, of course you were. Look, I wanted to apologize for my outburst a few weeks ago. I said some things that were inappropriate. Especially as it was strictly a family matter and shouldn't have been aired in front of others. I've asked God's forgiveness. And I'd like to ask yours, too."

Still flustered by having been caught with his arms around Janey, Thumper jokingly replied, "Oh, well, it's nice that you put me on the same level with the Almighty. Most people around here do think of me as a godlike presence."

Bob's usually stony face turned to granite. "I didn't come to you to hear the Lord's name blasphemed."

"Oh, no, of course not. I was just... you know me... joking." Thumper tried to squelch his desire to laugh at Bob's pompous piety. He mustered as much seriousness as possible. "I accept your apology. I hope whatever family matters are troubling you can be resolved to everyone's satisfaction."

"Thank you." Bob turned and walked away.

"Pretty uptight fellow," Janey observed.

Thumper noted Bob's rigid posture and determined gait. "Poor guy. Must not be getting any."

As she started untacking Bee, Thumper heard Janey mutter, "Someone needs to get him on a horse."

****

The post-hunt tailgate found Janey mobbed by new-found admirers and well-wishers, Ryman and Nardell prominently placed among them, congratulating her on losing her foxhunting virginity.

Thumper stood quietly and watched Ryman move away from Janey's side to welcome the Sensabaugh kids back to the fold. Ryman gave Beatrice a hug and Baden a firm handshake augmented by a smack on the shoulder. He then strode over to Bob and greeted him warmly. Bob accepted Ryman's offered hand, but his face revealed nothing more than flinty inscrutability.

Grantham Meisner made his way through the crowd to Thumper's side. "Sorry to sully this festive atmosphere," he said, "but I'm getting some flak about what Ryman's doing. It's starting to make some people—some rather influential people—uncomfortable."

Thumper thought about the fox effigy and its dire Old Testament warning. He was glad that neither Grantham nor Kirsten had been with them that morning.

Grantham continued. "It could be especially nasty if word of this gets around to the anti-hunting forces. Foxhunters putting their actions on par with religion. You know, not good for our broader public image."

"Perhaps you should talk to him about this," Thumper suggested.

"I think we both know what he thinks of me. His father was never a supporter of the association. If it had been up to Fergus, this would have been an unregistered farmers pack. It's always been because of the Billingtons that Montfair has continued to be part of NAFCA."

"The fact that my grandfather was one of the founding members of that association might have something to do with that."

"Precisely. And how do you think he'd feel about what's going on here?"

"Frankly, I have no idea. And that's not really relevant. The point is that I've already tried to talk to Ryman, asked him to at least tone things down some. But he obviously isn't listening to me either."

"You are the senior master, are you not? Surely you have some leverage here. Without your cooperation and support, I mean, let's be honest, there would be no Montfair Hunt. The McKendricks have never been able to provide the financial support a club like this requires. From your great-grandfather's day, a McKendrick was only allowed to be a master because of Billington noblesse oblige."

"There's more to being a hunt master than just shelling out money. The McKendricks have always brought something to the table. It's unfair of you to make it sound like we're just being kind to our poor relations."

"Thumper, really, I *am* your relation. So not just as head of NAFCA, but also as your dear cousin, I appeal to you to intercede here. If Ryman continues with this folly, the wider repercussions may be...well, unpleasant."

****

When the crowd around Janey began to thin out, Dan slipped up beside her.

"Today's experience must have added reams to your research," he said. "It's going to be quite a book."

"I certainly hope so. At some point I'm going to have to cloister myself and start going through everything, try to absorb the essence of all this so I can do it justice."

"A place for quiet meditation and reflection."

"Exactly. Too many distractions around my apartment, with all the neighbors and the noise. I did most of the work on my first two books at my family's lake cottage. Nice secluded spot, great place for writing. But there's no way I can pack up and go back to Minnesota this time. Guess I'll just have to tough it out."

"Has anyone mentioned The Cabin?"

"What cabin?"

"I assume not, then. *The* Cabin. It belongs to the Billington family, but they're very liberal about its use. Lovely spot, quite remote. I go there sometimes myself when I need to concentrate on a difficult sermon topic or spend time in prayer and meditation. Perhaps I can show it to you sometime. It's a bit difficult to find if you don't know the way, no paved road or signs showing you how to get there."

"Sure, that sounds great. But the way things are going, it might be awhile longer before I'm ready to move from research phase to writing."

"Whenever it suits you, I'm available to serve as your trail guide."

"Thanks. Oh, look, the Sensabaugh children are back. I guess their father relented."

"Yes, it appears he did. How nice."

****

Thumper intercepted Ryman as he made his way to the trailer. "Ry, a moment, please."

"Certainly, Brother Thumper. But if this is another one of your pleas for me to forsake Saint Hubert's calling, you're wasting your breath."

"Look, Ry, I'm just thinking about your own welfare here."

"Saint Hubert will see that all who call on him will be under his watchful care."

"Yeah, right. Well, the person who needs to do that more than anyone else right now is you. Whoever made that threat with the stuffed fox is serious. It took a lot of planning and execution to lay that drag line and hang that sign. It had to be someone who knows about hunting and has the woodsman skills to pull that off. No telling how far this person might go. People who think they're 'defending the faith' can be prone to act in some pretty unreasonable ways."

Ryman placed a hand gently on Thumper's shoulder. It was not knocked away this time. "Thumper, my oldest, bestest friend, I appreciate your concern. But I have faith that Saint Hubert will see me through whatever lies ahead. Be honest now. You've seen his power at work, haven't you?"

Thumper could not stop the reflexive nod he gave in reply.

"There, you see," Ryman said. "Your heart is not as hard as you might think. I knew our blessed Saint Hubert would open your eyes to the truth in good time."

"It's not about Saint Hubert, blessed or otherwise. If there's a burden on my heart, old buddy, it's strictly for you. I don't want to see you brought down to ridicule, maybe expelled from the hunting world, or… well, what could be even much worse. Can't you just concentrate on the hunting, cool it with the other stuff?"

"Saint Hubert revealed the 'Foxhunter's Faith' to me. He showed me how these ten articles are the founding scriptures. Their lessons must be imparted. And he showed me how the songs of the sport are hymns to the glory of the chase. They must be sung. I must lay the foundation as he's called me to do. I must complete the ten articles. After that, well, if it makes you feel any better, maybe he'll reveal another plan that's more to your liking."

"I just hope you make it to that point."

****

Back at Montfair, Thumper led Janey up to the attic. This time the mission was to pick out her kit for the opening of formal season the following Saturday.

"The breeches will be okay," he said. "And the helmet. But everything else changes. Let's start with the coat."

He picked up a black coat and motioned for Janey to turn around. He slipped it on her and then spun her back to face him. She buttoned up the front and did a quick, self-conscious modeling pose.

Satisfied that the coat would do, he then selected a white hunting shirt, white stock tie, plain gold stock pin, and black dress boots.

"Next step," he said, "a lesson in how to tie a stock."

He ushered her downstairs and into his bedroom. He slipped off the coat and placed her in front of the full-length mirror in his dressing area.

Standing behind her, he placed the midpoint of the folded fabric against the front of her neck, brought the ends around behind, then reached forward and draped them down her front where they hung like the strands of a long, thin scarf.

"Now, there are several different ways this can be done. But I'm going to show you the simplest and most traditional method."

He began to cross, tuck, and slip the two lengths of the tie, narrating his actions with "This goes here. Then cross this over and bring it underneath, keeping a finger there…" His arms rested against her shoulders as he worked, his chest pressed against her back, and his muttering instructions tickled her ear. He was not aware of how this might seem until he felt her leaning back against him.

He slowed his pace, playing with the tie, slipping one end into the opening he'd created and pulling it through a short way, then pulling it back the other way, then a little farther through, then back again.

"And that," he whispered, "is how you tie a stock. Let's see how it looks." He put his hands on her shoulders and turned her to face him. "Perfect."

The adrenalin rush from the morning's chase still lingered for Janey, the sensual freedom she felt to release all control and go with the moment. She slipped her arms around his waist and tilted her head back to receive his kiss. She wanted to stay in his arms, returning kiss for kiss, taking this wherever it led, just as she'd done a few hours earlier. The chase was on. And she was the fox.

But a small voice began to sound an alarm in her brain. Do not get personally involved with your subjects. Danger!

She pulled back and withdrew from Thumper's embrace.

"I'm sorry," he said, flustered and embarrassed. "You're absolutely right. I should be ashamed. Please forgive me."

"No, no. My fault. I… I may have led you on. I'm supposed to be the professional observer here. Totally my bad."

"And let's not forget that I'm a married man. Technically anyway." Thumper shook himself in an effort to lower his state of arousal. He thought of Bob Sensabaugh's stern, judgmental face and that did the trick. "But… um, if things were different."

"Yes," she said, undoing the stock tie and laying it atop the pile of formal hunting clothes, "if things were different."

"You're welcome to stay over again tonight," Thumper offered with a hopeful note. "I promise to be the perfect gentleman."

"You always are." She patted him on the chest. "But, no, I'd better be going."

"Right, yes. Well, we're still on for next weekend though, right? Big day for Opening Meet. You certainly won't want to miss that. Only happens once a year." He knew he was babbling but could not stop himself.

"Yes, I'll be here."

Chapter 59

"THOU SHALT NOT kill."

Reverend Dan cast a steely eye over the Sunday morning congregants. Attendance had swelled as word of the vicar's newfound vigor spread. Nominal members of the church who rarely set foot inside St. Cuthbert's except for Christmas and Easter services now sat in rapt attention to hear his preaching.

"Thou shalt not kill!" Dan repeated with more emphasis. Everyone's head lifted up and all eyes turned to him. "Or…?" A pensive thought creased his brow. "Does it say 'Thou shalt not *murder*?' The Hebrew word could be interpreted either way. So which is it? Does the Sixth Commandment forbid killing in any form? Or does it only forbid murder? And, if so, what then is the distinction? What about killing in war? The Israelites of Old Testament times were almost always at war with someone. Were they breaking the Lord's Commandment when they killed to protect the home He had promised them? Does it violate the Lord's Commandment to defend yourself against someone attempting to take your life, or the life of a loved one, even if you use lethal force to stop them? In the eyes of manmade law, self-defense can be a valid reason to take another person's life. And so it is in God's eyes too. When circumstances demand, we must rise up and fight."

Dan's hand came down on the lectern with a loud smack. "Rise up and fight! Yes, if your home is invaded, if your life is threatened, if the life of another is threatened. Rise up and defend what's right!"

He waited for the echo of his voice to subside in the small building, lingered in the dramatic silence a few seconds, then continued. "Defend what's right," he said softly. "Whatever it takes, no matter the cost. We must defend what's right."

****

"She's watching us like a hawk," Baden said.

"It's kinda creepy," Missy replied. "It's like she thinks we're gonna grab each other at any moment and just start fucking."

"Missy Winslow! Such language." The titter in Baden's voice revealed a surge of excitement at the sound of his girlfriend using the F-word in such a bold way.

"Yeah, what would your father say?"

She flashed him a come-hither smile and it was all he could do to keep from dragging her off somewhere and doing the deed. It was only the prison matron behavior of Dorcas—skulking around corners, appearing as if out of nowhere, staring at them whenever they were less than five feet apart—that restrained him.

"I think we know what my father would say." He deepened his voice to mimic Bob's and wagged a finger at an unseen audience. 'I won't have my son behaving that way! He'll never get into Harvard if he kisses girls.'"

"Or has sex with them."

"Even worse."

The sound of bootsteps in the barn aisle caused them to refocus on their tack cleaning duties. Dorcas appeared in the doorway of the tack room and found Missy diligently working on her bridle at one end of the room, Baden cleaning his at the other end. She stayed there for several seconds just observing them. Then she turned and walked away.

"Creepy," Missy said.

"Very creepy," Baden agreed.

"Maybe her brother showing up, like, weirded her out. Talk about creepy. He gave me a look that… I don't know. It was like he could see right through me, like I could feel everything he wanted to do to me. Compared to him, she's almost normal."

"Did he look at you like this?" Baden tried to appear scary-sexy.

With his youthful face, it looked to Missy more like stupid-silly. She started to giggle. "Oooo. I can tell what you want to do to me. You want to pull my boots off and chew on them."

The giggling ceased when they heard the rapid-fire stomp of Dorcas's boots marching back toward the tack room.

Chapter 60

NARDELL SAW THE dust cloud as a vehicle moved along the road to Worsham's farm. Hounds worked their quarry in that direction, still safely away from the Worsham property but close enough for a whipper-in to cover that side of the chase. As Nardell crested the rise next to the farm road, she saw Bar's truck rolling along, a flatbed trailer hitched behind. Their paths were on a course to meet at the road.

Bar pulled up when he saw her approaching. She maneuvered Gabby next to the driver's window.

"Going hunting?" she asked.

"Does it look like I'm going hunting?"

"You've got your rifle in the gun rack."

"So?"

"Well, I just thought…"

"You're really not the brightest bulb in the box, are you? First of all, it's ten-thirty in the morning, a bit late to be getting into the woods. Second, you really think I'd be hauling *that* around if I was going hunting?" He jerked his thumb at the piece of equipment secured to the trailer. "Turns out I not only have to cover the sales job for your idiot boyfriend, I also have to be out here on a Tuesday morning as delivery boy and field mechanic because hooking up and operating this new tiller Worsham ordered is too complicated for Tweedle Dumb and Tweedle Dumber. Now if you'll excuse me, one of us has work to do."

Indignant at Bar's insult to her intelligence, Nardell shot back, "Fine. But that doesn't explain why you're carrying that rifle around. Were you expecting to be highjacked by a marauding band of tractor part thieves?"

"Very funny. In case you've never noticed, I always keep that in the truck. Comes in handy when I find something that needs to be put down. People run into deer and just keep going, leavin' 'em injured on the side of the road. Cain't count how many I've had to finish off over the years. It's the humane thing to do, and keeps my birds well fed." He shifted into gear and started to release the clutch. "Well, been a real pleasure chattin' with you. Gotta run." He pulled away, leaving rider and horse enveloped in a cloud of gritty farm road dust.

****

"Just let me check my email first," Nardell said as she slipped from Ryman's attempted embrace.

"Ah, it can wait. I can't. Saint Hubert be praised! Another glorious morning afield and I'm invigorated!" He pulled her toward him and nuzzled the back of her neck. "Ready for another chase. A-wooooo!"

"I just have to see if... *oooh*... don't do that... if I have to go to.... *giggle*.... stop it... an appointment at... *mmmm*... okay, but then I have to get right back to...."

He swiveled her around and guided her down the hall.

An hour later she left Ryman snoring noisily, with Wycroft spooned beside him, and returned to the office. Opening her email, she saw a message from an unfamiliar address. The subject line read, "Be Careful Who You Live With." She thought about sending it to the spam folder. But curiosity overtook her. She opened the message.

> Jer 14:14 (NIV): "The prophets are prophesying lies in my name. I have not sent them or appointed them or spoken to them. They are prophesying to you false visions, divinations, idolatries, and the delusion of their own minds."
>
> Jer 23:16-18 (NIV): "This is what the Lord Almighty says: 'Do not listen to what the prophets are prophesying to you; they fill you with *false hopes.* They speak visions from their own minds, not from the mouth of the Lord.'"
>
> There is still time to save yourself. Do not be deceived. God is not mocked. Retribution is coming.
>
> The Defender of the Faith

She stared at the screen. This was not spam. It must be someone who knew her personally. But who? And what did he mean by "Retribution?" Should she tell Ryman? No, he must not be deterred from his mission. If he thought she was at risk, it might weaken his resolve. She must be strong, for his sake, and for the sake of blessed Saint Hubert. Glory to his name.

The sound of a snoring duet floated from the bedroom. Nardell hit "Delete" and moved on to her next message.

Chapter 61

TWO HOURS BEFORE Thursday's hunt, Thumper placed a call to Marva. "Sorry for the short notice, but we're going to have to change the fixture for today. Mildred just called, seems an underground spring erupted in their front pasture where we park. It's all a soggy mess. Derrick Philman's on his way with a backhoe but it's going to take a while to get it cleared up. I suggest we meet at Caleb's Forty. We haven't gone from there lately."

"That's pretty far back in the country. You think it will be okay?"

"Should be. Can you get that on the monitor right away? I've already told Ryman and Crispie. Hopefully everyone else will remember to check the monitor before they head out."

****

The report from a high-powered rifle broke the late morning stillness. Deer hunter, Ryman thought. A bit late for someone to still be at it. The deer would all be bedded down by now, especially on this chilly, drizzly October day. Unless hounds had roused them and driven them toward the hunter's stand. But the pack was working the other way, moving east. The shot had sounded from the west.

He continued to canter along the trail, skirting the pack as they pursued a crafty red. The cool temperature, moist ground, and low cloud ceiling made for ideal foxhunting conditions. The fox's scent clung to the forest's leafy floor, aided by the dampness. Absent sun, wind, and rising temperatures, the scent hung strong and low, perfectly positioned for the nose of a foxhound.

Ryman might just as well have been wearing camouflage. His tweed hacking jacket, an earthy green with muted mud-brown stripes, blended with the fall palette now at its peak. His rust colored breeches flowed into dull brown boots and even the bay horse he rode presented little visual disturbance to the autumnal landscape.

The second shot caught Ryman's attention. A split second later Ryman heard the hiss of a bullet whizzing by, inches in front of his face, then the thud of impact as it hit a tree just beside him. Splintered bark exploded from the point of impact. A few shards landed on Token's rump as he cantered past the tree.

Wow, Ryman thought as he continued to pace the hounds, that was close. I wonder who that was. Well, I reckon I'm hard to see in this drizzle and mist. He turned his eyes heavenward. "Thank you, blessed Saint Hubert, for your protection. Amen."

Ryman chose not to say anything about this incident at the tailgate. He felt sure it was an accident. A deer hunter's shot had missed its mark; that was all. Ryman and Token weren't exactly decked out in blaze orange, and even harder to see under the weather conditions that morning. Well, maybe it was an accident. Best, though, that Thumper not find out or he'd have a fit, insist someone was trying to kill Ryman because of his mission.

Ryman did, though, mention it to Nardell on the way home.

"What? Someone took a shot at you? Ryman, we have to report this. Maybe Thumper had a point about keeping the stuffed fox thing quiet. But this! You could have been killed. And whoever did it is still out there."

"Nah, I think we should handle it ourselves for now. Thumper's kind of right, although for a different reason. I don't think the church needs the negative attention. And if it was just an accident, then that'll mean stirring people up against not only foxhunting but against deer hunters too. The animal rights people will make a stink because it could have been Token who took the bullet. To hell with me. Humans aren't important to those wackos. And some of our followers might lose their enthusiasm for the Venatican Church if they think they could get shot for being part of it."

"So how, exactly, do we go about handling it ourselves?"

"Oh, y'know, ask around, try to find out who might have been deer hunting in that area about that time. Maybe just have a private, gentle conversation with whoever pulled the trigger."

"And if it happens again? Maybe with a worse outcome."

"Ah, you must have faith in our blessed Saint Hubert. All praises be to his name."

For once, Ryman's chief acolyte did not reply with her usual "Amen!"

****

Nardell stuck her head into Ryman's study. "I've got to run into town for a few things. Won't be long."

"Mmmph," he replied, not taking his eyes off the computer screen. Opening Day for formal season was four days away and there was much still to do to polish his sermon on Article Seven for the big event.

Nardell's first stop was at McKendrick and Sons. She entered the showroom to find Bar explaining to a customer why he needed the additional power of a 300 series riding mower rather than the much cheaper 100 series the man had in mind.

"Bar, I need to talk to you," she said.

"Sure thing, just be a few minutes. Why don't you have a seat in the office? I'm sure Muriel would love to catch up with you."

"Okay, yeah. But I can't wait long."

Muriel had nothing to catch up with Nardell about. Nor did Nardell have any interest in catching up with Muriel. The two women sat in awkward silence until Bar finally entered, after much longer than the few minutes Nardell expected.

"Sorry," he said, "only got a sec. An eager customer's waiting to close the deal."

Nardell jumped to her feet and blurted out, "Where were you this morning?"

The accusatory tone immediately put Bar on the defensive. "What the hell business is that of yours?"

"I have my reasons."

"You wanna tell me what they are?"

"No. But they're very good ones. So where were you?"

"I don't think I'm going to answer that, other than to say that I was taking care of business duties that your dumb ass boyfriend should have been doing. But, no, he's too wacked out for that, no thanks to you. If he's not going to be a part of this operation any more, than he's got no call to ask about where I am or what I'm doing. And neither do you."

"Fine. There are other ways I can find out. And I will."

"Go ahead, do whatever you want. But go do it somewheres else. Muriel and me got work to do." He turned to Muriel. "I convinced Carrington to go with the 300 DX. The 100's okay for basic lawn care, but it doesn't have the torque to pull a manure spreader without burning out the transmission. Can you get the paperwork started while I finish up the details?"

"Certainly," Muriel replied and swung around toward her computer, turning her back to Nardell.

Bar started toward the office door. "You still here?" he said. "Best you run along and play now, the adults are busy."

Nardell sped down Main Street and lurched to a stop in front of the General Store. If anyone knew Bar's whereabouts that morning, Luella Starett would. The store's proprietress was the Delphic Oracle of gossip and information for all of Paradise Gap and much of Crutchfield County. When there was a need to disseminate information quickly, the local wisdom was, "Don't telephone. Tell Luella."

Nardell stormed in to find Miles and Conway standing at the deli counter as Luella slapped together a couple of sandwiches for them.

"Ah," Nardell said, "just the people I need to see. Where was Bar this morning?"

All three blinked in surprise at this unexpected outburst.

Miles was the first to speak. His naturally combative nature immediately kicked in. "What business is that of yours?"

"I have my reasons."

"Yeah? Well, maybe I have my reasons for not telling you."

"Why are you covering up for him? That just makes me all the more suspicious."

"Suspicious about what?" Conway asked.

"Suspicious about who was out in the woods this morning, close to where we were hunting, and fired a shot that almost hit Ryman."

Luella's eyes lit up with a merry gleam. She stood on tiptoes to peer over the deli case, a slice of bread hanging limply in one hand. Nardell realized the entire county would now know about this before sunset.

"Wasn't Bar picking up some equipment this morning?" Luella asked the boys. "I think it was over toward Patrician Springs, though. Not where y'all were hunting."

"Maybe he was," Miles said. "So what? Besides, that's a long way from Montfair territory."

"If that's where he was," Nardell countered.

"Um, yeah," Conway said. "He, like, brought back a rotary rake that needed some repair work."

"And you know for a fact that this came from someplace over by Patrician Springs?"

"Um, well, gee, I guess so. It didn't, like, have an address or nothin' on it."

"So it could have come from anywhere."

"Look," Miles said, "it's bad enough we have to work for that damn freak because your boyfriend has flipped out and gone all religious. But at least he's trying to keep things going, keep me and Conway employed. And I hate to say it, but for a damn freak he ain't doing too bad. Besides, why the hell would Bar want to shoot Ryman? That don't make no sense. So maybe you just oughta go back to the farm and do some more praying with Ryman. Maybe Saint Herbert or whoever the hell he is will tell you who tried to take a potshot at his crazy ass preacher. You're barkin' up the wrong tree here."

"Fine," Nardell fired back. "But if anything happens to Ryman, and it turns out Bar's behind it, you won't be so damn smart then. Especially if it means the business folds. Bar Reinhardt doesn't own a splinter of that business. He's just the hired help, like you two. No Ryman McKendrick, no more McKendrick and Sons Farm Implements. You think about that." She spun around and stomped out.

Before the boys had taken the first bite of their sandwiches, Luella was already pounding out a text message: "Did you hear someone took a shot at Ryman McKendrick?"

****

Word reached Ryman by the time Nardell got home. He was pacing in the living room when she arrived. "What's the big idea blabbing about this to Luella? Now everyone knows. We were going to keep this quiet."

"You were the one who said we should handle this ourselves, ask around, try to find out who might have been in the woods this morning. That's exactly what I was doing."

"But Luella? C'mon, that's not exactly asking around. That's putting it on a fucking billboard."

"I didn't actually mean to tell her. It just sort of slipped out when I was asking Miles and Conway about where Bar was this morning."

"Bar? You don't seriously suspect Bar, do you?"

"Why not?"

"Well, let's see. Because he's one of my best friends, almost like a brother."

"And brothers never, ever take shots at each other, do they?"

"What the hell kind of motivation would he have? Without me, the shop goes down the toilet. And Ma would kick his ass off the farm before my body was cold. It makes no sense."

"Well, I'm still trying to sort that out. But he had the opportunity and he certainly has the ability."

"What's that supposed to mean?"

"It means I saw him driving to Worsham's on Tuesday with his rifle in his truck's gun rack. He gave me some bullshit story about having it handy to finish off injured deer. Right, like I believed that for a second."

"It's true. I've seen him do it. Done it a few times myself." Ryman pointed to an old lever-action Winchester .30-30 mounted above the fireplace mantel. "Main reason I keep that old piece around."

"Okay, so maybe he always has it with him, and I've just never noticed it. Not like I pay much attention to him and his old truck. But that just means he had the opportunity. Miles, Conway, and Luella all agreed he was away from the shop this morning. They said he was picking up something for repair in Patrician Springs. But that doesn't mean that's where he really was."

"Oh, c'mon, it's ridiculous to think Bar might..."

"*And*, if I may finish, he has the ability. I've been hearing everyone say for years what a marksman he is, how he won a bunch of awards when he was in the Marines, 'Best shot in the Corps,' your father used to say. And that even with one eye gone he could still 'hit a fly at fifty paces,' or some damn redneck phrase like that."

"It's exactly that ability that rules him out as a suspect. If it was Bar, I'd be a dead man right now, wouldn't I?"

"Not if he was just trying to scare you."

"Oh, for Christ sakes! This is pointless. Just makes me even more convinced it had to be an accident. Besides, even if he did have the opportunity and the ability… and I'm not saying I agree with you about that… you're still missing the most important thing—motive."

"I'm working on that."

"Well, don't bother wasting your time. I've prayed to Saint Hubert about this and he's given me a peace that it was just someone's careless mistake, and his hand was at work to keep me safe. Besides, formal season starts Saturday so I'll be wearing scarlet from here on. Much easier for everyone to see me."

"Yeah, and it makes you a much easier target too."

Ryman's cell phone rang. "Oh, great. It's Thumper. I'm sure Luella's info has reached him by now. Thanks to you." Ryman tried to sound nonchalant when he answered the call. "Hey, Brother Thumper, how's it going?"

"What's this crap about someone taking a shot at you? Why didn't you say something?"

"Oh, it was nothing. Had to just be a deer hunter who missed his mark. You know what it was like out there this morning, dark and drizzly, we were all wearing cubbing attire, hard to see us. And it wasn't all that close really. I didn't think it was worth mentioning."

Nardell spoke up. "You said it was right in front of your…"

Ryman raised a hand to shush her. "You know how Luella makes everything sound a lot more dramatic than it was. Nardell said she was just chatting with Miles and Conway at the store, happened to mention it to them, Luella must have overheard and taken it out of context."

Nardell stood with her arms crossed and glared at Ryman.

"Well," Thumper said, "I was thinking about canceling Opening Meet because of this. I was worried about something like that fox effigy. But that's pretty minor compared to a fanatic with a high-powered rifle. What if the shooter was this Defender of the Faith who seems to have it in for you?"

"Oh, gosh, Thumper, no need to cancel Opening Meet. This is all being blown out of proportion."

Nardell started to say something but Ryman raised his hand again to stop her.

"Well, if you think it's okay," Thumper said, "I'll trust your judgment. Luella has occasionally been known to take a grain of truth and blow it into a much bigger tale. But, y'know, most of her information is pretty reliable."

"I'm sure this is one of those exceptions. Had to just be someone taking a shot at a deer, couldn't hear with the rain falling or see me clearly. And from here on we'll be wearing scarlet so it'll be easier for people to see me coming."

"Right. Or it'll make you an easier target," Thumper said.

Nardell was close enough to hear Thumper's remark. As Ryman clicked off, she threw her hands up, stormed down the hallway, and slammed the bedroom door behind her.

Wycroft lifted his head off the sofa and looked at Ryman.

"It appears Mama ain't happy."

"Mmmmph." The old hound laid his head down and went back to sleep.

"Yes, have no fear. Our blessed Saint Hubert will allow no harm to come to any of us. We are his children, his chosen servants. Praises to his name!"

Chapter 62

WHEN JANEY ARRIVED at Montfair Friday evening, Thumper was on the front lawn, surrounded by caterers and farm workers, attending to the final details for Saturday's breakfast. She drove past the house and parked in the family area behind the kitchen. High-pitched voices and a mechanical buzzing sound came from the barn. She went to investigate. A line of horses stood in the aisle, secured by cross-ties. Four young women—Elizabeth and three of her classmates visiting for the weekend—and a middle-aged woman—Javier's wife Bettiana—hovered around them clipping, braiding, brushing, polishing, and chatting.

Janey left them to their duties and went to the kitchen where Natasha was hard at work preparing what appeared to be a dozen dishes. "I thought the caterers were handling everything," Janey said.

"Bah! Is not proper meal vithout food from Montfair kitchen. Caterers do not put love into food like I do." She added with a wink, "You be sure to try the curry chicken salad tomorrow."

Natasha bustled around the kitchen, humming the "Man in the Woolen Cap" tune. Janey continued on through the house, up the main staircase and down the hallway toward the corner guest room. As she passed Thumper's bedroom, she noticed the door was open and the sight of his formal hunting attire, laid out for the next morning, caught her eye. She could not resist the temptation to step inside and examine the garments: scarlet frock coat with the Montfair colors on the collar, the buttons emblazoned with the club's logo and buffed to a high sheen; sparkling white collarless shirt and matching four-fold stock tie; canary yellow vest with plain gold buttons; white breeches with a button-fly front and flared seat; black dress boots with brown tops, shined to perfection; a pair of white string gloves.

She knew the finishing touches—his black velvet-covered hardhat and leather hunt whip—were hanging in the mudroom, ready to be grabbed as he dashed out the door in the morning. Javier would be waiting by the mounting block, holding Lenny at the ready for the master's foot to step into the gleaming stirrup.

Janey set her overnight bag down and moved closer to Thumper's hunting kit. A few pieces looked new—shirt, stock tie, gloves—items more subject to wear from hard use. But the main components—coat, vest, breeches, boots—could have been his father's, or even grandfather's. They clearly had seen many hunt seasons, but with proper care remained as serviceable as the day they were made. Moreover, the style had not changed one whit. She thought back to the antique prints she had seen in the hotel and bank lobbies. Someone wearing these garments could have stepped into any of those paintings and looked perfectly in place.

And tomorrow she would be stepping into that scene herself.

She reached out and fondled the lapel of his coat. A sense of permanence flowed through her at the touch, a thread of tradition winding back centuries, a connection to the land, to family, to history. It was the same sensation she felt when she touched the Yir Yoront stone ax head. These were not mere inanimate objects. Spirits lived in them.

A sound from behind startled her and she turned to see Thumper standing in the doorway. A wide grin lit up his face.

Janey turned almost as scarlet as the coat. "I'm sorry. I didn't mean to intrude. The door was open, I couldn't resist a look…"

"I understand. Just doing some research, right? Examining the costumes we primitives wear for our pagan celebrations."

"It is a form of religion, isn't it? Even without Ryman's formality and emphasis on Saint Hubert. There's laity and clergy, clearly identified by the vestments. Specialized jargon, high holy days, a strong desire to pass the beliefs and practices onto the next generation. And, like most religions, there are others who disagree with those beliefs and practices, who feel you are warped and misleading others into sin and damnation."

"I'd like to think I let people find their own way into sin and damnation without any help from me. But, yes, I suppose you have a point." He stepped farther into the room and stood before his laid out hunting kit. "Is it religion? Or a strong cultural connection with religious overtones? The stone ax wasn't a religious element to the Yir Yoront. But it was the cultural mortar that held their society together. When it was replaced with factory made steel axes, social decay quickly followed. 'Foxhunting is the soul of country life,' Beckford said. It is, in a sense, our stone ax."

They stood together silently contemplating the significance of the cloth and leather arrayed before them.

Thumper broke the meditative mood. "I'm embarrassed to say I put you at risk last Saturday."

"Oh, you mean about jumping those logs? It was really pretty exciting. And Bee is so steady…"

"Not that kind of risk, although I should have thought that through better too. I mean legal risk. You're required to have a hunting license to chase foxes in Virginia. Good thing we didn't run into a game warden. You'll need to have one for tomorrow."

"How can I do that now? Here?"

"Not a problem. You can get one online and print it out. Costs a whopping twenty-three bucks for the whole season. We'll do that this evening."

Janey replied in melodramatic fashion, wiping her hand across her forehead. "Whew! And to think I might have been sent to foxhunters prison."

"Also, I've asked Elizabeth to give you a hand in the morning, putting everything together correctly… tying your stock." Janey blinked at the memory of the previous Saturday. "And she said she'd be happy to ride with you in second field, help you out in any way she can. Opening Meet can be a circus and Mildred's likely to have her hands full keeping order in the field. Elizabeth will see to it that you're well clear of any dust-ups."

"That's very nice of her. And of you."

"Right." He clapped his hands and rubbed them together. "Well, dinner should be ready soon. And then I'll make myself scarce so you can have my daughter and her friends all to yourself, squeeze out every detail about foxhunting from their generation's perspective that you can. But don't let them keep you up too late. See you downstairs in a few."

"Thumper."

He stopped midway through his exit. "Yes?"

"Thank you for all your help. And for letting me into your world. I don't take this privilege lightly."

It was the first time he'd heard her address him directly as "Thumper."

He replied with a curt nod and then was gone.

Chapter 63

THE SCENE ON the Montfair front lawn was indeed the foxhunting prints in hotel and bank lobbies come to life. Except Janey was no longer gazing at a frozen two-dimensional image from outside the frame. She was Alice gone through the Looking Glass, riding down the pebbled driveway between Thumper and Elizabeth, as much a part of the costumed pageant as any of the other players.

There appeared to be at least sixty or more mounted riders, ranging from small children on ponies, some secured to a lead-line held by an adult rider, to octogenarians such as Bing Sensabaugh. The group before her spanned four generations, from people old enough to recall the Great Depression and the days before television to those who could not imagine life without instant global communication at the push of a button. Yet here they all were, sharing this archaic sporting practice, arrayed in their finest hunting attire, ready to take part in the grand reenactment of the communal chase.

Thumper left Janey in Elizabeth's care and joined the other masters, staff, and hounds at the center of the tableau.

"Hark, please!"

All eyes turned to the senior master as he prepared to make the welcoming announcements. Along with the standard greeting, a moment of silence in memory of Fergus McKendrick was included.

The spotlight then shifted to Ryman. He squeezed Token a step forward and gazed around at the eager crowd. "Ah, Saint Hubert is surely well pleased. What a glorious display to his eternal honor."

Dan Davenport, watching from the crowd of spectators, snorted as a cloud of pipe smoke erupted from this mouth.

Grantham Meisner shifted in his saddle uneasily and shot a disapproving scowl toward Ryman. He then cast a look of disappointment at Thumper.

Oblivious to their displeasure, Ryman continued. "We come this morning to the seventh article from The Foxhunter's Faith." He held up an index card and read from it. "He who, of his own freewill, goes home before the hounds do, or who is displeased with the day, or who is not fully uplifted, joyful, and thankful because of the day, is an abomination." He slipped the card into the pocket of his scarlet coat and continued. "Now, what do we notice from this admonition? Well, first, there's the word 'freewill.' There are certainly times when someone has no choice but to retire early from the hunt field; lost shoes, injuries, ailments, emergencies—all legitimate reasons to pack it in while hounds continue to hunt on. What our blessed North-Country Hunting Parson is telling us here is that we dishonor our sport and Saint Hubert if we simply decide we're not having a good time, that the hunt's not going the way we'd like it to, or maybe we're angry with someone else and simply ride off in a huff. No, my friends, we should be ever mindful of the tremendous privilege we have, praise be to Saint Hubert, to be out here in this wonderful country, enjoying this fabulous sport.

"How could anyone not be uplifted, joyful and thankful? We've been enjoying some exceptionally good hunting the past couple of months. Will it always be like this? I'm afraid I can't predict that. I can only say that Saint Hubert's will shall be done. Maybe we'll have some days when the foxes just don't feel like playing. Why, maybe that will even happen today." He grinned and cocked his head. "Although I tend to doubt that, if you know what I mean." Several hunters and spectators chuckled and nodded back at him. "But even on such days, Saint Hubert still encourages us to remember how privileged we are to be doing this at all. I reckon you could put it this way: A bad day of foxhunting is... Wait a minute! There is no such thing as a bad day of foxhunting! Saint Hubert be praised!"

A thunderous chorus of "Amen!" erupted from the crowd.

"So, my friends, let us go forth today in that spirit. No matter what happens, may you all be uplifted, joyful, and thankful. And may no one, of his own freewill, go home before the hounds do!" He turned toward Crispie and the waiting pack. "Mister O'Rourke, let's go hunting."

****

If Saint Hubert planned to withdraw his blessings at some point, this was not the day. The action began with a warm-up run on a fox who took his time, made several leisurely loops around the territory, and went to ground in a handy spot for all to see. After a short breather, the second fox kicked up the action, the pace intensified, and an hour later a group of tired but exhilarated hunters stood around the den as Crispie blew "Gone to Ground."

With Elizabeth providing counsel about what to expect and who to steer away from, Janey stayed with the chase stride for stride. Her legs had been sore following her first hunt. Running had been tough the first couple of days. By mid-week the stiffness began to wear off. Now, though, she was feeling the strain again. But it was a satisfying ache, a sensory confirmation that she was mastering a new and challenging experience. And the adrenalin flow was back again, as strong as before, carrying her along on a tide of twisting, turning, thumping, bumping motion. And then the culmination of it all when the fox slipped out of sight.

If Danella Kernan could only see me now, she thought.

The last trills of Crispie's horn were twanging through Janey down to her toes as Ryman rode through the crowd exclaiming his pleasure and flashing the three-finger salute to each person. "Saint Hubert be praised! What a glorious morning of sport he has given us! A badge of glory to you! And to you, and to you, and to…" Grantham Meisner's glower stopped him cold. "Why Brother Grantham, are you not fully uplifted, joyful, and thankful because of this day?"

"I'll tell you what I am. I'm fed up with your 'Saint Hubert be praised' foolishness. And your 'badge of glory' bullshit too. This has gone way too far. You have no idea what trouble all your Venatican church crap is causing me. I shouldn't even be here this morning. By hunting with you it makes everyone think I'm endorsing your craziness." He turned to Kirsten. "Come on, we're going in!"

Heads, including Janey's, turned to catch this exchange.

"Brother Grantham," Ryman pleaded, "are you so upset that you would actually go home before the hounds do? Surely you don't want to be seen as an abomination in the eyes of our blessed Saint Hubert."

"Your blessed Saint Hubert can go to hell. This lunacy has got to stop. If you don't come to your senses, someone's going to have to make you."

The other riders sat in embarrassed silence and watched Grantham turn and ride away. Kirsten followed reluctantly.

Ryman appeared to be on the verge of tears. "Oh him of little faith," he muttered. He looked skyward and offered up a prayer. "May our dear Saint Hubert open his eyes to the truth before it's too late. Protect our brother, and our sister with him. Let no evil befall them. He knows not of what he speaks. Amen."

A few uncomfortable "Amens" were mumbled in response.

Ryman shook himself and tried to regain his merry composure. "Well, my friends. I don't think these wonderful hounds are ready to go home yet. I do believe another fox awaits our arrival. Mister O'Rourke, what say we cast over toward Gretchen's Bottom?"

Crispie sprang lightly back up onto his horse. "Aye, Master, Gretchen's Bottom it is." He blew a short note on his horn to get the hounds' attention. "C'mon, me beauties. Let's be away."

****

"Grantham!" Kirsten called as Meisner cantered off, "slow down. Let's just walk back from here, give the horses a break."

He ignored her pleas and pushed his horse harder. He headed toward a stiff three-feet-six-inch coop in the thick tree line ahead. A convenient hand gate was a short distance off to one side.

"Let's use the gate," Kirsten advised. "No need to jump that. Grantham! Listen to me!"

He spurred his horse on. Kirsten's horse drafted behind, tired but not willing to be left by his barnmate.

Grantham was about four strides from the jump when Kirsten saw something stir in the trees to the right of the coop. The movement revealed a large brown body bounding out from cover. The deer—a buck with a large rack—leapt across the landing path of the coop just as Grantham's horse closed the final strides and reached the take-off spot. The sudden appearance of the buck caused the horse to abort the jump. The forward momentum carried the animal sliding forward into the coop at which point the laws of physics brought the horse to a stop. Grantham, however, remained a body in motion. He was launched from the saddle and flew over the coop alone. The trajectory caused him to somersault as he left the horse. He landed hard on his back. His helmet smacked the firmly packed turf.

Kirsten caught only a fleeting glimpse of the deer; it passed so quickly across the small opening in the tree line and her view was partially blocked by Grantham and his horse. By the time she pulled her horse to a stop, leapt off and scaled the coop to where Grantham lay motionless on the ground, the buck was nowhere to be seen.

She heard the sound of vehicles and looked up to see the car-followers along the farm road at the edge of the field. The caravan stopped and a dozen people poured out of cars and trucks and ran across the field to render aid.

Chet Henderson had served as an EMT with the Paradise Gap volunteer fire department. Although now retired from that service, he was still frequently called on as a first responder for hunt field crashes, especially when Josh Preston wasn't readily available. Chet quickly determined that Grantham was breathing and there did not appear to be any obvious fractures. But beyond that it was impossible to tell the extent of his injuries. There was no doubt he was severely concussed, if not worse, and Chet wasted no time calling for the rescue squad. His knowledge of the procedures and familiarity with the terrain assured help would arrive soon.

Chet had just clicked off his phone when Grantham emitted a low moan. He opened his eyes and looked up at the crowd of people standing around him. His unfocused gaze drifted from face to face, each one vaguely familiar yet somehow strange. A morose man with a salt-and-pepper beard and a clerical collar stared down at him with an air of grave concern. Was the minister giving him his last rites? If he was dead, why did he really need to pee?

"Grantham! Grantham! Can you hear me?"

The voice had a comforting ring to it, an intimate sound, sharp, but feminine.

Yes, yes, I can hear you. The thought formed. But the words did not.

"Grantham!" The voice was stern this time, different, male and commanding. "Don't move. Don't try to get up. Lie still. You've had a bad fall. Help's on the way."

Grantham blinked in response.

"Do you know who I am?" the male voice asked.

A crease formed between his eyebrows. Chuck? Chip? Chet? Yes, it was Chet! "Che.."

"Yes, right! It's Chet."

"Oh, thank goodness!" Kirsten said.

"Do you know who *you* are?" Chet asked.

"Bom…"

"What? No, it wasn't a bomb. You've fallen from your horse."

"A bomin'…"

"Not a bombing, a riding accident. Can you tell me what your name is?"

"My name… my name is… 'Abomination.'"

****

Despite Grantham's injury, the post-hunt atmosphere on the Montfair front lawn was every bit as festive as an Opening Day breakfast should be. Thumper was accepting the expressions of gratitude from a band of appreciative revelers when Chet Henderson waved him over. He joined Chet and Ryman a short distance away from the crowd.

"Grantham sustained a pretty bad concussion," Chet said. "But it doesn't look like he suffered any other serious injuries, nothing broken anyway. I expect he'll be sore for quite awhile, especially his back."

"Any idea what happened?" Thumper asked.

"According to Kirsten it was Grantham's own fault. She tried to tell him not to take the jump, the horses were tired. But he wouldn't listen, just kept thrusting toward it. He was angry, upset, pushing his horse too hard."

"I tried to calm him down," Ryman said, as if Chet blamed him. "I even said a prayer to Saint Hubert for his safety."

Thumper placed a consoling hand on Ryman's shoulder. "Maybe if you hadn't, things would have been even worse." He didn't believe a word of what he was saying, but the distraught look on Ryman's face compelled him to offer comfort. Thumper turned his attention back to Chet. "I wonder why the horse refused. A tired horse might quit dirty like that, especially if it's being pushed too hard to the jump. But Grantham and Kirsten's horses are supremely fit, and very reliable jumpers."

"Kirsten said it all happened so fast she couldn't be certain, but she did see a deer break from the trees just beside the coop. It ran out into the landing area just as Grantham's horse was about to take off."

"A deer you say?" Thumper asked.

"Looked pretty big, she said. She caught a quick glimpse of the rack, enough to know it was a buck. By the time she got to Grantham it was gone."

Ryman's knees wobbled and he turned a sickly shade of pale.

"The strange thing," Chet continued, "is what he said when he regained consciousness. He kept saying 'Abomination' over and over. Said his name was 'Abomination,' said he was an 'Abomination.'" Chet looked at Ryman. "Seems your opening remarks this morning made quite an impression on him."

Thumper reached out to steady Ryman as he began to totter. "You okay, Ry?"

"I… I need to sit. Need a drink."

Marva appeared and told Chet his presence was required to schmooze some visiting guests. Thumper guided Ryman to a row of folding chairs under the tent canopy and they both sat.

"It's my fault," Ryman said. He bowed his head and rubbed his hands back and forth on his thighs. "I called a curse down on him."

"Ry, sorry to break the news to you old buddy, but that's complete bullshit. Okay, so maybe all your Saint Hubert crap pushed Grantham over the edge. I've been trying to tell you to tone it down. But what happened was purely Grantham's own fault. Or just one of those things that happens out here in the hunt field. Lots of people have been hurt much worse. Some even killed. You think that was all your fault too? Or that Saint Hubert was out to get them?"

"We're not talking about what's happened to others, at other times. I said he'd be an abomination if he went in before the hounds did. And look how it turned out. Saint Hubert even sent the buck to make sure it happened."

Thumper took a deep breath and twisted his neck to prepare for the distaste of the words that were about to come out of his mouth. "Maybe…

maybe Saint Hubert sent the buck to assure Grantham's foolishness didn't turn out much worse. Maybe that was the answer to your prayer. If Grantham had kept his cool, he'd have taken it slower, used the gate like Kirsten wanted. But, no, he had to be a hothead. Suppose… just suppose… that the horse had tried to take the jump, but, say, he hit the coop, flipped, and landed on Grantham."

What little color remained in Ryman's face drained as he conjured up that terrible image.

"Sad to say we've seen it happen," Thumper continued. "More than once over all the years we've been doing this. At least two or three headstones in the old church cemetery I can think of. So—and I'm just guessing here—maybe what happened was to assure Grantham didn't end up with anything more than a royal concussion and a sore back."

"You think?"

"Just guessing. But possible I reckon."

A faint smile lightened Ryman's face and a trace of color returned. "Yeah, possible. Saint Hubert be praised." It was more mumble than exultation.

Nardell appeared holding two flutes of champagne. "Ryman, the people are asking for you. Everyone's just thrilled with the day's sport. Three foxes, great runs. A little concerned about Grantham, of course, but the reports are all positive. Kirsten's sent some texts from the hospital, says he's awake, alert, no signs of injury other than the head bonk. They're going to keep him overnight for observation. Bing said he'd drive Grantham's truck and trailer back to their farm, take care of the horses. Marie will drive Bing's rig and follow him. So all is well." She handed him a glass. "Come on. Your people await."

He stood up, accepted the drink, and took a sip. He straightened his vest, squared his shoulders, and said, "Yes, yes. My people." The Prophet and his acolyte strode off to greet their growing body of believers.

****

Reverend Dan found Janey among the crowd. A stream of smoke meandered from the briar pipe clenched between his teeth as he sized up her hunting attire. "So you've gone native."

"Purely for research purposes. I've hunted in the Kalahari with the San Bushmen to better understand their way of life. Just doing the same thing here."

"Were you wearing nothing more than a loincloth when you hunted with the San?"

"Well, no, of course not. But that… well, that was different."

"Varying degrees of going native then?"

"Yes, I suppose you could say that."

****

Encouraged by Thumper's assurance that Grantham's accident was not the work of Saint Hubert, or that his prayer to the good saint may have even spared Grantham from worse injury, Ryman remained at the breakfast until the last guests were straggling off. Every attendee received the three-finger salute and the Jäger blessing, some multiple times.

As the host, Thumper had also stayed to bid good-bye to the last partiers and to then settle up with the caterers. A sense of obligation kept Janey there as well.

Ryman was blessing the catering crew when Janey asked Thumper, "Are you sure Grantham will be okay? From what I've heard, it was a pretty nasty fall."

"Grantham rode as an amateur on the steeplechase circuit for many years, both around here and in the UK. He's had his share of spills. Spent a good bit of time in the hospital as a result of some of them. This one seems fairly mild by comparison."

"You mentioned when we first met that he's your cousin. But he grew up in England. How'd he end up here?"

"Haven't you asked him that as part of your research?"

"He's been a bit stand-offish. I don't really know why, but when someone reacts negatively, I tend not to press too hard. Better to wait and give them time to warm up to me."

"Or try to get the information you want from someone else. Like, say, a cousin."

"You've found me out again. I can't fool you."

"I'd like to think you wouldn't try to."

"No, of course not. Never."

Thumper studied Janey's face, looking for even the slightest trace of duplicity, some remote flicker of the practiced spy. All he saw was genuine earnestness fueled by her professional curiosity.

"Okay, here's the thumbnail bio. His father was an executive with a British insurance company, an international firm. He hopped around from country to country, dragged the family along with him. Grantham's boyhood covered much of the globe. He spent his teen years at Tonbridge, a boarding school in the UK. When he finished there, his mother, one of the Richmond Crutchfields, insisted he get the rest of his schooling here in Virginia. I was in my third year at The University when he showed up. I took him under my wing and we became fast friends. He joined my fraternity and I was his big brother. The relationship only became shaky when he started outscoring me in polo matches. He went into association work after school, eventually parlayed that and his equestrian skills into the plum job with NAFCA. Done a helluva job for the sport. Will that do?"

"Very nicely. Thank you."

With no one left to bless, Ryman and Nardell joined them. They stood together on the Montfair lawn and watched the workers pack up the tables and chairs.

Nardell leaned against Ryman's side and he wrapped an arm around her. The rush of the morning's chases and the stimulation from the revelry that followed still stirred in their blood. A generous quantity of Thumper's champagne added a bubbling looseness in the joints.

Nardell turned her face up toward Ryman's with an unmistakable suggestion of what would soon follow. He responded with a passionate kiss. They remained in lip-lock as they swiveled toward each other, arms entwined around bodies. A slow grind began to flow in their hips.

Thumper caught their attention with an "Ahem!"

They stopped kissing but remained embraced.

"Oh, sorry," Ryman said, no trace of remorse on his leering face. "Forgot you guys were there." Addressing Janey, he said, "Ain't foxhunting the most stimulating thing you've ever experienced?"

"Um, well, it's certainly thrilling. While you're doing it anyway."

Nardell added her two cents. "Yes. And afterwards, and before, sometimes even during."

Thumper caught the flush of modesty on Janey's cheeks.

"Are you coming along for the joint meet next week?" Ryman asked Janey.

Thumper answered on her behalf. "She will be there but not mounted. You know what a circus joint meets can be. With only two hunts under her belt, I thought it best to stick to car-following. She'll ride again the following week when we're back in our home territory."

Ryman shrugged. "Makes sense, I suppose." He then returned his attention to Nardell. "Hey, darlin', what say we hightail it back to the shack?"

"Race you to the truck!" she replied and took off at a sprint.

"See ya, guys." Ryman waggled an eyebrow at Thumper and Janey, then sauntered along after Nardell. He jangled his keys in the air as a reminder that she wasn't going anywhere without him.

"Well," Thumper said, trying to sound matter-of-fact, "looks like we're finally done here." He glanced at his watch. "Damn, I didn't realize it was so late. You must be exhausted. Maybe a nap would be in order before dinner. You are staying, aren't you?"

"Oh, I appreciate the offer, but I don't want to overstay my welcome."

"You wouldn't be overstaying…"

"So much to do, busy day tomorrow. This has all been wonderful. But I really should be going."

Thumper thought of the evening ahead. Elizabeth and her guests had plans to meet other college-age friends at a bar in Warrenton. It would be well past midnight before they returned to Montfair. Natasha had left some light fare in the fridge and taken the rest of the day off. The house would be empty. If Janey stayed over, she and Thumper would be alone, the stimulation of the day's chase still teasing at their senses, no one to interrupt whatever might happen.

"Yes," he said. "Perhaps you're right. Until next week then."

****

Back at the cottage, Ryman found the keys to unlock a variety of pleasures. It was late evening before he and Nardell collapsed into exhausted slumber.

Arising later in the night to relieve himself, Ryman could not resist the lure of the office and went in to check his email. His chest swelled and he muttered "Saint Hubert be praised" repeatedly as he read through several congratulatory comments and favorable postings. But the glow faded into a cold shiver when he saw that another message awaited from The Defender. It took a minute of internal debate before he decided to give it a read.

> Proverbs 16:5: "Everyone who is arrogant in heart is an abomination to the Lord; be assured, he will not go unpunished."
>
> Proverbs 15:9: "The way of the wicked is an abomination to the Lord, but he loves him who pursues righteousness."
>
> Your arrogance and wickedness are leading you to destruction, and leading many innocents astray. You dare speak of "Abomination?" YOU are the abomination before the Lord. As His Word says, be assured, you will not go unpunished.
>
> The Defender of the Faith

Okay, Ryman thought, maybe this is getting serious. Should he write back? Perhaps Saint Hubert would guide his words so he could win this person over. Or would it be better to just ignore this crank? Was it possible to trace the email address and find out who was sending these messages?

He Googled "threatening anonymous emails," skimmed through a few web pages, and concluded that it would be difficult, likely impossible, to find out who this was without involving the authorities. And they could only help if the messages contained clear threats. He thought back over the string of emails he'd received and he couldn't really say they were overtly threatening. The messages were all taken directly from the Bible. Not like the sender himself was saying, "I'm personally going to harm you." More like "You're in trouble with God." Not exactly something the police would be interested in. And then there was Thumper's concern about bad publicity.

Ryman rubbed his hands over his face. His eyes were bleary and his mind fuzzy. No, let it go. Better not to engage. Not now anyway. Back to bed.

He found Nardell spooning with Wycroft. He curled himself against her other side and the three of them slept, two soundly, one not so much.

****

Bing sat uneasily listening to Reverend Davenport expound on the Seventh Commandment. It was long ago, but he'd replayed the details in his mind so many times over the years that he remembered everything as if it had been yesterday. True, he'd gone in before the hounds did. But with a good excuse—a nasty fall and an injured back. It plagued him still. The house was close, he just needed to rest, get some ice on the sore spot. He remembered the tender nursing, playful teasing, the shock of an icepack pressed against his back, the touch of her hand on his bare skin.

He should have seen it coming. They both should have. Their lighthearted banter masked the true nature of their feelings. Years of pent up verbal foreplay exploded in one afternoon of indiscretion. It might have been put away after that, kept forever secret between them. But they were found. And the results still rippled four decades later.

"And so, my friends," Dan said as he reached his conclusion, "I think we can all agree that this is a very straightforward commandment, easily understood, black and white, no room for alternative interpretation. Thou… shalt… not… commit… adultery! Let us pray."

As Bing bowed his head, a sharp twinge shot up his back.

Chapter 64

SOME CLUBS ENCOURAGE their members to dress up in costumes, for both rider and horse, when a hunting day falls on Halloween. Such frivolity was not observed at the venerable Montfair Hunt. On this subject Thumper and Ryman found a point of agreement, albeit for different reasons. Thumper's was his devotion to the traditions established by his great-grandfather and steadfastly observed through the succeeding generations. Ryman's was his belief that Saint Hubert did not want the holy message of the Venatican Church weakened by the practice of silly customs like Halloween.

To emphasize that position, Ryman led the post-hunt singing with even more than his usual vigor. The riders had enjoyed another Tuesday morning of exhilarating sport and all were eager participants in the songfest. All, that is, except Thumper who loaded up his horse and left before the singers had finished the second stanza of the first song. The absence of Baden and Beatrice on this school day left a noticeable gap in the choral quality, but Bing covered much of the shortcomings of his fellow choir members. And what those others lacked in vocal skill they amply made up for in enthusiasm.

Eventually, though, even Bing's talent could not drown out Nardell's screeching and Ryman called it quits. As he was heading to his trailer, Bing took him by the arm.

"A word please," Bing said as he guided Ryman away from Nardell and the others.

"I know, I know," Ryman said. "The rest of us can't hold a candle to you and the kids. Nardell especially. She so wants to be in the choir but, Saint Hubert forgive me, the woman can't carry a tune in a…"

"That's not what I need to talk to you about."

"…bucket. Mildred's not bad, though. Better than I expected. And Marie…"

"Ryman, listen to me. Focus here. This is serious."

"Well, yes, of course it is. We don't want to do anything that would dishonor Saint Hu…"

"This isn't about Saint Hubert. It's not about the choir and it's not about your church."

"Well, it isn't exactly *my* church. It's Saint Hubert's church. I'm just the..."

"Ryman, for Christ sakes, listen to me! This is about the shop. We've got a serious problem. *You've* got a serious problem. *Bob's* got a serious problem. Bob's problem is with the auditors. And if the auditors aren't happy, nobody's happy. The old times when your father and I could do business with a handshake are gone. Bob asked me to talk to you, let you know that if the credit line isn't paid down substantially, and soon, he'll have no choice but to begin... well, let's just say it's not going to be pleasant for anyone, on either side."

Ryman crumbled into his habitual slouch. "Ah, well, damn, Bing. What can I do, I mean, really? I'm sure things will turn around. Bar's doing a helluva job, but he's just getting started. Sheltie Lou's helping too, with a website and some marketing stuff. But that all takes time. If Bob could just give them... give us... a bit longer. Hell, no more than a few months. We're getting into the slow winter season now. Likely to be spring before we really start to see much improvement."

"I know Bob would do that if he could, Ry. If things aren't cleaned up to the satisfaction of the auditors, and quickly, they can downgrade the bank's rating. Bob has a fiduciary duty to the customers and the shareholders. He can't just blow off the auditors, tell them not to worry, good old McKendrick and Sons will come through eventually."

"How quickly?"

"Bob says he can give you two weeks."

"Two weeks? Holy shit. How much are we talking about?"

Bing quoted a figure.

Ryman whistled. "Man, that's more than I'd a thought. A lot more."

"Perhaps you didn't know just how bad the situation was."

"Daddy handled all the money stuff."

"And, I'm sorry to say, not particularly well these past few years. It seemed, at times, that he was stuck in the '50s, that he couldn't, or wouldn't, get a grip on how business is done today. And then, well, then he was gone. So now it's your ballgame, Ry."

"Daddy left the farm and all the personal assets to Ma. Pretty good life insurance policy too, I believe, although she hasn't shared any of the details with me. I've socked away a tiny bit over the years, figured that and some horse dealing would keep me going till the shop got back on its feet, so I could concentrate on what Saint Hubert's called me..." A tiny shred of doubt about his calling caused Ryman's posture to sag even more. Bing saw the look of confusion and pain in his pale green eyes. "But even if I plunked all of it into the business, it wouldn't put a dent in what's owed."

"I don't mean to get too personal here," Bing said, "but maybe your mother could help. And when the business gets on its feet again, she can be paid back."

A trace of hope lightened Ryman's face. But it quickly faded to despair when he realized what a deal with Rhetta would mean. "Can't you get us a bit more time? I know you're retired but you're still on the board, right?"

"It's just an honorary position, a bone tossed to an old man so he doesn't feel totally useless. It's not my place to deal with the auditors, nor to tell Bob what to do. It's his responsibility now."

"So how come it's not him giving me this bad news?"

"Well, you know, things are a bit, um, strained between you two just now, aren't they? Bob felt this would be better coming from me. And I think that was wise of him." Bing placed his hand on Ryman's arm. "This is hard for me too, Ry. You understand, don't you?"

Ryman nodded.

"Well," Bing said, "you've got two weeks. See what you can do."

****

Ryman sat in his office and stared blankly at the computer screen.

Nardell appeared in the doorway. "I've got to run out for a bit," she said, pulling on a jacket. "Won't be long."

"Yeah, okay," he said absently, without turning away from the computer.

Nardell pulled her braid loose from the jacket and paused to assess Ryman's distracted state. "Are you all right?"

"Huh? Oh, yeah. Just concentrating on my sermon for this Saturday. Big day coming, our first time out of Montfair territory this season. Want to be sure I do Saint Hubert proud."

"His name be praised."

"Yeah."

"You'll do fine. Those Marylanders will be thrilled to hear the good news of the Venatican Church."

"Yeah."

"You sure you're okay?"

"Fine. Just thinking, that's all."

"Well, don't push yourself too hard. Saint Hubert will guide you. He always has. Gotta run. Be back soon."

"Yeah."

Nardell drove off with conflicted thoughts. She was relieved to have gotten away without Ryman pestering her about where she had to go so late on Halloween night. But she might have preferred the pestering to the funk he appeared to be in, the lack of any concern about why she had to run out. She was also angry with herself. How could she have forgotten her earlier promise? It was almost midnight. The others would already be there, with ample time to cause mischief. Could she still stop them in time? She'd been so focused on the Venatican Church and her role as Ryman's chief helper that she'd put most other entanglements out of her mind. Maybe the others had forgotten too. She'd extended the offer months earlier. They might have made different plans. But the failure to get through on anyone's cell phone led her to assume they'd taken her up on it and were even now doing what she feared would happen.

She turned her Outback off Montfair Lane onto a rough farm road. Even with the high beams on it was hard to see where she was going. But she kept the pedal down, gripped the wheel, gritted her teeth, and drove on.

****

Ryman was still sitting where she'd left him when she returned to the cottage. Trying to control her breathing and sound as casual as possible, she called out from the living room. "I'm back, sweetheart."

"Mmmmph."

"Okay, I'm going to bed now. You should knock off and come get some sleep too."

"Mmmmph."

It was hardly a secret in Crutchfield County that the McKendrick business was in trouble. Miles Flanagan's big mouth was likely responsible for half the population knowing. And Luella Starett could have easily reached the other half. So the latest message from The Defender, received earlier that evening, may have had nothing to do with Bing's warning about the line of credit. Still, the double whammy sent Ryman spiraling even further into despair.

Could The Defender have been one of the people at the morning's hunt? Ryman had gone through the list of participants multiple times and no one stood out as a possibility. Bing had carefully taken him aside where no one else could have heard their conversation. Could Bing be The Defender? He didn't appear to have any problem with the Venatican Church. He was even serving as an essential part of the team by leading the choir. Ryman remembered something about the guy who betrayed Jesus being one of his trusted helpers. But Ryman's lack of formal church training left him a bit fuzzy on the details.

Nor could he recall having ever seen the two most recent Bible quotes from The Defender. But whether or not their timing was coincidental, their intent was plain.

> Proverbs 13:18 (NIV): Whoever disregards discipline comes to poverty and shame, but whoever heeds correction is honored.
>
> Proverbs 28:19 (NIV): Those who work their land will have abundant food, but those who chase fantasies will have their fill of poverty.

Poverty and shame. Such black marks awaited him in just two weeks if he could not figure out a way to stave off the bank before then. And wouldn't The Defender rejoice over that?

A night of deep thought and fervent prayer to Saint Hubert, focused to the point where he barely noticed Nardell's departure and return, yielded no answer.

It was nearly dawn before he finally crawled into bed. In his distracted state, he was oblivious to the fact that Nardell had not slept a wink either.

Chapter 65

BY WEDNESDAY EVENING no plan, whether from Saint Hubert or any other source, had been revealed to save the shop. Adding to Ryman's troubles was the need to prepare a special sermon for Saturday's hunt when Montfair would be travelling to Maryland for a joint meet with Tiber Creek Hounds. The schedule called for Article Eight from "The Foxhunter's Faith" to be the topic for that day:

> "Whosoever kills or takes a fox by other means save by hunting is an abomination; may his dwelling become desolate and his possessions a desert; may his mind be filled with bitterness and his body with pain."

Ryman had never violated this Article. Yet he felt the weight of these words as acutely as if they applied directly to him. A desolate dwelling, loss of possessions, and a mind filled with bitterness awaited him in less than a fortnight. Surely bodily pain would somehow follow as well.

The more he pondered the words of the North-Country Hunting Parson and the most recent quotes from The Defender, the more the Biblical tone began to gel in his mind. The Defender was using Bible quotes to convince him, in a threatening way, to abandon his service to Saint Hubert. The Parson mimicked Biblical form for his Articles. Perhaps the answer could be found in that same vein. Fight fire with fire. Play The Defender at his own game. Ryman's ability to call up Bible passages from memory was non-existent. But that gap in his education could be easily overcome. Ryman had a computer.

Having no idea where to start, it took several hours of searching, countless cyber trips down blind alleys, before he found something that struck a chord. It came from Luke, chapter 9, verse 62: "And Jesus said unto him, No man, having put his hand to the plough, and looking back, is fit for the kingdom of God."

Ryman didn't know much about Holy Scripture, but he knew a thing or two about plowing. And he knew what happened if you looked back instead of straight ahead. He'd learned to drive a tractor before he was old enough to drive a car. His father taught him the importance of plowing in a straight line. You pick a spot on the far side of the field—a fencepost, tree, rock, something stationary to serve as your guide—and you plow directly to that point. Take your eyes off that target, look back to see where you've been, and you'll veer off course. Neat, well-ordered furrows are plowed by those who know how to stay focused on the goal, those who, having put their hand to the task, do not look back.

Ryman fixed his eyes on the computer screen, put his hands to the keyboard, brought up his unfinished draft for Saturday's sermon, and plowed ahead.

****

A bounce had returned to Ryman's step by Thursday morning.

Thumper caught him just before he mounted Colby. "All ready for Saturday?"

"You betcha!"

"That's what I was afraid of. Look, I'd like to ask you, as a personal favor to me, to skip all the Saint Hubert stuff, the preaching, singing, blessing shenanigans for this joint meet."

"Why should I do that? This will be a wonderful opportunity to spread the word to those who…"

"Because we will be the guests. You wouldn't go into someone's home and just start preaching your Venatican Church nonsense. That would be rude."

"There's nothing rude about spreading the good word Saint Hubert wants people to hear. You've seen how our people are joyful and uplifted, how others are flocking to hear the news and enjoy the bountiful sport he's laid before us. And today's going to be just as grand. If we want the Saturday sport to be the same, we must honor his name."

"It's not up to us to show good sport on Saturday. That's up to the folks at Tiber Creek. It's their country, they've invited us to come along."

"We're bringing some of our hounds too."

"Yes, but it's still proper for us to defer to them as our hosts."

Ryman took a breath and considered Thumper's request. "My hand is on the plow. I must not look back."

Thumper blinked. "What's that supposed to mean?"

"It means I must keep to the straight path. A badge of glory awaits at the end of each furrow. No obstacle can block my way. If I swerve, I will not be worthy of Saint Hubert's calling. Fear not, my friend. Saint Hubert will allow no dishonor to befall the Montfair Hunt." He swung up onto his horse. Smiling down at a frustrated Thumper Billington, Ryman flashed the three-finger salute. "Now let's go hunting."

Chapter 66

TIBER CREEK HOUNDS boasted a history almost as stellar as Montfair's. Founded shortly after the turn of the Twentieth Century, it began as a club for the elite of Washington: congressmen, diplomats, military officers, jurists, and business leaders. Suburban development steadily pushed the sport farther out into the Maryland countryside. And only the rare personage of note—a former ambassador or retired general—now appeared among their members on a hunting day.

But while few, if any, of the current members were likely to find their names listed in a Bob Woodward index, they remained strong in number and devoted in spirit.

The bustle of pre-hunt preparation was well underway when Janey pulled into the field. Having attended the memorial hunt for Fergus McKendrick and the Montfair Opening Meet, she was already familiar with the extra measure of pageantry that goes into a special day, in this case a joint meet between two old and respected hunt clubs. Scarlet coats were in abundance, horses' manes, and even a few tails, were artfully braided, several women were decked out in shadbelly coats and top hats.

Riders mounted up and milled about exchanging friendly chatter. Volunteer servers moved through the crowd with trays of stirrup cup libations.

Scanning the scene through the lens of her video camera, Janey noticed two ladies riding sidesaddle. The sight of their flowing black skirts and veiled faces propelled Janey back to the hotel lobby where the seeds of her quest had first been sown. Here was the embodiment of those images from a lost time, figures she thought were trapped in frozen frames now brought to life before her.

She felt uncomfortably out of place in her plain modern clothes, a piece of electronic equipment in her hand. She wanted to be in the picture herself, as she had been at the Montfair Opening Meet. Was there any sidesaddle attire in the Billington attic? A saddle stored away somewhere on the estate? Was she really prepared to go native to that extent? It was certainly more appealing than wearing a loincloth with the Bushmen of the Kalahari.

One scarlet-coated gentleman peeled away from the others and guided his horse over toward Janey. She felt a shiver of anticipation.

"I'm glad you came," Thumper said, gallantly doffing his hunt cap. "Should be quite a spectacle."

She pointed to her video camera. "I'm ready for it."

"Crispie and Patti are looking forward to spending time with you tomorrow. Nothing Crispie enjoys more than bragging about his hounds. Be prepared to learn every name, each hound's character, and the miniscule details of the blood lines all the way back to General Washington and Thomas, the Sixth Lord Fairfax."

"Do they really go back that far?"

"Some claim so, and possibly even farther. Oh, and one other thing. Bring along your riding gear. If you're going to hunt with us again next Saturday, you need some saddle time in between. And old Bee needs to keep moving to stay fit. I've arranged for Patti to work with you in the ring. She's an excellent instructor."

"That's very kind." She looked over at the two sidesaddle ladies. "You wouldn't happen to have… I mean, there isn't any chance that there'd be…?"

The horn sounded as the Tiber Creek huntsman and staff moved off with hounds from the club's kennels and rode up toward the meet location.

"What?" Thumper asked.

Janey decided her request was a bit premature. "Oh, nothing. It can wait. You've got to go join the others now."

"Right, that I do. But there should be a splendid breakfast after. We can catch up on more then."

He rode off and joined the group just as the Montfair hounds were released from their trailer. The two packs mingled together, sniffing and wiggling in exuberant canine greeting. The two huntsmen and their staffs did essentially the same, albeit in a more restrained manner.

Janey darted about, videotaping and interviewing as many Tiber Creek members as possible. Thumper arranged for her to ride with the leader of the Tiber Creek car-followers when the hunt moved off.

All activity halted when the senior master of the host club called out "Hark, please!"

Welcoming announcements were made, honored guests were recognized, and the visiting masters and staff were introduced. When Ryman's turn came, he moved forward and took center stage.

"Thank you, Master," he began, tipping his cap to the Tiber Creek senior leader. "I'd like to take just a minute to share a thought from 'The Foxhunters Faith,' a wonderful piece written many years ago that reminds us of the reverence we should have for this sport we are all so blessed to enjoy."

His opening line did not strike anyone as out of place on this special occasion. But while the Tiber Creek people did not know where Ryman was going, Thumper did. He carefully moved closer to his joint-master, ready to intercede before the situation got out of hand.

"Article Eight of this statement of faith begins this way: 'Whosoever kills or takes a fox by any other means save by hunting, is an abomination.' Now I'm sure y'all are familiar with the ban on foxhunting in England. This misguided law has made it illegal to chase and kill a fox with a pack of hounds. But it says nothing about killing foxes through other means. Trapping, shooting, poisoning foxes? Oh, that's all okay. Only hounds are forbidden. How sad that England, the very home of our beloved sport, has gotten things completely turned around."

Thumper could hear a questioning murmur start to ripple through the crowd. He moved Lenny another step closer to Ryman.

"It's all those other means of killing foxes that should be considered an abomination," Ryman said. "Only hunting with hounds is right and honorable. Of course, we've taken it one more step here in America where we don't even seek to kill the fox, just enjoy a fun chase until the fox is ready to call it quits.

"Now as for what the author says about the consequences of taking a fox by any means other than by a fair and sporting hunt, he leaves no doubt what he thinks should befall such people. He says, 'may his dwelling become…"

"Thank you, Ryman!" Thumper said. "Those are very enlightening thoughts." He turned to the Tiber Creek senior master, leaving Ryman frozen in open-mouthed interruption. "Well, Master, shall we go hunting?"

The huntsmen called their hounds to attention and the combined pack began to move off. As Thumper started to follow, Ryman said, "I worked on this message for days. I was just getting to the serious part. Why'd you stop me?"

"You know damn well why. You were about to embarrass the Montfair Hunt in front of our hosts, who are old and dear friends. I can't let you do that." He reached over and patted Ryman's thigh. "You can finish your sermon at our Tuesday meet. I'm sure our members will want to hear the rest. They've gotten used to this nonsense."

Hounds worked well and a fox was up and away in short order. The chase coursed through the best part of the Tiber Creek country. The hunters savored an excellent run, with plenty of fences for the first field, rolling country and easy gates for the non-jumpers, and several views of the quarry as he managed to keep just ahead of hounds.

The car-followers enjoyed an equally good view of the action.

Riding shotgun with the group's leader, Janey was treated to a running commentary, including the names and hunting qualities of each hound in the Tiber Creek pack.

When the time came for Sir Charles to retire for the morning, he chose an unusual but seemingly effective spot. There had once been a gazebo in the backyard of an old house, now abandoned and fallen into decay. The upper portion of the gazebo was gone, but the floor remained, a deck-like platform of solid planks, just high enough for a fox to squirm under but no room for any portion of a hound more than its nose.

Seconds after the fox slipped into this safe haven, hounds swarmed the platform. Both huntsmen leapt from their horses and cheered their hounds, congratulating them on their excellent work. The first and second fields arrived and the whippers-in came in quickly from their flanking positions. The driveway to the old house was still sufficiently passable for the car-followers to pull in as well.

Crispie called his hounds off the platform and prepared to regroup and go in search of a second fox. The Tiber Creek huntsman, however, made an unexpected move. He jumped up onto the old gazebo floor and began stomping on the planks. "We'll get him out! C'mon, boys! Get at him!"

Ryman rode forward. "What are you doing?"

"Rousting him out! What does it look like I'm doing. I'll get this bugger."

"You can't do that. It isn't sporting. He's gone to ground, the chase is over. Let him be."

"I'll be damned if I'll let him be. My hounds are eager for blood. They'll taste his yet."

Ryman turned to the Tiber Creek senior master. "This isn't right. Aren't you going to stop him?"

"I let my huntsman hunt his foxes as he sees fit," he replied coolly.

The man continued to stomp and rage across the platform. Rotted planks began to collapse under the heavy blows of his booted feet. The Tiber Creek hounds became increasingly frantic, sensing what their leader was up to and catching the scent of distress wafting up from the fox as his shelter crumbled around him.

The Montfair hounds remained packed up to one side, excited and confused but held out of the fray by Crispie's steady hand. He, too, thought this behavior very unsporting, but if this was how the hosts conducted their hunting, he would not interfere with the master's wishes. Patti and Nardell moved to assist him, assuring their hounds would not take part in this travesty.

"Thumper!" Ryman pleaded. "We must stop him. In Saint Hubert's name, we can't allow this."

"He has a point," Thumper said to the Tiber Creek master. "Do we really want to see the fox broken up in this way? And in front of so many ladies and children?"

"When did you become opposed to accounting for a fox? Seems I've known your pack to take a few under your leadership."

"Yes, but most all of them when the fox was diseased or suffering and needed to be culled. And always where the fox had a sporting chance. This… this is simply vulpicide."

The host master flipped a hand and curtly dismissed Thumper's protestations.

The platform continued to cave in under the huntsman's pounding. His hounds were on the verge of riot as the fox slipped around just out of their grasp, seeking what last bits of cover remained, trying to forestall the inevitable moment when he would be forced to flee, his escape surely cut short by the jaws of the nearest hound.

Seeing no other recourse, Ryman moved quickly to the opposite side of the platform, where the edge of the yard ended in thick, tangled bushes. A nod to Nardell as he rode by the Montfair pack signaled her to join him. They took up sentry positions and awaited the fox's emergence.

Ryman mumbled a prayer. "Blessed Saint Hubert, let no harm befall our brother fox. Give him the courage to flee and the speed to succeed. May we, your servants, find the strength to stand our ground and protect our brother. Amen."

A few more tense seconds passed. The Tiber Creek huntsman stamped his feet and bellowed. His hounds were wild-eyed and frothing. Ryman gave Nardell another nod and they both withdrew their pistols. Just as the weapons cleared their holsters, the fox broke from his last bit of cover and darted straight toward his protectors. The hounds were so frantic that it took them a moment to realize the fox had fled. Only when the huntsman hollered, "There he is! On to him, lads! On to him!" did they spring from the platform and give chase.

The fox made a straight line for the bushes, running at full speed between Ryman and Nardell's horses. As hounds came on, two pistols let loose a double blast of birdshot into the ground in front of them. The pack immediately froze and went silent. The fox dived into the bushes and was safely away.

The Tiber Creek huntsman was anything but silent. "What the hell are you doing?" He jumped off the remains of the old gazebo floor and marched toward Ryman. "These are not your hounds! This is not your hunt! You son-of-a-bitch, you got a lot a goddamn nerve. No one interferes with my hounds. I oughta pull you off that horse and give you a thrashing you won't for…"

Ryman raised his pistol and pointed it at the man. "And I, sir, should give you a taste of your own medicine."

The huntsman froze along with his hounds. All the venom in his voice now concentrated in his eyes, wide and glaring with hatred.

"But I know Saint Hubert has his own reward in store for you," Ryman said. "You are an abomination before his eyes. As the scripture says, may your dwelling become desolate and your possessions a desert, may your mind be filled with bitterness and your body with pain."

Ryman lowered his pistol and looked toward Thumper. "I think we'd best go home now."

"Yes, I think you're right." He turned to the Tiber Creek master. "The Montfair Hunt will now retire from this field. I thank you for your hospitality. I hope you'll understand if we do not stay for the breakfast."

Chapter 67

"WHAT IS 'STEALING?'" Reverend Davenport asked. "The Eighth Commandment tells us we should not steal. Sounds pretty simple and straightforward, doesn't it? If someone breaks into your home and makes off with your possessions, that's stealing. If someone mugs you on the street and takes your wallet, that's stealing. Embezzling funds from your employer. Defrauding people out of their savings. Gaining access to someone's bank account and cleaning it out. Stealing, stealing, stealing.

"But can you be robbed of something more important than money? Most certainly. You can be robbed of your good reputation through slanderous gossip. You could be robbed of your livelihood by the deceitful practices of others, those who would turn away your customers, or your audience, with bait-and-switch tactics, shoddy merchandise, or fantastic promises. Oh, these tricks may fail in the end. But not before they've done real damage to those who strive to practice their professions with integrity and honor."

Reverend Dan paused to let his points sink in with his Sunday morning congregation.

"And what, then, should be done with the thief? He must be rooted out from among us! His ways of guile and deceit must be resisted, and shown for what they are. That he would rob people of their very souls by leading them astray with delusions and fantasies. Resist, my brothers and sisters! Resist the thief who bedazzles you with trickery and false claims. Resist!"

****

Janey had experienced many pungent and exotic smells in her travels. The aroma of a kennel that housed sixty-plus working foxhounds was a new one. It was not offensive, thanks to the diligent, daily work of Crispie, Patti, and Voytek. Although strong, it had a homey, comfortable musk about it, like grandmother's quilt.

After a lengthy session in which huntsman and whipper-in explained the finer details of their jobs and the breeding, training, and hunting of a pack of hounds, Patti excused herself to catch up on some office work, leaving Crispie to give Janey the kennel tour. She took notes as Crispie described the personality, vocal qualities, and hunting style of each hound. The bloodlines went back centuries, some of the purest bred canines in the world. He explained how the foxhound was close to what a dog should be in its natural state.

"Y'see, humans have misused selective breeding for their own amusement. Dogs with flat faces to look more like humans, but they can't breathe right. Giant breeds that don't live long and have hip trouble. Skulls that are too small to hold the brain. All sarts a silly things we've done to the poor beasts, and all just for human vanity.

"But you take the foxhound." He pointed to Hempstead. "Now that's what a dog should look like, sturdy, well-balanced, an animal that looks like a dog, not a stuffed toy, and is made to do its job like the true athlete it is."

"Among the people I've talked to in my research," Janey said, "several have said they're always called hounds, not dogs."

"Aye, as a group, yes. A male is a dog, and a female is a bitch. That was once the standard way of referring to any canine. But these days it's pretty much only hunters who still know that."

They strolled down the kennel's center aisle and into the open yard next to the cottage. Janey noticed a vegetable garden, now fully harvested and ready to rest for the winter. A white picket fence with a decorative flourish along the top bordered the garden on all four sides. A gate hung in an arched frame. "I'm surprised you have time for gardening with so much work to do taking care of all these animals, hounds and horses both."

"That's Patti's hobby, not much interest in it m'self. She says it makes the place feel more like a home. Important to a woman I suppose."

Janey thought about her own gypsy lifestyle, how she'd left behind the sense of closeness to the land that everyone else in her family valued. Her mother kept a vegetable garden, about the same size as Patti's. It too would now be going dormant for the long Minnesota winter.

There was a poorly repaired breach in the fence. "What happened here?" she asked.

"Lots a marauding critters around, always trying to get in and feast on whatever Patti's growing. If they can't climb it or slip under it, they'll try to knock it down. Gotta get this piece fixed better. Patti's been after me for that. A carse, now that the growing season's over, there ain't much urgency to it."

Janey stood looking at the damaged spot. After a long moment, she said, "Crispie, what's your honest opinion about what Ryman's doing?"

"Ah, lass, that's the question, ain't it? My honest opinion is… I'm not sure what to think. I thought it was a load a crap at first. But, well, you've seen a good bit of it yourself. The more things happen, the harder it is to think it's all just a bunch a coincidences. Don't get me wrong, now. I pride m'self on being a good huntsman, and we've an excellent pack a hounds here. Great country too, with plenty a healthy foxes just waitin' for the chase. I can honestly say I've not had a blank day, where we didn't get up at least one fox, in quite a long while, well before all this Saint Hubert stuff started. But the number we're getting up each time? And the runs they're giving us? Well, either Ryman's on to someting special, or I'm a much better huntsman then I give m'self credit for."

"Thumper… um, Mister Billington certainly thinks highly of you."

Crispie looked at the ground and did an aw-shucks shuffle. "That means a lot to me. He's a fine man, our master is."

"Yes, he certainly seems to be. Makes me wonder why his recent marriage failed. And the one before that too."

"That a subject of interest to you is it?"

"Everything here is of interest to me. You never know what might be relevant for the book."

"A carse."

****

Thumper told himself he was not a voyeur. He was simply assessing Janey's progress as an equestrienne while staying out of the way. His presence seemed to make her nervous and he didn't want to interfere with Patti's role as instructor. So he positioned himself at an upstairs window of the main house with a full view of the ring. Even from that distance he could tell the lesson was going well. Janey looked relaxed and confident. He couldn't hear what Patti was saying, but her gestures and the general sounds of encouragement were all positive.

When both rider and horse had enough, Janey dismounted with considerably more grace than she had shown before—she did not stumble and fall into Patti's arms. The two ladies then chatted jovially as they walked the horse back to the barn. Thumper checked his watch and determined the appropriate length of time to wait before he made his appearance.

Janey and Patti were just finishing up the tack cleaning when Thumper arrived. "How'd it go?" he asked, stepping into the tack room and feigning ignorance that he had witnessed any part of the lesson.

"Very well," Patti replied. "Not sure I'd say she's a natural, but she certainly has potential. Being a runner helps. Good core strength, flexibility, endurance."

Thumper turned to Janey. "Wonderful. I expect all that riding worked up an appetite. Can you stay for lunch?"

"I'd love to. But I've got so much work to do, between the book project and my regular teaching duties. Don't forget I still have a full time job all week long."

Thumper's disappointment was clearly visible as his smile faded. "Oh, sure, right. I understand. Been there many times myself, trying to find time for everything. Next weekend then. Two hunts down, two more to go before you've earned the big payoff."

Patti's expression indicated confusion about that remark.

"Nothing," Thumper said, catching the look. "Just a friendly challenge between Miss Musgrove and myself." Turning back to Janey he continued, "You're welcome to come out Friday and stay over if that would be easier. Maybe Patti could squeeze in another lesson that evening."

Patti hesitated for a moment, knowing how much she and Crispie had to do to prepare hounds and horses for Saturday's hunt. But the glow of eager anticipation in Thumper's eyes sparked her to say, "Absolutely. I'm sure we could find some time for a little more ring work."

"Oh, no, thank you both really. I have a prior commitment that evening. But I'll definitely be here Saturday morning."

Minutes later Thumper and Patti were standing in the stable yard watching Janey drive away.

"Did it really go that well?" he asked.

"Yes, it did," Patti replied. "I wasn't just saying that. Of course, Bee's a steady old guy, good school horse. I wouldn't put her on Ozzy any time soon."

"Hell, there are days when I don't want to be on Ozzy. I'm getting too old to work with these hot young Thoroughbreds."

"Yeah, hot young things can be a danger. Especially when they dump you and run off. Better to stick to something steady, dependable, and smart."

Thumper watched Janey's car turn onto Montfair Lane. "How right you are."

****

Bar's weekly updates to Shelton McKendrick detailed her father's increasingly odd behavior. There was little she could do about it from three thousand miles away, and this feeling of impotence, of abandoning her family, weighed on her heavily.

Alone in her apartment on Sunday evening, she was packing for another long week on the road in the Pacific Northwest when Astrid Stevenson's ringtone sounded.

"How are the moving plans coming?" Astrid asked.

"Working on them. But nothing definite yet."

"But you're serious? This might really happen?"

"It might."

"Wonderful. Will you be home for Thanksgiving? Will I see you then?"

"Yes, I'll be home. This will be the first holiday since my grandfather died. I have to be there for my grandmother. Our neighbor is hosting a big dinner."

"Oh, I see."

"Um, look, it's just that, well, it's very gracious of him to invite us. I wouldn't feel right asking if… y'know, if I could bring a guest."

"Oh, of course. I understand. But I'll see you sometime before you leave, right?"

"Definitely," Shelton said. "After Thursday, I'm free until I fly back on Sunday."

"So, um, you'll be spending Thanksgiving in your old girlhood haunts?"

"Yeah, that's where I'll be." Shelton grasped Astrid's implication. A memory of their night together after she had followed the memorial hunt for her grandfather brought a devilish smile to her lips. "Out there where all those old passions get stirred up," she added in a sultry voice.

"Excellent. Well, then, how about staying over at my place Friday and Saturday nights?"

"Wonderful."

Two loves drove Shelton's desire to move back to Virginia. What she hadn't figured out yet was how to keep those two incompatible loves from colliding once she got there.

Chapter 68

CECELIA BROADHURST FOLLOWED Rhetta's instructions to meet her at Bar's trailer late Tuesday afternoon. She arrived to find Rhetta, standing with Abel at her side in the bare front yard, waiting impatiently despite the fact that Cecelia was five minutes early.

"What's this about, Mrs. M?" Cecelia asked.

"Got some business for you. Maybe, anyways. Want to sell off about a five acre parcel here."

"You mean Bar's five acres?"

"There ain't no five acres here that belong to anyone but me. That person you mentioned is no more than a damned squatter. High time he made his own way, stopped moochin' off the kindness of others. I figger this piece would make a good spot for someone who wants a weekend place, build a little house here, nice view, country air, peace an' quiet. I hear there's city folk who like that sorta thing."

"I did a little research on your property after you asked me to meet you here," Cecelia said. "Are you familiar with the conservation easement Fergus put on the farm? You must have signed it too as the joint owner."

"Yeah, right, I remember that. Something about not developing the place, keeping it open land. He wanted to be sure the hunt could always come through here. Well, I ain't talking about no development. Just parceling off this one little patch, five acres outta seven hunnert, and replacing this ugly looking piece a crap with something nicer. Won't cause no problem for the hunt."

"The easement does allow for three residences, but no more than that. So, yes, you could build something here in place of the trailer. But what you can't do is sell part of the land to someone else. It has to remain as one intact parcel, all seven hundred acres. You could sell it all, or pass it along to your heirs. But you're legally restricted from splitting it up."

Rhetta knew that was part of the easement restriction. Rhetta McKendrick never signed any document without knowing exactly what it meant. What she'd hoped, though, was that enough time had passed since the original transaction, and with the other grantor now dead, that no one would notice that little detail and she could pull off the sale before anyone caught on. She realized now that she should have chosen a less experienced and knowledgeable realtor.

"Well," Rhetta said after quickly considering her options, "no matter. I reckon I can just have this piece cleared, get some nice little place built, and then rent it out. Would be good to have some rental income anyway."

"It might take awhile to recoup your investment, cover the costs involved with having a new house built, and start seeing any return from rental income."

"Mmmm, I reckon you might be right about that. Well, no one in his right mind would want to rent this pile a junk. But there's another place here that's already built. Would just need a bit of fancying up to make it a cozy little spot for someone. Start generating profit from the first rent payment."

"You mean Ryman's cottage?"

"It ain't Ryman's cottage, dammit! Any more than this is Ba… Ba… that other guy's trailer. Everything on this farm belongs to me. Bad enough him and his girlfriend living there for free before he started all this Saint What's-his-face crap, thinking he's got some church calling. But now, instead a stepping up and taking over the business after his daddy died, he's turned it over to other people who ain't McKendricks and shouldn't be running the place. Serve him right to have to go find another place to live. 'Specially after the business folds up 'cause he's too busy chasing foxes and thinking it's some kinda religion."

"I'm a little skeptical about the religion part myself," Cecelia admitted. "But there's certainly something going on with the fox chasing part. We had another fabulous hunt this morning. I've been following hounds for longer than I care to admit, and I've never seen anything like this."

"So ain't that just wonderful," Rhetta said with a smirk. "Instead a tending to business, y'all are gallivantin' around the country chasing some poor critter and thinking that's the best thing in life. And that fool son a mine is leading the party."

"I don't think that's fair, Mrs. M. If you and Ryman have a problem about the shop, that's your business. But as for the rest of us, we're not neglecting our other duties. Plenty of people have a sports interest that takes a lot of time, but no one criticizes them for it. I know folks who spend as much time, if not more, whacking a little ball around a golf course, or sailing their boats, riding their motorcycles. Even more who waste much of their time just sitting in front of the boob tube. For me, especially at my age, getting out with hounds a couple of times a week keeps me fit and focused. And the kind of sport we've had the past couple of months really gets the blood pumping, puts a real spring in the old step."

"Yeah, well, that may be true for some of you. A fine hunting day always put Fergus in a good mood. But that don't explain my crazy-ass son thinking some old saint is speaking to him, telling him to drop all his other responsibilities and do nothing else, parade around every day in his hunting clothes, thinking he can talk to foxes and such."

Rhetta reached down and gave Abel a scratch behind his ear. "I thank you for your time. Sorry it don't look like we can do business." Just before Cecelia closed her car door, Rhetta added, "But if you know anyone who might be interested in renting a nice, cozy cottage out here in the country, give me a shout."

****

Rhetta hoped Ryman would take notice of the two vehicles passing by the cottage, either on the way to Bar's trailer or returning from it. He would likely recognize Cecelia's car, ask his mother what was going on, and she could then level more threats at him to drop his Church of Foxhunting silliness and attend to business.

But Ryman was oblivious to what was happening outside. Nardell was away on massage appointments and Ryman was parked in front of his computer, reading the disturbing chain of postings on Foxhunters Connected.

> Did you hear about the huntsman at Tiber Creek? Nasty leg break, compound fracture. He's out for the season.
>
> I was there. It was awful. His horse slipped going around a corner, the horse landed on his right leg, then twisted. It was deep in the country, too muddy to get the ambulance there. They had to haul him out in the bed of a pick-up truck. He was in a lot of pain. It was pretty ugly.
>
> Serves him right after what he did on Saturday.
>
> I guess that'll teach him not to mess with Ryman McKendrick.

In the heat of the moment, Ryman had been ready to call down hellfire and brimstone on that man. But after a few days his indignation at such unsporting conduct eased. Moreover, he now had only a week left to either figure out a way to save the shop—preferably without asking his mother for the money—or let it go under and trust Saint Hubert to provide. He was no closer to a more palatable solution, and this reality filled most of his waking thoughts. The incident on Saturday had faded to a gauzy memory, of little importance compared to the bank's impending deadline. Or so it was until he read about his adversary's accident.

Chapter 69

BY THURSDAY IT still seemed Ryman's only options were to either abandon his calling to serve Saint Hubert or accept the poverty and shame predicted by The Defender. Neither, now that the reality of the latter lay just a few days away, held much appeal. The injury to the Tiber Creek huntsman further darkened his mood. He'd stopped logging on to Foxhunters Connected to avoid the steady stream of comments about the Saturday incident and the ongoing debate about whether or not Ryman had called down a curse on the man.

The only bright spot for him during the week was the time he spent hunting Thursday morning. Saint Hubert had not withdrawn his blessing. Foxes played and hounds chased, riders were shown good sport, and Ryman kept up a positive façade. He praised the venerable saint and delivered a badge of glory salute to everyone.

But those who knew him well were not fooled. The downcast pull had returned to his sad green eyes, his shoulders succumbed to the habitual slouch.

Sensing his anxiety, and now having some insight into its cause, Cecelia Broadhurst did not want to burden him further with more bad news. But she felt it best to warn him about his mother's plans.

Catching him between the kennel truck and his trailer after all hounds were on, she rode up alongside. "Ryman, I assume you know about my meeting with your mother the other day."

"Huh? No. You had a meeting with Ma?"

"We drove right past your cottage, back to Bar's trailer. Your truck was parked in front of your place. I figured you must have seen us."

"Oh, well, I was kinda busy that afternoon. Working on this Saturday's sermon, you know. Takes a lot of time and focus."

"I'm sure it does. Look, I don't want to cause you any heartache, and it might be just a bunch of bluffing on your mother's part, but, well, she was talking about selling off the land where Bar's trailer sits, letting someone build a weekend place there."

"What? She can't do that. That's been Bar's home for…"

"You're right she can't do it. But not because Bar has any legal rights to it. It's because the conservation easement she and your father put on the property won't allow it."

"Well, that's a relief."

"Yes, I suppose in some ways it is. But when I pointed that out to her, even though I suspect she already knew it, she came up with another idea."

"I can't wait to hear what that was."

"Turn your cottage into a rental unit."

Ryman took a deep breath. He rubbed his hand over his face and scratched at his four-day stubble. "Let her do as she pleases. Saint Hubert will provide. Better that Nardell and I have to move than Bar."

"Um, it gets worse."

Ryman sighed again and waited for the rest of Cecelia's report.

"You know Derrick Philman, who owns Philman Excavation?"

"Sure. Known Derrick for years. We've done a lot of work on his equipment. Always been a good customer."

"I ran into him at the post office yesterday. He said he'd just come from Fair Enough Farm, Rhetta called him to come over and look at an old dumpsite she wanted cleared. When he got there she took him back to Bar's trailer, said she wanted it hauled away. Derrick asked if Bar was planning to move. She said, yes, he was moving. He just didn't know it yet. Derrick got kind of upset. He said Bar's the best mechanic to ever work on his equipment, and a good friend. He couldn't possibly do something like that without Bar knowing about it and saying it was okay. Your mother didn't want to hear that, gave poor Derrick a good piece of her mind. When I saw him at the post office, he was still red-faced and shaking. Big, rough guy like that is still no match for your dear mother."

"Tell me about it."

"Derrick may have refused, but he's not the only contractor around who could do that kind of work. And the others aren't likely to have as much loyalty to Bar."

As Ryman was mulling this over, Cecelia's cell phone beeped with an incoming text message. She pulled the phone from her coat pocket and took a look. Her eyes widened and her face turned pale.

"What is it?" Ryman asked.

"From a friend who hunts with Tiber Creek. Fire at the kennels. Huntsman's house and stables too. Total loss."

Ryman teetered in his saddle, started to say something to Cecelia, but the sky began to spin above him. She watched in horror as his eyes rolled back and he fell to the ground.

****

When he came to, a crowd of familiar faces stood above him. Thumper knelt at his side.

"I… I… didn't mean to," Ryman stuttered, "… didn't mean any harm. I was… was just quoting Article Eight. Not my words. They can't blame me… for… for…"

"No one's blaming you, Ry," Thumper said, although he knew many probably were. "Must have been some kind of accident. Grantham just called. He says the early report is that all hounds, horses, and humans are okay. The hounds were in the kennel yard, horses in the pasture, and the huntsman's still in the hospital. The kennelman was there, and the huntsman's family. They got the hounds and horses to safety, but the buildings went up too fast to get anything else out."

"His… his dwelling desolate and… and his possessions a desert."

"Don't worry yourself about that. Not your fault. These things happen. Old buildings, bad wiring, someone forgets to turn off a heater. Who knows? Anyway, you were miles away, not even in the same state. Just a coincidence." The sound of that final word rang in Thumper's mind. He'd used it too many times the past couple of months.

Chapter 70

A PROFUSION OF children and ponies greeted Thumper and Janey as they rode down to Montfair's front lawn Saturday morning for the season's second Juniors Day. The sea of bright, youthful faces formed a stark contrast to the troubled, worn appearance of Ryman McKendrick and Nardell Raithby. They rode over from Fair Enough Farm, slumped in their saddles, both showing the effects of some rough nights. Even their horses looked listless.

As Ryman steered Token over toward Bing's trailer, Thumper intercepted Nardell. There were dark circles under her eyes. Just as Thumper stopped her, she let loose a wide yawn.

"Sorry," she said. "Didn't get hardly any sleep last night. Or the night before. Ryman was tossing and turning, mumbling to himself, kept getting up and pacing around."

"The happenings at Tiber Creek are bothering him that much?"

"Yes. But he won't talk about it. Just sits at his computer staring at the screen. Like he's waiting for some message to arrive."

"It seems everything was fine when the lucky streak was going his way. But it's a different story when it looks like his power includes getting people hurt and setting buildings on fire. Not that I believe for one minute that he had anything to do with that."

"You still think it's all just luck and coincidence?" Indignation fueled a spark. She sat erect, her head high, and a trace of color returned to her cheeks. "You don't believe, even after all you've seen. Well, I can tell you, it's all real. I've been searching for this all my life. Everything else before has left me empty and dissatisfied. But this is truth. Whatever's going on with Ryman, it's not just luck or coincidence. You'll come to see. I'll pray especially hard to Saint Hubert that he opens your eyes."

With that, energized in a way Thumper had never before seen her, she turned her horse and rode off at a brisk trot to join Ryman.

At the staff confab, everyone looked to Ryman for his choice of the morning's first draw. "Ah, gee, I dunno." He rubbed his hand over his face and looked with weary, bloodshot eyes out toward the horizon.

"What do y'all think?"

Thumper was quick to respond. "Not quite up to your usual spritely self, huh, Ry? Okay, then, I say we draw to Gretchen's Bottom."

This was met with a general murmur of agreement.

Nardell reached over and placed a hand on Ryman's arm. "Sweetheart, you need to pull yourself together now. It's time for Article Nine. Your people are waiting."

"Maybe we should just skip that today," Thumper suggested.

"No!" Nardell shot back. "We can't. Ryman, honey, Saint Hubert will give you the strength. Just read the article, make a few comments. Then we'll go hunting."

He reached into his coat pocket, pulled out a piece of paper, and handed it to Nardell. "Why don't you read it? This is as much your ministry as it is mine."

"Me? Oh, no, I couldn't… not in public… in front of people…"

"Where's *your* faith then?" Ryman shot back.

Nardell looked out at the crowd of hunters, an expectant audience that appeared to her as if it numbered in the thousands. Her mouth went dry. She'd have rather jumped into a pit of copperheads than be forced into public speaking.

Thumper's exasperation was climbing by the second. "Oh, for Christ sakes! Give me that damn paper." He snatched it from Nardell's hand and turned to face the crowd of adults and children. "Sorry for the delay folks. I'm afraid Ryman's not feeling well this morning. Seems to have a bit… a bit of a… a sore throat. So it looks like I'll be covering for him. I'm afraid there won't be any brilliantly crafted sermon for you. Just a quick read from this." He held up the note card.

"Okay. So this would be from The Foxhunter's Faith, Article Nine. 'Whoever lives as a cheerful good neighbor, striving to help and encourage his friends at all times, and who hunts on foot if he has no horse, and by whose behavior the scarlet is never brought into dishonor; may he live long and be happy and may his possessions be'"—Thumper felt himself getting into the spirit of the moment, held a dramatic pause to heighten the climax, and concluded with an oratorical flourish—"'as the sand of the seashore for multitude!'"

The congregation responded with a polite, if somewhat restrained, smattering of "Amens."

A relieved senior master called to the huntsman, "Mister O'Rourke, let's go hunting."

Moving off toward Gretchen's Bottom, they approached the dirt road between the main farm complex and the intended destination. Thumper raised a hand to signal his followers to a halt when he saw the vehicle parked on the road, directly blocking the path. He recognized the SUV, emblazoned on the side with the emblem of the Virginia Department of Game and Inland Fisheries, the policing agency for hunting and fishing. Leaning against the vehicle, awaiting their approach, was a uniformed conservation officer or, as most people still called them, a game warden.

Thumper's scalp prickled under his hunt cap. Shortly before the season began, Marva sent out the standard reminder to the membership about hunting licenses. Thumper usually would have made at least a couple of additional announcements to further reinforce the importance of having the proper license tucked in a helmet or pocket. But the distractions caused by Ryman's Saint Hubert antics had knocked that detail off his radar screen. He now had a sinking feeling that some folks were about to get nailed.

As it turned out, there were even more miscreants than he expected. At least he and Janey were not among them. The embarrassment would have been far worse if the senior master had failed to set the proper example for himself and his guest. But the officer had plenty of opportunity to write out citations to others, including Baden who at sixteen was no longer considered a "junior" in the eyes of Virginia DGIF. Beatrice was still below the age requirement for a hunting license.

Thumper doubted, though, that this would make much difference to Bob. His dark blue Yukon was shrouded in a swirl of farm road dust as he barreled toward the forestalled hunters. He slid to an abrupt stop, was out of the vehicle and marching forward before the first dust particle settled. Kitty jumped out from the passenger seat and followed him, pleading for restraint.

"What's going on here?" Bob demanded.

Bing intercepted him and tried to explain, said it was no big deal, just an oversight by some folks who forgot about the hunting license requirement. When Bob discovered that his son was among those in violation, he erupted in a fit of rage.

"No big deal?" he shouted. "No big deal? Maybe not to you. But this is my son we're talking about here. Barely sixteen, and now he'll have a record. Do you know what that will mean for his future? For college? For his career?"

"Bob, please," Bing said, "it's not like that at all. This doesn't even rise to the level of a parking ticket."

The conservation officer paused in mid-ticketing and arched an eyebrow.

"Look, son," Bing continued, "this is my fault. I forgot that Baden needed a license once he turned sixteen."

"Damn right it's your fault."

"But, really, this is not going to spell the difference between Harvard and Podunk Community College."

"So you say. But the sight of *my* son being charged with a violation, hunting laws or any other kind, is more than I care to witness." Turning to the children, he said, "You two get off those horses right now. We're going home."

"But Daddy," Beatrice protested, "I'm not in any trouble. I can still go hunting. Please!"

"I'm not leaving you out here alone. It's not safe."

"But I'll be with Grandpa."

"Right, until he hurts his back again and can't ride. Then who'll look after you? Get off that horse, young lady. You're coming with me. Grandpa and Miss Marie will lead your horses back to the trailer and take them home. Won't you, Grandpa?"

Bing nodded and mumbled an apology to Marie. She reached over and gave him an understanding pat on the shoulder.

The kids slid off their horses and shuffled toward the Yukon. Kitty placed herself between them, a protective arm around each child, and tried to offer consolation.

As the warden continued to work through the crowd of mounted hunters, finding about every other one to be in violation, Crispie and his staff held the hounds off to the side waiting for the day's sport to resume. The hunting day was over for those without a license, but the rest could go on.

Thumper noticed Crispie looked a little uneasy as the officer approached the staff. Ryman and Nardell also exchanged nervous glances. The senior master's sinking feeling sunk even lower.

"Shall we be off now, Master?" Crispie called out as he gathered up his reins and signaled the others to get ready.

"Hold on a minute," the officer said. "I'll need to see your licenses too."

The huntsman and his three whippers-in were all silent. The officer started writing out four more citations.

Thumper rode over to them. "Do you mean to tell me that *none* of you remembered to get your hunting license?" The frustration in his voice would have been apparent even to Saint Hubert himself in his thirteen-hundred-year-old grave.

A garbled response of "sorry… I forgot… busy… slipped my mind" was accompanied by shrugs and sheepish grins.

"I don't believe this," Thumper hissed. "Ryman and Nardell I can understand. The two of you have been so off in the clouds with your Saint Hubert bullshit that you couldn't be bothered with such piddling real world details as getting your goddamn hunting licenses." He then focused his displeasure on Crispie. "But you! You're the professional here. Or at least you're supposed to be. And you too," he added with a flash toward

Patti. "What? You've been so busy shagging each other that you didn't have the energy left to drag yourself to the computer and order your license?"

All four of them sat on their horses in dejected silence, their faces crimson.

"May I apologize on behalf of my staff," Thumper said to the game warden. He turned an angry eye toward Ryman. "Including my joint-master, who, of all people, should have known better."

"Well," the officer replied with practiced law enforcement neutrality, "don't let it happen again."

"No, we certainly won't. We respect the laws and understand the importance of your job."

The officer allowed a quick smile to pass across his face and gave Thumper a curt nod.

"You certainly hit the jackpot with us today," Thumper said. "Just a lucky guess to cruise down this particular farm road this morning, huh?"

"Looking for bow hunters," the officer replied. "Had some complaints about them tracking wounded deer onto properties where they don't have permission to go. Heard the horn over this way, figured I'd check it out."

"Well, if you folks have a quota, I expect you've made yours for the rest of the year."

He did not respond. He handed the final citation to Crispie, told them all to have a nice day in the ironic tone cops use for that hackneyed phrase, returned to his SUV and drove away.

"Looks like the day's over for everyone now," Thumper said. "I suggest you get hounds back to kennels as quickly as possible, and you'd better hope they don't get any game up on the way. We'll have some caps to return to all of our guests. And some very disappointed children who were expecting great sport today and will now have to be sent home."

As the staff slunk away with a confused pack of foxhounds, wondering why they were being taken home and not on to the first draw, Thumper looked upon an even sadder scene: a pack of dejected children. The kids looked to Dorcas. Dorcas looked to Thumper.

A solution came to him. "Tell you what," he said brightly. "How about a game of fox-and-hounds? You all know how to play that, right?"

The children all nodded.

Raising his voice, Thumper addressed the full assembly. "Look, folks, I'm really sorry about this. Everyone who paid a cap fee to be here this morning will have that returned. Without the hounds, we can't have a real foxhunt. But we can still have some fun this morning." He surveyed the group of children and settled on Missy Winslow. She and her horse had won the Junior Field Hunter Championship the year before. Thumper knew her to be one of the best riders among Dorcas's students, and her horse was steady and bold. "Missy, how'd you like to be our fox this morning?"

"Yeah, sure. I can do that."

"Great. Okay, and all you other kids, the jumpers anyway, can be the hounds. Dorcas, how's that sound?"

"Wonderful idea, Master. We play that game often on our schooling rides. And I have a jacket in the trailer that whoever plays the fox wears. Missy, ride over to the trailer and put that on. You know where it is, right?"

"Yes, ma'am."

Thumper continued as Missy went to get the jacket. "All right everyone. If you'd still like to get in a little sport this morning, please come along. Missy will pretend to be the fox and the kids playing the hounds will try to follow her. The rest of us will follow them as we'd normally follow the pack, jumpers with me, second field with Mildred."

Missy returned wearing the jacket, a reddish-brown windbreaker with the image of a fox's head emblazoned on the back.

"Okay, then," Thumper said. "Off you go, Missy. We'll give you a good head start. Kids, you watch where she goes. Then when I give the signal, raise your voices and give chase."

Missy was away quickly. When she was just about to go out of sight, Thumper hollered, "Tally-ho!"

The children raised their voices in a high-pitched imitation of baying hounds and sprang off at a gallop. The sound and sight gave a rush of delight to everyone present.

Thumper looked over at Mildred's followers and saw Janey wearing a huge smile. He stood up in his stirrups, yelled "Forrard!" and led his field in pursuit of the "hounds."

****

Thumper and Janey left the horses in Javier's care and strolled across the front lawn toward the tailgate gathering.

"That was great," she said. "Those kids are incredible. Absolutely fearless."

"The invincibility of youth."

"Not only invincible, but fit too. I counted eighteen kids, from the little ones on ponies to the teenagers. Not a fat one among them. All this talk we hear about the epidemic of childhood obesity, it doesn't appear to have reached Crutchfield County."

"Not among the Pony Club set anyway. These kids are not sitting around for hours watching TV, playing video games, and eating junk food. If every kid in America lived that kind of outdoor, active lifestyle, that epidemic would cease."

"Maybe. But that's not really an option for most kids today, is it? These children are very fortunate. I hope they realize that."

"I'd like to think most do. Although I can think of one young man who's probably not feeling very fortunate right now, thanks to the absence of his hunting license."

"What will happen to the people who were issued citations?"

"Not much. Bing was pretty close to it when he said it amounts to about the same thing as a parking ticket."

"So," Janey asked, "does this count as my third hunt?"

Thumper stopped and thought about that for a moment. He shook his head and said, "Nope, I'm afraid not."

"You mean I still have to do this *twice* more before I can learn the secret of your nickname?" She tried to look disappointed, but it was an obvious mockery.

"The deal was four 'hunts.' This was, more or less, a trail ride. Simulated hunting. Can't count that."

"So if foxhunting is simulated sex, what's simulated foxhunting?"

"My goodness, that's an interesting question. Mounted masturbation maybe?"

"So I was riding a twelve-hundred pound vibrator?"

Thumper's eyes widened, his lips parted but no words come out.

"Why, Mister Billington," Janey teased, "I do believe I've embarrassed you." She adopted the Southern belle accent. "Ah do apologize, suh, if ah have offended your gentle sensibilities."

He scoffed it off. "Pshaw. Not at all. But perhaps I take the sex analogy a bit too far."

"From what little I've seen, I think not." She placed a hand on his chest. "I'm going to catch up with Dorcas, find out more about her work with the kids." As she walked away, she looked back over her shoulder. "Research you know. The reason I'm here."

Thumper arrived at the food spread to find Natasha in her glory, hovering over the serving platters, assuring there was plenty for everyone, and soaking up the praises for her culinary talents.

Cecelia Broadhurst slipped up to Thumper's side. "Brilliant idea," she said, "to come up with the fox-and-hounds game. The kids were great. It was almost as much fun watching them as it would have been following real hounds. You saved the day."

"The kids saved the day," he replied. Spooning a heaping portion of homemade coleslaw onto his plate, he added, "Actually, I was just trying to save the tailgate. Can you imagine what my life would have been like if everyone had left? Natasha's been preparing for this all week. Forget about losing the hunting day. If there'd been no breakfast, if all this had gone to waste, I'd have never heard the end of it."

Cecelia noticed Janey in deep conversation with Dorcas. "So your new friend's taken up hunting. How nice."

"Purely for research purposes."

"Who's researching who?"

"It's strictly professional, I assure you."

"You don't need to assure me of anything. She does, though, seem very nice. And, I might add, well, I'd say she's more your type."

"Really? You know what my 'type' is?"

"More like what your type isn't. I'd say the two previous marriages fit that bill."

"The real estate business is so slow you've decided to take up matchmaking?" He formed his hands to suggest a sign frame. "Cecelia Broadhurst, the Yenta of Crutchfield County."

"Shadchanit," she corrected.

"What?"

"My third husband was Jewish. It drove him crazy when people misused the word 'yenta.' That means a busybody, an old gossipy woman. A female matchmaker is a 'shadchanit.' If there's a Yenta of Crutchfield County, it's Luella Starett."

"Thank you for the vocabulary lesson. I'll be sure to remember it the next time someone tries to suggest a certain person and I would make a good match."

They continued to work their way down the food table.

A burst of laughter from Dorcas at something Janey said caught their attention.

"It's good to see Dorcas in such high spirits," Cecelia remarked.

"What do you mean?"

"You heard about her father passing away, didn't you?"

"Um, yeah, I guess so. Can't say I took much notice of it."

"It hit her pretty hard. Seems they were estranged for many years. Dorcas always held out hope that they'd reconcile one day. But then he up and dropped dead. It's been a rough patch for her dealing with that."

"She seems to be handling it okay from what I can see."

"Yes, well, some of us see more than others."

Cecelia took her lightly filled plate and walked away.

Janey's conversation with Dorcas ended and she rejoined Thumper at the beverage end of the food table.

He lifted a bottle of wine and a plastic cup. "Care for some refreshment?"

"I'd love to. But I'd better not if I'm going to drive home this afternoon. I have a dim recollection of you offering me wine at a previous social function. Next thing I knew I was waking up in one of your guest rooms."

Thumper slowly poured some wine into two cups. "Why not do that again? Not the too-much-wine part, but the guest room part."

"Oh, I don't know. I don't want to impose on your…"

"Tell me this, Professor Musgrove," he said with the stern tone of a prosecutor grilling a witness. "When you were studying the San Bushmen of the Kalahari, did you go home to your apartment every night?"

"No, of course not. I was…"

"And with the Yanomamö along the Orinoco? Or the Igbo of Burkina Faso?"

"Well, no, but there was no way…"

"No way you could drive home to your cozy apartment and leave the natives to their primitive, cloistered world. But just because you have that option here, we do not receive the same level of your personal involvement as did those others. Frankly, Professor Musgrove, I am disappointed." He pursed his lips and shook his head slowly to express his grave displeasure. "I thought you to be a more dedicated professional than this easy nod to your personal convenience would suggest."

She reached out and took the cup from his hand. Replying in the same satirical vein, she said. "You are right, Hunt Master Billington. I have been shortchanging the depth of my research for the sake of my own comfort. I owe it to my future readers to bear whatever burdens are necessary to reach the heart of the story I must tell. Even if it means spending more nights suffering under the Spartan conditions of your guest room."

"A wise decision, Professor Musgrove. You may consider that space your personal hut on the barren plains of Crutchfield County. Bathrobe included free of charge."

"I accept, with just one caveat."

"What's that?"

"Bathrobes are fine. But I draw the line at loincloths."

That caught Thumper off guard.

"It's a Bushmen joke," she explained. "I guess you had to be there."

****

Warwick paced along the kennel fence. He looked up at Patti and his eyes showed his frustration. *Why didn't we go hunting? Why'd we come back so soon? There was a fox waiting for us in Gretchen's Bottom. It would have been a glorious chase.*

"I'm sorry, buddy," she said. "We screwed up. We'll make it up to you on Tuesday."

Crispie stepped up beside her. "I can't believe you forgot to get our licenses."

"Oh, it's all my fault, huh?" Patti snapped. "Maybe if you'd learn to use a computer, you could help out with that sort of thing."

"That's your area, mine's hounds and hunting."

"Maybe if you hadn't kept grabbing me every time I tried to sit down at the computer, I'd have had time to get the licenses. And just how, exactly, does Thumper know about our… our… that we've been… you know… a lot?"

"I've said nothing to 'im."

"Well, I certainly haven't."

"Maybe Voytek said something."

"Voytek! How would he know anything? Unless you…"

Crispie's weather-reddened face turned redder still. "I've not said a word to 'im neither. It's just that, well, I was thinking, y'know, he's around the kennels, helping out and all. Maybe sometime when we were… y'know… he might have heard, or even seen…"

"Seen! You think Voytek might have seen us? Oh, my God. How embarrassing."

"I'm not saying he did, lass. I'm just kinda, well, speculatin' is all."

Patti shuddered at the thought of Voytek the Voyeur, watching her and Crispie wearing out the old sofa in the kennel office. "I'm going to go order our hunting licenses," she said curtly. "Maybe you can keep your hands off me long enough for me to get that done."

"I'll try, lass."

"Good. And since your hands have nothing else to do today, maybe you can try again to fix the fence around my garden."

"I think we've used up all the wood and wire that were in the shed."

"Then go get some more. And I want those nice decorative pickets, like the others. Don't come home with some plain old straight piece of wood and tell me they don't have any more." She turned sharply and headed for the kennel office.

Crispie looked down at Warwick. "It would appear she's a wee bit pissed at me."

The hound's eyes said *She's not the only one, pal.*

****

Marie Hardesty was luxuriating in a relaxing shower, soothing away the disappointments of the morning and the efforts she'd expended helping Bing get over his sense of guilt at having forgotten to get a hunting license for Baden. He'd been too embarrassed by his own son's tirade to stay for the fox-and-hounds game.

The trick turned out to be swapping stories from their many years of foxhunting, even acting out some scenes, imitating the voices of people they knew, and laughing until they fell onto the couch exhausted but almost as exhilarated as if the hunt had actually taken place that day.

She'd left Bing napping on the couch when she went to take a shower. Now, though, she sensed a presence in the bathroom, saw a hand grasp the shower curtain and slide it back, and in stepped a naked Bing Sensabaugh.

"Well, hello there," Marie said. Glancing down, she added, "My goodness, look at you."

"I thought you might want some help scrubbing your back."

"How considerate."

"And anything else that might need attention."

"Sure you're feeling okay? No back problems?"

"I'm fit as a fiddle and ready to play."

"Then rosin up your bow and let the music begin."

Bing grabbed a bar of soap and went to work.

Chapter 71

RYMAN SPENT THAT Saturday afternoon shut in his office. He'd made it plain to Nardell that he didn't want to be disturbed. She tried to keep herself busy by tackling some long-neglected household cleaning chores. Mostly she fretted about what Ryman was doing in there. By late afternoon she couldn't stand it any longer.

"Honey," she said as she knocked on the door, "are you okay?"

"Fine," came the terse reply.

"May I come in now?"

"Yeah, sure, whatever."

She found Ryman seated at his computer. A stocky, square-shaped bottle containing a brown liquid was on the desk next to his keyboard. He lifted the bottle and took a drink.

"What are you doing?" Nardell asked from the doorway.

"What does it look like I'm doing?"

"Is that Jägermeister?"

"It ain't iced tea."

"Where'd you get that?"

"Um, the ABC store? *Hello*."

"Do you think this is a good idea?"

"Of course it's not a good idea. It wasn't a good idea to forget about our hunting licenses. It wasn't a good idea for me to think the old man had things under control at the shop. And maybe it wasn't a good idea for me to think… to think that I… that I'd been…" He stood up abruptly. "I gotta go discuss some things with Bar. I'll be back after awhile."

As he closed the front door behind him, Nardell looked back in the office. She noticed an email message on the computer screen. She took a step closer and leaned over to read it.

> Jeremiah 23:25-26 (NIV): "I have heard what the prophets say who prophesy lies in my name. They say, 'I had a dream! I had a dream!' How long will this continue in the hearts of these lying prophets, who prophesy the delusions of their own minds?"

Ryman's inbox showed another email from the same sender. Nardell hesitated. The cursor hovered over it. She clicked the mouse and read:

> Deuteronomy 13:5 (NIV): "That prophet or dreamer must be put to death, because he preached rebellion against the Lord your God... He has tried to turn you from the way the Lord your God commanded you to follow. You must purge the evil from among you."

Nardell looked at the open bottle of Jäger and then out the window as Ryman's truck threw up dust heading for the road to Bar's trailer.

Ryman didn't bother to call first. He knew the big man would be there. Where else would he be on a Saturday evening? Or any evening?

Bar grabbed a six-pack of beer and the two men sat down outside, Bar in his lawn chair, Ryman on the one all-purpose kitchen chair he carried out from the trailer.

The air was turning chilly. Shafts of light cut through the trees as the sun's descent settled toward the western mountains.

Ryman sat sipping a beer and staring straight ahead.

"You look like crap, bro," Bar said.

"We got a problem."

"Maybe you got a problem, shit-for-brains. My life is totally care-free."

"The shop could go under."

"Well, damn shame. But no major sweat off my fat hairy ass." Bar looked around at his trailer. "I could use some free time to fix things up here. The place is gettin' kinda tawdry." He gestured with his beer bottle toward a spot next to the woods. "Might plant me a garden. Make things more homey, doncha think?"

"This ain't the time for your sarcasm."

"Me? Sarcastic? I'm dead serious. Maybe I'll finally start that research project into the cause of terminal stupidity. You can be my first subject."

"There's only one way to save McKendrick and Sons."

"Good. Then you ain't gotta stay up nights deciding what to do."

"I gotta ask Ma for the money. Otherwise, we're done."

"Damn, bro, I don't envy you that. But, hey, I ain't gettin' into your family affairs."

"There will be conditions."

"There always are."

"I'll have to put aside my calling to do Saint Hubert's work. Ma's likely to insist on that. She doesn't understand that this isn't crazy talk.

It's real, I know it is. Or at least I… I think it is."

"Well, hell, if it is real, things will work out, right? Just get the shop up and going again, then when you've paid off the old ba… your dear mama… you can get back to your church foolishness. Sheltie Lou can help with the marketing stuff. Not the same as having her right here but she can do all that online in her spare time. And I can do whatever you need, cover the sales floor some days, work in the shop others. May never get back to like it was with your old man at the helm, but we can make a go of it."

"Yeah, well, y'see, here's the problem with that. I'm pretty sure that she'll have one other condition. She'll, ah, well, what she'll want to see go is… you."

"What you mean?"

"She's been angling to get you off the farm ever since Daddy died. I've been trying my best to keep her from doing anything like that. She was talking to Cecelia Broadhurst about how she wanted to sell off this parcel, let some city folks build a weekend retreat here. When Cecelia talked her out of that, she called Derrick Philman, told him she wanted this lot cleared, and your trailer hauled away. I wasn't sure I should say anything, but now you see how serious this is."

Bar grunted. "Crazy old bitch. Damned if I know why she's had it in for me all these years. No offense, man, but your mama just ain't right."

"You don't have to tell me that. But right or not, the fact is Ma's gonna do whatever she can to send you packing. The only leverage I got is that you living here has always been tied to your job at the shop, the deal you and Daddy made when he first hired you. And as long as I'm calling the shots for the business, I got the power to honor that agreement, keep things like they've always been.

"But if I gotta go beggin' to Ma for the money we need to keep the shop open, she'll have me over a barrel. And you and I both know she'll take every advantage of that. So I reckon it's what they call a lose-lose situation. If I borrow the money from Ma, she's gonna insist you get fired. And that I give up the work Saint Hubert's called me to do. If I don't, the shop's gonna go under. Then none of us got a job. Either way, you won't be working for McKendrick and Sons any more, and there won't be any way of keeping her from kicking you off the farm."

"How much we talking here?"

Ryman quoted a figure.

Bar whistled. "That's a lot."

"A lot more than I can scrape up in the next week or so. More than we're gonna sell any time soon. I know you're off to a great start handling sales. And I'm sure Sheltie Lou's got some really good ideas about marketing. But there just ain't time. Daddy left things in pretty bad shape."

"And you never bothered to get involved yourself. Just assumed an eighty-five-year-old man was on top of everything, same as he'd been all your life."

"Well, why shouldn't I? He seemed as sharp as ever to me. Didn't he to you?"

"Yeah, I gotta admit I didn't see anything different. But, still, you shoulda…"

"Look, 'shoulda' and 'woulda' ain't gonna do us any good now. The old man's gone and it is what it is. I don't like it. I don't like it one damn bit. But what the hell can I do? We're both fucked. If I let the shop go under, everyone's out of a job. Not only that, but I reckon I've got some responsibility to my old man's memory, and to the family name. Shoulda been Teedy running things, not me. But it didn't work out that way. Most of all, though, is my responsibility to Saint Hubert. I'm the one he's chosen for this honor. But Ma doesn't believe it. And I know she'll tell me I gotta quit doing his work if she's gonna put up the money. It kills me to think about letting him down."

"Look, man, get a grip. There is no Saint Hubert and no one's calling you to do a damn thing. We got enough churches in the world already. Too many, if you ask me. We don't need your wacky foxhunting church crap. You people are bat-shit crazy enough as it is without thinking chasing foxes is some kinda religion. This might be your wake-up call to get back to reality."

"You don't understand. Many don't yet. But others do believe. And those who don't will come around in time. This isn't some weird new church thing. What Saint Hubert has revealed to me is the ancient truth. It's what ties us to the world, to nature, to all living creatures. It gets past all the fake stuff about modern life. I don't know why Saint Hubert chose me, but I'm sure he did. I just… it's just that… does he want me to cut all ties and go on faith? I'm being tested now. I can see that. And the tests are coming from different directions. I let him down today. I was not worthy. And I'm ashamed for that. I'm being tested because of my failures in the past. And now someone… some wacko is sending… making threats..."

"Man, you're the one who's wacked out. You think you're being tested now? You don't know shit. Your ass is gonna be in sorry shape before long. You're gonna have no shop, no business, no income. And when you realize your Saint Hubert is all bullshit, then what? You're gonna end up driving a feed truck, or something worse. That'll make the big time master of the Montfair Hunt look swell, won't it? Or maybe Nardell can support you. She's got a real reliable employment record, don't she? Or maybe your dear mama will take pity on you and give you an allowance, like when you were twelve. I ain't too thrilled about getting kicked outta here. Fuck the job though. That's just something to fill my time anyway. I got other options. But I sure as hell wouldn't want to be in your sorry shoes, all wacked out, and nowhere to go. Saint Hubert my ass."

"I'm not wacked out, man. I'm not. I've been chosen. I know I have. But I gotta admit, it's kinda scary. Damn scary, actually. The shop's been there all my life. You've been here most of my life. Am I worthy of this calling? Do I have the strength to do Saint Hubert's work? Or will I end up disappointing him? Like I've disappointed most everyone else. I'm sorry about this, man. Sorry that, whatever else happens, you gotta move. But, hey, y'know, there's lots of other places around here like this, maybe not trailers but cottages, small tenant houses and such. And always folks looking for reliable help. Hell, someone with your mechanical skills and work record, you'll get snapped up in a jiffy. You even speak English, sorta."

"Might be kinda hard finding a place with a liberal pets policy."

"Hell, the county's full of vultures."

"Not like mine."

"Well, look, man, I'm real sorry to have to dump this on you. Seems the old man left us both in a tight spot. I gotta think things through on my end, decide just what I'm gonna do. But unless Saint Hubert can work some kind of miracle here, I reckon you'd better start looking around for another place to live."

****

Janey settled into the guest room for the evening, parked in a lumpy wingback chair, blazing away on her laptop. Thumper sat alone in his man-cave, working on his second tumbler of Talisker single malt, a stack of notes on the Jefferson Bible gathering dust on his desk, when Grantham Meisner called.

"Hey," Thumper said, "I guess you heard about what happened this morning. On behalf of my members and staff, let me apologize for…"

"Yeah, I heard about the license bust. A minor annoyance, it'll blow over. The reason I'm calling is about Ryman. I'm in Massachusetts for the All New England Joint Meet. All I'm hearing about up here is him and his Venatican Church foolishness. Some people are going as far as to suggest he's somehow responsible for what happened at Tiber Creek. I'm sorry Thumper, but I can't put this off any longer. I've given you ample opportunity to squelch this, talk some sense to him. I was really hoping you could get through to him, that the association wouldn't have to get involved."

Thumper took a sip of whiskey. "By the way, Brother Grantham, how are your head and back feeling these days? Been sent flying over any coops lately?"

He heard Meisner take a breath. "Look, Thumper, you don't really think Ryman had anything to do with that, do you? I admit it was my own fault. I'm embarrassed I went off on him like I did, especially in front of so many guests and young children. I shouldn't have tried to take that coop. Although it probably would have been just fine if that deer hadn't spooked my horse at the last second."

"Yes, certainly a case of bad timing, or good timing, depending on your view. So you no longer consider yourself an abomination?"

"About that, I was, after all, rather badly concussed. Simply the power of suggestion, the last thing I'd heard before… well, before things went a bit fuzzy. I refuse to believe Ryman had anything to do with that. Just as I don't believe he had anything to do with the Tiber Creek situation. But what I believe or don't believe isn't the point. There are others who are increasingly displeased with what he's doing, people I have to answer to. Puts me in a difficult position. I need your help here, dear cousin."

"I've tried talking to him, but nothing I've said..."

"You obviously haven't tried enough. Bottom line is this: You've got one more chance, a couple of days at most, to get Montfair Hunt back to just plain old everyday foxhunting, put a lid on this Venatican Church thing, or, well, I hate to say it, but the association will have no choice but to intervene. And I hate to think what your grandfather would have had to say about that."

****

"Thumper!" Nardell exclaimed when she answered his knock. "What a nice surprise." She grabbed his arm and pulled him through the doorway. Her brightly welcoming tone changed to one of quietly deep concern. "Ryman could use some cheering up. If you thought he was down this morning, he's much worse now. He's just come back from Bar's. I don't know what went on—he won't tell me a thing—but he's, like, big-time depressed. He's in his office, knocking back Jägermeister. And someone sent him, well, I shouldn't have been prying, but…"

"Sorry to tell you this, but I'm not here to cheer him up. If anything, what I have to tell him will likely upset him even more."

Her face hardened and she reached for the doorknob. "Then maybe you'd better just go. He doesn't need any more…"

"Hey, Thumper," Ryman said. He shuffled out from the hallway and raised a limp hand in greeting. The sight of him almost made Thumper agree with Nardell, turn around, and leave. He'd been running his hands through is hair to the point where it looked like it had been styled with a manure rake. His pupils were dull green pods floating in a sea of red. His face was pale and drawn, his posture slumped more than Thumper had ever seen it. He'd removed his stock tie but otherwise he still wore his hunting attire from the morning, right down to his boots, suggesting he'd been unable to muster the energy to pull them off.

As haggard and vulnerable as he looked, Thumper hesitated to pile on yet more bad news. But it had to be done.

"We need to talk," he said.

"Do we? Shit, everyone needs to talk. Bing needs to talk, you need to talk, I need to talk. I'm gettin' pretty much talked out." He dropped into his recliner. Slouched in the big chair, he looked small and old.

"This won't take long."

Nardell stood at attention, her arms folded across her chest, darts of displeasure shooting from her eyes.

"I got a call from Grantham. He's getting a lot of heat about what happened at Tiber Creek. It's bullshit, of course, completely unfounded, but a lot of people are promoting the belief that you called down a curse on the huntsman."

"I was just quoting Article Eight," Ryman offered as a weak defense. "I had no idea it would actually happen."

"Of course you didn't. Because that's not why the huntsman broke his leg and two days later his house and kennels burned down. Just bad timing. But not everyone sees it that way, and all the rumors are putting Grantham in an awkward position."

"Well, if it's not my fault, why do I need to apologize?"

"No one's asking you to apologize. What Grantham's asking, what I'm asking, is for you to see the bigger picture, the problems you're causing for others."

With some effort Ryman pushed himself up from his recliner. "Thumper, I appreciate your concern. I'll give this some thought. Now, if you don't mind, I've got a lot to think about and I could use some…"

"Sweetheart," Nardell said, "you must have faith that Saint Hubert will provide a way through this. We know he's called you, that he's construed you with special powers. He won't let his church fail. You must be strong."

"Look, Ry" Thumper said, "this whole thing is clearly taking a toll on you. Why not take a break, put everything on hold for a while, let life get back to normal, get some rest. I'm sure Saint Hubert will understand."

Nardell turned on him with the protective passion of a mother bear. "What do you know about Saint Hubert? You don't even believe. You think this is all a joke, that Ryman's crazy. Your legalistic, rational mind can't explain the things you've seen, so you just ignore it, reject it, or say it's all just coincidences. But we have faith. And faith will see us through. I think you'd better leave now. Ryman and I need time to pray, to seek Saint Hubert's guidance. And we don't need your negative attitude bringing us down." She pulled the door open and pointed to the exit as the final exclamation to her statement.

"Fine. I've said what I came to say." He addressed Ryman once more before taking his leave. "Pray all you want. But while you're at it, think about the impact your actions have on others. If this goes any farther, you may find yourself out on your own. Remember, Montfair Hunt is not your private party. You sully the reputation of this club, and I'll personally see to it that your status as a master is withdrawn and if that's not enough you can be expelled completely. What you do on McKendrick property is your own business. But you don't have free rein to do whatever you think your Saint Hubert is telling you to do on mine or on the property of other landowners." He shot a hard stare at Nardell. She was doing her best to maintain her defiant stance, but Thumper could see that his words hit home. "You both think about that. Good night."

He was only a split second through the portal when Nardell slammed the door closed. The force rattled the cottage windows and sent a sharp report thundering over the fields of Fair Enough Farm.

****

Janey heard Thumper's car speeding up the driveway. Seconds later the sound of another slamming door sounded as he stormed through the mudroom. This was followed by stomping footsteps and one more door slam—the door to his study.

She debated for several minutes whether to stay in her room or go investigate. Her purpose in being there—or at least so she kept telling herself—was to get closer to the inner dynamics of this community. That was the point of Thumper's offer for her to stay over. She wouldn't learn anything by hiding in the guest room.

She went downstairs and tapped lightly on his study door.

"What?" came the sharp reply.

She opened the door slowly. "Are you okay?"

He was seated at his desk, a highball glass with a double portion of scotch in his hand. "Me? Oh, hell yeah. I'm just dandy. Never mind that my best, oldest friend and joint-master has gone bat-shit crazy. That the whole damn North American hunting community is buzzing about the wacky stuff going on around here. That I might have to expel Ryman from the hunt. Other than that, what could possibly be wrong?" He took a stiff gulp of single malt.

"You're upset. Maybe I should leave you alone to work this out."

"Hell, no. C'mon in." He waved for her to enter with a disjointed sweep of his arm. "You might as well get all this down for your book." He flipped his hand in a shooing gesture. "Go get your video camera and record the senior master having a meltdown. That's the kind of thing that'll make for compelling reading, right? The tension between the crazy cult leader and the established hierarchy? I'm giving you a helluva gift here. This should be good for at least a chapter or two."

"I think I'd better leave you alone." She started to retreat out the door.

"Yeah, maybe that's best. You've seen and heard enough by now anyway." He turned and looked up at the portrait of Thaddeus the First. "Whatcha think, Great-Grandpa? You and Fingal started this club. There's never been a time since without a Billington-McKendrick dyad in charge. Have we reached the end of that run, thanks to some imagined deer with a strange object floating above its head. Is that strange object our steel axe?" He raised his glass to the image of his great-grandfather. "It was fun while it lasted, old boy. Good thing you're not still around to see it all going to hell."

He turned back toward the door. "You getting all this down?"

But Janey was gone.

Chapter 72

THE SUNDAY MORNING sunrise found Bar still in his lawn chair, empty beer bottles strewn around him. He awakened with a start from a cold, fitful sleep to the comforting sounds of *whoosh-whoosh-whoosh*. He glanced at his watch. Still the middle of the night on the West Coast. The phone call he'd decided to make would have to wait a few more hours.

****

Thumper awoke at the same time but to a different sound. He heard a car starting up, then the crunch of tires on the driveway. By the time he pulled himself out of bed and stumbled to the window, all he could see were the taillights of Janey's car as she passed through the front entrance pillars and turned onto Montfair Lane.

****

Nardell rolled over and draped an arm around the figure beside her. She spooned against her bedmate's back, soaking up the comforting warmth and familiar odor. A thick wet tongue began to lick her hand.

She arose and left Wycroft stretched out across the bed alone. She put on her robe and went to Ryman's office where a light shown into the hallway. "Have you been up all night?" she asked.

"Pretty much."

She saw an empty bottle of Jägermeister on the desk. Next to it sat a bottle of Bowman's scotch, half its contents gone. "Sweetheart, you need to go easy on that stuff. Saint Hubert doesn't object to alcohol, but he does want us to be responsible…"

"What the hell do you know about what Saint Hubert wants?"

The bitterness in his voice and the anger in his eyes when he turned to face her caused Nardell to take a frightened step backward. She was struck mute as he launched into a foul-tempered tirade.

"What do *I* know? What does anyone know? Saint Hubert… phfft! I thought I'd been called, that I'd been given special powers, that everyone would rejoice and we'd all restore the true faith together." He pointed to the computer screen. "Well, not everyone's rejoicing. In fact, a lot of folks aren't rejoicing. Foxhunters Connected is buzzing. Some of it's good, but a lot of people are saying it's crazy, over the top, dangerous even. And these are people I know and respect, leaders in the hunting world."

Her voice was small and timid as she tried to calm him down. "They just need time. We must be patient and faithful. Saint Hubert will…"

"And then there's this guy. 'The Defender of the Faith.' Defender my ass! He's no defender. He's becoming an attacker. Get this." Ryman brought up a saved email. "He says this is from the Book of Deuter… Deuter… romneus."

She started to correct him but thought it best not to. Nor could she admit that she'd read his emails while he was with Bar the evening before.

"'That prophet or dreamer must be put to death, because he preached rebellion against the Lord your God... He has tried to turn you from the way the Lord your God commanded you to follow. You must purge the evil from among you.' Ain't that just swell? Some asshole out there wants me purged." He reached for the bottle of scotch and took a swig.

"Maybe my old man had it right." He passed a hand over the scattered piles of books. "Foxhunting mighta been a kind of religion to him. But he kept that to himself. He ran the shop, sold his tractors and stuff, still found plenty of time to hunt. But he didn't go preaching about it. Didn't get all—whatcha call it?—evangelical about it. Maybe that's what I should do. Be more like my old man, instead of some wacked-out weirdo who thinks he's hearing voices, that an ancient saint and a bunch of animals are talking to me."

Seeing Ryman's anger deflate into self-focused sullenness, Nardell's courage returned. "What you should do is honor the special calling you've been given. Don't you see? Your father was chosen to prepare the way for you. He had all this ready because it was part of Saint Hubert's plan. Sure, not everyone understands. Some never will. And the True Faith is a threat to them. Anything that makes them confront their own misguided beliefs is a threat. But you have to believe Saint Hubert will protect you. He wouldn't have called you if he didn't want to see his work fulfilled."

Ryman sat slumped in his chair, the bottle of scotch resting on his thigh. "Goddamn Defender of the Faith," he muttered to himself and took another long drink. "I don't need this shit. Ma's on the warpath about the shop. And she's got good cause to be. We're gonna lose it unless I go groveling to her. Either way, she's gonna kick Bar off the farm. Thumper, Grantham, all the foxhunting bigwigs are telling me to tone it down." Another swig. Wiping the back of his hand across his mouth, he continued, "Oh, yeah. And let's not forget our friend The Defender out there somewhere saying I must be put to death."

Nardell reached out and grasped the neck of the bottle. "Let's put this away. You're upset. You're exhausted. And this isn't helping any. You need to rest, then you'll feel better and we'll work through this. You can't hear Saint Hubert's voice when you're all full of this…"

Ryman pulled the bottle away as she tried to lift it from him. "I can hear just fine! And I can read too!" He stood up quickly, knocking the chair over and stumbling to keep his balance, almost dropping the bottle. "It's you that's not hearing. They're out to get me. They're all out to get me. Someone wants to fucking kill me! Do you get that? Some asshole actually wants to kill me." He cradled the bottle to his chest and looked at her with red, flaky, pleading eyes. His breath sent her back a step. He needed a shower and a change of clothes badly. His voice sunk into a childish whimper. "Saint fucking Hubert. I'm gonna get killed over this. Is that what you want? Huh?"

"Of course that's not what I want, sweetheart. Now just give me the bottle and we'll…"

"No!"

They stood at an impasse. Ryman clutched the bottle tightly. Nardell reached out gently and waited for him to surrender it.

After a tense standoff, she threw up her arms. "Fine! I should have known you wouldn't see it through. You never see anything through. You know what your problem is?"

"Yeah, that someone wants to kill…"

"No! Your problem is commitment. You've never been able to stick to anything in your life. I've known you since we were in Pony Club. Did you finish the program? No, you dropped out at C level. Then you quit college. You never got serious about the shop. The stockboy knows more about the business than you do. You never made a commitment to Karen. You were just stuck with her because of Sheltie Lou. And as soon as the kid went off to college, Karen was out of here. And you didn't do a damn thing to stop her. And me? I've been living with you for seven years now. Seven years, three months, two and a half weeks, to be precise. Not that anyone's counting. And what have I got to show for it?" She held up her left hand. "A bare finger, that's what. You won't commit to me. And now you won't commit to the one true thing you've finally been called to do. Oh, I'm okay just being your 'lady friend,'" she added with a smirk. "But I won't stand by and watch you let Saint Hubert down. Maybe I don't deserve better, but he does."

"Look, sweetheart, you don't understand." He reached out a hand toward her. But he didn't release the bottle. "Y'see, it's just that I…"

"I understand perfectly. You're drunk and you're feeling sorry for yourself. Did you really think this was going to be all fun and games? That there wouldn't be challenges, tough times, opposition?"

"Well, I... I thought... I mean everything happened so fast... and it was going so well... but now..."

"It's pointless talking to you when you're like this." She turned and walked briskly back to the bedroom. He followed her, trying to make her understand his predicament. She ignored him, was dressed in less than a minute, threw a few necessities into a bag, and headed for the door. Ryman and Wycroft trotted after her. "Call me when you're sober and ready to make a commitment. Until then, I'll be... well, I don't know where I'll be. But not here." She left the cottage, fired up her Subaru, and drove away.

Ryman flopped down on the sofa and looked at Wycroft. "It's all going to hell, buddy." He took another drink of scotch. "All because of Saint Hubert and that fucking deer. I wish I'd never seen that goddamn deer. How could a buck that big, with a rack like that, and a damn Celtic cross floating above its head not get his ass shot in this county? Every goddamn deer hunter around here has been looking for a trophy like that his whole life. And we've got some first rate shots in these parts. How come I'm the only one who's seen him?"

Wycroft looked up, his rheumy old eyes now clear and sparkling. "Rrrrnnnn? Kllll?"

"Don't you start that shit again." Ryman tried to ignore the image forming in his mind, but the mental scene would not be banished. He was Wycroft, in the midst of a pack of hounds. He felt the exhilaration of the chase, his muscles strong and lithe as he ran over open ground, his nostrils filled with an intoxicating scent that pulled him onward.

Wycroft let out a long, exuberant *A-wooooooo!*

Ryman shook the image away. "Stop it, goddamn it, stop it! I don't want this. That goddamn deer." Another image caught his eye, the old Winchester 94 mounted above the fireplace. It wasn't much good as a hunting rifle; lever action, short barrel, no scope. And Ryman wasn't much of a shot. He kept it around mostly for show, some occasional target shooting, and to scare away any marauding varmint. But a well-placed slug from a .30-30 made a big hole. Big enough to bring down a fourteen-pointer.

Chapter 73

THE SHELLS WERE not in the sideboard drawer where they were usually kept. Ryman pulled the other drawers open, rummaged through them, came up empty. Where did he leave the box of .30-30 shells? Kitchen cupboard? Bedroom dresser? Pantry shelf? He checked, rechecked, even triple checked every place in the cottage where they could possibly be. No box of shells. A sleepless night and heavy drinking blurred his memory for details—never strong on a good day—into an opaque haze.

He sat on the couch, head in hands, and tried to recall where he'd seen them last. His fingers spread apart and his eyes opened wide. The Cabin! He'd gone up there with Crispie and Thumper for some target shooting one summer afternoon. They stacked up hay bales in the paddock and plinked away at cans and paper targets with an assortment of firearms, including his old Winchester 94. When it started raining, they hauled everything inside quickly, broke out the beer, and spent the rest of the day, and well into the evening, drinking, smoking cigars, and swapping yarns about guns, horses, hounds, hunting, and women. When they finally packed up, Ryman must have left the box of shells behind. That was the only place they could be.

"C'mon," he said to Wycroft. "Let's go get some bullets. Then find us that goddamn deer."

"Woof!"

****

Reverend Dan stood by the church's front door and soaked up the compliments as the parishioners slowly disgorged from Saint Cuthbert's.

Even Bob Sensabaugh was smiling as he gripped Dan's hand firmly. "Well done, Reverend. I don't know where you found this new inspiration, but I'm sure enjoying your series on the Commandments." His smile faded as he continued. "I just wish you'd gotten inspired a lot sooner. The diocese is still pressuring us and if we don't..." Bob realized there were still many people waiting in line behind him. "Well, now's not the time. Let's talk later."

"Any time at your convenience," Dan replied. He then reached out to greet the next person.

"Wonderful service, Reverend!"

****

Ryman was in no condition to be handling a high-powered rifle, nor even driving a truck for that matter. But he at least had the good judgment to leave the nearly empty bottle of scotch at home. Wycroft sat on the front seat, looking straight ahead. As the truck bounced along the rough dirt road leading to The Cabin, Ryman began to sense the futility of his mission. Crutchfield County encompassed almost three hundred square miles, much of it heavy forest. What was the likelihood of finding one specific buck in all that territory? Damn slim. The buck might not even be in Crutchfield County anymore. Two months had passed since Ryman saw him. Assuming he really did see him and it hadn't been just a concussion-conjured mirage. The rut was in full swing; thousands of does were perfuming the air with estrus-laden love messages. A big alpha buck could be traipsing through a half dozen counties in his quest to father as many Bambis as possible. Or his rack could now be adorning some lucky hunter's living room wall, the rest of him chilling out in neatly wrapped packages in someone's freezer.

But maybe the buck wasn't real. If no one had seen him except Ryman—three times in one crazy day, then nothing since—perhaps it truly was a vision sent from Saint Hubert. If he wasn't flesh and blood, he couldn't be shot. If he was a vision, maybe Saint Hubert would make him appear again. If he did, there was one way to find out for sure. All Ryman needed to do was locate the box of shells, load up the rifle, and get that sumbitch in his sights.

As they neared The Cabin, Wycroft stood up on all fours on the front seat, his ears cocked forward, his eyes bright.

The hair on the back of Ryman's neck bristled. "You feel it too?" he asked.

"Woof!"

There seemed to be a force drawing him toward The Cabin. It was almost as if he didn't need to steer or press the accelerator, that the truck was being borne forward by something other than its engine. Ryman and Wycroft were both fixated on The Cabin as it loomed ahead, still another mile up the old mountain logging road.

Between his thoughts about the deer and now this increasing sense of purpose to what had first seemed a harebrained folly, Ryman had not noticed the vehicle following his truck. It was obvious to the other driver where Ryman was going; the road only led to one place. The other vehicle slowed and the driver watched as Ryman's F250 rumbled over the rippled terrain.

Ryman pulled up in front of The Cabin, hopped out and held the door while Wycroft descended from the seat. Looking around, he saw the stack of hay bales still in the split rail paddock next to the building. A few bits of tattered paper target clung to one bale. He thought back to youthful visits to this secluded spot, sometimes by car or truck, other times on horseback. He and his friends had downed a lot of beer in this place when they were teenagers. And several Crutchfield County kids had experienced their signal passage into adulthood here. From the perspective of forty years later, he realized now that not all of those encounters had turned out well.

Still, though, the place held many special memories for him. And, he hoped, it also held a box of .30-30 shells.

When he and Wycroft entered, he was surprised by what he saw. "Someone's been doing some redecorating," he said. "What do you suppose is up with all these drawings on the walls?"

The dog did not answer.

"Probably kids messing around. Halloween maybe?"

He shrugged—the appearance of The Cabin's interior was not his concern—and looked around for the shells. Not seeing them in plain sight, he began opening drawers and cabinets. He found the shells in a kitchen cupboard. He was sure he hadn't put them there. Someone must have done some tidying up since his summer visit.

Standing in the small kitchen, still holding the handle of the knotty pine cupboard door, another prickle danced across his neck, stronger this time.

Wycroft looked up at him, barked, pranced toward the door, and began to scratch.

The prickling grew more insistent. He lifted his shoulders and shuddered.

Gripping the box of bullets, Ryman went to the door. Wycroft shot out the split second it was opened. The hound had barely taken two strides when Ryman saw him freeze in his tracks.

Man and dog stared past the truck, toward the edge of the woods that lined the small parking area. Head erect and chest swelled, the buck stared back at them.

The Celtic cross was still there, floating between the deer's impressive rack. But it seemed somehow diminished from the way Ryman remembered it; a little tilted to one side, the bright white sheen faded to an ashen gray and marred by several dark scratches. Was there a jagged piece missing near the top? It was hard to tell for sure with the buck framed against the woods behind him. Ryman's lack of sleep and lingering drunkenness did nothing to improve his eyesight.

The deer, clearly sober and seemingly on a mission of his own, locked his large brown eyes on Ryman. "Hubbbbtttttt!"

Wycroft lifted a front paw. "Rrrrnnnn?"

"No," Ryman whispered. "Leave it."

Wycroft dropped his paw.

"Good hound."

"*Hubbbbttttt!*"

Ryman realized he'd left the rifle in the truck. He expected to go searching for the deer, not for the deer to come to him. He felt the box of shells in his hand. They had served their purpose. They were the draw that brought him to The Cabin. Surely Saint Hubert had arranged it. He wanted Ryman here so he could ease his mind, strengthen his resolve, a secluded spot where the buck would appear to no one else. This was Ryman's Forty Hours in the Wilderness, the answer to his Moment of Doubt and Pain.

The ringing cell phone startled him so much that he dropped the box of shells. It burst open on impact. Bullets scattered across the rocky, hard packed earth.

Wycroft took advantage of the distraction and sprang forward. "Rnnnnnn! Klllllll!"

Ryman's "Leave it!" command, throttled by a dry tightness in his throat, came out no louder than a whispered croak.

The hound ran on, unrestrained.

The buck did not move.

Faced with a three hundred pound animal, a nasty fourteen-point weapon on its head, Wycroft stopped his assault. He stood looking at the deer. The deer looked down at him. The buck snorted and pawed the ground. Wycroft took a step back.

Ryman remained where he was, watching this standoff, his phone still ringing. Unable to resist the temptation, he pulled the phone from its holster and glanced at the screen. It showed Crispie's name as the caller. He remembered now that he'd promised to help with some kennel chores. Crispie must be wondering where he was. He clicked the call to voicemail.

When he glanced up, there was only Wycroft. Rifle shells crunched under his feet as Ryman ran to where the deer had stood only a second before. "Where'd he go?"

Wycroft appeared as confused as Ryman.

Looking left and right, he saw nothing. Could the buck have already gotten out of sight into the woods? The woods were thick, but thick enough to conceal an animal that large so quickly? Ryman strained to listen for any sounds of a body moving through the brush. Nothing.

"Well, that does it. Saint Hubert be praised! I now know what I must do. Whatta ya say, buddy? Are you with me?"

"Woof!"

As he drove back down the mountain road, Ryman was so focused on his rekindled mission that he failed to notice the vehicle parked up a side logging path, only partially hidden from view. The driver watched him go by. When Ryman's truck was safely out of sight, the vehicle pulled out from its hiding place and turned toward The Cabin.

****

There was a metallic crunch underfoot as The Defender stepped from the vehicle. Two-dozen large caliber bullets lay scattered on the ground. But the greater surprise was yet to come. Stepping through the door of The Cabin, The Defender beheld the walls covered with weird symbols. What were these? Eyes, stars, triangles, half moons, a square intersecting four curved quadrants, a circle with a cog-like figure inside, and something that looked like a cross except at the top was an egg-shaped circle. The room was full of candles, most of them burned down to the nub. Hardened wax drippings covered tabletops, counters, the hearth, and the mantelpiece.

The Defender walked around the room, studying the symbols. Passing by the coffee table, The Defender's foot struck something protruding from beneath the adjacent sofa. It made a clanking sound. Looking down, a pointed silver blade could be seen. Not wishing to touch the object, The Defender used a leg to push the sofa back just enough to get a better view. An ornate dagger lay on the floor, its long black handle inlaid with a symbol similar to the cross with the egg-shaped circle. Where had something like this been seen before? Ah, yes, on the cards Ryman and Nardell had been handing out, part of the logo for the Ancient and Venerable Church of Ars Venatica.

The Defender was sure now that this was the hidden lair of Ryman's church. It was where they came for their pagan rituals. And the evidence here showed that it was even worse than might have been imagined. Oh, sure, they tried to put on a nice public face. It was just about foxhunting, they said, having fun, honoring a little known Christian saint, no harm in that. Now The Defender's suspicions were confirmed, the truth was clear. Ryman was surely a false prophet, the kind Holy Scripture warned of, a dangerous dreamer seeking to lead the people astray. If there'd been any doubt before, it was all washed away now. The Defender knew what had to be done. Ryman must be stopped.

****

Baden walked back to the barn after turning out the horse he'd ridden that afternoon. Dorcas, with Missy assisting her, was in the ring working with several of the younger children. Cecelia's Mercedes came flying down the driveway from the main house and jerked to an abrupt halt in the barnyard. The driver's window descended and Cecelia beckoned Baden over to her. She handed him a cardboard box filled with an array of bottles in a variety of shapes and sizes.

"Here," she said, "I picked these up from the vet's office two days ago and forgot I'd left them in the car. I'm running late for an appointment to show a property. Would you be a love and put them in the office? Dorcas will know what to do with them."

"Yes, ma'am."

Baden headed on to the barn as Cecelia sped away. He put the box down on the desk and began idly pulling up random bottles just to see what they were. He was familiar with most of the medications—the commonly used compounds found at every horse facility. They ranged from mild over-the-counter supplements to stringently controlled drugs.

He was holding a bottle in the latter category when Dorcas entered the office. He'd heard her coming, but felt no cause for alarm.

The look of panic on her face surprised him. The intensity of her stare quickly turned his reaction from alarm to confusion and then to fear.

"What are you doing?" she demanded. "Where did you get that?"

She crossed the room in an instant and grabbed the bottle out of his hand. It almost fell to the floor in the clumsy exchange, but she caught it in time.

"I was just…" Baden stuttered. "Mrs. Broadhurst asked me to… to put these here for you to put away."

"And you saw this as your chance. I know what you were going to do with this. I've been watching you. I knew you couldn't be trusted. I knew it!"

Baden's fear morphed into indignation, the righteousness of a teenager falsely accused. "You've got a problem! Missy and I are fed up with you creeping around, spying on us, trying to watch everything we do. You're not our mother. You're not anybody's mother. You're just a lonely woman who lives in a barn and likes to play with children. I don't know what you thought I was going to do with this stuff, but I wasn't going to do anything." He pointed at the bottle Dorcas held. "Besides, if I did want to get at this stuff, there's some in my grandfather's barn. But it's just for horses. What else would anyone do with it?"

"Don't play innocent with me. You know exactly what to do with it. I've seen you… seen the way you look… seen what you're thinking."

"You're weird. Too weird." He stepped around her and moved

toward the door. "Missy and I are leaving. And I don't think we're coming back. My sister either. I don't want her around someone like you."

He left Dorcas standing in the office, cradling the bottle against her chest, and mumbling to herself. "Good riddance. I've done all I can do. Not my responsibility. Not their mother. He's right. Not anyone's mother." She slipped the bottle back into the box. She then pulled it back up again and studied the label. An idea began to form.

Chapter 74

NARDELL REACHED UP and straightened Ryman's stock tie. She brushed a few bits of hound hair from his vest, then stepped back to take in the full view. He stood by the front door, perfectly turned out in full formal hunting attire. A good night's sleep, thorough grooming, and time to let the alcohol pass from his system had restored him to clarity of mind and cleanliness of body.

"You look wonderful," she said. "Saint Hubert is surely pleased."

"Praised be his name. Um, look, about yesterday, I'm sorry I… it's just that… with all the…"

She placed a finger gently on his lips. "You had to go through that. Saint Hubert needed to strengthen your resolve for what's to come. If anything, it was selfish of me to bring our relationship into it. It's not about me, not about you. Is it?"

He leaned over, kissed her, and pulled her tightly against him with his hands on the small of her back. "Well, in some ways, it *is* about you."

"Oh, go on," she said, wiggling away but smiling and smacking him on the chest. "You need to get out of here. Saint Hubert's work awaits."

Ryman drew himself up, took a breath, and stepped through the cottage door.

He was soon seated in one of the guest chairs in the office of McKendrick and Sons. Muriel sat at her desk, Bar at his.

"I wanted to talk to the two of you first," Ryman began, "before I break the news to Miles and Conway. I now clearly see the path I must follow. I have been called to a special purpose. I don't know why. I'm certainly not worthy. But Saint Hubert has called me, and I must obey."

Muriel stiffened. "Hmmph!"

"Oh, I don't expect you to understand," Ryman continued. "Either one of you. I don't really understand myself. But the point is that in order to honor my calling, I have to let the shop go. I won't take a dime from my mother. And I can see no other way to hold off the bank. It's the end of McKendrick and Sons."

"Mister Ryman," Muriel said, "I'll be sad to see the business go. But not one bit for myself. No, sir. Oh, it's been a blessing in many ways working here all these years. And I'll miss it. Yes, I surely will. But my heart is breaking right now because of you. I know you mean well, that you're sincere in what you feel. But, oh, Mister Ryman, you've been led so terribly astray." She leaned across her small desk and reached her hands out to him. "There is no Saint Hubert calling you. You're blaspheming. And there's nothing more dangerous to your eternal soul than blasphemy. The Bible says, in First Timothy, chapter two, verse five, 'For there is one God, and one mediator between God and men, the man Christ Jesus.' Because I loved your father in the Lord, and I love you in the Lord as well, I beg you, Mister Ryman, come to your senses. Let Jesus into your heart and know the joy of eternal salvation through His blood."

Ryman reached out and took Muriel's petite hands in his. "Oh, Muriel, that's sweet. And I know you mean well too. But you haven't seen what I've seen. You haven't heard or felt what I have. This is no easy decision, trust me. But I know what I have to do. My main concern, though, is that you'll be okay if the shop's not here anymore."

"Don't you worry about that. The Lord will take care of me. He always has. But, Mister Ryman, you…"

He squeezed her hands, released them, and sat back. "Good. I'm sure he will. Saint Hubert will help see to that." He turned his attention to Bar. "How about you, Mister Executive Sales Manager?"

Bar sat silently for a long moment staring back at Ryman. Ryman began to feel his armpits moistening as Bar's one crystal blue eye held him in an unblinking gaze. When Ryman had reached the point of sufficiently visible discomfort, Bar spoke. "I may be just as crazy as you are, boss man. But I'm not gonna let it happen."

"Bar, it's not your call to make. I know the shop means a lot to you, and living at the farm even more. Believe me, this has been the hardest part of my decision. But I know Saint Hubert will…"

"Saint Hubert my fat hairy ass!" Bar brought a massive hand down on his desk so hard the computer bounced into the air. Muriel and Ryman both sat agape at the outburst. Having gotten their attention, Bar continued in a calmer tone. "I appreciate Muriel's concern over your eternal soul. But I'm more interested in the here and now. The shop is still here, and now's the time to make sure it stays here."

"Look, man, I know this is harder on you than anyone else, but there's no point discussing…"

"I'm not discussing. I'm telling. The bank's not going to call the note, and John Deere's not going to pull the franchise."

"And how, exactly, is that not going to happen?"

"Because me and Sheltie Lou are putting up the money. Mostly me."

"You're what? You know how much we're talking about here? What it'll take to keep this place afloat?"

"Yeah, I know, dumb ass. Remember? You came to my place two nights ago and unburdened your eternally lost soul. Or has that already gone flittering out of your messed up brain?" Bar fluttered one hand beside the scarred side of his head.

"But how could you possibly…? I mean I appreciate the thought, man. I really do. But this is a shitload… er…" Ryman sensed Muriel's disapproval. He realized that Bar's language was extremely mild compared to his usual pattern. "…a boatload of money. What did you do? Rob a bank over the weekend?"

"What do you think I've been doing back there in the woods for all these years? What have you seen me spending money on since I showed up here?"

Ryman thought hard. "Um, beer?"

"Okay, beer. And cheap stuff at that. I've never made much working here, but my overhead's been practically nothing. And at least the government was kind enough to compensate me for some lost body parts. I'm even still driving the same truck that brought me here in the first place. Your old man let me work on it in the shop in my spare time. He even let me order the parts and put 'em on the company account. I obviously ain't spent much on my wardrobe. Until now anyway." He tugged at his clean white overalls. "Never took a vacation. Hell, I even get my pet food for free. It's amazing what frugality, diligence, and patience can do over time."

"You mean…" Ryman stammered, "…you mean you've saved that much dough…"

"Yeah, that much and a good bit more. And not just saved it. It's called 'investing,' something you've obviously never caught on to. I saw what Muriel and Ben were doing shortly after I came here. They didn't earn a lot, but I saw how they handled things, always careful with their money and thinking about the future. Figured it might be worth a try, instead of blowin' it all on booze, weed, and women. Kind of became a hobby. I started subscribing to a bunch of money management magazines and newsletters. Helped a bunch when it became possible to do everything online. About the only thing I've spent more than a few dollars on is computers."

Muriel sat beaming at the big man beside her. She had no idea she and her late husband had been an inspiration to him. She was as surprised as Ryman that he'd amassed enough to cover the shop's shortfall.

"I figured I was just building up a nest egg for when I retired," Bar went on. "Y'know, so I could continue to live in the gracious manner I've become accustomed to. But, well, some priorities have changed lately."

"Like what?" Ryman asked.

"Man, you are one dense sumbitch, ain't you? Oh, let's see. Like the business that's been the anchor of my life for about forty years going down the shi…down the toilet. The place I've come to every day, the devotion I've poured into my trade, trying to be the best darn tractor mechanic I could be." Bar paused. His face darkened and his focus wavered. "Like maybe there was some reason I… I survived when all those other men didn't. Like since maybe your brother didn't make it back, I was supposed to, I dunno, not take his place, exactly, but somehow, y'know, be here and… and…" His voice trailed off. After a pause, he cleared his throat, squared his shoulders and continued. "'Course, Teedy ain't the only McKendrick to inspire me to do this."

"Oh, man, I can't tell you how much it means to me that you'd do this for…"

"Not you, dumb ass." Bar turned to Muriel. "It's okay to say 'ass,' ain't it? I mean, ain't there 'ass' mentioned in the Bible? I remember in Sunday school we all giggled about the story of Bedlam's Ass."

"Balaam," Muriel said.

"Yeah, that."

She smiled indulgently and waved a hand. "It's okay. You go on."

"Right. So anyways, like I was saying to Balaam's dumb ass here, it ain't about you. I'm talking about your dear mama, the crazy old bat. I don't want her to have the satisfaction of thinking she's won. I reckon it'll always be a mystery to me why she hates my guts. Nothin' I've ever done to her that I can think of. But I'd gladly give up every dime I've saved just to keep her from getting her way about kicking me off the farm. Besides," he added with what passed for a smile on his mangled face, "the birds deserve it."

"I… I don't know what to say…"

"I'll tell you what you're gonna say. You're gonna say, 'Thank you, Mister Reinhardt. Yes, I accept your offer.' And the terms are that I'm coming into the business as a full partner. I ain't had time to get the papers drawn up yet, but whatever I put in front of you, you're gonna put your John Hancock on. Oh, and it ain't gonna be a neat fifty-fifty arrangement."

"Well, if you want a bigger share, I reckon I can't really…"

"That ain't what I'm saying. It's forty for me, forty for you, ten for Sheltie Lou, and the other ten percent goes to Muriel."

"What?" Muriel said. "No, Barstow. That's most exceedingly thoughtful and generous of you. But I can't allow you to do that. If I could contribute something, then maybe, but I'm not in a position…"

"You've contributed more than enough already. If it wasn't for you, the old man would have run the shop into ruin long before this. And I wouldn't be sitting here today able to do what I'm doing. So, please, do as dumb… as Mister McKendrick here is doing. Say 'Thank you' and put your name on the documents when I put them in front of you."

Muriel nodded, reached across the small divide between their desks, and patted Bar on his arm. "Thank you," she whispered.

Bar turned back to Ryman. "So, boss man, are these terms acceptable to you?"

"Yes, certainly! Saint Hubert be…"

"*And* one more thing. You're not gonna say this is anyone's doing but mine and Sheltie Lou's. Don't you go trying to say your imaginary saint did this. Muriel may think that's blasphemy and will damn your eternal soul. I got a more immediate type of punishment in mind." Bar balled one hand into a fist and raised it slightly off the desk, just enough for Ryman to get the point.

Ryman wanted to jump up and shout praises to Saint Hubert. But he gripped the seat of his chair, bit his lip, and managed to restrain himself. "Yes, I agree. Thank you. Thank you more than I can say." He arose, grabbed Bar's hand, and pumped it frantically. "Thank you!" He stopped pumping and a questioning look contorted his face. "But, um, how did Sheltie Lou get involved in this? I'm not sure I want her risking her money. She couldn't have all that much saved."

"She ain't risking much. More like a token gesture, show her support for the cause. Mostly, she's gonna help put the extra cash to good use, got some great ideas for new marketing plans, change things around. 'Rebranding' she called it. You send a kid off to college for a business degree and an MBA, and look how she turns out. Anyways, me and her been talking things over. Even before you stopped by the other night and gave me the details, it's been pretty obvious things ain't been going well around here. Hell, she's even startin' to weaken a bit about the idea of moving back home. Seems California ain't turned out to be quite the Promised Land she was expecting."

"Wow, wouldn't that be great!" It took all Ryman's resolve to keep from shouting out praises to you-know-who.

"Better her than having to look at your ugly ass around here every day. And speaking of that ugly ass, maybe it's time you got it out of here. Me and Muriel have work to do." He fluttered one hand in a shooing motion. "You go on and play now. The grown-ups are busy."

Ryman restrained himself until he was outside. Standing next to his truck, he threw his arms into the air and shouted, "Saint Hubert be praised! Blessed be his name!"

Chapter 75

RHETTA AND ABEL stormed across the front lawn to where the riders were assembling for Tuesday's hunt. Ryman saw her coming and, mounted on Clyde, calmly stood his ground in the face of the impending assault.

The hazel fire flared in Rhetta's eyes. "What's this wild story I heard about you taking on the freak and that prissy little colored woman as partners?"

Ryman replied coolly, "The news traveled fast. You musta been talking to Luella when you were doing your Monday errands."

"Then it's true." She threw her hands up in disgust. "You're beyond stark ravin' mad. There ain't been no one outside the family to own a piece a that business since your great-granddaddy started it. And here you go giving it away to them two."

"First of all, Ma, I did not give it away. The business was seriously in need of cash. It was either accept Bar's offer to make up the sizeable shortfall, or as of tomorrow there'd be no more McKendrick and Sons."

Rhetta tried to adopt a hurt, suffering-mother tone. "Gosh, son, why didn't you come to me?" The effort caused her ears to turn red and the veins in her neck to pulse under the strain of such artificiality. "I'd a been happy to help. And we'd a kept everything in the family."

Ryman scoffed. "Yeah, right. And with what kinda conditions attached?"

His flippant tone set her off again. "Conditions? I'll tell you what conditions I'm makin' now. I want y'all off my property. The lot of you. Get these damn horses back on the trailers and get the hell outta here. You want to go wasting your time chasing foxes around the countryside instead a tending to what y'all should be doing? Fine, that's your business. Just go do it somewheres else."

She stalked through the field, ordering everyone to leave. She stopped short when she came to Bing and Marie, just preparing to mount their horses. "Especially you, Harry Sensabaugh. You got a lot a nerve bein' here anyways, after what you done."

Bing replied softly, "That was a long time ago, Henrietta. Haven't we both suffered enough since?"

"Enough? What do you know about enough suffering? I lost a son. When's enough suffering for something like that? You still got Bob, sitting at the bank this very morning, running the business, like Teedy should a been doing at ours. Instead I got this crazy, good-for-nothing excuse for a son, thinks he's getting messages from some saint or somebody who ain't even real. Suffering? Hell, you don't know… don't know…" Her lip began to quiver and a faint mist clouded her eyes. "Just… git," she said as she turned away.

Some of the hunters obeyed her command and were loading their horses back onto the trailers. Others stood where they were, unsure of what to do, looking to Ryman for his lead.

He guided Clyde to a central spot where all could hear and said, "Y'all just stay where you are. Nobody's leaving. We're here for sport and sport we will have."

Rhetta froze. The mist cleared, her mouth drew tight. "Like hell you will. I want all you yay-hoos outta here. My farm, my rules."

Ryman moved to where Rhetta stood. He stopped with his knee next to her head, leaned over from the saddle, and said quietly, "Ma, I love you, and I wouldn't want any harm to come to you. Perhaps it's best you not get on the bad side of our blessed Saint Hubert."

"You threatening me, boy?" she hissed back. "You think I'm afraid of you or your imaginary saint person? I ain't afraid a you, I ain't afraid a ghosts, I ain't afraid a nothing."

"I know you ain't, Ma. And I admire that about you. But, well, I'm just saying, maybe you should have a little chat with Grantham Meisner. Or the folks over at Tiber Creek. See what they all think about the wisdom of going against Saint Hubert."

She started to open her mouth, but nothing came out. Thanks to Luella, everyone in Crutchfield County knew about Grantham's fall and the double tragedies at the Maryland hunt. The gossip included a strong line of thought that led straight back to Ryman's pronouncements preceding each incident.

"You think I… that I'd be afraid of you and your damned old Saint What's-his…" She gave Ryman one final defiant glare. Without looking down she said, "C'mon, dog."

Thumper arrived just then, still timing his arrival on Ozzy as close to the hunting start as possible to minimize the horse's misbehavior. He expected to find everyone mounted and the sport ready to commence. Instead he came upon a frozen tableau with Ryman at the center, some people standing motionless next to their horses, others with their horses on the trailers as if they'd just arrived. The only figures moving were Rhetta and Abel marching toward the main house.

"What's going on?" Thumper asked. "How come you all aren't ready to hunt?"

Ryman returned a nonchalant reply. "Oh, me and Ma just had a couple of things to discuss. Kind of put us off schedule I reckon." He looked around the field. "C'mon, y'all. Get those horses ready, get yourselves mounted up, and let's go have some sport." He turned to Crispie. "Mister O'Rourke, prepare to draw to Blackberry Covert. There's a little vixen waiting there for us, the one who introduced herself to Patti a couple of months ago. Saint Hubert be praised!"

Chapter 76

JANEY STEPPED OUT of Krug Hall following her Wednesday afternoon class. She stopped in mid-stride when she saw Thumper sitting on a bench along the quad at GMU's Fairfax campus. He arose as she walked toward him.

"Just happened to be in the neighborhood?" she asked.

"Oh, you know, cruising around, nothing much to do, next thing I know I'm driving right past good old GMU. Thought I'd stop by and say 'hi.'"

"And you knew which building I'd be coming out of and when?"

"Lucky guess."

"Right."

"Okay, I looked up the course schedule online. Pretty easy actually."

They began walking along, an aimless stroll in the general direction of the Fenwick Library.

"This isn't, like, a stalking thing, is it?"

"I certainly hope it doesn't look that way," he said, realizing to his discomfort that it could. "I'm terribly embarrassed about my behavior Saturday night. It was rude, ungentlemanly, completely inappropriate. I don't blame you for not sticking around. Nor for not wanting to return."

"Who said I didn't want to return?"

"Oh, well, I assumed, I mean, the way you left, that you…"

"I thought you needed some space. And I figured you might feel a bit uncomfortable the next morning."

"You figured right."

"I didn't want to put you through the displeasure of that, so I thought it best if I gave you some time to be alone, deal with the hunt's problems without me being there to make things worse."

"You're not making things worse. It's just that…"

"Yes, I am making it worse for you. Bad enough you have to deal with Ryman, Grantham, and all that. But for me to be there, chronicling everything and preparing to share it with the world, well, yes, that makes it worse."

"So what are you saying? That you're willing to suspend your research and hold off on the book until we get all this Church of Foxhunting bullshit sorted out?"

"Maybe back off for just a bit, yes." She stopped walking and turned to face him. "I'm afraid I'm losing my objectivity. The truth is, I've gotten too close to my subject."

Thumper was flummoxed. "I don't know what to say. You've got a lot riding on this book. Danella made that clear. And here we've given you a golden opportunity with Ryman getting himself 'construed.'"

They both smiled.

"I'd hate to be the cause of you missing out on that," Thumper said. "Or at least having to wait on it, running the risk that it'll play itself out and become old news. Or that someone else might beat you to the punch."

Janey felt a twinge at that last thought. She hadn't considered the possibility of anyone else getting in on this, or that someone could get to the market before her work was ready. She'd assumed it was strictly her good fortune to have stumbled into this unique confluence of sport and religion—better still, with a dash of sex appeal—and thus her work would be the first and unquestionably the definitive word on the subject. But for all she knew, there might already be another investigator looking into this, or even someone on the inside planning to co-opt her idea.

"Who could possibly be in a position to do that?" she asked, a defensive quiver in her voice.

"Hell, I don't know. Probably nobody. I'm just saying that, well, I'd like to re-extend my offer for you to camp out at Montfair. And I promise I'll behave, in all respects this time."

They resumed walking again, veering toward the statue of the school's namesake.

"Is that why you tracked down my schedule and drove all the way here?"

"Gosh, no. Like I said, I was just in the neighborhood and… okay, yes, that's why I'm here."

"You could have just called. Emailed. Even texted."

"Too impersonal, too easy. My misbehavior demanded a more substantive apology. Besides, I still can't accept the use of the word 'text' as a verb, let alone use that disembodied method to convey a personal request for forgiveness."

"Well, I think you've done your penance. And I appreciate the gesture."

They stopped walking again. Both knew this would have been the moment to face each other, drop the forced formality, and express themselves physically. But a public display of affection would have been inappropriate for a professor on the grounds of the university, with hundreds of students all around them, especially locking lips with the subject of her personal research. Even more so that this particular research subject was, technically, married.

Still, he'd made a special trip to apologize. And she'd agreed to return to Montfair. At least there was that.

He cleared his throat and they resumed their stroll.

"So then," Thumper said, "how about coming back out to Montfair Friday after your classes. Saturday's meet is at the Prestons' farm."

"That will make three hunts. Assuming there isn't another license bust."

"I can assure you that won't happen. And then the following week is Thanksgiving. I assume you have plans, going home to Minnesota."

"No, actually, I'd planned to stay here. I'd like to see my family, but it's just such a hassle traveling on holidays like that."

Thumper thought it odd that a world traveler like Janey couldn't deal with a quick holiday trip back to little old Clara City. But he decided it best not to question her about this.

She realized it was a lame excuse, easy to see through. But she wasn't about to admit that her limited funds would not permit such an extravagance. She'd explained to her mother that the pressing demands of this hot book project meant she had to stay in Virginia and burn the midnight oil. Her mother hadn't been any more convinced than Thumper was. But she had the good judgment to accept the excuse and not insult her only daughter by offering to pay for the airfare.

"Well, then," Thumper said, "may I invite you to stay over for Thanksgiving? It's a High Holy Day, if you'll excuse the phrase, for foxhunting. There will be the Blessing of the Hounds, which, oddly enough, is done in the name of Saint Hubert. You won't want to miss that."

"Wonderful. All the more reason to be there that day."

"I was thinking maybe you could make it for more than just that day. With the holiday and all, why not the whole week?"

"Because I still have classes to teach on Monday and Tuesday. The holiday break doesn't start until Wednesday."

"Maybe someone would be willing to cover for you. You do have some reciprocal arrangements for that, right?"

"Yes, we do. I can ask. But I can't promise anything."

"Okay. But this Friday evening and the weekend for sure. And, if nothing else, at least come back after your Tuesday classes and stay for the holiday."

"Yes, certainly. And by the time the holiday's over, I shall know the secret of your nickname."

"That alone should make the visit worthwhile."

Chapter 77

PATTI'S LITTLE VIXEN had indeed been waiting again in Blackberry Covert where Ryman said she'd be and provided another morning of entertainment on Tuesday. Two of her cousins took up the baton on Thursday and played a tag-team game that ended at a well-used den in the field next to the meet, a most obliging conclusion for the large group of tired but happy hunters.

By Saturday morning the autumnal foliage was past its peak, the trees half naked, a mid-November warning of winter's barrenness to come. The air was chilly, dampened by a fine mist that stubbornly resisted the sun's weak efforts to burn it away. But the spirits of the hunters remained as brilliant and warm as they had been since the season's first day.

"Hark, please!" Everyone turned to Ryman as he called the assembly to order. "We come now, on this glorious Saturday morning, to the tenth and final Article of our Foxhunter's Faith, as handed down to us by our beloved North-Country Hunting Parson. He concludes the foundational articles for our Ancient and Venerable Church of Ars Venatica with this: 'And may all men, rich and poor, have equal rights and pleasures in "the chase" if they devoutly agree to these articles.'"

Nardell added the requisite "Amen" and the crowd echoed it back with a vigorous reply.

"Ah, my brothers and sisters," Ryman continued, "it's about the chase, isn't it? And that's true for everyone. We're all chasing something, aren't we? It may not be foxes. And it may not be with hounds and horses. What are we chasing, then? We may be chasing after an education, a certain degree we want to earn. The 'paper chase' some people call it. Why, Brother Thumper has put so many degrees to ground, he needs extra large business cards just to fit in all the letters after his name."

Thumper smiled and bowed to a polite ripple of laughter.

"Others are chasing their career, chasing a relationship, chasing a cause they believe in, chasing a better place to live, chasing a nest egg to retire on. It's the chase that makes us human, that gives us a reason to be alive, to get up every morning with a purpose, a goal to strive toward. Unhappy people are those who have lost the joy of the chase. Life is mere drudgery, no challenge, just getting by day to day. That's no way to live. Oh, the chase may not always end successfully. And what then? Well, take a breath, regroup, then cast your hounds and try again. And if the whole day is a blank, don't worry. There will be another day, and another chase.

"What we do out here, three days a week for seven months out of the year, is more than just mindless sport. Much more. It's a reminder of what life's about on a grander scale. Foxhunters are some of the happiest, most well-balanced people on the planet. Oh, not because, like many people wrongly think, we're all a bunch of idle rich, spoiled trust fund brats. You all here this morning know that's not true."

Even without Nardell's prompting, a few spontaneous "Amens" sounded from the crowd.

"No, it's because we understand that life is a chase. By acting it out in this manner, by challenging ourselves against a wily opponent, against the forces of nature, and against our own weaknesses, we know that we can face whatever obstacles life throws at us. That's the message Saint Hubert would have us take from all this. And tell others, rich or poor, no matter who they are, where they live, or what they do. Life is about the pleasures of the chase. Glory to his name!"

Even Thumper and Grantham, the chief Pharisees, as well as Janey the neutral Scribe-Gone-Native, joined the Amen Chorus. Only Dan the High Priest and Bob the Moneychanger remained silent.

"And now, Brother Crispie, if you will, let's be about the chase!"

****

Janey fell in behind Mildred as they moved off. Crispie took hounds to the first draw and the riders gathered on a small rise that afforded a full view of the covert. Mildred motioned for Janey to come up next to her. Cecelia slipped up on Janey's other side.

As hounds worked below, Janey shivered. She wasn't sure if it was from the morning chill or the anticipation of what she now knew was soon to happen: hounds would open, the cry would send a galvanizing bolt through riders and horses, muscles would tense, adrenalin would surge, and the hunters would sweep away in single-minded pursuit.

The mental image caused another shiver.

Mildred noticed it. "Are you cold, deah?" she asked quietly.

"A little. Mostly just nervous, I think."

"The anticipation," Cecelia said. "Still gets to me after all these years. It's like… like when you're on your way to meet a man. You know what's going to happen. But you don't know just how it's going to unfold. Might be okay. Might be spectacular. But there's some risk. You might get hurt. It's the knowing, but the not knowing that gets you revved up. Does me anyway."

Mildred looked around Janey to reply to Cecelia. "That's so true." She thought about the trail of clothing she'd left for Josh, how she felt while waiting for him in the bedroom, lying there naked, listening to his footsteps through the house, then pounding up the stairs and down the hallway. When he finally reached her, she was already close to orgasm at his first touch. Similar post-hunt games had been played many times since.

Janey and Cecelia both caught the far-away gleam in Mildred's eyes. She was too lost in her thoughts of what afternoon pleasures awaited to notice the small reddish creature creeping from one end of the covert. The fox stayed low to the ground, trying to slip away without being noticed as hounds worked to sort out his jumbled line of scent in the heavy thicket. Thumper had the first field placed to watch the other end of the covert. No one with him could see the fox. The stealthy critter did not, however, escape Janey's eye.

She tapped Mildred on the arm and whispered, "Look, there goes the fox."

Mildred snapped back to the moment. She smiled at Janey and whispered in reply, "I believe that's 'Tally-ho.'"

"Is this when you say that?"

"It is. And you're the one to say it. Shout it out, like you mean it, and point toward the fox. Go ahead. Let it rip."

Janey was unprepared to be the center of attention. But she had to trust Mildred. Her nerves jangling, she steeled herself, stood up in her stirrups, pointed toward the escaping fox, and shouted for all she was worth, "Tally-HOOOOOO!"

The response was immediate. Crispie looked to Janey, then saw the fox. The fox knew he'd been discovered and the chase was on. He abandoned the attempt to slink away and kicked into gear.

"C'mon, now!" Crispie called to his hounds. "On to 'im!" He blew the cavalry charge notes of "Gone Away." The pack surged as one force from the covert and swarmed onto the fresh line of scent. They were away, Crispie right behind encouraging them on.

"Well done," Mildred said as she gathered her reins and prepared to move out. "That's your fox now. Janey's fox."

The first field took off and then the second field swept down from the rise and joined the action.

Janey felt the thrilling anticipation of knowing what was coming, while not fully knowing. The fox would decide. Would it be a quickie? Fun, but over too soon, the hunters left craving more? Or would Reynard string it out, tempt and tease, flirt with a climax but then make an unexpected move and continue on, wait until the other players neared their limit, breath short, strength almost gone, expectation pushing them into a frenzy of desire. And then… a riotous, boisterous, bumping, straining end. Hounds swarming the den, horses panting and pawing, riders red-faced and gasping, huge smiles gleaming from every face.

It would be good. That she knew. Would it be great? That was up to the fox. Either way, Janey was caught up in the irresistible flow toward the known yet unknown, carried along on an unstoppable tide of anticipation in pursuit of the craftiest—and sexiest—creature there is.

****

Back at the Prestons' pasture, Janey and Thumper relived the morning's action as they untacked their horses. Each twist and turn was acted out with animated gestures and the enthusiasm still showed on their glowing faces. It had been a one-fox day. But that one fox—Janey's fox—had given a gold medal solo performance.

It was too outlandish for Janey to admit to Thumper, but there had been a moment when hounds faltered on the scent and the fox stopped to size up his pursuers. For a fleeting instant, Janey felt the fox look right at her. Then a hound opened and the fox was off again.

As Lenny and Bee rested comfortably with hay and water, the senior master and now three-time foxhunter headed for the tailgate spread. Mildred and Cecelia stood watching them approach, still laughing and talking about the chase. Janey failed to notice a large hoof-shaped divot in the pasture, stepped into it, lost her balance, and tilted against Thumper's shoulder. He reached out to steady her. This caused them to laugh even harder.

"Damn fool," Cecelia said. "Could there be anything worse than a morally upright lawyer? That gal is ready for a good shagging. What the hell's he waiting for?"

"How do you know they're not?" Mildred asked. "She's staying at Montfair. Plenty of opportunity."

"Oh, c'mon. Isn't it obvious? They're still in the circling phase, haven't come in for the landing yet. He's very careful where he places his hands, because permission has not yet been given. Did you see how he reacted when she bumped into him? The barrier's still there. Once that's broken, it's a whole 'nuther ballgame."

"I suppose you're right."

"Of course I'm right. There are two things I know about, foxhunting and men."

"You've certainly had plenty of experience with both."

Cecelia took that in the complimentary way it was meant.

"Well," Mildred continued, "I've done my part, inviting her to take your place at our dinnah party, then hustling her off with him afterward when she'd had too much wine. But I guess nothing came of that."

"A start anyway. I'll tell you this, though, Sister Mildred. When those two finally do break that barrier, you'll hear it all the way from Montfair to Moscow."

****

Grantham reached around Bob to grab another spicy chicken wing from the tailgate table. "I got the official report on the fire at Tiber Creek," he said to Thumper. "Faulty wiring, bad design, cheap construction. The master's skinflint ways finally caught up with him. No indication of foul play or anything like… any other… well, nothing out of the ordinary."

"You mean," Thumper said, "such as inexplicable spontaneous combustion, or fire and brimstone raining down from above on that one accursed spot?"

"Yes, nothing like that."

"Well, serves the old cheapskate right. And thankfully no one—humans, hounds, or horses—were hurt in the fire. Any update on how the huntsman's broken leg is doing?"

"He's out of the hospital, but no permanent home to go to. The pack has been split up and taken in by various members. No sport over there for now, likely won't be for awhile."

They both stood and watched Ryman working his way through the crowd, accepting praise and bestowing blessings.

"There doesn't seem to be quite the urgency to shut him down as there was when we spoke last Sunday," Thumper said.

"I suppose the report on Tiber Creek will back some folks off. Of course, Ryman has plenty of his supporters and defenders too."

"And perhaps a few who've seen what might happen if you get on his bad side."

Ryman joined them around the jam-packed tailgate table. "Another badge of glory to all," he said, inserting himself between Billington and Meisner, a hand firmly gripping each man's shoulder. "A great morning of sport. Saint Hubert be praised!"

"So, your Holiness," Thumper said, "now that you've finished the ten articles, what brilliantly crafted sermonettes will we be regaled with next?"

"Well, the next one is kind of a no brainer, Thanksgiving and the Blessing of the Hounds. That message will pretty much write itself. After that, well, I'm sure Saint Hubert will provide me with the right inspiration."

Thumper noticed Janey engaged in a private conversation with Dan off on the far fringes of the crowd. "Y'know, the Blessing is traditionally given by a member of the recognized clergy. That should be Reverend Davenport's role."

"Oh, yeah, right. I'll speak to him about that. I'm sure he won't mind sharing a bit of the limelight."

"The question is, will *you* be willing to share that limelight?"

"Of course, Brother Thumper. I'm not seeking any glory here. Saint Hubert works through us all. Even you, just as he did last Saturday when you gave such an inspiring reading of Article Nine."

"I was just trying to get the hunt underway. You and Nardell had already held things up long enough."

Ryman smiled. "Sure, whatever you say."

"Look, just make sure the good Reverend is fully included in the ceremonies. We blew it with Opening Day, none of us remembered to ask him to deliver the invocation."

"I will, don't you worry. And I have a favor to ask of you. I'm still having some issues with Colby. I need someone with a steady jumper to go along on some schooling rides, give him a lead over fences, help him settle into the job. Nardell's going out with me tomorrow, but I'd like to go again Monday and she's got a full day of massage appointments. Any chance you could bring Lenny and ride out with me Monday morning?"

"Ah, gee, I don't know. I'm way behind on my Jefferson Bible project. I told my editor I'd have a decent first draft turned in before the holiday. Now I've got some major cranking to do if I'm going to make that. I'd probably better not."

"I could ride out with you," a voice behind them said.

The two men turned to see Dorcas standing close by.

"There you go," Thumper said to Ryman. "What better partner than someone who's used to dealing with those of a childlike mind."

The barb eluded Ryman. "Oh, well, I don't think… I mean, I'm sure you're really busy with everything you have to do at Cecelia's. I guess I can just work with him myself."

"I have to get Waylon, Cecelia's main hunter, out for some exercise before Thursday," Dorcas explained. "I was planning to take him out Monday morning anyway. He's the most reliable jumper in the barn, perfect for giving a young horse a lead. If you want to trailer Colby to Kimber Farm, we can go work him over the fences I use to school the kids."

Thumper added his input. "Sounds perfect to me, Ry." He turned to Dorcas. "What time should he be there?"

"How about nine o'clock?"

"Fine. Looks like you and Colby got a date." Thumper gave Ryman a pat on the back and walked off to socialize with some other tailgaters.

Ryman and Dorcas stood awkwardly alone.

"Look," Ryman said, "about that other thing… when you came to my place…"

Dorcas brushed off the remark. "I was out of line, and I'm sorry. Won't happen again, I promise. Just thought I could offer some help, that's all."

"Okay, well, I appreciate the offer. But I'm not sure it would be a good idea for us to…"

Ryman had been so focused on this uncomfortable exchange with Dorcas that he hadn't noticed Nardell approaching.

"What's going on?" she asked.

Dorcas answered. "Ryman said he needed some help schooling Colby over fences. I offered to ride out with him Monday."

"Oh, that's a wonderful idea," Nardell said. "I'm booked up all day, everyone wants their horses in top form for Thursday. That's great if you can help."

Ryman expected Nardell's feminine radar to be on full alert, that she'd come up with some excuse to get him off the hook. But if she didn't sense anything amiss, maybe he was overreacting. The thought of being alone with Dorcas aside, there was great appeal to schooling Colby behind Cecelia's number one hunter.

"Okay, then," Ryman said. "I'll see you Monday. Is it okay if I bring Wycroft? The old boy could use some exercise too."

"Sure." She then added in a voice low enough that Nardell did not hear, "He can be our chaperone."

****

Thumper went out of his way to be the perfect gentleman throughout the weekend when he and Janey were alone in the house. Perhaps a bit too gentlemanly for Janey's comfort level as his stiff formality and physical caution made her feel like an unwelcomed intruder, a burden that had to be borne rather than a guest whose company could be enjoyed. But she understood the motivation behind it and to ease the tension they spent as much time as possible in their respective rooms working on their writing projects.

For Janey, her presence at Montfair deepened the sense of immersion into her subject, far more than if she tried to write about foxhunting in the sterile environment of a suburban apartment.

But while the atmosphere of Montfair inspired her prose, the passages she composed only further fueled her desire to cast off the restraints of a neutral observer. The more she wrote about what she'd seen and experienced over the past several weeks, the more she wanted to fully embrace this newfound community as her own. She'd never felt that with any other subject of her studies. She admired the San Bushmen for their peaceful, non-judgmental philosophy. But she never felt the slightest desire to abandon her Western attire and spend the rest of her life living in a hut and scavenging for survival on the unforgiving Kalahari. The Yanomamö were a fascinating study. But she feared for her safety every minute she was with them. And so it went, whether homegrown cult or ancient culture, the routine was always the same: swoop in, do the research, go home, write the story.

Now, though, when she tried to write about the passion, the challenge, the stimulating excitement of riding a horse in pursuit of a pack of foxhounds in full cry, the wild sensuality of it all came flooding back over her.

She found it difficult to stay in her assigned guest room, her only company the spirit of Uncle Josiah.

To lessen the discomfort, she made plans to be away for at least part of Sunday. She would spend the earlier part of the day attending her first service at Saint Cuthbert's. She then had plans for the afternoon to take another lesson in the ring with Patti followed by a guided trail ride.

Thumper claimed his looming deadline as the excuse not to join her for either church in the morning or riding in the afternoon.

Chapter 78

"TODAY BRINGS US to the tenth and final Commandment," Reverend Dan announced. "And it brings me to a confession. I have been guilty of violating this commandment." He looked down at the text before him. His bushy, upturned eyebrows shielded much of his face. "'You shall not covet your neighbor's house; you shall not covet your neighbor's wife, nor his male servant, nor his female servant, nor his ox, nor his donkey, nor anything that is your neighbor's.'"

Dan slowly raised his head and with misty eyes looked out upon the packed pews of Saint Cuthbert's-in-the-Woods. His gaze held for several seconds on Janey Musgrove, seated with the Sensabaugh family.

"Some of you here this morning may have had problems with coveting. Some may still be having such problems even now. My confession, though, is not about material things. No, mine comes under the 'anything' category. As a young priest, I envisioned myself rising in the church to a position of great leadership, to be widely acclaimed among the faithful, to be ministering to thousands, hundreds of thousands even. But here I am in middle age, serving a tiny congregation where we count ourselves not by the thousands nor even by the hundreds but by the dozens. And until recently, barely even by that. Oh, I'm gratified to see so many here this morning. But I fear this outpouring has come too late." He looked down at the Sensabaughs and an ironic smile ignited a suffering, beatific glow on his pale, drawn face.

"I will be moving on soon, perhaps to serve in an even smaller role somewhere else. I confess, this has troubled me. Particularly in light of what else has been transpiring in our community, a mockery of true faith that has taken many in by its appeal to the sensual, aided by what some have seen as mystical signs and wonders. I have warned you about this heresy, have I not? And yet it continues to grow. I have striven to reinforce the foundational elements of our faith so that you might be strengthened to withstand any false prophets that come among you.

"But my time draws to a close soon. And before that time arrives, I felt I must unburden my soul of the covetous feelings that have plagued me. I am but an instrument of our Lord. Whatever lies ahead, His will must be done."

****

Those seated in the front pews had an exceptionally long wait to exit the building that morning as those ahead of them took their time shaking Dan's hand, thanking him for his service to the church, expressing their sorrow at his impending departure, and wondering how that sad outcome might yet be avoided.

By the time Bob Sensabaugh's turn came, Dan's arm was tired and his hand was starting to cramp. He winced slightly at Bob's forceful grip.

"Too bad you didn't find this spark of spiritual fire sooner, Reverend. If we'd been seeing attendance like this consistently for the past two or three years, we wouldn't be in this predicament. Funny how it took something like Ryman McKendrick's malarkey to finally get you to drop those boring, heavy, philosophical sermons and get down to where people really live."

Dan had become so lulled by the constant stream of favorable comments and best wishes that he was not prepared for Bob's critical remarks. Before he could formulate an answer, Bob had moved on. Dan watched his accuser bounce down the front steps to where Kitty and the children waited for him. Turning back to the receiving line, he found himself facing Janey Musgrove.

"Oh, I'm so glad you finally came," he said, trying to regain his composure and put forth a positive attitude. "Limited engagement, you know, only a few performances left."

"Have you found out where you'll go from here?"

"Not yet. I need time to think this through, consider my options. You know, it would help to have someone to kick some thoughts around with. And I still haven't made good on my promise to show you The Cabin. Do you have to go back to Fairfax today?"

"Actually, I'm staying out here until tomorrow evening. I arranged for someone to cover my Monday classes, but not Tuesday. But I'll be back right after that. Thump…um, Mister Billington invited me to stay at Montfair for the Thanksgiving holiday, have some quiet time to work on the notes for my book. Much better than trying to concentrate in an apartment surrounded by noisy neighbors."

"How thoughtful of him. And I'm sure the company is pleasant as well."

"He spends most of his time in his study working on his Jefferson Bible project, I'm upstairs at the other end of the house concentrating on my work. Other than chatting over meals, it's mostly about having plenty of space and productive quiet time for both of us. Two writers, lost in their own worlds."

Janey conveniently omitted the part about the after-dinner time spent in Thumper's study the previous two evenings, with the fire blazing in the stone hearth, sipping cocktails and talking late into the night. Neither seemed willing to end the chat session and face the awkwardness of trudging upstairs to their separate rooms. The barrier was still there.

"Sounds like an ideal arrangement," Dan said. "So if you can be pulled away from your productive time for just a quick trip, what say we take a drive up to The Cabin tomorrow? You can consider it yet another bullet point on your research list. Pick you up, say, ten o'clock?"

"Okay, yes, it's a date."

Chapter 79

RYMAN TRIED TO focus on the back of Dorcas's helmet. It was difficult to keep his gaze from dropping lower, especially when she flexed into jumping position at each fence. The late November morning was cool and damp, perfect Barbour jacket weather. But Dorcas had opted for a quilted vest that only reached the small of her back. Rather than the blue jeans she often wore on exercise rides, she sported a pair of form fitting breeches. And that form was giving Ryman fits.

Colby was relaxed and comfortable following along behind Waylon, Cecelia's big, steady hunter. The experienced horse took each jump at an even pace, arching over the highest, most challenging obstacles as if they were nothing more than tiny logs. It was much more pleasurable for Ryman than dealing with his youngster out alone, trying to keep him straight going into a jump and convincing him that he didn't have to sprint away on the landing as if he was still on the racetrack.

Ryman fell into the rhythm as Dorcas chose the route. The syncopation of the hoof beats and the gentle motion of the horse's movements soothed him into a mildly hypnotic state. With his mind freed from the need to manage his horse, he let his eyes drift down toward the alluring curvature ahead of him, perfectly sculpted muscle and flesh squeezed into flesh-tone fabric.

It took a while before he assessed his surroundings and realized they had covered the full expanse of Kimber Farm's back acreage, crossed onto Montfair land, and worked themselves partway up the wooded hillside below The Cabin.

Finally taking stock of the situation, Ryman saw that Colby was winded and Wycroft was nearing exhaustion.

Dorcas pulled Waylon to a stop and turned around. "Maybe we should give these guys a break," she said.

"Good idea," he replied. "Poor old Wycroft looks like he could use a rest, and maybe a drink too. But no creeks around here, so I guess he'll have to wait."

"There's running water just up above."

"Huh?"

"The Cabin's right up this trail." She pointed to a path, rarely used but still passable, that led through the woods, along the edge of the ravine, and emerged at The Cabin.

Wycroft's tongue hung out far to one side and his panting intensified.

"Oh, yeah, so it is," Ryman said. "Perfect."

They guided their horses up the trail. Once at the secluded structure, they dismounted, put the horses in the makeshift paddock, and loosened the girths.

"This gate's a bear," Dorcas said as she struggled with the rusty, misaligned latch.

"Doesn't get used much," Ryman said. "We used to ride up here a lot. Now when folks come here they pretty much all drive. We mostly just use the old paddock for target practice."

"Well, you're going to have to help me get this open when we leave. Too hard for my weak little hands."

"Yeah, right," Ryman scoffed.

Dorcas went inside and came back carrying a large bowl of water. With her back toward Ryman, she bent over and placed it on the ground. Wycroft eagerly lapped away.

"Looks tempting, doesn't it?" Dorcas asked.

Ryman was unsure what she meant. He'd been staring at temptation for the past hour.

"The water," Dorcas said. "I'm a bit dry myself. You?"

"Oh, yeah. Now that you mention it, I could use a drink. Reckon I'll step inside and get one."

"No need for that." She reached into her vest and withdrew a flask. "I forgot I had this. Must have put it in here after Saturday's hunt to keep it out of sight of the kids. Don't want to set a bad example in front of them." She gave it a shake. "Still plenty left." She unscrewed the cap and handed it to Ryman.

He tilted his head back and took a long swig. "Mmmm. Good stuff. Can't quite place it though." He smacked his lips. "Schnapps maybe? Orange liqueur?"

She motioned for him to take another sip. "You're close. Keep trying."

He swilled some around in his mouth, then swallowed. His brow furrowed. "Something in there's familiar. But something else I can't quite place. And I know my booze flavors, believe me."

"It's a special recipe I got from my brother."

"He a bartender?"

"More like a chemist."

"Chemist, huh? Well, he knows… he knows how to… to mix…"

Dorcas's face blurred. The logs in The Cabin's front wall began to undulate as if they were thick brown snakes. The bare ground beneath him rolled like ocean waves. He reached out a hand toward her. She stood rigid, expressionless, and watched him collapse at her feet.

****

"And where is the Squire of Montfair this morning?" Dan asked as Janey settled into the passenger seat of his Mini Cooper.

"Holed up in his study. Nothing fuels a writer's juices like a looming deadline."

"In my own way, I know the feeling well. I face one every Sunday."

"He's hoping to get it finished this morning so he can get on Ozzy for some schooling work. The horse just needs a lot more mileage away from the track to settle into his new job as a hunter."

"You seem to be picking up the lingo pretty quickly."

She chuckled at her own casual use of the terminology. "All just part of the research."

Dan steered his car down the Montfair driveway. "And now, m'lady, let us sally forth to The Cabin."

****

Janey gripped the dashboard as Dan's car bounced over the rough road. "You do have a spare, right?"

Dan smiled and flipped a hand. "Fear not."

To Janey's relief, and mild surprise, they made it to The Cabin without incident. As they approached the clearing along the mountainside, she could see the appeal this remote, elevated location offered.

She could also see two horses in the paddock and a hound scratching at The Cabin's door.

"'Allo! What's all this then?" Dan said, mimicking the chief inspector from a 1930s British murder mystery.

They got out of the car and looked around.

"Isn't that the young horse Ryman's been riding?" Janey asked.

"Can't say I take much notice of such things. They all look pretty much alike to me."

"I think I've seen Cecelia riding that big dark bay."

"You are observant, aren't you?"

"It's what I do, observe things. Remember?"

"My, my, Cecelia and Ryman alone here at The Cabin," Dan mused. "This could be interesting. Let's go do some observing."

When Dan opened the door, Wycroft shot past him. But the hound, as well as the two humans, stopped short at what they saw.

Ryman lay naked, strapped down to the coffee table. He appeared to be semi-conscious, moaning softly as he slowly rolled his head from side to side. Dorcas stood over him, holding what appeared to be a small dagger.

Dan was the first to find his voice. "What, in God's name, is going on here?"

Righteous fire flared in Dorcas's eyes as she replied. "God's Word says, 'Without the shedding of blood, there can be no forgiveness of sin.' Hebrews 9:22."

"Dorcas," Janey said gently, "you don't need to shed any blood. Everything's fine. Let's all just relax. Put down the knife."

"No!" Dorcas replied. "I must protect the faith, defend it against heresy and blasphemy. I won't let you stop me! Either one of you." Holding the dagger handle with both hands, she raised it higher, directly above Ryman's heart, and prepared to plunge it into him.

Before either Janey or Dan could move to stop her, Wycroft sprang forward. He made two quick bounds, leapt up, and hurled his seventy pounds against her. The impact knocked her into the front edge of the sofa. The dagger fell from her hand as she hit the floor and lay motionless. The effort to protect his master was all the old hound had left after the morning's exertions. He flopped on his side and panted heavily.

Still stunned by what they'd encountered, Janey and Dan were too slow to react when Dorcas stirred. She was on her feet in an instant, the wildly demonic blaze in her eyes now even brighter. She saw the dagger lying at her feet, reached down, and grabbed it. She drew her arm back into a striking pose and lunged at the person closest to her.

Realizing he was her target, Dan's face lost what little color it had and his mouth went dry. He let out a high-pitched squeak of desperation as Dorcas came at him.

Certain the dagger was about do its damnedest, Dan's eye caught sight of a hand coming from his side. The hand intercepted Dorcas's wrist a fraction of an inch before the blade found its mark. The blade tilted upward, then swung back. Dorcas let out a cry of pain as the dagger dropped to the floor.

"Quick!" Janey urged. "Get the knife!"

Dan, dazed, saw Janey twisting Dorcas's hand, forcing her arm into an agonizingly contorted position.

"Now! I can't hold her like this forever."

Dan regained enough attention to follow her command. He stooped down and picked up the dagger.

"Get some rope!" Janey ordered.

"Wh… where? I don't know… maybe in the…"

Janey looked around the room. "The window blind cord! Just grab that."

"Oh, right. The blind cord." He stepped over to the window and took hold of the cord. "But how do I… I mean it's attached to…"

Janey could feel Dorcas starting to fight through the pain. The hold Janey had on her would eventually make the hand and arm go numb. Then she'd be even harder to hold.

"The knife! Use the goddamn knife."

Dan looked at the dagger in his hand. "Oh, yes, of course, the knife."

It took some effort to cut through the cord, but Dan got the job done with enough time left for him and Janey to get Dorcas's hands bound securely behind her back. Janey did most of the tying, using knots unfamiliar to Dan.

Once done, Janey pushed Dorcas down onto a chair where she sat grimacing as feeling slowly returned to her arm. Given the apparently lethal intent of her actions, Janey thought it best to use another length of cord to tie Dorcas to the chair.

She then pulled out her phone and called Thumper. "There's a situation at your Cabin. You need to get here right away. No, too hard to explain. Just come, now."

Dan looked at Janey, her face flush, strands of hair twirling out at random angles, her breath quick, the hint of a triumphant smile on her lips.

"How did you do that?" he asked. "Where did you learn that move?"

"While studying the Yanomamö of the Amazon, a fierce warrior tribe. Well, that and growing up with three brothers in Minnesota." She turned to Dorcas. "What were you and Ryman doing here? And what were you going to do to him with that knife?"

"I'm not telling you anything," Dorcas replied. "I think you've broken my arm, maybe done serious nerve damage. You'll be hearing from my lawyer. And I have nothing else to say until he's been contacted."

"I guess the Yanomamö of the Amazon don't have to worry about personal injury lawyers," Dan said.

"No, mostly just huge snakes, poisonous insects, man-eating plants, and other Yanomamö trying to kill them."

"Heavenly. At least the 'no lawyers' part."

For the first time, Janey and Dan began to take in the symbols that had been painted on the walls.

"What do you think all this is?" Dan asked.

"It's Wicca," Janey replied. She noticed several candles around the room, burned down to stubs. "It looks like some kind of ceremony has been held here. All Hallows Eve maybe. Let me see that dagger."

Dan handed it to her.

She looked closely at the symbol set into the handle, a cross with an egg-shaped figure above it. "This is definitely Wicca, what they call an anthame. This isn't making much sense."

Ryman let out a long, loud moan.

Ignoring the man's nakedness, Janey went to him. "Ryman, are you okay? Can you hear me? Are you hurt anywhere?"

"Wha… wha' happened? Drink. Something in the… in the…"

"You're okay now," she said. "Dan and I are here."

Janey and Dan looked toward the front door at the sound of an approaching vehicle.

"Thumper couldn't have gotten here this quickly," Janey said.

Dan looked at Dorcas and asked, "Were you expecting an accomplice? Someone to help you dispose of the body?"

Dorcas sat muttering to herself, now lost in her own world. Her head bobbed in a rhythmic cadence and Janey thought she heard snatches of an old gospel hymn.

Dan looked through the blinds and saw a faded green, mud-splattered Subaru Outback. The vehicle stopped before it reached the parking area, as if the sight of Dan's car had startled the driver.

"That's Nardell's car," Dan said. "She couldn't be in league with Dorcas, could she?" As the car started to back away, Dan stepped outside and waved his arms to get her attention. He motioned for her to pull up. Nardell stopped, paused for a moment, then drove forward slowly.

"Hey there," she said, reluctantly stepping out of the car and trying to sound nonchalant. "I just, um, came to do some housekeeping, tidy the place up a bit."

Dan noticed what looked like several cans of paint, along with brushes and trays, in the back of Nardell's car. A stepladder was strapped to the roof rack.

"I didn't think anyone else would be here," she said.

"Neither did we."

"'We?'" Nardell asked.

"Janey and me." Just then the two horses moved around from the side of the paddock that The Cabin blocked from view. Nardell saw the horses as Dan added, "And Ryman and Dorcas."

"What? Ryman's here with *Dorcas*?" She rushed past Dan and burst through the door. Dan followed at a more measured pace.

Nardell was not prepared for the scene that awaited her. Dorcas sat tied to a chair with her arms positioned oddly behind her, babbling incoherently. Ryman lay naked, still tied to the coffee table. Janey leaned over him holding a knife.

"What the hell's going here?" Nardell demanded.

"That's exactly what we've been trying to find out," Janey replied.

"You and Dan, Ryman and Dorcas. Ropes and a knife, these two tied up, him naked." Nardell looked at Janey with shocked disgust. "What kind of weirdness are you in to? And here everyone thought you were so respectable, a little prudish even. And the *Reverend*!"

"I beg your pardon!" Dan exclaimed.

"No, no!" Janey protested. "It's nothing like that. Dan and I just came up here so I could finally see this famous Cabin. And we found Ryman this way with Dorcas holding this blade over him, like she was going to… going to… Well, now that I think about it, maybe they were just role-playing. No, I'm sure Dorcas meant to harm Ryman. Even kill him the way she was holding the knife. And it didn't look like Ryman was exactly, um, enjoying things, if you know what I mean. If it hadn't been for Wycroft, she probably would have stabbed him. And then she tried to attack Dan."

"Actually," Dan said to Nardell, "I think you've also got some explaining to do. The paint cans and painting tools you brought up here, the tidying up you planned to do when no one else was here. That wouldn't have anything to do with these symbols painted on the walls, would it?"

"Oh, well," Nardell began, "y'see…" She stopped, let out a long, slow breath, and then confessed. "I forgot I'd told the Coven that they could use The Cabin for their All Hallows Eve ceremony. This was, like, back in August. Ryman had his visions right after that, and I got so focused on helping him with the Venatican church that everything about Wicca just left my mind. I only remembered on Halloween night but by then it was too late. I drove up here to try and stop them, but the ceremony was already underway and they'd… they'd painted the walls with all these symbols."

Dorcas snapped back to a semblance of lucidity and shouted, "Liar! You, Ryman, and your evil followers have been using this place for your orgies and animal sacrifices. I even found the knife you used, with its symbol of wickedness."

Nardell replied with wide-eyed surprise, "What? Orgies and animal sacrifices? A knife? Where would you get such silly ideas?"

"I knew it the moment I saw the signs of your wickedness when I followed Ryman up here. I tried to warn you. But you wouldn't listen. You left me no choice."

Waving the dagger around at the walls, Janey asked Nardell, "Did you tell your Wicca friends they could do this?"

"I might have… um, well, maybe I said something about them doing whatever they wanted. I was a new member of the Coven, and I guess… I guess I wanted to make a good impression, be part of the group. But when

I remembered what I'd offered, it struck me that Thumper probably wouldn't approve. I tried to call them, but they all turn their phones off during ceremonies."

Dan chimed in. "Wish I could get some of my parishioners to do that."

Ignoring him, Nardell went on. "So I had to drive up here. But it was too late. I got pretty upset, told them all to get out. It was a critical moment in the ceremony, they weren't very happy with me breaking the mood. But they packed up their stuff and left." She took a closer look at the dagger in Janey's hand. "That looks like an anthame, the ritual knife. Where did you get it?"

Janey pointed the blade toward Dorcas. "From her hand."

"It must have gotten left behind when I was kicking them all out of here. They were packing up and leaving in a hurry." She rested her head in one hand and massaged her temples. "This is all too weird."

"Yes, it certainly is," Janey agreed.

Dan pulled out his cell phone. "Shouldn't we call the police?"

"No!" Janey and Nardell said in unison.

The two women looked at each other and, also in perfect synch, asked, "Why not?"

"You first," Janey insisted.

Nardell hesitated. She looked to Dan hoping he might offer a way out. But he made a "c'mon" gesture that endorsed Janey's demand. Realizing she was outnumbered, she said, "Okay, fine. I came up here hoping to get all this painted over before Thumper saw it, clean the place up some, get all these candles out of here. If you call the police, Thumper will know what happened before I can fix everything."

"Might be too late for that now," Janey suggested. "I've already called him. He's on his way."

Nardell groaned and rubbed her temples harder.

Dan still held his phone, ready to press 911. "What's your reason?" he asked Janey.

"This is Thumper's property after all. I think we should wait for him to get here and decide how he wants this handled."

Nardell was the first to hear the sound of a truck rumbling up the road. She brushed Dan aside and rushed out to intercept Thumper.

"I can explain," she said. "I'm sorry about the walls. I'll paint over everything, make them good as new."

"What are you talking about?" he asked. "What walls? Is this what Janey called me about? She said it was urgent. And I thought you told Ryman you had a full day of appointments."

"Oh, um, yeah, I did say that. Well, y'see, this was one of them. Only not a massage appointment, just something else I had to do."

Thumper looked at the Mini Cooper. "This is Dan's car. What the hell's going on here?"

"Dan and Janey are also here," Nardell said. "And Ryman and Dorcas. Wycroft too. It's all very confusing. Maybe you should go inside and try to figure this out."

"Yes," Thumper replied, "perhaps I should."

Thumper surveyed the strange scene around him. Ryman, naked, still lay on the coffee table. Janey stood over him coiling up a length of heavy rope. "Somebody who makes at least a modicum of sense want to tell me what the hell's going on here?" His eyes settled on Janey. "You, perhaps?"

She filled him in on the reason for her and Dan being there, what they found when they arrived, and what had happened to that point.

By the time she finished, Ryman was standing up and getting dressed. Though still woozy, he'd regained enough consciousness to function and converse reasonably well. He stretched out his limbs and shook himself. Then he looked at Dorcas. "You drugged me. You tried to… to kill me! Ah, but Saint Hubert stepped in, didn't he? His name be praised!"

"Blasphemer!" Dorcas shouted. "False visions, divinations, idolatries, and the delusion of your own mind! The false prophet must be put to death, because he preached rebellion against the Lord your God... He has tried to turn you from the way the Lord your God commanded you to follow. You must purge the evil from among you."

Dan took the opportunity to display his encyclopedic knowledge of scripture. "Deuteronomy 13:5."

Dorcas looked at Dan. "Daddy?"

"What? No, I'm Reverend Davenport."

Her face contorted and her eyes watered. "Daddy, I'm sorry. I'm so sorry. I should never have left… left you, left your church. All these years… when I should have been serving God, like you wanted. Instead I was wasting my substance with riotous living." Tears flowed freely and she continued to stare at Dan. "And then… and then you were gone. I never had the chance to make it up. But now… now I can. I can purge the evil from our midst, drive out the false prophet, he who is worthy of death because he turns the people away from the True God. I can still serve, Daddy."

Thumper stepped forward and drew her attention. "Dorcas. It's Thumper. Your friend, Thumper Billington. Do you know who I am?"

"Thumper? What are you doing here? Are you a false prophet too?"

"Dorcas, listen carefully. Are you taking any medications?"

"What?"

"Medications. Pills. Are you taking any?"

"Pills? Oh, no. God doesn't want me to. I must rely on him, not pills. Pills are the Devil's work. Satan's candy."

Nardell chimed in. "Maybe it wouldn't be a bad idea to call the police. We've got attempted murder here. Maybe kidnapping too. I saw an episode on 'Law and Order' where this guy…"

Thumper cut her off. "No. No police. Dorcas has a serious problem, a mental problem. She didn't know what she was doing. She needs help." He pulled out his phone. "I'm calling Cecelia. Maybe she knows what's going on, what should be done." He looked at his phone screen. "Damn. I can't get a signal in here. Maybe outside will be better." He noticed Dorcas glaring at Ryman. "Ry, why don't you come with me? Your presence seems to make Dorcas uneasy."

"Not half as much as hers makes me," he replied.

****

The cell signal was stronger outside and Cecelia answered Thumper's call. He gave her a quick rundown of the situation.

"Oh, my God! She did what? I was afraid something like this might happen, that she'd go off her meds. She's been doing so well the past two years. I knew I was taking a chance on her, but… but this! It's all my fault. I should have listened to Andrea."

"Who?"

"The master she worked for in Florida, Andrea Mercando. You know her."

"Oh, yeah, right. I thought you said Andrea gave her a decent reference."

"Well, maybe 'decent' wasn't exactly the best choice of words. Andrea tried to warn me. But you know how I am. I've got this big soft spot for kids, strays, and sad cases. And her case was pretty sad."

"So do we call the cops? If we turn her in, she'll likely be facing attempted murder, aggravated assault, and kidnapping."

"Oh, God, no! We can't do that. I'll take responsibility for her. I know an excellent place where she can go. She'll get the best treatment and they won't ask any, shall we say, *uncomfortable* questions. I'll cover everything."

"Hang on one second. There's someone else who has a say in this." Thumper turned to Ryman. "Whatcha think, Ry? Cecelia says she'll take care of her, pack her off someplace. I assume some private, no-questions-asked rehab joint. You're the victim here. Do you want to press charges, have this all exposed, make a big field day for the press out it?"

Ryman understood what Thumper meant. Did he want the Venatican

Church held up to the ridicule this would bring? Headlines like, "Crazy foxhunting cult leader almost killed by even crazier follower. Naked man saved by hound at last second."

"Well," Ryman replied, "I guess if Cecelia wants to take care of her, that's okay with me. Just as long as she's far away and safely locked up, at least until we're sure she's got her head straight."

Thumper spoke back into his phone. "Ryman's good with it. So do what you gotta do, but do it quickly."

"I'll have someone there within the hour, someone responsible and discreet. Just try to keep her comfortable until then."

"We'll bring her milk and cookies."

Ryman tossed in his final two cents as Thumper ended the call. "Just keep the crazy bitch tied up until the men in white suits get here."

"I reckon this clears things up about the fox effigy," Thumper said. "The hunt she worked for in Florida is a drag pack. She probably learned how to lay a drag line there. And she would have had time that morning to lay the line, hang the stuffed fox, and get back to the barn just before the hunt started."

"Yeah, that makes sense."

Both men turned toward the sound of whining and scratching as Wycroft pleaded to be let out. A rustling noise at the wood's edge pulled their attention away from The Cabin. A large buck stood staring back at them. The object between its antlers was more battered, faded, and askew then when Ryman saw it a week earlier. But it was still there, and clearly resembled the Celtic cross.

Nardell opened the door and Wycroft bolted out, baying in full voice. He darted between Thumper and Ryman and headed straight toward the buck. The buck lowered his rack and raised one front hoof as if about to paw the ground in warning. But Wycroft was not going to be deterred this time. Sensing his attacker's determination, the deer did what any prudent herbivore would do: he turned and fled back into the woods.

Thumper and Ryman stood in frozen silence for a few seconds. Then Ryman shouted, "To the horses!"

Janey, Dan, and Nardell stepped outside to see what was happening. Dorcas remained tied to the chair, once again lost in the private world of her damaged mind.

Ryman dashed to the paddock, vaulted over the rail fence, and grabbed Colby's reins. The young horse shied at the commotion. Ryman had to hold the reins tightly to keep him from getting away. Despite the lingering effects of being slipped a date rape drug, he had enough presence of mind to check the girth.

Thumper tried the gate but couldn't open the latch. He climbed the fence with a bit less athleticism than Ryman. Having planned to get in a quick ride on Ozzy later that morning, he'd arrived at The Cabin wearing boots and breeches. He recognized Waylon as Cecelia's number one hunting mount, a horse much like his own Lenny. He figured Cecelia could have no objection to him borrowing the horse under the circumstances.

Colby's antics had Waylon on edge but the well-disciplined horse was compliant enough that Thumper had the girth tightened and was in the saddle while Ryman was still trying to mount.

"Go!" Ryman commanded. "Follow him! Catch him! Do something. I'll be right behind you."

"Ryman!" Nardell hollered. "Your helmet!"

"No time for that," he called back.

She ran inside and looked for his helmet. She had no idea where Dorcas might have put it. It hadn't been among the pile of Ryman's clothes. And Dorcas wasn't in the mood to offer any help.

Janey and Dan watched and wondered what was going on.

Thumper trotted Waylon toward the fence, gave him a firm squeeze with his legs and a light hand on the reins, and the athletic bay glided over the rails. While Thumper started down the trail after the deer, Ryman finally managed to scramble onto Colby. Wide-eyed and shaking, the youngster desperately wanted to follow his new companion. But doing so meant jumping a rail fence that to his frazzled mind now looked ten feet tall. Ryman had ample experience taking green horses over fences. But his desire to get after the buck caused him to push the horse to the jump with too much aggression and not enough focus. The animal sprinted the few strides from one side of the paddock to the other, changed his mind at the last split-second, and slammed on the brakes as his chest touched the top rail.

Nardell found Ryman's helmet behind the sofa. Holding it aloft, she emerged from the cabin just in time to see the horse refuse and send his rider sailing over the fence. Ryman, bare-headed, landed with a thud on the rocky mountainside ground.

****

Wycroft was back in top hunting form, his aching joints revitalized by the thrill of chasing live quarry, although this particular quarry was supposed to be off limits. He'd always been steady on deer, well aware that the only acceptable game was the fox. But absent the restraining voice of a huntsman, this deer was his. The embarrassment of being turned back by the buck the week before still stung and he would have his canine pride avenged or die trying.

Thumper also knew that running deer with dogs was against the state law. But this was an exceptional situation. He pressed Waylon on, up the slippery, rock-strewn slope, staying with Wycroft stride-for-stride. The buck's flight took them where there was no trail. Low hanging branches and thick brambles smacked Thumper's face and tore at his Barbour coat. He had to detour around heavier brush that the deer jumped and Wycroft slipped through. But Waylon had the speed and stamina to quickly close the gap. He instinctively knew his job was to stay with the hound no matter what it took.

Wycroft gained steadily on the panicked deer.

The buck, not breaking stride, looked back over his shoulder as the hound drew nearer. He picked the wrong moment to assess his pursuers. A tangle of heavy vines snagged his massive rack. His forward momentum lifted his legs off the ground, swung his body into the air, and he slid on his side into an intertwined mass of scrub brush.

Thumper arrived seconds later to find Wycroft barking and snarling at his fallen prey, giving the vanquished deer what-for in hound speak.

"Leave it!" Thumper commanded. "Good hound, good job. Now leave it."

Wycroft added a final insult for emphasis. The adrenalin rush then faded, exhaustion overtook him, and the old hound flopped over and gasped for air.

The buck's legs were caught in the brush and his rack was firmly secured by two-inch thick vines. He lay still, the only movement the rapid heaving of his sides. His large brown eyes revealed a sense of resignation to his fate.

Thumper looked down at the trapped animal. "Well, I'll be damned." He hopped off Waylon, pulled his Swiss Army knife from his jacket pocket, and went to work.

****

"Ryman! Ryman! Oh, my God, he's really hurt this time." Nardell, kneeling over Ryman, turned to Janey. "We need an ambulance."

Ryman opened his eyes. "The buck! Gotta catch that buck."

"Oh, thank goodness!" Nardell exclaimed. "He's awake."

Ryman pushed her aside and jumped up from the ground. "I gotta go! Open the gate!"

Nardell protested. "Ryman, no. You've had a bad fall. And a serious concussion. Another one. You can't get back on a horse."

"Like hell I can't. I have to find that buck. Bring me my damn horse. I ain't gonna try jumping that fence again."

Nardell shoved Ryman's helmet into his chest. "Fine! Go get yourself killed. At least wear your damn helmet this time. And get your own fucking horse!"

Ryman used the helmet to force the dilapidated gate latch open. He left the gate hanging by one hinge and tossed the battered helmet aside. He then led Colby from the paddock, used a tree stump as a mounting block to swing back on the horse, and galloped away up the mountain trail.

****

Thumper heard the sound of horse hooves clattering over the rocky hillside below.

"Thumper!" Ryman cried out. "Where are you?"

Wycroft lifted his head at the sound of his human's voice. Thumper whispered to him, "Okay, buddy. This is just between us. No blabbing to Ryman. Got that?"

"Woof!"

"I have no idea what that means, but I'm going to keep my fingers crossed that you won't tell your master what just happened here."

"Woof!"

Closer this time, Ryman cried out again. "Thumper! Are you up here? Is that Wycroft? Where the hell are you?"

"You're on the right track, Ry. Just keep coming forward."

As Colby struggled up the difficult slope, Thumper saw the unfocused gaze in his old friend's eyes. "Oh, crap, Ry. You got bonked again, didn't you? And without a helmet this time."

"No big deal, Thumper. Hell, you're not wearing one either."

"No, but I'm not riding a green horse with a history of dumping its rider on his head."

"Ah, just a little snafu jumping out of the paddock. I'm okay. The important thing is, where's the buck?"

"Keep coming and you'll see when you get up here."

Ryman finished negotiating the last stretch of the challenging terrain. When he reached Thumper and Wycroft, he saw the deer, still caught in the vines and bushes. It looked like the same buck, a fourteen pointer for sure. But there was nothing between that impressive rack. Only empty space where he'd seen the sign of Saint Hubert.

"I don't understand," Ryman said, dismounting from Colby. "Where is it? You saw it, didn't you, Thumper? When we were standing outside The Cabin. You saw it too, right?"

"Gosh, Ry, I'm not sure what I saw. It all happened so fast. I didn't get a good look before Wycroft scared the deer away."

"Well, I saw it. I know I saw it. Just like I'd seen it before. I saw him in that same spot a week ago. We stood there looking at each other, and that thing was there. Didn't look quite like it did when I first saw it, but it was there all right."

"I'm not saying you didn't, Ry. But there's definitely nothing there now. Just a big buck with a nice rack, the damn thing trapped and scared. The right thing to do is get him free, let him go."

Ryman stood silently staring at the helpless buck. He waited, hoping to see the mouth move, to hear the animal make the noise that sounded like "Hhhhhbbbbuttt!" He looked down at Wycroft. Exhausted and sore, the hound lay on his side, panting softly. "What do you think, buddy? Rrrrnnnn? Hnnnnttt?" Wycroft did not respond.

"I think if we cut the vine about there," Thumper said pointing to a spot a few feet away from the buck's head, "that'll release the hold enough for him to get free. And we can stay safely out of the way. I don't especially care to get too close to that rack or those hooves when this big fellah comes up off the ground."

"Huh? Oh, yeah, I suppose you're right. So we're just gonna... let him go?"

"What else do you suggest? Maybe he'll follow you home like a puppy and be your personal pet. Look, Ry, he's a wild animal. He deserves to go free, take his chances out there in the cruel world of nature."

"Yeah, and with the deer hunters."

"Yep, them too. But he hasn't lived to grow a rack like that without knowing a trick or two about how to survive. C'mon, hold this vine steady while I cut it. Might be a bit tough getting through it with just my pocket knife, but I think with some work we can get it done."

Thumper hacked at the vine as Ryman kept it steady. After a few minutes, it was severed. The deer's head dropped as the tension relaxed. He lay still for several seconds, then slowly lifted his head. Realizing he was free from that restraint, he pushed against the ground with his shoulder and slid his legs out from the bushes. The encumbrances at both ends gone, he stumbled to his feet, still shaky from the traumatic experience. He looked at the two men, took a downward glance at the hound, pawed the ground once, and made a defiant snort. He then turned, bounded away, and was quickly out of sight.

Chapter 80

WITH THE HORSES returned to the paddock, six stunned and confused people stood and watched the plain, unassuming vehicle pull away from The Cabin. No red light flashed, no siren wailed. No men in white suits had swaddled Dorcas in a straightjacket and manhandled her into a padded wagon. She had obeyed Cecelia's urging to take the offered sedative and was now quietly on her way to medicated redemption thanks to Cecelia's largesse, fueled in part by her sense of guilt. She knew she was a sucker for hard cases, but her do-gooder efforts had never before put someone's life at risk.

Thumper breathed out a heavy sigh. "Anybody care for a drink?"

Five relieved and eager voices sounded their acceptance.

Everyone found a seat inside and to the delight of all Thumper produced a bottle of Wasmund's Virginia whiskey from a hiding place known only to him. Glasses were passed around and greedily filled.

Thumper directed his opening question to Cecelia. "You said on the phone you were afraid something like this might happen. You want to tell us about that?"

Cecelia stiffened, took a drink, and composed herself. "She left her job in Florida under a cloud. A rather nasty, dark cloud. It was mostly her brother's doing, but she tried to shield him, and she let him get away."

She took another sip of whiskey before she went on. "Their childhood was, from what I understand, rather difficult." Cecelia looked at Janey. "Their father would have made an interesting study for you. Dorcas only told me so much. But I did some digging on my own. Well, okay, I hired a private investigator. Mister Stanhope, er, *Reverend* Stanhope"—she cast a glance first at Reverend Davenport and then at Ryman—"had his own church, independent, non-denominational. The House of God's Love and Everlasting Life, or something like that. He was a real fire-and-brimstone holy-roller type. He believed an angel spoke to him regularly, told him what God wanted him to do. He'd go into fits, or trances, speak in tongues.

"It was a pretty crazy childhood for his two children. Did it contribute to the way they turned out? Who can say, really? Plenty of people from normal families turn out like… well, I mean, even my own daughter has some… but that's another matter. The point is, both Dorcas and her brother Enoch suffer from some serious, deep-seated problems."

When she paused, Thumper gave her a prompt. "Such as?"

Cecelia steeled herself for what she was about to say. "Enoch likes young girls. Not little girls, but mid-teens. Still under age anyway. And he mostly likes to have his way with them while they're in... in a... defenseless state."

"Drugged," Thumper said.

"Yes," Cecelia confirmed. "Seems he's developed quite a skill at mixing certain concoctions. He's particularly adept with one of the most common sedatives we use on horses."

"Ace?" Nardell asked.

"No," Cecelia replied. "Too mild. He uses Dormosedan."

All eyes widened.

Thumper let out a low whistle. "Holy shit. That's powerful stuff. Doesn't take much to send a twelve hundred pound horse off to laa-laa land. And pretty quickly too. Probably kill a human with a small amount."

"I'm sure it could," Cecelia agreed. "I don't know the details, but from what my investigator was able to find out, Enoch knew just the right amount to use, mixed with something harmless, to render a person—and specifically a young girl—immobile long enough for him to, um, have his fun and then be on his way."

"Didn't he get caught?" Janey asked. "That's a serious offense. Like life sentence level from what I understand."

"It was the 'on his way' part that kept him from getting nabbed," Cecelia explained. "After the first episode back in Arkansas, he hit the road. Been a drifter ever since. He's a good looking, charismatic young man. That allows him to get away with a lot. You all know the type."

Nardell snorted. "Don't I though."

Everyone looked at her quizzically.

"Oh, nothing," she said. "Never mind. Long time ago. Please, Cecelia, what happened next?"

"Before I get to that," she replied, "let me fill in some background on Dorcas. It seems this very odd upbringing may have had an effect on her too. In a different way, of course, but still problematic. She has a personality disorder that's sort of a love-hate thing. She finds herself attracted to a man, but then the attraction turns to hatred. And sometimes it turns violent. Maybe it goes back to all that Bible thumping from her father, that she feels the natural impulses of a woman, but then hates herself for it, thinking she's letting God down or some such crap, and takes her frustration out on the man instead. She did some time in a psych ward. A good bit of time actually. She came out better, mostly thanks to good medication. As long as she remembered to take it.

"As part of her therapy, it was suggested she try working with horses. Sort of a way to learn patience, take care of another creature. It was arranged for her to live and work on a horse farm back in Arkansas. Turns out she took to it very well, had some real talent for both riding and barn management. And the place she was working at had a lot of kids riding there. It was much safer for her to be around children than around handsome, virile adult males."

"Not many of them in the horse world," Thumper scoffed.

"Sadly, no," Cecelia agreed. "And the few that are often turn out to be gay." She continued, "So Dorcas worked her way through a succession of barns, landed at one that was in a foxhunting community, and really found that to be a good match for her. She eventually made her way to Florida where she was hired as kennelman and whip. It's a drag hunt down there, and overrun with young girls. A great place for her. But for her brother? Not so much."

"He showed up, did he?" Thumper asked.

"Unfortunately, yes. No one there knew about the warrants he'd skipped out on in other states. I don't think Dorcas was very happy to see him, but out of sibling loyalty she recommended him for a job on the Mercandos' farm. Andrea and her husband have quite a spread, they need lots of help keeping the place running. Enoch was willing to do hard manual labor. And he spoke English. Hard to pass up that rare combination."

"I assume the 'overrun with young girls' part was especially to his liking," Thumper said.

"That's how it all went to hell," Cecelia answered. "Dorcas walked in on him just in time. Enoch had the girl in the feed room. She was already drugged and he was just about to do the deed. Dorcas stopped him, told him to hit the road, said she'd try to cover for him, at least give him a head start. But she never wanted to see him again, it was the last straw for her.

"When the kid came too, she fingered Enoch, of course. Dorcas tried to make it seem like an accident, or that her brother was just pulling a prank, didn't mean any harm. But it was a weak attempt and it didn't take much for the Mercandos to figure out the truth. They could have had her arrested for obstruction of justice, aiding and abetting, some stuff like that. I'm not a lawyer." She looked over at Thumper.

"Yes," he said, "something like that."

Cecelia continued. "But Andrea's got a soft heart. Maybe not as soft as mine, but she felt sorry for Dorcas. And she'd been a really solid employee before her brother showed up. Andrea couldn't give her a good reference, but she at least allowed her to split before the girl's parents called the cops."

"And you knew all this when you hired her?" Thumper asked.

Cecelia held the cool highball glass against her forehead. "Enough of it. I knew I was taking a chance, but I didn't think it would affect anyone else. She was doing a great job, and really getting along with the kids. Then she got word her father died. That started the spiral. Seems they'd been estranged for many years. She went 'worldly,' left home as soon as she was old enough, and turned her back on religion, especially her father's rather outré brand of it."

"It appears you got to know this woman pretty well," Thumper observed.

"Oh, you know me," Cecelia replied with a flip of her hand. "Mother figure to all. We had some late night heart-to-hearts up in her apartment. She was really trying to keep herself straight, stay on the right meds. I guess she felt she could confide in me as I knew about the incident in Florida but still gave her a chance anyway. The news about her father hit her hard. Came unexpectedly, and ended any possibility that they could reconcile some day. And then her brother showed up."

"What?" Thumper exclaimed. "The brother showed up here? Around our juniors?"

"Oh, I sent him packing in short order. Told him he had two minutes to get off my property or I'd call the sheriff."

Thumper was incredulous. "Yes, but with his history, a predator like that. You didn't think it might be a good idea to turn him in?"

"I didn't know the full extent of his history until later. I knew there'd been an incident in Florida but I thought it was a one-time thing. Andrea thought that too, which was why she let Dorcas leave without calling the cops on her. But after he showed up at my place, that's when I had my investigator start digging into things back in Arkansas. If I'd known all that then, I'd have probably shot the son-of-a-bitch myself. That was also when I found out more about Dorcas's history, the love-hate thing, how she'd come on to men and then turn violent towards them."

Ryman squirmed in his chair, finished his drink, and reached for the bottle to refill his glass.

"Well," Thumper said, "she was certainly about to do some violence to Ryman." He looked over at his old friend. "How about the coming on part, Ry? Had there been any of that?"

"Uh, well, gee, I dunno. Not really, I guess." He could feel Nardell's eyes boring into him.

"So just how did you end up here with her," Nardell asked, "all alone, and conveniently naked?"

"It was just an exercise and schooling ride. You know that. Wycroft was really thirsty, and we were close to The Cabin. So we stopped off to get him some water. She offered me her flask, I didn't see any harm in that. Next thing I know, I'm strapped to that board and she's about to stab me in the heart. Honest." He saw no point in mentioning the time she showed up at their cottage and offered herself to him.

Thumper retrieved the whiskey bottle from Ryman and offered everyone else a refill. "That 'Defender of the Faith' thing, the Bible quote on the fox effigy. What do you think that was all about?"

Cecelia shrugged.

Ryman and Nardell looked at each other. She gestured to him to tell the others about the emails.

"Um, well," he began, "y'see, that was just one of a bunch of messages she sent. The others were all emails. Oh, and there was one on a song sheet I found in my truck."

Nardell's head jerked. "You didn't tell me about that."

"Didn't want to worry you, sweetheart. Anyway, I kept getting these emails from this Defender person, all Bible quotes about false prophets, leading people astray, saying the false prophet must be put to death." He waggled his hands in the air for emphasis. "I had some suspicions about who might be sending them." He cast a sideways glance at Dan. "But I'd have never figured Dorcas for being the one."

"Still one thing that all this doesn't explain," Thumper said. He turned to Ryman. "Someone took a shot at you. Dorcas was hunting with us that morning, close behind me, schooling one of Cecelia's greenies. Couldn't have been her."

"Oh, that," Ryman said casually. "I'm sure it was just an accident. Some hunter who didn't see me in the rain and fog."

"Yeah, maybe. Or someone else who thinks the false prophet should be put to death is still out there."

Chapter 81

THUMPER REARRANGED HIS man-cave; he moved the two gentlemen's club chairs off to a corner and placed a small sofa in front of the fireplace where he and Janey could sit together.

On this damp, chilly November evening the fire felt especially curative as it soothed away the rigors of an exceptional day. The double portion of Talisker single malt scotch that Thumper sipped further eased the strains of a hard ride and a difficult decision.

Janey set her glass of wine down on the end table and turned to Thumper. "Those are some nasty scratches," she said, reaching over and lightly touching his face.

"I've had worse. Left a few bits of flesh out there in the woods over the years, a piece of ear here, a slice of nose there."

"It's only added to your rugged handsomeness."

"Chicks dig scars?"

"Some do. For what it's worth, I think you made the right call, going along with Cecelia, not bringing in the police. It's better to handle something like this as quietly as possible within the tribal structure."

"'Tribal structure?' You see the whole world through that lens, don't you?"

"It's really how the world functions at its core. The problem is that most people don't understand that. They think all seven billion people on the planet should be able to get along as one big, happy, cooperative family. The reality of human nature suggests otherwise."

"I suppose."

They sat in a long easy silence, nursing their drinks and watching the sparks crackle and pop in the fireplace.

Janey was the first to speak again. "Any more thoughts about telling me what happened when you went after the deer?"

"Still thinking about that." He glanced at his watch. "It's getting late. Been a long damn day. And we're still hunting tomorrow, want to keep all appearances as routine as possible."

"And I have to get an early start if I'm going to be on time for my first class."

"Damn shame you couldn't get someone to cover for you."

"At least I only have a couple of morning classes to teach. A lot of others wanted to leave early for the holiday. I was lucky to get today off."

"And isn't it grand you did. Otherwise, Ryman would probably be dead. If Dorcas had plunged that dagger into his heart, or into Dan's, we'd have had a pretty hard time keeping that inside the 'tribal structure.'"

"I'm just glad I was able to be here."

"Yes, you being here is a good thing." He arose, slowly and stiffly, turned to Janey and offered her a hand. She accepted and he pulled her up with a firm, gentle motion. They stood face-to-face, inches apart, drained from the pressures of the day, drowsily comforted by the warmth of the fire and the closeness of their bodies. He reflexively slipped a hand around her waist. She placed a hand on his shoulder.

Pulling back slightly, he said, "I'm still a married man."

"Yes, you are. And I am the neutral observer, not a part of your tribal structure. This would be wrong."

"Very wrong," he agreed. "You would never do such a thing with a San Bushman."

She leaned away and said with a coy smile, "How do you know I haven't?"

"Hmmm… I suppose I don't. A moonlit night on the open Kalahari, a soft breeze carries the sound of a lonely hyena, a cozily inviting hut, your nearly naked paramour's bronze skin glowing in the fire's blazing flames. Who could blame you if…"

She took a step back and fanned her face. "My goodness. Maybe you should quit writing about dead white men, take up romance novels instead."

"More money in that I suppose."

They stood uneasily, a safe distance apart.

"So," Janey said, "goodnight then?"

"Yes, goodnight."

****

Ryman slid a footstool in front of the old sofa and sat down. Wycroft was stretched out across all three cushions, dead to the world.

Ryman sat staring at the hound for a long time.

Nardell finally interrupted his vigil. "Anything?"

"Nope, nothing."

"Maybe it doesn't work when the animal's sleeping."

"Yeah, maybe that's it."

"Well, I think it's time you got to bed. You can check on Wycroft in the morning when you're both rested. He's exhausted and you had a pretty hard fall, hit that ground without a helmet. You should have listened to me."

"I always should. But no harm done. I'm okay. You go on to bed, sweetheart. I'm going to wait a little longer."

"Ryman, it's been over three hours. We have to hunt in the morning. You need some sleep."

"I'm okay. I won't be able to sleep anyway until I know Wycroft's okay."

"Ryman, sweetheart, tell me what you saw when you went after the deer."

"I already told you. It sure looked like the same buck, but there was no sign of Saint Hubert's symbol, no lips moving, no voice speaking to me. Just a big old scared deer, couldn't wait to get away from us."

"I'm not sure I believe you."

"I'm not sure what I believe now myself." He returned his focus to the tired old hound.

"I'm going to bed," she said.

"Fine. I'll be along directly."

Chapter 82

RYMAN'S ALL NIGHT vigil was rewarded when, just before dawn, Wycroft stirred. Still lying on his side, the old hound stretched his legs out and emitted a sleepy "Mmmmpph." He raised his head and looked at Ryman who, unshaven and crusty-eyed, smiled at him.

"Back with the living, huh? You had me worried for awhile."

The mental connection was weak, but Ryman could feel it again. Wycroft's thoughts were fuzzy from the exertion of the day before and the long slumber after.

As the hound began to awaken more fully, Ryman tried to tap into the images he'd seen when alone with Thumper and the deer. Thumper's attempt to swear the hound to secrecy was pointless. Deceit is a human art, dependent on the ability to manipulate language—spoken, written, or body—to one's selfish advantage. The old hound could only revisit the images he had seen in his mind's eye. Falsehood was a foreign concept.

Those images floated through a hazy mist into Ryman's mind. He saw the buck turn to look back at Wycroft, saw the thick vines snag the antlers, and the deer's body crash into the heavy brush. He could see something between the antlers, but the image was indistinct. Wycroft was nearing the point of exhaustion by then. Ryman could make out the form of Thumper dismounting and standing over the deer, then withdrawing something from his pocket. Wycroft collapsed at that point and the scene went blank.

A new image now formed, this one accompanied by a corresponding bodily urge. "Yeah," Ryman said. "I expect you do have to pee. Now that you mention it, me too. C'mon."

Ryman rose from the footstool and walked toward the door. Wycroft climbed off the couch slowly and joined him. The November air was crisp and fresh. The first hint of sunrise cast a pink sliver of light along the eastern horizon. In the stillness of the deep country morning, Ryman could sense the rhythm of life all around him. The diurnal world was waking as the nocturnal creatures returned home from their nightly labors—the twice-daily change of shifts when the world is most alive, when the cycle begins anew—the hunters and gatherers versus the hunted and gathered.

One sensation stood out above the rest, the approach of a familiar presence. Human and hound stood side-by-side relieving themselves; Ryman onto a sparse strip of grass, Wycroft with his leg lifted on a tree trunk. The presence drew closer. Ryman could make out a small figure coming toward them. In the dim light he saw a fox trotting along the cottage driveway. As the animal came nearer, Ryman could see it was a large fellow, with a thick, lustrous coat, black points, and a bright white tip on his brush. A mouse hung limply in the fox's mouth.

When the fox was just a few feet away, he stopped. The three friendly enemies stood frozen in place. Ryman and Wycroft were still peeing. The fox looked at them with an air of amusement. After a few seconds, the fox lifted his leg and joined them. When the last droplet trickled to the ground, the fox gave Ryman a jaunty catch-me-if-you-can smirk and then pranced on his way.

Still unzipped, Ryman looked down at Wycroft. "Saint Hubert works in wondrous ways."

The old hound looked up at his two-legged partner, a canine grin on his graying face.

****

Thumper arrived at the Tuesday morning meet to find Ryman and Nardell already there, mounted and working through the crowd with effusive greetings and Jäger blessings. When Nardell saw Thumper, she peeled away and caught him as he emerged from his truck.

"Good morning, Master," she said cheerily.

Thumper returned the welcome with a cocked head and raised eyebrow. "And good morning to you. You seem awfully chipper." He looked over at Ryman who burst out in laughter at something another rider said to him. "His Wackiness too. Appears he's okay after yesterday's adventure."

"Oh, more than okay. He was up all night with Wycroft. I hardly slept either, I was so worried about him. Both of them actually. But I finally fell asleep and then about dawn he came tearing into the bedroom, all worked up, leaping around, praising Saint Hubert. Ryman was, um, stimulated I guess you'd say." A dainty blush colored her cheeks and brightened her smile; an unusually demure look for the typically brash Nardell Raithby.

As Nardell moved off to confer with Crispie and Patti, who also appeared to be in high spirits, Thumper thought of his morning, waking alone, then sharing an early breakfast with Janey before she dressed and drove back to Fairfax. He, too, had felt a sense of stimulation looking at her across the breakfast table. She wore a Minnesota Vikings sweatshirt with faded striped pajama bottoms and sat with one leg tucked under the opposite thigh in a lithely relaxed manner. She fit nicely into his house, at his table, in his life. During breakfast they talked at length over the events of the day before. But nothing was said about the way the evening had ended; a faint spark quickly doused. Mature responsibility and gentlemanly honor had their drawbacks.

An ember still burned that morning. Perhaps if he'd bounded into her bedroom, leapt around, and praised Saint Hubert...

"Brother Thumper!" Ryman called out as he approached. "What a glorious morning!"

"Huh? Oh, yes it is. You feeling okay?"

"Never better. Why should I be feeling anything less than tiptop?"

"Well, you did have a rough time yesterday. And Nardell said you were up all night with Wycroft."

"True enough. But the morning brought a great... a great... epipenifery."

"Epiphany?"

"Yeah, that."

"So you're still on the Saint Hubert kick."

"Why shouldn't I be?"

"Well, y'know, after the incident with the buck..."

Ryman flipped a hand in a dismissive gesture. "Ah, well, that wasn't *the* buck, was it? Might have looked a lot like Saint Hubert's stag, but it obviously was just your plain old, run-of-the-mill buck."

"With a fourteen point rack?"

"A rarity, yes, but not unheard of."

"You still think your imagined buck with the sign of Saint Hubert above its head is out there somewhere?"

"No reason to believe otherwise. But does that really matter? Perhaps Saint Hubert has finished with that particular vision. And now we're on to other things."

"Such as?"

"Well, I had a visitor this morning. He brought me a new message. I'm still mulling over the details, but I'll fill you in as soon as it's all sorted out."

"Not another vision," Thumper moaned.

"A vision? No, I wouldn't say it was a vision. A sign? Yeah, maybe a sign. But the message was clear."

"Don't you think you got enough of a message yesterday? You're treading into some dangerous turf here. One of mankind's favorite pastimes is killing others in the name of religion. You came within a hair's breadth from finding yourself on the wrong end of that passion. Are you sure you want to keep pushing this envelope?"

"Ah, but St. Hubert intervened, didn't he? And through his most trusted servant, a faithful old hound."

"Well, there were some others involved in saving your sorry ass. You might allow a nod to Janey and Dan for showing up when they did."

"All arranged by our beloved patron saint. Blessed be his name!"

Thumper covered his eyes with his hand and shook his head in frustration.

"And now," Ryman continued, "what say we go enjoy this glorious day he has provided for us?"

****

Ryman's hand was on Nardell's eagle tattoo as he ushered her through the cottage door. "Great sport this morning."

"Wonderful. Haven't we seen that fox before?"

"We certainly have. Some of us have seen him pretty recently."

"What do you mean?"

He continued to press her forward, through the living room and toward the hallway. "Oh, lets just say he and I are… sort of… old friends. Pissin' pals you might say."

She gave him a quizzical look over her shoulder. "Are you taking me where I think you're taking me?"

"You are most perceptive, madam."

"This morning wasn't enough?" she asked with an expectant smile.

"Never enough with you, darlin'. Not when the sport is running hot and the game is afoot."

She trotted down the hallway. "Yip, yip, yeeee!"

"A-wooooo!"

****

By the time Thumper returned from Tuesday's hunt, Janey had finished her teaching duties and was back at Montfair. He found her parked in the wingback chair, surrounded by stacks of notes, pounding away on her laptop. She wore blue jeans and a baggy plaid flannel shirt with the tail out.

"How'd it go?" she asked.

"Another good day. We got a fox up in Gretchen's Bottom, looked a lot like that one we chased on the first day of cub hunting. Surely a dog fox, nice coat, big white tip on his brush. Gave us a good run."

"Sorry I missed it. Would have been my fourth hunt. And then…"

"Yes, it would. But you'll have another chance on Thursday." He paused and took a deep breath. "Look, um, about last night… I was thinking… well…"

Natasha's unmistakable footfalls echoed down the hall. Her large presence appeared in the doorway. Addressing Janey she said, "I am leaving now. You are ready, yes?"

"Be right there." She closed her computer and organized her notes.

"Going somewhere?" Thumper asked.

"Natasha has to run into Warrenton for some last minute necessities for Thanksgiving dinner. She invited me to go along. Give us a chance to get to know each other better." Setting her computer aside, she hopped up from the chair, gave him a peck on the cheek, and whispered, "Hold that thought." Then she followed Natasha out the door.

****

Thumper stood with his hand against his cheek where she'd planted the quick kiss. He then turned to the window and watched as the two women left in Janey's car. When they were out of sight, he regained his composure, checked his watch, and calculated when they would likely return. A minute later he was racing down the driveway in his truck.

A fast, bouncy ride had him at The Cabin in record time. The climb up the steep hillside was even more strenuous on foot than it had been on horseback the day before. The misty weather made the thin soil and prominent rocks especially slippery. Other than exchanging his scarlet coat for his Barbour jacket, there'd been no time to switch out of his hunting clothes. Struggling through the brambly scrub growth added a few more rips to his already damaged Barbour. His slick-soled riding boots were ill suited for this terrain and he stumbled several times, leaving deep mud stains on his white breeches. He hoped Natasha would not ask about that when she found them in the dirty clothes hamper.

The trail created by Waylon's hooves was clear enough for Thumper to follow and eventually he reached the spot where he'd found the trapped deer. The object was still where he'd hidden it, tucked behind a fallen log, safely out of Ryman's sight.

The return was no easier, and by the time he reached The Cabin there were mud stains on the seat of his breeches to match those on the knees.

Once back in his study, he placed the object on his desk and examined it carefully. Its possession posed a number of difficult questions. Did its material presence alone relate to the significance behind its appearance? The power of the Yir Yoront stone ax lay not in its use as a common tool, but in the meanings attached to it. When that cohesive force was lost, social order crumbled. This relic—as the faithful were likely to consider it—might simply be the physical manifestation of a deeper truth, nothing more than a marker pointing to the larger mystical verities that can only be known by faith.

Faith itself may be ethereal. But humans, being such frail creatures, forever seek a tangible embodiment of faith, a Piece of the Cross to hold in their hands.

Was this the modern day equivalent of a Piece of the Cross that Thumper now held in his scratched and soiled hands? If he revealed it to others, would it become an object of worship or the subject of ridicule? If Ryman knew the truth, would his powers evaporate? Did he even have any powers? Had it all just been coincidence and what Thumper held was nothing more than a piece of chipped, faded wood and a tangle of metal wires? Or had this device been a guide to put Ryman on the path to those powers and something had transpired that Thumper could not explain?

Lost in these thoughts, he'd not been aware of Janey's car coming up the driveway. When he heard the laughing chatter of the two women as they came through the mudroom door, he realized he still wore his mud stained hunting clothes. He hastily thrust the object into a desk drawer and ran upstairs to change.

****

Shelton was worn out by the time she finished the last leg of her journey and turned her rental car off Montfair Lane and onto the Fair Enough Farm driveway. She entered the house to find Rhetta waiting in the front foyer, hands on her hips and displeasure on her face.

"What's the big idea going in with that freak to bail out the shop?"

"Nice to see you too, Grandma," Shelton said as she dropped her bags with a thud. "It's been a very long trip. Any chance I could freshen up, maybe have some coffee, before we get into this?"

Rhetta conceded but without softening her confrontational stance.

They reconvened over coffee at the kitchen table.

"My plan," Rhetta said, "was to force your old man back into his rightful duties, stop this silly church nonsense. Then you come along and help him. Worse yet, you did it with that damned freak who now thinks he's running things, him and that prissy colored woman."

"I thought you might be pleased that there'd still be a McKendrick involved."

"Yeah, but not you. You got your own career, another life far away from here, way out there in California." To Rhetta's mind, the entire state of California was one continuous expanse of Hollywood, a place where everyone was in the movie industry, where song-and-dance numbers could break out anytime, anywhere. She imagined her granddaughter hobnobbing with film stars and crooners. The real life of a veterinary pharmaceuticals rep covering the Pacific Northwest coast was far less glamorous.

"Grandma, Bar was going to do this anyway, with or without me. It was pretty much all his money that paid down what was owed to the bank. I thought it would be best if someone from the family stayed involved."

"How involved are you gonna be when you're three thousand miles away?"

Gazing down into her coffee cup, Shelton's response was barely audible. "Yeah, well, that might not be the case for much longer."

"What? You getting another promotion? Moving somewheres else?"

"Something like that."

"Well, ain't that wonderful. I sure am proud of you, child. I know your granddaddy would be too if he was still alive."

"I hope so."

The two women sat in silence for several minutes. Sensing that Rhetta's mood was softening, Shelton said, "Grandma, I don't know what it is about Bar that sets you off. I can only assume you have a valid reason. But I've known him all my life. He's been there for me many times. Times when Daddy wasn't. Even some times when Grandpa wasn't." She wanted to include Rhetta in that list, but thought better. "Believe me, the shop's in good hands. And that goes for Muriel too."

"Yeah, well, they ain't McKendrick hands."

"I don't think you need to worry about that."

"But I do need to worry about your daddy and all his crazy talk. Now I got nothing over him, 'cept to maybe kick him and his girlfriend and their freak pal off the farm. But he don't seem too concerned about that."

"Can I ask one thing, Grandma?"

"You can ask."

"Don't do anything just yet. This might all work out okay. Give it a few days at least."

"For you, child. But don't expect me to put up with your old man's foolishness forever." She gave her granddaughter a careful assessment. "You look right peaked. Maybe you oughta go up and take a nap."

Shelton agreed that was a good idea.

She awoke two hours later to the sound of piano music coming from the parlor. The playing was competent, although several keys were out of tune. Shelton went downstairs and found Rhetta seated at the old upright. She stopped playing when she sensed Shelton's presence.

Without turning around, Rhetta said, "It was his voice." There was a long pause as she stared at the sheet music before her. "He coulda been a movie star. Had the looks for it too. But here we both were, stuck in Crutchfield County, family duties holding us down. But that voice. It took me away, made me forget about all this." She flipped a hand toward the window and the open countryside beyond. "Made me think about California out there where you live. All them people singing and dancing, having a fine time. All that was in his voice. Singing at church, singing here on hunting days and at parties.

"I shoulda seen it coming, shoulda been stronger. But it just happened, kinda natural like. That day he hurt his back and ended up here. We both knew it was wrong, probably coulda gone on as usual after that, put it behind us and got back to real life. But then *he* showed up."

She paused again, long enough for Shelton to offer a prompt. "Who showed up? Bar?"

"Nah, not him. That came later. Your Uncle Teedy."

The reference sounded foreign to Shelton's ear. She'd never known her uncle, never thought of him as "Uncle Teedy," only as a revered family memory, an historical figure spoken of in sadly hushed tones. Now she tried to envision him as a real person, finding his mother and Bing in… in an embarrassing… as she thought about it, the image of her grandmother and Mister Sensabaugh in that position was equally hard to imagine.

Rhetta continued. "His horse had gone lame and he'd come in early. We didn't hear him coming in from the barn, through the back door. All of a sudden, there he was." She plunked a couple of notes on the piano as she struggled to maintain her composure. "That's what sent him off to the war. *I* sent him off to the war 'cause a what I done. He was young, too proud and hotheaded. I tried to make him understand, pleaded with him to find some forgiveness. But he wouldn't listen. Said he couldn't be in the same house with me after that, couldn't look at me the same any more, not as his mother. So he quit school and went off and joined the Marines. Figured that would make his daddy proud and would make me suffer. Well, he was right on both counts."

"I'm sorry, Grandma. I never knew."

"No, a course you didn't, child. Nobody knew. That was the whole point. Bing and me were never gonna say nothing to nobody. And to this day we never have. Least I never have, up until telling you now, and I'm pretty sure he ain't neither. But there's one other person who might know."

"Who?"

She looked out the parlor window for a while before she replied. "It was well after we got the news about Teedy. I wouldn't say things was back to normal. I reckon things ain't never the same after something like that, losing your child in some stupid war that lots a folks thought we shouldn't been fighting anyways. Even worse that your child didn't have to go, only did it to spite you. But we were dealing with it, trying to get on as best we could.

"Then one day this big freaky looking thing shows up at the door, half his face tore up. Tells your granddaddy he and Teedy were best friends over there, spent all their time together. Says he was with him when it happened, whole platoon got wiped out, only he survived. Then he looked down at me with that eye. That damned eye. Sent a cold chill down my back, like there was blue ice shooting out of it, right through me. He knew. He musta known. Soldier pals tell each other all kinds a things, don't they? Sitting there in the foxhole, baring their souls to each other. Like they done in all them war movies. Figure if they're likely to get killed, they want to 'fess up first. There was something in the way he was looking at me with that one eye that said, 'I know what you done. I know why Teedy went off and got hisself killed. It was your fault.'

"Well, I 'bout fainted at that point. It was all my legs could do to carry me upstairs to my bedroom. Then your granddaddy, not knowing any a this, goes and offers him a job and a place to live. I couldn't tell him the truth about why I didn't want him around. But I been seeing that eye ever since, the way it was staring down at me and what it was saying about what I done. It ain't the missing eye that bothers me. It's the one he's still got."

Shelton crossed the room and placed her hands on Rhetta's shoulders. "It was one indiscretion, Grandma. Happens to lots of people. You don't need to keep paying for it your whole life."

"I appreciate that, child. But nothing's ever gonna bring Teedy back. So I'm paying for it whether I want to or not. Cain't change that."

"Maybe not. But I do think you're wrong about Bar. I have no way of knowing what he and Uncle Teedy might have shared with each other. But I'm pretty sure that even if he does know, he's never told anyone."

"Hell, child, you weren't born yet when he showed up here. You got no way a knowing what he might a done, who he might a told."

"True. But I know Bar better than most folks do. In fact, probably no one except maybe Daddy knows him better. If he had a mind to blab about this, I think it would have come out by now."

"Yeah, but that eye. There was something in that eye sayin'…"

"I know what you mean. I've seen that look too. Countless times. But it's just something he does, and most of the time I don't think he even realizes how spooky it seems. You may not be able to bring Teedy back, but you still have time to change your attitude about Bar. He's a bit rough around the edges, but there's a good heart inside that big, damaged body."

"Well, I reckon you'd know about that better than most." Rhetta flipped through the sheet music, selected a song, and placed it in front of her. As her hands hovered over the keys, she said, "I'll think about it. But I ain't promising nothing."

The tune she began to play was familiar, quick and bouncy, but Shelton couldn't place it at first. *One-two-three-AND-one-two-three.* The image of an old movie began to form. Colorful costumes, an elaborate set, a barefoot bald man in shiny red and gold pajamas prancing about. Then the words started to come:

On the clear understanding
That this kind of thing can happen,
Shall we dance?
Shall we dance?
Shall we dance?

Chapter 83

"FRANK!" LUELLA CALLED out as Worsham stepped into the General Store. "Haven't seen you in ages."

"Been busy. The wife sent me in to pick up a couple of last minute things for tomorrow."

Worsham wanted nothing more than to pay for the few items he needed and be on his way. But Luella had paragraphs of gossip to fill him in on and in the interest of community harmony he politely stood and listened. When she got to the part about someone taking a shot at Ryman, he snapped out of his head-bobbing stupor.

"When did you say that happened, and where?" he asked.

She repeated the details.

"Huh," he mumbled, "ain't that something."

"You know anything about that, Frank?"

"Me? Nah. Well, I gotta run. Good to catch up with you, Luella." He grabbed his bag of groceries and hustled out the door.

Ryman was just walking back to his cottage from the barn when he saw Frank's truck coming down the Fair Enough driveway. The F350 came to a stop and Worsham jumped out.

"Ry," he said, "glad I caught you. Got a minute?"

"For you, always, Frank."

"Um, look man, I gotta… well, I guess I gotta apologize. I've just come from the store and Luella was filling me in on what's been happening lately. I been kinda outta the loop. She said someone took a shot at you, or shot close to you, something like that."

As much as Ryman tried to scoff it off as an accident, a lingering fear remained that perhaps there was a second "Defender" still out there, biding his time, and waiting to strike again, with more accuracy on the next attempt.

Worsham continued. "When she told me when and where this happened, well, I gotta admit I was in a tree stand around there that morning. It might have been me."

"But Frank, you always check to see where we're hunting to make sure there's no risk of that."

"Yeah, I do. And y'all weren't supposed to be there that morning. I checked the monitor before I headed out. It said y'all were meeting at the Prestons'."

The light dawned for Ryman. "Holy shit! We changed at the last minute. The Prestons had a problem in their pasture, an underground spring or something. You must have called before Marva changed the message. But the shot happened kinda late in the morning. Are you sure you would have still been there?"

"It was a slow day, drizzly, foggy, chilly. The deer weren't moving much. I'd been in the stand a long time, hadn't gotten a decent shot. I kept thinking I should pack it in, but figured I'd wait just a little longer, maybe something would turn up. You know how it is."

Ryman nodded his agreement.

"It was, like, eleven o'clock or later when I finally saw a legal buck. Big damn sucker too. Hard to tell how many points for sure what with the fog and drizzle and all, but he had a helluva rack on him. I had him sighted for a perfect heart-lung shot. I squeezed the trigger and fired. That sumbitch just stood there looking back at me, like he was daring me to take another shot. I couldn't believe I'd missed him. So I fired a second time, slow and steady. When I looked again, he was gone. I thought maybe I'd wounded him. I climbed down and went to the spot where he'd been. No blood, nothing. He'd got clean away. I know I shouldn't have taken that second shot. It must have been the one that damn near hit you. I never did see you, I was so focused on that buck. And, like I said, y'all weren't supposed to be there that morning."

"That's all right, Frank. Not your fault, and no harm done."

"Thanks, Ry. I appreciate that." Worsham shook his head. "Still, though, I can't believe I missed him. I'm a pretty good shot. About the best around here, except for maybe Bar. And I had two good chances and missed him clean. I tell you what, though, I'm gonna be looking for that sumbitch. I got a special spot on my trophy wall just waiting for that rack."

Ryman smiled and put a hand on Worsham's shoulder. "Best of luck to you, old buddy. You're gonna need it."

****

Bing and Reverend Dan sat facing each other, perched on the edge of two small guest chairs in the musty, pipe-smoke-scented living room of the vicarage.

"You understand," Bing said, "that this is only a temporary reprieve. The diocese leaders, particularly the bishop, are pleased with this recent turnaround in the church's fortunes. Not just the increase in offerings, but the vocal support from the membership."

"I am most gratified. But I give all the glory to the hand of God."

"Well, not to take anything away from the Almighty, but you might give a word of thanks to Bob as well. It was his endorsement that finally tipped the scales in your favor. As head of the finance committee, that carried a lot of weight."

"I'll be sure to express my gratitude."

"We're all glad that St. Cuthbert's doors will remain open, at least for now anyway. The diocese will keep a close eye on things, and if attendance begins to flag again, well, they're not going to wait for the situation to become critical."

"I understand. I'm sure they were also pleased to hear the choir is being, um, shall we say, 'resurrected.' And under your talented leadership, along with the admirable talents of your grandchildren, your friend Marie, and others."

"I suppose we have to thank Ryman for that," Bing said. "At least giving us the inspiration to start singing again as a group. In fact, it seems his Venatican Church idea just happened to coincide with the start of your newfound fervor."

"Imagine that."

Bing arose. Dan took the cue and did the same.

"Well, Reverend," Bing said, "we're all trusting in you. Don't let us down."

Dan stood in the vicarage doorway and watched him drive away. His eyes followed a trail of smoke as it curled lazily from the bowl of his pipe. With a sardonic grin, Dan said to himself, "Saint Hubert be praised."

Chapter 84

JANEY WAS ACCUSTOMED to a bustle of activity on the evening before Thanksgiving. But the action around Montfair rose to a level akin to battle preparations. Field Marshall Thumper gave her the choice of a kitchen or stable assignment. She opted for the stable, which left Elizabeth to serve as Natasha's sous chef. Crispie and Patti snagged Voytek to help with the preparations at kennels.

Janey joined Javier and Bettiana in the barn to assist with getting the horses ready for the big day. The Ledesmas had this down to a smooth routine and needed no help. But they accommodated Thumper's wishes and found a few menial tasks for Janey to perform. She applied herself to the job, watched diligently, and learned a few valuable tricks about horse grooming and tack cleaning. Most of all, just being immersed in this antiquarian world—infused with the odor of hay, horse manure, mane and body shampoo, leather cleaner, boot polish—stimulated her senses and gave her the satisfaction of physical accomplishment.

As the evening wore on, she looked out the open barn doors into the surrounding darkness. Inside the barn, where the ceiling lights cast stark shadows around large horses and small people, she felt as if she was in an ark adrift in a sea of blackness. It was both comforting and unnerving in a way she'd never known, another manifestation of the yin and yang of country life. There was a constant tension between risk and reward, challenge and achievement, victory and defeat, even life and death. It demanded determination and commitment, and in return granted moments of ecstasy unknown to the poor souls trapped in the mind-numbing monotony of suburban life.

It made her feel fully alive in every part of her body as she bent, reached, stretched, lifted, carried, brushed, and buffed.

As she dusted a few loose hairs off Bee's neck, she felt the flutter of anticipation Thumper had spoken of, the one he said he still felt the night before a special hunt. She understood what Cecelia meant, about the knowing and the not knowing, the giddiness just before the chase begins. She had a sense about what was behind Mildred's dreamy stare. There was something deeper there than just following hounds after a fox.

Somewhere in Mildred's eyes Janey had seen a glimmer of the way a woman thinks about a man, a man she knows—and wants to know—in a certain way.

****

The following morning the flutter blossomed into a roiling rumble down to Janey's core as she rode between Thumper and Elizabeth, heading toward the front lawn where another time-warp scene waited for her to become part of the pageantry. As she'd seen at the Tiber Creek joint meet, she noticed two ladies riding sidesaddle, decked out in the accompanying top hat, veil, and flowing black skirt. She hadn't yet broached the sidesaddle question with Thumper. But the desire was still there, now refreshed by the sight of these elegantly turned out ladies.

Equally striking was the sight of the Reverend Doctor Daniel T. Davenport, standing on the lawn, his red-trimmed white clerical robes fluttering in the cool November breeze.

Several children were present, including Baden and Beatrice. With Dorcas gone, Cecelia offered to fill in for her. She sat mounted among the children, Baden to one side, Missy Winslow to the other. The club leaders were glad for her help. Some suspected the children might get a bit more of an education beyond just horsemanship. Especially Baden and Missy.

As Thumper made the welcoming announcements, Ryman considered the scene before him. Every Thanksgiving Day of Ryman McKendrick's life had included this ancient tradition. But it had become so routine that he barely thought of it beyond the rote performance. Now he understood the deeper meanings, the link to the past, the bond to community. His mother stood where she always had, where she had cradled him in her arms as an infant. And she looked just as disapproving as always. Where he had once stood beside her as a toddler, his grown daughter now stood. Thumper sat mounted beside him, his hunt cap off in anticipation of the blessing, just as their fathers had done, as Billington and McKendrick men had done for generations before them.

Thumper wrapped up the greeting and turned the spotlight over to Ryman.

"Friends, on Saturday I spoke of the tenth and final article from 'The Foxhunter's Faith,' which says, 'And may all men, rich and poor, have equal rights and pleasures in "the chase" if they devoutly agree to these articles.' Two words in that article have been on my mind the past few days: 'all men.' Now, of course, we know 'men' here means all people, men and women, children too. But what about the 'all' part? Saint Hubert has given us wonderful blessings these past few months, and I'm confident he'll continue to do so. Yet we are but a small group. There are many more who need to hear Saint Hubert's message, that life is about 'the chase.'

"I ask each of you to pray that Saint Hubert will open their minds and their hearts to his words. Will y'all do that for me?"

His request was answered with a rumble of weak and bewildered affirmations.

"Good," Ryman said. "And whatever else happens, wherever I might be, I know Saint Hubert will continue to watch over every one of you here. So now let me turn things over to our own Reverend Davenport. Okay, Padre, take it away!"

Dan shook his head and sighed. He drew himself up to an oratorical posture and his voice rang strong and clear across the fields of Montfair. "The traditional blessing for this special day: 'Bless, O Lord, rider and horse, and hounds that run, in their running, and shield them from danger to life and limb. May Thy children who ride, and Thy creatures who carry, come to the close of the day unhurt and give thanks to Thee with grateful hearts. Bless those over whose lands we hunt, and grant that no deed or omission of ours may cause them hurt or trouble. Bless the foxes who partake in the chase, that they may run straight and true and may find their destiny in Thee. Bless the hounds to our use and their joyful part in Thy service. O God, who of Thy love sanctifieth all things by Thy Word, pour down Thy mercy upon these Thy servants, their horses and their hounds; to all who shall take part in the hunt, grant protection of body and soul; make us all ever mindful of, and responsive to, the needs of others that the spirit of true sportsmanship may prevail in all that we do.'"

And the people all said, "Amen!"

****

Typical of a High Holy Day, when many riders of less than admirable skill show up to be seen, Janey was crowded out from staying with Mildred as others vied for a place of honor at the front. Some did so mainly because they couldn't control their horses well enough to keep them further back in the group.

No matter though. Janey was getting the hang of this hunting thing. And Bee knew what he was doing even if several riders around him didn't. Janey noticed one rider ahead whose horse had a red ribbon tied to its tail. She recalled Thumper's explanation of the ribbon convention, that green was used if the horse was inexperienced in the hunt field, red meant the horse was a kicker. He'd also said that proper etiquette required known kickers to be kept to the rear, safely behind the other horses. A particularly dangerous animal should not be brought to the hunt field at all.

This woman had apparently not gotten that information. Or willfully chose to ignore it for her own convenience.

Hounds opened, tentatively, and began to work a faint line. As they moved across the open ground, the followers picked up a trot. Janey sensed the chaos about to unfold around her. Several riders were struggling to control their horses. Even to Janey's untrained eye she could see the difference between the steadiness of an experienced rider, one who remained calm and in command no matter what the horse did, and some of the people who were having problems. The more a horse objected, the more nervous its rider became. This, in turn, fueled the horse's meltdown, which sent the rider into an even deeper panic. Janey could tell the end result was likely to be unpleasant.

Having seen this countless times, Bee had the sense to stay clear of the worst offenders. But as more horses became infected with the spreading chaos, the harder that became.

Janey felt Bee dodge to his left as a dark bay with a wide butt started backing toward him. A split second later she caught the fleeting sight of a red ribbon, followed by an airborne rear hoof aimed straight at Bee's neck. The experienced hunt horse did what any animal would do in that situation; he spun away to avoid the kick.

Janey was thrust forward and to the side by the momentum. She had a glimpse of a chestnut shoulder from a horizontal angle, then came the impact with the ground as she landed flat on her back.

The attempted kick was the last straw for Bee. Steady as he was, self-preservation took over and he cantered away, up toward first field and the safety of saner horses and better riders.

Mildred signaled for her field to stop and several horses behind her crashed into each other as the riders tried to obey.

Someone shouted "Loose horse!"

At the sound of that call, Thumper's only thought was, *Not Bee. Please not Bee.* When a flash of motion to his left caught his eye, he turned to see a familiar chestnut, riderless, stirrups flapping loosely.

"Shit!" he said. "Grantham, take the field." Without waiting for reply, he turned Lenny around and cantered back to where second field stood milling around. Mildred was off her horse and kneeling beside the fallen rider.

"Don't try to get up," he heard Mildred say as he vaulted off Lenny.

"No, really," Janey insisted, "I'm fine. All parts working okay."

Thumper felt a surge of relief when he heard that.

"Are you sure, deah? If you've hurt your neck or your back, it could cause…"

"Please," Janey said. "Not to worry. Just a light tumble." She rose to a sitting position. "See. No problem." She got to her feet. "Is Bee okay?

Did that other horse kick him? It looked like it came so close."

"What other horse?" Thumper demanded. "What happened here?"

"Several horses were acting up," Janey explained. "One of them, one with a red ribbon, struck out at Bee. He ducked away to keep from getting kicked. Next thing I knew, I was on the ground. But no harm done."

Thumper's face grew increasingly crimson with anger at the sound of each word. "Which horse was it?"

Janey looked at the two-dozen riders arrayed around her. She pointed to one of them. "That one, I think."

"I might have known!" Thumper turned his wrath on a certain woman who was trying to look inconspicuous in the crowd. "How many times have you been told? Do you think the rules of common courtesy and safety don't apply to you? You keep that damn horse to the back. And you either get that kicking behavior under control, or that horse will be excused from the hunt field." His voice rose in a final damnation. "And you too if you don't do as I say!"

It wasn't often the Squire of Montfair revealed a reminder of just how much power he held over every detail of foxhunting in Crutchfield County. It took an offense of significant severity. And, as those around him clearly saw, putting Janey Musgrove at risk of injury was such an offense.

Les Peterson arrived leading Bee. "Your mount, m'lady," he said with a courtly nod.

"Are you sure you want to continue on?" Thumper asked as Janey thanked Les and took the reins.

"Are you kidding? It hasn't been an hour yet."

"Really, I can make an exception. You've earned the right to know my…"

She raised a hand to silence him. "A deal's a deal. And I am a woman of honor. Now help me get back on the horse. We have to catch up with hounds."

Thumper gave her a leg up. He leapt back onto Lenny, he and Les cantered away to rejoin first field, and the day's sport resumed.

****

A large hand tapped lightly on Muriel's door. When she opened it, the sound of adult laughter and children squealing in playful delight poured out. The aroma of roasting turkey wafted from the kitchen. The small, tidy house was packed and the man at the door wondered if there'd be room for him. He tugged on the stiff collar of his denim shirt and struggled to straighten his clean white overalls.

Muriel looked up with a welcoming smile. "I'm so glad you could join us, Barstow. Please, come on in."

****

The post-hunt festivities at Montfair were equally joyous, although the participants were a much more eclectic group than were those at the Hudkins', where Bar was the sole non-family guest. Besides Thumper, Janey, and Elizabeth, the Montfair celebrants included Ryman, Nardell, Rhetta, Shelton, Dan, Crispie, Patti, Grantham, Kirsten, Natasha, Voytek, Javier, and Bettiana: three continents, and a variety of faiths or lack thereof, were represented around the formal dining room table.

The highlight of the table talk was Janey's first fall. Despite the tumble, she finished the hunt, right up to when the gentlemanly fox went to ground in time for everyone to get home for their big dinners. The grass and mud stains down the back of Claudette's old hunt coat were a badge of honor for Janey, a cause for congratulatory remarks from others in whose eyes her credibility as a promising foxhunter, and not just a snooping wannabe, had risen considerably.

Elizabeth, seated next to her, remarked teasingly, "The old saying is that you have to fall off at least twenty times before you're a real horseperson."

Ryman said, "I'd always heard it was fifty. They must have lowered the bar since Nardell and me were in Pony Club."

Rhetta scoffed. "Ah, you kids don't know shit. It's a hunnert."

No one was willing to contest Rhetta's pronouncement. So "a hunnert" it was.

Janey turned to Thumper and said with a challenging smile, "Well, one down, ninety-nine to go. And I've now completed four full hunts. So, how about it? Are you ready to tell me?"

Thumper ducked his head and lowered his voice. "Not in front of all these people."

Elizabeth heard that. "Tell her what?"

"It's just between Janey and me," he said to his daughter. "Besides, you already know. But not everyone here does." He turned back to Janey and whispered, "I'll tell you later, when we're alone. You've earned it."

"Ooooh," Elizabeth teased. "Whatever could it be?" She flashed a conspiratorial wink at Janey.

As the guests were getting up from the table, patting their bellies, and making the obligatory comments about how they were near to exploding, Ryman caught Thumper's eye and waved him over. "What say you and me take a little stroll, walk off some of that excellent dinner."

Thumper's curiosity was aroused by this unexpected overture, spiced with a look of devilment in Ryman's eyes.

The two men left through the mudroom and walked along the pebbled path from the main barn in the general direction of the huntsman's residence and kennels.

"I need to ask you a serious question," Ryman said. He stopped and turned to face Thumper squarely. "You know there was something above that deer's head, don't you? You saw it too when he appeared to us at The Cabin. Just exactly what did you find when you caught up with him? What happened before I got there?"

Thumper did his best to appear earnest. Lying was abhorrent to him. But he was also a lawyer. "I told you, Ry. The buck was there by the woods in front of The Cabin for just an instant, and then it was gone. Once I was on the horse, all I could do was follow the sound of Wycroft's baying. By the time I caught up, the deer was on the ground, snagged in the vines." What he said was true, up to that point.

"And there was nothing in its rack? No cross, no circle, nothing?"

"Hell, Ry, you saw it when you got there. Did you see anything?"

Ryman studied his old friend's face. He'd never known Thumper Billington to tell an untruth. "No, nothing."

"Well, there you go."

Ryman pursed his lips, then nodded.

The two men began strolling along again, silently for a time.

"I'm still worried about that shooting incident," Thumper said. "Dorcas accounts for everything else, but not that."

"Oh! I forgot to tell you. Frank came by yesterday and 'fessed up. Like I figured, just an accident. A rainy day, he didn't know we were hunting around there because we changed the plans on short notice. All just a coincidence."

"Been a lot of that going around lately."

"So you say."

"I do say. But at least that's one less thing to be concerned about."

"You remember what I said to you Tuesday morning?" Ryman asked. "That I'd had an epi… epipen…?"

"Epiphany?"

"Yeah, that. I believe Saint Hubert sent another message, just at sunrise that morning."

"Still woozy from the Dormosedan were you?" Thumper's tone was heavy with frustration. "That plus another smack on the noggin without your helmet? No telling what crazy shit is swirling around in that damaged, scotch-soaked brain of yours."

Ryman ignored these remarks with patient forbearance. "I know what I must do next, what Saint Hubert's plan is now that I've gone through all ten articles here."

"And that plan is…?"

"Ah, all in good time, my friend. But I can assure you that you'll be the first to know when the time is right. And that time will be very soon."

****

After everyone else had left Montfair—most back to their own homes, Elizabeth off to stay over with friends—Thumper and Janey settled in before the fire in the study.

"Are you sure you're okay?" Thumper asked. "A bit sore from that tumble?"

"Everything seems to be fine. If the other ninety-nine falls go this well, I'll be a real horseperson in no time."

"I doubt Claudette's old hunting kit will hold up for ninety-nine more tumbles. We'll have to get you to Warrenton, pay a visit to my favorite store, Horse Country Saddlery, and have you properly outfitted."

"I'm not much of a shopper. You'll have to be my guide."

"It will be my pleasure."

She reached over, took his chin in her hand, and turned his head to one side and then the other. "Your scratches from Monday's adventure seem to be healing up well. Losing the aura of your rugged handsomeness though." She released his chin and leaned back.

They both sat silently, watching the fire.

Thumper took a generous swig of scotch and then said, "It happened when I was in the ninth grade at the Woodberry Forest School for Boys." He looked down, swirled the ice around in his highball glass, and continued in a confessional voice. "There was this guy, fellow named Fred. He was a year ahead of me, a big fellah who knew how to throw his weight around. He was from up north, the son of a self-made man and the first in his family to attend a private school. Fred didn't particularly like Woodberry Forest, didn't like being stuck in an all-boys school in the middle of nowhere, hated Virginia, and, most of all, hated me."

"What did you do to deserve that?"

"I made the mistake of being born into a wealthy old Virginia family, of being the current young man from a long line of young men who had attended the school. The founder was a Civil War veteran, served with Mosby's Rangers, and was a passing acquaintance of my Uncle Josiah." He gestured toward the brace of Navy Colt .44s.

"To Fred I was the embodiment of everything he hated about Virginia in general and Woodberry Forest in particular. I did my best to ignore his taunts and insults, in part because I did not want to blemish my record at the school and disgrace my family. And perhaps in greater part because, well, Fred was significantly larger, stronger, and clearly had been in a scrape or two in his young life."

"Nothing wrong with sizing up your opponent and knowing when not to engage," Janey offered.

"Right. I did so for as long as I could. But then Fred found the hot button."

"Which was?"

"He impugned the virtue of my mother and sisters."

"Ouch!"

"My family's honor was on the line and I could not let that insult go unchallenged. In my youthful haze of righteous indignation, and with a bit of silly theatrical flair, I shouted, 'You Yankee swine! I'll give you the solid thumping you deserve.'"

Janey grinned as she realized where this tale was going.

"Fred stood there smirking and said, 'Oh, yeah? Think you can give me a thumping, you spoiled little prick? C'mon then. Let's see what kind of thumper you are.'"

He paused, took another sip of scotch, and gazed into the fire.

"And…?" Janey asked.

"He beat the crap out of me."

She reached over and placed her hand on his arm in a gesture of sympathy. Her gentle touch sent a warm glow up to his shoulders. Without meaning to do so, she squeezed a little harder, as if her body wanted to confirm that the hardness she felt was really flesh.

"Unfortunately," he continued, "several other boys witnessed this, heard what was said, and by the next day all the boys at Woodberry Forest were calling me 'Thumper.' Several of them continued on with me to The University, some even joined the same fraternity, so I couldn't get away from the name there. But by then I'd gotten used to it, figured it could have been worse."

"And now," Janey said, "gentleman that you are, you have met your obligation."

"And woman of integrity that you are, I'm confident you will maintain your agreement as well to never share that information with another soul without my express permission."

She held up the three-finger salute. "Scout's honor."

The faint sound of a vehicle clattering up the main driveway caught their attention. They went to the front porch and saw Ryman's truck approaching. Its headlights cast a spectral path in the evening mist. Janey shivered as she felt the chill of late November.

As the truck drew closer, the trailer behind came into view. In place of Ryman's usual two-horse rig was a stock trailer loaded with four horses.

Ryman pulled to a stop at the base of the porch steps. He and Nardell hopped out. They were full of animated energy and wore their best cubbing attire.

"We've come to say good-bye," Ryman announced. "We must be about the chase over different fields. The foundation has been laid here. But there are thousands more, tens or hundreds of thousands even, who need to hear the words of Saint Hubert. As Article Ten says, the blessings of the chase apply to all men, not just foxhunters and not just the folks here in Crutchfield County."

"So you're packing up your medicine show and hitting the road," Thumper said with a flippantly annoyed tone.

"Precisely. Well, I wouldn't put it quite that way. But, yes, Nardell and me are going to spread the word far and wide. It's what Saint Hubert's called us to do."

"And you're leaving now?" Janey asked. "On Thanksgiving night?"

"What better time?" Ryman replied. "This will become known as Saint Hubert's Day on the Venatican calendar, the time when we give thanks for his many blessings, not just over us but over the foxes and hounds and our horses too. Praises be unto his name!"

"Amen!" Nardell sang out.

"And," Ryman continued, "this will be known as the day I, his Prophet, and Nardell, his Apostle, began our holy mission."

"What you're beginning is wholly insane. You can't just up and split," Thumper protested. "Especially not for something as harebrained as this. You've got responsibilities here. To the hunt, to the shop."

"All will be fine. Y'all don't really need me and Nardell whipping-in now. Crispie and Patti can handle things. Our hounds are under the watchful care of Saint Hubert. Better him than a dozen whips. Bar and Muriel have the shop covered. And it looks like Sheltie Lou's decided to move back here and satisfy Ma's big stink about having at least one McKendrick taking care of the business. Our blessed Saint Hubert has provided for everything, don't you see. Nardell and me are really excited about this. We can't wait to get going and spread the good word."

"And just where are you going?" Thumper asked.

"We feel Saint Hubert wants us to start with our friends at Brookside. They're hunting tomorrow and we'll be there to share the good news. Then we'll move on as he leads us. The plan is to visit every hunt club in North America. With Saint Hubert's guidance and blessing, the Ancient and Venerable Church of Ars Venatica will soon be flourishing from coast to coast, from Texas to Canada. His name be praised!"

"Hallelujah!" Nardell added.

As Nardell lifted her hands in exultation, Janey noticed a small band on Nardell's left ring finger where no such adornment had been previously.

"You're in for a hard time ahead, old friend," Thumper said.

Ryman's demeanor took on a more serious cast. "I've been adrift all my life. You know that as well as anyone. A problem with commitment some folks say. I can't explain it exactly, but I've finally found something I know I've been called to do. As my oldest, bestest friend, you might show some support."

"As your oldest, bestest friend, I've been trying to talk some sense into you. But, okay, if you're determined to do this and it makes you feel like you've found some purpose, I guess all I can do is wish you well. And let you know I'll be here for you when you come back."

"Thanks, man."

"Yeah, well, don't say I didn't warn you when this crazy-ass venture doesn't go quite as well as you expect."

With a flurry of hugs and handshakes, the Prophet and his Apostle took their leave and rumbled off to begin their mission.

Thumper turned to Janey the Scribe and said, "There's something I'd like to show you. I've been trying to decide what to do with it. And now I think I know. Come with me."

They returned to his study where he opened a desk drawer and took out the object in question.

"Is that what I think it is?" she asked.

"It is indeed."

"It's just wood and wires."

"Yes. And The Cross was just wood and nails."

"Are you suggesting this rises to the same level of significance?"

"Hardly. But some might consider it to have a certain value, either positive or negative depending on their personal view."

"Yes, I see. Perhaps the myth is stronger when the truth can never be known."

"The truth is rarely as appealing as the myth."

She reached out and touched it. The same sensation surged through her as when she held the stone ax head. Thumper, his fingers on the other end, felt the flow of energy as well.

Janey's mind swirled with the action of the morning; the fear when the horses around her became uncontrollable, the jarring impact with the ground followed by the realization that she was unhurt, the desire to remount and get on with the chase, the exhilaration of galloping to catch up with hounds, charged by the freedom that she had crossed an important barrier—her first fall—and she could ride on with confidence knowing that another part of the initiation was behind her.

Thumper's thoughts went back to his panic when he saw the loose horse and realized Janey had fallen. The continuation of the hunt ceased to be of any importance to him then; his only concern was her safety. He saw himself giving her a leg up onto Bee, his left hand supporting her knee and his right hand cupped under her derriere. He recalled the feel of her butt muscles tightening as she sprang from his grasp and landed lightly in the saddle.

As if by an irresistible force, drawn by the object they both held, Thumper leaned forward and kissed her. With one hand still gripping the object, Janey placed her other hand behind his neck, pulled him closer, and embraced the same sense of abandon she'd felt in the hunt field.

Thumper whispered in her ear, "There's something else I'd like to show you."

"I'll bet there is," she teased.

He set the object down and lifted a piece of paper from his desk. "This arrived in the mail yesterday, from a solicitor in Ireland. I am no longer a legally married man."

Janey looked up with a nervous grin. "Saint Hubert be praised! Let the chase begin."

"A-woooooo!"

****

It was around two o'clock when Thumper arose, slipped on his robe, left Janey sleeping peacefully in his dark bedroom, and went quietly downstairs. He lifted the object from his desk, tiptoed back up the stairs, passed as silently as possible by the bedroom door, on to the end of the hallway, and up the narrow set of stairs to the attic.

He switched on the light and felt the eerie dead-of-night presence of dust-covered detritus entombed in this third storey catacomb. Making his way carefully through centuries of Billington family cast-offs, he came to an old trunk tucked under the edge of the slanted rafters. The trunk was his Uncle Josiah's. To avoid detection of certain contraband items—such as a brace of Navy Colt revolvers—by Union authorities, a false bottom had been installed.

Thumper carefully lifted the folded garments and personal trinkets—Josiah's final worldly possessions—then removed the panel that concealed the hidden compartment. He placed the object inside, put everything back just as it had been, and closed the lid.

His work on Jefferson's cut-and-paste Bible had sharpened his knowledge of New Testament passages. One in particular stuck in his mind, the words of the Apostle Paul:

> Hebrews 11:1 "Faith is the substance of things hoped for,
> the evidence of things not seen."

He muttered those two-thousand-year-old words under his breath, then made his way through the attic obstacle course, switched off the light, and bounced down the stairs.

As he reached the last step, his pace accelerated and he began to sing. "*Hark, hark, forward! Tally-ho, tally-ho, tally-ho!*"

Janey awoke and listened to the sound in the hallway. Thumper trotted along, as if following hounds, closing in on the quarry. She surprised herself with a nervous giggle, accompanied by a shiver that sent her snuggling under the covers. Her breath quickened and her body quivered with each fall of his eager feet. For the first time in her life, as Thumper's hand found the knob and the door began to open, Janey Musgrove knew what "foxy" felt like.

Chapter 85

THUMPER AWOKE BEFORE dawn. Janey stood by the window, gazing toward the driveway. He slipped out of bed and went to her. He saw the desire in her eyes. He could feel the waves of anticipation flowing from her body.

He steeled himself, then asked the question. "You have to follow them, don't you?"

"It's the chance of a lifetime. This is my chase, the story is my fox. I have to go wherever it leads, do whatever it takes." She looked at him with an elfin grin. "A badge of glory awaits at the end."

He turned his face away from hers. They stood together in silence for a long moment. "I guess you'd better get your stuff. If you leave now, you can just make it to Brookside in time for the hunt."

Cast of Characters

Elizabeth Billington: Thumper Billington's daughter, a third year student at the University of Virginia.

Shelagh (pronounced "Sheila") Billington: Thumper's current wife, away in Ireland attending to the affairs of her recently deceased father.

Thaddeus Augustus "Thumper" Billington IV: Joint-master of the Montfair Hunt, owner of the Montfair estate.

Cecelia Broadhurst: Owner of Kimber Farm, patron of the juniors riding program.

Reverend Daniel T. Davenport: Vicar of Saint-Cuthbert's-in-the-Woods Episcopal Church.

Miles Flanagan: Parts counter worker and delivery driver for McKendrick and Sons Farm Implements.

Marie Hardesty: Visiting from Brookside Hunt, Bing Sensabaugh's new companion.

Chet Henderson: Leader of the car-followers on hunting days (Marva Henderson's husband).

Marva Henderson: Montfair Hunt's honorary secretary.

Muriel Hudkins: Office manager for McKendrick and Sons.

Danella Kernan: Literary agent, her clients include Thumper Billington and Janey Musgrove.

Kirsten Kettering: Professional horse trainer, Grantham Meisner's significant other.

Bettiana Ledesma: Javier Ledesma's wife, part of Montfair's full-time farm staff.

Javier Ledesma: Thumper Billington's horse groom and assistant farm manager.

Rhetta McKendrick: Ryman McKendrick's mother, owner of Fair Enough Farm.

Ryman McKendrick: Joint-master of the Montfair Hunt, believes he's been chosen by Saint Hubert to establish The Ancient and Venerable Church of Ars Venatica.

Shelton "Sheltie Lou" McKendrick: Ryman's daughter, a veterinary pharmaceuticals rep working in the Pacific Northwest.

Grantham Meisner: Executive director of the North American Fox Chasers Association (NAFCA).

Janey Musgrove: Author and professor, an authority on fringe religions and primitive cultures.

Natasha Nutchenko: Thumper Billington's housekeeper and cook.

Voytek Nutchenko: Natasha's husband, Montfair farm manager and kennelman.

Crispian "Crispie" O'Rourke: Professional huntsman for the Montfair Hunt.

Lester Peterson: A recent member of Montfair Hunt.

Dr. Josh Preston: Family practice physician, owner (with his wife Mildred) of BoSox Farm.

Mildred Preston: Joint-master of the Montfair Hunt, originally from Boston, MA, owner (with her husband Dr. Josh Preston) of BoSox Farm.

Conway Purvis: Assistant mechanic, McKendrick and Sons.

Nardell Raithby: Ryman McKendrick's significant other, an equine massage therapist.

Barstow "Bar" Reinhardt: Head mechanic for McKendrick and Sons.

Baden and Beatrice Sensabaugh: Bob and Kitty Sensabaugh's teenage children.

Bob Sensabaugh: Son of Harry "Bing" Sensabaugh, husband of Kitty Sensabaugh, current president of Crutchfield County Bank.

Harry "Bing" Sensabaugh: Retired president of the Crutchfield County Bank, widower, and lifelong foxhunter.

Dorcas Stanhope: Cecelia Broadhurst's barn manager, runs the local juniors riding program as part of her employment.

Enoch Stanhope: Dorcas Stanhope's estranged brother.

Luella Starett: Owner of the Paradise Gap General Store.

Astrid Stevenson: Shelton McKendrick's lover, head of People Against Cruelty to Animals (PACA).

Patti Vestor: Crispie O'Rourke's significant other, first whipper-in for Montfair Hunt.

Missy Winslow: Baden Sensabaugh's girlfriend.

Frank Worsham: Crutchfield County farmer, customer of McKendrick and Sons.